THE NEW
MACHIAVELLI
&
THE FOOD OF
THE GODS

THE NEW MACHIAVELLI

and

THE FOOD OF THE GODS

by

H. G. WELLS

ODHAMS PRESS LIMITED
LONDON, W.C.2

Printed in Great Britain

THE NEW
MACHIAVELLI

" A closer examination . . . shows that Abelard was a Nominalist under a new name."   G. H. LEWES, *History of Philosophy*.

" It suffices for our immediate purpose that tender-minded and tough-minded people . . . do both exist." WILLIAM JAMES, *Pragmatism*.

CONTENTS

Book One

The Making of a Man

Book Two

Margaret

Book Three

The Heart of Politics

CONTENTS

Book Four

Isabel

Book One

The Making of a Man

CHAPTER ONE

CONCERNING A BOOK THAT WAS NEVER WRITTEN

§ 1

SINCE I came to this place I have been restless, wasting my energies in the futile beginning of ill-conceived books. One does not settle down very easily at two-and-forty to a new way of living, and I have found myself with the teeming interests of the life I have abandoned still buzzing like a swarm of homeless bees in my head. My mind has been full of confused protests and justifications. In any case I should have found difficulties enough in expressing the complex thing I have to tell, but it has added greatly to my trouble that a certain Niccolo Machiavelli chanced to fall out of politics at very much the age I have reached, and wrote a book to engage the restlessness of his mind very much as I have wanted to do. He wrote about the relation of the great constructive spirit in politics to individual character and weaknesses, and so far his achievement lies like a deep rut in the road of my intention. It has taken me far astray. It is a matter of many weeks now—diversified indeed by some long drives into the mountains behind us and a memorable sail to Genoa across the blue and purple waters that drowned Shelley—since I began a laboured and futile imitation of *The Prince*. I sat up late last night with the jumbled accumulation ; and at last made a little fire of olive twigs and burned it all, sheet by sheet—to begin again clear this morning.

But incidentally I have re-read most of Machiavelli, not excepting those scandalous letters of his to Vettori, and it seems to me, now that I have released myself altogether from his literary precedent, that he still has his use for me. In spite of his vast prestige I claim kindred with him and set his name upon my title-page, in partial intimation of the matter of my story. He takes me with sympathy not only by reason of the dream he pursued and the humanity of his politics, but by the mixture of his nature. His vices come in, essential to my issue. He is dead and gone, all his immediate correlations to party and faction have faded to insignificance, leaving only on the one hand his broad method and conceptions, and upon the other his intimate living personality, exposed down to its salacious corners as the soul of no contemporary can ever be exposed. Of those double strands it is I have to write, of the subtle protesting perplexing play of instinctive passion and desire against too abstract a dream of statesmanship. But things that seemed to lie very far apart in Machiavelli's time have come near to one another ; it is no simple story of white passions struggling against the red that I have to tell.

The state-making dream is a very old dream indeed in the world's history. It plays too small a part in novels. Plato and Confucius are but the highest of a great host of minds that have had a kindred aspiration, have dreamt of a world of men better ordered, happier, finer, securer. They imagined cities grown more powerful and peoples made rich and multitudinous by their efforts, they thought in terms of harbours and shining navies, great roads engineered marvellously, jungles cleared and deserts conquered, the ending of muddle and diseases and dirt and misery ; the ending of confusions that waste human possibilities ; they thought of these things with passion and desire as other men think of the soft lines and tender beauty of women. Thousands of men there are to-day almost mastered by this white passion of state-craft, and in nearly every one who reads and thinks you could find, I suspect, some sort of answering response. But in every one it presents itself extraordinarily entangled and mixed up with other, more intimate things.

So it was with Machiavelli. I picture him at San Casciano as he lived in retirement upon his property after the fall of the Republic, perhaps with a twinge of the torture that punished his conspiracy still lurking in his limbs. Such twinges could not stop his dreaming. Then it was *The Prince* was written. All day he went about his personal affairs, saw homely neighbours, dealt with his family, gave vent to everyday passions. He would sit in the shop of Donato del Corno gossiping curiously among vicious company, or pace the lonely woods of his estate, book in hand, full of bitter meditations. In the evening he returned home and went to his study. At the entrance, he says, he pulled off his peasant clothes covered with the dust and dirt of that immediate life, washed himself, put on his " noble court dress," closed the door on the world of toiling and getting, private loving, private hating and personal regrets, sat down with a sigh of contentment to those wider dreams.

I like to think of him so, with brown books before him lit by the light of candles in silver candlesticks, or heading some new chapter of *The Prince*, with a grey quill in his clean fine hand.

So writing, he becomes a symbol for me, and none the less because of his animal humour, his queer indecent side, and because of such lapses into utter meanness as that which made him sound the note of the begging-letter writer even in his " Dedication," reminding His Magnificence very urgently, as if it were the gist of his matter, of the continued malignity of fortune in his affairs. These flaws complete him. They are my reason for preferring him as a symbol to Plato, of whose indelicate side we know nothing, and whose correspondence with Dionysius of Syracuse has perished ; or to Confucius who travelled China in search of a Prince he might instruct, with lapses and indignities now lost in the mists of ages. They have achieved the apotheosis of individual forgetfulness, and

Plato has the added glory of that acquired beauty, that bust of the Indian Bacchus which is now indissolubly mingled with his tradition.   They have passed into the world of the ideal, and every humbug takes his freedoms with their names.   But Machiavelli, more recent and less popular, is still all human and earthly, a fallen brother—and at the same time that nobly dressed and nobly dreaming writer at the desk.

That vision of the strengthened and perfected state is protagonist in my story.   But as I re-read *The Prince* and thought out the manner of my now abandoned project, I came to perceive how that stir and whirl of human thought one calls by way of embodiment the French Revolution, has altered absolutely the approach to such a question.   Machiavelli, like Plato and Pythagoras and Confucius two hundred odd decades before him, saw only one method by which a thinking man, himself not powerful, might do the work of state building, and that was by seizing the imagination of a Prince.   Directly these men turned their thoughts towards realisation, their attitudes became—what shall I call it ?—secretarial.   Machiavelli, it is true, had some little doubts about the particular Prince he wanted, whether it was Cæsar Borgia or Giuliano or Lorenzo, but a Prince it had to be.   Before I saw clearly the differences of our own time I searched my mind for the modern equivalent of a Prince.   At various times I redrafted a parallel dedication to the Prince of Wales, to the Emperor William, to Mr. Evesham, to a certain newspaper proprietor who was once my schoolfellow at City Merchants', to Mr. J. D. Rockefeller—all of them men in their several ways and circumstances and possibilities, princely.   Yet in every case my pen bent of its own accord towards irony because—because, although at first I did not realise it, I myself am just as free to be a prince.   The appeal was unfair.   The old sort of Prince, the old little principality has vanished from the world.   The commonweal is one man's absolute estate and responsibility no more.   In Machiavelli's time it was indeed to an extreme degree one man's affair.   But the days of the Prince who planned and directed and was the source and centre of all power are ended.   We are in a condition of affairs infinitely more complex, in which every prince and statesman is something of a servant and every intelligent human being something of a Prince.   No magnificent pensive Lorenzos remain any more in this world for secretarial hopes.

In a sense it is wonderful how power has vanished, in a sense wonderful how it has increased.   I sit here, an unarmed discredited man, at a small writing-table in a little defenceless dwelling among the vines, and no human being can stop my pen except by the deliberate self-immolation of murdering me, nor destroy its fruits except by theft and crime.   No King, no council, can seize and torture me ; no Church, no nation silence me.   Such powers of ruthless and complete suppression

have vanished.   But that is not because power has diminished,
but because it has increased and become multitudinous,
because it has dispersed itself and specialised.   It is no longer
a negative power we have, but positive ; we cannot prevent,
but we can do.   This age, far beyond all previous ages, is full
of powerful men, men who might, if they had the will for it,
achieve stupendous things.

The things that might be done to-day !   The things indeed
that are being done !   It is the latter that give one so vast a
sense of the former.   When I think of the progress of physical
and mechanical science, of medicine and sanitation during the
last century, when I measure the increase in general education
and average efficiency, the power now available for human
service, the merely physical increment, and compare it with
anything that has ever been at man's disposal before, and
when I think what a little straggling, incidental, undisciplined
and unco-ordinated minority of inventors, experimenters,
educators, writers and organisers has achieved this development of human possibilities, achieved it in spite of the disregard and aimlessness of the huge majority, and the passionate
resistance of the active dull, my imagination grows giddy with
dazzling intimations of the human splendours the justly organised state may yet attain.   I glimpse for a bewildering instant
the heights that may be scaled, the splendid enterprises made
possible. . . .

But the appeal goes out now in other forms, in a book that
catches at thousands of readers for the eye of a Prince diffused.
It is the old appeal indeed for the unification of human effort,
the ending of confusions, but instead of the Machiavellian
deference to a flattered lord, a man cries out of his heart to the
unseen fellowship about him.   The last written dedication of
all those I burned last night, was to no single man, but to the
socially constructive passion—in any man. . . .

There is, moreover, a second great difference in kind between
my world and Machiavelli's.   We are discovering women.   It
is as if they had come across a vast interval since his time,
into the very chamber of the statesman.

§ 2

In Machiavelli's outlook the interest of womanhood was in
a region of life almost infinitely remote from his statecraft.
They were the vehicle of children, but only Imperial Rome
and the new world of to-day have ever had an inkling of the
significance that might give them in the state.   They did
their work, he thought, as the ploughed earth bears its crops.
Apart from their function of fertility they gave a humorous
twist to life, stimulated worthy men to toil, and wasted the
hours of Princes.   He left the thought of women outside with
his other dusty things when he went into his study to write,
dismissed them from his mind.   But our modern world is

burthened with its sense of the immense, now half articulate,
significance of women. They stand now, as it were, close
beside the silver candlesticks, speaking as Machiavelli writes,
until he stays his pen and turns to discuss his writing with
them.

It is this gradual discovery of sex as a thing collectively
portentous that I have to mingle with my statecraft if my
picture is to be true, which has turned me at length from a
treatise to the telling of my own story. In my life I have
paralleled very closely the slow realisations that are going
on in the world about me. I began life ignoring women, they
came to me at first perplexing and dishonouring ; only very
slowly and very late in my life and after misadventure, did I
gauge the power and beauty of the love of man and woman
and learn how it must needs frame a justifiable vision of the
ordered world. Love has brought me to disaster, because my
career had been planned regardless of its possibility and value.
But Machiavelli, it seems to me, when he went into his study,
left not only the earth of life outside but its unsuspected
soul. . . .

§ 3

Like Machiavelli at San Casciano, if I may take this analogy
one step further, I too am an exile. Office and leading are
closed to me. The political career that promised so much for
me is shattered and ended for ever.

I look out from this vine-wreathed verandah under the
branches of a stone pine ; I see wide and far across a purple
valley whose sides are terraced and set with houses of pink and
ivory, the Gulf of Liguria gleaming sapphire blue, and cloud-
like baseless mountains hanging in the sky, and I think of lank
and coaly steamships heaving on the grey rollers of the English
Channel and darkling streets wet with rain, I recall as if I were
back there the busy exit from Charing Cross, the cross and the
money-changers' offices, the splendid grime of giant London
and the crowds going perpetually to and fro, the lights by
night and the urgency and eventfulness of that great rain-
swept heart of the modern world.

It is difficult to think we have left that—for many years if
not for ever. In thought I walk once more in Palace Yard
and hear the clink and clatter of hansoms and the quick quiet
whirr of motors ; I go in vivid recent memories through the
stir in the lobbies, I sit again at eventful dinners in those old
dining-rooms like cellars below the House—dinners that ended
with shrill division bells, I think of huge clubs swarming and
excited by the bulletins of that electoral battle that was for
me the opening opportunity. I see the stencilled names and
numbers go up on the green baize, constituency after constituency, amidst murmurs or loud shouting. . . .

It is over for me now and vanished. That opportunity will

come no more. Very probably you have heard already some crude inaccurate version of our story and why I did not take office, and have formed your partial judgment on me. And so it is I sit now at my stone table, half out of life already, in a warm, large, shadowy leisure, splashed with sunlight and hung with vine tendrils, with paper before me to distil such wisdom as I can, as Machiavelli in his exile sought to do, from the things I have learned and felt during the career that has ended now in my divorce.

I climbed high and fast from small beginnings. I had the mind of my party. I do not know where I might not have ended, but for this red blaze that came out of my unguarded nature and closed my career for ever.

CHAPTER TWO

BROMSTEAD AND MY FATHER

§ 1

I DREAMT first of states and cities and political things
when I was a little boy in knickerbockers.

When I think of how such things began in my mind,
there comes back to me the memory of an enormous bleak
room with its ceiling going up to heaven and its floor covered
irregularly with patched and defective oilcloth and a dingy mat
or so and a " surround " as they call it, of dark stained wood.
Here and there against the wall are trunks and boxes. There
are cupboards on either side of the fireplace and bookshelves
with books above them, and on the wall and rather tattered
is a large yellow-varnished geological map of the South of
England. Over the mantel is a huge lump of white coral
rock and several big fossil bones, and above that hangs the
portrait of a brainy gentleman, sliced in half and displaying
an interior of intricate detail and much vigour of colouring.
It is the floor I think of chiefly ; over the oilcloth of which,
assumed to be land, spread towns and villages and forts of
wooden bricks ; there are steep square hills (geologically,
volumes of Orr's *Cyclopædia of the Sciences*) and the cracks and
spaces of the floor and the bare brown surround were the water
channels and open sea of that continent of mine.

I still remember with infinite gratitude the great-uncle to
whom I owe my bricks. He must have been one of those
rare adults who have not forgotten the chagrins and dreams of
childhood. He was a prosperous west of England builder ;
including my father he had three nephews, and for each of
them he caused a box of bricks to be made by an out-of-work
carpenter, not the insufficient supply of the toyshop, you
understand, but a really adequate quantity of bricks made out
of oak and shaped and smoothed, bricks about five inches by
two and a half by one, and half-bricks and quarter-bricks to
correspond. There were hundreds of them, many hundreds.
I could build six towers as high as myself with them, and there
seemed quite enough for every engineering project I could
undertake. I could build whole towns with streets and houses
and churches and citadels ; I could bridge every gap in the
oilcloth and make causeways over crumpled spaces (which I
feigned to be morasses), and on a keel of whole bricks it was
possible to construct ships to push over the high seas to the
remotest port in the room. And a disciplined population,
that rose at last by sedulous begging on birthdays and all convenient occasions to well over two hundred, of lead sailors
and soldiers, horse, foot and artillery, inhabited this world.

Justice has never been done to bricks and soldiers by those who write about toys. The praises of the toy theatre have been a common theme for essayists, the planning of the scenes, the painting and cutting out of the caste, penny plain twopence coloured, the stink and glory of the performance and the final conflagration. I had such a theatre once, but I never loved it nor hoped for much from it ; my bricks and soldiers were my perpetual drama. I recall an incessant variety of interests. There was the mystery and charm of the complicated buildings one could make, with long passages and steps and windows through which one peeped into their intricacies, and by means of slips of card one could make slanting ways in them, and send marbles rolling from top to base and thence out into the hold of a waiting ship. Then there were the fortresses and gun emplacements and covered ways in which one's soldiers went. And there was commerce ; the shops and markets and storerooms full of nasturtium seed, thrift-seed, lupin beans and suchlike provender from the garden ; such stuff one stored in match-boxes and pill-boxes, or packed in sacks of old glove fingers tied up with thread and sent off by waggons along the great military road to the beleaguered fortress on the Indian frontier beyond the worn places that were dismal swamps. And there were battles on the way.

That great road is still clear in my memory. I was given, I forget by what benefactor, certain particularly fierce Red Indians of lead—I have never seen such soldiers since—and for these my father helped me to make tepees of brown paper, and I settled them in a hitherto desolate country under the frowning nail-studded cliffs of an ancient trunk. Then I conquered them and garrisoned their land. (Alas ! they died, no doubt through contact with civilisation—one my mother trod on—and their land became a wilderness again and was ravaged for a time by a clockwork crocodile of vast proportions.) And out towards the coal-scuttle was a region near the impassable thickets of the rugged hearthrug where lived certain china Zulus brandishing spears, and a mountain country of rudely piled bricks concealing the most devious and enchanting caves and several mines of gold and silver paper. Among these rocks a number of survivors from a Noah's Ark made a various, dangerous, albeit frequently invalid and crippled fauna, and I was wont to increase the uncultivated wildness of this region further by trees of privet-twigs from the garden hedge and box from the garden borders. By these territories went my Imperial Road carrying produce to and fro, bridging gaps in the oilcloth, tunnelling through Encyclopædic hills—one tunnel was three volumes long—defended as occasion required by camps of paper tents or brick block-houses, and ending at last in a magnificently engineered ascent to a fortress on the cliffs commanding the Indian reservation.

My games upon the floor must have spread over several years

and developed from small beginnings, incorporating now this suggestion and now that. They stretch, I suppose, from seven to eleven or twelve. I played them intermittently, and they bulk now in the retrospect far more significantly than they did at the time. I played them in bursts, and then forgot them for long periods ; through the spring and summer I was mostly out of doors, and school and classes caught me early. And in the retrospect I see them all not only magnified and transfigured, but fore-shortened and confused together. A clockwork railway, I seem to remember, came and went ; one or two clockwork boats, toy sailing-ships that, being keeled, would do nothing but lie on their beam ends on the floor ; a detestable lot of cavalrymen, undersized and gilt all over, given me by a maiden aunt, and very much what one might expect from an aunt, that I used as Nero used his Christians to ornament my public buildings ; and I finally melted some into fratricidal bullets, and therewith blew the rest to flat splashes of lead by means of a brass cannon in the garden.

I find this empire of the floor much more vivid and detailed in my memory now than many of the owners of the skirts and legs and boots that went gingerly across its territories. Occasionally, alas ! they stooped to scrub, abolishing in one universal destruction the slow growth of whole days of civilised development. I still remember the hatred and disgust of these catastrophes. Like Noah I was given warnings. Did I disregard them, coarse red hands would descend, plucking garrisons from fortresses and sailors from ships, jumbling them up in their wrong boxes, clumsily so that their rifles and swords were broken, sweeping the splendid curves of the Imperial Road into heaps of ruins, casting the jungle growth of Zululand into the fire.

"Well, Master Dick," the voice of this cosmic calamity would say, "you ought to have put them away last night. No ! I can't wait until you've sailed them all away in ships. I got my work to do, and do it I will."

And in no time all my continents and lands were swirling water and swiping strokes of house-flannel.

That was the worst of my giant visitants, but my mother too, dear lady, was something of a terror to this microcosm. She wore spring-sided boots, a kind of boot now vanished, I believe, from the world, with dull bodies and shiny toes, and a silk dress with flounces that were very destructive to the more hazardous viaducts of the Imperial Road. She was always, I seem to remember, fetching me ; fetching me for a meal, fetching me for a walk or, detestable absurdity ! fetching me for a wash and brush-up, and she never seemed to understand anything whatever of the political systems across which she came to me. Also she forbade all toys on Sundays except the bricks for church-building and the soldiers for church parade, or a Scriptural use of the remains of the Noah's Ark mixed up with a wooden Swiss dairy farm.   But she really did not know whether a thing was a church or not unless it positively bristled with cannon, and many a Sunday afternoon have I played Chicago (with the fear of God in my heart) under an infidel pretence that it was a new sort of ark rather elaborately done.

Chicago, I must explain, was based upon my father's description of the pig slaughterings in that city and certain pictures I had seen.   You made your beasts—which were all the ark lot really, provisionally conceived as pigs—go up elaborate approaches to a central pen, from which they went down a cardboard slide four at a time, and dropped most satisfyingly down a brick shaft, and pitter-litter over some steep steps to where a head slaughterman (*né* Noah) strung a cotton loop round their legs and sent them by pin hooks along a wire to a second slaughterman with a chipped foot (formerly Mrs. Noah), who, if I remember rightly, converted them into Army sausage by means of a portion of the inside of an old alarum clock.

My mother did not understand my games, but my father did.   He wore bright-coloured socks and carpet slippers when he was indoors—my mother disliked boots in the house—and he would sit down on my little chair and survey the microcosm on the floor with admirable understanding and sympathy.

It was he who gave me most of my toys and, I more than suspect, most of my ideas. "Here's some corrugated iron," he would say, "suitable for roofs and fencing," and hand me a lump of that stiff crinkled paper that is used for packing medicine bottles.   Or, "Dick, do you see the tiger loose near the Imperial Road ?—won't do for your cattle ranch."   And I would find a bright new lead tiger like a special creation at large in the world, and demanding a hunting expedition and much elaborate effort to get him safely housed in the city menagerie beside the captured dragon crocodile, tamed now, and his key lost and the heart and spring gone out of him.

And to the various irregular reading of my father I owe the inestimable blessing of never having a boy's book in my boyhood except those of Jules Verne.   But my father used to get books for himself and me from the Bromstead Institute, Fenimore Cooper and Mayne Reid and illustrated histories ; one of the Russo-Turkish war and one of Napier's expedition to Abyssinia I read from end to end ; Stanley and Livingstone, lives of Wellington, Napoleon and Garibaldi, and back volumes of *Punch* from which I derived conceptions of foreign and domestic politics it has taken years of adult reflection to correct.   And at home permanently we had Wood's *Natural History*, a brand-new illustrated Green's *History of the English People*, Irving's *Companions of Columbus*, a great number of unbound parts of some geographical work, a *Voyage Round the World* I think it was called, with pictures of foreign places, and Clarke's *New Testament* with a map of Palestine, and a variety of other informing books bought at sales.   There was a Sowerby's *Botany* also, with thousands of carefully tinted pictures of British plants, and one or two other important works in the sitting-room. I was allowed to turn these over and even lie on the floor with them on Sundays and other occasions of exceptional cleanliness.

And in the attic I found one day a very old forgotten map after the fashion of a bird's-eye view, representing the Crimea, that fascinated me and kept me for hours navigating its waters with a pin.

§ 2

My father was a lank-limbed man in easy shabby tweed clothes and with his hands in his trouser pockets. He was a science teacher, taking a number of classes at the Bromstead Institute in Kent under the old Science and Art Department, and " visiting " various schools ; and our resources were eked out by my mother's income of nearly a hundred pounds a year, and by his inheritance of a terrace of three palatial but structurally unsound stucco houses near Bromstead Station.

They were big clumsy residences in the earliest Victorian style, interminably high and with deep damp basements and downstairs coal-cellars and kitchens that suggested an architect vindictively devoted to the discomfort of the servant class. If so, he had overreached himself and defeated his end, for no servant would stay in them unless for exceptional wages or exceptional tolerance of inefficiency or exceptional freedom in repartee. Every storey in the house was from twelve to fifteen feet high (which would have been cool and pleasant in a hot climate), and the stairs went steeply up, to end at last in attics too inaccessible for occupation. The ceilings had vast plaster cornices of classical design, fragments of which would sometimes fall unexpectedly, and the wall-papers were bold and gigantic in pattern and much variegated by damp and ill-mended rents.

As my father was quite unable to let more than one of these houses at a time, and that for the most part to eccentric and undesirable tenants, he thought it politic to live in one of the two others, and devote the rent he received from the let one, when it was let, to the incessant necessary repairing of all three. He also did some of the repairing himself and, smoking a bull-dog pipe the while, which my mother would not allow him to do in the house, he cultivated vegetables in a sketchy, unpunctual and not always successful manner in the unoccupied gardens. The three houses faced north, and the back of the one we occupied was covered by a grape-vine that yielded, I remember, small green grapes for pies in the spring, and imperfectly ripe black grapes in favourable autumns for the purposes of dessert. The grape-vine played an important part in my life, for my father broke his neck while he was pruning it when I was thirteen.

My father was what is called a man of ideas, but they were not always good ideas. My grandfather had been a private schoolmaster and one of the founders of the College of Preceptors, and my father had assisted him in his school until increasing competition and diminishing attendance had made it evident that the days of small private schools kept by unqualified persons were numbered. Thereupon my father had roused himself and had qualified as a science teacher under the Science and Art Department, which in those days had charge of the scientific and artistic education of the mass of the English population, and had thrown himself into science teaching and the earning of government grants therefor with great if transitory zeal and success.

I do not remember anything of my father's earlier and more energetic time. I was the child of my parents' middle years ; they married when my father was thirty-five and my mother past forty, and I saw only the last decadent phase of his educational career.

The Science and Art Department has vanished altogether from the world, and people are forgetting it now with the utmost readiness and generosity. Part of its substance and staff and spirit survive, more or less completely digested into the Board of Education. . . . The world does move on, even in its government. It is wonderful how many of the clumsy and limited governing bodies of my youth and early manhood have given place now to more scientific and efficient machinery. When I was a boy, Bromstead, which is now a borough, was ruled by a strange body called a Local Board—it was the Age of Boards—and I still remember indistinctly my father rejoicing at the breakfast-table over the liberation of London from the corrupt and devastating control of a Metropolitan Board of Works. Then there were also School Boards ; I was already practically in politics before the London School Board was absorbed by the spreading tentacles of the London County Council.

It gives a measure of the newness of our modern ideas of the State to remember that the very beginnings of public education lie within my father's lifetime, and that many most intelligent and patriotic people were shocked beyond measure at the State doing anything of the sort. When he was born, totally illiterate people who could neither read a book nor write more than perhaps a clumsy signature, were to be found everywhere in England ; and great masses of the population were getting no instruction at all. Only a few schools flourished upon the patronage of exceptional parents ; all over the country the old endowed grammar schools were to be found sinking and dwindling ; many of them had closed altogether. In the new great centres of population multitudes of children were sweated in the factories, darkly ignorant and wretched, and the under-equipped and under-staffed National and British schools, supported by voluntary contributions and sectarian rivalries, made an ineffectual fight against this festering darkness. It was a condition of affairs clamouring for remedies, but there was an immense amount of indifference and prejudice to be overcome before any remedies were possible. Perhaps some day some industrious and lucid historian will disentangle all the muddle of impulses and antagonisms, the commercialism, utilitarianism, obstinate conservatism, humanitarian enthusiasm, out of which our present educational organisation arose. I have long since come to believe it necessary that all new social institutions should be born in confusion, and that at first they should present chiefly crude and ridiculous aspects. The distrust of government in the Victorian days was far too great, and the general intelligence far too low, to permit the State to go about the new business it was taking up in a business-like way, to train teachers, build and equip schools, endow pedagogic research, and provide properly written school-books. These things it was felt *must* be provided by individual and local effort, and since it was manifest that it was individual and local effort that were in default, it was reluctantly agreed to stimulate them by money payments. The State set up a machinery of examination both in Science and Art and for the elementary schools ; and payments, known technically as grants, were made in accordance with the examination results attained, to such schools as Providence might see fit to send into the world. In this way it was felt the Demand would be established that would, according to the beliefs of that time, inevitably ensure the Supply. An industry of " Grant earning " was created, and this would give education as a necessary by-product.

In the end this belief was found to need qualification, but Grant-earning was still in full activity when I was a small boy. So far as the Science and Art Department and my father are concerned, the task of examination was entrusted to eminent scientific men, for the most part quite unaccustomed to teaching. You see, if they also were teaching classes similar to those they examined, it was feared that injustice might be done. Year after year these eminent persons set questions and employed subordinates to read and mark the increasing thousands of answers that ensued, and having no doubt the national ideal of fairness well developed in their minds, they were careful each year to re-read the preceding papers before composing the current one, in order to see what it was usual to ask. As a result of this, in the course of a few years the recurrence and permutation of questions became almost calculable, and since the practical object of the teaching was to teach people not science, but how to write answers to these questions, the industry of Grant-earning assumed a form easily distinguished from any kind of genuine education whatever.

Other remarkable compromises had also to be made with

the spirit of the age. The unfortunate conflict between
Religion and Science prevalent at this time was mitigated, if
I remember rightly, by making graduates in arts and priests
in the established church Science Teachers *ex officio*, and
leaving local and private enterprise to provide schools,
diagrams, books, material, according to the conceptions of
efficiency prevalent in the district. Private enterprise made a
particularly good thing of the books. A number of competing
firms of publishers sprang into existence specialising in Science
and Art Department work ; they set themselves to produce
text-books that should supply exactly the quantity and
quality of knowledge necessary for every stage of each of five-
and-twenty subjects into which desirable science was divided,
and copies and models and instructions that should give precisely the method and gestures esteemed as proficiency in art.
Every section of each book was written in the idiom found to
be most satisfactory to the examiners, and test questions extracted from papers set in former years were appended to every
chapter. By means of these last the teacher was able to train
his class to the highest level of grant-earning efficiency, and
very naturally he cast all other methods of exposition aside.
First he posed his pupils with questions and then dictated
model replies.

That was my father's method of instruction. I attended his
classes as an elementary Grant-earner from the age of ten until
his death, and it is so I remember him, sitting on the edge of a
table, smothering a yawn occasionally and giving out the in-
fallible formulæ to the industriously scribbling class sitting in
rows of desks before him. Occasionally he would slide to his
feet and go to a blackboard on an easel and draw on that very
slowly and deliberately in coloured chalks a diagram for the
class to copy in coloured pencils, and sometimes he would display a specimen or arrange an experiment for them to see.
The room in the Institute in which he taught was equipped
with a certain amount of apparatus prescribed as necessary for
subject this and subject that by the Science and Art Department, and this my father would supplement with maps and
diagrams and drawings of his own.

But he never really did experiments, except that in the
class in systematic botany he sometimes made us tease common
flowers to pieces. He did not do experiments if he could
possibly help it, because in the first place they used up time
and gas for the Bunsen burner and good material in a ruinous
fashion, and in the second they were, in his rather careless and
sketchy hands, apt to endanger the apparatus of the Institute
and even the lives of his students. Then thirdly, real experiments involved washing up. And moreover they always
turned out wrong, and sometimes misled the too observant
learner very seriously and opened demoralising controversies.
Quite early in life I acquired an almost ineradicable sense of

the unscientific perversity of Nature and the impassable gulf that is fixed between systematic science and elusive fact. I knew, for example, that in science, whether it be subject XII., Organic Chemistry, or subject XVII., Animal Physiology, when you blow into a glass of lime water it instantly becomes cloudy, and if you continue to blow it clears again, whereas in truth you may blow into the stuff from the lime-water bottle until you are crimson in the face and painful under the ears, and it never becomes cloudy at all. And I knew, too, that in science if you put potassium chlorate into a retort and heat it over a Bunsen burner, oxygen is disengaged and may be collected over water, whereas in real life if you do anything of the sort the vessel cracks with a loud report, the potassium chlorate descends sizzling upon the flame, the experimenter says "Oh! Damn!" with astonishing heartiness and distinctness, and a lady student in the back seats gets up and leaves the room.

Science is the organised conquest of Nature, and I can quite understand that ancient libertine refusing to co-operate in her own undoing. And I can quite understand, too, my father's preference for what he called an illustrative experiment, which was simply an arrangement of the apparatus in front of the class with nothing whatever by way of material, and the Bunsen burner clean and cool, and then a slow luminous description of just what you did put in it when you were so ill-advised as to carry the affair beyond illustration, and just exactly what ought anyhow to happen when you did. He had considerable powers of vivid expression, so that in this way he could make us see all he described. The class, freed from any unpleasant nervous tension, could draw this still life without flinching, and if any part was too difficult to draw, then my father would produce a simplified version on the blackboard to be copied instead. And he would also write on the blackboard any exceptionally difficult but grant-earning words, such as "empyreumatic" or "botryoidal."

Some words in constant use he rarely explained. I remember once sticking up my hand and asking him in the full flow of description, "Please, sir, what is flocculent?"

"The precipitate is."

"Yes, sir, but what does it mean?"

"Oh! flocculent!" said my father, "flocculent! Why—" he extended his hand and arm and twiddled his fingers for a second in the air. "Like that," he said.

I thought the explanation sufficient, but he paused for a moment after giving it. "As in a flock bed, you know," he added, and resumed his discourse.

§ 3

My father, I am afraid, carried a natural incompetence in practical affairs to an exceptionally high level. He combined

practical incompetence, practical enterprise, and a thoroughly
sanguine temperament in a manner that I have never seen
paralleled in any human being.   He was always trying to do
new things in the briskest manner, under the suggestion of
books or papers or his own spontaneous imagination, and as he
had never been trained to do anything whatever in his life
properly, his futilities were extensive and thorough.   At one
time he nearly gave up his classes for intensive culture, so
enamoured was he of its possibilities ; the peculiar pungency
of the manure he got, in pursuit of a chemical theory of his
own, has scarred my olfactory memories for a lifetime.   The
intensive culture phase is very clear in my memory ; it came
near the end of his career and when I was between eleven and
twelve.   I was mobilised to gather caterpillars on several
occasions, and assisted in nocturnal raids upon the slugs by
lantern-light that wrecked my preparation work for school
next day.   My father dug up both lawns, and trenched and
manured in spasms of immense vigour alternating with periods
of paralysing distaste for the garden.   And for weeks he talked
about eight hundred pounds an acre at every meal.

A garden, even when it is not exasperated by intensive
methods, is a thing as exacting as a baby, its moods have to
be watched ; it does not wait upon the cultivator's convenience,
but has times of its own.   Intensive culture greatly increases
this disposition to trouble mankind ; it makes a garden touchy
and hysterical, a drugged and demoralised and over-irritated
garden.   My father got at cross-purposes with our two patches
at an early stage.   Everything grew wrong from first to last,
and if my father's manures intensified nothing else, they certainly intensified the Primordial Curse.   The peas were eaten
in the night before they were three inches high, the beans bore
nothing but blight, the only apparent result of a spraying of
the potatoes was to develop a penchant in the cat for being ill
indoors, the cucumber frames were damaged by the catapulting
of boys going down the lane at the back, and all our cucumbers
were mysteriously embittered.   That lane with its occasional
passers-by did much to wreck the intensive scheme, because
my father always stopped work and went indoors if any one
watched him.   His special manure was apt to arouse a troublesome spirit of inquiry in hardy natures.

In digging his rows and shaping his patches he neglected
the guiding string and trusted to his eye altogether too much,
and the consequent obliquity and the various wind-breaks
and scare-crows he erected, and particularly an irrigation
contrivance he began and never finished by which everything
was to be watered at once by means of pieces of gutter from
the roof and outhouses of Number 2, and a large and particularly obstinate clump of elder-bushes in the abolished hedge
that he had failed to destroy entirely either by axe or by fire,
combined to give the gardens under intensive culture a singu-

larly desolate and disorderly appearance. He took steps towards the diversion of our house drain under the influence of the Sewage Utilisation Society; but happily he stopped in time. He hardly completed any of the operations he began; something else became more urgent or simply he tired; a considerable area of the Number 2 territory was never even dug up.

In the end the affair irritated him beyond endurance. Never was a man less horticulturally-minded. The clamour of these vegetables he had launched into the world for his service and assistance wore out his patience. He would walk into the garden the happiest of men after a day or so of disregard, talking to me of history perhaps or social organisation, or summarising some book he had read. He talked to me of anything that interested him, regardless of my limitations. Then he would begin to note the growth of the weeds. "This won't do," he would say and pull up a handful.

More weeding would follow and the talk would become fragmentary. His hands would become earthy, his nails black, weeds would snap off in his careless grip, leaving the roots behind. The world would darken. He would look at his fingers with disgusted astonishment. "*Curse* these weeds!" he would say from his heart. His discourse was at an end. . . .

I have memories, too, of his sudden unexpected charges into the tranquillity of the house, his hands and clothes intensively enriched. He would come in like a whirlwind. "This damned stuff all over me and the Agricultural Chemistry Class at six! Bah! *Aaaaaah!*"

My mother would never learn not to attempt to break him off swearing on such occasions. She would remain standing a little stiffly in the scullery, refusing to assist him to the adjectival towel he sought.

"If you say such things——"

He would dance with rage and hurl the soap about. "The towel!" he would cry, flicking suds from his fingers in every direction; "the towel! I'll let the blithering class slide if you don't give me the towel! I'll give up everything, I tell you—everything!" . . .

At last with the failure of the lettuces came the breaking-point. I was in the little arbour learning Latin irregular verbs when it happened. I can see him still, his peculiar tenor voice still echoes in my brain, shouting his opinion of intensive culture for all the world to hear, and slashing away at that abominable mockery of a crop with a hoe. We had tied them up with bast only a week or so before, and now half were rotten and half had shot up into tall slender growths. He had the hoe in both hands and slogged. Great wipes he made, and at each stroke he said, "Take that!"

The air was thick with flying fragments of abortive salad. It was a fantastic massacre. It was the French Revolution of that cold tyranny, the vindictive overthrow of the pampered vegetable aristocrats. After he had assuaged his passion upon them, he turned for other prey ; he kicked holes in two of our noblest marrows, flicked off the heads of half a row of artichokes, and shied the hoe with a splended smash into the cucumber frame. Something of the awe of that moment returns to me as I write of it.

"Well, my boy, " he said, approaching with an expression of beneficent happiness, " I've done with gardening. Let's go for a walk like reasonable beings. I've had enough of this "—his face was convulsed for an instant with bitter resentment—" Pandering to cabbages."

§ 4

That afternoon's walk sticks in my memory for many reasons. One is that we went farther than I had ever been before ; far beyond Keston and nearly to Sevenoaks, coming back by train from Dunton Green, and the other is that my father as he went along talked about himself, not so much to me as to himself, and about life and what he had done with it. He monologued so that at times he produced an effect of weird world-forgetfulness. I listened puzzled, and at that time not understanding many things that afterwards became plain to me. It is only in recent years that I have discovered the pathos of that monologue ; how friendless my father was and uncompanioned in his thoughts and feelings, and what a hunger he may have felt for the sympathy of the undeveloped youngster who trotted by his side.

" I'm no gardener," he said, " I'm no anything. Why the devil did I start gardening ?

" I suppose man was created to mind a garden. . . . But the Fall let us out of that ! What was *I* created for ? God ! what was *I* created for ? . . .

" Slaves to matter ! Minding inanimate things ! It doesn't suit me, you know. I've got no hands and no patience. I've mucked about with life. Mucked about with life." He suddenly addressed himself to me, and for an instant I started like an eavesdropper discovered. " Whatever you do, boy, whatever you do, make a Plan. Make a good Plan and stick to it. Find out what life is about—*I* never have—and set yourself to do—whatever you ought to do. I admit it's a puzzle. . . .

" Those damned houses have been the curse of my life. Stucco white elephants ! Beastly cracked stucco with stains of green—black and green. Conferva and soot. . . . Property, they are ! . . . Beware of Things, Dick, beware of Things ! Before you know where you are you are waiting on them and minding them. They'll eat your life up. Eat up your hours and your blood and energy! When those houses came to me, I ought to have sold them—or fled the country. I ought to have cleared out. Sarcophagi—eaters of men! Oh! the hours and days of work, the nights of anxiety those vile houses have cost me! The painting! It worked up my arms; it got all over me. I stank of it. It made me ill. It isn't living—it's minding. . . .

"Property's the curse of life. Property! Ugh! Look at this country all cut up into silly little parallelograms, look at all those villas we passed just now and those potato patches and that tarred shanty and the hedge! Somebody's minding every bit of it like a dog tied to a cart's tail. Patching it and bothering about it. Bothering! Yapping at every passer-by. Look at that notice-board! One rotten worried little beast wants to keep us other rotten little beasts off *his* patch —God knows why! Look at the weeds in it. Look at the mended fence! . . . There's no property worth having, Dick, but money. That's only good to spend. All these things. Human souls buried under a cartload of blithering rubbish. . . .

"I'm not a fool, Dick. I have qualities, imagination, a sort of go. I ought to have made a better thing of life.

"I'm sure I could have done things. Only the old people pulled my leg. They started me wrong. They never started me at all. I only began to find out what life was like when I was nearly forty.

"If I'd gone to a university; if I'd had any sort of sound training, if I hadn't slipped into the haphazard places that came easiest. . . .

"Nobody warned me. Nobody. It isn't a world we live in, Dick; it's a cascade of accidents; it's a chaos exasperated by policemen! *You* be warned in time, Dick. You stick to a plan. Don't wait for any one to show you the way. Nobody will. There isn't a way till you make one. Get education, get a good education. Fight your way to the top. It's your only chance. I've watched you. You'll do no good at digging and property minding. There isn't a neighbour in Bromstead won't be able to skin you at such-like games. You and I are the brainy unstable kind, topside or nothing. And if ever those blithering houses come to you—don't have 'em. Give them away! Dynamite 'em—and off! *Live*, Dick! I'll get rid of them for you if I can, Dick, but remember what I say." . . .

So it was my father discoursed, if not in those particular words, yet exactly in that manner, as he slouched along the southward road, with resentful eyes becoming less resentful as he talked, and flinging out clumsy illustrative motions at the outskirts of Bromstead as we passed along them. That afternoon he hated Bromstead, from its foot-tiring pebbles up. He had no illusions about Bromstead or himself. I have the clearest impression of him in his garden-stained tweeds with a deer-stalker hat on the back of his head and presently a pipe sometimes between his teeth and sometimes in his gesticulating hand, as he became diverted by his talk from his original exasperation. . . .

This particular afternoon is no doubt mixed up in my memory with many other afternoons ; all sorts of things my father said and did at different times have got themselves referred to it ; it filled me at the time with a great unprecedented sense of fellowship and it has become the symbol now for all our intercourse together. If I didn't understand the things he said, I did the mood he was in. He gave me two very broad ideas in that talk and the talks I have mingled with it ; he gave them to me very clearly and they have remained fundamental in my mind ; one a sense of the extraordinary confusion and waste and planlessness of the human life that went on all about us ; and the other of a great ideal of order and economy which he called variously Science and Civilisation, and which, though I do not remember that he ever used that word, I suppose many people nowadays would identify with Socialism—as the Fabians expound it.

He was not very definite about this Science, you must understand, but he seemed always to be waving his hand towards it,—just as his contemporary Tennyson seems always to be doing—he belonged to his age and mostly his talk was destructive of the limited beliefs of his time, he led me to infer rather than actually told me that this Science was coming, a spirit of light and order, to the rescue of a world groaning and travailing in muddle for the want of it. . . .

§ 5

When I think of Bromstead nowadays I find it inseparably bound up with the disorders of my father's gardening, and the odd patchings and paintings that disfigured his houses. It was all of a piece with that.

Let me try and give something of the quality of Bromstead and something of its history. It is the quality and history of a thousand places round and about London, and round and about the other great centres of population in the world. Indeed it is in a measure the quality of the whole of this modern world from which we who have the statesman's passion struggle to evolve, and dream still of evolving order.

First, then, you must think of Bromstead a hundred and fifty years ago, as a narrow irregular little street of thatched houses strung out on the London and Dover Road, a little mellow sample unit of a social order that had a kind of completeness, at its level, of its own. At that time its population numbered a little under two thousand people, mostly engaged in agricultural work or in trades serving agriculture. There was a blacksmith, a saddler, a chemist, a doctor, a barber, a linen-draper (who brewed his own beer), a veterinary surgeon, a hardware shop, and two capacious inns. Round and about it were a number of pleasant gentlemen's seats, whose owners went frequently to London town in their coaches along the very tolerable high-road. The church was big enough to hold the whole population, were people minded to go to church ; and indeed a large proportion did go, and all who married were married in it, and everybody, to begin with, was christened at its font and buried at last in its yew-shaded graveyard. Everybody knew everybody in the place. It was, in fact, a definite place and a real human community in those days. There was a pleasant old market-house in the middle of the town with a weekly market, and an annual fair at which much cheerful merrymaking and homely intoxication occurred ; there was a pack of hounds which hunted within five miles of London Bridge, and the local gentry would occasionally enliven the place with valiant cricket matches for a hundred guineas a side, to the vast excitement of the entire population. It was very much the same sort of place that it had been for three or four centuries. A Bromstead Rip van Winkle from 1550 returning in 1750 would have found most of the old houses still as he had known them, the same trades a little improved and differentiated one from the other, the same roads rather more carefully tended, the Inns not very much altered, the ancient familiar market-house. The occasional wheeled traffic would have struck him as the most remarkable difference, next perhaps to the swaggering painted stone monuments instead of brasses and the protestant severity of the communion-table in the parish church—both from the material point of view very small things. A Rip van Winkle from 1350, again, would have noticed scarcely greater changes ; fewer clergy, more people, and particularly more people of the middling sort ; the glass in the windows of many of the houses, the stylish chimneys springing up everywhere would have impressed him, and such-like details. The place would have had the same boundaries, the same broad essential features, would have been still itself in the way that a man is still himself after he has " filled out " a little and grown a longer beard and changed his clothes.

But after 1750 something got hold of the world, something that was destined to alter the scale of every human affair.

That something was machinery, and a vague energetic disposition to improve material things. In another part of England ingenious people were beginning to use coal in smelting-iron, and were producing metal in abundance and metal castings in sizes that had hitherto been unattainable. Without warning or preparation, increment involving countless possibilities of further increment was coming to the strength of horses and men. " Power," all unsuspected, was flowing like a drug into the veins of the social body.

Nobody seems to have perceived this coming of power, and

nobody had calculated its probable consequences. Suddenly, almost inadvertently, people found themselves doing things that would have amazed their ancestors. They began to construct wheeled vehicles much more easily and cheaply than they had ever done before, to make up roads and move things about that had formerly been esteemed too heavy for locomotion, to join woodwork with iron nails instead of wooden pegs, to achieve all sorts of mechanical possibilities, to trade more freely and manufacture on a larger scale, to send goods abroad in a wholesale and systematic way, to bring back commodities from overseas, not simply spices and fine commodities, but goods in bulk. The new influence spread to agriculture, iron appliances replaced wooden, breeding of stock became systematic, paper-making and printing increased and cheapened. Roofs of slate and tile appeared amidst and presently prevailed over the original Bromstead thatch, the huge space of Common to the south was extensively enclosed, and what had been an ill-defined horse-track to Dover, only passable by adventurous coaches in dry weather, became the Dover Road, and was presently the route first of one and then of several daily coaches. The High Street was discovered to be too tortuous for these awakening energies, and a new road cut off its worst contortions. Residential villas appeared occupied by retired tradesmen and widows, who esteemed the place healthy, and by others of a strange new unoccupied class of people who had money invested in joint-stock enterprises. First one and then several boys' boarding-schools came, drawing their pupils from London—my grandfather's was one of these. London, twelve miles to the north-west, was making itself felt more and more.

But this was only the beginning of the growth period, the first trickle of the coming flood of mechanical power. Away in the north they were casting iron in bigger and bigger forms, working their way to the production of steel on a large scale, applying power in factories. Bromstead had almost doubled in size again long before the railway came ; there was hardly any thatch left in the High Street, but instead were houses with handsome brass-knockered front doors and several windows, and shops with shop-fronts all of square glass panes, and the place was lighted publicly now by oil lamps—previously only one flickering lamp outside each of the coaching inns had broken the nocturnal darkness. And there was talk, it long remained talk—of gas. The gasworks came in 1834, and about that date my father's three houses must have been built convenient for the London Road. They mark nearly the beginning of the real suburban quality ; they were let at first to City people still engaged in business.

And then hard on the gasworks had come the railway and cheap coal ; there was a wild outbreak of brickfields upon the claylands to the east, and the Great Growth had begun in

earnest. The agricultural placidities that had formerly come
to the very borders of the High Street were broken up north,
west, and south, by new roads. This enterprising person and
then that began to "run up" houses, irrespective of every
other enterprising person who was doing the same thing. A
Local Board came into existence, and with much hesitation
and pennywise economy inaugurated drainage works. Rates
became a common topic, a fact of accumulating importance.
Several chapels of zinc and iron appeared, and also a white
new church in commercial Gothic upon the common, and
another of red brick in the residential district out beyond the
brickfields towards Chessington.

The population doubled again and doubled again, and
became particularly teeming in the prolific "working-class"
district about the deep-rutted, muddy, coal-blackened roads
between the gasworks, Blodgett's laundries, and the railway
goods-yard. Weekly properties, that is to say small houses
built by small property owners and let by the week, sprang
up also in the Cage Fields, and presently extended right up the
London Road. A single national school in an inconvenient
situation set itself inadequately to collect subscriptions and
teach the swarming, sniffing, grimy offspring of this dingy new
population to read. The villages of Beckington, which used
to be three miles to the west, and Blamely four miles to the
east of Bromstead, were experiencing similar distensions and
proliferations, and grew out to meet us. All effect of locality
or community had gone from these places long before I was
born ; hardly any one knew any one ; there was no general
meeting-place any more, the old fairs were just common
nuisances haunted by gypsies, van showmen, Cheap Jacks
and London roughs, the churches were incapable of a quarter
of the population. One or two local papers of shameless
venality reported the proceedings of the local Bench and the
local Board, compelled tradesmen who were interested in these
affairs to advertise, used the epithet " Bromstedian " as one
expressing peculiar virtues, and so maintained in the general
mind a weak tradition of some local quality that embraced
us all. Then the parish graveyard filled up and became a
scandal, and an ambitious area with an air of appetite was
walled in by a Bromstead Cemetery Company, and planted
with suitably high-minded and sorrowful varieties of conifer.
A stone-mason took one of the earlier villas with a front
garden at the end of the High Street, and displayed a supply
of urns on pillars and headstones and crosses in stone, marble,
and granite that would have sufficed to commemorate in
elaborate detail the entire population of Bromstead as one
found it in 1750.

The cemetery was made when I was a little boy of five or
six ; I was in the full tide of building and growth from the
first ; the second railway with its station at Bromstead North

and the drainage followed when I was ten or eleven, and all my childish memories are of digging and wheeling, of woods invaded by building, roads gashed open and littered with iron pipes amidst a fearful smell of gas, of men peeped at and seen toiling away deep down in excavations, of hedges broken down and replaced by planks, of wheelbarrows and builders' sheds, of rivulets overtaken and swallowed up by drain-pipes. Big trees, and especially elms, cleared of undergrowth and left standing amid such things, acquired a peculiar tattered dinginess rather in the quality of needy widow women who have seen happier days.

The Ravensbrook of my earlier memories was a beautiful stream. It came into my world out of a mysterious Beyond, out of a garden, splashing brightly down a weir which had once been the weir of a mill. (Above the weir and inaccessible there were bulrushes growing in splendid clumps, and beyond that, pampas grass, yellow and crimson spikes of hollyhock, and blue suggestions of wonderland.) From the pool at the foot of this initial cascade it flowed in a leisurely fashion beside a footpath—there were two pretty thatched cottages on the left, and here were ducks, and there were willows on the right— and so came to where great trees grew on high banks on either hand and bowed closer, and at last met overhead. This part was difficult to reach because of an old fence, but a little boy might glimpse that long cavern of greenery by wading. Either I have actually seen kingfishers there, or my father has described them so accurately to me that he inserted them into my memory. I remember them there anyhow. Most of that overhung part I never penetrated at all, but followed the field path with my mother and met the stream again, where beyond there were flat meadows, Roper's meadows. The Ravens- brook went meandering across the middle of these, now between steep banks and now with wide shallows at the bends where the cattle waded and drank. Yellow and purple loose- strife and ordinary rushes grew in clumps along the bank, and now and then a willow. On rare occasions of rapture one might see a rat cleaning his whiskers at the water's edge. The deep places were rich with tangled weeds, and in them fishes lurked—to me they were big fishes—water-boatmen and water-beetles traversed the calm surface of these still deeps ; in one pool were yellow lilies and water-soldiers, and in the shoaly places hovering fleets of small fry basked in the sun- shine—to vanish in a flash at one's shadow. In one place, too, were Rapids, where the stream woke with a start from a dreamless brooding into foaming panic and babbled and hastened. Well do I remember that half-mile of rivulet ; all other rivers and cascades have their reference to it for me. And after I was eleven, and before we left Bromstead, all the delight and beauty of it was destroyed.

The volume of its water decreased abruptly—I suppose the

new drainage works that linked us up with Beckington, and made me first acquainted with the geological quality of the London clay, had to do with that—until only a week uncleansing trickle remained. That at first did not strike me as a misfortune. An adventurous small boy might walk dryshod in places hitherto inaccessible. But hard upon that came the pegs, the planks and carts and devastation. Roper's meadows, being no longer in fear of floods, were now to be slashed out into parallelograms of untidy road, and built upon with rows of working-class cottages. The roads came—horribly ; the houses followed. They seemed to rise in the night. People moved into them as soon as the roofs were on, mostly workmen and their young wives, and already in a year some of these raw houses stood empty again from defaulting tenants, with windows broken and wood-work warping and rotting. The Ravensbrook became a dump for old iron, rusty cans, abandoned boots and the like, and was a river only when unusual rains filled it for a day or so with an inky flood of surface water. . . .

That indeed was my most striking perception in the growth of Bromstead. The Ravensbrook had been important to my imaginative life ; that way had always been my first choice in all my walks with my mother, and its rapid swamping by the new urban growth made it indicative of all the other things that had happened just before my time, or were still, at a less dramatic pace, happening. I realised that building was the enemy. I began to understand why in every direction out of Bromstead one walked past scaffold-poles into litter, why fragments of broken brick and cinder mingled in every path, and the significance of the universal notice-boards, either white and new or a year old and torn and battered, promising sites, proffering houses to be sold or let, abusing and intimidating passers-by for fancied trespass, and protecting rights of way.

It is difficult to disentangle now what I understood at this time, and what I have since come to understand, but it seems to me that even in those childish days I was acutely aware of an invading and growing disorder. The serene rhythms of the old-established agriculture, I see now, were everywhere being replaced by cultivation under notice and snatch crops ; hedges ceased to be repaired, and were replaced by cheap iron railings or chunks of corrugated iron ; more and more hoardings sprang up, and contributed more and more to the nomad tribes of filthy paper scraps that flew before the wind and overspread the country. The outskirts of Bromstead were a maze of exploitation roads that led nowhere, that ended in tarred fences studded with nails (I don't remember barbed wire in those days ; I think the Zeitgeist did not produce that until later), and in trespass boards that used vehement language. Broken glass, tin cans, and ashes and paper abounded. Cheap glass, cheap tin, abundant fuel, and a free untaxed Press had rushed upon a world quite unprepared to dispose of these blessings when the fulness of enjoyment was past.

I suppose one might have persuaded oneself that all this was but the replacement of an ancient tranquillity, or at least an ancient balance, by a new order. Only to my eyes, quickened by my father's intimations, it was manifestly no order at all. It was a multitude of inco-ordinated fresh starts, each more sweeping and destructive than the last, and none of them ever really worked out to a ripe and satisfactory completion. Each left a legacy of products, houses, humanity, or what not, in its wake. It was a sort of progress that had bolted ; it was change out of hand, and going at an unprecedented pace nowhere in particular.

No, the Victorian epoch was not the dawn of a new era ; it was a hasty, trial experiment, a gigantic experiment of the most slovenly and wasteful kind. I suppose it was necessary ; I suppose all things are necessary. I suppose that before men will discipline themselves to learn and plan, they must first see in a hundred convincing forms the folly and muddle that come from headlong, aimless and haphazard methods. The nineteenth century was an age of demonstrations, some of them very impressive demonstrations, of the powers that have come to mankind ; but of permanent achievement, what will our descendants cherish ? It is hard to estimate what grains of precious metal may not be found in a mud torrent of human production on so large a scale, but will any one, a hundred years from now, consent to live in the houses the Victorians built, travel by their roads or railways, value the furnishings they made to live among or esteem, except for curious or historical reasons, their prevalent art and the clipped and limited literature that satisfied their souls ?

That age which bore me was indeed a world full of restricted and undisciplined people, overtaken by power, by possessions and great new freedoms, and unable to make any civilised use of them whatever ; stricken now by this idea and now by that, tempted first by one possession and then another to ill-considered attempts ; it was my father's exploitation of his villa gardens on the wholesale level. The whole of Bromstead as I remember it, and as I saw it last—it is a year ago now—is a dull useless boiling-up of human activities, an immense clustering of futilities. It is as unfinished as ever ; the builders' roads still run out and end in mid-field in their old fashion ; the various enterprises jumble in the same hopeless contradiction, if anything intensified. Pretentious villas jostle slums, and public-house and tin tabernacle glower at one another across the cat-haunted lot that intervenes. Roper's meadows are now quite frankly a slum ; back doors and sculleries gape towards the railway, their yards are hung with tattered washing unashamed ; and there seem to be more boards by the railway every time I pass, advertising pills and pickles, tonics and condiments, and suchlike solicitudes of a people with no natural health nor appetite left in them. . . .

Well, we have to do better. Failure is not failure nor waste wasted if it sweeps away illusion and lights the road to a plan.

§ 6

Chaotic indiscipline, ill-adjusted effort, spasmodic aims, these give the quality of all my Bromstead memories. The crowning one of them all rises to desolating tragedy. I remember now the wan spring sunshine of that Sunday morning, the stiff feeling of best clothes and aggressive cleanliness and formality, when I and my mother returned from church to find my father dead. He had been pruning the grape-vine. He had never had a ladder long enough to reach the sill of the third-floor windows—at house-painting times he had borrowed one from the plumber who mixed his paint—and he had in his own happy-go-lucky way contrived a combination of the garden fruit ladder with a battered kitchen-table that served all sorts of odd purposes in an outhouse. He had stayed up this arrangement by means of the garden roller, and the roller had at the critical moment—rolled. He was lying close by the garden door with his head queerly bent back against a broken and twisted rain-water pipe, an expression of pacific contentment on his face, a bamboo curtain rod with a table-knife tied to the end of it, still gripped in his hand. We had been rapping for some time at the front door unable to make him hear, and then we came round by the door in the side trellis into the garden and so discovered him.

" Arthur ! " I remember my mother crying with the strangest break in her voice. " What are you doing there ? Arthur ! And—*Sunday* ! "

I was coming behind her, musing remotely, when the quality of her voice roused me. She stood as if she could not go near him. He had always puzzled her so, he and his ways, and this seemed only another enigma. Then the truth dawned on her, she shrieked as if afraid of him, ran a dozen steps back towards the trellis door and stopped and clasped her ineffectual gloved hands, leaving me staring blankly, too astonished for feeling, at the carelessly flung limbs.

The same idea came to me also. I ran to her. " Mother ! " I cried, pale to the depths of my spirit, " *Is he dead ?* "

I had been thinking two minutes before of the cold fruit pie that glorified our Sunday dinner-table, and how I might perhaps get into the tree at the end of the garden to read in the afternoon. Now an immense fact had come down like a curtain and blotted out all my childish world. My father was lying dead before my eyes. . . . I perceived that my mother was helpless and that things must be done.

" Mother ! " I said, " we must get Doctor Beaseley—and carry him indoors."

CHAPTER THREE

SCHOLASTIC

§ I

MY formal education began in a small preparatory school in Bromstead. I went there as a day boy. The charge for my instruction was mainly set off by the periodic visits of my father with a large bag of battered fossils to lecture to us upon geology. I was one of those fortunate youngsters who take readily to school-work, I had a good memory, versatile interests and a considerable appetite for commendation, and when I was barely twelve I got a scholarship at the City Merchants School and was intrusted with a scholar's railway season ticket to Victoria. After my father's death a large and very animated and solidly built uncle in tweeds from Staffordshire, Uncle Minter, my mother's sister's husband, with a remarkable accent and remarkable vowel sounds, who had plunged into the Bromstead home once or twice for the night but who was otherwise unknown to me, came on the scene, sold off the three gaunt houses with the utmost gusto, invested the proceeds and my father's life-insurance money, and got us into a small villa at Penge within sight of that immense façade of glass and iron, the Crystal Palace. Then he retired in a mood of good-natured contempt to his native habitat again. We stayed at Penge until my mother's death.

School became a large part of the world to me, absorbing my time and interest, and I never acquired that detailed and intimate knowledge of Penge and the hilly villadom round about, that I have of the town and outskirts of Bromstead.

It was a district of very much the same character, but it was more completely urbanised and nearer to the centre of things ; there were the same unfinished roads, the same occasional disconcerted hedges and trees, the same butcher's horse grazing under a builder's notice-board, the same incidental lapses into slum. The Crystal Palace grounds cut off a large part of my walking radius to the west with impassable fences and forbiddingly expensive turnstiles, but it added to the ordinary spectacle of meteorology a great variety of gratuitous fireworks which banged and flared away of a night after supper and drew me abroad to see them better. Such walks as I took, to Croydon, Wimbledon, West Wickham, and Greenwich, impressed upon me the interminable extent of London's residential suburbs ; mile after mile one went, between houses, villas, rows of cottages, streets of shops, under railway arches, over railway bridges. I have forgotten the detailed local characteristics—if there were any—of much of that region altogether. I was there only two years and half my perambulations occurred at dusk or after dark. But with Penge I associate my first realisations of the wonder and beauty of twilight and night, the effect of dark walls reflecting lamp-light, and the mystery of blue haze-veiled hillsides of houses, the glare of shops by night, the glowing steam and streaming sparks of railway trains and railway signals lit up in the darkness. My first rambles in the evening occurred at Penge—I was becoming a big and independent-spirited boy—and I began my experience of smoking during these twilight prowls with the threepenny packets of American cigarettes then just appearing in the world.

My life centred upon the City Merchants School. Usually I caught the eight-eighteen for Victoria, I had a midday meal and tea; four nights a week I stayed for preparation, and often I was not back home again until within an hour of my bedtime. I spent my half-holidays at school in order to play cricket and football. This, and a pretty voracious appetite for miscellaneous reading which was fostered by the Penge Middleton Library, did not leave me much leisure for local topography. On Sundays also I sang in the choir at St. Martin's Church, and my mother did not like me to walk out alone on the Sabbath afternoon; she herself slumbered, so that I wrote or read at home. I must confess I was at home as little as I could contrive.

Home, after my father's death, had become a very quiet and uneventful place indeed. My mother had either an unimaginative temperament or her mind was greatly occupied with private religious solicitudes; and I remember her talking to me but little, and that usually upon topics I was anxious to evade. I had developed my own view about low-Church theology long before my father's death, and my meditation upon that event had finished my secret estrangement from my mother's faith. My reason would not permit even a remote chance of his being in hell, he was so manifestly not evil, and this religion would not permit him a remote chance of being out of it. When I was a little boy my mother had taught me to read and write and pray and had done many things for me, indeed she persisted in washing me and even in making my clothes until I rebelled against these indignities. But our minds parted very soon. She never began to understand the mental processes of my play, she never interested herself in my school life and work, she could not understand things I said; and she came, I think, quite insensibly to regard me with something of the same hopeless perplexity she had felt towards my father.

Him she must have wedded under considerable delusions. I do not think he deceived her, indeed, nor do I suspect him of mercenariness in their union; but no doubt he played up to her requirements in the half-ingenious way that was and still is the quality of most wooing, and presented himself as a very brisk and orthodox young man. I wonder why nearly all love-making has to be fraudulent. Afterwards he must have disappointed her cruelly by letting one aspect after another of his careless, sceptical, experimental temperament appear. Her mind was fixed and definite, she embodied all that confidence in church and decorum and the assurances of the pulpit which was characteristic of the large mass of the English people—for after all, the rather low-Church section *was* the largest single mass—in early Victorian times. She had dreams, I suspect, of going to church with him side by side ; she in a poke bonnet and a large flounced crinoline, all mauve and magenta and starched under a little lace-trimmed parasol, and he in a tall silk hat and peg-top trousers and a roll-collar coat, and looking rather like the Prince Consort— white angels almost visibly raining benedictions on their amiable progress. Perhaps she dreamed gently of much-belaced babies and an interestingly pious (but not too dissent-ing or fanatical) little girl or boy or so, also angel-haunted. And I think, too, she must have seen herself ruling a seemly " home of taste," with a vivarium in the conservatory that opened out of the drawing-room, or again, making preserves in the kitchen. My father's science-teaching, his diagrams of disembowelled humanity, his pictures of prehistoric beasts that contradicted the Flood, his disposition towards soft shirts and loose tweed suits, his inability to use a clothes brush, his spasmodic reading fits and his bulldog pipes, must have jarred cruelly with her rather unintelligent anticipations. His wild moments of violent temper when he would swear and smash things, absurd almost lovable storms that passed like summer thunder, must have been starkly dreadful to her. She was constitutionally inadaptable, and certainly made no attempt to understand or tolerate these outbreaks. She tried them by her standards, and by her standards they were wrong. Her standards hid him from her. The blazing things he said rankled in her mind unforgettably.

As I remember them together they chafed constantly. Her attitude to nearly all his moods and all his enterprises was a sceptical disapproval. She treated him as something that belonged to me and not to her. " *Your* father," she used to call him, as though I had got him for her.

She had married late and she had, I think, become mentally self-subsisting before her marriage. Even in those Penge days I used to wonder what was going on in her mind, and I find that old speculative curiosity return as I write this. She took a considerable interest in the housework that our generally servantless condition put upon her—she used to have a char-woman in two or three times a week—but she did not do it with any great skill. She covered most of our furniture with flouncey ill-fitting covers, and she cooked plainly and without very much judgment. The Penge house, as it contained nearly all our Bromstead things, was crowded with furniture, and is chiefly associated in my mind with the smell of turpentine, a condiment she used very freely upon the veneered mahogany pieces. My mother had an equal dread of "blacks" by day and the "night air," so that our brightly clean windows were rarely open.

She took a morning paper, and she would open it and glance at the headlines, but she did not read it until the afternoon and then, I think, she was interested only in the more violent crimes, and in railway and mine disasters and in the minutest domesticities of the Royal Family. Most of the books at home were my father's, and I do not think she opened any of them. She had one or two volumes that dated from her own youth, and she tried in vain to interest me in them ; there was Miss Strickland's *Queens of England*, a book I remember with particular animosity, and *Queechy* and the *Wide Wide World*. She made these books of hers into a class apart by sewing outer covers upon them of calico and figured muslin. To me in these habiliments they seemed not so much books as confederated old ladies.

My mother was also very punctual with her religious duties, and rejoiced to watch me in the choir.

On winter evenings she occupied an arm-chair on the other side of the table at which I sat, head on hand, reading, and she would be darning stockings or socks or the like. We achieved an effect of rather stuffy comfortableness that was soporific, and in a passive way I think she found these among her happy times. On such occasions she was wont to put her work down on her knees and fall into a sort of thoughtless musing that would last for long intervals and rouse my curiosity. For like most young people I could not imagine mental states without definite forms.

She carried on a correspondence with a number of cousins and friends, writing letters in a slanting Italian hand and dealing mainly with births, marriages, and deaths, business starts (in the vaguest terms) and the distresses of bankruptcy.

And yet, you know, she did have a curious intimate life of her own that I suspected nothing of at the time, that only now becomes credible to me. She kept a diary that is still in my possession, a diary of fragmentary entries in a miscellaneous collection of pocket-books. She put down the texts of the sermons she heard, and queer stiff little comments on casual visitors—" Miss G. and much noisy shrieking talk about games and such frivolities and *croquay*. A. delighted and *very attentive*." Such little human entries abound. She had an odd way of never writing a name, only an initial ; my father is always " A.," and I am always " D." It is manifest she followed the domestic events in the life of the Princess of Wales, who is now Queen Mother, with peculiar interest and sympathy.   ' 'Pray G. all may be well," she writes in one such crisis."

But there are things about myself that I still find too poignant to tell easily, certain painful and clumsy circumstances of my birth in very great detail, the distresses of my infantile ailments.   Then later I find such things as this : " Heard D. s——."   The " s " is evidently " swear "—" G. bless and keep my boy from evil."   And again, with the thin handwriting shaken by distress : " D. would not go to church, and hardened his heart and said wicked infidel things, much disrespect of the clergy.   The anthem is tiresome ! ! !   That men should set up to be wiser than their maker ! ! ! "   Then trebly underlined : " *I fear his father's teaching.*"   Dreadful little tangle of misapprehensions and false judgments !   More comforting for me to read, " D. very kind and good.   He grows more thoughtful every day."   I suspect myself of forgotten hypocrisies.

At just one point my mother's papers seem to dip deeper. I think the death of my father must have stirred her for the first time for many years to think for herself.   Even she could not go on living in any peace at all, believing that he had indeed been flung headlong into hell.   Of this gnawing solicitude she never spoke to me, never, and for her diary also she could find no phrases.   But on a loose half-sheet of notepaper between its pages I find this passage that follows, written very carefully.   I do not know whose lines they are nor how she came upon them.   They run :

> " And if there be no meeting past the grave ;
> If all is darkness, silence, yet 'tis rest.
> Be not afraid ye waiting hearts that weep,
> For God still giveth His beloved sleep,
> And if an endless sleep He wills, so best."

That scrap of verse amazed me when I read it.   I could even wonder if my mother really grasped the import of what she had copied out.   It affected me as if a stone-deaf person had suddenly turned and joined in a whispered conversation. It set me thinking how far a mind in its general effect quite hopelessly limited, might range.   After that I went through all her diaries, trying to find something more than a conventional term of tenderness for my father.   But I found nothing. And yet somehow there grew upon me the realisation that there had been love. . . . Her love for me, on the other hand, was abundantly expressed.

I knew nothing of that secret life of feeling at the time ; such expression as it found was all beyond my schoolboy range. I did not know when I pleased her and I did not know when I distressed her.   Chiefly I was aware of my mother as rather dull company, as a mind thorny with irrational conclusions and incapable of explication, as one believing quite wilfully and irritatingly in impossible things. So I suppose it had to be ; life was coming to me in new forms and with new requirements. It was essential to our situation that we should fail to understand. After this space of years I have come to realisations and attitudes that dissolve my estrangement from her, I can pierce these barriers, I can see her and feel her as a loving and feeling and desiring and muddle-headed person. There are times when I would have her alive again, if only that I might be kind to her for a little while and give her some return for the narrow intense affection, the tender desires, she evidently lavished so abundantly on me. But then again I ask how I could make that return ? And I realise the futility of such dreaming. Her demand was rigid, and to meet it I should need to act and lie.

So she whose blood fed me, whose body made me, lies in my memory as I saw her last, fixed, still, infinitely intimate, infinitely remote. . . .

My own case with my mother, however, does not awaken the same regret I feel when I think of how she misjudged and irked my father, and turned his weaknesses into thorns for her own tormenting. I wish I could look back without that little twinge to two people who were both in their different quality so good. But goodness that is narrow is a pedestrian and ineffectual goodness. Her attitude to my father seems to me one of the essentially tragic things that have come to me, personally, one of those things that nothing can transfigure, that *remain* sorrowful, that I cannot soothe with any explanation, for as I remember him he was indeed the most lovable of weak spasmodic men. But my mother had been trained in a hard and narrow system that made evil out of many things not in the least evil, and inculcated neither kindliness nor charity. All their estrangement followed from that.

These cramping cults do indeed take an enormous toll of human love and happiness, and not only that but what we Machiavellians must needs consider, they make frightful breaches in human solidarity. I suppose I am a deeply religious man, as men of my quality go, but I hate more and more, as I grow older, the shadow of intolerance cast by religious organisations. All my life has been darkened by irrational intolerance, by arbitrary irrational prohibitions and exclusions. Mohammedanism with its fierce proselytism has, I suppose, the blackest record of uncharitableness, but most of the Christian sects are tainted, tainted to a degree beyond any of the anterior paganisms, with this same hateful quality. It is their exclusive claim that sends them wrong, the vain ambition that inspires them all to teach a uniform one-sided God and be the one and only gateway to salvation. Deprecation of all outside the household of faith, an organised undervaluation of heretical goodness and lovableness, follows necessarily. Every petty difference is exaggerated to the quality of a saving grace or a damning defect. Elaborate precautions are taken to shield the believer's mind against broad or amiable suggestions; the faithful are deterred by dark allusions, by sinister warnings, from books, from theatres, from worldly conversation, from all the kindly instruments that mingle human sympathy. For only by isolating its flock can the organisation survive.

Every month there came to my mother a little magazine called, if I remember rightly, the *Home Churchman*, with the combined authority of print and clerical commendation. It was the most evil thing that ever came into the house, a very devil, a thin pamphlet with one woodcut illustration on the front page of each number; now the uninviting visage of some exponent of the real and only doctrine and attitudes, now some coral strand in act of welcoming the missionaries of God's mysterious preferences, now a new church in the Victorian Gothic. The vile rag it was! A score of vices that shun the policeman have nothing of its subtle wickedness. It was an outrage upon the natural kindliness of men. The contents were all admirably adjusted to keep a spirit in prison. Their force of sustained suggestion was tremendous. There would be dreadful intimations of the swift retribution that fell upon individuals for Sabbath-breaking, and upon nations for weakening towards Ritualism, or treating Roman Catholics as tolerable human beings; there would be great rejoicings over the alleged conversion of Jews, and terrible descriptions of the death-beds of prominent infidels with boldly invented last words—the most unscrupulous lying; there would be the appallingly edifying careers of "early piety" lusciously described, or stories of condemned criminals who traced their final ruin unerringly to early laxities of the kind that leads people to give up subscribing to the *Home Churchman*.

Every month that evil spirit brought about a slump in our mutual love. My mother used to read the thing and become depressed and anxious for my spiritual welfare, used to be stirred to unintelligent pestering. . . .

§ 2

A few years ago I met the editor of this same *Home Churchman*. It was at one of the weekly dinners of that Fleet Street dining club, the Blackfriars.

I heard the paper's name with a queer little shock and surveyed the man with interest. No doubt he was only a successor of the purveyor of discords who darkened my boyhood. It was amazing to find an influence so terrible embodied in a creature so palpably petty. He was seated some way down a table at right angles to the one at which I sat, a man of mean appearance with a greyish complexion, thin, with a square nose, a heavy wiry moustache and a big Adam's apple sticking out between the wings of his collar. He ate with considerable appetite and unconcealed relish, and as his jaw was underhung, he chummed and made the moustache wave like reeds in the swell of a steamer. It gave him a conscientious look. After dinner he a little forced himself upon me. At that time, though the shadow of my scandal was already upon me, I still seemed to be shaping for great successes, and he was glad to be in conversation with me and anxious to intimate political sympathy and support. I tried to make him talk of the *Home Churchman* and the kindred publications he ran, but he was manifestly ashamed of his job so far as I was concerned.

"One wants," he said, pitching himself as he supposed in my key, "to put constructive ideas into our readers, but they are narrow, you know, very narrow. Very." He made his moustache and lips express judicious regret. "One has to consider them carefully, one has to respect their attitudes. One dare not go too far with them. One has to feel one's way."

He chummed and the moustache bristled.

A hireling, beyond question, catering for a demand. I gathered there was a home in Tufnell Park, and three boys to be fed and clothed and educated. . . .

I had the curiosity to buy a copy of his magazine afterwards, and it seemed much the same sort of thing that had worried my mother in my boyhood. There was the usual Christian hero, this time with mutton-chop whiskers and a long bare upper lip. The Jesuits, it seemed, were still hard at it, and Heaven frightfully upset about the Sunday opening of museums and the falling birth-rate, and as touchy and vindictive as ever. There were two vigorous paragraphs upon the utter damnableness of the Rev. R. J. Campbell, a contagious damnableness I gathered, one wasn't safe within a mile of Holborn Viaduct, and a foul-mouthed attack on poor little Wilkins the novelist —who was being baited by the moralists at that time for making one of his women characters, not being in holy wedlock, desire a baby and say so. . . .

The broadening of human thought is a slow and complex process. We do go on, we do get on. But when one thinks that people are living and dying now, quarrelling and sulking, misled and misunderstanding, vaguely fearful, condemning and thwarting one another in the close darknesses of these narrow cults—— Oh, God ! one wants a gale out of Heaven, one wants a great wind from the sea !

§ 3

While I lived at Penge two little things happened to me, trivial in themselves and yet in their quality profoundly significant. They had this in common, that they pierced the texture of the life I was quietly taking for granted and let me see through it into realities—realities I had indeed known about before but never realised. Each of these experiences left me with a sense of shock, with all the values in my life perplexingly altered, attempting readjustment. One of these disturbing and illuminating events was that I was robbed of a new pocket-knife, and the other that I fell in love. It was altogether surprising to me to be robbed. You see, as an only child I had always been fairly well looked after and protected, and the result was an amazing confidence in the practical goodness of the people one met in the world. I knew there were robbers in the world, just as I knew there were tigers ; that I was ever likely to meet robber or tiger face to face seemed equally impossible.

The knife as I remember it was a particularly jolly one with all sorts of instruments in it, tweezers and a thing for getting a stone out of the hoof of a horse, and a corkscrew ; it had cost me a carefully accumulated half-crown, and amounted indeed to a new experience in knives. I had had it for two or three days, and then one afternoon I dropped it through a hole in my pocket on a footpath crossing a field between Penge and Anerley. I heard it fall in the way one does without at the time appreciating what had happened, then later, before I got home, when my hand wandered into my pocket to embrace the still dear new possession, I found it gone, and instantly that memory of something hitting the ground sprang up into consciousness. I went back and commenced a search. Almost immediately I was accosted by the leader of a gang of four or five extremely dirty and ragged boys of assorted sizes and slouching carriage who were coming from the Anerley direction.

" Lost anythink, Matey ? " said he.

I explained.

" 'E's dropped 'is knife," said my interlocutor, and joined in the search.

" What sort of 'andle was it, Matey ? " said a small white-faced sniffing boy in a big bowler hat.

I supplied the information. His sharp little face scrutinised the ground about us.

" *Got* it," he said, and pounced.

" Give it 'ere," said the big boy hoarsely, and secured it.

I walked towards him serenely confident that he would hand it over to me, and that all was for the best in the best of all possible worlds.

" No bloomin' fear ! " he said, regarding me obliquely. " Oo said it was your knife ? "

Remarkable doubts assailed me. " Of course it's my knife," I said. The other boys gathered round me.

" This ain't your knife," said the big boy, and spat casually.

" I dropped it just now."

" Findin's keepin's, *I* believe," said the big boy.

" Nonsense," I said. " Give me my knife."

" 'Ow many blades it got ? "

" Three."

" And what sort of 'andle ? "

" Bone."

" Got a corkscrew like ? "

" Yes."

" Ah ! This ain't you knife no'ow. See ? "

He made no offer to show it to me. My breath went.

" Look here ! " I said. " I saw that kid pick it up. It *is* my knife."

" Rot ! " said the big boy, and slowly, deliberately put my knife into his trouser pocket.

I braced my soul for battle. All civilisation was behind me, but I doubt if it kept the colour in my face. I buttoned my jacket and clenched my fists and advanced on my antagonist —he had, I suppose, the advantage of two years of age and three inches of height. " Hand over that knife," I said.

Then one of the smallest of the band assailed me with extra-ordinary vigour and swiftness from behind, had an arm round my neck and a knee in my back before I had the slightest intimation of attack, and so got me down. " I got 'im, Bill," squeaked this amazing little ruffian. My nose was flattened by a dirty hand, and as I struck out and hit something like sacking, some one kicked my elbow. Two or three seemed to be at me at the same time. Then I rolled over and sat up to discover them all making off, a ragged flight, footballing my cap, my City Merchants' cap, amongst them. I leaped to my feet in a passion of indignation and pursued them.

But I did not overtake them. We are beings of mixed com-position, and I doubt if mine was a single-minded pursuit. I knew that honour required me to pursue, and I had a vivid impression of having just been down in the dust with a very wiry and active and dirty antagonist of disagreeable odour and incredible and incalculable unscrupulousness, kneeling on me and gripping my arm and neck. I wanted of course to be even with him, but also I doubted if catching him would necessarily involve that. They kicked my cap into the ditch at the end of the field, and made off compactly along a cinder lane while I turned aside to recover my dishonoured head-dress. As I knocked the dust out of that and out of my jacket, and brushed my knees and readjusted my very crumpled collar, I tried to focus this startling occurrence in my mind.

I had vague ideas of going to a policeman or of complaining at a police station, but some boyish instinct against informing prevented that. No doubt I entertained ideas of vindictive pursuit and murderous reprisals. And I was acutely enraged whenever I thought of my knife. The thing indeed rankled in my mind for weeks and weeks, and altered all the flavour of my world for me. It was the first time I glimpsed the simple brute violence that lurks and peeps beneath our civilisation. A certain kindly complacency of attitude towards the palpably lower classes was qualified for ever.

§ 4

But the other experience was still more cardinal. It was the first clear intimation of a new motif in life, the sex motif, that was to rise and increase and accumulate power and enrichment and interweave with and at last dominate all my life.

It was when I was nearly fifteen this happened. It is inseparably connected in my mind with the dusk of warm September evenings. I never met the girl I loved by daylight, and I have forgotten her name. It was some insignificant name.

Yet the peculiar quality of the adventure keeps it shining darkly like some deep-coloured gem in the common setting of my memories. It came as something new and strange, something that did not join on to anything else in my life or connect with any of my thoughts or beliefs or habits ; it was a wonder, a mystery, a discovery about myself, a discovery about the whole world. Only in after years did sexual feeling lose that isolation and spread itself out to illuminate and pervade and at last possess the whole broad vision of life.

It was in that phase of an urban youth's development, the phase of the cheap cigarette, that this thing happened. One evening I came by chance on a number of young people promenading by the light of a row of shops towards Beckington, and, with all the glory of a glowing cigarette between my lips, I joined their strolling number. These twilight parades of young people, youngsters chiefly of the lower middle-class, are one of the odd social developments of the great suburban growths—unkindly critics, blind to the inner meanings of things, call them, I believe, Monkeys' Parades—the shop apprentices, the young work-girls, the boy clerks and so forth, stirred by mysterious intimations, spend their first-earned money upon collars and ties, chiffon hats, smart lace collars, walking-sticks, sunshades or cigarettes, and come valiantly into the vague transfiguring mingling of gaslight and evening, to walk up and down, to eye meaningly, even to accost and make friends. It is a queer instinctive revolt from the narrow limited friendless homes in which so many find themselves, a going out towards something, romance if you will, beauty, that has suddenly become a need—a need that hitherto has lain dormant and unsuspected. They promenade.

Vulgar !—it is as vulgar as the spirit that calls the moth abroad in the evening and lights the body of the glow-worm in the night. I made my way through the throng, rather contemptuously as became a public schoolboy, my hands in my pockets—none of your cheap canes for me !—and very careful of the lie of my cigarette upon my lips. And two girls passed me, one a little taller than the other, with dim warm-tinted faces under clouds of dark hair and with dark eyes like pools reflecting stars.

I half turned, and the shorter one glanced back at me over her shoulder—I could draw you now the pose of her cheek and neck and shoulder—and instantly I was as passionately in love with the girl as I have ever been before or since, as any man ever was with any woman. I turned about and followed them, I flung away my cigarette ostentatiously and lifted my school cap and spoke to them.

The girl answered shyly with her dark eyes on my face. What I said and what she said I cannot remember, but I have no doubt it was something absolutely vapid. It really did not matter ; the thing was we had met. I felt as I think a new-hatched moth must feel when suddenly its urgent headlong searching brings it in tremulous amazement upon its mate.

We met, covered from each other, with all the nets of civilisation keeping us apart. We walked side by side.

It led to scarcely more than that. I think we met four or five times altogether, and always with her nearly silent elder sister on the other side of her. We walked on the last two occasions arm in arm, furtively caressing each other's hands, we went away from the glare of the shops into the quiet roads of villadom, and there we whispered instead of talking and looked closely into one another's warm and shaded face. "Dear," I whispered very daringly, and she answered, "Dear ! " We had a vague sense that we wanted more of that quality of intimacy and more. We wanted each other as one wants beautiful music again or to breathe again the scent of flowers.

And that is all there was between us. The events are nothing, the thing that matters is the way in which this experience stabbed through the common stuff of life and left it pierced, with a light, with a huge new interest shining through the rent.

When I think of it I can recall even now the warm mystery of her face, her lips a little apart, lips that I never kissed, her soft shadowed throat, and I feel again the sensuous stir of her proximity. . . .

Those two girls never told me their surname nor let me approach their house. They made me leave them at the corner of a road of small houses near Penge Station. And quite abruptly, without any intimation, they vanished and came to the meeting-place no more, they vanished as a moth goes out of a window into the night, and left me possessed of an intolerable want. . . .

The affair pervaded my existence for many weeks. I could not do my work and I could not rest at home. Night after night I promenaded up and down that Monkeys' Parade full of an unappeasable desire, with a thwarted sense of something just begun that ought to have gone on. I went backwards and forwards on the way to the vanishing place, and at last explored the forbidden road that had swallowed them up. But

I never saw her again, except that later she came to me, my symbol of womanhood, in dreams. How my blood was stirred! I lay awake of nights whispering in the darkness for her. I prayed for her.

Indeed that girl, who probably forgot the last vestiges of me when her first real kiss came to her, ruled and haunted me, gave a Queen to my imagination and a texture to all my desires until I became a man.

I generalised her at last. I suddenly discovered that poetry was about her and that she was the key to all that had hitherto seemed nonsense about love. I took to reading novels, and if the heroine could not possibly be like her, dusky and warm and starlike, I put the book aside. . . .

I hesitate and add here one other confession. I want to tell this thing because it seems to me we are altogether too restrained and secretive about such matters. The cardinal thing in life sneaks in to us darkly and shamefully like a thief in the night.

One day during my Cambridge days—it must have been in my first year before I knew Hatherleigh—I saw in a print-shop window near the Strand an engraving of a girl that reminded me sharply of Penge and its dusky encounter. It was just a half-length of a bare-shouldered, bare-breasted Oriental with arms akimbo, smiling faintly. I looked at it, went my way, then turned back and bought it. I felt I must have it. The odd thing is that I was more than a little shamefaced about it. I did not have it framed and hung in my room open to the criticism of my friends, but I kept it in the drawer of my writing-table. And I kept that drawer locked for a year. It speedily merged with and became identified with the dark girl of Penge. That engraving became in a way my mistress. Often when I had sported my oak and was supposed to be reading, I was sitting with it before me.

Obeying some instinct I kept the thing very secret indeed. For a time nobody suspected what was locked in my drawer nor what was locked in me. I seemed as sexless as my world required.

§ 5

These things stabbed through my life, intimations of things above and below and before me. They had an air of being no more than incidents, interruptions.

The broad substance of my existence at this time was the City Merchants School. Home was a place where I slept and read, and the mooning explorations of the south-eastern postal district which occupied the restless evenings and spare days of my vacations mere interstices, giving glimpses of enigmatical lights and distant spaces between the woven threads of a schoolboy's careeer. School life began for me every morning at Herne Hill, for there I was joined by three or four other boys and the rest of the way we went together. Most of the streets and roads we traversed in our morning's walk from Victoria are still intact, the storms of rebuilding that have submerged so much of my boyhood's London have passed and left them, and I have revived the impression of them again and again in recent years as I have clattered dinnerward in a hansom or hummed along in a motor cab to some engagement. The main gate still looks out with the same expression of ancient well-proportioned kindliness upon St. Margaret's Close. There are imposing new science laboratories in Chambers Street indeed, but the old playing-fields are unaltered except for the big electric trams that go droning and spitting blue flashes along the western boundary. I know Ratten, the new Head, very well, but I have not been inside the school to see if it has changed at all since I went up to Cambridge.

I took all they put before us very readily as a boy, for I had a mind of vigorous appetite, but since I have grown mentally to man's estate and developed a more and more comprehensive view of our national process and our national needs, I am more and more struck by the oddity of the educational methods pursued, their aimless disconnectedness from the constructive forces in the community. I suppose if we are to view the public school as anything more than an institution that has just chanced to happen, we must treat it as having a definite function towards the general scheme of the nation, as being in a sense designed to take the crude young male of the more or less responsible class, to correct his harsh egotisms, broaden his outlook, give him a grasp of the contemporary developments he will presently be called upon to influence and control, and send him on to the university to be made a leading and ruling social man. It is easy enough to carp at schoolmasters and set up for an Educational Reformer, I know, but still it is impossible not to feel how infinitely more effectually—given certain impossibilities perhaps—the job might be done.

My memory of school has indeed no hint whatever of that quality of elucidation it seems reasonable to demand from it. Here all about me was London, a vast inexplicable being, a vortex of gigantic forces, that filled and overwhelmed me with impressions, that stirred my imagination to a perpetual vague inquiry ; and my school not only offered no key to it, but had practically no comment to make upon it at all. We were within three miles of Westminster and Charing Cross, the government offices of a fifth of mankind were all within an hour's stroll, great economic changes were going on under our eyes, now the hoardings flamed with election placards, now the Salvation Army and now the unemployed came trailing in procession through the winter-grey streets, now the newspaper placards outside news-shops told of battles in strange places, now of amazing discoveries, now of sinister crimes, abject squalor and poverty, imperial splendour and luxury,

Buckingham Palace, Rotten Row, Mayfair, the slums of
Pimlico, garbage-littered streets of bawling costermongers,
the inky silver of the barge-laden Thames—such was the background of our days. We went across St. Margaret's Close and
through the school gate into a quiet puerile world apart from
all these things. We joined in the earnest acquirement of all
that was necessary for Greek epigrams and Latin verse, and for
the rest played games. We dipped down into something
clear and elegantly proportioned and time-worn and for all its
high resolve of stalwart virility a little feeble, like our blackened
and decayed portals by Inigo Jones.

Within, we were taught as the chief subjects of instruction,
Latin and Greek. We were taught very badly because the
men who taught us did not habitually use either of these
languages, nobody uses them any more now except perhaps for
the Latin of a few Levantine monasteries. At the utmost
our men read them. We were taught these languages because
long ago Latin had been the language of civilisation ; the one
way of escape from the narrow and localised life had lain in
those days through Latin, and afterwards Greek had come in
as the vehicle of a flood of new and amazing ideas. Once these
two languages had been the sole means of initiation to the
detached criticism and partial comprehension of the world. I
can imagine the fierce zeal of our first Heads, Gardener and
Roper, teaching Greek like passionate missionaries, as a progressive Chinaman might teach English to the boys of Pekin,
clumsily, impatiently, with rod and harsh urgency, but sin-
cerely, patriotically, because they felt that behind it lay
revelations, the irresistible stimulus to a new phase of history.
That was long ago. A new great world, a vaster Imperialism
had arisen about the school, had assimilated all these once
incredible ideas, had gone on to new and yet more astounding
developments of its own. But the City Merchants School still
made the substance of its teaching Latin and Greek, still, with
no thought of rotating crops, sowed in a dream amidst the
harvesting.

There is no fierceness left in the teaching now. Just after
I went up to Trinity, Gates, our Head, wrote a review article in
defence of our curriculum. In this, among other indiscre-
tions, he asserted that it was impossible to write good English
without an illuminating knowledge of the classic tongues, and
in saying so, he split an infinitive and failed to button up a
sentence. His main argument conceded every objection a
reasonable person could make to the City Merchants' curriculum. He admitted that translation had now placed all the
wisdom of the past at a common man's disposal, that scarcely
a field of endeavour remained in which modern work had not
long since passed beyond the ancient achievement. He dis-
claimed any utility. But there was, he said, a peculiar magic
in these grammatical exercises possessed by no other subjects

of instruction. Nothing else provided the same strengthening and orderly discipline for the mind.

He said that, knowing the Senior Classics he did, himself a Senior Classic !

Yet in a dim confused way I think he was making out a case. In schools as we knew them, and with the sort of assistant available, the sort of assistant who has been trained entirely on the old lines, he could see no other teaching so effectual in developing attention, restraint, sustained constructive effort and various yet systematic adjustment. And that was as far as his imagination could go.

It is infinitely easier to begin organised human affairs than end them ; the curriculum and the social organisation of the English public school are the crowning instances of that. They go on because they have begun. Schools are not only immortal institutions but reproductive ones. Our founder, Jabez Arvon, knew nothing, I am sure, of Gates' pedagogic values and would, I feel certain, have dealt with them disrespectfully. But public schools and university colleges sprang into existence correlated, the scholars went on to the universities and came back to teach the schools, to teach as they themselves had been taught, before they had ever made any real use of the teaching ; the crowd of boys herded together, a crowd perpetually renewed and unbrokenly the same, adjusted itself by means of spontaneously developed institutions. In a century, by its very success, this revolutionary innovation of Renascence public schools had become an immense tradition woven closely into the fabric of the national life. Intelligent and powerful people ceased to talk Latin or read Greek, they had got what was wanted, but that only left the schoolmaster the freer to elaborate his point. Since most men of any importance or influence in the country had been through the mill, it was naturally a little difficult to persuade them that it was not quite the best and most ennobling mill the wit of man could devise. And, moreover, they did not want their children made strange to them. There was all the machinery and all the men needed to teach the old subjects, and none to teach whatever new the critic might propose. Such science instruction as my father gave seemed indeed the uninviting alternative to the classical grind. It was certainly at that time an altogether inferior instrument.

So it was I occupied my mind with the exact study of dead languages for seven long years. It was the strangest of detachments. We would sit under the desk of such a master as Topham like creatures who had fallen into an enchanted pit, and he would do his considerable best to work us up to enthusiasm for, let us say, a Greek play. If we flagged he would lash himself to revive us. He would walk about the class-room mouthing great lines in a rich roar, and asking us with a flushed face and shining eyes if it was not " *glorious*." The very sight of Greek letters brings back to me the dingy, faded, ink-splashed quality of our class-room, the banging of books, Topham's disordered hair, the sheen of his alpaca gown, his deep unmusical intonations and the wide striding of his creaking boots. Glorious ! And being plastic human beings we would consent that it was glorious, and some of us even achieved an answering reverberation and a sympathetic flush. I at times responded freely. We all accepted from him unquestioningly that these melodies, these strange sounds, exceeded any possibility of beauty that lay in the Gothic intricacy, the splash and glitter, the jar and recovery, the stabbing lights, the heights and broad distances of our English tongue. That indeed was the chief sin of him. It was not that he was for Greek and Latin, but that he was fiercely against every beauty that was neither classic nor deferred to classical canons.

And what exactly did we make of it, we seniors who understood it best ? We visualised dimly through the bookish dust and the grammatical fog, the spectacle of the chorus chanting grotesquely, helping out protagonist and antagonist, masked and buskined, with the telling of incomprehensible parricides, of inexplicable incest, of gods faded beyond symbolism, of that Relentless Law we did not believe in for a moment, that no modern western European can believe in. We thought of the characters in the unconvincing wigs and costumes of our school performances. No Gilbert Murray had come as yet to touch these things to life again. It was like the ghost of an antiquarian's toy theatre, a ghost that crumbled and condensed into a gritty dust of construing as one looked at it.

Marks, shindies, prayers and punishments, all flavoured with the leathery stuffiness of time-worn Big Hall. . . .

And then out one would come through our grey old gate into the evening light and the spectacle of London hurrying like a cataract, London in black and brown and blue and gleaming silver, roaring like the very loom of Time. We came out into the new world no teacher has yet had the power and courage to grasp and expound. Life and death sang all about one, joys and fears on such a scale, in such an intricacy as never Greek nor Roman knew. The interminable procession of horse omnibuses went lumbering past, bearing countless people we knew not whence, we knew not whither. Hansoms clattered, foot passengers jostled one, a thousand appeals of shop and hoarding caught the eye. The multi-coloured lights of window and street mingled with the warm glow of the declining day under the softly flushing London skies ; the ever-changing placards, the shouting news-vendors, told of a kaleidoscopic drama all about the globe. One did not realise what had happened to us, but the voice of Topham was suddenly drowned and lost, he and his minute, remote gesticulations. . . .

That submerged and isolated curriculum did not even join

on to living interests where it might have done so. We were left absolutely to the hints of the newspapers, to casual political speeches, to the cartoons of the comic papers or a chance reading of some Socialist pamphlet for any general ideas whatever about the wide swirling world process in which we found ourselves. I always look back with particular exasperation to the cessation of our modern history at the year 1815. There it pulled up abruptly, as though it had come upon something indelicate. . . .

But, after all, what would Topham or Flack have made of the huge adjustments of the nineteenth century? Flack was the chief cricketer on the staff; he belonged to that great cult which pretends that the place of this or that county in the struggle for the championship is a matter of supreme importance to boys. He obliged us to affect a passionate interest in the progress of county matches, to work up unnatural enthusiasms. What a fuss there would be when some well-trained boy, panting as if from Marathon, appeared with an evening paper! "I say, you chaps, Middlesex all out for a hundred and five!"

Under Flack's pressure I became, I confess, a cricket humbug of the first class. I applied myself industriously year by year to mastering scores and averages; I pretended that Lords or the Oval were the places nearest Paradise for me. (I never went to either.) Through a slight mistake about the county boundary I adopted Surrey for my loyalty, though as a matter of fact we were by some five hundred yards or so in Kent. It did quite as well for my purposes. I bowled rather straight and fast, and spent endless hours acquiring the skill to bowl Flack out. He was a bat in the Corinthian style, rich and voluminous, and succumbed very easily to a low shooter or an unexpected Yorker, but usually he was caught early by long leg. The difficulty was to bowl him before he got caught. He loved to lift a ball to leg. After one had clean bowled him at the practice nets one deliberately gave him a ball to leg just to make him feel nice again.

Flack went about a world of marvels dreaming of leg hits. He has been observed, going across the Park on his way to his highly respectable club in Piccadilly, to break from profound musings into a strange brief dance that ended with an imaginary swipe with his umbrella, a roofer, over the trees towards Buckingham Palace. The hit accomplished, Flack resumed his way.

Inadequately instructed foreigners would pass him in terror, needlessly alert.

§ 6

These schoolmasters move through my memory as always a little distant and more than a little incomprehensible. Except when they wore flannels, I saw them almost always in old college caps and gowns, a uniform which greatly increased their detachment from the world of actual men. Gates, the Head, was a lean loose-limbed man, rather stupid I discovered when I reached the Sixth and came into contact with him, but honest, simple, and very eager to be liberal-minded. He was bald with an almost conical baldness, with a grizzled pointed beard, small featured and, under the stresses of a Zeitgeist that demanded liberality, with an expression of puzzled but resolute resistance to his own unalterable opinions. He made a tall dignified figure in his gown. In my junior days he spoke to me only three or four times, and then he annoyed me by giving me a wrong surname ; it was a sore point because I was an outsider and not one of the old school families, the Shoesmiths, the Naylors, the Marklows, the Tophams, the Pevises, and such-like, who came generation after generation. I recall him most vividly against the background of faded brown book-backs in the old library in which we less destructive seniors were trusted to work, with the light from the stained-glass window falling in coloured patches on his face. It gave him the appearance of having no colour of his own. He had a habit of scratching the beard on his cheek as he talked, and he used to come and consult us about things and invariably do as we said. That, in his phraseology, was " maintaining the traditions of the school."

He had indeed an effect not of a man directing a school, but of a man captured and directed by a school. Dead and gone Elizabethans had begotten a monster that could carry him about in its mouth.

Yet being a man, as I say, with his hair a little stirred by a Zeitgeist that made for change, Gates did at times display a disposition towards developments. City Merchants had no modern side, and utilitarian spirits were carping in the *Pall Mall Gazette* and elsewhere at the omissions from our curriculum, and particularly at our want of German. Moreover, four classes still worked together with much clashing and uproar in the old Big Hall that had once held in a common tumult the entire school. Gates used to come and talk to us older fellows about these things.

" I don't wish to innovate unduly," he used to say, " but we ought to get in some German, you know—for those who like it. The army men will be wanting it some of these days."

He referred to the organisation of regular evening preparation for the lower boys in Big Hall as a " revolutionary change," but he achieved it, and he declared he began the replacement of the hacked wooden tables, at which the boys had worked since Tudor days, by sloping desks with safety inkpots and scientifically adjustable seats, " with grave misgivings." And though he never birched a boy in his life, and was, I am convinced, morally incapable of such a scuffle, he retained the block and birch in the school through all his term of office, and spoke at the Headmasters' Conference in temperate approval of corporal chastisement, comparing it, dear soul! to the power of the sword. . . .

I wish I could, in some measure and without tediousness, convey the effect of his discourses to General Assembly in Big Hall. But that is like trying to draw the obverse and reverse of a sixpence worn to complete illegibility. His tall fine figure stood high on the daïs, his thoughtful tenor filled the air as he steered his hazardous way through sentences that dragged inconclusive tails and dropped redundant prepositions. And he pleaded ever so urgently, ever so finely, that what we all knew for Sin was sinful, and on the whole best avoided altogether, and so went on with deepening notes and even with short arresting gestures of the right arm and hand, to stir and exhort us towards goodness, towards that modern, unsectarian goodness, goodness in general and nothing in particular, which the Zeitgeist seemed to indicate in those transitional years.

§ 7

The school never quite got hold of me. Partly I think that was because I was a day-boy and so freer than most of the boys, partly because of a temperamental disposition to see things in my own way and have my private dreams, partly because I was a little antagonised by the family traditions that ran through the school. I was made to feel at first that I was a rank outsider, and I never quite forgot it. I suffered very little bullying, and I never had a fight—in all my time there were only three fights—but I followed my own curiosities. Before I was fifteen I was already a very keen theologian and politician. I was also intensely interested in modern warfare. I read the morning papers in the Reading Room during the midday recess, never missed the illustrated weeklies, and often when I could afford it I bought a *Pall Mall Gazette* on my way home.

I do not think that I was very exceptional in that ; most intelligent boys, I believe, want naturally to be men, and are keenly interested in men's affairs. There is not the universal passion for a magnified puerility among them it is customary to assume. I was indeed a voracious reader of everything but boys' books—which I detested—and fiction. I read histories, travel, popular science and controversy with particular zest, and I loved maps. School work and school games were quite subordinate affairs for me. I worked well and made a passable figure at games, and I do not think I was abnormally insensitive to the fine quality of our school, to the charm of its mediæval nucleus, its Gothic cloisters, its scraps of Palladian and its dignified Georgian extensions ; the contrast of the old quiet, that in spite of our presence pervaded it everywhere, with the rushing and impending London all about it, was

indeed a continual pleasure to me. But these things were
certainly not the living and central interests of my life.

I had to conceal my wider outlook to a certain extent—
from the masters even more than from the boys. Indeed I
only let myself go freely with one boy, Britten, my especial
chum, the son of the Agent-General for East Australia. We
two discovered in a chance conversation à *propos* of a map in
the library that we were both of us curious why there were
Malays in Madagascar, and how the Mecca pilgrims came from
the East Indies before steamships were available. Neither
of us had suspected that there was any one at all in the school
who knew or cared a rap about the Indian Ocean, except as
water on the way to India. But Britten had come up through
the Suez Canal, and his ship had spoken a pilgrim ship on the
way. It gave him a startling quality of living knowledge.
From these pilgrims we got to a comparative treatment of
religions, and from that, by a sudden plunge, to entirely
sceptical and disrespectful confessions concerning Gates' last
outbreak of simple piety in School Assembly. We became
congenial intimates from that hour.

The discovery of Britten happened to me when we were
both in the Lower Fifth. Previously there had been a water-
tight compartment between the books I read and the thoughts
they begot on the one hand and human intercourse on the
other. Now I really began my higher education, and aired
and examined and developed in conversation the doubts, the
ideas, the interpretations that had been forming in my mind.
As we were both day-boys with a good deal of control over our
time, we organised walks and expeditions together, and my
habit of solitary and rather vague prowling gave way to much
more definite joint enterprises. I went several times to his
house. He was the youngest of several brothers, one of whom
was a medical student and let us assist at the dissection of a
cat, and once or twice in vacation time he came to Penge, and
we went with parcels of provisions to do a thorough day in the
grounds and galleries of the Crystal Palace, ending with the
fireworks at close quarters. We went in a river steamboat
down to Greenwich, and fired by that made an excursion to
Margate and back ; we explored London docks and Bethnal
Green Museum, Petticoat Lane, and all sorts of out-of-the-way
places together.

We confessed shyly to one another a common secret vice,
" Phantom warfare." When we walked alone, especially in
the country, we had both developed the same practice of
fighting an imaginary battle about us as we walked. As we
went along we were generals, and our attacks pushed along
on either side, crouching and gathering behind hedges, cresting
ridges, occupying copses, rushing open spaces, fighting from
house to house. The hillsides about Penge were honey-
combed in my imagination with the pits and trenches I had

created to check a victorious invader coming out of Surrey. For him West Kensington was chiefly important as the scene of a desperate and successful last stand of insurrectionary troops (who had seized the Navy, the Bank and other advantages) against a royalist army—reinforced by Germans—advancing for reasons best known to themselves by way of Harrow and Ealing. It is a secret and solitary game, as we found when we tried to play it together. We made a success of that only once. All the way down to Margate, we schemed defences and assailed and fought them as we came back against the sunset. Afterwards we recapitulated all that conflict by means of a large-scale map of the Thames and little paper ironclads in plan cut out of paper.

A subsequent revival of these imaginings was brought about by Britten's luck in getting, through a friend of his father's, admission for us both to the spectacle of volunteer officers fighting the war game in Caxton Hall. We developed a war game of our own at Britten's home with nearly a couple of hundred lead soldiers, some excellent spring cannons that shot hard and true at six yards, hills of books and a constantly elaborated set of rules. For some months that occupied an immense proportion of our leisure. Some of our battles lasted several days. We kept the game a profound secret from the other fellows. They would not have understood.

And we also began, it was certainly before we were sixteen, to write, for the sake of writing. We liked writing. We had discovered Lamb and the best of the middle articles in such weeklies as the *Saturday Gazette*, and we imitated them. Our minds were full of dim uncertain things we wanted to drag out into the light of expression. Britten had got hold of "In Memoriam," and I had disinterred Pope's "Essay on Man" and "Rabbi Ben Ezra," and these things had set our theological and cosmic solicitudes talking. I was somewhere between sixteen and eighteen, I know, when he and I walked along the Thames Embankment confessing shamefully to one another that we had never read Lucretius. We thought every one who mattered had read Lucretius.

When I was nearly sixteen my mother was taken ill very suddenly, and died of some perplexing complaint that involved a post-mortem examination; it was, I think, the trouble that has since those days been recognised as appendicitis. This led to a considerable change in my circumstances; the house at Penge was given up, and my Staffordshire uncle arranged for me to lodge during school terms with a needy solicitor and his wife in Vicars Street, S.W., about a mile and a half from the school. So it was I came right into London; I had almost two years of London before I went to Cambridge.

Those were our great days together. Afterwards we were torn apart; Britten went to Oxford, and our circumstances never afterwards threw us continuously together until the days of the *Blue Weekly*.

As boys, we walked together, read and discussed the same books, pursued the same inquiries. We got a reputation as inseparables and the nickname of the Rose and the Lily, for Britten was short and thick-set with dark close curling hair and a ruddy Irish type of face ; I was lean and fair-haired and some inches taller than he. Our talk ranged widely and yet had certain very definite limitations. We were amazingly free with politics and religion, we went to that little meeting-house of William Morris's at Hammersmith and worked out the principles of Socialism pretty thoroughly, and we got up the Darwinian theory with the help of Britten's medical-student brother and the galleries of the Natural History Museum in Cromwell Road. Those wonderful cases on the ground floor illustrating mimicry, dimorphism and so forth, were new in our time, and we went through them with earnest industry and tried over our Darwinism in the light of that. Such topics we did exhaustively. But on the other hand I do not remember any discussion whatever of human sex or sexual relationships. There, in spite of intense secret curiosities, our lips were sealed by a peculiar shyness. And I do not believe we ever had occasion either of us to use the word "love." It was not only that we were instinctively shy of the subject, but that we were mightily ashamed of the extent of our ignorance and uncertainty in these matters. We evaded them elaborately with an assumption of exhaustive knowledge.

We certainly had no shyness about theology. We marked the emancipation of our spirits from the frightful teachings that had oppressed our boyhood, by much indulgence in blasphemous wit. We had a secret literature of irreverent rhymes, and a secret art of theological caricature. Britten's father had delighted his family by reading aloud from Dr. Richard Garnett's *Twilight of the Gods*, and Britten conveyed the precious volume to me. That and the *Bab Ballads* were the inspiration of some of our earliest lucubrations.

For an imaginative boy the first experience of writing is like a tiger's first taste of blood, and our literary flowerings led very directly to the revival of the school magazine, which had been comatose for some years. But there we came upon a disappointment.

§ 8

In that revival we associated certain other of the Sixth Form boys, and notably one for whom our enterprise was to lay the foundations of a career that has ended in the House of Lords, Arthur Cossington, now Lord Paddockhurst. Cossington was at that time a rather heavy, rather good-looking boy who was chiefly eminent in cricket, an outsider even as we were and preoccupied, no doubt, had we been sufficiently detached to observe him, with private imaginings very much of the same quality and spirit as our own. He was, we were inclined to think, rather a sentimentalist, rather a poseur, he affected a concise emphatic style, played chess very well, betrayed a belief in will-power, and earned Britten's secret hostility, Britten being a sloven, by the invariable neatness of his collars and ties. He came into our magazine with a vigour that we found extremely surprising and unwelcome.

Britten and I had wanted to write. We had indeed figured our project modestly as a manuscript magazine of satirical, liberal and brilliant literature by which in some rather inexplicable way the vague tumult of ideas that teemed within us was to find form and expression ; Cossington, it was manifest from the outset, wanted neither to write nor writing, but a magazine. I remember the inaugural meeting in Shoesmith major's study—we had had great trouble in getting it together —and how effectually Cossington bolted with the proposal.

" I think we fellows ought to run a magazine," said Cossington. " The school used to have one. A school like this ought to have a magazine."

" The last one died in '84," said Shoesmith from the hearth-rug. " Called the *Observer*. Rot rather."

" Bad title," said Cossington.

" There was a *Tatler* before that," said Britten, sitting on the writing-table at the window that was closed to deaden the cries of the Lower School at play, and clashing his boots together.

" We want something suggestive of City Merchants."

" *City Merchandise*," said Britten.

" Too fanciful. What of *Arvonian* ? Richard Arvon was our founder, and it seems almost a duty——"

" They call them all -usians or -onians," said Britten.

" I like *City Merchandise*," I said. " We could probably find a quotation to suggest—oh ! mixed good things."

Cossington regarded me abstractedly.

" Don't want to put the accent on the City, do we ? " said Shoesmith, who had a feeling for county families, and Naylor supported him by a murmur of approval.

" We ought to call it the *Arvonian*," decided Cossington, " and we might very well have underneath, ' With which is incorporated the *Observer*.' That picks up the old traditions, makes an appeal to old boys and all that, and it gives us something to print under the title."

I still held out for *City Merchandise*, which had taken my fancy. " Some of the chaps' people won't like it," said Naylor, " certain not to. And it sounds Rum."

" Sounds Weird," said a boy who had not hitherto spoken.

" We aren't going to do anything Queer," said Shoesmith, pointedly not looking at Britten.

The question of the title had manifestly gone against us.

" Oh, *have* it *Arvonian*," I said.

" And next, what size shall we have ? " said Cossington.

" Something like *Macmillan's Magazine*—or *Longmans'* ; *Longmans'* is better because it has a whole page, not columns. It makes no end of difference to one's effects."

" What effects ? " asked Shoesmith abruptly.

" Oh ! a pause or a white line or anything. You've got to write closer for a double column. It's nuggetty. You can't get a swing on your prose." I had discussed this thoroughly with Britten.

" If the fellows are going to write——" began Britten.

" We ought to keep off fine writing," said Shoesmith. " It's cheek. I vote we don't have any."

" We shan't get any," said Cossington, and then as an olive branch to me, "unless Remington does a bit. Or Britten. But it's no good making too much space for it."

" We ought to be very careful about the writing," said Shoesmith. " We don't want to give ourselves away."

" I vote we ask old Topham to see us through," said Naylor.

Britten groaned aloud and every one regarded him. " Greek epigrams on the fellows' names," he said. " Small beer in ancient bottles. Let's get a stuffed broody hen to *sit* on the magazine."

" We might do worse than a Greek epigram," said Cossington. " One in each number. It—it impresses parents and keeps up our classical tradition. And the masters *can* help. We don't want to antagonise them. Of course—we've got to departmentalise. Writing is only one section of the thing. The *Arvonian* has to stand for the school. There's questions of space and questions of expense. We can't turn out a great chunk of printed prose like—like wet cold toast and call it a magazine."

Britten writhed, appreciating the image.

" There's to be a section of sports. *You* must do that."

" I'm not going to do any fine writing," said Shoesmith.

" What you've got to do is just to list all the chaps and put a note to their play : ' Naylor minor must pass more. Football isn't the place for extreme individualism.' ' Ammersham shapes well as half-back.' Things like that."

" I could do that all right," said Shoesmith, brightening and manifestly becoming pregnant with judgments.

" One great thing about a magazine of this sort," said Cossington, " is to mention just as many names as you can in each number. It keeps the interest alive. Chaps will turn it over looking for their own little bit. Then it all lights up for them."

" Do you want any reports of matches ? " Shoesmith broke from his meditation.

" Rather. With comments."

"Naylor surpassed himself and negotiated the lemon safely home," said Shoesmith.

"Shut it," said Naylor modestly.

"Exactly," said Cossington. "That gives us three features," touching them off on his fingers, "Epigram, Literary Section, Sports. Then we want a section to shove anything into, a joke, a notice of anything that's going on. So on. Our Note Book."

"Oh, Hell!" said Britten, and clashed his boots, to the silent disapproval of every one.

"Then we want an editorial."

"A *what*?" cried Britten, with a note of real terror in his voice.

"Well, don't we? Unless we have our Note Book to begin on the front page. It gives a scrappy effect to do that. We want something manly and straightforward and a bit thoughtful, about Patriotism, say, or *Esprit de Corps*, or After-Life."

I looked at Britten. Hitherto we had not considered Cossington mattered very much in the world.

He went over us as a motor-car goes over a dog. There was a sort of energy about him, a new sort of energy to us; we had never realised that anything of the sort existed in the world. We were hopelessly at a disadvantage. Almost instantly he had developed a clear and detailed vision of a magazine made up of everything that was most acceptable in the magazines that flourished in the adult world about us, and had determined to make it a success. He had by a kind of instinct, as it were, synthetically plagiarised every successful magazine and breathed into this dusty mixture the breath of life. He was elected at his own suggestion managing director, with the earnest support of Shoesmith and Naylor, and conducted the magazine so successfully and brilliantly that he even got a whole back page of advertisements from the big sports shop in Holborn, and made the printers pay at the same rate for a notice of certain books of their own which they said they had inserted by inadvertency to fill up space. The only literary contribution in the first number was a column by Topham in faultless stereotyped English in depreciation of some fancied evil called Utilitarian Studies and ending with that noble old quotation :—

"To the glory that was Greece and the grandeur that was Rome."

And Flack crowded us out of number two with a bright little paper on the "Humours of Cricket," and the Head himself was profusely thoughtful all over the editorial under the heading of "The School Chapel ; and How it Seems to an Old Boy."

Britten and I found it difficult to express to each other with any grace or precision what we felt about that magazine.

CHAPTER FOUR

ADOLESCENCE

§ 1

I FIND it very difficult to trace how form was added to form and interpretation followed interpretation in my ever-spreading, ever-deepening, ever-multiplying and enriching vision of this world into which I had been born. Every day added its impressions, its hints, its subtle explications to the growing understanding. Day after day the living interlacing threads of a mind weave together. Every morning now for three weeks and more (for to-day is Thursday and I started on a Tuesday) I have been trying to convey some idea of the factors and early influences by which my particular scrap of subjective tapestry was shaped, to show the child playing on the nursery floor, the son perplexed by his mother, gazing aghast at his dead father, exploring interminable suburbs, touched by first intimations of the sexual mystery, coming in with a sort of confused avidity towards the centres of the life of London. It is only by such an effort to write it down that one realises how marvellously crowded, how marvellously analytical and synthetic those years must be. One begins with the little child to whom the sky is a roof of blue, the world a screen of opaque and disconnected facts, the home a thing eternal, and "being good" just simple obedience to unquestioned authority ; and one comes at last to the vast world of one's adult perception, pierced deep by flaring searchlights of partial understanding, here masked by mists, here refracted and distorted through half-translucent veils, here showing broad prospects and limitless vistas and here impenetrably dark.

I recall phases of deep speculation, doubts and even prayers by night, and strange occasions when by a sort of hypnotic contemplation of nothingness I sought to pierce the web of appearances about me. It is hard to measure these things in receding perspective, and now I cannot trace, so closely has mood succeeded and overlaid and obliterated mood, the phases by which an utter horror of death was replaced by the growing realisation of its necessity and dignity. Difficulty of the imagination with infinite space, infinite time, entangled my mind ; and moral distress for the pain and suffering of bygone ages that made all thought of reformation in the future seem but the grimmest irony upon now irreparable wrongs. Many an intricate perplexity of these broadening years did not so much get settled as cease to matter. Life crowded me away from it.

I have confessed myself a temerarious theologian, and in that passage from boyhood to manhood I ranged widely in my search for some permanently satisfying Truth. That, too, ceased after a time to be urgently interesting. I came at last into a phase that endures to this day, of absolute tranquillity, of absolute confidence in whatever that Incomprehensible Comprehensive which must needs be the substratum of all things, may be. Feeling *of it*, feeling *by it*, I cannot feel afraid of it. I think I had got quite clearly and finally to that adjustment long before my Cambridge days were done. I am sure that the evil in life is transitory and finite like an accident or distress in the nursery ; that God is my Father and that I may trust Him, even though life hurts so that one must needs cry out at it, even though it shows no consequence but failure, no promise but pain. . . .

But while I was fearless of theology I must confess it was comparatively late before I faced and dared to probe the secrecies of sex. I was afraid of sex. I had an instinctive perception that it would be a large and difficult thing in my life, but my early training was all in the direction of regarding it as an irrelevant thing, as something disconnected from all the broad significances of life, as hostile and disgraceful in its quality. The world was never so emasculated in thought, I suppose, as it was in the Victorian time. . . .

I was afraid to think either of sex or (what I have always found inseparable from a kind of sexual emotion) beauty. Even as a boy I knew the thing as a haunting and alluring mystery that I tried to keep away from. Its dim presence obsessed me none the less for all the extravagant decency, the stimulating silences of my upbringing. . . .

The plaster Venuses and Apollos that used to adorn the vast aisle and huge grey terraces of the Crystal Palace were the first intimations of the beauty of the body that ever came into my life. As I write of it I feel again the shameful attraction of those gracious forms. I used to look at them not simply, but curiously and askance. Once at least in my later days at Penge, I spent a shilling in admission chiefly for the sake of them. . . .

The strangest thing of all my odd and solitary upbringing seems to me now that swathing up of all the splendours of the flesh, that strange combination of fanatical terrorism and shyness that fenced me about with prohibitions. It caused me to grow up, I will not say blankly ignorant, but with an ignorance blurred and dishonoured by shame, by enigmatical warnings, by cultivated aversions, an ignorance in which a fascinated curiosity and desire struggled like a thing in a net. I knew so little and I felt so much. There was indeed no Aphrodite at all in my youthful Pantheon, but instead there was a mysterious and minatory gap. I have told how at last a new Venus was born in my imagination out of gas-lamps and the twilight, a Venus with a cockney accent and dark eyes shining out of the dusk, a Venus who was a warm, passion-stirring atmosphere

rather than incarnate in a body.   And I have told, too, how
I bought a picture.

All this was a thing apart from the rest of my life, a locked
avoided chamber. . . .

It was not until my last year at Trinity that I really broke
down the barriers of this unwholesome silence and brought
my secret broodings to the light of day.   Then a little set of
us plunged suddenly into what we called at first sociological
discussion.   I can still recall even the physical feeling of those
first tentative talks.   I remember them mostly as occurring in
the rooms of Ted Hatherleigh, who kept at the corner by Trinity
great gate, but we also used to talk a good deal at a man's in
King's, a man named, if I remember rightly, Redmayne.   The
atmosphere of Hatherleigh's rooms was a haze of tobacco
smoke against a background brown and deep.   He professed
himself a socialist with anarchistic leanings—he had suffered
the martyrdom of ducking for it—and a huge French May-day
poster displaying a splendid proletarian in red and black on a
barricade against a flaring orange sky, dominated his decorations.   Hatherleigh affected a fine untidiness, and all the place,
even the floor, was littered with books, for the most part open
and face downward ;   deeper darknesses were supplied by a
discarded gown, and our caps all conscientiously battered,
Hatherleigh's flopped like an elephant's ear, and inserted quill
pens supported the corners of mine ;   the high lights of the
picture came chiefly as reflections from his chequered blue
mugs full of audit ale.   We sat on oak chairs, except the four
or five who crowded on a capacious settle, we drank a lot of
beer and were often fuddled, and occasionally quite drunk, and
we all smoked reckless-looking pipes—there was a transient
fashion among us for corn cobs for which Mark Twain, I think,
was responsible.   Our little excesses with liquor were due far
more to conscience than appetite, indicated chiefly a resolve
to break away from restraints that we suspected were keeping
us off the instructive knife-edges of life.   Hatherleigh was a
good Englishman of the premature type with a red face, a lot
of hair, a deep voice and an explosive plunging manner, and
it was he who said one evening—Heaven knows how we got
to it—" Look here, you know, it's all Rot, this Shutting Up
about Women.   We *ought* to talk about them.   What are we
going to do about them ?   It's got to come.   We're all festering inside about it.   Let's out with it.   There's too much
Decency altogether about this Infernal University ! "

We rose to his challenge a little awkwardly and our first talk
was clumsy, there were flushed faces and red ears, and I
remember Hatherleigh broke out into a monologue on decency.
" Modesty and Decency," said Hatherleigh,   " are Oriental
vices.   The Jews brought them to Europe.   They're Semitic,
just like our monasticism here and the seclusion of women and
mutilating the dead on a battlefield.   And all that sort of thing."

Hatherleigh's mind progressed by huge leaps, leaps that were usually wildly inaccurate, and for a time we engaged hotly upon the topic of those alleged mutilations and the Semitic responsibility for decency. Hatherleigh tried hard to saddle the Semitic race with the less elegant war customs of the Soudan and the north-west frontier of India, and quoted Doughty, at that time a little-known author, and Cunninghame Graham to show that the Arab was worse than a county-town spinster in his regard for respectability. But his case was too preposterous, and Esmeer, with his shrill penetrating voice and his way of pointing with all four long fingers flat together, carried the point against him. He quoted Cato and Roman law and the monasteries of Thibet.

"Well, anyway," said Hatherleigh, escaping from our hands like an intellectual frog, "Semitic or not, I've got no use for decency."

We argued points and Hatherleigh professed an unusually balanced and tolerating attitude. "I don't mind a certain refinement and dignity," he admitted generously. "What I object to is this spreading out of decency until it darkens the whole sky, until it makes a man's father afraid to speak of the most important things, until it makes a man afraid to look a frank book in the face or think—even think ! until it leads to our coming to—to the business at last with nothing but a few prohibitions, a few hints, a lot of dirty jokes and, and "—he waved a hand and seemed to seek and catch his image in the air—" oh, a confounded buttered slide of sentiment, to guide us. I tell you I'm going to think about it and talk about it until I see a little more daylight than I do at present. I'm twenty-two. Things might happen to me anywhen. You men can go out into the world if you like, to sin like fools and marry like fools, not knowing what you are doing and ashamed to ask. You'll take the consequences, too, I expect, pretty meekly, sniggering a bit, sentimentalising a bit, like—like Cambridge humorists. . . . *I* mean to know what I'm doing."

He paused to drink, and I think I cut in with ideas of my own. But one is apt to forget one's own share in a talk, I find, more than one does the clear-cut objectivity of other people's, and I do not know how far I contributed to this discussion that followed. I am, however, pretty certain that it was then that ideal that we were pleased to call aristocracy and which soon became the common property of our set was developed. It was Esmeer, I know, who laid down and maintained the proposition that so far as minds went there were really only two sorts of man in the world, the aristocrat and the man who subdues his mind to other people's.

" ' I couldn't *think* of it, Sir,' " said Esmeer in his elucidatory tones ; " that's what a servant says. His mind even is broken in to run between fences, and he admits it. *We've* got to be able to think of anything. And ' such things aren't for the

Likes of Us!' That's another servant's saying. Well, everything *is* for the Likes of Us. If we see fit, that is."

A small fresh-coloured man in grey objected.

"Well," exploded Hatherleigh, "if that isn't so, what the deuce are we up here for ? Instead of working in mines ? If some things aren't to be thought about ever ! We've got the privilege of all these extra years for getting things straight in our heads, and then we won't use 'em. Good God ! what do you think a university's for ?" . . .

Esmeer's idea came with an effect of real emancipation to several of us. We were not going to be afraid of ideas any longer, we were going to throw down every barrier of prohibition and take them in and see what came of it. We became for a time even intemperately experimental, and one of us, at the bare suggestion of an eminent psychic investigator, took hashish and very nearly died of it within a fortnight of our great elucidation.

The chief matter of our interchanges was of course the discussion of sex. Once the theme had been opened it became a sore place in our intercourse ; none of us seemed able to keep away from it. Our imaginations got astir with it. We made up for lost time and went round it and through it and over it exhaustively. I recall prolonged discussion of polygamy on the way to Royston, muddy November tramps to Madingley, when amidst much profanity from Hatherleigh at the serious treatment of so obsolete a matter, we weighed the reasons, if any, for the institution of marriage. The fine dim night-time spaces of the Great Court are bound up with the inconclusive finales of mighty hot-eared wrangles ; the narrows of Trinity Street and Petty Cury and Market Hill have their particular associations for me with that spate of confession and free speech, that almost painful gaol delivery of long pent and cramped and sometimes cripple1 ideas.

And we went on a reading party that Easter to a place called Pulborough in Sussex, where there is a fishing inn and a river that goes under a bridge. It was a late Easter and a blazing one, and we boated and bathed and talked of being Hellenic and the beauty of the body until at moments it seemed to us that we were destined to restore the Golden Age by the simple abolition of tailors and outfitters.

Those undergraduate talks ! how rich and glorious they seemed, how splendidly new the ideas that grew and multiplied in our seething minds ! We made long afternoon and evening raids over the Downs towards Arundel, and would come tramping back through the still keen moonlight singing and shouting. We formed romantic friendships with one another, and grieved more or less convincingly that there were no splendid women fit to be our companions in the world. But Hatherleigh, it seemed, had once known a girl whose hair was gloriously red. " My God ! " said Hatherleigh to convey the

quality of her ; just simply and with projectile violence :
" My God ! "

Benton had heard of a woman who lived with a man refusing
to be married to him—we thought that splendid beyond
measure—I cannot now imagine why. She was " like a
tender goddess," Benton said.   A sort of shame came upon us
in the dark in spite of our liberal intentions when Benton
committed himself to that.   And after such talk we would fall
upon great pauses of emotional dreaming, and if by chance we
passed a girl in a governess-cart, or some farmer's daughter
walking to the station, we became alertly silent or obstreper-
ously indifferent to her.   For might she not be just that one
exception to the banal decency, the sickly pointless conven-
tionality, the sham modesty of the times in which we lived ?

We felt we stood for a new movement, not realising how
perennially this same emancipation returns to those ancient
courts beside the Cam.   We were the anti-decency party, we
discovered a catch phrase that we flourished about in the
Union and made our watchword, namely, " stark fact."   We
hung nude pictures in our rooms much as if they had been
flags, to the earnest concern of our bedders, and I disinterred
my long-kept engraving and had it framed in fumed oak, and
found for it a completer and less restrained companion, a
companion I never cared for in the slightest degree. . . .

This efflorescence did not prevent, I think indeed it rather
helped, our more formal university work, for most of us took
firsts, and three of us got Fellowships in one year or another.
There was Benton who had a Research Fellowship and went to
Tubingen, there was Esmeer and myself who both became
Residential Fellows.   I had taken the Mental and Moral
Science Tripos (as it was then), and three years later I got a
lectureship in political science.   In those days it was disguised
in the cloak of Political Economy.

§ 2

It was our affectation to be a little detached from the main
stream of undergraduate life.   We worked pretty hard, but
by virtue of our beer, our socialism, and such-like heterodoxy,
held ourselves to be differentiated from the swatting reading
man.   None of us except Baxter, who was a rowing blue, a
rather abnormal blue with an appetite for ideas, took games
seriously enough to train, and on the other hand we intimated
contempt for the . rather mediocre, deliberately humorous,
consciously gentlemanly and consciously wild undergraduate
men who made up the mass of Cambridge life.   After the
manner of youth we were altogether too hard on our contemporaries.   We battered our caps and tore our gowns
lest they should seem new, and we despised these others
extremely for doing exactly the same things ; we had an

idea of ourselves and resented beyond measure a similar weakness in these our brothers.

There was a type, or at least there seemed to us to be a type—I'm a little doubtful at times now whether after all we didn't create it—for which Hatherleigh invented the nickname the "Pinky Dinkys," intending thereby both contempt and abhorrence in almost equal measure. The Pinky Dinky summarised all that we particularly did not want to be, and also, I now perceive, much of what we were and all that we secretly dreaded becoming.

But it is hard to convey the Pinky Dinky idea, for all that it meant so much to us. We spent one evening at least during that reading-party upon the Pinky Dinky ; we sat about our one fire after a walk in the rain—it was our only wet day— smoked our excessively virile pipes, and elaborated the natural history of the Pinky Dinky. We improvised a sort of Pinky Dinky litany, and Hatherleigh supplied deep notes for the responses.

" The Pinky Dinky extracts a good deal of amusement from life," said some one.

" Damned prig ! " said Hatherleigh.

" The Pinky Dinky arises in the Union and treats the question with a light gay touch. He makes the weird ones mad. But sometimes he cannot go on because of the amusement he extracts."

" I want to shy books at the giggling swine," said Hatherleigh.

" The Pinky Dinky says suddenly while he is making the tea, ' We're all being frightfully funny. It's time for *you* to say something now.' "

" The Pinky Dinky shakes his head and says : ' I'm afraid I shall never be a responsible being.' And he really *is* frivolous."

" Frivolous but not vulgar," said Esmeer.

" Pinky Dinkys are chaps who've had their buds nipped," said Hatherleigh. " They're Plebs and they know it. They haven't the Guts to get hold of things. And so they worry up all those silly little jokes of theirs to carry it off." . . .

We tried bad ones for a time, viciously flavoured.

" Pinky Dinkys are due to over-production of the type that ought to keep outfitters' shops. Pinky Dinkys would like to keep outfitters' shops with whimsy 'scriptions on the boxes and make your bill out funny, and not be snobs to customers, no !—not even if they had titles."

" Every Pinky Dinky's people are rather good people, and better than most Pinky Dinky's people. But he does not put on side."

" Pinky Dinkys become playful at the sight of women."

" ' Croquet's my game,' said the Pinky Dinky, and felt a man condescended."

" But what the devil do they think they're up to, any-how ? " roared old Hatherleigh suddenly, dropping plump into bottomless despair.

We felt we had still failed to get at the core of the mystery of the Pinky Dinky.

We tried over things about his religion. "The Pinky Dinky goes to King's Chapel, and sits and feels in the dusk. Solemn things ! Oh, *hush* ! He wouldn't tell you——"

" He *couldn't* tell you."

" Religion is so sacred to him he never talks about it, never reads about it, never thinks about it. Just feels ! "

" But in his heart of hearts, oh ! ever so deep, the Pinky Dinky has a doubt——"

Some one protested.

" Not a vulgar doubt," Esmeer went on, " but a kind of hesitation whether the Ancient of Days is really exactly what one would call good form. . . . There's a lot of horrid coarse-ness got into the world somehow. *Somebody* put it there. . . . And anyhow there's no particular reason why a man should be seen about with Him. He's jolly Awful of course and all that——"

" The Pinky Dinky for all his fun and levity has a clean mind."

" A thoroughly clean mind. Not like Esmeer's—the Pig ! "

" If once he began to think about sex, how could he be comfortable at croquet ? "

" It's their Damned Modesty," said Hatherleigh suddenly, " that's what's the matter with the Pinky Dinky. It's Mental Cowardice dressed up as a virtue and taking the poor dears in. Cambridge is soaked with it ; it's some confounded local bacillus. Like the thing that gives a flavour to Havana cigars. He comes up here to be made into a man and a ruler of the people, and he thinks it shows a nice disposition not to take on the job ! How the Devil is a great Empire to be run with men like him ? "

" All his little jokes and things," said Esmeer regarding his feet on the fender, " it's just a nervous sniggering—because he's afraid. . . . Oxford's no better."

" What's he afraid of ? " said I.

" God knows ! " exploded Hatherleigh and stared at the fire.

" *Life* ! " said Esmeer. " And so in a way are we," he added, and made a thoughtful silence for a time.

" I say," began Carter, who was doing the Natural Science Tripos, " what is the adult form of the Pinky Dinky ? "

But there we were checked by our ignorance of the world.

" What is the adult form of any of us ? " asked Benton, voicing the thought that had arrested our flow.

§ 3

I do not remember that we ever lifted our criticism to the dons and the organisation of the University. I think we took them for granted. When I look back at my youth I am always astonished by the multitude of things that we took for granted. It seemed to us that Cambridge was in the order of things, for all the world like having eyebrows or a vermiform appendix. Now with the larger scepticism of middle age I can entertain very fundamental doubts about these old universities. Indeed I had a scheme——

I do not see what harm I can do now by laying bare the purpose of the political combinations I was trying to effect.

My educational scheme was indeed the starting-point of all the big project of conscious public reconstruction at which I aimed. I wanted to build up a new educational machine altogether for the governing class out of a consolidated system of special public service schools. I meant to get to work upon this whatever office I was given in the new government. I could have begun my plan from the Admiralty or the War Office quite as easily as from the Education Office. I am firmly convinced it is hopelsss to think of reforming the old public schools and universities to meet the needs of a modern state, they send their roots too deep and far, the cost would exceed any good that could possibly be effected, and so I have sought a way round this invincible obstacle. I do think it would be quite practicable to side-track, as the Americans say, the whole system by creating hard-working, hard-living, modern and scientific boys' schools, first for the Royal Navy and then for the public departments generally, and as they grew, opening them to the public without any absolute obligation to subsequent service. Simultaneously with this it would not be impossible to develop a new college system with strong faculties in modern philosophy, modern history, European literature and criticism, physical and biological science, education and sociology.

We could in fact create a new liberal education in this way, and cut the umbilicus of the classical languages for good and all. I should have set this going, and trusted it to correct or kill the old public schools and the Oxford and Cambridge tradition altogether. I had men in my mind to begin the work, and I should have found others. I should have aimed at making a hard-trained, capable, intellectually active, proud type of man. Everything else would have been made subservient to that. I should have kept my grip on the men through their vacation, and somehow or other I would have contrived a young woman to match them. I think I could have seen to it effectually enough that they didn't get at croquet and tennis with the vicarage daughters, nor discover sex in the Peeping Tom fashion as I did, and that they realised quite early in life that it isn't really virile to reek of tobacco. I should have had military manœuvres, training-ships, aeroplane work, mountaineering and so forth, in the place of the solemn trivialities of games, and I should have fed and housed my men clean and very hard—where there wasn't any audit ale, no credit tradesmen, and plenty of high-pressure douches. . . .

I have revisited Cambridge and Oxford time after time since I came down, and so far as the Empire goes, I want to get clear of those two places. . . .

Always I renew my old feelings, a physical oppression, a sense of lowness and dampness almost exactly like the feeling of an underground room where paper moulders and leaves the wall, a feeling of ineradicable contagion in the Gothic buildings, in the narrow ditch-like rivers, in those roads and roads of stuffy little villas. Those little villas have destroyed all the good of the old monastic system and none of its evil. . . .

Some of the most charming people in the world live in them, but their collective effect is below the quality of any individual among them. Cambridge is a world of subdued tones, of excessively subtle humours, of prim conduct and free thinking ; it fears the Parent, but it has no fear of God ; it offers amidst surroundings that vary between disguises and antiquarian charm the inflammation of literature's purple draught ; one hears there a peculiar thin scandal like no other scandal in the world—a covetous scandal—so that I am always reminded of Ibsen in Cambridge. In Cambridge and the plays of Ibsen alone does it seem appropriate for the heroine before the great crisis of life to " enter, take off her overshoes, and put her wet umbrella upon the writing-desk." . . .

We have to make a new Academic mind for modern needs, and the last thing to make it out of, I am convinced, is the old Academic mind. One might as soon try to fake the old *Victory* at Portsmouth into a line-of-battleship again. Besides which the old Academic mind, like those old bathless, damp Gothic colleges, is much too delightful in its peculiar and distinctive way to damage by futile patching.

My heart warms to a sense of affectionate absurdity as I recall dear old Codger, surely the most " unleaderly " of men. No more than from the old Schoolmen, his kindred, could one get from him a School for Princes. Yet apart from his teaching he was as curious and adorable as a good Netsuké. Until quite recently he was a power in Cambridge, he could make and bar and destroy, and in a way he has become the quintessence of Cambridge in my thoughts.

I see him on his way to the morning's lecture, with his plump childish face, his round innocent eyes, his absurdly non-prehensile fat hand carrying his cap, his grey trousers braced up much too high, his feet a trifle inturned, and going across Great Court with a queer tripping pace that seemed cultivated even to my naïve undergraduate eye. Or I see him lecturing. He lectured walking up and down between the desks, talking in a fluting rapid voice, and with the utmost lucidity. If he could not walk up and down he could not lecture. His mind and voice had precisely the fluid quality of some clear subtle liquid ; one felt it could flow round anything and overcome nothing. And its nimble eddies were wonderful ! Or again I recall him drinking port with little muscular movements in his neck and cheek and chin and his brows knit—very judicial, very concentrated, preparing to say the apt just thing ; it was the last thing he would have told a lie about.

When I think of Codger I am reminded of an inscription I saw on some occasion in Regent's Park above two eyes scarcely more limpidly innocent than his—" Born in the Menagerie." Never once since Codger began to display the early promise of scholarship at the age of eight or more, had he been outside the bars. His utmost travel had been to lecture here and lecture there. His student phase had culminated in papers of quite exceptional brilliance, and he had gone on to lecture with a cheerful combination of wit and mannerism that had made him a success from the beginning. He has lectured ever since. He lectures still. Year by year he has become plumper, more rubicund and more and more of an item for the intelligent visitor to see. Even in my time he was pointed out to people as part of our innumerable enrichments, and obviously he knew it. He has become now almost the leading Character in a little donnish world of much too intensely appreciated Characters.

He boasted he took no exercise, and also of his knowledge of port wine. Of other wines he confessed quite frankly he had no " special knowledge." Beyond these things he had little pride except that he claimed to have read every novel by a woman writer that had ever entered the Union Library. This, however, he held to be remarkable rather than ennobling, and such boasts as he made of it were tinged with playfulness. Certainly he had a scholar's knowledge of the works of Miss Marie Corelli, Miss Braddon, Mrs. Elinor Glyn and Madame Sarah Grand that would have astonished and flattered those ladies enormously, and he loved nothing so much in his hours of relaxation as to propound and answer difficult questions upon their books. Tusher of King's was his ineffectual rival in this field, their bouts were memorable and rarely other than glorious for Codger ; but then Tusher spread himself too much, he also undertook to rehearse whole pages out of Bradshaw, and tell you with all the changes how to get from any station to any station in Great Britain by the nearest and cheapest routes. . . .

Codger lodged with a little deaf innocent old lady, Mrs. Araminta Mergle, who was understood to be herself a very redoubtable Character in the Gyp-Bedder class ; about her he related quietly absurd anecdotes. He displayed a marvellous invention in ascribing to her plausible expressions of opinion entirely identical in import with those of the Oxford and Harvard Pragmatists, against whom he waged a fierce obscure war. . . .

It was Codger's function to teach me philosophy—philosophy! the intimate wisdom of things. He dealt in a variety of Hegelian stuff like nothing else in the world, but marvellously consistent with itself. It was a wonderful web he spun out of that queer big active childish brain that had never lusted nor hated nor grieved nor feared nor passionately loved—a web of iridescent threads. He had luminous final theories about Love and Death and Immortality, odd matters they seemed for him to think about ! and all his woven thoughts lay across my perception of the realities of things, as flimsy and irrelevant and clever and beautiful, oh !—as a dew-wet spider's web slung in the morning sunshine across the black mouth of a gun. . . .

§ 4

All through those years of development I perceive now there must have been growing in me, slowly, irregularly, assimilating to itself all the phrases and forms of patriotism, diverting my religious impulses, utilising my æsthetic tendencies, my dominating idea, the statesman's idea, that idea of social service which is the protagonist of my story, that real though complex passion for Making, making widely and greatly, cities, national order, civilisation, whose interplay with all those other factors in life I have set out to present. It was growing in me—as one's bones grow, no man intending it.

I have tried to show how, quite early in my life, the fact of disorderliness, the conception of social life as being a multitudinous confusion out of hand, came to me. One always of course simplifies these things in the telling, but I do not think I ever saw the world at large in any other terms. I never at any stage entertained the idea which sustained my mother, and which sustains so many people in the world—the idea that the universe, whatever superficial discords it may present, is as a matter of fact " all right," is being steered to definite ends by a serene and unquestionable God. My mother thought that Order prevailed, and that disorder was just incidental and foredoomed rebellion ; I feel and have always felt that order rebels against and struggles against disorder, that order has an uphill job, in gardens, experiments, suburbs, everything alike ; from the very beginnings of my experience I discovered hostility to order, a constant escaping from control.

The current of living and contemporary ideas in which my mind was presently swimming made all in the same direction ; in place of my mother's attentive, meticulous but occasionally extremely irascible Providence, the talk was all of the Struggle for Existence and the survival not of the Best—that was nonsense—but of the fittest to survive.

The attempts to rehabilitate Faith in the form of the Individualist's *laissez faire* never won upon me. I disliked Herbert Spencer all my life until I read his autobiography, and then I laughed a little and loved him. I remember as early as the City Merchants' days how Britten and I scoffed at that pompous question-begging word " Evolution," having, so to speak, found it out. Evolution, some illuminating talker had remarked at the Britten lunch-table, had led not only to man, but to the liver-fluke and skunk, obviously it might lead anywhere ; order came into things only through the struggling mind of man. That lit things wonderfully for us. When I went up to Cambridge I was perfectly clear that life was a various and splendid disorder of forces that the spirit of man sets itself to tame. I have never since fallen away from that persuasion.

I do not think I was exceptionally precocious in reaching these conclusions and a sort of religious finality for myself by eighteen or nineteen. I know men and women vary very much in these matters, just as children do in learning to talk. Some will chatter at eighteen months and some will hardly speak until three, and the thing has very little to do with their subsequent mental quality. So it is with young people ; some will begin their religious, their social, their sexual interests at fourteen, some not until far on in the twenties. Britten and I belonged to one of the precocious types, and Cossington very probably to another. It wasn't that there was anything priggish about any of us ; we should have been prigs to have concealed our spontaneous interests and ape the theoretical boy.

The world of man centred for my imagination in London, it still centres there ; the real and present world, that is to say, as distinguished from the wonderlands of atomic and microscopic science and the stars and future time. I had travelled scarcely at all, I had never crossed the Channel, but I had read copiously and I had formed a very good working idea of this round globe with its mountains and wildernesses and forests and all the sorts and conditions of human life that were scattered over its surface. It was all alive, I felt, and changing every day ; how it was changing, and the changes men might bring about, fascinated my mind beyond measure.

I used to find a charm in old maps that showed The World as Known to the Ancients, and I wish I could now without any suspicion of self-deception write down compactly the world as it was known to me at nineteen. So far as extension went it was, I fancy, very like the world I know now at forty-two ; I had practically all the mountains and seas, boundaries and races, products and possibilities that I have now. But its intension was very different. All the interval has been increasing and deepening my social knowledge, replacing crude and second-hand impressions by felt and realised distinctions.

In 1895—that was my last year with Britten, for I went up

to Cambridge in September—my vision of the world had much the same relation to the vision I have to-day that an ill-drawn daub of a mask has to the direct vision of a human face. Britten and I looked at our world and saw—what did we see ? Forms and colours side by side that we had no suspicion were interdependent. We had no conception of the roots of things nor of the reaction of things. It did not seem to us, for example, that business had anything to do with government, or that money and means affected the heroic issues of war. There were no waggons in our war game, and where there were guns, there it was assumed the ammunition was gathered together. Finance again was a sealed book to us ; we did not so much connect it with the broad aspect of human affairs as regard it as a sort of intrusive nuisance to be earnestly ignored by all right-minded men. We had no conception of the quality of politics, nor how " interests " came into such affairs ; we believed men were swayed by purely intellectual convictions and were either right or wrong, honest or dishonest (in which case they deserved to be shot), good or bad. We knew nothing of mental inertia, and could imagine the opinion of a whole nation changed by one lucid and convincing exposition. We were capable of the most incongruous transfers from the scroll of history to our own times, we could suppose Brixton ravaged and Hampstead burned in civil wars for the succession to the throne, or Cheapside a lane of death and the front of the Mansion House set about with guillotines in the course of an accurately transposed French Revolution. We rebuilt London by Act of Parliament, and once in a mood of hygienic enterprise we transferred its population *en masse* to the North Downs by an order of the Local Government Board. We thought nothing of throwing religious organisations out of employment or superseding all the newspapers by freely distributed bulletins. We could contemplate the possibility of laws abolishing whole classes ; we were equal to such a dream as the peaceful and orderly proclamation of Communism from the steps of St. Paul's Cathedral, after the passing of a simply worded bill—a close and not unnaturally an exciting division carrying the third reading. I remember quite distinctly evolving that vision. We were then fully fifteen and we were perfectly serious about it. We were not fools ; it was simply that as yet we had gathered no experience at all of the limits and powers of legislation and conscious collective intention. . . .

I think this statement does my boyhood justice, and yet I have my doubts. It is so hard now to say what one understood and what one did not understand. It isn't only that every day changed one's general outlook, but also that a boy fluctuates between phases of quite adult understanding and phases of tawdrily magnificent puerility. Sometimes I myself was in those tumbrils that went along Cheapside to the Mansion

House, a Sydney Cartonesque figure, a white defeated Mira-
beau ; sometimes it was I who sat judging and condemning and
ruling (sleeping in my clothes and feeding very simply) the
soul and autocrat of the Provisional Government, which
occupied, of all inconvenient places ! the General Post Office at
St. Martin's-le-Grand ! . . .

I cannot trace the development of my ideas at Cambridge,
but I believe the mere physical fact of going two hours'
journey away from London gave that place for the first time
an effect of unity in my imagination. I got outside London.
It became tangible instead of being a frame almost as universal
as sea and sky.

At Cambridge my ideas ceased to live in a duologue ; in
exchange for Britten, with whom, however, I corresponded
lengthily, stylishly and self-consciously for some years, I had
now a set of congenial friends. I got talk with some of the
younger dons, I learned to speak in the Union, and in my little
set we were all pretty busily sharpening each other's wits and
correcting each other's interpretations. Cambridge made
politics personal and actual. At City Merchants' we had had
no sense of effective contact ; we boasted, it is true, an under-
secretary and a colonial governor among our old boys, but
they were never real to us ; such distinguished sons as returned
to visit the old school were allusive and pleasant in the best
Pinky Dinky style, and pretended to be in earnest about
nothing but our football and cricket, to mourn the abolition
of " water," and find a shuddering personal interest in the
ancient swishing block. At Cambridge I felt for the first time
that I touched the thing that was going on. Real living
statesmen came down to debate in the Union, the older dons
had been their college intimates, their sons and nephews ex-
pounded them to us and made them real to us. They invited
us to entertain ideas ; I found myself for the first time in my
life expected to read and think and discuss, my secret vice had
become a virtue.

That combination-room world is at least larger and more
populous and various than the world of schoolmasters. The
Shoesmiths and Naylors who had been the aristocracy of City
Merchants' fell into their place in my mind ; they became an
undistinguished mass on the more athletic side of Pinky
Dinkyism, and their hostility to ideas and to the expression of
ideas ceased to limit and trouble me. The brighter men of
each generation stay up ; these others go down to propagate
their tradition, as the fathers of families, as mediocre professional men, as assistant masters in schools. Cambridge
which perfects them is by the nature of things least oppressed
by them—except when it comes to a vote in Convocation.

We were still in those days under the shadow of the great
Victorians. I never saw Gladstone (as I never set eyes on the
old Queen), but he had resigned office only a year before I went

up to Trinity, and the Combination Rooms were full of personal gossip about him and Disraeli and the other big figures of the gladiatorial stage of Parliamentary history, talk that leaked copiously into such sets as mine. The ceiling of our guest chamber at Trinity was glorious with the arms of Sir William Harcourt, whose Death Duties had seemed at first like a socialist dawn. Mr. Evesham we asked to come to the Union every year, Masters, Chamberlain and the old Duke of Devonshire ; they did not come indeed, but their polite refusals brought us all, as it were, within personal touch of them. One heard of cabinet councils and meetings at country houses. Some of us, pursuing such interests, went so far as to read political memoirs and the novels of Disraeli and Mrs. Humphry Ward. From gossip, example and the illustrated newspapers one learned something of the way in which parties were split, coalitions formed, how permanent officials worked and controlled their ministers, how measures were brought forward and projects modified.

And while I was getting the great leading figures on the political stage, who had been presented to me in my schooldays not so much as men as the pantomimic monsters of political caricature, while I was getting them reduced in my imagination to the stature of humanity and their motives to the quality of impulses like my own, I was also acquiring in my Tripos work a constantly developing and enriching conception of the world of men as a complex of economic, intellectual and moral processes. . . .

§ 5

Socialism is an intellectual Proteus, but to the men of my generation it came as the revolt of the workers. Rodbertus we never heard of and the Fabian Society we did not understand ; Marx and Morris, the Chicago Anarchists, *Justice* and the Social Democratic Federation (as it was then) presented socialism to our minds. Hatherleigh was the leading exponent of the new doctrines in Trinity, and the figure upon his wall of a huge-muscled, black-haired toiler swaggering sledgehammer in hand across a revolutionary barricade, seemed the quintessence of what he had to expound. Landlord and capitalist had robbed and enslaved the workers, and were driving them quite automatically to inevitable insurrection. They would arise and the capitalist system would flee and vanish like the mists before the morning, like the dews before the sunrise, giving place in the most simple amd obvious manner to an era of Right and Justice and Virtue and Well-Being, and in short a Perfectly Splendid Time.

I had already discussed this sort of socialism under the guidance of Britten, before I went up to Cambridge. It was all mixed up with ideas about freedom and natural virtue and a great scorn for kings, titles, wealth and officials, and it was symbolised by the red ties we wore. Our simple verdict on existing arrangements was that they were " all wrong." The rich were robbers and knew it, kings and princes were usurpers and knew it, religious teachers were impostors in league with power, the economic system was an elaborate plot on the part of the few to expropriate the many. We went about feeling scornful of all the current forms of life, forms that esteemed themselves solid, that were, we knew, no more than shapes painted on a curtain that was presently to be torn aside. . . .

It was Hatherleigh's poster and his capacity for overstating things, I think, that first qualified my simple revolutionary enthusiasm. Perhaps also I had met with Fabian publications, but if I did I forget the circumstances. And no doubt my innate constructiveness with its practical corollary of an analytical treatment of the material supplied, was bound to push me on beyond this melodramatic interpretation of human affairs.

I compared that Working Man of the poster with any sort of working man I knew. I perceived that the latter was not going to change, and indeed could not under any stimulus whatever be expected to change, into the former. It crept into my mind as slowly and surely as the dawn creeps into a room that the former was not, as I had at first rather glibly assumed, an "ideal," but a complete misrepresentation of the quality and possibilities of things.

I do not know now whether it was during my schooldays or at Cambridge that I first began not merely to see the world as a great contrast of rich and poor, but to feel the massive effect of that multitudinous majority of people who toil continually, who are for ever anxious about ways and means, who are restricted, ill clothed, ill fed and ill housed, who have limited outlooks and continually suffer misadventures, hardships and distresses through the want of money. My lot had fallen upon the fringe of the possessing minority ; if I did not know the want of necessities I knew shabbiness, and the world that let me go on to a university education intimated very plainly that there was not a thing beyond the primary needs that my stimulated imagination might demand that it would not be an effort for me to secure. A certain aggressive radicalism against the ruling and propertied classes followed almost naturally from my circumstances. It did not at first connect itself at all with the perception of a planless disorder in human affairs that had been forced upon me by the atmosphere of my upbringing, nor did it link me in sympathy with any of the profounder realities of poverty. It was a personal independent thing. The dingier people one saw in the back streets and lower quarters of Bromstead and Penge, the drift of dirty children, ragged old women, street loafers, grimy workers that made the social background of London, the stories one heard of privation and sweating, only joined up very slowly with the general propositions I was making about life. We could become splendidly eloquent about the social revolution and the triumph of the Proletariat after the class war, and it was only by a sort of inspiration that it came to me that my bedder, a garrulous old thing with a dusty black bonnet over one eye and an ostentatiously clean apron outside the dark mysteries that clothed her, or the cheeky little ruffians who yelled papers about the streets, were really material to such questions.

Directly any of us young socialists of Trinity found ourselves in immediate contact with servants or cadgers or gyps or bedders or plumbers or navvies or cabmen or railway porters we became unconsciously and unthinkingly aristocrats. Our voices altered, our gestures altered. We behaved just as all the other men, rich or poor, swatters or sportsmen or Pinky Dinkys, behaved, and exactly as we were expected to behave. On the whole it is a population of poor quality round about Cambridge, rather stunted and spiritless and very difficult to idealise. That theoretical Working Man of ours !—if we felt the clash at all we explained it, I suppose, by assuming that he came from another part of the country ; Esmeer, I remember, who lived somewhere in the Fens, was very eloquent about the Cornish fishermen, and Hatherleigh, who was a Hampshire man, assured us we ought to know the Scottish miner. My private fancy was for the Lancashire operative because of his co-operative societies, and because what Lancashire thinks to-day England thinks to-morrow. . . . And also I had never been in Lancashire.

By little increments of realisation it was that the profounder verities of the problem of socialism came to me. It helped me very much that I had to go down to the Potteries several times to discuss my future with my uncle and guardian ; I walked about and saw Bursley Wakes and much of the human aspects of organised industrialism at close quarters for the first time. The picture of a splendid Working Man cheated out of his innate glorious possibilities and presently to arise and dash this scoundrelly and scandalous system of private ownership to fragments, began to give place to a limitless spectacle of inefficiency, to a conception of millions of people not organised as they should be, not educated as they should be, not simply prevented from but incapable of nearly every sort of beauty, mostly kindly and well-meaning, mostly incompetent, mostly obstinate, and easily humbugged and easily diverted. Even the tragic and inspiring idea of Marx, that the poor were nearing a limit of painful experience and awakening to a sense of intolerable wrongs, began to develop into the more appalling conception that the poor were simply in a witless uncomfortable inconclusive way—" muddling along " ; that they wanted nothing very definitely nor very urgently, that mean fears enslaved them and mean satisfactions decoyed them, that they took the very gift of life itself with a spiritless lassitude, hoarding it, being rather anxious not to lose it than to use it in any way whatever.

The complete development of that realisation was the work of many years. I had only the first intimations at Cambridge. But I did have intimations. Most acutely do I remember the doubts that followed the visit of Chris Robinson. Chris Robinson was heralded by such heroic anticipations, and he was so entirely what we had not anticipated.

Hatherleigh got him to come, arranged a sort of meeting for him at Redmayne's rooms in King's, and was very proud and proprietorial. It failed to stir Cambridge at all profoundly. Beyond a futile attempt to screw up Hatherleigh made by some inexpert duffers who used nails instead of screws and gimlets, there was no attempt to rag. Next day Chris Robinson went and spoke at Bennett Hall in Newnham College, and left Cambridge in the evening amidst the cheers of twenty men or so. Socialism was at such a low ebb politically in those days that it didn't even rouse men to opposition.

And there sat Chris under that flamboyant and heroic Worker of the poster, a little wrinkled grey-bearded apologetic man in ready-made clothes, with watchful innocent brown eyes and a persistent and invincible air of being out of his element. He sat with his stout boots tucked up under his chair, and clung to a teacup and saucer and looked away from us into the fire, and we all sat about on tables and chair-arms and window-sills and boxes and anywhere except upon chairs after the manner of young men. The only other chair whose seat was occupied was the one containing his knitted woollen comforter and his picturesque old beach-photographer's hat. We were all shy and didn't know how to take hold of him now we had got him, and, which was disconcertingly unanticipated, he was manifestly having the same difficulty with us. We had expected to be gripped.

"I'll not be knowing what to say to these Chaps," he repeated with a north-country quality in his speech.

We made reassuring noises.

The Ambassador of the Workers stirred his tea earnestly through an uncomfortable pause.

"I'd best tell 'em something of how things are in Lancashire, what with the new machines and all that," he speculated at last with red reflections in his thoughtful eyes.

We had an inexcusable dread that perhaps he would make a mess of the meeting.

But when he was no longer in the unaccustomed meshes of refined conversation, but speaking with an audience before him, he became a different man. He declared he would explain to us just exactly what socialism was, and went on at once to an impassioned contrast of social conditions. "You young men," he said, "come from homes of luxury; every need you feel is supplied——"

We sat and stood and sprawled about him, occupying every inch of Redmayne's floor space except the hearthrug-platform, and we listened to him and thought him over. He was the voice of wrongs that made us indignant and eager. We forgot for a time that he had been shy and seemed not a little incompetent, his provincial accent became a beauty of his earnest speech, we were carried away by his indignations. We looked with shining eyes at one another and at the various dons who had dropped in and were striving to maintain a front of judicious severity. We felt more and more that social injustice must cease, and cease forthwith. We felt we could not sleep upon it. At the end we clapped and murmured our applause and wanted badly to cheer.

Then like a lancet stuck into a bladder came the heckling. Denson, that indolent, liberal-minded sceptic, did most of the questioning. He lay contorted in a chair, with his ugly head very low, his legs crossed and his left boot very high, and he pointed his remarks with a long thin hand and occasionally adjusted the unstable glasses that hid his watery eyes. "I don't want to carp," he began. "The present system, I admit, stands condemned. Every present system always *has* stood condemned in the minds of intelligent men. But where it seems to me you get thin, is just where everybody has been thin, and that's when you come to the remedy."

"Socialism," said Chris Robinson, as if it answered everything, and Hatherleigh said "Hear! Hear!" very resolutely.

"I suppose I *ought* to take that as an answer," said Denson, getting his shoulder-blades well down to the seat of his chair; "but I don't. I don't, you know. It's rather a shame to cross-examine you after this fine address of yours "—Chris Robinson on the hearthrug made acquiescent and inviting noises—" but the real question remains how exactly are you going to end all these wrongs? There are the administrative questions. If you abolish the private owner, I admit you abolish a very complex and clumsy way of getting businesses run, land controlled and things in general administered, but you don't get rid of the need of administration, you know."

"Democracy," said Chris Robinson.

"Organised somehow," said Denson. "And it's just the How perplexes me. I can quite easily imagine a socialist state administered in a sort of scrambling tumult that would be worse than anything we have got now."

"Nothing could be worse than things are now," said Chris Robinson. "I have seen little children——"

"I submit life on an ill-provisioned raft, for example, could easily be worse—or life in a beleaguered town."

Murmurs.

They wrangled for some time, and it had the effect upon me

of coming out from the glow of a good matinée performance into the cold daylight of late afternoon. Chris Robinson did not shine in conflict with Denson ; he was an orator and not a dialectician, and he missed Denson's points and displayed a disposition to plunge into untimely pathos and indignation. And Denson hit me curiously hard with one of his shafts. " Suppose," he said, " you found yourself prime minister——"

I looked at Chris Robinson, bright-eyed and his hair a little ruffled and his whole being rhetorical, and measured him against the huge machine of government muddled and mysterious. Oh ! but I was perplexed !

And then we took him back to Hatherleigh's rooms and drank beer and smoked about him while he nursed his knee with hairy-wristed hands that protruded from his flannel shirt, and drank lemonade under the cartoon of that emancipated Worker, and we had a great discursive talk with him.

" Eh ! you should see our big meetings up north ! " he said.

Denson had ruffled him and worried him a good deal, and ever and again he came back to that discussion. " It's all very easy for your learned men to sit and pick holes," he said, " while the children suffer and die. They don't pick holes up north. They mean business."

He talked, and that was the most interesting part of it all, of his going to work in a factory when he was twelve—" when you Chaps were all with your mammies "—and how he had educated himself of nights until he would fall asleep at his reading.

" It's made many of us keen for all our lives," he remarked, " all that clemming for education. Why ! I longed all through one winter to read a bit of Darwin. I must know about this Darwin if I die for it, I said. And I couldno' get the book."

Hatherleigh made an enthusiastic noise and drank beer at him with round eyes over the mug.

" Well, anyhow I wasted no time on Greek and Latin," said Chris Robinson. " And one learns to go straight at a thing without splitting straws. One gets hold of the Elementals."

(Well, did they ? That was the gist of my perplexity.)

" One doesn't quibble," he said, returning to his rankling memory of Denson, " while men decay and starve."

" But suppose," I said, suddenly dropping into opposition, " the alternative is to risk a worse disaster—or do something patently futile ? "

" I don't follow that," said Chris Robinson. " We don't propose anything futile, so far as I can see."

§ 6

The prevailing force in my undergraduate days was not Socialism but Kiplingism. Our set was quite exceptional in its socialistic professions. And we were all, you must understand, very distinctly Imperialists also, and professed a vivid sense of the "White Man's Burden."

It is a little difficult now to get back to the feelings of that period ; Kipling has since been so mercilessly and exhaustively mocked, criticised and torn to shreds ;—never was a man so violently exalted and then, himself assisting, so relentlessly called down. But in the middle 'nineties this spectacled and moustached little figure with its heavy chin and its general effect of vehement gesticulation, its wild shouts of boyish enthusiasm for effective force, its lyric delight in the sounds and colours, in the very odours of empire, its wonderful dis-covery of machinery and cotton-waste and the under officer and the engineer, and "shop" as a poetic dialect, became almost a national symbol. He got hold of us wonderfully, he filled us with tinkling and haunting quotations, he stirred Britten and myself to futile imitations, he coloured the very idiom of our conversation. He rose to his climax with his "Recessional," while I was still an undergraduate.

What did he give me exactly ?

He helped to broaden my geographical sense immensely, and he provided phrases for just that desire for discipline and devotion and organised effort the Socialism of our time failed to express, that the current socialist movement still fails, I think, to express. The sort of thing that follows, for example, tore something out of my inmost nature and gave it a shape, and I took it back from him shaped and let much of the rest of him, the tumult and the bullying, the hysteria and the impatience, the incoherence and inconsistency, go uncriticised for the sake of it :—

"Keep ye the Law—be swift in all obedience—
Clear the land of evil, drive the road and bridge the ford,
Make ye sure to each his own
That he reap where he hath sown ;
By the peace among Our peoples let men know we serve the Lord ! "

And then again, and for all our later criticism, this sticks in my mind, sticks there now as quintessential wisdom :

"The 'eathen in 'is blindness bows down to wood an' stone ;
'E don't obey no orders unless they is 'is own ;
'Ee keeps 'is side-arms awful : 'e leaves 'em all about ;
An' then comes up the regiment an' pokes the 'eathen out.
    All along o' dirtiness, all along o' mess,
    All along o' doin' things rather-more-or-less,
    All along of abby-nay, kul, an' hazar-ho,
    Mind you keep your rifle an' yourself jus' so ! "

It is after all a secondary matter that Kipling, not having been born and brought up in Bromstead and Penge, and the war in South Africa being yet in the womb of time, could quite

honestly entertain the now remarkable delusion that England
had her side-arms at that time kept anything but "awful."
He learned better, and we all learned with him in the dark
years of exasperating and humiliating struggle that followed,
and I do not see that we fellow-learners are justified in turning
resentfully upon him for a common ignorance and assumption. . . .

South Africa seems always painted on the back cloth of my
Cambridge memories. How immense those disasters seemed
at the time, disasters our facile English world has long since
contrived in any edifying or profitable sense to forget ! How
we thrilled to the shouting newspaper sellers as the first false
flush of victory gave place to the realisation of defeat. Far
away there our army showed itself human, mortal and human
in the sight of all the world, the pleasant officers we had
imagined would change to wonderful heroes at the first crackling of rifles, remained the pleasant, rather incompetent men
they had always been, failing to imagine, failing to plan and
co-operate, failing to grip. And the common soldiers, too,
they were just what our streets and country-side had made
them, no sudden magic came out of the war bugles for them.
Neither splendid nor disgraceful were they—just ill-trained
and fairly plucky and wonderfully good-tempered men—paying
for it. And how it lowered our vitality all that first winter
to hear of Nicholson's Nek, and then presently close upon one
another, to realise the bloody waste of Magersfontein, the
shattering retreat from Stromberg, Colenso—Colenso, that
blundering battle, with White, as it seemed, in Ladysmith
near the point of surrender ! and so through the long unfolding
catalogue of bleak disillusionments, of aching, unconcealed
anxiety lest worse should follow. To advance upon your
enemy singing about his lack of cleanliness and method went
out of fashion altogether ! The dirty retrogressive Boer
vanished from our scheme of illusion.

All through my middle Cambridge period, the guns boomed
and the rifles crackled away there on the veldt, and the horsemen rode and the tale of accidents and blundering went on.
Men, mules, horses, stores and money poured into South
Africa, and the convalescent wounded streamed home. I see
it in my memory as if I had looked at it through a window
instead of through the pages of the illustrated papers ; I recall
as if I had been there the wide open spaces, the ragged hillsides, the open order attacks of helmeted men in khaki, the
scarce visible smoke of the guns, the wrecked trains in great
lonely places, the burned isolated farms, and then the block-
houses and the fences of barbed wire uncoiling and spreading
for endless miles across the desert, netting the elusive enemy
until at last, though he broke the meshes again and again, we
had him in the toils. If one's attention strayed in the lecture-
room it wandered to those battlefields.

And that imagined panorama of war unfolds to an accompaniment of yelling newsboys in the narrow old Cambridge streets, of the flicker of papers hastily bought and torn open in the twilight, of the doubtful reception of doubtful victories, and the insensate rejoicings at last that seemed to some of us more shameful than defeats. . . .

§ 7

A book that stands out among these memories, that stimulated me immensely so that I forced it upon my companions, half in the spirit of propaganda and half to test it by their comments, was Meredith's *One of Our Conquerors*. It is one of the books that have made me. In that I got a supplement and corrective of Kipling. It was the first detached and adverse criticism of the Englishman I had ever encountered. It must have been published already, nine or ten years when I read it. The country had paid no heed to it, had gone on to the expensive lessons of the war because of the dull aversion our people feel for all such intimations, and so I could read it as a book justified. The war endorsed its every word for me, underlined each warning indication of the gigantic dangers that gathered against our system across the narrow seas. It discovered Europe to me, as watching and critical.

But while I could respond to all its criticism of my country's intellectual indolence, of my country's want of training and discipline and moral courage, I remember that the idea that on the Continent there were other peoples going ahead of us, mentally alert while we fumbled, disciplined while we slouched, aggressive and preparing to bring our Imperial pride to a reckoning, was extremely novel and distasteful to me. It set me worrying of nights. It put all my projects for social and political reconstruction upon a new uncomfortable footing. It made them no longer merely desirable but urgent. Instead of pride and the love of making one might own to a baser motive. Under Kipling's sway I had a little forgotten the continent of Europe, treated it as a mere envious echo to our own world-wide display. I began now to have a disturbing sense as it were of busy searchlights over the horizon. . . .

One consequence of the patriotic chagrin Meredith produced in me was an attempt to belittle his merit. " It isn't a good novel, anyhow," I said.

The charge I brought against it was, I remember, a lack of unity. It professed to be a study of the English situation in the early 'nineties, but it was all deflected, I said, and all the interest was confused by the story of Victor Radnor's fight with society to vindicate the woman he had loved and never married. Now in the retrospect and with a mind full of bitter enlightenment, I can do Meredith justice, and admit the conflict was not only essential but cardinal in his picture, that the terrible inflexibility of the rich aunts and the still more terrible claim of Mrs. Burman Radnor, the "infernal punctilio," and Dudley Sowerby's limitations, were the central substance of that inalertness the book set itself to assail. So many things have been brought together in my mind that were once remotely separated. A people that will not valiantly face and understand and admit love and passion can understand nothing whatever. But in those days what is now just obvious truth to me was altogether outside my range of comprehension. . . .

§ 8

As I seek to recapitulate the interlacing growth of my apprehension of the world, as I flounder among the half-remembered developments that found me a crude schoolboy and left me a man, there comes out, as if it stood for all the rest, my first holiday abroad. That did not happen until I was twenty-two. I was a fellow of Trinity, and the Peace of Vereeniging had just been signed.

I went with a man named Willersley, a man some years senior to myself, who had just missed a fellowship and the higher division of the Civil Service, and who had become an enthusiastic member of the London School Board, upon which the cumulative vote and the support of the "advanced" people had placed him. He had, like myself, a small independent income that relieved him of any necessity to earn a living, and he had a kindred craving for social theorising and some form of social service. He had sought my acquaintance after reading a paper of mine (begotten by the visit of Chris Robinson) on the limits of pure democracy. It had marched with some thoughts of his own.

We went by train to Spiez on the Lake of Thun, then up the Gemmi, and hence with one or two halts and digressions and a little modest climbing we crossed over by the Antrona pass (on which we were benighted) into Italy, and by way of Domo D'ossola and the Santa Maria Maggiore valley to Cannobio, and thence up the lake to Locarno (where, as I shall tell, we stayed some eventful days) and so up the Val Maggia and over to Airolo and home.

As I write of that long tramp of ours, something of its freshness and enlargement returns to me. I feel again the faint pleasant excitement of the boat-train, the trampling procession of people with hand baggage and laden porters along the platform of the Folkstone pier, the scarcely perceptible swaying of the moored boat beneath our feet. Then, very obvious and simple, the little emotion of standing out from the homeland and seeing the long white Kentish cliffs recede. One walked about the boat doing one's best not to feel absurdly adventurous, and presently a movement of people directed one's attention to a white lighthouse on a cliff to the east of us, coming up suddenly ; and then one turned to scan the little

different French coast villages, and then, sliding by in a pale
sunshine came a long wooden pier with oddly dressed children
upon it, and the clustering town of Boulogne.

One took it all with the outward calm that became a young
man of nearly three-and-twenty, but one was alive to one's
finger-tips with pleasing stimulations. The custom-house
examination excited one, the strangeness of a babble in a
foreign tongue ; one found the French of City Merchants' and
Cambridge a shy and viscous flow, and then one was standing
in the train as it went slowly through the rail-laid street to
Boulogne Ville, and one looked out at the world in French,
porters in blouses, workmen in enormous purple trousers,
police officers in peaked caps instead of helmets and romanti-
cally cloaked, big carts, all on two wheels instead of four, green-
shuttered casements instead of sash windows, and great
numbers of neatly dressed women in economical mourning.

" Oh ! there's a priest ! " one said, and was betrayed into
suchlike artless cries.

It was a real other world, with different government and
different methods, and in the night one was roused from uneasy
slumbers and sat blinking and surly, wrapped up in one's
converture and with one's *oreiller* all awry, to encounter a new
social phenomenon, the German official, so different in manner
from the British ; and when one woke again after that one
had come to Bâle, and out one tumbled to get coffee in
Switzerland. . . .

I have been over that route dozens of times since, but it
still revives a certain lingering youthfulness, a certain sense of
cheerful release in me.

I remember that I and Willersley became very sociological
as we ran on to Spiez, and made all sorts of generalisations
from the steeply sloping fields on the hillsides, and from the
people we saw on platforms and from little differences in the
way things were done.

The clean prosperity of Bâle and Switzerland, the big clean
stations, filled me with patriotic misgivings as I thought of the
vast dirtiness of London, the mean dirtiness of Cambridge-
shire. It came to me that perhaps my scheme of international
values was all wrong, that quite stupendous possibilities and
challenges for us and our empire might be developing here—
and I recalled Meredith's Skepsey in France with a new
understanding.

Willersley had dressed himself in a world-worn Norfolk suit
of greenish-grey tweeds that ended unfamiliarly at his rather
impending, spectacled, intellectual visage. I didn't, I remember, like the contrast of him with the drilled Swiss and
Germans about us. Convict-coloured stockings and vast hob-
nail boots finished him below, and all his luggage was a
borrowed rucksac that he had tied askew. He did not want
to shave in the train, but I made him at one of the Swiss

stations—I dislike these Oxford slovenlinesses—and then, confound him ! he cut himself and bled. . . .

Next morning we were breathing a thin exhilarating air that seemed to have washed our very veins to an incredible cleanliness, and eating hard-boiled eggs in a vast clear space of rime-edged rocks, snow-mottled, above a blue-gashed glacier. All about us the monstrous rock surfaces rose towards the shining peaks above, and there were winding moraines from which the ice had receded, and then dark clustering fir-trees far below.

I had an extraordinary feeling of having come out of things, of being outside.

"But this is the round world ! " I said, with a sense of never having perceived it before ; "this is the round world ! "

§ 9

That holiday was full of big comprehensive effects ; the first view of the Rhone valley and the distant Valaisian Alps, for example, which we saw from the shoulder of the mountain above the Gemmi, and the early summer dawn breaking over Italy as we moved from our night's crouching and munched bread and chocolate and stretched our stiff limbs among the tumbled and precipitous rocks that hung over Lake Cingolo, and surveyed the winding tiring rocky track going down and down to Antronapiano.

And our thoughts were as comprehensive as our impressions. Willersley's mind abounded in historical matter ; he had an inaccurate abundant habit of topographical reference ; he made me see and trace and see again the Roman Empire sweep up these winding valleys, and the coming of the first great Peace among the warring tribes of men. . . .

In the retrospect each of us seems to have been talking about our outlook almost continually. Each of us, you see, was full of the same question, very near and altogether predominant to us, the question : "What am I going to do with my life ? " He saw it almost as importantly as I, but from a different angle, because his choice was largely made and mine still hung in the balance.

"I feel we might do so many things," I said, " and everything that calls one, calls one away from something else."

Willersley agreed without any modest disavowals.

"We have got to think out," he said, " just what we are and what we are up to. We've got to do that now. And then—it's one of those questions it is inadvisable to reopen subsequently."

He beamed at me through his glasses. The sententious use of long words was a playful habit with him, that and a slight deliberate humour, habits occasional Extension Lecturing was doing very much to intensify.

"You've made your decision ? "

He nodded with a peculiar forward movement of his head.
" How would you put it ? "

" Social Service—education. Whatever else matters or
doesn't matter, it seems to me there is one thing we *must* have
and increase, and that is the number of people who can think
a little—and have "—he beamed again—" an adequate sense
of causation."

" You're sure it's worth while."

" For me—certainly. I don't discuss that any more."

" I don't limit myself too narrowly," he added. " After
all, the work is all one. We who know, we who feel, are building the great modern state, joining wall to wall and way to
way, the new great England rising out of the decaying old . . .
we are the real statesmen—I like that use of ' statesmen.' . . ."

" Yes," I said with many doubts. " Yes, of course. . . ."

Willersley is middle-aged now, with silver in his hair and a
deepening benevolence in his always amiable face, and he has
very fairly kept his word. He has lived for social service and
to do vast masses of useful, undistinguished, fertilising work.
Think of the days of arid administrative plodding and of contention still more arid and unrewarded, that he must have
spent ! His little affectations of gesture and manner, imi-
tative affectations for the most part, have increased, and the
humorous beam and the humorous intonations have become
a thing he puts on every morning like an old coat. His
devotion is mingled with a considerable whimsicality, and
they say he is easily flattered by subordinates and easily
offended into opposition by colleagues ; he has made mistakes
at times and followed wrong courses, still there he is, a flat
contradiction to all the ordinary doctrine of motives, a man
who has foregone any chances of wealth and profit, foregone
any easier paths to distinction, foregone marriage and parentage, in order to serve the community. He does it without any
fee or reward except his personal self-satisfaction in doing this
work, and he does it without any hope of future joys and
punishments, for he is an implacable Rationalist. No doubt
he idealises himself a little, and dreams of recognition. No
doubt he gets his pleasure from a sense of power, from the
spending and husbanding of large sums of public money, and
from the inevitable proprietorship he must feel in the fair,
fine, well-ordered schools he has done so much to develop.
" But for me," he can say, " there would have been a Job
about those diagrams, and that subject or this would have
been less ably taught." . . .

The fact remains that for him the rewards have been ad-
dequate, if not to content at any rate to keep him working.
Of course he covets the notice of the world he has served,
as a lover covets the notice of his mistress. Of course he
thinks somewhere, somewhen, he will get credit. Only last
year I heard some men talking of him, and they were noting,

with little mean smiles, how he had shown himself self-conscious while there was talk of some honorary degree-giving or other ; it would, I have no doubt, please him greatly if his work were to flower into a crimson gown in some Academic parterre. Why shouldn't it ? But that is incidental vanity at the worst ; he goes on anyhow. Most men don't.

But we had our walk twenty years and more ago now. He was oldish even then as a young man, just as he is oldish still in middle age. Long may his industrious elderliness flourish for the good of the world ! He lectured a little in conversation then ; he lectures more now and listens less, toilsomely disentangling what you already understand, giving you in detail the data you know ; these are things like callosities that come from a man's work.

Our long three weeks' talk comes back to me as a memory of ideas and determinations slowly growing all mixed up with a smell of wood smoke and pine woods and huge precipices and remote gleams of snow-fields and the sound of cascading torrents rushing through deep gorges far below. It is mixed, too, with gossips with waitresses and fellow-travellers, with my first essays in colloquial German and Italian, with disputes about the way to take, and other things that I will tell of in another section. But the white passion of human service was our dominant theme. Not simply perhaps nor altogether unselfishly, but quite honestly, and with at least a frequent self-forgetfulness, did we want to do fine and noble things, to help in their developing, to lessen misery, to broaden and exalt life. It is very hard—perhaps it is impossible—to present in a page or two the substance and quality of nearly a month's conversation, conversation that is casual and discursive in form, that ranges carelessly from triviality to immensity, and yet is constantly resuming a constructive process, as workmen on a wall loiter and jest and go and come back, and all the while build.

We got it more and more definite that the core of our purpose beneath all its varied aspects must needs be order and discipline. "Muddle," said I, "is the enemy." That remains my belief to this day. Clearness and order, light and foresight, these things I know for Good. It was muddle had just given us all the still freshly painful disasters and humiliations of the war, muddle that gives us the visibly sprawling disorder of our cities and industrial country-side, muddle that gives us the waste of life, the limitations, wretchedness and unemployment of the poor. Muddle ! I remember myself quoting Kipling—

"All along o' dirtiness, all along o' mess,
All along o' doin' things rather-more-or-less."

"We build the state," we said over and over again. "That is what we are for—servants of the new reorganisation ! "

We planned half in earnest and half Utopianising, a League of Social Service.

We talked of the splendid world of men that might grow out of such unpaid and ill-paid work as we were setting our faces to do. We spoke of the intricate difficulties, the monstrous passive resistances, the hostilities to such a development as we conceived our work subserved, and we spoke with that underlying confidence in the invincibility of the causes we adopted that is natural to young and scarcely tried men.

We talked much of the detailed life of politics so far as it was known to us, and there Willersley was more experienced and far better informed than I ; we discussed possible combinations and possible developments, and the chances of some great constructive movement coming from the heart-searchings the Boer war had occasioned. We would sink to gossip—even at the Suetonius level. Willersley would decline towards illuminating anecdotes that I capped more or less loosely from my private reading. We were particularly wise, I remember, upon the management of newspapers, because about that we knew nothing whatever. We perceived that great things were to be done through newspapers. We talked of swaying opinion and moving great classes to massive action.

Men are egotistical even in devotion. All our splendid projects were thickset with the first personal pronoun. We both could write, and all that we said in general terms was reflected in the particular in our minds ; it was ourselves we saw, and no others, writing and speaking that moving word. We had already produced manuscript and passed the initiations of proof-reading ; I had been a frequent speaker in the Union, and Willersley was an active man on the School Board. Our feet were already on the lower rungs that led up and up. He was six-and-twenty, and I twenty-two. We intimated our individual careers in terms of bold expectation. I had prophetic glimpses of walls and hoardings clamorous with " Vote for Remington," and Willersley no doubt saw himself chairman of this committee and that, saying a few slightly ironical words after the declaration of the poll, and then sitting friendly beside me on the government benches. There was nothing impossible in such dreams. Why not the Board of Education for him ? My preference at that time wavered between the Local Government Board—I had great ideas about town-planning, about revisions of municipal areas and reorganised internal transit—and the War Office. I swayed strongly towards the latter as the journey progressed. My educational bias came later.

The swelling ambitions that have tramped over Alpine passes ! How many of them, like mine, have come almost within sight of realisation before they failed ?

There were times when we posed like young gods (of unassuming exterior), and times when we were full of the absurdest little solicitudes about our prospects. There were times when one surveyed the whole world of men as if it was a little thing at one's feet, and by way of contrast I remember once lying in bed—it must have been during this holiday, though I cannot for the life of me fix where—and speculating whether perhaps some day I might not be a K.C.B., Sir Richard Remington, K.C.B., M.P.

But the big style prevailed. . . .

We could not tell from minute to minute whether we were planning for a world of solid reality, or telling ourselves fairy-tales about this prospect of life. So much seemed possible, and everything we could think of so improbable. There were lapses when it seemed to me I could never be anything but just the entirely unimportant and undistinguished young man I was for ever and ever. I couldn't even think of myself as five-and-thirty.

Once I remember Willersley going over a list of failures, and why they had failed—but young men in the twenties do not know much about failures.

§ 10

Willersley and I professed ourselves Socialists, but by this time I knew my Rodbertus as well as my Marx, and there was much in our socialism that would have shocked Chris Robinson as much as anything in life could have shocked him. Socialism as a simple democratic cry we had done with for ever. We were socialists because Individualism for us meant muddle, meant a crowd of separated, undisciplined people all obstinately and ignorantly doing things jarringly, each one in his own way. " Each," I said, quoting words of my father's that rose apt in my memory, " snarling from his own little bit of property, like a dog tied to a cart's tail."

" Essentially," said Willersley, " essentially we're for conscription, in peace and war alike. The man who owns property is a public official and has to behave as such. That's the gist of socialism as I understand it."

" Or be dismissed from his post," I said, " and replaced by some better sort of official. A man's none the less an official because he's irresponsible. What he does with his property affects people just the same. Private! No one is really private but an outlaw. . . ."

Order and devotion were the very essence of our socialism, and a splendid collective vigour and happiness its end. We projected an ideal state, an organised state as confident and powerful as modern science, as balanced and beautiful as a body, as beneficent as sunshine, the organised state that should end muddle for ever ; it ruled all our ideals and gave form to all our ambitions.

Every man was to be definitely related to that, to have his

predominant duty to that. Such was the England renewed we had in mind, and how to serve that end, to subdue undisciplined worker and undisciplined wealth to it, and make the Scientific Commonweal, King, was the continuing substance of our intercourse.

§ 11

Every day the wine of the mountains was stronger in our blood, and the flush of our youth deeper. We would go in the morning sunlight along some narrow Alpine mule-path shouting large suggestions for national reorganisation, and weighing considerations as lightly as though the world was wax in our hands. " Great England," we said in effect, over and over again, " and we will be among the makers ! England renewed ! The country has been warned ; it has learned its lesson. The disasters and anxieties of the war have sunk in. England has become serious. . . . Oh ! there are big things before us to do ; big enduring things ! "

One evening we walked up to the loggia of a little pilgrimage church, I forget its name, that stands out on a conical hill at the head of a winding stair above the town of Locarno. Down below the houses clustered amidst a confusion of heat-bitten greenery. I had been sitting silently on the parapet, looking across to the purple mountain masses where Switzerland passes into Italy, and the drift of our talk seemed suddenly to gather to a head.

I broke into speech, giving form to the thoughts that had been accumulating. My words have long since passed out of my memory, the phrases of familiar expression have altered for me, but the substance remains as clear as ever. I said how we were in our measure emperors and kings, men undriven, free to do as we pleased with life ; we classed among the happy ones, our bread and common necessities were given us for nothing, we had abilities—it wasn't modesty but cowardice to behave as if we hadn't—and Fortune watched us to see what we might do with opportunity and the world.

" There are so many things to do, you see," began Willersley, in his judicial lecturer's voice.

" So many things we may do," I interrupted, " with all these years before us. . . . We're exceptional men. It's our place, our duty, to do things.

" Here anyhow," I said, answering the faint amusement of his face, " I've got no modesty. Everything conspires to set me up. Why should I run about like all those grubby little beasts down there, seeking nothing but mean vanities and indulgences—and then take credit for modesty ? I *know* I am capable. I *know* I have imagination. Modesty ! I know if I don't attempt the very biggest things in life I am a damned shirk. The very biggest ! Somebody has to attempt them.

I feel like a loaded gun that is only rather perplexed because it has to find out just where to aim itself. . . ."

The lake and the frontier villages, a white puff of steam on the distant railway to Luino, the busy boats and steamers trailing triangular wakes of foam, the long vista eastward towards battlemented Bellinzona, the vast mountain distances, now tinged with sunset light, behind this nearer landscape, and the southward waters with remote coast towns shining dimly, waters that merged at last in a luminous golden haze, made a broad panoramic spectacle. It was as if one surveyed the world—and it was like the games I used to set out upon my nursery floor. I was exalted by it ; I felt larger than men. So kings should feel.

That sense of largeness came to me then, and it has come to me since, again and again, a splendid intimation or a splendid vanity. Once, I remember, when I looked at Genoa from the mountain crest behind the town and saw that multitudinous place in all its beauty of width and abundance and clustering human effort, and once as I was steaming past the brown low hills of Staten Island towards the towering vigour and clamorous vitality of New York City, that mood rose to its quintessence. And once it came to me, as I shall tell, on Dover cliffs. And a hundred times when I have thought of England as our country might be, with no wretched poor, no wretched rich, a nation armed and ordered, trained and purposeful amidst its vales and rivers, that emotion of collective ends and collective purposes has returned to me. I felt as great as humanity. For a brief moment I was humanity, looking at the world I had made and had still to make. . . .

§ 12

And mingled with these dreams of power and patriotic service there was another series of a different quality and a different colour, like the antagonistic colour of a shot silk. The white life and the red life contrasted and interchanged, passing swiftly at a turn from one to another, and refusing ever to mingle peacefully one with the other. I was asking myself openly and distinctly : what are you going to do for the world ? What are you going to do with yourself ? and with an increasing strength and persistence Nature in spite of my averted attention was asking me in penetrating undertones : what are you going to do about this other fundamental matter, the beauty of girls and women and your desire for them ?

I have told of my sisterless youth and the narrow circumstances of my upbringing. It made all womankind mysterious to me. If it had not been for my Staffordshire cousins I do not think I should have known any girls at all until I was twenty. Of Staffordshire I will tell a little later. But I can remember still how through all those ripening years, the thought of women's beauty, their magic presence in the world beside me and the unknown, untried reactions of their intercourse, grew upon me and grew, as a strange presence grows in a room when one is occupied by other things. I busied myself and pretended to be wholly occupied, and there the woman stood, full half of life neglected, and it seemed to my averted mind sometimes that she was there clad and dignified and divine, and sometimes Aphrodite shining and commanding, and sometimes that Venus who stoops and allures.

This travel abroad seemed to have released a multitude of things in my mind ; the clear air, the beauty of the sunshine, the very blue of the glaciers made me feel my body and quickened all those disregarded dreams. I saw the sheathed beauty of women's forms all about me, in the cheerful waitresses at the inns, in the pedestrians one encountered in the tracks, in the chance fellow-travellers at the hotel tables. " Confound it ! " said I, and talked all the more zealously of that greater England that was calling us.

I remember that we passed two Germans, an old man and a tall fair girl, father and daughter, who were walking down from Saas. She came swinging and shining towards us, easy and strong. I worshipped her as she approached.

" Gut Tag ! " said Willersley, removing his hat.

" Morgen ! " said the old man, saluting.

I stared stockishly at the girl, who passed with an indifferent face.

That sticks in my mind as a picture remains in a room, it has kept there bright and fresh as a thing seen yesterday, for twenty years. . . .

I flirted hesitatingly once or twice with comely serving-girls, and was a little ashamed lest Willersley should detect the keen interest I took in them, and then as we came over the pass from Santa Maria Maggiore to Cannobio, my secret preoccupation took me by surprise and flooded me and broke down my pretences.

The women in that valley are very beautiful—women vary from valley to valley in the Alps and are plain and squat here and divinities five miles away—and as we came down we passed a group of five or six of them resting by the wayside. Their burthens were beside them, and one like Ceres held a reaping hook in her brown hand. She watched us approaching and smiled faintly, her eyes at mine.

There was some greeting, and two of them laughed together. We passed.

" Glorious girls they were," said Willersley, and suddenly an immense sense of boredom enveloped me. I saw myself striding on down that winding road, talking of politics and parties and bills of parliament and all sorts of desiccated things. That road seemed to me to wind on for ever down to dust and infinite dreariness. I knew it for a way of death. Reality was behind us.

Willersley set himself to draw a sociological moral. " I'm not so sure," he said in a voice of intense discriminations, " after all, that agricultural work isn't good for women."

" Damn agricultural work ! " I said, and broke out into a vigorous cursing of all I held dear. " Fettered things we are ! " I cried. " I wonder why I stand it ! "

" Stand what ? "

" Why don't I go back and make love to those girls and let the world and you and everything go hang ? Deep breasts and rounded limbs—and we poor emasculated devils go tramping by with the blood of youth in us ! . . ."

" I'm not quite sure, Remington," said Willersley, looking at me with a deliberately quaint expression over his glasses, " that picturesque scenery is altogether good for your morals."

That fever was still in my blood when we came to Locarno.

§ 13

Along the hot and dusty lower road between the Orrido of Traffiume and Cannobio, Willersley had developed his first blister. And partly because of that and partly because there was a bag at the station that gave us the refreshment of clean linen and partly because of the lazy lower air into which we had come, we decided upon three or four days' sojourn in the Empress Hotel.

We dined that night at a table-d'hôte, and I found myself next to an Englishwoman who began a conversation that was resumed in the hotel lounge. She was a woman of perhaps thirty-three or thirty-four, slenderly built, with a warm reddish skin and very abundant fair golden hair, the wife of a petulant-looking heavy-faced man of perhaps fifty-three, who smoked a cigar and dozed over his coffee and presently went to bed. " He always goes to bed like that," she confided startlingly. " He sleeps after all his meals. I never knew such a man to sleep."

Then she returned to our talk, whatever it was.

We had begun at the dinner-table with itineraries and the usual topographical talk, and she had envied our pedestrian travel. " My husband doesn't walk," she said. " His heart is weak and he cannot manage the hills."

There was something friendly and adventurous in her manner ; she conveyed she liked me, and when presently Willersley drifted off to write letters our talk sank at once to easy confidential undertones. I felt enterprising, and indeed it is easy to be daring with people one has never seen before and may never see again. I said I loved beautiful scenery and all beautiful things, and the pointing note in my voice made her laugh. She told me I had bold eyes, and so far as I can remember I said she made them bold. " Blue they are," she remarked, smiling archly. " I like blue eyes."

Then I think we compared ages, and she said she was the Women of Thirty, " George Moore's Woman of Thirty."

I had not read George Moore at the time, but I pretended to understand.

That, I think, was our limit that evening. She went to bed, smiling good-night quite prettily down the big staircase, and I and Willersley went out to smoke in the garden. My head was full of her, and I found it necessary to talk about her. So I made her a problem in sociology. " Who the deuce are these people ? " I said, " and how do they get a living ? They seem to have plenty of money. He strikes me as being— Willersley, what is a drysalter ? I think he's a retired drysalter."

Willersley theorised while I thought of the woman and that provocative quality of dash she had displayed. The next day at lunch she and I met like old friends. A huge mass of private thinking during the interval had been added to our effect upon one another. We talked for a time of insignificant things.

" What do you do," she asked rather quickly, " after lunch ? Take a siesta ? "

" Sometimes," I said, and hung for a moment eye to eye.

We hadn't a doubt of each other, but my heart was beating like a steamer propeller when it lifts out of the water.

" Do you get a view from your room ? " she asked after a pause.

" It's on the third floor, Number Seventeen, near the staircase. My friend's next door."

She began to talk of books. She was interested in Christian Science, she said, and spoke of a book. I forget altogether what that book was called, though I remember to this day with the utmost exactness the purplish magenta of its cover. She said she would lend it to me, and hesitated.

Willersley wanted to go for an expedition across the lake that afternoon, but I refused. He made some other proposals that I rejected abruptly. " I shall write in my room," I said.

" Why not write down here ? "

" I shall write in my room," I snarled like a thwarted animal, and he looked at me curiously. " Very well," he said ; " then I'll make some notes and think about that order of ours out under the magnolias."

I hovered about the lounge for a time buying postcards and feverishly restless, watching the movements of the other people. Finally I went up to my room and sat down by the windows, staring out. There came a little tap at the unlocked door and in an instant, like the go of a taut bowstring, I was up and had it open.

" Here is that book," she said, and we hesitated.

" *Come in* ! " I whispered, trembling from head to foot.

" You're just a boy," she said in a low tone.

I did not feel a bit like a lover, I felt like a burglar with the safe-door nearly opened. "Come in," I said almost impatiently, for any one might be in the passage, and I gripped her wrist and drew her towards me.

"What do you mean?" she answered with a faint smile on her lips, and awkward and yielding.

I shut the door behind her, still holding her with one hand, then turned upon her—she was laughing nervously—and without a word drew her to me and kissed her. And I remember that as I kissed her she made a little noise almost like the purring miaow with which a cat will greet one, and her face, close to mine, became solemn and tender.

She was suddenly a different being from the discontented wife who had tapped a moment since on my door, a woman transfigured. . . .

That evening I came down to dinner a monster of pride, for behold! I was a man. I felt myself the most wonderful and unprecedented of adventurers. It was hard to believe that any one in the world before had done as much. My mistress and I met smiling, we carried things off admirably, and it seemed to me that Willersley was the dullest old dog in the world. I wanted to give him advice. I wanted to give him derisive pokes. After dinner and coffee in the lounge I was too excited and hilarious to go to bed, I made him come with me down to the café under the arches by the pier, and there drank beer and talked extravagant nonsense about everything under the sun, in order not to talk about the happenings of the afternoon. All the time something shouted within me : " I am a man! I am a man!" . . .

"What shall we do to-morrow?" said he.

"I'm for loafing," I said. "Let's row in the morning and spend to-morrow afternoon just as we did to-day."

"They say the church behind the town is worth seeing."

"We'll go up about sunset ; that's the best time for it. We can start about five."

We heard music, and went farther along the arcade to discover a place where girls in operatic Swiss peasant costume were singing and dancing on a creaking, protesting little stage. I eyed their generous display of pink neck and arm with the seasoned eye of a man who has lived in the world. Life was perfectly simple and easy, I felt, if one took it the right way.

Next day Willersley wanted to go on, but I delayed. Altogether I kept him back four days. Then abruptly my mood changed, and we decided to start early the following morning. I remember, though indistinctly, the feeling of my last talk with that woman whose surname, odd as it may seem, either I never learned or I have forgotten. (Her Christian name was Milly.) She was tired and rather low-spirited, and disposed to be sentimental, and for the first time in our intercourse I found myself liking her for the sake of her own personality. There was something kindly and generous appearing behind the veil of naïve and uncontrolled sensuality she had worn. There was a curious quality of motherliness in her attitude to me that something in my nature answered and approved. She didn't pretend to keep it up that she had yielded to my initiative. "I've done you no harm," she said a little doubtfully, an odd note for a man's victim! And, "We've had a good time. You have liked me, haven't you?"

She interested me in her lonely dissatisfied life; she was childless and had no hope of children, and her husband was the only son of a rich meat salesman, very mean, a mighty smoker —"he reeks of it," she said, "always"—and interested in nothing but golf, billiards (which he played very badly), pigeon shooting, convivial Free Masonry and Stock Exchange punting. Mostly they drifted about the Riviera. Her mother had contrived her marriage when she was eighteen. They were the first samples I ever encountered of the great multitude of functionless property owners which encumbers modern civilisation—but at the time I didn't think much of that aspect of them. . . .

I tell all this business as it happened without comment, because I have no comment to make. It was all strange to me, strange rather than wonderful, and it may be some dream of beauty died for ever in those furtive meetings; it happened to me, and I could scarcely have been more irresponsible in the matter or controlled events less if I had been suddenly pushed over a cliff into water. I swam, of course—finding myself in it. Things tested me, and I reacted, as I have told. The bloom of my innocence, if ever there had been such a thing, was gone. And here is the remarkable thing about it; at the time and for some days I was over-weeningly proud; I have never been so proud before or since; I felt I had been promoted to virility; I was unable to conceal my exultation from Willersley. It was a mood of shining shameless ungracious self-approval. As he and I went along in the cool morning sunshine by the rice-fields in the throat of the Val Maggia a silence fell between us.

"You know?" I said abruptly—"about that woman?"

Willersley did not answer for a moment. He looked at me over the corner of his spectacles.

"Things went pretty far?" he asked.

"Oh! all the way!" and I had a twinge of fatuous pride in my unpremeditated achievement.

"She came to your room?"

I nodded.

"I heard her. I heard her whispering. . . . The whispering and rustling and so on. I was in my room yesterday. . . . Any one might have heard you. . . ."

I went on with my head in the air.

"You might have been caught, and that would have meant endless trouble. You might have incurred all sorts of conse-

quences. What did you know about her ? . . . We have
wasted four days in that hot, close place. When we found
that League of Social Service we were talking about," he said
with a determined eye upon me, " chastity will be first among
the virtues prescribed."

" I shall form a rival league," I said, a little damped.   " I'm
hanged if I give up a single desire in me until I know why."

He lifted his chin and stared before him through his glasses
at nothing.   " There are some things," he said, " that a man
who means to work—to do great public services—*must* turn
his back upon.   I'm not discussing the rights or wrongs of
this sort of thing.   It happens to be the conditions we work
under.   It will probably always be so.   If you want to experiment in that way, if you want even to discuss it—out you
go from political life.   You must know that's so. . . . You're
a strange man, Remington, with a kind of kink in you.   You've
a sort of force.   You might happen to do immense things. . . .
Only——"

He stopped.   He had said all that he had forced himself to
say.

" I mean to take myself as I am," I said.   " I'm going to get
experience for humanity out of all my talents—and bury
nothing."

Willersley twisted his face to its humorous expression.   " I
doubt if sexual proclivities," he said dryly, " come within the
scope of the parable."

I let that go for a little while.   Then I broke out.   " Sex,"
said I, " is a fundamental thing in life.   We went through all
this at Trinity.   I'm going to look at it, experience it, think
about it—and get it square with the rest of life.   Career and
Politics must take their chances of that.   It's part of the
general English slackness that they won't look this in the face.
Gods ! what a muffled time we're coming out of !   Sex means
breeding, and breeding is a necessary function in a nation.
The Romans broke up upon that.   The Americans fade out
amidst their successes.   Eugenics——"

" *That* wasn't Eugenics," said Willersley.

" It was a woman," I said after an interval, feeling oddly
that I had failed altogether to answer him, and yet had a strong
dumb case against him.

Book Two

Margaret

CHAPTER ONE

MARGARET IN STAFFORDSHIRE

§ 1

I MUST go back a little way with my story. In the previous book I have described the kind of education that happens to a man of my class nowadays, and it has been convenient to leap a phase in my experience that I must now set out at length. I want to tell in this second book how I came to marry, and to do that I must give something of the atmosphere in which I first met my wife and some intimations of the forces that went to her making. I met her in Staffordshire while I was staying with that uncle of whom I have already spoken, the uncle who sold my father's houses and settled my mother in Penge. Margaret was twenty then and I was twenty-two.

It was just before the walking tour in Switzerland that opened up so much of the world to me. I saw her once, for an afternoon, and circumstances so threw her up in relief that I formed a very vivid memory of her. She was in the sharpest contrast with the industrial world about her ; she impressed me as a dainty blue flower might do, come upon suddenly on a clinker heap. She remained in my mind at once a perplexing interrogation and a symbol. . . .

But first I must tell of my Staffordshire cousins and the world that served as a foil for her.

§ 2

I first went to stay with my cousins when I was an awkward youth of sixteen, wearing deep mourning for my mother. My uncle wanted to talk things over with me, he said, and if he could, to persuade me to go into business instead of going up to Cambridge.

I remember that visit on account of all sorts of novel things, but chiefly, I think, because it was the first time I encountered anything that deserves to be spoken of as wealth. For the first time in my life I had to do with people who seemed to have endless supplies of money, unlimited good clothes, numerous servants ; whose daily life was made up of things that I had hitherto considered to be treats or exceptional extravagances. My cousins of eighteen and nineteen took cabs, for instance, with the utmost freedom, and travelled first-class in the local trains that run up and down the district of the Five Towns with an entire unconsciousness of the magnificence, as it seemed to me, of such a proceeding.

The family occupied a large villa in Newcastle, with big lawns before it and behind, a shrubbery with quite a lot of shrubs, a coach-house and stable, and subordinate dwelling-places for the gardener and the coachman.   Every bedroom contained a gas-heater and a canopied brass bedstead, and had a little bathroom attached equipped with the porcelain baths and fittings my uncle manufactured, bright and sanitary and stamped with his name, and the house was furnished throughout with chairs and tables in bright shining wood, soft and prevalently red Turkish carpets, cosy corners, curtained archways, gold-framed landscapes, overmantels, a dining-room sideboard like a palace, with a large Tantalus, and electric-light fittings of a gay and expensive quality.   There was a fine billiard-room on the ground floor with three comfortable sofas and a rotating bookcase containing an excellent collection of the English and American humorists from *Three Men in a Boat* to the penultimate Mark Twain.   There was also a conservatory opening out of the drawing-room, to which the gardener brought potted flowers in their season. . . .

My aunt was a little woman with a scared look and a cap that would get over one eye, not very like my mother and nearly eight years her junior ; she was very much concerned with keeping everything nice, and unmercifully bullied by my two cousins, who took after their father and followed the imaginations of their own hearts.   They were tall, dark, warmly flushed girls, handsome rather than pretty.   Gertrude, the eldest and tallest, had eyes that were almost black ; Sibyl was of a stouter build, and her eyes, of which she was shamelessly proud, were dark blue.   Sibyl's hair waved, and Gertrude's was severely straight.   They treated me on my first visit with all the contempt of the adolescent girl for a boy younger and infinitely less expert in the business of life than herself.   They were very busy with the writing of notes and certain mysterious goings and comings of their own, and left me very much to my own devices.   Their speech in my presence was full of unfathomable allusions.   They were the sort of girls who will talk over and through an uninitiated stranger with the pleasantest sense of superiority.

I met them at breakfast and at lunch and at the half-past six o'clock high tea that formed the third chief meal of the day. I heard them rattling off the compositions of Chaminade and Moskowski with great decision and effect, and hovered on the edge of tennis foursomes where it was manifest to the dullest intelligence that my presence was unnecessary.   Then I went off to find some readable book in the place, but apart from miscellaneous popular novels, some veterinary works, a number of comic books, old bound volumes of *The Illustrated London News* and a large, popular illustrated History of England, there was hardly anything to be found.   My aunt talked to me in a casual feeble way, chiefly about my mother's last illness.   The two had seen very little of each other for many years ; she made no secret of it that the ineligible qualities of my father were the cause of the estrangement.   The only other society in the house during the day was an old and rather decayed Skye terrier in constant conflict with what were no doubt imaginary fleas. I took myself off for a series of walks, and acquired a considerable knowledge of the scenery and topography of the Potteries.

It puzzled my aunt that I did not go westward, where it was country-side and often quite pretty, with hedgerows and fields and copses and flowers. But always I went eastward, where in a long valley industrialism smokes and sprawls. That was the stuff to which I turned by nature, to the human effort, and the accumulation and jar of men's activities. And in such a country as that valley social and economic relations were simple and manifest. Instead of the limitless confusion of London's population, in which no man can trace any but the most slender correlation between rich and poor, in which every one seems disconnected and adrift from every one, you can see here the works, the pot-bank or the ironworks or what not, and here close at hand the congested, meanly-housed workers, and at a little distance a small middle-class quarter, and again remoter, the big house of the employer. It was like a very simplified diagram—after the untraceable confusion of London.

I prowled alone, curious and interested, through shabby back streets of mean little homes ; I followed canals, sometimes canals of mysteriously heated waters with ghostly wisps of steam rising against blackened walls or a distinct prospect of dustbin-fed vegetable gardens, I saw the women pouring out from the pot-banks, heard the hooters summoning the toilers to work, lost my way upon slag heaps as big as the hills of the south country, dodged trains at manifestly dangerous level-crossings, and surveyed across dark intervening spaces, the flaming uproar, the gnome-like activities of iron foundries. I heard talk of strikes and rumours of strikes, and learned from the columns of some obscure labour paper I bought one day, of the horrors of the lead poisoning that was in those days one of the normal risks of certain sorts of pottery workers. Then back I came, by the ugly groaning and clanging steam tram of that period, to my uncle's house and lavish abundance of money and more or less furtive flirtations and the tinkle of Moskowski and Chaminade. It was, I say, diagrammatic. One saw the expropriator and the expropriated—as if Marx had arranged the picture. It was as jumbled and far more dingy and disastrous than any of the confusions of building and development that had surrounded my youth at Bromstead and Penge, but it had a novel quality of being explicable. I found great virtue in the word " exploitation."

There stuck in my mind as if it was symbolical of the whole thing the twisted figure of a man whose face had been horribly scalded—I can't describe how, except that one eye was just expressionless white—and he ground at an organ bearing a card which told in weak and bitterly satirical phrasing that he had been scalded by the hot water from the tuyeres of the blast furnace of Lord Pandram's works. He had been scalded and quite inadequately compensated and dismissed. And Lord Pandram was worth half a million.

That upturned sightless white eye of his took possession of my imagination. I don't think that even then I was swayed by any crude melodramatic conception of injustice. I was quite prepared to believe the card wasn't a punctiliously accurate statement of fact, and that a case could be made out for Lord Pandram. Still there in the muddy gutter, painfully and dreadfully, was the man, and he was smashed and scalded and wretched and he ground his dismal hurdy-gurdy with a weary arm, calling upon Heaven and the passer-by for help, for help and some sort of righting—one could not imagine quite what. There he was as a fact, as a by-product of the system that heaped my cousins with trinkets and provided the comic novels and the abundant cigars and spacious billiard-room of my uncle's house. I couldn't disconnect him and them.

My uncle on his part did nothing to conceal the state of war that existed between himself and his workers, and the mingled contempt and animosity he felt for them.

§ 3

Prosperity had overtaken my uncle. So quite naturally he believed that every man who was not as prosperous as he was had only himself to blame. He was rich and he had left school and gone into his father's business at fifteen, and that seemed to him the proper age at which every one's education should terminate. He was very anxious to dissuade me from going up to Cambridge, and we argued intermittently through all my visit.

I had remembered him as a big and buoyant man, striding destructively about the nursery floor of my childhood, and saluting my existence by slaps, loud laughter, and questions about half-herrings and half-eggs subtly framed to puzzle and confuse my mind. I didn't see him for some years until my father's death, and then he seemed rather smaller, though still a fair size, yellow instead of red and much less radiantly aggressive. This altered effect was due not so much to my own changed perspectives, I fancy, as to the facts that he was suffering for continuous cigar smoking, and being taken in hand by his adolescent daughters who had just returned from school.

During my first visit there was a perpetual series of—the only word is rows, between them and him. Up to the age of fifteen or thereabouts, he had maintained his ascendency over them by simple old-fashioned physical chastisement. Then after an interlude of a year it had dawned upon them that power had mysteriously departed from him. He had tried stopping their pocket-money, but they found their mother financially amenable ; besides which it was fundamental to my uncle's attitude that he should give them money freely. Not to do so would seem like admitting a difficulty in making it. So that after he had stopped their allowances for the fourth time Sybil and Gertrude were prepared to face beggary without a qualm. It had been his pride to give them the largest allowance of any girls at the school, not even excepting the grand-daughter of Fladden the Borax King, and his soul recoiled from this discipline as it had never recoiled from the ruder method of the earlier phase. Both girls had developed to a high pitch in their mutual recriminations a gift for damaging retort, and he found it an altogether deadlier thing than the power of the raised voice that had always cowed my aunt. Whenever he became heated with them, they frowned as if involuntarily, drew in their breath sharply, said : " Daddy, you really must not say——" and corrected his pronunciation. Then, at a great advantage, they resumed the discussion. . . .

My uncle's views about Cambridge, however, were perfectly clear and definite. It was waste of time and money. It was all damned foolery. Did they make a man a better business man ? Not a bit of it. He gave instances. It spoiled a man for business by giving him " false ideas." Some men said that at college a man formed useful friendships. What use were friendships to a business man ? He might get to know lords, but, as my uncle pointed out, a lord's requirements in his line of faïence were little greater than a common man's. If college introduced him to hotel proprietors there might be something in it. Perhaps it helped a man into Parliament, Parliament still being a confused retrogressive corner in the world where lawyers and such-like sheltered themselves from the onslaughts of common-sense behind a fog of Latin and Greek and twaddle and tosh ; but I wasn't the sort to go into Parliament, unless I meant to be a lawyer. Did I mean to be a lawyer ? It cost no end of money, and was full of uncertainties, and there were no judges nor great solicitors among my relations. " Young chaps think they get on by themselves," said my uncle. " It isn't so. Not unless they take their coats off. I took mine off before I was your age by nigh a year."

We were at cross-purposes from the outset, because I did not think men lived to make money ; and I was obtuse to the hints he was throwing out at the possibilities of his own pot-bank, not wilfully obtuse, but just failing to penetrate his meaning. Whatever City Merchants' had or had not done for me, Flack, Topham and old Gates had certainly barred my mistaking the profitable production and sale of lavatory basins and bath-room fittings for the highest good. It was only upon reflection that it dawned upon me that the splendid chance for a young fellow with my uncle, " me, having no son of my own," was anything but an illustration for comparison with my own chosen career.

I still remember very distinctly my uncle's talk—he loved

to speak " reet Staffordshire "—his rather flabby face with the mottled complexion that told of crude ill-regulated appetites, his clumsy gestures—he kept emphasising his points by prodding at me with his finger—the ill-worn, costly, grey tweed clothes, the watch-chain of plain solid gold, and soft felt hat thrust back from his head. He tackled me first in the garden after lunch, and then tried to raise me to enthusiasm by taking me to his pot-bank and showing me its organisation, from the dusty grinding mills in which whitened men worked and coughed, through the highly ventilated glazing-room in which strangely masked girls looked ashamed of themselves—"They'll risk death, the fools, to show their faces to a man," said my uncle, quite audibly—to the firing kilns and the glazing kilns, and so round the whole place to the railway siding and the gratifying spectacle of three trucks laden with executed orders.

Then we went up a creaking outside staircase to his little office, and he showed off before me for a while, with one or two subordinates and the telephone.

" None of your Gas," he said, " all this. It's Real every bit of it. Hard cash and hard glaze."

" Yes," I said, with memories of a carelessly read pamphlet in my mind, and without any satirical intention, " I suppose you *must* use lead in your glazes ? "

Whereupon I found I had tapped the ruling grievance of my uncle's life. He hated leadless glazes more than he hated anything, except the benevolent people who had organised the agitation for their use. " Leadless glazes ain't only fit for buns," he said. " Let me tell you, my boy——"

He began in a voice of bland persuasiveness that presently warmed to anger, to explain the whole matter. I hadn't the rights of the thing at all. Firstly, there was practically no such thing as lead poisoning. Secondly, not every one was liable to lead poisoning, and it would be quite easy to pick out the susceptible types—as soon as they had it—and put them to other work. Thirdly, the evil effects of lead poisoning were much exaggerated. Fourthly, and this was in a particularly confidential undertone, many of the people liked to get lead poisoning, especially the women, because it caused abortion. I might not believe it, but he knew it for a fact. Fifthly, the work-people simply would not learn the gravity of the danger, and would eat with unwashed hands, and incur all sorts of risks, so that as my uncle put it : " the fools deserve what they get." Sixthly, he and several associated firms had organised a simple and generous insurance scheme against lead-poisoning risks. Seventhly, he never wearied in rational (as distinguished from excessive, futile and expensive) precautions against the disease. Eighthly, in the ill-equipped shops of his minor competitors lead poisoning was a frequent and virulent evil, and people had generalised from these exceptional cases. The small shops, he hazarded, looking out of the cracked and dirty window at distant chimneys, might be advantageously closed. . . .

" But what's the good of talking ? " said my uncle, getting off the table on which he had been sitting. " Seems to me there'll come a time when a master will get fined if he don't run round the works blowing his girls' noses for them. That's about what it'll come to."

He walked to the black mantelpiece and stood on the threadbare rug, and urged me not to be misled by the stories of prejudiced and interested enemies of our national industries.

" They'll get a strike one of these days, of employers, and then we'll see a bit," he said. " They'll drive Capital abroad and then they'll whistle to get it back again." . . .

He led the way down the shaky wooden steps and cheered up to tell me of his way of checking his coal consumption. He exchanged a ferocious greeting with one or two work-people, and so we came out of the factory gates into the ugly narrow streets, paved with a peculiarly hard diapered brick of an unpleasing inky-blue colour, and bordered with the mean and squalid homes of his workers. Doors stood open and showed grimy interiors, and dirty ill-clad children played in the kennel.

We passed a sickly-looking girl with a sallow face, who dragged her limbs and peered at us dimly with painful eyes. She stood back, as partly blinded people will do, to allow us to pass, although there was plenty of room for us.

I glanced back at her.

" *That's* ploombism," said my uncle casually.

" What ? " said I.

" Ploombism. And the other day I saw a fool of a girl, and what d'you think ? She'd got a basin that hadn't been fired, a cracked piece of biscuit it was, up on the shelf over her head, just all over glaze, killing glaze, man, and she was putting up her hand if you please, and eating her dinner out of it. Got her dinner in it !

" Eating her dinner out of it," he repeated in loud and bitter tones, and punched me hard in the ribs.

" And then they comes to *that*—and grumbles. And the fools up in Westminster want you to put in fans here and fans there—the Longton fools have. . . . And they eating their dinners out of it all the time ! " . . .

At high tea that night—my uncle was still holding out against evening dinner—Sibyl and Gertrude made what was evidently a concerted demand for a motor-car.

" You've got your mother's brougham," he said, " that's good enough for you." But he seemed shaken by the fact that some Burslem rival was launching out with the new invention. " He spoils his girls," he remarked. " He's a fool," and became thoughtful.

Afterwards he asked me to come with him into his study ;

it was a room with a writing-desk and full of pieces of earthen-
ware and such-like litter, and we had our great row about
Cambridge.

" Have you thought things over, Dick ? " he said.

" I think I'll go to Trinity, Uncle," I said firmly.   " I want
to go to Trinity.   It is a great college."

He was manifestly chagrined.   " You're a fool," he said.

I made no answer.

" You're a damned fool," he said.   " But I suppose you've
got to do it.   You could have come here—that don't matter,
though, now. . . .   You'll have your time and spend your
money, and be a poor half-starved clergyman, mucking about
with the women all the day and afraid to have one of your
own ever, or you'll be a schoolmaster or some such fool for the
rest of your life.   Or some newspaper chap.   That's what
you'll get from Cambridge.   I'm half a mind not to let you.
Eh ?   More than half a mind. . . .

" You've got to do the thing you can," he said, after a
pause, " and likely it's what you're fitted for."

§ 4

I paid several short visits to Staffordshire during my Cambridge days, and always these relations of mine produced the
same effect of hardness.   My uncle's thoughts had neither
atmosphere nor mystery.   He lived in a different universe
from the dreams of scientific construction that filled my mind.
He could as easily have understood Chinese poetry.   His
motives were made up of intense rivalries with other men of
his class and kind, a few vindictive hates springing from real
and fancied slights, a habit of acquisition that had become a
second nature, a keen love both of efficiency and display in his
own affairs.   He seemed to me to have no sense of the state,
no sense and much less any love of beauty, no charity and no
sort of religious feeling whatever.   He had strong bodily
appetites, he ate and drank freely, smoked a great deal, and
occasionally was carried off by his passions for a " bit of a
spree " to Birmingham or Liverpool or Manchester.   The
indulgences of these occasions were usually followed by a
period of reaction, when he was urgent for the suppression of
nudity in the local Art Gallery and a harsh and forcible eleva-
tion of the superficial morals of the valley.   And he spoke
of the ladies who ministered to the delights of his jolly-dog
period, when he spoke of them at all, by the unprintable
feminine equivalent.   My aunt he treated with a kindly contempt and considerable financial generosity, but his daughters
tore his heart ; he was so proud of them, so glad to find them
money to spend, so resolved to own them, so instinctively
jealous of every man who came near them.

My uncle has been the clue to a great number of men for
me.   He was an illuminating extreme.   I have learned what

not to expect from them through him, and to comprehend resentments and dangerous sudden antagonisms I should have found incomprehensible in their more complex forms, if I had not first seen them in him in their feral state.

With his soft felt hat at the back of his head, his rather heavy, rather mottled face, his rationally thick boots and slouching tweed-clad form, a little round-shouldered and very obstinate looking, he strolls through all my speculations sucking his teeth audibly, and occasionally throwing out a shrewd aphorism, the intractable unavoidable ore of the new civilisation.

Essentially he was simple. Generally speaking, he hated and despised in equal measure whatever seemed to suggest that he personally was not the most perfect human being conceivable. He hated all education after fifteen because he had had no education after fifteen, he hated all people who did not have high tea until he himself under duress gave up high tea, he hated every game except football, which he had played and could judge, he hated all people who spoke foreign languages because he knew no language but Staffordshire, he hated all foreigners because he was English, and all foreign ways because they were not his ways. Also he hated particularly, and in this order, Londoners, Yorkshiremen, Scotch, Welsh and Irish, because they were not "reet Staffordshire," and he hated all other Staffordshire men as insufficiently "reet." He wanted to have all his own women inviolate, and to fancy he had a call upon every other woman in the world. He wanted to have the best cigars and the best brandy in the world to consume or give away magnificently, and every one else to have inferior ones. (His billiard table was an extra large size, specially made and very inconvenient.) And he hated Trade Unions because they interfered with his autocratic direction of his works, and his work-people because they were not obedient and untiring mechanisms to do his bidding. He was, in fact, a very naïve, vigorous human being. He was about as much civilised, about as much tamed to the ideas of collective action and mutual consideration as a Central African negro.

There are hordes of such men as he throughout all the modern industrial world. You will find the same type with the slightest modifications in the Pas de Calais or Rhenish Prussia or New Jersey or North Italy. No doubt you would find it in New Japan. These men have raised themselves up from the general mass of untrained, uncultured, poorish people in a hard industrious selfish struggle. To drive others they have had first to drive themselves. They have never yet had occasion nor leisure to think of the state or social life as a whole, and as for dreams or beauty, it was a condition of survival that they should ignore such cravings. All the distinctive qualities of my uncle can be thought of as dictated by his conditions ; his success and harshness, the extravagances that expressed his pride in making money, the uncongenial luxury that sprang from rivalry, and his self-reliance, his contempt for broad views, his contempt for everything that he could not understand.

His daughters were the inevitable children of his life. Queer girls they were ! Curiously "spirited " as people phrase it, and curiously limited. My uncle, though he still resented my refusal to go into his business, was also in his odd way proud of me. I was his nephew and poor relation, and yet there I was, a young gentleman learning all sorts of unremunerative things in the grandest manner, "Latin and mook," while the sons of his neighbours, not nephews merely, but sons, stayed unpolished in their native town. Every time I went down I found extensive changes and altered relations, and before I had settled down to them off I went again. I don't think I was one person to them ; I was a series of visitors. There is a gulf of ages between a gaunt schoolboy of sixteen in unbecoming mourning and two vividly self-conscious girls of eighteen and nineteen, but a Cambridge " man " of two-and-twenty with a first and good tennis and a growing social experience, is a fair contemporary for two girls of twenty-three and twenty-four.

A motor-car appeared, I think in my second visit ; a bottle-green affair that opened behind, had dark purple cushions, and was controlled mysteriously by a man in shiny black costume and a flat cap. The high tea had been shifted to seven and rechristened dinner, but my uncle would not dress nor consent to have wine ; and after one painful experiment, I gathered, and a scene, he put his foot down and prohibited any but high-necked dresses.

" Daddy's perfectly impossible," Sybil told me.

The foot had descended vehemently ! " My own daughters ! " he had said, " dressed up like "— and had arrested himself and fumbled and decided to say—" actresses, and showin' their fat arms for every fool to stare at ! " Nor would he have any people invited to dinner. He didn't, he had explained, want strangers poking about in his house when he came home tired. So such calling as occurred went on during his absence in the afternoon.

One of the peculiarities of the life of these ascendant families of the industrial class to which wealth has come, is its tremendous insulations. There were no customs of intercourse in the Five Towns. All the isolated prosperities of the district sprang from economising, hard-driven homes, in which there was neither time nor means for hospitality. Social intercourse centred very largely upon the church or chapel, and the chapels were better at bringing people together than the Establishment to which my cousins belonged. Their chief outlet to the wider world lay therefore through the acquaint-

ances they had formed at school, and through two much less
prosperous families of relations who lived at Longton and
Hanley. A number of gossiping friendships with old school-
mates were "kept up," and my cousins would "spend the
afternoon" or even spend the day with these ; such occasions
led to other encounters and interlaced with the furtive cor-
respondences and snatched meetings that formed the emotional
thread of their lives. When the billiard-table had been new,
my uncle had taken to asking in a few approved friends for
an occasional game, but mostly the billiard-room was for
glory and the girls. Both of them played very well. They
never, so far as I know, dined out, and when at last after bitter
domestic conflicts they began to go to dances, they went with
the quavering connivance of my aunt, and changed into ball
frocks at friends' houses on the way. There was a tennis club
that formed a convenient afternoon rendezvous, and I recall
that in the period of my earlier visits the young bloods of the
district found much satisfaction in taking girls for drives in
dog-carts and such-like high-wheeled vehicles, a disposition that
died in tangled tandems at the apparition of motor-cars.

My aunt and uncle had conceived no plans in life for their
daughters at all. In the undifferentiated industrial community from which they had sprung, girls got married somehow, and it did not occur to them that the concentration of
property that had made them wealthy, had cut their children
off from the general social sea in which their own awkward
meeting had occurred, without necessarily opening any other
world in exchange. My uncle was too much occupied with
the works and his business affairs and his private vices to
philosophise about his girls ; he wanted them just to keep
girls, preferably about sixteen, and to be a sort of animated
flowers and make home bright and be given things. He was
irritated that they would not remain at this, and still more
irritated that they failed to suppress altogether their natural
interest in young men. The tandems would be steered by
weird and devious routes to evade the bare chance of his
bloodshot eye. My aunt seemed to have no ideas whatever
about what was likely to happen to her children. She had
indeed no ideas about anything ; she took her husband and
the days as they came.

I can see now the pathetic difficulty of my cousins' position
in life ; the absence of any guidance or instruction or provision
for their development. They supplemented the silences of
home by the conversation of schoolfellows and the suggestions
of popular fiction. They had to make what they could out of
life with such hints as these. The church was far too modest
to offer them any advice. It was obtruded upon my mind
upon my first visit that they were both carrying on corre-
spondences and having little furtive passings and seeings and
meetings with the mysterious owners of certain initials, S. and

L. K., and, if I remember rightly, "the R. N.," brothers and
cousins, I suppose, of their friends. The same thing was going
on, with a certain intensification, at my next visit, excepting
only that the initials were different. But when I came again
their methods were maturer or I was no longer a negligible
quantity, and the notes and the initials were no longer
flaunted quite so openly in my face.

My cousins had worked it out from the indications of their
universe that the end of life is to have a "good time." They
used the phrase. That and the drives in dog-carts were only
the first of endless points of resemblance between them and
the commoner sort of American girl. When some years ago I
paid my first and only visit to America I seemed to recover my
cousins' atmosphere as soon as I entered the train at Euston.
There were three girls in my compartment supplied with huge
decorated cases of sweets and being seen off by a company of
friends, noisily arch and eager about the "steamer letters"
they would get at Liverpool ; they were the very soul-sisters
of my cousins. The chief elements of a good time, as my
cousins judged it, as these countless thousands of rich young
women judge it, are a petty eventfulness, laughter, and to
feel that you are looking well and attracting attention.
Shopping is one of its leading joys. You buy things, clothes
and trinkets for yourself and presents for your friends. Presents always seemed to be flying about in that circle ; flowers
and boxes of sweets were common currency. My cousins were
always getting and giving, my uncle caressed them with parcels
and cheques. They kissed him and he exuded sovereigns as a
stroked *Aphis* exudes honey. It was like the new language
of the Academy of Lagado to me, and I never learned how to
express myself in it, for nature and training make me feel
encumbered to receive presents and embarrassed in giving
them. But then, like my father, I hate and distrust possessions.

Of the quality of their private imagination I never learned
anything ; I suppose it followed the lines of the fiction they
read and was romantic and sentimental. So far as marriage
went, the married state seemed to them at once very attractive
and dreadfully serious, composed in equal measure of becoming
important and becoming old. I don't know what they thought
about children. I doubt if they thought about them at all.
It was very secret if they did.

As for the poor and dingy people all about them, my cousins
were always ready to take part in a Charitable Bazaar. They
were unaware of any economic correlation of their own prosperity and that circumambient poverty, and they knew of
Trade Unions simply as disagreeable external things that upset
my uncle's temper. They knew of nothing wrong in social
life at all except that there were "Agitators." It surprised
them a little, I think, that Agitators were not more drastically
put down. But they had a sort of instinctive dread of social

discussion as of something that might breach the happiness of their ignorance. . . .

§ 5

My cousins did more than illustrate Marx for me ; they also undertook a stage of my emotional education. Their method in that as in everything else was extremely simple, but it took my inexperience by surprise.

It must have been on my third visit that Sybil took me in hand. Hitherto I seemed to have seen her only in profile, but now she became almost completely full face, manifestly regarded me with those violet eyes of hers. She passed me things I needed at breakfast—it was the first morning of my visit—before I asked for them.

When young men are looked at by pretty cousins, they become intensely aware of those cousins. It seemed to me that I had always admired Sybil's eyes very greatly, and that there was something in her temperament congenial to mine. It was odd I had not noted it on my previous visits.

We walked round the garden somewhen that morning, and talked about Cambridge. She asked quite a lot of questions about my work and my ambitions. She said she had always felt sure I was clever.

The conversation languished a little, and we picked some flowers for the house. Then she asked if I could run. I conceded her various starts and we raced up and down the middle garden path. Then, a little breathless, we went into the new twenty-five-guinea summer-house at the end of the herbaceous border.

We sat side by side, pleasantly hidden from the house, and she became anxious about her hair, which was slightly and prettily disarranged, and asked me to help her with the adjustment of a hairpin. I had never in my life been so near the soft curly hair and the dainty eyebrow and eyelid and warm soft cheek of a girl, and I was stirred——

It stirs me now to recall it.

I became a battleground of impulses and inhibitions.

"Thank you," said my cousin, and moved a little away from me.

She began to talk about friendship, and lost her thread and forgot the little electric stress between us in a rather meandering analysis of her principal girl friends.

But afterwards she resumed her purpose.

I went to bed that night with one proposition overshadowing everything else in my mind, namely, that kissing my cousin Sybil was a difficult but not impossible achievement. I do not recall any shadow of a doubt whether on the whole it was worth doing. The thing had come into my existence, disturbing and interrupting its flow exactly as a fever does. Sybil had infected me with herself.

The next day matters came to a crisis in the little upstairs sitting-room which had been assigned me as a study during my visit. I was working up there, or rather trying to work in spite of the outrageous capering of some very primitive elements in my brain, when she came up to me, under the transparent pretext of looking for a book.

I turned round and then got up at the sight of her. I quite forget what our conversation was about, but I know she led me to believe I might kiss her. Then when I attempted to do so she averted her face.

" How *could* you ? " she said ; " I didn't mean that ! "

That remained the state of our relations for two days. I developed a growing irritation with and resentment against cousin Sybil, combined with an intense desire to get that kiss for which I hungered and thirsted. Cousin Sybil went about in the happy persuasion that I was madly in love with her, and her game, so far as she was concerned, was played and won. It wasn't until I had fretted for two days that I realised that I was being used for the commonest form of excitement possible to a commonplace girl ; that dozens perhaps of young men had played the part of Tantalus at cousin Sybil's lips. I walked about my room at nights, damning her and calling her by terms which on the whole she rather deserved, while Sybil went to sleep pitying " poor old Dick ! "

" Damn it ! " I said, " I *will* be equal with you."

But I never did equalise the disadvantage, and perhaps it's as well, for I fancy that sort of revenge cuts both people too much for a rational man to seek it. . . .

" Why are men so silly ? " said cousin Sybil next morning, wriggling back with down-bent head to release herself from what should have been a compelling embrace.

" Confound it ! " I said with a flash of clear vision. " You *started* this game."

" Oh ! "

She stood back against a hedge of roses, a little flushed and excited and interested, and ready for the delightful defensive if I should renew my attack.

" Beastly hot for scuffling," I said, white with anger. " I don't know whether I'm so keen on kissing you, Sybil, after all. I just thought you wanted me to."

I could have whipped her, and my voice stung more than my words.

Our eyes met, a real hatred in hers leaping up to meet mine.

" Let's play tennis," I said, after a moment's pause.

" No," she answered shortly, " I'm going indoors."

" Very well."

And that ended the affair with Sybil.

I was still in the full glare of this disillusionment when Gertrude awoke from some preoccupation to an interest in my existence. She developed a disposition to touch my hand by accident, and let her fingers rest in contact with it for a moment —she had pleasant soft hands;—she began to drift into summer-houses with me, to let her arm rest trustfully against mine, to ask questions about Cambridge. They were much the same questions that Sybil had asked. But I controlled myself and maintained a profile of intelligent and entirely civil indifference to her blandishments.

What Gertrude made of it came out one evening in some talk—I forget about what—with Sybil.

" Oh, Dick ! " said Gertrude a little patiently, " Dick's Pi."

And I never disillusioned her by any subsequent levity from this theory of my innate and virginal piety.

§ 6

It was against this harsh and crude Staffordshire background that I think I must have seen Margaret for the first time. I say I think, because it is quite possible that we had passed each other in the streets of Cambridge, no doubt with that affectation of mutual disregard which was once customary between undergraduates and Newnham girls. But if that was so I had noted nothing of the slender graciousness that shone out so pleasingly against the bleaker midland surroundings.

She was a younger schoolfellow of my cousins', and the stepdaughter of Seddon, a prominent solicitor of Burslem. She was not only not in my cousins' generation but not in their set, she was one of a small hard-working group who kept immaculate notebooks, and did as much as is humanly possible of that insensate pile of written work that the Girls' Public School movement has inflicted upon schoolgirls. She really learned French and German admirably and thoroughly, she got as far in mathematics as an unflinching industry can carry any one with no great natural aptitude, and she went up to Bennett Hall, Newnham, after the usual conflict with her family, to work for the History Tripos.

There in her third year she made herself thoroughly ill through overwork, so ill that she had to give up Newnham altogether and go abroad with her step-mother. She made herself ill, as so many girls do in those university colleges, through the badness of her home and school training. She thought study must needs be a hard straining of the mind. She worried her work, she gave herself no leisure to see it as a whole, she felt herself not making headway and she cut her games and exercise in order to increase her hours of toil, and worked into the night. She carried a knack of laborious thoroughness into the blind alleys and essentials of her subject. It didn't need the badness of the food for which Bennett Hall is celebrated and the remarkable dietary of nocturnal cocoa, cakes and soft biscuits with which the girls have supplemented it, to ensure her collapse. Her mother brought her home, fretting and distressed, and then finding her hopelessly un-

happy at home, took her and her half-brother, a rather ailing
youngster of ten who died three years later, for a journey to
Italy.

Italy did much to assuage Margaret's chagrin. I think all
three of them had a very good time there. At home Mr.
Seddon, her step-father, played the part of a well-meaning
blight by reason of the moods that arose from nervous dys-
pepsia. They went to Florence, equipped with various introductions and much sound advice from sympathetic Cambridge
friends, and having acquired an ease in Italy there, went on
to Siena, Orvieto, and at last Rome. They returned, if I
remember rightly, by Pisa, Genoa, Milan and Paris. Six
months or more they had had abroad, and now Margaret was
back in Burslem, in health again and consciously a very
civilised person.

New ideas were abroad, it was Maytime and a spring of
abundant flowers—daffodils were particularly good that year
—and Mrs. Seddon celebrated her return by giving an afternoon reception at short notice, with the clear intention of
letting every one out into the garden if the weather held.

The Seddons had a big old farmhouse modified to modern
ideas of comfort on the road out towards Misterton, with an
orchard that had been rather pleasantly subdued from use to
ornament. It had rich blossoming cherry and apple trees.
Large patches of grass full of nodding yellow trumpets had
been left amidst the not too precisely mown grass, which was
as it were grass path with an occasional lapse into lawn or
glade. And Margaret, hatless, with the fair hair above her
thin, delicately pink face very simply done, came to meet our
rather too consciously dressed party—we had come in the
motor four strong, with my aunt in grey silk. Margaret wore
a soft flowing flowered blue dress of diaphanous material, all
unconnected with the fashion and tied with pretty ribbons,
like a slenderer, unbountiful Primavera.

It was one of those May days that ape the light and heat of
summer, and I remember disconnectedly quite a number of
brightly lit figures and groups walking about, and a white gate
between orchard and garden and a large lawn with an oak
tree and a red Georgian house with a verandah and open
French windows, through which the tea drinking had come
out upon the moss-edged flagstones even as Mrs. Seddon had
planned.

The party was almost entirely feminine except for a little
curate with a large head, a good voice and a radiant manner, who
was obviously attracted by Margaret, and two or three young
husbands still sufficiently addicted to their wives to accompany
them. One of them I recall as a quite romantic figure with
abundant blond curly hair on which was poised a grey felt
hat encircled by a refined black band. He wore, moreover,
a loose rich shot-silk tie of red and purple, a long frock-coat,

grey trousers and brown shoes, and presently he removed his hat and carried it in one hand. There were two tennis-playing youths besides myself. There was also one father with three daughters in anxious control, a father of the old school scarcely half broken in, reluctant, rebellious and consciously and conscientiously " reet Staffordshire." The daughters were all alert to suppress the possible plungings, the undesirable humorous impulses of this almost feral guest. They nipped his very gestures in the bud. The rest of the people were mainly mothers with daughters—daughters of all ages, and a scattering of aunts, and there was a tendency to clotting, parties kept together and regarded parties suspiciously. Mr. Seddon was in hiding, I think, all the time, though not formally absent.

Matters centred upon the tea in the long room of the French windows, where four trim maids went to and fro busily between the house and the clumps of people seated or standing before it ; and tennis and croquet were intermittently visible and audible beyond a bank of rockwork rich with the spikes and cups and bells of high spring.

Mrs. Seddon presided at the tea-urn, and Margaret partly assisted and partly talked to me and my cousin Sibyl—Gertrude had found a disused and faded initial and was partnering him at tennis in a state of gentle revival—while their mother exercised a divided chaperonage from a seat near Mrs. Seddon. The little curate, stirring a partially empty cup of tea, mingled with our party, and preluded, I remember, every observation he made by a vigorous resumption of stirring.

We talked of Cambridge, and Margaret kept us to it. The curate was a Selwyn man and had taken a pass degree in theology, but Margaret had come to Gaylord's lecturers in Trinity for a term before her breakdown, and understood these differences. She had the eagerness of an exile to hear the old familiar names of places and personalities. We capped familiar anecdotes and were enthusiastic about King's Chapel and the Backs, and the curate, addressing himself more particularly to Sybil, told a long confused story illustrative of his disposition to reckless devilry (of a pure-minded kindly sort) about upsetting two canoes quite needlessly on the way to Grantchester.

I can still see Margaret as I saw her that afternoon, see her fresh fair face with the little obliquity of the upper lip and her brow always slightly knitted, and her manner as of one breathlessly shy but determined. She had rather open blue eyes, and she spoke in an even musical voice with the gentlest of stresses and the ghost of a lisp. And it was true, she gathered, that Cambridge still existed. " I went to Grantchester," she said, " last year, and had tea under the apple-blossom. I didn't think then I should have to come down." (It was that started the curate upon his anecdote.)

" I've seen a lot of pictures, and learned a lot about them—
at the Pitti and the Brera—the Brera is wonderful—wonderful
places—but it isn't like real study," she was saying presently.
. . . " We bought bales of photographs," she said.

I thought the bales a little out of keeping.

But fair-haired and quite simply and yet graciously and
fancifully dressed, talking of art and beautiful things and a
beautiful land, and with so much manifest regret for learning
denied, she seemed a different kind of being altogether from
my smart, hard, high-coloured, black-haired and resolutely
hatted cousins ; she seemed translucent beside Gertrude.
Even the little twist and droop of her slender body was a grace
to me.

I liked her from the moment I saw her, and set myself to
interest and please her as well as I knew how.

We recalled a case of ragging that had rustled the shrubs of
Newnham, and then Chris Robinson's visit—he had given a
talk to Bennett Hall also—and our impression of him.

" He disappointed me, too," said Margaret.

I was moved to tell Margaret something of my own views in
the matter of social progress, and she listened—oh ! with a
kind of urged attention, and her brow a little more knitted,
very earnestly.   The curate desisted from the appendices and
refuse heaps and general débris of his story, and made himself
look very alert and intelligent.

" We did a lot of that when I was up in the 'eighties," he said.
" I'm glad Imperialism hasn't swamped you fellows altogether."

Gertrude, looking bright and confident, came to join our
talk from the shrubbery ; the initial, a little flushed and evidently in a state of refreshed relationship, came with her, and a
cheerful lady in pink and more particularly distinguished by a
pink bonnet joined our group.   Gertrude had been sipping
admiration and was not disposed to play a passive part in the
talk.

" Socialism ! " she cried, catching the word.   " It's well Pa
isn't here.   He has Fits when people talk of socialism.   Fits ! "

The initial laughed in a general kind of way.

The curate said there was socialism and socialism, and looked
at Margaret to gauge whether he had been too bold in this
utterance.   But she was all, he perceived, for broad-minded-
ness, and he stirred himself (and incidentally his tea) to still
more liberality of expression.   He said the state of the poor
was appalling, simply appalling ; that there were times when he
wanted to shatter the whole system, " only," he said, turning
to me appealingly, " what have we got to put in its place ? "

" The thing that exists is always the more evident alternative," I said.

The little curate looked at it for a moment.   " Precisely," he
said explosively, and turned stirring and with his head on one
side, to hear what Margaret was saying.

Margaret was saying, with a swift blush and an effect of daring, that she had no doubt she was a socialist.

" And wearing a gold chain ! " said Gertrude, " and drinking out of eggshell ! I like that ! "

I came to Margaret's rescue. " It doesn't follow that because one's a socialist one ought to dress in sackcloth and ashes."

The initial coloured deeply, and having secured my attention by prodding me slightly with the wrist of the hand that held his teacup, cleared his throat and suggested that " one ought to be consistent."

I perceived we were embarked upon a discussion of the elements. We began an interesting wrangle, one of those crude discussions of general ideas that are dear to the heart of youth. I and Margaret supported one another as socialists, Gertrude and Sybil and the initial maintained an anti-socialist position, the curate attempted a cross-bench position with an air of intending to come down upon us presently with a casting vote. He reminded us of a number of useful principles too often overlooked in argument, that in a big question like this there was much to be said on both sides, that if every one did his or her duty to every one about them there would be no difficulty with social problems at all, that over and above all enactments we needed moral changes in people themselves. My cousin Gertrude was a difficult controversialist to manage, being unconscious of inconsistency in statement and absolutely impervious to reply. Her standpoint was essentially materialistic ; she didn't see why she shouldn't have a good time because other people didn't ; they would have a good time, she was sure, if she didn't. She said that if we did give up everything we had to other people, they wouldn't very likely know what to do with it. She asked if we were so fond of work-people, why we didn't go and live among them, and expressed the inflexible persuasion that if we *had* socialism, everything would be just the same again in ten years' time. She also threw upon us the imputation of ingratitude for a beautiful world by saying that so far as she was concerned she didn't want to upset everything. She was contented with things as they were, thank you.

The discussion led in some way that I don't in the least recall now, and possibly by abrupt transitions, to a croquet foursome in which Margaret involved the curate without involving herself, and then stood beside me on the edge of the lawn while the others played. We watched silently for a moment.

" I *hate* that sort of view," she said suddenly in a confidential undertone, with her delicate pink flush returning.

" It's want of imagination," I said.

" To think we are just to enjoy ourselves," she went on ; " just to go on dressing and playing and having meals and spending money ! " She seemed to be referring not simply to my cousins, but to the whole world of industry and property about us. " But what is one to do ? " she asked. " I do wish I had not had to come down. It's all so pointless here. There seems to be nothing going forward, no ideas, no dreams. No one here seems to feel quite what I feel, the sort of need there is for *meaning* in things. I hate things without meaning."

" Don't you do—local work ? "

" I suppose I shall. I suppose I must find something. Do you think—if one were to attempt some sort of propaganda ? "

" Could you—— ? " I began a little doubtfully.

" I suppose I couldn't," she answered, after a thoughtful moment. " I suppose it would come to nothing. And yet I feel there is so much to be done for the world, so much one ought to be doing. . . . I want to do something for the world."

I can see her now as she stood there with her brows nearly frowning, her blue eyes looking before her, her mouth almost petulant. " One feels that there are so many things going on —out of one's reach," she said.

I went back in the motor-car with my mind full of her, the quality of delicate discontent, the suggestion of exile. Even a kind of weakness in her was sympathetic. She told tremendously against her background. She was, I say, like a protesting blue flower upon a cinder-heap. It is curious, too, how she connects and mingles with the furious quarrel I had with my uncle that very evening. That came absurdly. Indirectly Margaret was responsible. My mind was running on ideas she had revived and questions she had set clamouring, and quite inadvertently in my attempt to find solutions I talked so as to outrage his profoundest feelings. . . .

§ 7

What a preposterous shindy that was !

I sat with him in the smoking-room, propounding what I considered to be the most indisputable and non-contentious propositions conceivable—until, to my infinite amazement, he exploded and called me a " damned young puppy."

It was seismic.

" Tremendously interesting time," I said, " just in the beginning of making a civilisation."

" Ah ! " he said, with an averted face, and nodded, leaning forward over his cigar.

I had not the remotest thought of annoying him.

"Monstrous muddle of things we have got," I said, " jumbled streets, ugly population, ugly factories——"

" You'd do a sight better if you had to do with it," said my uncle, regarding me askance.

" Not me. But a world that had a collective plan and knew where it meant to be going would do a sight better, anyhow. We're all swimming in a flood of ill-calculated chances——"

" You'll be making out I organised that business down there—by chance—next," said my uncle, his voice thick with challenge.

I went on as though I was back in Trinity.

" There's a lot of chance in the making of all great businesses," I said.

My uncle remarked that that showed how much I knew about businesses. If chance made businesses, why was it that he always succeeded and grew while those fools Ackroyd and Sons always took second place ? He showed a disposition to tell the glorious history of how once Ackroyd's overshadowed him, and how now he could buy up Ackroyd's three times over. But I wanted to get out what was in my mind.

" Oh ! " I said, " as between man and man and business and business, some of course get the pull by this quality or that—but it's forces quite outside the individual case that make the big part of any success under modern conditions. *You* never invented pottery, nor any process in pottery that matters a rap in your works ; it wasn't *your* foresight that joined all England up with railways and made it possible to organise production on an altogether different scale. You really at the utmost can't take credit for much more than being the sort of man who happened to fit what happened to be the requirements of the time, and who happened to be in a position to take advantage of them——"

It was then my uncle cried out and called me a damned young puppy, and became involved in some unexpected trouble of his own.

I woke up as it were from my analysis of the situation to discover him bent over a splendid spittoon, cursing incoherently, retching a little, and spitting out the end of his cigar which he had bitten off in his last attempt at self-control, and withal fully prepared as soon as he had cleared for action to give me just all that he considered to be the contents of his mind upon the condition of mine.

Well, why shouldn't I talk my mind to him ? He'd never had an outside view of himself for years, and I resolved to stand up to him. We went at it hammer and tongs ! It became clear that he supposed me to be a socialist, a zealous, embittered hater of all ownership—and also an educated man of the vilest, most pretentiously superior description. His principal grievance was that I thought I knew everything ; to that he recurred again and again. . . .

We had been maintaining an armed truce with each other since my resolve to go up to Cambridge, and now we had out all that had accumulated between us. There had been stupendous accumulations. . . .

The particular things we said and did in that bawling encounter matter nothing at all in this story. I can't now estimate how near we came to fisticuffs. It ended with my saying, after a pungent reminder of benefits conferred and re-membered, that I didn't want to stay another hour in his house. I went upstairs, in a state of puerile fury, to pack and go off to the Railway Hotel, while he, with ironical civility, telephoned for a cab.

"Good riddance!" shouted my uncle, seeing me off into the night.

On the face of it our row was preposterous, but the under-lying reality of our quarrel was the essential antagonism, it seemed to me, in all human affairs, the antagonism between ideas and the established method, that is to say, between ideas and the rule of thumb. The world I hate is the rule-of-thumb world, the thing I and my kind of people exist for primarily is to battle with that, to annoy it, disarrange it, reconstruct it. We question everything, disturb anything that cannot give a clear justification to our questioning, because we believe in-herently that our sense of disorder implies the possibility of a better order. Of course we are detestable. My uncle was of that other vaster mass who accept everything for the thing it seems to be, hate inquiry and analysis as a tramp hates washing, dread and resist change, oppose experiment, despise science. The world is our battleground; and all history, all literature that matters, all science, deals with this conflict of the thing that is and the speculative " if " that will destroy it.

But that is why I did not see Margaret Seddon again for five years.

CHAPTER TWO

MARGARET IN LONDON

§ 1

I WAS twenty-seven when I met Margaret again, and the intervening five years had been years of vigorous activity for me, if not of very remarkable growth. When I saw her again, I could count myself a grown man. I think, indeed, I counted myself more completely grown than I was. At any rate, by all ordinary standards, I had " got on " very well, and my ideas, if they had not changed very greatly, had become much more definite and my ambitions clearer and bolder.

I had long since abandoned my fellowship and come to London. I had published two books that had been talked about, written several articles, and established a regular relationship with the *Weekly Review* and the *Evening Gazette*. I was a member of the Eighty Club and learning to adapt the style of the Cambridge Union to larger uses. The London world had opened out to me very readily. I had developed a pleasant variety of social connections. I had made the acquaintance of Mr. Evesham, who had been attracted by my *New Ruler*, and who talked about it and me, and so did a very great deal to make a way for me into the company of prominent and amusing people. I dined out quite frequently. The glitter and interest of good London dinner-parties became a common experience. I liked the sort of conversation one got at them extremely, the little glow of duologues burning up into more general discussions, the closing-in of the men after the going of the women, the sage, substantial masculine gossiping, the later resumption of effective talk with some pleasant woman, graciously at her best. I had a wide range of houses ; Cambridge had linked me to one or two correlated sets of artistic and literary people, and my books and Mr. Evesham had opened to me the big vague world of " society." I wasn't aggressive nor particularly snobbish nor troublesome, sometimes I talked well, and if I had nothing interesting to say I said as little as possible, and I had a youthful gravity of manner that was liked by hostesses. And the other side of my nature that first flared through the cover of restraints at Locarno, that too had had opportunity to develop along the line London renders practicable. I had had my experiences and secrets and adventures among that fringe of ill-mated or erratic or discredited women the London world possesses. The thing had long ago ceased to be a matter of magic or mystery, and had become a question of appetites and excitement, and among other things the excitement of not being found out.

I write rather doubtfully of my growing during this period. Indeed I find it hard to judge whether I can say that I grew at all in any real sense of the word, between three-and-twenty and twenty-seven. It seems to me now to have been rather a phase of realisation and clarification. All the broad lines of my thought were laid down, I am sure, by the date of my Locarno adventure, but in those five years I discussed things over and over again with myself and others, filled out with concrete fact forms I had at first apprehended sketchily and conversationally, measured my powers against my ideals and the forces in the world about me. It was evident that many men no better than myself and with no greater advantages than mine had raised themselves to influential and even decisive positions in the worlds of politics and thought. I was gathering the confidence and knowledge necessary to attack the world in the large manner ; I found I could write, and that people would let me write if I chose, as one having authority and not as the scribes. Socially and politically and intellectually I knew myself for an honest man, and that quite without any deliberation on my part this showed and made things easy for me. People trusted my good faith from the beginning— for all that I came from nowhere and had no better position than any adventurer.

But the growth process was arrested, I was nothing bigger at twenty-seven than at twenty-two, however much saner and stronger, and any one looking closely into my mind during that period might well have imagined growth finished altogether. It is particularly evident to me now that I came no nearer to any understanding of women during that time. That Locarno affair was infinitely more to me than I had supposed. It ended something—nipped something in the bud perhaps— took me at a stride from a vague, fine, ignorant, closed world of emotion to intrigue and a perfectly definite and limited sensuality. It ended my youth, and for a time it prevented my manhood. I had never yet even peeped at the sweetest, profoundest thing in the world, the heart and meaning of a girl, or dreamt with any quality of reality of a wife or any such thing as a friend among womanhood. My vague anticipation of such things in life had vanished altogether. I turned away from their possibility. It seemed to me I knew what had to be known about womankind. I wanted to work hard, to get on to a position in which I could develop and forward my constructive projects. Women, I thought, had nothing to do with that. It seemed clear I could not marry for some years ; I was attractive to certain types of women, I had vanity enough to give me an agreeable confidence in love-making, and I went about seeking a convenient mistress quite deliberately, some one who should serve my purpose and say in the end, like that kindly first mistress of mine, " I've done you no harm," and so release me. It seemed the only wise way of disposing of urgencies that might otherwise entangle and wreck the career I was intent upon.

I don't apologise for, or defend my mental and moral phases. So it was I appraised life and prepared to take it, and so it is a thousand ambitious men see it to-day. . . .

For the rest these five years were a period of definition. My political conceptions were perfectly plain and honest. I had one constant desire ruling my thoughts. I meant to leave England and the empire better ordered than I found it, to organise and discipline, to build up a constructive and controlling State out of my world's confusions. We had, I saw, to suffuse education with public intention, to develop a new better-living generation with a collectivist habit of thought, to link now chaotic activities in every human affair, and particularly to catch that escaped, world-making, world-ruining, dangerous thing, industrial and financial enterprise, and bring it back to the service of the general good. I had then the precise image that still serves me as a symbol for all I wish to bring about, the image of an engineer building a lock in a swelling torrent—with water pressure as his only source of power. My thoughts and acts were habitually turned to that enterprise ; it gave shape and direction to all my life. The problem that most engaged my mind during those years was the practical and personal problem of just where to apply myself to serve this almost innate purpose. How was I, a child of this confusion, struggling upward through the confusion, to take hold of things ? Somewhere between politics and literature my grip must needs be found, but where ? Always I seem to have been looking for that in those opening years, and disregarding everything else to discover it.

§ 2

The Baileys, under whose auspices I met Margaret again, were in the sharpest contrast with the narrow industrialism of the Staffordshire world. They were indeed at the other extreme of the scale, two active self-centred people excessively devoted to the public service. It was natural I should gravitate to them, for they seemed to stand for the maturer, more disciplined, better informed expression of all I was then urgent to attempt to do. The bulk of their friends were politicians or public officials, they described themselves as publicists—a vague yet sufficiently significant term. They lived and worked in a hard little house in Chambers Street, Westminster, and made a centre for quite an astonishing amount of political and social activity.

Willersley took me there one evening. The place was almost pretentiously matter-of-fact and unassuming. The narrow passage-hall, papered with some ancient yellowish paper, grained to imitate wood, was choked with hats and cloaks and an occasional feminine wrap. Motioned rather than announced by a tall Scotch woman servant, the only domestic I ever remember seeing there, we made our way up a narrow staircase past the open door of a small study packed with blue-books, to discover Altiora Bailey receiving before the fireplace in her drawing-room. She was a tall commanding figure, splendid but a little untidy in black silk and red beads, with dark eyes that had no depths, with a clear hard voice that had an almost visible prominence, aquiline features and straight black hair that was apt to get astray, that was now astray like the head feathers of an eagle in a gale. She stood with her hands behind her back, and talked in a high tenor of a projected Town Planning Bill with Blupp, who was practically in those days the secretary of the Local Government Board. A very short broad man with thick ears and fat white hands writhing intertwined behind him, stood with his back to us, eager to bark interruptions into Altiora's discourse. A slender girl in pale blue, manifestly a young political wife, stood with one foot on the fender listening with an expression of entirely puzzled propitiation. A tall sandy-bearded bishop with the expression of a man in a trance completed this central group.

The room was one of those long apartments once divided by folding-doors, and reaching from back to front, that are common upon the first floors of London houses. Its walls were hung with two or three indifferent water-colours, there was scarcely any furniture but a sofa or so and a chair, and the floor, severely carpeted with matting, was crowded with a curious medley of people, men predominating. Several were in evening dress, but most had the morning garb of the politician ; the women were either severely rational or radiantly magnificent. Willersley pointed out to me the wife of the Secretary of State for War, and I recognised the Duchess of Clynes, who at that time cultivated intellectuality. I looked round, identifying a face here or there, and stepping back trod on some one's toe, and turned to find it belonged to the Right Hon. G. B. Mottisham, dear to the *Punch* caricaturists. He received my apology with that intentional charm that is one of his most delightful traits, and resumed his discussion. Beside him was Esmeer of Trinity, whom I had not seen since my Cambridge days. . . .

Willersley found an ex-member of the School Board for whom he had affinities, and left me to exchange experiences and comments upon the company with Esmeer. Esmeer was still a don ; but he was nibbling, he said, at certain negotiations with *The Times* that might bring him down to London. He wanted to come to London. " We peep at things from Cambridge," he said.

" This sort of thing," I said, " makes London necessary. It's the oddest gathering."

" Every one comes here," said Esmeer. " Mostly we hate them like poison—jealousy—and little irritations—Altiora can be a horror at times—but we *have* to come."

" Things are being done ? "

" Oh !—no doubt of it.   It's one of the parts of the British machinery—that doesn't show. . . . But nobody else could do it.

"Two people," said Esmeer, "who've planned to be a power—in an original way.   And by Jove ! they've done it ! "

I did not for some time pick out Oscar Bailey, and then Esmeer showed him to me in elaborately confidential talk in a corner with a distinguished-looking stranger wearing a ribbon. Oscar had none of the fine appearance of his wife ; he was a short sturdy figure with a rounded protruding abdomen and a curious broad, flattened, clean-shaven face that seemed nearly all forehead.   He was of Anglo-Hungarian extraction, and I have always fancied something Mongolian in his type.   He peered up with reddish swollen-looking eyes over gilt-edged glasses that were divided horizontally into portions of different refractive power, and he talked in an ingratiating undertone, with busy thin lips, an eager lisp and nervous movements of the hands.

People say that thirty years before at Oxford he was almost exactly the same eager, clever little man he was when I first met him.   He had come up to Balliol bristling with extraordinary degrees and prizes captured in provincial and Irish and Scotch universities—and had made a name for himself as the most formidable dealer in exact fact the rhetoricians of the Union had ever had to encounter.   From Oxford he had gone on to a position in the Higher Division of the Civil Service, I think in the War Office, and had speedily made a place for himself as a political journalist.   He was a particularly neat controversialist, and very full of political and sociological ideas. He had a quite astounding memory for facts and a mastery of detailed analysis, and the time afforded scope for these gifts. The later 'eighties were full of politico-social discussion, and he became a prominent name upon the contents list of the *Nineteenth Century*, the *Fortnightly* and *Contemporary*, chiefly as a half-sympathetic but frequently very damaging critic of the socialism of that period.   He won the immense respect of every one specially interested in social and political questions, he soon achieved the limited distinction that is awarded such capacity, and at that I think he would have remained for the rest of his life if he had not encountered Altiora.

But Altiora Macvitie was an altogether exceptional woman, an extraordinary mixture of qualities, the one woman in the world who could make something more out of Bailey than that. She had much of the vigour and handsomeness of a slender impudent young man, and an unscrupulousness altogether feminine.   She was one of those women who are wanting in— what is the word ?—muliebrity.   She had courage and initiative and a philosophical way of handling questions, and she could be bored by regular work like a man.   She was entirely unfitted for her sex's sphere.   She was neither uncertain, coy, nor hard to please, and altogether too stimulating and aggressive for any gentleman's hours of ease. Her cookery would have been about as sketchy as her handwriting, which was generally quite illegible, and she would have made, I feel sure, a shocking bad nurse. Yet you mustn't imagine she was an inelegant or unbeautiful woman, and she is inconceivable to me in high collars or any sort of masculine garment. But her soul was bony, and at the base of her was a vanity gaunt and greedy ! When she wasn't in a state of personal untidiness that was partly a protest against the waste of hours exacted by the toilet and partly a natural disinclination, she had a gypsy splendour of black and red and silver all her own. And somewhen in the early 'nineties she met and married Bailey.

I know very little about her early years. She was the only daughter of Sir Deighton Macvitie, who applied the iodoform process to cotton, and only his subsequent unfortunate attempts to become a Cotton King prevented her being a very rich woman. As it was she had a tolerable independence. She came into prominence as one of the more able of the little shoal of young women who were led into politico-philanthropic activities by the influence of the earlier novels of Mrs. Humphry Ward—the Marcella crop. She went " slumming " with distinguished vigour, which was quite usual in those days—and returned from her experiences as an amateur flower girl with clear and original views about the problem—which is and always had been unusual. She had not married, I suppose, because her standards were high, and men are cowards and with an instinctive appetite for muliebrity. She had kept house for her father by speaking occasionally to the housekeeper, butler and cook her mother had left her, and gathering the most interesting dinner parties she could, and had married off four orphan nieces in a harsh and successful manner. After her father's smash and death she came out as a writer upon social questions and a scathing critic of the Charity Organisation Society ; and she was three-and-thirty and a little at loose ends when she met Oscar Bailey, so to speak, in the *Contemporary Review*. The lurking woman in her nature was fascinated by the ease and precision with which the little man rolled over all sorts of important and authoritative people, she was the first to discover a sort of imaginative bigness in his still growing mind, the forehead perhaps carried him off physically, and she took occasion to meet and subjugate him and, so soon as he had sufficiently recoevered from his abject humility and a certain panic at her attentions, marry him.

This had opened a new phase in the lives of Bailey and herself. The two supplemented each other to an extraordinary extent. Their subsequent career was, I think, almost entirely her invention. She was aggressive, imaginative, and had a great capacity for ideas, while he was almost destitute of initiative, and could do nothing with ideas except remember and discuss them. She was, if not exact, at least

indolent, with a strong disposition to save energy by sketching
—even her handwriting showed that—while he was inex-
haustibly industrious with a relentless invariable caligraphy
that grew larger and clearer as the years passed by. She had
a considerable power of charming ; she could be just as nice to
people—and incidentally just as nasty—as she wanted to be.
He was always just the same, a little confidential and *sotto voce*,
artlessly rude and egoistic in an undignified way. She had
considerable social experience, good social connections, and
considerable social ambition, while he had none of these things.
She saw in a flash her opportunity to redeem his defects, use
his powers, and do large, novel, rather startling things. She
ran him. Her marriage, which shocked her friends and
relations beyond measure—for a time they would only speak of
Bailey as " that gnome "—was a stroke of genius, and forthwith they proceeded to make themselves the most formidable
and distinguished couple conceivable. P.B.P., she boasted,
was engraved inside their wedding rings, Pro Bono Publico,
and she meant it to be no idle threat. She had discovered very
early that the last thing influential people will do is to work.
Everything in their lives tends to make them dependent upon
a supply of confidently administered detail. Their business
is with the window and not the stock behind, and in the end
they are dependent upon the stock behind for what goes into
the window. She linked with that the fact that Bailey had a
mind as orderly as a museum, and an invincible power over
detail. She saw that if two people took the necessary pains to
know the facts of government and administration with precision,
to gather together knowledge that was dispersed and confused,
to be able to say precisely what had to be done and what avoided
in this eventuality or that, they would necessarily become a
centre of reference for all sorts of legislative proposals and
political expedients, and she went unhesitatingly upon that.

Bailey, under her vigorous direction, threw up his post in
the Civil Service and abandoned sporadic controversies, and
they devoted themselves to the elaboration and realisation
of this centre of public information she had conceived as their
rôle. They set out to study the methods and organisation and
realities of government in the most elaborate manner. They did
the work as no one had ever hitherto dreamt of doing it. They
planned the research on a thoroughly satisfying scale, and arranged their lives almost entirely for it. They took that house
in Chambers Street and furnished it with severe economy, they discovered that Scotch domestic who is destined to be the guardian
and tyrant of their declining years, and they set to work. Their
first book, *The Permanent Official*, fills three plump volumes, and
took them and their two secretaries upwards of four years to do.
It is an amazingly good book, an enduring achievement. In
a hundred directions the history and the administrative treatment of the public service was clarified for all time. . . .

They worked regularly every morning from nine to twelve, they lunched lightly but severely, in the afternoon they " took exercise " or Bailey attended meetings of the London School Board, on which he served, he said, for the purposes of study— he also became a railway director for the same end. In the late afternoon Altiora was at home to various callers, and in the evening came dinner or a reception or both.

Her dinners and gatherings were a very important feature in their scheme. She got together all sorts of interesting people in or about the public service, she mixed the obscurely efficient with the ill-instructed famous and the rudderless rich, got together in one room more of the factors in our strange jumble of a public life than had ever met easily before. She fed them with a shameless austerity that kept the conversation brilliant, on a soup, a plain fish, and mutton or boiled fowl and milk pudding, with nothing to drink but whisky and soda, and hot and cold water, and milk and lemonade. Everybody was soon very glad indeed to come to that. She boasted how little her housekeeping cost her, and sought constantly for fresh economies that would enable her, she said, to sustain an additional private secretary. Secretaries were the Baileys' one extravagance, they loved to think of searches going on in the British Museum, and letters being cleared up and précis made overhead, while they sat in the little study and worked together, Bailey with a clockwork industry, and Altiora in splendid flashes between intervals of cigarettes and meditation. " All efficient public careers," said Altiora, " consist in the proper direction of secretaries."

" If everything goes well I shall have another secretary next year," Altiora told me. " I wish I could refuse people dinner napkins. Imagine what it means in washing ! I dare most things. . . . But as it is, they stand a lot of hardship here."

" There's something of the miser in both these people," said Esmeer, and the thing was perfectly true. For, after all, the miser is nothing more than a man who either through want of imagination or want of suggestion misapplies to a base use a natural power of concentration upon one end. The concentration itself is neither good nor evil, but a power that can be used in either way. And the Baileys gathered and reinvested usuriously not money, but knowledge of the utmost value in human affairs. They produced an effect of having found themselves—completely. One envied them at times extraordinarily. I was attracted, I was dazzled—and at the same time there was something about Bailey's big wrinkled forehead, his lisping broad mouth, the gestures of his hands and an uncivil preoccupation I could not endure. . . .

§ 3

Their effect upon me was from the outset very considerable. Both of them found occasion on that first visit of mine to talk to me about my published writings and particularly about my then just published book, *The New Ruler*, which had interested them very much. It fell in indeed so closely with their own way of thinking that I doubt if they ever understood how independently I had arrived at my conclusions. It was their weakness to claim excessively. That irritation, however, came later. We discovered each other immensely ; for a time it produced a tremendous sense of kindred and co-operation.

Altiora, I remember, maintained that there existed a great army of such constructive-minded people as ourselves—as yet undiscovered by one another.

" It's like boring a tunnel through a mountain," said Oscar, " and presently hearing the tapping of the workers from the other end."

" If you didn't know of them beforehand," I said, " it might be a rather badly joined tunnel."

" Exactly," said Altiora with a high note, " and that's why we all want to find out each other. . . ."

They didn't talk like that on our first encounter, but they urged me to lunch with them next day, and then it was we went into things. A woman Factory Inspector and the Educational Minister for New Banksland and his wife were also there, but I don't remember they made any contribution to the conversation. The Baileys saw to that. They kept on at me in an urgent litigious way.

" We have read your book," each began—as though it had been a joint function. " And we consider——"

" Yes," I protested, " *I* think——"

That was a secondary matter.

They did not consider, said Altiora, raising her voice and going right over me, that I had allowed sufficiently for the inevitable development of an official administrative class in the modern state.

" Nor of its importance," echoed Oscar.

That, they explained in a sort of chorus, was the cardinal idea of their lives, what they were up to, what they stood for. " We want to suggest to you," they said—and I found this was a stock opening of theirs—" that from the mere necessities of convenience elected bodies *must* avail themselves more and more of the services of expert officials. We have that very much in mind. The more complicated and technical affairs become, the less confidence will the elected official have in himself. We want to suggest that these expert officials must necessarily develop into a new class and a very powerful class in the community. We want to organise that. It may be *the* power of the future. They will necessarily have to have very much of a common training. We consider ourselves as amateur unpaid precursors of such a class." . . .

The vision they displayed for my consideration as the aim of public-spirited endeavour, seemed like a harder, narrower,

more specialised version of the idea of a trained and disciplined
state that Willersley and I had worked out in the Alps.   They
wanted things more organised, more correlated with government
and a collective purpose, just as we did, but they saw it not in
terms of a growing collective understanding, but in terms of
functionaries, legislative change, methods of administration. . . .

It wasn't clear at first how we differed.   The Baileys were
very anxious to win me to co-operation, and I was quite
prepared at first to identify their distinctive expressions with
phrases of my own, and so we came readily into an alliance
that was to last some years, and break at last very painfully.
Altiora manifestly liked me, I was soon discussing with her
the perplexity I found in placing myself efficiently in the
world, the problem of how to take hold of things that occupied my
thoughts, and she was sketching out careers for my consideration, very much as an architect on his first visit sketches houses,
considers requirements, and puts before you this example and
that of the more or less similar thing already done. . . .

§ 4

It is easy to see how much in common there was between
the Baileys and me, and how natural it was that I should
become a constant visitor at their house and an ally of theirs
in many enterprises.   It is not nearly so easy to define the
profound antagonism of spirit that also held between us.
There was a difference in texture, a difference in quality.   How
can I express it ?   The shapes of our thoughts were the same,
but the substance quite different.   It was as if they had made
in china or cast-iron what I had made in transparent living
matter.   (The comparison is manifestly from my point of
view.)   Certain things never seemed to show through their
ideas that were visible, refracted perhaps and distorted, but
visible always through mine.

I thought for a time the essential difference lay in our
relation to beauty.   With me beauty is quite primary in life ;
I like truth, order and goodness, wholly because they are
beautiful or lead straight to beautiful consequences.   The
Baileys either hadn't got that or they didn't see it.   They
seemed at times to prefer things harsh and ugly.   That
puzzled me extremely.   The æsthetic quality of many of their
proposals, the " manners " of their work, so to speak, were at
times as dreadful as—well, War Office barrack architecture.
A caricature by its exaggerated statements will sometimes
serve to point a truth by antagonising falsity and falsity.   I
remember talking to a prominent museum official in need of
more public funds for the work he had in hand.   I mentioned
the possibility of enlisting Bailey's influence.

" Oh, we don't want Philistines like that infernal Bottle-Imp
running us," he said hastily, and would hear of no concerted action
for the end he had in view.   " I'd rather not have the extension.

"You see," he went on to explain, "Bailey's wanting in the essentials."

"What essentials?" said I.

"Oh! he'd be like a nasty oily efficient little machine for some merely subordinate necessity among all my delicate stuff. He'd do all we wanted no doubt in the way of money and powers—and he'd do it wrong and mess the place for ever. Hands all black, you know. He's just a means. Just a very aggressive and unmanageable means. This isn't a plumber's job. . . ."

I stuck to my argument.

"I don't *like* him," said the official conclusively, and it seemed to me at the time he was just blind prejudice speaking. . . .

I came nearer the truth of the matter as I came to realise that our philosophies differed profoundly. That isn't a very curable difference—once people have grown up. Theirs was a philosophy devoid of *finesse*. Temperamentally the Baileys were specialised, concentrated, accurate, while I am urged either by some inner force or some entirely assimilated influence in my training, always to round off and shadow my outlines. I hate them hard. I would sacrifice detail to modelling always, and the Baileys, it seemed to me, loved a world as flat and metallic as Sidney Cooper's cows. If they had the universe in hand I know they would take down all the trees and put up stamped tin green shades and sunlight accumulators. Altiora thought trees hopelessly irregular and sea cliffs a great mistake. . . . I got things clearer as time went on. Though it was an Hegelian mess of which I had partaken at Codger's table by way of a philosophical training, my sympathies have always been Pragmatist. I belong almost by nature to that school of Pragmatism that, following the mediæval Nominalists, bases itself upon a denial of the reality of classes, and of the validity of general laws. The Baileys classified everything. They were, in the scholastic sense—which so oddly contradicts the modern use of the word—"Realists." They believed classes were *real* and independent of their individuals. This is the common habit of all so-called educated people who have no metaphysical aptitude and no metaphysical training. It leads them to a progressive misunderstanding of the world. It was a favourite trick of Altiora's to speak of everybody as a "type"; she saw men as samples moving; her dining-room became a chamber of representatives. It gave a tremendously scientific air to many of their generalisations, using "scientific" in its nineteenth-century uncritical Herbert Spencer sense, an air that only began to disappear when you thought them over again in terms of actuality and the people one knew. . . .

At the Bailey's one always seemed to be getting one's hands on the very strings that guided the world. You heard legislation projected to affect this "type" and that; statistics marched by you with sin and shame and injustice and misery reduced to quite manageable percentages, you found men who were to frame or amend bills in grave and intimate exchange with Bailey's omniscience, you heard Altiora canvassing approaching resignations and possible appointments that might make or mar a revolution in administrative methods, and doing it with a vigorous directness that manifestly swayed the decision ; and you felt you were in a sort of signal-box with levers all about you, and the world outside there, albeit a little dark and mysterious beyond the window, running on its lines in ready obedience to these unhesitating lights, true and steady to trim termini.

And then with all this administrative fizzle, this pseudo-scientific administrative chatter, dying away in your head, out you went into the limitless grimy chaos of London streets and squares, roads and avenues lined with teeming houses, each larger than the Chambers Street house and at least equally alive, you saw the chaotic clamour of hoardings, the jumble of traffic, the coming and going of mysterious myriads, you heard the rumble of traffic like the noise of a torrent ; a vague incessant murmur of cries and voices, wanton crimes and accidents bawled at you from the placards ; imperative unaccountable fashions swaggered triumphant in dazzling windows of the shops ; and you found yourself swaying back to the opposite conviction that the huge formless spirit of the world it was that held the strings and danced the puppets on the Bailey stage. . . .

Under the lamps you were jostled by people like my Staffordshire uncle out for a spree, you saw shy youths conversing with prostitutes, you passed young lovers pairing with an entire disregard of the social suitability of the " types " they might blend or create, you saw men leaning drunken against lamp-posts whom you knew for the " type " that will charge with fixed bayonets into the face of death, and you found yourself unable to imagine little Bailey achieving either drunkenness or the careless defiance of annihilation. You realised that quite a lot of types were under-represented in Chambers Street, that feral and obscure and altogether monstrous forces must be at work, as yet altogether unassimilated by those neat administrative reorganisations.

§ 5

Altiora, I remember, preluded Margaret's reappearance by announcing her as a " new type."

I was accustomed to go early to the Baileys' dinners in those days, for a preliminary gossip with Altiora in front of her drawing-room fire. One got her alone, and that early arrival was a little sign of appreciation she valued. She had every woman's need of followers and servants.

" I'm going to send you down to-night," she said, " with a

very interesting type indeed—one of the new generation of
serious gals. Middle-class origin—and quite well off. Rich,
in fact. Her stepfather was a solicitor and something of an
entrepreneur towards the end, I fancy—in the Black Country.
There was a little brother died, and she's lost her mother quite
recently. Quite on her own, so to speak. She's never been
out into society very much, and doesn't seem really very
anxious to go. . . . Not exactly an intellectual person, you
know, but quiet, and great force of character. Came up to
London on her own and came to us—some one had told her
we were the sort of people to advise her—to ask what to do.
I'm sure she'll interest you. . . ."

"What *can* people of that sort do ? " I asked. "Is she
capable of investigation ? "

Altiora compressed her lips and shook her head. She
always did shake her head when you asked that of any one.

"Of course what she ought to do," said Altiora, with her
silk dress pulled back from her knee before the fire, and with
a lift of her voice towards a chuckle at her daring way of
putting things, " is to marry a member of Parliament and see
he does his work. . . . Perhaps she will. It's a very exceptional gal who can do anything by herself—quite exceptional.
The more serious they are—without being exceptional—the
more we want them to marry."

Her exposition was truncated by the entry of the type in
question.

"Well ! " cried Altiora turning, and with a high note of
welcome, " *Here* you are ! "

Margaret had gained in dignity and prettiness by the lapse
of five years, and she was now very beautifully and richly and
simply dressed. Her fair hair had been done in some way
that made it seem softer and more abundant than it was in
my memory, and a gleam of purple velvet-set diamonds
showed amidst its mist of little golden and brown lines. Her
dress was of white and violet, the last trace of mourning for
her mother, and confessed the gracious droop of her tall and
slender body. She did not suggest Staffordshire at all, and
I was puzzled for a moment to think where I had met her.
Her sweetly shaped mouth with the slight obliquity of the lip
and the little kink in her brow were extraordinarily familiar
to me. But she had either been prepared by Altiora or she
remembered my name. "We met," she said, " while my step-
father was alive—at Misterton. You came to see us " ; and
instantly I recalled the sunshine between the apple blossom
and a slender pale-blue girlish shape among the daffodils, like
something that had sprung from a bulb itself. I recalled at
once that I had found her very interesting, though I did not
clearly remember how it was she had interested me.

Other guests arrived—it was one of Altiora's boldly blended
mixtures of people with ideas and people with influence or

money who might perhaps be expected to resonate to them. Bailey came down late with an air of hurry, and was introduced to Margaret and said absolutely nothing to her—there being no information either to receive or impart and nothing to do—but stood scratching his left cheek until I rescued him and her, and left him free to congratulate the new Lady Snape on her husband's K.C.B.

I took Margaret down. We achieved no feats of mutual expression, except that it was abundantly clear we were both very pleased and interested to meet again, and that we had both kept memories of each other. We made that Misterton tea-party and the subsequent marriages of my cousins and the world of Burslem generally, matter for quite an agreeable conversation until at last Altiora, following her invariable custom, called me by name imperatively out of our duologue. " Mr. Remington," she said, " we want your opinion——" in her entirely characteristic effort to get all the threads of conversation into her own hands for the climax that always wound up her dinners. How the other women used to hate those concluding raids of hers ! I forget most of the other people at that dinner, nor can I recall what the crowning rally was about. It didn't in any way join on to my impression of Margaret.

In the drawing-room of the matting floor I rejoined her, with Altiora's manifest connivance, and in the interval I had been thinking of our former meeting.

" Do you find London," I asked, " gives you more opportunity for doing things and learning things than Burslem ? "

She showed at once she appreciated my allusion to her former confidences. " I was very discontented then," she said and paused. " I've really only been in London for a few months. It's so different. In Burslem, life seems all business and getting—without any reason. One went on and it didn't seem to mean anything. At least anything that mattered. . . . London seems to be so full of meanings—all mixed up together."

She knitted her brows over her words and smiled appealingly at the end as if for consideration for her inadequate expression, appealingly and almost humorously.

I looked understandingly at her. " We have all," I agreed, " to come to London."

" One sees so much distress," she added, as if she felt she had completely omitted something, and needed a codicil.

" What are you doing in London ? "

" I'm thinking of studying. Some social question. I thought perhaps I might go and study social conditions as Mrs. Bailey did, go perhaps as a work-girl or see the reality of living-in, but Mrs. Bailey thought perhaps it wasn't quite my work."

" Are you studying ? "

" I'm going to a good many lectures, and perhaps I shall take up a regular course at the Westminster School of Politics and

Sociology. But Mrs. Bailey doesn't seem to believe very much in that either."

Her faintly whimsical smile returned. " I seem rather indefinite," she apologised, " but one does not want to get entangled in things one can't do. One—one has so many advantages, one's life seems to be such a trust and such a responsibility——"

She stopped.

" A man gets driven into work," I said.

" It must be splendid to be Mrs. Bailey," she replied with a glance of envious admiration across the room.

" *She* has no doubts, anyhow," I remarked.

" She *had*," said Margaret with the pride of one who has received great confidences.

§ 6

" You've met before ? " said Altiora, a day or so later.

I explained when.

" You find her interesting ? "

I saw in a flash that Altiora meant to marry me to Margaret. Her intention became much clearer as the year developed. Altiora was systematic even in matters that evade system. I was to marry Margaret, and freed from the need of making an income I was to come into politics—as an exponent of Baileyism. She put it down with the other excellent and advantageous things that should occupy her summer holiday. It was her pride and glory to put things down and plan them out in detail beforehand, and I'm not quite sure that she did not even mark off the day upon which the engagement was to be declared. If she did, I disappointed her. We didn't come to an engagement, in spite of the broadest hints and the glaring obviousness of everything, that summer.

Every summer the Baileys went out of London to some house they hired or borrowed, leaving their secretaries toiling behind, and they went on working hard in the mornings and evenings and taking exercise in the open air in the afternoon. They cycled assiduously and went for long walks at a trot, and raided and studied (and incidentally explained themselves to) any social " types " that lived in the neighbourhood. One invaded type, resentful under research, described them with a dreadful aptness as Donna Quixote and Sancho Panza—and himself as a harmless windmill, hurting no one and signifying nothing. She did rather tilt at things. This particular summer they were at a pleasant farmhouse in level country near Pangbourne, belonging to the Hon. Wilfrid Winchester, and they asked me to come down to rooms in the neighbourhood—Altiora took them for a month for me in August—and board with them upon extremely reasonable terms ; and when I got there I found Margaret in a hammock, sitting at Altiora's feet. Lots of people, I gathered, were coming and going in the neighbourhood, the Ponts were in a villa on the river, and the Rickhams' house-boat was to moor for some days ; but these irruptions did not impede a great deal of duologue between Margaret and myself.

Altiora was efficient rather than artistic in her match-making. She sent us off for long walks together—Margaret was a fairly good walker—she exhumed some defective croquet things and incited us to croquet, not understanding that de-testable game is the worst stimulant for lovers in the world. And Margaret and I were always getting left about, and finding ourselves for odd half-hours in the kitchen garden with nothing to do except talk, or we were told with a wave of the hand to run away and amuse each other.

Altiora even tried a picnic in canoes, knowing from fiction rather than imagination or experience the conclusive nature of such excursions. But there she fumbled at the last moment, and elected at the river's brink to share a canoe with me. Bailey showed so much zeal and so little skill—his hat fell off and he became miraculously nothing but paddle-clutching hands and a vast wrinkled brow—that at last he had to be paddled ignominiously by Margaret, while Altiora, after a phase of rigid discretion, as nearly as possible drowned herself—and me no doubt into the bargain—with a sudden lateral gesture of the arm to emphasise the high note with which she dismissed the efficiency of the Charity Organisation Society. We shipped about an inch of water and sat in it for the rest of the time, an inconvenience she disregarded heroically. We had difficulties in landing Oscar from his frail craft upon the ait of our feasting—he didn't balance sideways and was much alarmed, and afterwards, as Margaret had a pain in her back, I took him in my canoe, let him hide his shame with an in-effectual but not positively harmful paddle, and towed the other by means of the joined painters. Still it was the fault of the inadequate information supplied in the books and not of Altiora that that was not the date of my betrothal.

I find it not a little difficult to state what kept me back from proposing marriage to Margaret that summer, and what urged me forward at last to marry her. It is so much easier to re-member one's resolutions than to remember the moods and suggestions that produced them.

Marrying and getting married was, I think, a pretty simple affair to Altiora ; it was something that happened to the adolescent and unmarried when you threw them together under the circumstances of health, warmth and leisure. It happened with the kindly and approving smiles of the more experienced elders who had organised these proximities. The young people married, settled down, children ensued, and father and mother turned their minds, now decently and properly dis-illusioned, to other things. That to Altiora was the normal sexual life, and she believed it to be the quality of the great bulk of the life about her.

One of the great barriers to human understanding is the wide temperamental difference one finds in the values of things relating to sex. It is the issue upon which people most need training in charity and imaginative sympathy. Here are no universal standards at all, and indeed for no single man nor woman does there seem to be any fixed standard, so much do the accidents of circumstances and one's physical phases affect one's interpretations. There is nothing in the whole range of sexual fact that may not seem supremely beautiful or humanly jolly or magnificently wicked or disgusting or trivial or utterly insignificant, according to the eye that sees or the mood that colours. Here is something that may fill the skies and every waking hour or be almost completely banished from a life. It may be everything on Monday and less than nothing on Saturday. And we make our laws and rules as though in these matters all men and women were commensurable one with another, with an equal steadfast passion and an equal constant duty. . . .

I don't know what dreams Altiora may have had in her schoolroom days, I always suspected her of suppressed and forgotten phases, but certainly her general effect now was of an entirely passionless worldliness in these matters. Indeed so far as I could get at her, she regarded sexual passion as being hardly more legitimate in a civilised person than—let us say —homicidal mania. She must have forgotten—and Bailey too. I suspect she forgot before she married him. I don't suppose either of them had the slightest intimation of the dimensions sexual love can take in the thoughts of the great majority of people with whom they came in contact. They loved in their way—an intellectual way it was and a fond way —but it had no relation to beauty and physical sensation— except that there seemed a decree of exile against these things. They got their glow in high moments of altruistic ambition— and in moments of vivid worldly success. They sat at opposite ends of their dinner-table with so-and-so " captured," and so-and-so, flushed with a mutual approval. They saw people in love forgetful and distraught about them, and just put it down to forgetfulness and distraction. At any rate Altiora manifestly viewed my situation and Margaret's with an abnormal and entirely misleading simplicity. There was the girl, rich, with an acceptable claim to be beautiful, shiningly virtuous, quite capable of political interests, and there was I, talented, ambitious and full of political and social passion, in need of just the money, devotion and regularisation Margaret could provide. We were both unmarried—white sheets of uninscribed paper. Was there ever a simpler situation ? What more could we possibly want ?

She was even a little offended at the inconclusiveness that did not settle things at Pangbourne. I seemed to her, I suspect, to reflect upon her judgment and good intentions.

§ 7

I didn't see things with Altiora's simplicity.

I admired Margaret very much, I was fully aware of all that she and I might give each other ; indeed so far as Altiora went we were quite in agreement.   But what seemed solid ground to Altiora and the ultimate footing of her emasculated world, was to me just the superficial covering of a gulf—oh ! abysses of vague and dim, and yet stupendously significant things.

I couldn't dismiss the interests and the passion of sex as Altiora did.   Work, I agreed, was important ; career and success ;   but deep unanalysable instincts told me this pre-occupation was a thing quite as important ; dangerous, inter-fering, destructive indeed, but none the less a dominating interest in life.   I have told how flittingly and uninvited it came like a moth from the outer twilight into my life, how it grew in me with my manhood, how it found its way to speech and grew daring, and led me at last to experience.   After that adventure at Locarno sex and the interests and desires of sex never left me for long at peace.   I went on with my work and my career, and all the time it was like—like some one talking ever and again in a room while one tries to write.

There were times when I could have wished the world a world all of men, so greatly did this unassimilated series of motives and curiosities hamper me ; and times when I could have wished the world all of women.   I seemed always to be seeking something in women, in girls, and I was never clear what it was I was seeking.   But never—even at my coarsest—was I moved by physical desire alone.   Was I seeking help and fellowship ?   Was I seeking some intimacy with beauty ?   It was a thing too formless to state, that I seemed always desiring to attain and never attaining.   Waves of gross sensuousness arose out of this preoccupation, carried me to a crisis of grati-fication or disappointment that was clearly not the needed thing ; they passed and left my mind free again for a time to get on with the permanent pursuits of my life.   And then presently this solicitude would have me again, an irrelevance as it seemed, and yet a constantly recurring demand.

I don't want particularly to dwell upon things that are dis-agreeable for others to read, but I cannot leave them out of my story and get the right proportions of the forces I am balancing. I was no abnormal man, and that world of order we desire to make must be built of such stuff as I was and am and can beget. You cannot have a world of Baileys; it would end in one orderly generation.   Humanity is begotten in Desire, lives by Desire.

> " Love which is lust, is the Lamp in the Tomb ;
>   Love which is lust, is the Call from the Gloom."

I echo Henley.

I suppose the life of celibacy which the active, well-fed, well-exercised and imaginatively stirred young man of the educated classes is supposed to lead from the age of nineteen or twenty, when Nature certainly meant him to marry, to thirty or more, when civilisation permits him to do so, is the most impossible thing in the world. We deal here with facts that are kept secret and obscure, but I doubt for my own part if more than one man out of five in our class satisfies that ideal demand. The rest are even as I was, and Hatherleigh and Esmeer and all the men I knew. I draw no lessons and offer no panacea ; I have to tell the quality of life, and this is how it is. This is how it will remain until men and women have the courage to face the facts of life.

I was no systematic libertine, you must understand ; things happened to me and desire drove me. Any young man would have served for that Locarno adventure, and after that what had been a mystic and wonderful thing passed rapidly into a gross, manifestly misdirected and complicating one. I can count a meagre tale of five illicit loves in the days of my youth, to include that first experience, and of them all only two were sustained relationships. Besides these five " affairs," on one or two occasions I dipped so low as the inky dismal sensuality of the streets, and made one of those pairs of correlated figures, the woman in her squalid finery sailing homeward, the man modestly aloof and behind, that every night in the London year flit by the score of thousands across the sight of the observant. . . .

How ugly it is to recall ; ugly and shameful now without qualification ! Yet at the time there was surely something not altogether ugly in it—something that has vanished, some fine thing mortally ailing.

One such occasion I recall as if it were a vision deep down in a pit, as if it had happened in another state of existence to some one else. And yet it is the sort of thing that has happened, once or twice at least, to half the men in London who have been in a position to make it possible. Let me try and give you its peculiar effect. Man or woman, you ought to know of it.

Figure to yourself a dingy room, somewhere in that network of streets that lies about Tottenham Court Road, a dingy bedroom lit by a solitary candle and carpeted with scraps and patches, with curtains of cretonne closing the window, and a tawdry ornament of paper in the grate. I sit on a bed beside a weary-eyed, fair-haired, sturdy young woman, half undressed, who is telling me in broken German something that my knowledge of German is at first inadequate to understand. . .

I thought she was boasting about her family, and then slowly the meaning came to me. She was a Lett from near Libau in Courland, and she was telling me—just as one tells something too strange for comment or emotion—how her father had been shot and her sister outraged and murdered before her eyes.

It was as if one had dipped into something primordial and stupendous beneath the smooth and trivial surfaces of life. There was I, you know, the promising young don from Cambridge, who wrote quite brilliantly about politics and might presently get into Parliament, with my collar and tie in my hand, and a certain sense of shameful adventure fading out of my mind.

"Ach Gott!" she sighed by way of comment, and mused deeply for a moment before she turned her face to me, as to something forgotten and remembered, and assumed the half-hearted meretricious smile.

"Bin ich eine hübsche?" she asked like one who repeats a lesson.

I was moved to crave her pardon and come away.

"Bin ich eine hübsche?" she asked a little anxiously, laying a detaining hand upon me, and evidently not understanding a word of what I was striving to say.

§ 8

I find it extraordinarily difficult to recall the phases by which I passed from my first admiration of Margaret's earnestness and unconscious daintiness to an intimate acquaintance. The earlier encounters stand out clear and hard, but then the impressions become crowded and mingle not only with each other but with all the subsequent developments of relationship, the enormous evolutions of interpretation and comprehension between husband and wife. Dipping into my memories is like dipping into a ragbag, one brings out this memory or that, with no intimation of how they came in time or what led to them and joined them together. And they are all mixed up with subsequent associations, with sympathies and discords, habits of intercourse, surprises and disappointments and discovered misunderstandings. I know only that always my feelings for Margaret were complicated feelings, woven of many and various strands.

It is one of the curious neglected aspects of life how at the same time and in relation to the same reality we can have in our minds streams of thought at quite different levels. We can be at the same time idealising a person and seeing and criticising that person quite coldly and clearly, and we slip unconsciously from level to level and produce all sorts of inconsistent acts. In a sense I had no illusions about Margaret; in a sense my conception of Margaret was entirely poetic illusion. I don't think I was ever blind to certain defects of hers, and quite as certainly they didn't seem to matter in the slightest degree. Her mind had a curious want of vigour, "flatness" is the only word; she never seemed to escape from her phrase; her way of thinking, her way of doing was indecisive; she remained in her attitude, it did not flow out to easy, confirmatory action.

I saw this quite clearly, and when we walked and talked together I seemed always trying for animation in her and never finding it. I would state my ideas. " I know," she would say, " I know."

I talked about myself and she listened wonderfully, but she made no answering revelations. I talked politics, and she remarked with her blue eyes wide and earnest : " Every *word* you say seems so just."

I admired her appearance tremendously but—I can only express it by saying I didn't want to touch her. Her fair hair was always delectably done. It flowed beautifully over her pretty small ears, and she would tie its fair coilings with fillets of black or blue velvet that carried pretty buckles of silver and paste. The light, the faint down on her brow and cheek was delightful. And it was clear to me that I made her happy.

My sense of her deficiencies didn't stand in the way of my falling at last very deeply in love with her. Her very short-comings seemed to offer me something. . . .

She stood in my mind for goodness—and for things from which it seemed to me my hold was slipping.

She seemed to promise a way of escape from the deepening opposition in me between physical passions and the constructive career, the career of wide aims and human service, upon which I had embarked. All the time that I was seeing her as a beautiful, fragile, rather ineffective girl, I was also seeing her just as consciously as a shining slender figure, a radiant reconciliation, coming into my darkling disorders of lust and impulse. I could understand clearly that she was incapable of the most necessary subtleties of political thought, and yet I could contemplate praying to her and putting all the intricate troubles of my life at her feet.

Before the reappearance of Margaret in my world at all an unwonted disgust with the consequences and quality of my passions had arisen in my mind. Among other things that moment with the Lettish girl haunted me persistently. I would see myself again and again sitting amidst those sluttish surroundings, collar and tie in hand, while her heavy German words grouped themselves to a slowly apprehended meaning. I would feel again, with a fresh stab of remorse, that this was not a flash of adventure, this was not seeing life in any permissible sense, but a dip into tragedy, dishonour, hideous degradation, and the pitiless cruelty of a world as yet uncontrolled by any ordered will.

" Good God ! " I put it to myself, " that I should finish the work those Cossacks had begun ! I who want order and justice before everything ! There's no way out of it, no decent excuse ! If I didn't think, I ought to have thought ! " . . .

" How did I get to it ? " . . . I would ransack the phases of my development from the first shy unveiling of a hidden

wonder to the last extremity as a man will go through muddled
account books to find some disorganising error. . . .

I was also involved at that time—I find it hard to place
these things in the exact order of their dates because they
were so disconnected with the regular progress of my work and
life—in an intrigue, a clumsy, sensuous, pretentious, artificially
stimulated intrigue, with a Mrs. Larrimer, a woman living
separated from her husband. I will not go into particulars of
that episode, nor how we quarrelled and chafed one another.
She was at once unfaithful and jealous and full of whims about
our meetings ; she was careless of our secret, and vulgarised
our relationship by intolerable interpretations ; except for
some glowing moments of gratification, except for the recurrent and essentially vicious desire that drew us back to
each other again, we both fretted at a vexatious and unexpectedly binding intimacy. The interim was full of the quality
of work delayed, of time and energy wasted, of insecure precautions against scandal and exposure. Disappointment is
almost inherent in illicit love. I had, and perhaps it was part
of her recurrent irritation also, a feeling as though one had
followed something fine and beautiful into a net—into bird
lime ! These furtive scuffles, this sneaking into shabby
houses of assignation, was what we had made out of the
suggestion of pagan beauty ; this was the reality of our vision
of nymphs and satyrs dancing for the joy of life amidst incessant sunshine. We had laid hands upon the wonder and
glory of bodily love and wasted them. . . .

It was the sense of waste, of finely beautiful possibilities
getting entangled and marred for ever that oppressed me. I
had missed, I had lost. I did not turn from these things after
the fashion of the Baileys, as one turns from something low
and embarrassing. I felt that these great organic forces were
still to be wrought into a harmony with my constructive passion.
I felt too that I was not doing it. I had not understood the
forces in this struggle nor its nature, and as I learned I failed.
I had started wrong, I had gone on wrong, in a world that was
muddled and confused, full of false counsel and erratic shames
and twisted temptations. I learned to see it so by failures
that were perhaps destroying any chance of profit in my
lessons. Moods of clear keen industry alternated with moods
of relapse and indulgence and moods of dubiety and remorse.
I was not going on as the Baileys thought I was going on.
There were times when the blindness of the Baileys irritated
me intensely. Beneath the ostensible success of those years
between twenty-three and twenty-eight, this rottenness,
known to scarcely any one but myself, grew and spread. My
sense of the probability of a collapse intensified. I knew
indeed now, even as Willersley had prophesied five years
before, that I was entangling myself in something that might
smother all my uses in the world. Down there among those

incommunicable difficulties, I was puzzled and blundering.
I was losing my hold upon things ; the chaotic and adventurous element in life was spreading upward and getting the
better of me, overmastering me and all my will to rule and
make. . . . And the strength, the drugging urgency of the
passion ! . . .

Margaret shone at times in my imagination like a radiant
angel in a world of mire and disorder, in a world of cravings
hot and dull red like scars inflamed. . . .

I suppose it was because I had so great a need of such help
as her whiteness proffered, that I could ascribe impossible
perfections to her, a power of intellect, a moral power and
patience to which she, poor fellow mortal, had indeed no claim.
If only a few of us *were* angels and freed from the tangle of
effort, how easy life might be ! I wanted her so badly, so
very badly, to be what I needed. I wanted a woman to save
me. I forced myself to see her as I wished to see her. Her
tepidities became infinite delicacies, her mental vagueness an
atmospheric realism. The harsh precisions of the Baileys
and Altiora's blunt directness threw up her fineness into relief
and made a grace of every weakness.

Mixed up with the memory of times when I talked with
Margaret as one talks politely to those who are hopelessly
inferior in mental quality, explaining with a false lucidity,
welcoming and encouraging the feeblest response, when possible
moulding and directing, are times when I did indeed, as the
old phrase goes, worship the ground she trod on. I was
equally honest and unconscious of inconsistency at each extreme. But in neither phase could I find it easy to make love
to Margaret. For in the first I did not want to, though I
talked abundantly to her of marriage and so forth, and was a
little puzzled at myself for not going on to some personal application, and in the second she seemed inaccessible, I felt I
must make confessions and put things before her that would
be the grossest outrage upon the whole purity I attributed
to her.

§ 9

I went to Margaret at last to ask her to marry me, wrought
up to the mood of one who stakes his life on a cast. Separated
from her, and with the resonance of an evening of angry recriminations with Mrs. Larrimer echoing in my mind, I discovered myself to be quite passionately in love with Margaret.
Last shreds of doubt vanished. It has always been a feature
of our relationship that Margaret absent means more to me
than Margaret present ; her memory distils from its dross
and purifies in me. All my criticisms and qualifications of
her vanished into some dark corner of my mind. She was the
lady of my salvation ; I must win my way to her or perish.

I went to her at last, for all that I knew she loved me, in

passionate self-abasement, white and a-tremble. She was staying with the Rockleys at Woking, for Shena Rockley had been at Bennett Hall with her and they had resumed a close intimacy ; and I went down to her on an impulse, unheralded. I was kept waiting for some minutes, I remember, in a little room upon which a conservatory opened, a conservatory full of pots of large mauve-edged, white cyclamens in flower. And there was a big lacquer cabinet, a Chinese thing I suppose, of black and gold against the red-toned wall. To this day the thought of Margaret is inseparably bound up with the sight of a cyclamen's back-turned petals.

She came in looking pale, and drooping rather more than usual. I suddenly realised that Altiora's hint of a disappointment leading to positive illness was something more than a vindictive comment. She closed the door and came across to me, and took and dropped my hand and stood still. " What is it you want with me ? " she asked.

The speech I had been turning over and over in my mind on the way vanished at the sight of her.

" I want to talk to you," I answered lamely.

For some seconds neither of us said a word.

" I want to tell you things about my life," I began.

She answered with a scarcely audible " yes."

" I almost asked you to marry me at Pangbourne," I plunged. " I didn't. I didn't because—because you had too much to give me."

" Too much ! " she echoed, " to give you ! " She had lifted her eyes to my face and the colour was coming into her cheeks.

" Don't misunderstand me," I said hastily. " I want to tell you things, things you don't know. Don't answer me. I want to tell you."

She stood before the fireplace with her ultimate answer shining through the quiet of her face. " Go on," she said, very softly. It was so pitilessly manifest she was resolved to idealise the situation whatever I might say. I began walking up and down the room between those cyclamens and the cabinet. There were little gold fishermen on the cabinet fishing from little islands that each had a pagoda and a tree, and there were also men in boats or something, I couldn't determine what, and some obscure sub-office in my mind concerned itself with that quite intently. Yet I seem to have been striving with all my being to get words for the truth of things. " You see," I emerged, " you make everything possible to me. You can give me help and sympathy, support, understanding. You know my political ambitions. You know all that I might do in the world. I do so intensely want to do constructive things, big things perhaps, in this wild jumble. . . . Only you don't know a bit what I am. I want to tell you what I am. I'm complex. . . . I'm streaked."

I glanced at her, and she was regarding me with an expression of blissful disregard for any meaning I was seeking to convey.

"You see," I said, "I'm a bad man."

She sounded a note of valiant incredulity.

Everything seemed to be slipping away from me. I pushed on to the ugly facts that remained over from the wreck of my interpretation. "What has held me back," I said, "is the thought that you could not possibly understand certain things in my life. Men are not pure as women are. I have had love affairs. I mean I have had affairs. Passion—desire. You see, I have had a mistress, I have been entangled——"

She seemed about to speak, but I interrupted. "I'm not telling you," I said, "what I meant to tell you. I want you to know clearly that there is another side to my life, a dirty side. Deliberately I say, dirty. It didn't seem so at first——"

I stopped blankly. "Dirty," I thought, was the most idiotic choice of words to have made.

I had never in any tolerable sense of the word been dirty.

"I drifted into this—as men do," I said after a little pause and stopped again.

She was looking at me with her wide blue eyes.

"Did you imagine," she began, "that I thought you—that I expected——"

"But how can you know?"

"I know. I do know."

"But——" I began.

"I know," she persisted, dropping her eyelids. "Of course I know," and nothing could have convinced me more completely that she did not know.

"All men——" she generalised. "A woman does not understand these temptations."

I was astonished beyond measure at her way of taking my confession. . . .

"Of course," she said, hesitating over a transparent difficulty, "it is all over and past."

"It's all over and past," I answered.

There was a little pause.

"I don't want to know," she said. "None of that seems to matter now in the slightest degree."

She looked up and smiled as though we had exchanged some acceptable commonplaces. "Poor dear!" she said, dismissing everything, and put out her arms, and it seemed to me that I could hear the Lettish girl in the background—doomed safety-valve of purity in this intolerable world!—telling something in indistinguishable German—I knew not what nor why. . . .

I took Margaret in my arms and kissed her. Her eyes were wet with tears. She clung to me and was near, I felt, to sobbing.

"I have loved you," she whispered presently, "Oh! ever since we met in Misterton—six years and more ago."

CHAPTER THREE

MARGARET IN VENICE

§ 1

THERE comes into my mind a confused memory of conversations with Margaret; we must have had dozens altogether, and they mix in now for the most part inextricably not only with one another, but with later talks and with things we discussed at Pangbourne. We had the immensest anticipations of the years and opportunities that lay before us. I was now very deeply in love with her indeed. I felt not that I had cleaned up my life but that she had. We called each other " confederate," I remember, and made during our brief engagement a series of visits to the various legislative bodies in London, the County Council, the House of Commons, where we dined with Villiers, and the St. Pancras Vestry, where we heard Shaw speaking. I was full of plans and so was she of the way in which we were to live and work. We were to pay back in public service whatever excess of wealth beyond his merits old Seddon's economic advantage had won for him from the toiling people in the potteries. The end of the Boer War was so recent that that blessed word " efficiency " echoed still in people's minds and thoughts. Lord Rosebery in a memorable oration had put it into the heads of the big outer public, but the Baileys with a certain show of justice claimed to have set it going in the channels that took it to him—if as a matter of fact it was taken to him. But then it was their habit to make claims of that sort. They certainly did their share to keep " efficiency " going. Altiora's highest praise was " thoroughly efficient." We were to be a " thoroughly efficient " political couple of the " new type." She explained us to herself and Oscar, she explained us to ourselves, she explained us to the people who came to her dinners and afternoons until the world was highly charged with explanation and expectation, and the proposal that I should be the Liberal candidate for the Kinghamstead Division seemed the most natural development in the world.

I was full of the ideal of hard restrained living and relentless activity, and throughout a beautiful November at Venice, where chiefly we spent our honeymoon, we turned over and over again and discussed in every aspect our conception of a life tremendously focussed upon the ideal of social service.

Most clearly there stands out a picture of ourselves talking in a gondola on our way to Torcello. Far away behind us the smoke of Murano forms a black stain upon an immense shining prospect of smooth water, water as unruffled and luminous as the sky above, a mirror on which rows of posts and distant

black high-stemmed, swan-necked boats with their minutely **clear** swinging gondoliers, float aerially. Remote and low **before** us rises the little tower of our destination. Our men **swing** together and their oars swirl leisurely through the water, **bump** back in the rowlocks, splash sharply and go swishing **back** again. Margaret lies back on cushions, with her face shaded by a holland parasol, and I sit up beside her.

"You see," I say, and in spite of Margaret's note of perfect acquiescence I feel myself reasoning against an indefinable antagonism, "it is so easy to fall into a slack way with life. There may seem to be something priggish in a meticulous discipline, but otherwise it is so easy to slip into indolent habits—and to be distracted from one's purpose. The country, the world, wants men to serve its constructive needs, to work out and carry out plans. For a man who has to make a living the enemy is immediate necessity ; for people like ourselves it's—it's the constant small opportunity of agreeable things."

"Frittering away," she says, "time and strength."

"That is what I feel. It's so pleasant to pretend one is simply modest, it looks so foolish at times to take one's self too seriously. We've *got* to take ourselves seriously."

She endorses my words with her eyes.

"I feel I can do great things with life."

"I *know* you can."

"But that's only to be done by concentrating one's life upon one main end. We have to plan our days, to make everything subserve our scheme."

"I feel," she answers softly, "we ought to give—every hour."

Her face becomes dreamy. "I *want* to give every hour," she adds.

§ 2

That holiday in Venice is set in my memory like a little artificial lake in uneven confused country, as something very bright and skylike, and discontinuous with all about it. The faded quality of the very sunshine of that season, the mellow discoloured palaces and places, the huge, time-ripened paintings of departed splendours, the whispering, nearly noiseless passage of hearse-black gondolas, for the horrible steam launch had not yet ruined Venice, the stilled magnificences of the depopulated lagoons, the universal autumn, made me feel altogether in recess from the teeming uproars of reality. There was not a dozen people all told, no Americans and scarcely any English, to dine in the big cavern of a dining-room, with its vistas of separate tables, its distempered walls and its swathed chandeliers. We went about seeing beautiful things, accepting beauty on every hand, and taking it for granted that all was well with ourselves and the world. It

was ten days or a fortnight before I became fretful and anxious
for action ; a long tranquillity for such a temperament as mine.

Our pleasures were curiously impersonal, a succession of
shared æsthetic appreciation threads all that time.   Our
honeymoon was no exultant coming together, no mutual shout
of "*you* ! "   We were almost shy with one another, and felt
the relief of even a picture to help us out.   It was entirely in
my conception of things that I should be very watchful not
to shock or distress Margaret or press the sensuous note.   Our
love-making had much of the tepid smoothness of the lagoons.
We talked in delicate innuendo of what should be glorious
freedoms.   Margaret had missed Verona and Venice in her
previous Italian journey—fear of the mosquito had driven her
mother across Italy to the westward route—and now she could
fill up her gaps and see the Titians and Paul Veroneses she
already knew in colourless photographs, the Carpaccios (the
St. George series delighted her beyond measure), the Basaitis
and that great statue of Bartolomeo Colleoni that Ruskin
praised.

But since I am not a man to look at pictures and architectural effects day after day, I did watch Margaret very
closely and store a thousand memories of her.   I can see her
now, her long body drooping a little forward, her sweet face
upraised to some discovered familiar masterpiece and shining
with a delicate enthusiasm.   I can hear again the soft cadences
of her voice murmuring commonplace comments, for she had
no gift of expressing the shapeless satisfaction these things
gave her.

Margaret, I perceived, was a cultivated person, the first
cultivated person with whom I had ever come into close contact.   She was cultivated and moral, and I, I now realise,
was never either of these things.   She was passive, and I am
active.   She did not simply and naturally look for beauty but
she had been incited to look for it at school, and took perhaps a
keener interest in books and lectures and all the organisation
of beautiful things than she did in beauty itself ; she found
much of her delight in being guided to it.   Now a thing ceases
to be beautiful to me when some finger points me out its
merits.   Beauty is the salt of life, but I take my beauty as a
wild beast gets its salt, as a constituent of the meal. . . .

And besides, there was that between us that should have
seemed more beautiful than any picture. . . .

So we went about Venice tracking down pictures and spiral
staircases and so on, and my brains were busy all the time with
such things as a comparison of Venice and its nearest modern
equivalent, New York, with the elaboration of schemes of
action when we returned to London, with the development of a
theory of Margaret.

Our marriage had done this much at least, that it had fused
and destroyed those two independent ways of thinking about

her that had gone on in my mind hitherto. Suddenly she had become very near to me and a very big thing, a sort of comprehensive generalisation behind a thousand questions, like the sky or England. The judgments and understandings that had worked when she was, so to speak, miles away from my life, had now to be altogether revised. Trifling things began to matter enormously, that she had a weak and easily fatigued back, for example, or that when she knitted her brows and stammered a little in talking, it didn't really mean that an exquisite significance struggled for utterance.

We visited pictures in the morning chiefly. In the afternoon, unless we were making a day-long excursion in a gondola, Margaret would rest for an hour while I prowled about in search of English newspapers, and then we would go to tea in the Piazza San Marco, and watch the drift of people feeding the pigeons and going into the little doors beneath the sunlit arches and domes of Saint Mark's. Then perhaps we would stroll on the Piazzetta, or go out into the sunset in a gondola. Margaret became very interested in the shops that abound under the colonnades and decided at last to make an extensive purchase of table-glass. "These things," she said, "are quite beautiful, and far cheaper than anything but the most ordinary looking English ware." I was interested in her idea, and a good deal charmed by the delightful qualities of tinted shape, slender handle and twisted stem. I suggested we should get not simply tumblers and wine-glasses but bedroom water-bottles, fruit- and sweet-dishes, water-jugs, and in the end we made quite a business-like afternoon of it.

I was beginning now to long quite definitely for events. Energy was accumulating in me, and worrying me for an outlet. I found *The Times* and the *Daily Telegraph* and the other papers I managed to get hold of, more and more stimulating. I nearly wrote to the former paper one day in answer to a letter by Lord Grimthorpe—I forget now upon what point. I chafed secretly more and more against this life of tranquil appreciations. I found my attitudes of restrained and delicate affection for Margaret increasingly difficult to sustain. I surprised myself and her by little gusts of irritability, gusts like the catspaws before a gale. I was alarmed at these symptoms.

One night when Margaret had gone up to her room, I put on a light overcoat, went out into the night and prowled for a long time through the narrow streets, smoking and thinking. I returned and went and sat on the edge of her bed to talk to her.

"Look here, Margaret," I said ; "this is all very well, but I'm restless."

"Restless ! " she said with a faint surprise in her voice.

"Yes. I think I want exercise. I've got a sort of feeling—I've never had it before—as though I was getting fat."

" My dear ! " she cried.

" I want to do things ;—ride horses, climb mountains, take the devil out of myself."

She watched me thoughtfully.

" Couldn't we *do* something ? " she said.

" Do what ? "

" I don't know. Couldn't we perhaps go away from here soon—and walk in the mountains—on our way home ? "

I thought. " There seems to be no exercise at all in this place."

" Isn't there some walk ? "

" I wonder," I answered. " We might walk to Chioggia perhaps, along the Lido." And we tried that, but the long stretch of beach fatigued Margaret's back and gave her blisters, and we never got beyond Malamocco. . . .

A day or so after we went out to those pleasant black-robed, bearded Armenians in their monastery at Saint Lazzaro, and returned towards sundown. We fell into silence. " *Piu lento*," said Margaret to the gondolier, and released my accumulated resolution.

" Let us go back to London," I said abruptly.

Margaret looked at me with surprised blue eyes.

" This is beautiful beyond measure, you know," I said, sticking to my point, " but I have work to do."

She was silent for some seconds. " I had forgotten," she said.

" So had I," I sympathised, and took her hand. " Suddenly I have remembered."

She remained quite still. " There is so much to be done," I said, almost apologetically.

She looked long away from me across the lagoon and at last sighed, like one who has drunk deeply, and turned to me.

" I suppose one ought not to be so happy," she said. " Everything has been so beautiful and so simple and splendid. And clean. It has been just With You—the time of my life. It's a pity such things must end. But the world is calling you, dear. . . . I ought not to have forgotten it. I thought you were resting—and thinking. But if you are rested—— Would you like us to start to-morrow ? "

She looked at once so fragile and so devoted that on the spur of the moment I relented, and we stayed in Venice four more days.

CHAPTER FOUR

THE HOUSE IN WESTMINSTER

§ 1

MARGARET had already taken a little house in Radnor Square, Westminster, before our marriage, a house that seemed particularly adaptable to our needs as public-spirited efficients; it had been very pleasantly painted and papered under Margaret's instructions, white paint and clean open purples and green predominating, and now we set to work at once upon the interesting business of arranging and—with our Venetian glass as a beginning—furnishing it. We had been fairly fortunate with our wedding presents, and for the most part it was open to us to choose just exactly what we would have and just precisely where we would put it.

Margaret had a sense of form and colour altogether superior to mine, and so quite apart from the fact that it was her money equipped us, I stood aside from all these matters and obeyed her summons to a consultation only to endorse her judgment very readily. Until everything was settled I went every day to my old rooms in Vincent Square and worked at a series of papers that were originally intended for the *Fortnightly Review*, the papers that afterwards became my fourth book, *New Aspects of Liberalism*.

I still remember as delightful most of the circumstances of getting into 79 Radnor Square. The thin flavour of indecision about Margaret disappeared altogether in a shop ; she had the preciset ideas of what she wanted, and the devices of the salesman did not sway her. It was very pleasant to find her taking things out of my hands with a certain masterfulness, and showing the distinctest determination to make a house in which I should be able to work in that great project of " doing something for the world."

" And I do want to make things pretty about us," she said. " You don't think it wrong to have things pretty ? "

" I want them so."

" Altiora has things hard."

" Altiora," I answered, " takes a pride in standing ugly and uncomfortable things. But I don't see that they help her. Anyhow they won't help me."

So Margaret went to the best shops and got everything very simple and very good. She bought some pictures very well indeed ; there was a Sussex landscape, full of wind and sunshine, by Nicholson, for my study, that hit my taste far better than if I had gone out to get some such expression for myself.

" We will buy a picture just now and then," she said, " sometimes—when we see one."

I would come back through the January mire or fog from Vincent Square to the door of 79, and reach it at last with a quite childish appreciation of the fact that its solid Georgian proportions and its fine brass furnishings belonged to *my* home ; I would use my latch-key and discover Margaret in the warm-lit, spacious hall with a partially opened packing-case, fatigued but happy, or go up to have tea with her out of the right tea-things, "come at last," or be told to notice what was fresh there.   It wasn't simply that I had never had a house before, but I had really never been, except in the most transitory way, in any house that was nearly so delightful as mine promised to be.   Everything was fresh and bright, and softly and harmoniously toned.   Downstairs we had a green dining-room with gleaming silver, dark oak, and English colour-prints ; above was a large drawing-room that could be made still larger by throwing open folding-doors, and it was all carefully done in greys and blues, for the most part with real Sheraton supplemented by Sheraton so skilfully imitated by an expert Margaret had discovered as to be indistinguishable except to a minute scrutiny.   And for me, above this and next to my bedroom, there was a roomy study, with specially thick stair-carpet outside and thick carpets in the bedroom overhead and a big old desk for me to sit at and work between fire and window, and another desk specially made for me by that expert if I chose to stand and write, and open bookshelves and bookcases and every sort of convenient fitting.   There were electric heaters beside the open fire, and everything was put for me to make tea at any time—electric kettle, infuser, biscuits and fresh butter, so that I could get up and work at any hour of the day or night.   I could do no work in this apartment for a long time, I was so interested in the perfection of its arrangements.   And when I brought in my books and papers from Vincent Square, Margaret seized upon all the really shabby volumes and had them re-bound in a fine official-looking leather.

I can remember sitting down at that desk and looking round me and feeling with a queer effect of surprise that after all even a place in the Cabinet, though infinitely remote, was nevertheless in the same large world with these fine and quietly expensive things.

On the same floor Margaret had a " den," a very neat and pretty den with good colour-prints of Botticelli's and Car-paccio's, and there was a third apartment for secretarial purposes should the necessity for them arise, with a severe-looking desk equipped with patent files.   And Margaret would come flitting into the room to me, or appear noiselessly stand-ing, a tall gracefully drooping form, in the wide open doorway.
" Is everything right, dear ? " she would ask.

" Come in," I would say, " I'm sorting out papers."

She would come to the hearthrug.

" I mustn't disturb you," she would remark.

" I'm not busy yet."

" Things are getting into order. Then we must make out a time-table as the Baileys do, and *begin* ! "

Altiora came in to see us once or twice, and a number of serious young wives known to Altiora called and were shown over the house, and discussed its arrangements with Margaret. They were all tremendously keen on efficient arrangements.

" A little pretty," said Altiora, with the faintest disapproval, " still——"

It was clear she thought we should grow out of that.

From the day of our return we found other people's houses open to us and eager for us. We went out of London for week-ends and dined out, and began discussing our projects for reciprocating these hospitalities. As a single man un-attached, I had had a wide and miscellaneous social range, but now I found myself falling into place in a set. For a time I acquiesced in this. I went very little to my clubs, the Climax and the National Liberal, and participated in no bachelor dinners at all. For a time, too, I dropped out of the garrulous literary and journalistic circles I had frequented. I put up for the Reform, not so much for the use of the club as a sign of serious and substantial political standing. I didn't go up to Cambridge, I remember, for nearly a year, so occupied was I with my new adjustments.

The people we found ourselves among at this time were people, to put it roughly, of the Parliamentary candidate class, or people already actually placed in the political world. They ranged between very considerable wealth and such a hard, bare independence as old Willersley and the sister who kept house for him possessed. There were quite a number of young couples like ourselves, a little younger and more artless, or a little older and more established. Among the younger men I had a sort of distinction because of my Cambridge reputation and my writing, and because, unlike them, I was an adventurer and had won and married my way into their circles instead of being naturally there. They couldn't quite reckon upon what I should do ; they felt I had reserves of experience and incal-culable traditions. Close to us were the Cramptons ; Willie Crampton, who has since been Postmaster-General, rich and very important in Rockshire, and his younger brother Edward, who has specialised in history and become one of those un-imaginative men of letters who are the glory of latter-day England. Then there was Lewis, further towards Kensington, where his cousins the Solomons and the Hartsteins lived, a brilliant representative of his race, able, industrious and in-variably uninspired, with a wife a little in revolt against the racial tradition of feminine servitude and inclined to the suffragette point of view, and Bunting Harblow, an old Blue, and with an erratic disposition well under the control of the able little cousin he had married. I had known all these men, but now (with Altiora floating angelically in benediction) they opened their hearts to me and took me into their order. They were all like myself, prospective Liberal candidates, with a feeling that the period of wandering in the wilderness of opposition was drawing near its close. They were all tremendously keen upon social and political service, and all greatly under the sway of the ideal of a simple, strenuous life, a life finding its satisfactions in political achievements and distinctions. The young wives were as keen about it as the young husbands, Margaret most of all, and I—whatever elements in me didn't march with the attitudes and habits of this set were very much in the background during that time.

We would give little dinners and have evening gatherings at which everything was very simple and very good, with a slight but perceptible austerity ; and there was more good fruit and flowers and less perhaps in the way of savouries, patties and entrées than was customary. Sherry we banished, and Marsala and liqueurs, and there was always good home-made lemonade available. No men waited, but very expert parlourmaids. Our meat was usually Welsh mutton—I don't know why, unless that mountains have ever been the last refuge of the severer virtues. And we talked politics and books and ideas and Bernard Shaw (who was a department by himself and supposed in those days to be ethically sound at bottom), and mingled with the intellectuals—I myself was, as it were, a promoted intellectual.

The Cramptons had a tendency on their less frequented receptions, to read good things aloud, but I have never been able to participate submissively in this hyper-digestion of written matter, and generally managed to provoke a disruptive debate. We were all very earnest to make the most of ourselves and to be and do, and still at times, with an unassuaged perplexity, I wonder how it is that in that phase of utmost earnestness I have always seemed to myself to be most remote from reality.

§ 2

I look back now across the detaching intervention of sixteen crowded years, critically and I fancy almost impartially, to those beginnings of my married life. I try to recall something near to their proper order the developing phases of relationship. I am struck most of all by the immense unpremeditated, generous-spirited insincerities upon which Margaret and I were building.

It seems to me that here I have to tell perhaps the commonest experience of all among married educated people, the deliberate, shy, complex effort to fill the yawning gaps in temperament as they appear, the sustained, failing attempt to bridge abysses, level barriers, evade violent pressures. I have come these latter years of my life to believe that it is possible for a man and woman to be absolutely real with one another, to stand naked-souled to each other, unashamed and unafraid, because of the natural all-glorifying love between them.   It is possible to love and be loved untroubling, as a bird flies through the air.   But it is a rare and intricate chance that brings two people within sight of that essential union, and for the majority marriage must adjust itself on other terms. Most coupled people never really look at one another.   They look a little away to preconceived ideas.   And each from the first days of love-making *hides* from the other, is afraid of disappointing, afraid of offending, afraid of discoveries in either sense.   They build not solidly upon the rock of truth, but upon arches and pillars and queer provisional supports that are needed to make a common foundation, and below in the imprisoned darknesses, below the fine fabric they sustain together, begins for each of them a cavernous hidden life. Down there things may be prowling that scarce ever peep out to consciousness except in the grey half-light of sleepless nights, passions that flash out for an instant in an angry glance and are seen no more, starved victims and beautiful dreams bricked up to die.   For the most of us there is no jail delivery of those inner depths, and the life above goes on to its honourable end.

I have told you how I loved Margaret and how I came to marry her.   Perhaps already unintentionally I have indicated the quality of the injustice our marriage did us both.   There was no kindred between us and no understanding.   We were drawn to one another by the unlikeness of our quality, by the things we misunderstood in each other.   I know a score of couples who have married in that fashion.

Modern conditions and modern ideas, and in particular the intenser and subtler perceptions of modern life, press more and more heavily upon a marriage tie whose fashion comes from an earlier and less discriminating time.   When the wife was her husband's subordinate, meeting him simply and uncritically for simple ends, when marriage was a purely domestic relationship, leaving thought and the vivid things of life almost entirely to the unencumbered man, mental and temperamental incompatibilities mattered comparatively little. But now the wife, and particularly the loving childless wife, unpremeditatedly makes a relentless demand for a complete association, and the husband exacts unthought-of delicacies of understanding and co-operation.   These are stupendous demands.   People not only think more fully and elaborately about life than they ever did before, but marriage obliges us to make that ever more accidented progress a three-legged race of carelessly assorted couples. . . .

Our very mental texture was different.   I was toughminded, to use the phrase of William James, primary and

intuitive and illogical ; she was tender-minded, logical, refined
and secondary. She was loyal to pledge and persons, sentimental and faithful ; I am loyal to ideas and instincts,
emotional and scheming. My imagination moves in broad
gestures ; hers was delicate with a real dread of extravagance.
My quality is sensuous and ruled by warm impulses ; hers was
discriminating and essentially inhibitory. I like the facts of
the case and to mention everything ; I like naked bodies and
the jolly smells of things. She abounded in reservations, in
circumlocutions and evasions, in keenly appreciated secondary
points. Perhaps the readers knows that Tintoretto in the
National Gallery, the " Origin of the Milky Way." It is an
admirable test of temperamental quality. In spite of my early
training I have come to regard that picture as altogether
delightful ; to Margaret it has always been " needlessly
offensive." In that you have our fundamental breach. She
had a habit, by no means rare, of damning what she did not
like or find sympathetic in me on the score that it was not my
" true self," and she did not so much accept the universe as
select from it and do her best to ignore the rest. And also I
had far more initiative than had she. This is no catalogue of
rights and wrongs, or superiorities and inferiorities ; it is a
catalogue of differences between two people linked in a
relationship that constantly becomes more intolerant of
differences.

This is how we stood to each other, and none of it was clear
to either of us at the outset. To begin with, I found myself
reserving myself from her, then slowly apprehending a jarring
between our minds and what seemed to me at first a queer
little habit of misunderstanding in her. . . .

It did not hinder my being very fond of her. . . .

Where our system of reservation became at once most usual
and most astounding was in our personal relations. It is not
too much to say that in that regard we never for a moment
achieved sincerity with one another during the first six years
of our life together. It goes even deeper than that, for in my
effort to realise the ideal of my marriage I ceased even to
attempt to be sincere with myself. I would not admit my
own perceptions and interpretations. I tried to fit myself to
her thinner and finer determinations. There are people who
will say with a note of approval that I was learning to conquer
myself. I record that much without any note of approval. . . .

For some years I never deceived Margaret about any concrete fact nor, except for the silence about my earlier life that
she had almost forced upon me, did I hide any concrete fact
that seemed to affect her, but from the outset I was guilty of
immense spiritual concealments, my very marriage was based,
I see now, on a spiritual subterfuge ; I hid moods from her,
pretended feelings. . . .

§ 3

The interest and excitement of setting-up a house, of walking about it from room to room and from floor to floor, or sitting at one's own dinner-table and watching one's wife control conversation with a pretty, timid resolution, of taking a place among the secure and free people of our world, passed almost insensibly into the interest and excitement of my Parliamentary candidature for the Kinghamstead Division, that shapeless chunk of agricultural midland between the Great Western and the North-Western railways. I was going to " take hold " at last, the Kinghamstead Division was my appointed handle. I was to find my place in the rather indistinctly sketched constructions that were implicit in the minds of all our circle. The precise place I had to fill and the precise functions I had to discharge were not as yet very clear, but all that, we felt sure, would become plain as things developed.

A few brief months of vague activities of " nursing " gave place to the excitements of the contest that followed the return of Campbell-Bannerman to power in 1906. So far as the Kinghamstead Division was concerned it was a depressed and tepid battle. I went about the constituency making three speeches that were soon threadbare, and an odd little collection of people worked for me ; two solicitors, a cheap photographer, a democratic parson, a number of dissenting ministers, the Mayor of Kinghamstead, a Mrs. Bulger, the widow of an old Chartist who had grown rich through electric traction patents, Sir Roderick Newton, a Jew who had bought Calersham Castle, and old Sir Graham Rivers, that sturdy old soldier, were among my chief supporters. We had headquarters in each town and village, mostly there were empty shops we leased temporarily, and there at least a sort of fuss and a coming and going were maintained. The rest of the population stared in a state of suspended judgment as we went about the business. The country was supposed to be in a condition of intellectual conflict and deliberation, in history it will no doubt figure as a momentous decision. Yet except for an occasional flare of bill-sticking or a bill in a window or a placard-plastered motor-car or an argumentative group of people outside a public-house or a sluggish movement towards the schoolroom or village hall, there was scarcely a sign that a great empire was revising its destinies. Now and then one saw a canvasser on a doorstep. For the most part people went about their business with an entirely irresponsible confidence in the stability of the universe. At times one felt a little absurd with one's flutter of colours and one's air of saving the country.

My opponent was a quite undistinguished Major-General who relied upon his advocacy of Protection, and was particularly anxious we should avoid " personalities " and fight the constituency in a gentlemanly spirit. He was always writing me notes, apologising for excesses on the part of his supporters, or pointing out the undesirability of some course taken by mine.

My speeches had been planned upon broad lines, but they lost touch with these as the polling approached. To begin with I made a real attempt to put what was in my mind before the people I was to supply with a political voice. I spoke of the greatness of our Empire and its destinies, of the splendid projects and possibilities of life and order that lay before the world, of all that a resolute and constructive effort might do at the present time. "We are building a state," I said, "secure and splendid, we are in the dawn of the great age of mankind." Sometimes that would get a solitary "'Ear, 'ear!'" Then having created, as I imagined, a fine atmosphere, I turned upon the history of the last Conservative administration and brought it into contrast with the wide occasions of the age ; discussed its failure to control the grasping financiers in South Africa, its failure to release public education from sectarian squabbles, its misconduct of the Boer War, its waste of the world's resources. . . .

It soon became manifest that my opening and my general spaciousness of method bored my audiences a good deal. The richer and wider my phrases the thinner sounded my voice in these non-resonating gatherings. Even the platform supporters grew restive unconsciously, and stirred and coughed. They did not recognise themselves as mankind. Building an empire, preparing a fresh stage in the history of humanity, had no appeal for them. They were mostly everyday, toiling people, full of small personal solicitudes and they came to my meetings, I think, very largely as a relaxation. This stuff was not relaxing. They did not think politics was a great constructive process, they thought it was a kind of dog-fight. They wanted fun, they wanted spice, they wanted hits, they wanted also a chance to say "'Ear, 'ear!'" in an intelligent and honourable manner and clap their hands and drum with their feet. The great constructive process in history gives so little scope for clapping and drumming and saying "'Ear, 'ear!'" One might as well think of hounding on the solar system.

So after one or two attempts to lift my audiences to the level of the issues involved, I began to adapt myself to them. I cut down my review of our imperial outlook and destinies more and more, and developed a series of hits and anecdotes and—what shall I call them ?—"crudifications" of the issue. My helpers congratulated me on the rapid improvement of my platform style. I ceased to speak of the late Prime Minister with the respect I bore him, and began to fall in with the popular caricature of him as an artful rabbit-witted person intent only on keeping his leadership, in spite of the vigorous attempts of Mr. Joseph Chamberlain to oust him therefrom.

I ceased to qualify my statement that Protection would make food dearer for the agricultural labourer. I began to speak of Mr. Alfred Lyttelton as an influence at once insane and diabolical, as a man inspired by a passionate desire to substitute manacled but still criminal Chinese for honest British labourers throughout the world. And when it came to the mention of our own kindly leader, of Mr. John Burns or any one else of any prominence at all on our side I fell more and more into the intonation of one who mentions the high gods. And I had my reward in brighter meetings and readier and readier applause.

One goes on from phase to phase in these things.

"After all," I told myself, "if one wants to get to Westminster one must follow the road that leads there," but I found the road nevertheless rather unexpectedly distasteful. "When one gets there," I said, "then it is one begins."

But I would lie awake at nights with that sore throat and headache and fatigue which come from speaking in ill-ventilated rooms, and wondering how far it was possible to educate a whole people to great political ideals. Why should political work always rot down to personalities and personal appeals in this way ? Life is, I suppose, to begin with and end with a matter of personalities, from personalities all our broader interests arise and to personalities they return. All our social and political effort, all of it, is like trying to make a crowd of people fall into formation. The broader lines appear, but then come a rush and excitement and irrelevancy, and forthwith the incipient order has vanished and the marshals must begin the work over again !

My memory of all that time is essentially confusion. There was a frightful lot of tiresome locomotion in it ; for the King-hamstead Division is extensive, abounding in ill-graded and badly metalled cross-roads and vicious little hills, and singularly unpleasing to the eye in a muddy winter. It is sufficiently near to London to have undergone the same process of ill-regulated expansion that made Bromstead the place it is. Several of its overgrown villages have developed strings of factories and sidings along the railway lines, and there is an abundance of petty villas. There seemed to be no place at which one could take hold of more than this or that element of the population. Now we met in a meeting-house, now in a Masonic Hall or Drill Hall ; I also did a certain amount of open-air speaking in the dinner-hour outside gas-works and groups of factories. Some special sort of people was, as it were, secreted in response to each special appeal. One said things carefully adjusted to the distinctive limitations of each gathering. Jokes of an incredible silliness and shallowness drifted about us. Our advisers made us declare that if we were elected we would live in the district, and one hasty agent had bills printed, " If Mr. Remington is elected he will live here." The enemy obtained a number of these bills and stuck them on outhouses, pigstyes, dog-kennels ; you cannot imagine how irksome the repetition of that jest became. The vast drifting indifference in between my meetings impressed me more and more. I realised the vagueness of my own plans as I had never done before I brought them to the test of this experience. I was perplexed by the riddle of just how far I was, in any sense of the word, taking hold at all, how far I wasn't myself flowing into an accepted groove.

Margaret was troubled by no such doubts. She was clear I had to go into Parliament on the side of Liberalism and the light, as against the late Government and darkness. Essential to the memory of my first contest, is the memory of her clear bright face, very resolute and grave, helping me consciously, steadfastly, with all her strength. Her quiet confidence, while I was so dissatisfied, worked curiously towards the alienation of my sympathies. I felt she had no business to be so sure of me. I had moments of vivid resentment at being thus marched towards Parliament.

I seemed now always to be discovering alien forces of character in her. Her way of taking life diverged from me more and more. She sounded amazing, independent notes. She bought for the campaign some particularly costly furs that roused enthusiasm whenever she appeared. She also made me a birthday present in November of a heavily fur-trimmed coat ; and this she would make me remove as I went on to the platform, and hold over her arm until I was ready to resume it. It was fearfully heavy for her and she liked it to be heavy for her. That act of servitude was in essence a towering self-assertion. I would glance sideways while some chairman floundered through his introduction and see the clear blue eye with which she regarded the audience, which existed so far as she was concerned merely to return me to Parliament. It was a friendly eye, provided they were not silly or troublesome. But it kindled a little at the hint of a hostile question. After we had come so far and taken so much trouble !

She constituted herself the dragoman of our political travels. In hotels she was serenely resolute for the quietest and the best, she rejected all their proposals for meals and substituted a severely nourishing dietary of her own, and even in private houses she astonished me by her tranquil insistence upon special comforts and sustenance. I can see her face now as it would confront a hostess, a little intent, but sweetly resolute and assured.

Since our marriage she had read a number of political memoirs, and she had been particularly impressed by the career of Mrs. Gladstone. I don't think it occurred to her to compare and contrast my quality with that of Mrs. Gladstone's husband. I suspect her of a deliberate intention of achieving parallel results by parallel methods. I was to be Gladstonised.

Gladstone it appeared used to lubricate his speeches with a mixture—if my memory serves me right—of egg beaten up in sherry, and Margaret was very anxious I should take a leaf from that celebrated book. She wanted, I know, to hold the glass in her hand while I was speaking.

But here I was firm. " No," I said, very decisively, " simply I won't stand that. It's a matter of conscience. I shouldn't feel—democratic. I'll take my chance of the common water in the carafe on the chairman's table."

" I *do* wish you wouldn't," she said, distressed. . . .

It was absurd to feel irritated ; it was so admirable of her, a little childish, infinitely womanly and devoted and fine—and I see now how pathetic. But I could not afford to succumb to her. I wanted to follow my own leading, to see things clearly, and this reassuring pose of a high destiny, of an almost terribly efficient pursuit of a fixed end when as a matter of fact I had a very doubtful end and an aim as yet by no means fixed, was all too seductive for dalliance. . . .

§ 4

And into all these things with the manner of a trifling and casual incident comes the figure of Isabel Rivers. My first impressions of her were of a rather ugly and ungainly, extra-ordinarily interesting schoolgirl with a beautiful quick flush under her warm brown skin, who said and did amusing and surprising things. When first I saw her she was riding a very old bicycle downhill with her feet on the fork of the frame—it seemed to me to the public danger, but afterwards I came better to understand the quality of her nerve—and on the third occasion she was for her own private satisfaction climbing a tree. On the intervening occasion we had what seems now to have been a long sustained conversation about the political situation and the books and papers I had written.

I wonder if it was.

What a delightful mixture of child and grave woman she was at that time, and how little I reckoned on the part she would play in my life ! And since she has played that part, how impossible it is to tell now of those early days ! Since I wrote that opening paragraph to this section my idle pen has been, as it were, playing by itself and sketching faces on the blotting-pad—one impish wizened visage is oddly like little Bailey—and I have been thinking cheek on fist amidst a limitless wealth of memories. She sits below me on the low wall under the olive trees with our child in her arms. She is now the central fact in my life. It still seems a little incredible that that should be so. She has destroyed me as a politician, brought me to this belated re-beginning of life. When I sit down and try to make her a girl again, I feel like the Arabian fisherman who tried to put the genius back into the pot from which it had spread gigantic across the skies. . . .

I have a very clear vision of her rush downhill past our
labouring ascendant car—my colours fluttered from handle-
bar and shoulder-knot—and her waving hand and the sharp
note of her voice. She cried out something, I don't know
what, some greeting.

"What a pretty girl!" said Margaret.

Parvill, the cheap photographer, that industrious organiser
for whom by way of repayment I got those magic letters, that
knighthood of the underlings, "J.P.," was in the car with us
and explained her to us, "One of the best workers you have,"
he said. . . .

And then after a toilsome troubled morning we came,
rather cross from the strain of sustained amiability, to Sir
Graham Rivers' house. It seemed all softness and quiet—I
recall dead-white panelling and oval mirrors horizontally set
and a marble fireplace between white marble-blind Homer and
marble-blind Virgil, very grave and fine—and how Isabel came
into lunch in a shapeless thing like a blue smock that made her
bright quick-changing face seem yellow under her cloud of
black hair. Her step-sister was there, Miss Gamer, to whom
the house was to descend, a well-dressed lady of thirty, amiably
disavowing responsibility for Isabel in every phrase and
gesture. And there was a very pleasant doctor, an Oxford
man, who seemed on excellent terms with every one. It was
manifest that he was in the habit of sparring with the girl, but
on this occasion she wasn't sparring and refused to be teased
into a display in spite of the taunts either of him or of her
father. She was, they discovered with rising eyebrows, shy.
It seemed an opportunity too rare for them to miss. They
proclaimed her enthusiasm for me in a way that brought a
flush to her cheek and a look into her eye between appeal and
defiance. They declared she had read my books, which I
thought at the time was exaggeration, their dry political
quality was so distinctly not what one was accustomed to
regard as schoolgirl reading. Miss Gamer protested to protect
her. "When once in a blue moon Isabel is well-behaved. . . . !"

Except for these attacks I do not remember much of the
conversation at table ; it was, I know, discursive and concerned with the sort of topographical and social and electioneering fact natural to such a visit. Old Rivers struck me as a
delightful person, modestly unconscious of his doubly-earned
V.C. and the plucky defence of Kardin-Bergat that won his
baronetcy. He was that excellent type, the soldier radical,
and we began that day a friendship that was only ended by his
death in the hunting-field three years later. He interested
Margaret into a disregard of my plate and the fact that I had
secured the illegal indulgence of Moselle. After lunch we went
for coffee into another low room, this time brown panelled and
looking through French windows on a red-walled garden,
graceful even in its winter desolation. And there the conversa-

tion suddenly picked up and became good. It had fallen to a pause, and the doctor, with an air of definitely throwing off a mask and wrecking an established tranquillity, remarked : " Very probably you Liberals will come in, though I'm not sure you'll come in so mightily as you think, but what you'll do when you do come in passes my comprehension."

" There's good work sometimes," said Sir Graham, " in undoing."

" You can't govern a great empire by amending and repealing the Acts of your predecessors," said the doctor.

There came that kind of pause that happens when a subject is broached too big and difficult for the gathering. Margaret's blue eyes regarded the speaker with quiet disapproval for a moment, and then came to me in the not too confident hope that I would snub him out of existence with some prompt rhetorical stroke. A voice spoke out of the big arm-chair.

" We'll do things," said Isabel.

The doctor's eye lit with the joy of the fisherman who strikes his fish at last. " What will you do ? " he asked her.

" Every one knows we're a mixed lot," said Isabel.

" Poor old chaps like me ! " interjected the general.

" But that's not a programme," said the doctor.

" But Mr. Remington has published a programme," said Isabel.

The doctor cocked half an eye at me.

" In some review," the girl went on. " After all, we're not going to elect the whole Liberal party in the Kinghamstead Division. I'm a Remington-ite ! "

" But the programme," said the doctor, " the programme——"

" In front of Mr. Remington ! "

" Scandal always comes home at last," said the doctor. " Let him hear the worst."

" I'd like to hear," I said. " Electioneering shatters convictions and enfeebles the mind."

" Not mine," said Isabel stoutly. " I mean—— Well, anyhow I take it Mr. Remington stands for constructing a civilised state out of this muddle."

" *This* muddle," protested the doctor with an appeal of the eye to the beautiful long room and the ordered garden outside the bright clean windows.

" Well, *that* muddle, if you like ! There's a slum within a mile of us already. The dust and blacks get worse and worse, don't they, Sissie ? "

" They do," agreed Miss Gamer.

" Mr. Remington stands for construction, order, education, discipline."

" And you ? " said the doctor.

" I'm a good Remington-ite."

" Discipline ! " said the doctor.

" Oh ! " said Isabel.   " At times one has to be—Napoleonic. They want to libel me, Mr. Remington.   A political worker can't always be in time for meals, can she ?   At times one has to make—splendid cuts."

Miss Gamer said something indistinctly.

" Order, education, discipline," said Sir Graham.   " Excellent things !   But I've a sort of memory—in my young days —we talked about something called liberty."

" Liberty under the law," I said with an unexpected approving murmur from Margaret, and took up the defence. " The old Liberal definition of liberty was a trifle uncritical. Privilege and legal restrictions are not the only enemies of liberty.   An uneducated, underbred and underfed propertyless man is a man who has lost the possibility of liberty.   There's no liberty worth a rap for him.   A man who is swimming hopelessly for life wants nothing but the liberty to get out of the water ;   he'll give every other liberty for it—until he gets out."

Sir Graham took me up and we fell into a discussion of the changing qualities of Liberalism.   It was a good give-and-take talk, extraordinarily refreshing after the nonsense and crowding secondary issues of the electioneering outside.   We all contributed more or less except Miss Gamer ;   Margaret followed with knitted brows and occasional interjections.   " People won't *see* that," for example, and " It all seems so plain to me." The doctor showed himself clever but unsubstantial and inconsistent.   Isabel sat back with her black mop of hair buried deep in the chair looking quickly from face to face.   Her colour came and went with her vivid intellectual excitement ; occasionally she would dart a word, usually a very apt word, like a lizard's tongue into the discussion.   I remember chiefly that a chance illustration betrayed that she had read Bishop Burnet. . . .

After that it was not surprising that Isabel should ask for a lift in our car as far as the Lurky Committee Room, and that she should offer me quite sound advice *en route* upon the intellectual temperament of the Lurky gasworkers. . . .

On the third occasion that I saw Isabel she was, as I have said, climbing a tree—and a very creditable tree—for her own private satisfaction.   It was a lapse from the high seriousness of politics, and I perceived she felt that I might regard it as such and attach too much importance to it.   I had some difficulty in reassuring her.   And it's odd to note now—it has never occurred to me before—that from that day to this I do not think I have ever reminded Isabel of that encounter.

After that memory she seems to be flickering about always in the election, an inextinguishable flame ;   now she flew by on her bicycle, now she dashed into committee rooms, now she appeared on doorsteps in animated conversation with dubious voters ;   I took every chance I could to talk to her—I had never met anything like her before in the world, and she interested me immensely—and before the polling day she and I had become, in the frankest simplicity, fast friends. . . .

That, I think, sets out very fairly the facts of our early relationship. But it is hard to get it true, either in form or texture, because of the bright, translucent, coloured, and refracting memories that come between. One forgets not only the tint and quality of thoughts and impressions through that intervening haze, one forgets them altogether. I don't remember now that I ever thought in those days of passionate love or the possibility of such love between us. I may have done so again and again. But I doubt it very strongly. I don't think I ever thought of such aspects. I had no more sense of any danger between us, seeing the years and things that separated us, than I could have had if she had been an intelligent bright-eyed bird. Isabel came into my life as a new sort of thing ; she didn't join on at all to my previous experiences of womanhood. They were not, as I have laboured to explain, either very wide or very penetrating experiences, on the whole " strangled dinginess " expresses them, but I do not believe they were narrower or shallower than those of many other men of my class. I thought of women as pretty things and beautiful things, pretty rather than beautiful, attractive, and at times disconcertingly attractive, often bright and witty but, because of the vast reservations that hid them from me, wanting, subtly and inevitably wanting, in understanding. My idealisation of Margaret had evaporated insensibly after our marriage. The shrine I had made for her in my private thoughts stood at last undisguisedly empty. But Isabel did not for a moment admit of either idealisation or interested contempt. She opened a new sphere of womanhood to me. With her steady amber-brown eyes, her unaffected interest in impersonal things, her upstanding waistless blue body, her energy, decision and courage, she seemed rather some new and infinitely finer form of boyhood than a feminine creature, as I had come to measure femininity. She was my perfect friend. Could I have foreseen, had my world been more wisely planned, to this day we might have been such friends.

She seemed at that time unconscious of sex, though she has told me since how full she was of protesting curiosities and restrained emotions. She spoke, as indeed she has always spoken, simply, clearly and vividly ; schoolgirl slang mingled with words that marked ample voracious reading, and she moved quickly with the directness of some graceful young animal. She took many of the easy freedoms a man or a sister might have done with me. She would touch my arm, lay a hand on my shoulder as I sat, adjust the lapel of a breast-pocket as she talked to me. She says now she loved me always from the beginning. I doubt if there was a suspicion of that in her mind in those days. I used to find her regarding me with the clearest steadiest gaze in the world, exactly like the gaze of some nice healthy innocent animal in a forest, interested, inquiring, speculative, but singularly untroubled. . . .

§ 5

Polling day came after a last hoarse and dingy crescendo. The excitement was not of the sort that makes one forget one is tired out. The waiting for the end of the count has left a long blank mark on my memory, and then every one was shaking my hand and repeating : " Nine hundred and seventy-six."

My success had been a foregone conclusion since the afternoon, but we all behaved as though we had not been anticipating this result for hours, as though any other figures but nine hundred and seventy-six would have meant something entirely different. " Nine hundred and seventy-six ! " said Margaret. " They didn't expect three hundred."

" Nine hundred and seventy-six," said a little short man with a paper. " It means a big turnover. Two dozen short of a thousand, you know."

A tremendous hullaboo began outside, and a lot of fresh people came into the room.

Isabel, flushed but not out of breath, Heaven knows where she had sprung from at that time of night ! was running her hand down my sleeve almost caressingly, with the innocent bold affection of a girl. " Got you in ! " she said. " It's been no end of a lark."

" And now," said I, " I must go and be constructive."

" Now you must go and be constructive," she said.

" You've got to live here," she added.

" By Jove ! yes," I said. " We'll have to house hunt."

" I shall read all your speeches."

She hesitated.

" I wish I was you," she said, and said it as though it was not exactly the thing she was meaning to say.

" They want you to speak," said Margaret with something unsaid in her face.

" You must come out with me," I answered, putting my arm through hers, and felt some one urging me to the French windows that gave on the balcony.

" If you think——" she said, yielding gladly.

" Oh, *rather* ! " said I.

The Mayor of Kinghamstead, a managing little man with no great belief in my oratorical powers, was sticking his face up to mine.

" It's all over," he said, " and you've won. Say all the nice things you can and say them plainly."

I turned and handed Margaret out through the window and stood looking over the Market-place, which was more than half filled with swaying people. The crowd set up a roar of approval at the sight of us, tempered by a little booing. Down in one corner of the square a fight was going on for a flag, a fight that even the prospect of a speech could not instantly check. " Speech ! " cried voices, " Speech ! " and then a brief " boo-oo-oo " that was drowned in a cascade of shouts and cheers. The conflict round the flag culminated in the smashing of a pane of glass in the chemist's window and instantly sank to peace.

" Gentlemen voters of the Kinghamstead Division," I began.

" Votes for Women ! " yelled a voice, amidst laughter—the first time I remember hearing that memorable war-cry.

" Three cheers for Mrs. Remington ! "

" Mrs. Remington asks me to thank you," I said, amidst further uproar and reiterated cries of " Speech ! "

Then silence came with a startling swiftness.

Isabel was still in my mind, I suppose. " I shall go to Westminster," I began. I sought for some compelling phrase and could not find one. " To do my share," I went on, " in building up a great and splendid civilisation."

I paused, and there was a weak gust of cheering, and then a renewal of booing.

" This election," I said, " has been the end and the beginning of much. New ideas are abroad——"

" Chinese labour," yelled a voice, and across the square swept a wildfire of hooting and bawling.

It is one of the few occasions when I quite lost my hold on a speech. I glanced sideways and saw the Mayor of Kinghamstead speaking behind his hand to Parvill. By a happy chance Parvill caught my eye.

" What do they want ? " I asked.

" Eh ? "

" What do they want ? "

" Say something about general fairness—the other side," prompted Parvill, flattered but a little surprised by my appeal. I pulled myself hastily into a more popular strain with a gross eulogy of my opponent's good taste.

" Chinese labour ! " cried the voice again.

" You've given that notice to quit," I answered.

The Market-place roared delight, but whether that delight expressed hostility to Chinamen or hostility to their practical enslavement no student of the General Election of 1906 has ever been able to determine. Certainly one of the most effective posters on our side displayed a hideous yellow face, just that and nothing more. There was not even a legend to it. How it impressed the electorate we did not know, but that it impressed the electorate profoundly there can be no disputing.

§ 6

Kinghamstead was one of the earliest constituencies fought, and we came back—it must have been Saturday—triumphant but very tired, to our house in Radnor Square. In the train we read the first intimations that the victory of our party was likely to be a sweeping one.

Then came a period when one was going about receiving and giving congratulations and watching the other men arrive, very like a boy who has returned to school with the first batch after the holidays. The London world reeked with the General Election ; it had invaded the nurseries. All the children of one's friends had got big maps of England divided up into squares to represent constituencies, and were busy sticking gummed blue labels over the conquered red of Unionism that had hitherto submerged the country. And there were also orange labels, if I remember rightly, to represent the new Labour party, and green for the Irish. I engaged myself to speak at one or two London meetings, and lunched at the Reform, which was fairly tepid, and dined and spent one or two tumultuous evenings at the National Liberal Club, which was in active eruption. The National Liberal became feverishly congested towards midnight as the results of the counting came dropping in. A big green baize screen had been fixed up at one end of the large smoking-room with the names of the constituencies that were voting that day, and directly the figures came to hand, up they went, amidst cheers that at last lost their energy through sheer repetition, whenever there was record of a Liberal gain. I don't remember what happened when there was a Liberal loss ; I don't think that any were announced while I was there.

How packed and noisy the place was, and what a reek of tobacco and whisky fumes we made ! Everybody was excited and talking, making waves of harsh confused sound that beat upon one's ears, and every now and then hoarse voices would shout for some one to speak. Our little set was much in evidence. Both the Cramptons were in, Lewis, Bunting Harblow. We gave brief addresses attuned to this excitement and the late hour, amidst much enthusiasm.

" Now we can *do* things ! " I said amidst a rapture of applause. Men I did not know from Adam held up glasses and nodded to me in solemn fuddled approval as I came down past them into the crowd again.

Men were betting whether the Unionists would lose more or less than two hundred seats.

" I wonder just what we shall do with it all," I heard one sceptic speculating. . . .

After these orgies I would get home very tired and excited, and find it difficult to get to sleep. I would lie and speculate about what it was we *were* going to do. One hadn't anticipated quite such a tremendous accession to power for one's party. Liberalism was swirling in like a flood. . . .

I found the next few weeks very unsatisfactory and distressing. I don't clearly remember what it was I had expected ; I suppose the fuss and strain of the General Election had built up a feeling that my return would in some way put power into my hands, and instead I found myself a mere undistinguished unit in a vast but rather vague majority. There were moments when I felt very distinctly that a majority could be too big a crowd altogether. I had all my work still before me, I had achieved nothing as yet but opportunity, and a very crowded opportunity it was at that. Every one about me was chatting Parliament and appointments ; one breathed distracting and irritating speculations as to what would be done and who would be asked to do it. I was chiefly impressed by what was unlikely to be done and by the absence of any general plan of legislation to hold us all together. I found the talk about Parliamentary procedure and etiquette particularly trying. We dined with the elder Cramptons one evening, and old Sir Edward was lengthily sage about what the House liked, what it didn't like, what made a good impression and what a bad one. " A man shouldn't speak more than twice in his first session, and not at first on too contentious a topic," said Sir Edward. " No."

" Very much depends on manner. The House hates a lecturer. There's a sort of airy earnestness——"

He waved his cigar to eke out his words.

" Little peculiarities of costume count for a great deal. I could name one man who spent three years living down a pair of spatterdashers. On the other hand—a thing like that— if it catches the eye of the *Punch* man, for example, may be your making."

He went off into a lengthy speculation of why the House had come to like an originally unpopular Irishman named Biggar. . . .

The opening of Parliament gave me some peculiar moods. I began to feel more and more like a branded sheep. We were sworn in in batches, dozens and scores of fresh men, trying not to look too fresh under the inspection of policemen and messengers, all of us carrying new silk hats and wearing magisterial coats. It is one of my vivid memories from this period, the sudden outbreak of silk hats in the smoking-room of the National Liberal Club. At first I thought there must have been a funeral. Familiar faces that one had grown to know under soft felt hats, under bowlers, under liberal-minded wide brims, and above artistic ties and tweed jackets, suddenly met one, staring with the stern gaze of self-consciousness, from under silk hats of incredible glossiness. There was a disposition to wear the hat much too forward, I thought, for a good parliamentary style.

There was much play with the hats all through; a tremendous competition to get in first and put hats on coveted seats. A memory hangs about me of the House in the early afternoon, an inhumane desolation inhabited almost entirely by silk hats. The current use of cards to secure seats came later. There were yards and yards of empty green benches with hats and hats and hats distributed along them, resolute-looking top hats, lax top hats with a kind of shadowy grin under them, sensible top hats brim upward, and one scandalous incontinent that had rolled from the front Opposition bench right to the middle of the floor. A headless hat is surely the most soulless thing in the world, far worse even than a skull. . . .

At last, in a leisurely muddled manner we got to the Address; and I found myself packed in a dense elbowing crowd to the right of the Speaker's chair; while the attenuated Opposition, nearly leaderless after the massacre, tilted its brim to its nose and sprawled at its ease amidst its empty benches.

There was a tremendous hullabaloo about something, and I craned to see over the shoulder of the man in front. "Order, order, order!"

"What's it about?" I asked.

The man in front of me was clearly no better informed, and then I gathered from a slightly contemptuous Scotchman beside me that it was Chris Robinson had walked between the honourable member in possession of the House and the Speaker. I caught a glimpse of him blushingly whispering about his misadventure to a colleague. He was just that same little figure I had once assisted to entertain at Cambridge, but grey-haired now, and still it seemed with the same knitted muffler he had discarded for a reckless half-hour while he talked to us in Hatherleigh's rooms.

It dawned upon me that I wasn't particularly wanted in the House, and that I should get all I needed of the opening speeches next day from *The Times*.

I made my way out and was presently walking rather aimlessly through the outer lobby.

I caught myself regarding the shadow that spread itself out before me, multiplied itself in blue tints of various intensity, shuffled itself like a pack of cards under the many lights, the square shoulders, the silk hat, already worn with a parliamentary tilt backward; I found I was surveying this statesmanlike outline with a weak approval. "A *member*!" I felt the little cluster of people that were scattered about the lobby must be saying.

"Good God!" I said in hot reaction, "what am I doing here?"

It was one of those moments infinitely trivial in themselves, that yet are cardinal in a man's life. It came to me with extreme vividness that it wasn't so much that I had got hold of something as that something had got hold of me. I distinctly recall the rebound of my mind.   Whatever happened in this Parliament, I at least would attempt something.   " By God ! " I said, " I won't be overwhelmed.   I am here to do something, and do something I will ! "

But I felt that for the moment I could not remain in the House.

I went out by myself with my thoughts into the night.   It was a chilling night, and rare spots of rain were falling.   I glanced over my shoulder at the lit windows of the Lords.   I walked, I remember, westward, and presently came to the Grosvenor Embankment and followed it, watching the glittering black rush of the river and the dark, dimly lit barges round which the water swirled.   Across the river was the hunched sky-line of Doulton's potteries, and a kiln flared redly.   Dimly luminous trams were gliding amidst a dotted line of lamps, and two little trains crawled into Waterloo station.   Mysterious black figures came by me and were suddenly changed to the commonplace at the touch of the nearer lamps.   It was a big confused world, I felt, for a man to lay his hands upon.

I remember I crossed Vauxhall Bridge and stood for a time watching the huge black shapes in the darkness under the gas-works.   A shoal of coal barges lay indistinctly on the darkly shining mud and water below, and a colossal crane was perpetually hauling up coal into mysterious blacknesses above, and dropping the empty clutch back to the barges.   Just one or two minute black featureless figures of men toiled amidst these monster shapes.   They did not seem to be controlling them but only moving about among them.   These gas-works have a big chimney that belches a lurid flame into the night, a livid shivering bluish flame, shot with strange crimson streaks. . . .

On the other side of Lambeth Bridge broad stairs go down to the lapping water of the river ; the lower steps are luminous under the lamps and one treads unwarned into thick soft Thames mud.   They seem to be purely architectural steps, they lead nowhere, they have an air of absolute indifference to mortal ends.

Those shapes and large inhuman places—for all of mankind that one sees at night about Lambeth is minute and pitiful beside the industrial monsters that snort and toil there—mix up inextricably with my memories of my first days as a legislater.   Black figures drift by me, heavy vans clatter, a newspaper rough tears by on a bicycle, and presently, on the Albert Embankment, every seat has its one or two outcasts huddled together and slumbering.

" These things come, these things go," a whispering voice urged upon me, " as once those vast unmeaning Saurians whose bones encumber museums came and went rejoicing noisily in fruitless lives." . . .

Fruitless lives !—was that the truth of it all ? . . .

Later I stood within sight of the Houses of Parliament in

front of the colonnades of St. Thomas's Hospital.   I leaned on the parapet close by a lamp-stand of twisted dolphins—and I prayed !

I remember the swirl of the tide upon the water, and how a string of barges presently came swinging and bumping round as high-water turned to ebb.   That sudden change of position and my brief perplexity at it, sticks like a paper pin through the substance of my thoughts.   It was then I was moved to prayer.   I prayed that night that life might not be in vain, that in particular I might not live in vain.   I prayed for strength and faith, that the monstrous blundering forces in life might not overwhelm me, might not beat me back to futility and a meaningless acquiescence in existent things.   I knew myself for the weakling I was, I knew that nevertheless it was set for me to make such order as I could out of these disorders, and my task cowed me, gave me at the thought of it a sense of yielding feebleness.

"Break me, O God," I prayed at last, " disgrace me, torment me, destroy me as you will, but save me from self-complacency and little interests and little successes and the life that passes like the shadow of a dream."

Book Three

The Heart of Politics

CHAPTER ONE

THE RIDDLE FOR THE STATESMAN

§ 1

I HAVE been planning and replanning, writing and re-writing, this next portion of my book for many days. I perceive I must leave it raw edged and ill joined. I have learned something of the impossibility of History. For all I have had to tell is the story of one man's convictions and aims and how they reacted upon his life ; and I find it too subtle and involved and intricate for the doing. I find it taxes all my powers to convey even the main forms and forces in that development. It is like looking through moving media of changing hue and variable refraction at something vitally unstable. Broad theories and generalisations are mingled with personal influences, with prevalent prejudices ; and not only coloured but altered by phases of hopefulness and moods of depression. The web is made up of the most diverse elements, beyond treatment mutitudinous. . . . For a week or so I desisted altogether, and walked over the mountains and returned to sit through the warm soft mornings among the shaded rocks above this little perched-up house of ours, dis-cussing my difficulties with Isabel and I think on the whole complicating them further in the effort to simplify them to manageable and stateable elements.

Let me, nevertheless, attempt a rough preliminary analysis of this confused process. A main strand is quite easily trace-able. This main strand is the story of my obvious life, my life as it must have looked to most of my acquaintances. It presents you with a young couple, bright, hopeful and ener-getic, starting out under Altiora's auspices to make a career. You figure us well dressed and active, running about in motor-cars, visiting in great people's houses, dining amidst brilliant companies, going to the theatre, meeting in the lobby. Margaret wore hundreds of beautiful dresses. We must have had an air of succeeding meritoriously during that time.

We did very continually and faithfully serve our joint career. I thought about it a great deal, and did and re-frained from doing ten thousand things for the sake of it. I kept up a solicitude for it, as it were by inertia, long after things had happened and changes occurred in me that rendered its completion impossible. Under certain very artless pre-tences, we wanted steadfastly to make a handsome position in the world, achieve respect, *succeed*. Enormous unseen changes had been in progress for years in my mind and the realities of my life, before our general circle could have had any inkling of their existence, or suspected the appearances of our life.

Then suddenly our proceedings began to be deflected, our outward unanimity visibly strained and marred by the insurgence of these so long-hidden developments.

That career had its own hidden side, of course ; but when I write of these unseen factors I do not mean that but something altogether broader. I do not mean the everyday pettinesses which gave the cynical observer scope and told of a narrower, baser aspect of the fair but limited ambitions of my ostensible self. This " sub-careerist " element noted little things that affected the career, made me suspicious of the rivalry of so-and-so, propitiatory to so-and-so, whom as a matter of fact I didn't respect or feel in the least sympathetic towards ; guarded with this man, who for all his charm and interest wasn't helpful, and a little touchy at the appearance of neglect from that. No, I mean something greater and not something smaller when I write of a hidden life.

In the ostensible self who glowed under the approbation of Altiora Bailey, and was envied and discussed, praised and depreciated, in the House and in smoking-room gossip, you really have as much of a man as usually figures in a novel or an obituary notice. But I am tremendously impressed now in the retrospect by the realisation of how little that frontage represented me, and just how little such frontages do represent the complexities of the intelligent contemporary. Behind it, yet struggling to disorganise and alter it altogether, was a far more essential reality, a self less personal, less individualised, and broader in its references. Its aims were never simply to get on ; it had an altogether different system of demands and satisfactions. It was critical, curious, more than a little unfeeling—and relentlessly illuminating.

It is just the existence and development of this more generalised self-behind-the-frontage that is making modern life so much more subtle and intricate to render, and so much more hopeful in its relations to the perplexities of the universe. I see this mental and spiritual hinterland vary enormously in the people about me, from a type which seems to keep, as people say, all its goods in the window, to others who, like myself, come to regard the ostensible existence more and more as a mere experimental feeder and agent for that greater personality behind. And this back-self has its history of phases, its crises and happy accidents and irrevocable conclusions, more or less distinct from the adventures and achievements of the ostensible self. It meets persons and phrases, it assimilates the spirit of a book, it is startled into new realisations by some accident that seems altogether irrelevant to the general tenor of one's life. its increasing independence of the ostensible career makes it the organ of corrective criticism ; it accumulates disturbing energy. Then it breaks our overt promises and repudiates our pledges, coming down at last like an overbearing mentor upon the small engagements of the pupil.

In the life of the individual it takes the rôle that the growth of philosophy, science and creative literature play in the development of mankind.

§ 2

It is curious to recall how Britten helped shatter that obvious, lucidly explicable presentation of myself upon which I had embarked with Margaret. He returned to revive a memory of adolescent dreams and a habit of adolescent frankness ; he reached through my shallow frontage as no one else seemed capable of doing, and dragged that back-self into relation with it.

I remember very distinctly a dinner and a subsequent walk with him which presents itself now as altogether typical of the quality of his influence.

I had come upon him one day while lunching with Somers and Sutton at the Playwrights' Club, and on the spur of the moment had asked him to dinner. He was oddly the same curly-headed, red-faced ventriloquist and oddly different, rather seedy as well as untidy, and at first a little inclined to make comparisons with my sleek successfulness. But that disposition presently evaporated, and his talk was good and fresh and provocative. And something that had long been straining at its checks in my mind flapped over, and he and I found ourselves of one accord.

Altiora wasn't at this dinner. When she came matters were apt to become confusedly strenuous. There was always a slight and ineffectual struggle at the end on the part of Margaret to anticipate Altiora's overpowering tendency to a rally and the establishment of some entirely unjustifiable conclusion by a *coup-de-main*. When, however, Altiora was absent, the quieter influence of the Cramptons prevailed ; temperance and information for its own sake prevailed excessively over dinner and the play of thought. . . . Good Lord ! what bores the Cramptons were ! I wonder I endured them as I did. They had all of them the trick of lying in wait conversationally ; they had no sense of the self-exposures, the gallant experiments in statement that are necessary for good conversation. They would watch one talking with an expression exactly like peeping through bushes. Then they would, as it were, dash out dissent succinctly, contradict some secondary fact, and back to cover. They gave one twilight nerves. Their wives were easier but still difficult at a stretch ; they talked a good deal about children and servants, but with an air caught from Altiora of making observations upon sociological types. Lewis gossiped about the House in an entirely finite manner. He never raised a discussion ; nobody ever raised a discussion. He would ask what we thought of Evesham's question that afternoon, and Edward would say it was good, and Mrs. Willie, who had been behind the grille,

would think it was very good, and then Willie, parting the
branches, would say rather conclusively that he didn't think
it was very much good, and I would deny hearing the question
in order to evade a profitless statement of views in that vacuum,
and then we would cast about in our minds for some other topic
of equal interest. . . .

On this occasion Altiora was absent, and to qualify our
Young Liberal bleakness we had Mrs. Millingham, with her
white hair and her fresh mind and complexion, and Esmeer.
Willie Crampton was with us, but not his wife, who was having
her third baby on principle ; his brother Edward was present,
and the Lewises, and of course the Bunting Harblows.   There
was also some other lady.   I remember her as pale blue, but
for the life of me I cannot remember her name.

Quite early there was a slight breeze between Edward
Crampton and Esmeer, who had ventured an opinion about the
partition of Poland.   Edward was at work then upon the
seventh volume of his monumental *Life of Kosciusko*, and
a little impatient with views perhaps not altogether false
but betraying a lamentable ignorance of accessible literature.
At any rate, his correction of Esmeer was magisterial.   After
that there was a distinct and not altogether delightful pause,
and then some one, it may have been the pale-blue lady, asked
Mrs. Lewis whether her aunt Lady Carmixter had returned
from her rest-and-sun-cure in Italy.   That led to a rather
anxiously sustained talk about regimen, and Willie told us
how he had profited by the no-breakfast system.   It had
increased his power of work enormously.   He could get through
ten hours a day now without inconvenience.

" What do you do ? " said Esmeer abruptly.

" Oh ! no end of work.   There's all the estate and looking
after things."

" But publicly ? "

" I asked three questions yesterday.   And for one of
them I had to consult nine books ! "

We were drifting, I could see, towards Doctor Haig's system
of dietary, and whether the exclusion or inclusion of fish and
chicken were most conducive to high efficiency, when Britten,
who had refused lemonade and claret and demanded Burgundy,
broke out, and was discovered to be demanding in his throat
just what we Young Liberals thought we were up to ?

" I want," said Britten, repeating his challenge a little
louder, " to hear just exactly what you think you are doing
in Parliament ? "

Lewis laughed nervously, and thought we were " Seeking
the Good of the Community."

" *How ?* "

" Beneficent Legislation," said Lewis.

" Beneficent in what direction ? " insisted Britten.   " I
want to know where you think you are going."

" Amelioration c fSocial Conditions," said Lewis.

" That's only a phrase ! "

" You wouldn't have me sketch bills at dinner ? "

" I'd like you to indicate directions," said Britten, and waited.

" Upward and On," said Lewis with conscious neatness, and turned to ask Mrs. Bunting Harblow about her little boy's French.

For a time talk frothed over Britten's head, but the natural mischief in Mrs. Millingham had been stirred, and she was presently echoing his demand in lisping, quasi-confidential undertones. " What *are* we Liberals doing ? " Then Esmeer fell in with the revolutionaries.

To begin with, I was a little shocked by this clamour for fundamentals—and a little disconcerted. I had the experience that I suppose comes to every one at times of discovering oneself together with two different sets of people with whom one has maintained two different sets of attitudes. It had always been, I perceived, an instinctive suppression in our circle that we shouldn't be more than vague about our political ideals. It had almost become part of my morality to respect this convention. It was understood we were all working hard, and keeping ourselves fit, tremendously fit, under Altiora's inspiration, Pro Bono Publico. Bunting Harblow had his undersecretaryship, and Lewis was on the verge of the Cabinet, and these things we considered to be in the nature of confirmations. . . . It added to the discomfort of the situation that these plunging inquiries were being made in the presence of our wives.

The rebel section of our party forced the talk.

Edward Crampton was presently declaring—I forget in what relation : " The country is with us."

My long-controlled hatred of the Crampton's stereotyped phrases about the Country and the House got the better of me. I showed my cloven hoof to my friends for the first time.

" We don't respect the Country as we used to do," I said. " We haven't the same belief we used to have in the will of the people. It's no good, Crampton, trying to keep that up. We Liberals know as a matter of fact—nowadays every one knows—that the monster that brought us into power has, among other deficiencies, no head. We've got to give it one —if possible with brains and a will. That lies in the future. For the present if the country is with us, it means merely that we happen to have hold of its tether."

Lewis was shocked. A " mandate " from the Country was sacred to his system of pretences.

Britten wasn't subdued by his first rebuff ; presently he was at us again. There were several attempts to check his outbreak of interrogation ; I remember the Cramptons asked questions about the welfare of various cousins of Lewis who

were unknown to the rest of us, and Margaret tried to engage
Britten in a sympathetic discussion of the Arts and Crafts
exhibition.   But Britten and Esmeer were persistent, Mrs.
Millingham was mischievous, and in the end our rising hopes
of Young Liberalism took to their thickets for good, while we
talked all over them of the prevalent vacuity of political
intentions.   Margaret was perplexed by me.   It is only now I
perceive just how perplexing I must have been.   " Of course,"
she said with that faint stress of apprehension in her eyes,
" one must have aims."   And, " it isn't always easy to put
everything into phrases."   " Don't be long," said Mrs.
Edward Crampton to her husband as the wives trooped out.
And afterwards when we went upstairs I had an indefinable
persuasion that the ladies had been criticising Britten's share
in our talk in an altogether unfavourable spirit.   Mrs. Edward
evidently thought him aggressive and impertinent, and
Margaret with a quiet firmness that brooked no resistance,
took him at once into a corner and showed him Italian
photographs by Coburn.   We dispersed early.

I walked with Britten along the Chelsea back streets towards
Battersea Bridge—he lodged on the south side.

" Mrs. Millingham's a dear," he began.

" She's a dear."

" I liked her demand for a hansom because a four-wheeler
was too safe."

" She was worked up," I said.   " She's a woman of faultless character, but her instincts, as Altiora would say, are
anarchistic—when she gives them a chance."

" So she takes it out in hansom cabs."

" Hansom cabs."

" She's wise," said Britten. . . .

" I hope, Remington," he went on after a pause, " I didn't
rag your other guests too much.   I've a sort of feeling at
moments—Remington, those chaps are so infernally not—not
bloody.   It's part of a man's duty sometimes at least to eat
red beef and get drunk.   How is he to understand government if he doesn't ?   It scares me to think of your lot—by a
sort of misapprehension—being in power.   A kind of neuralgia
in the head, by way of government.   I don't understand
where *you* come in.   Those others—they've no lusts.   Their
ideal is anæmia.   You and I, we had at least a lust to take
hold of life and make something of it.   They—they want to
take hold of life and make nothing of it.   They want to cut
out all the stimulants.   Just as though life was anything else
but a reaction to stimulation ! " . . .

He began to talk of his own life.   He had had ill-fortune
through most of it.   He was poor and unsuccessful, and a girl
he had been very fond of had been attacked and killed by a
horse in a field in a horrible manner.   These things had
wounded and tortured him, but they hadn't broken him.

They had, it seemed to me, made a kind of crippled and ugly demigod of him. He was, I began to perceive, so much better than I had any right to expect. At first I had been rather struck by his unkempt look, and it made my reaction all the stronger. There was about him something, a kind of raw and bleeding faith in the deep things of life, that stirred me profoundly as he showed it. My set of people had irritated him and disappointed him. I discovered at his touch how they irritated him. He reproached me boldly. He made me feel ashamed of my easy acquiescences as I walked in my sleek tall neatness beside his rather old coat, his rather battered hat, his sturdier shorter shape, and listened to his denunciations of our self-satisfied New Liberalism and Progressivism.

" It has the same relation to progress—the reality of progress—that the things they paint on door panels in the suburbs have to art and beauty. There's a sort of filiation. . . . Your Altiora's just the political equivalent of the ladies who sell traced cloth for embroidery ; she's a dealer in Refined Social Reform for the Parlour. The real progress, Remington, is a graver thing and a painfuller thing and a slower thing altogether. Look ! *that* "—and he pointed to where under a hoarding in the light of a gas-lamp a dingy prostitute stood lurking—" was in Babylon and Nineveh. Your little lot make-believe there won't be anything of the sort after this Parliament ! They're going to vanish at a few top notes from Altiora Bailey ! Remington !—it's foolery. It's prigs at play. It's make-believe, make-believe ! Your people there haven't got hold of things, aren't beginning to get hold of things, don't know anything of life at all, shirk life, avoid life, get in bright clean rooms and talk big over your bumpers of lemonade while the Night goes by outside—untouched. Those Crampton fools slink by all this,"—he waved at the woman again—" pretend it doesn't exist, or is going to be banished root and branch by an Act to keep children in the wet outside public-houses. Do you think they really care, Remington ? *I* don't. It's make-believe. What they want to do, what Lewis wants to do, what Mrs. Bunting Harblow wants her husband to do, is to sit and feel very grave and necessary and respected on the Government benches. They think of putting their feet out like statesmen, and tilting shiny hats with becoming brims down over their successful noses. Presentation portrait to a club at fifty. That's their Reality. That's their scope. They don't, it's manifest, *want* to think beyond that. The things there *are*, Remington, they'll never face ! the wonder and the depth of life—lust, and the night-sky—pain."

" But the good intention," I pleaded, " the Good Will ! "

" Sentimentality," said Britten. " No Good Will is anything but dishonesty unless it frets and burns and hurts and destroys a man. That lot of yours have nothing but a good will to think they have good will. Do you think they lie

awake of nights searching their hearts as we do ? Lewis ?
Crampton ? Or those neat, admiring, satisfied wives ? See
how they shrank from the probe ! "

" We all," I said, " shrink from the probe."

" God help us ! " said Britten. . . .

" We are but vermin at the best, Remington," he broke
out, " and the greatest saint only a worm that has lifted its
head for a moment from the dust. We are damned, we are
meant to be damned, coral animalculæ building upward, upward in a sea of damnation. But of all the damned things
that ever were damned, your damned shirking, temperate,
sham-efficient, self-satisfied, respectable, make-believe, Fabian-
spirited Young Liberal is the utterly damnedest." He paused
for a moment, and resumed in an entirely different note :
" Which is why I was so surprised, Remington, to find *you*
in this set ! "

" You're just the old plunger you used to be, Britten," I
said. " You're going too far with all your might for the sake
of the damns. Like a donkey that drags its cart up a bank to
get thistles. There's depths in Liberalism——"

" We were talking about Liberals."

" Liberty ! "

" Liberty ! What do *your* little lot know of liberty ? "

" What does any little lot know of liberty ? "

" It waits outside, too big for our understanding. Like the
night and the stars. And lust, Remington ! lust and bitterness ! Don't I know them ? with all the sweetness and hope
of life bitten and trampled, the dear eyes and the brain that
loved and understood—and my poor mumble of a life going
on ! I'm within sight of being a drunkard, Remington ! I'm
a failure by most standards ! Life has cut me to the bone.
But I'm not afraid of it any more. I've paid something of
the price, I've seen something of the meaning."

He flew off at a tangent. " I'd rather die in delirium
tremens," he cried, " than be a Crampton or a Lewis. . . ."

" Make-believe. Make-believe." The phrase and Britten's
squat gestures haunted me as I walked homeward alone. I
went to my room and stood before my desk and surveyed
papers and files and Margaret's admirable equipment of me.

I perceived in the lurid light of Britten's suggestions that
so it was Mr. George Alexander would have mounted a statesman's private room. . . .

§ 3

I was never at any stage a loyal party man. I doubt if
party will ever again be the force it was during the eighteenth
and nineteenth centuries. Men are becoming increasingly
constructive and selective, less patient under tradition and
the bondage of initial circumstances. As education becomes
more universal and liberating, men will sort themselves more

and more by their intellectual temperaments and less and less by their accidental associations. The past will rule them less ; the future more. It is not simply party but school and college and county and country that lose their glamour. One does not hear nearly as much as our forefathers did of the " old Harrovian," " old Arvonian," " old Etonian " claim to this or that unfair advantage or unearned sympathy. Even the Scotch and the Devonians weaken a little in their clannishness. A widening sense of fair play destroys such things. They follow freemasonry down—freemasonry of which one is chiefly reminded nowadays in England by propitiatory symbols outside shady public-houses. . . .

There is, of course, a type of man who clings very obstinately to party ties. These are the men with strong reproductive imaginations and no imaginative initiative, such men as Cladingbowl, for example, or Dayton. They are the scholars-at-large in life. For them the fact that the party system has been essential in the history of England for two hundred years gives it an overwhelming glamour. They have read histories and memoirs, they see the great grey pile of Westminster not so much for what it is as for what it was, rich with dramatic memories, populous with glorious ghosts, phrasing itself inevitably in anecdotes and quotations. It seems almost scandalous that new things should continue to happen, swamping with strange qualities the savour of these old associations.

That Mr. Ramsay MacDonald should walk through Westminster Hall, thrust himself, it may be, through the very piece of space that once held Charles the Martyr pleading for his life, seems horrible profanation to Dayton, a last posthumous outrage ; and he would, I think, like to have the front benches left empty now for ever, or at most adorned with laureated ivory tablets : " Here Dizzy sat," and " On this Spot William Ewart Gladstone made his First Budget Speech." Failing this, he demands, if only as signs of modesty and respect on the part of the survivors, meticulous imitation. " Mr. G.," he murmurs, " would not have done that," and laments a vanished subtlety even while Mr. Evesham is speaking. He is always gloomily disposed to lapse into wonderings about what things are coming to, wonderings that have no grain of curiosity. His conception of perfect conduct is industrious persistence along the worn-down, well-marked grooves of the great recorded days. So infinitely more important to him is the documented, respected thing than the elusive present.

Cladingbowl and Dayton do not shine in the House, though Cladingbowl is a sound man on a committee, and Dayton keeps the *Old Country Gazette*, the most gentlemanly paper in London. They prevail, however, in their clubs at lunch-time. There, with the pleasant consciousness of a morning's work free from either zeal or shirking, they mingle with permanent officials, prominent lawyers, even a few of the soberer type of business men, and relax their minds in the discussion of the morning paper, of the architecture of the West End, and of the latest public appointments, of golf, of holiday resorts, of the last judicial witticisms and forensic " crushers." The New Year and Birthday Honours lists are always very sagely and exhaustively considered, and anecdotes are popular and keenly judged. They do not talk of the things that are really active in their minds, but in the formal and habitual manner they suppose to be proper to intelligent but still honourable men. Socialism, individual money matters, and religion are forbidden topics, and sex and women only in so far as they appear in the law courts. It is to me the strangest of conventions, this assumption of unreal loyalties and traditional respects, this repudiation and concealment of passionate interests. It is like wearing gloves in summer fields, or bathing in a gown, or falling in love with the heroine of a novel, or writing under a pseudonym, or becoming a masked Tuareg. . . .

It is not, I think, that men of my species are insensitive to the great past that is embodied in Westminster and its traditions ; we are not so much wanting in the historical sense as alive to the greatness of our present opportunities and the still vaster future that is possible to us. London is the most interesting, beautiful and wonderful city in the world to me, delicate in her incidental and multitudinous littleness, and stupendous in her pregnant totality ; I cannot bring myself to use her as a museum or an old book-shop. When I think of Whitehall that little affair on the scaffold outside the Banqueting Hall seems trivial and remote in comparison with the possibilities that offer themselves to my imagination within the great grey Government buildings close at hand.

It gives me a qualm of nostalgia even to name those places now. I think of St. Stephen's tower streaming upwards into the misty London night and the great wet quadrangle of New Palace Yard, from which the hansom cabs of my first experiences were ousted more and more by taxicabs as the second Parliament of King Edward the Seventh aged ; I think of the Admiralty and War Office with their tall Marconi masts sending out invisible threads of direction to the armies in the camps, to great fleets about the world. The crowded, darkly shining river goes flooding through my memory once again, on to those narrow seas that part us from our rival nations ; I see quadrangles and corridors of spacious grey-toned offices in which undistinguished little men and little files of papers link us to islands in the tropics, to frozen wildernesses gashed for gold, to vast temple-studded plains, to forest worlds and mountain worlds, to ports and fortresses and lighthouses and watch-towers and grazing lands and corn lands all about the globe. Once more I traverse Victoria Street, grimy and dark, where the Agents of the Empire jostle one another, pass the big embassies in the West End with their flags and scutcheons, follow the broad avenue that leads to Buckingham Palace, witness the coming and going of troops and officials and guests along it from every land on earth. . . . Interwoven in the texture of it all, mocking, perplexing, stimulating beyond measure, is the gleaming consciousness, the challenging knowledge : " You and your kind might still, if you could but grasp it here, mould all the destiny of Man ! "

§ 4

My first three years in Parliament were years of active discontent. The group of younger Liberals to which I belonged was very ignorant of the traditions and qualities of our older leaders, and quite out of touch with the mass of the party. For a time Parliament was enormously taken up with moribund issues and old quarrels. The early Educational legislation was sectarian and unenterprising, and the Licensing Bill went little further than the attempted rectification of a Conservative mistake. I was altogether for the nationalisation of the public-houses, and of this end the Bill gave no intimations. It was just beer-baiting. I was recalcitrant almost from the beginning, and spoke against the Government so early as the second reading of the first Education Bill, the one the Lords rejected in 1906. I went rather beyond my intention in the heat of speaking—it is a way with inexperienced men. I called the Bill timid, narrow, a mere sop to the jealousies of sects and small-minded people. I contrasted its aim and methods with the manifest needs of the time.

I am not a particularly good speaker ; after the manner of a writer I worry to find my meaning too much ; but this was one of my successes. I spoke after dinner and to a fairly full House, for people were already a little curious about me because of my writings. Several of the Conservative leaders were present and stayed, and Mr. Evesham, I remember, came ostentatiously to hear me, with that engaging friendliness of his, and gave me at the first chance an approving " Hear, Hear ! " I can still recall quite distinctly my two futile attempts to catch the Speaker's eye before I was able to begin, the nervous quiver of my rather too prepared opening, the effect of hearing my own voice and my subconscious wonder as to what I could possibly be talking about, the realisation that I was getting on fairly well, the immense satisfaction afterwards of having on the whole brought it off, and the absurd gratitude I felt for that encouraging cheer.

Addressing the House of Commons is like no other public speaking in the world. Its semi-colloquial methods give it an air of being easy, but its shifting audience, the comings and goings and hesitations of members behind the chair—not mere audience units, but men who matter—the desolating emptiness that spreads itself round the man who fails to interest, the little compact, disciplined crowd in the strangers'

gallery, the light, elusive, flickering movements high up
behind the grille, the wigged, attentive, weary Speaker, the
table and the mace and the chapel-like Gothic background
with its sombre shadows, conspire together, produce a confused, uncertain feeling in me as though I was walking upon
a pavement full of trap-doors and patches of uncovered morass.
A misplaced, well-meant " Hear, Hear ! " is apt to be extraordinarily disconcerting, and under no other circumstances
have I had to speak with quite the same sideways twist that
the arrangement of the House imposes.   One does not recognise one's own voice threading out into the stirring brown.
Unless I was excited or speaking to the mind of some particular person in the House, I was apt to lose my feeling of an
auditor.   I had no sense of whither my sentences were going,
such as one has with a public meeting well under one's eye.
And to lose one's sense of an auditor is for a man of my temperament to lose one's sense of the immediate, and to become
prolix and vague with qualifications.

§ 5

My discontents with the Liberal party and my mental exploration of the quality of party generally is curiously mixed
up with certain impressions of things and people in the National
Liberal Club.   The National Liberal Club is Liberalism made
visible in the flesh—and Doultonware.   It is an extraordinary
big club done in a bold, wholesale, shiny, marbled style, richly
furnished with numerous paintings, steel engravings, busts
and full-length statues of the late Mr. Gladstone ; and its
spacious dining-rooms, its long, hazy, crowded smoking-room
with innumerable little tables and groups of men in arm-
chairs, its magazine room and library upstairs, have just that
undistinguished and unconcentrated diversity which is for me
the Liberal note.   The pensive member sits and hears perplexing dialects and even fragments of foreign speech, and
among the clustering masses of less insistent whites his roving
eye catches profiles and complexions that send his mind afield
to Calcutta or Rangoon or the West Indies or Sierra Leone
or the Cape. . . .
    I was not infrequently that pensive member.   I used to go
to the Club to doubt about Liberalism.
    About two o'clock in the day the great smoking-room is
crowded with countless little groups.   They sit about small
round tables or in circles of chairs, and the haze of tobacco
seems to prolong the great narrow place, with its pillars and
bays, to infinity.   Some of the groups are big, as many as a
dozen men talk in loud tones ; some are duologues, and there
is always a sprinkling of lonely, dissociated men.   At first
one gets an impression of men going from group to group and
as it were linking them, but as one watches closely one finds
that these men just visit three or four groups at the outside,

and know nothing of the others.   One begins to perceive more
and more distinctly that one is dealing with a sort of human
mosaic ;   that each patch in that great place is of a different
quality and colour from the next and never to be mixed with
it.   Most clubs have a common link, a lowest common de-
nominator in the Club Bore, who spares no one, but even the
National Liberal bores are specialised and sectional.   As one
looks round one sees here a clump of men from the North
Country or the Potteries, here an island of South London
politicians, here a couple of young Jews ascendant from White-
chapel, here a circle of journalists and writers, here a group of
Irish politicians, here two East Indians, here a priest or so,
here a clump of old-fashioned Protestants, here a knot of
eminent Rationalists indulging in a blasphemous story *sotto
voce*.   Next them are a group of anglicised Germans and
highly specialised chess-players, and then two of the oddest-
looking persons—bulging with documents and intent upon
extraordinary business transactions over long cigars. . . .

I would listen to a stormy sea of babblement, and try to
extract some constructive intimations.   Every now and then
I got a whiff of politics.   It was clear they were against the
Lords—against plutocrats—against Cossington's newspapers
—against the brewers. . . .   It was tremendously clear what
they were against.   The trouble was to find out what on
earth they were for ! . . .

As I sat and thought, the streaked and mottled pillars and
wall, the various views, aspects, and portraits of Mr. and Mrs.
Gladstone, the partitions of polished mahogany, the yellow-
vested waiters, would dissolve and vanish, and I would have a
vision of this sample of miscellaneous men of limited, diverse
interests and a universal littleness of imagination enlarged,
unlimited, no longer a sample but a community, spreading,
stretching out to infinity—all in little groups and duologues
and circles, all with their special and narrow concerns, all with
their backs to most of the others.

What but a common antagonism would ever keep these
multitudes together ?   I understood why modern electioneering is more than half of it denunciation.   Let us condemn, if
possible, let us obstruct and deprive, but not let us do.   There
is no real appeal to the commonplace mind in " Let us do."
That calls for the creative imagination, and few have been
accustomed to respond to that call.   The other merely needs
jealousy and hate, of which there are great and easily accessible
reservoirs in every human heart. . . .

I remember very vividly that vision of endless, narrow,
jealous individuality.   A seething limitlessness it became at
last, like a waste place covered by crawling locusts that men
sweep up by the sackload and drown by the million in
ditches. . . .

Grotesquely against it came the lean features, the sidelong

shy movements of Edward Crampton, seated in a circle of talkers close at hand. I had a whiff of his strained, unmusical voice, and behold ! he was saying something about the " Will of the People. . . ."

The immense and wonderful disconnectednesses of human life ! I forgot the smoke and jabber of the club altogether ; I became a lonely spirit flung aloft by some queer accident, a stone upon a ledge in some high and rocky wilderness, and below as far as the eye could reach stretched the swarming infinitesimals of humanity, like grass upon the field, like pebbles upon unbounded beaches. Was there ever to be in human life more than that endless struggling individualism ? Was there indeed some giantry, some immense valiant synthesis still to come—or present it might be and still unseen by me, or was this the beginning and withal the last phase of mankind ? . . .

I glimpsed for a while the stupendous impudence of our ambitions, the tremendous enterprise to which the modern statesman is implicitly addressed. I was as it were one of a swarm of would-be reef builders looking back at the teeming slime upon the ocean floor. All the history of mankind, all the history of life, has been and will be the story of something struggling out of the indiscriminated abyss, struggling to exist and prevail over and comprehend individual lives—an effort of insidious attraction, an idea of invincible appeal. That something greater than ourselves, which does not so much exist as seek existence, palpitating between being and not-being, how marvellous it is ! It has worn the form and visage of ten thousand different gods, sought a shape for itself in stone and ivory and music and wonderful words, spoken more and more clearly of a mystery of love, a mystery of unity, dabbling meanwhile in blood and cruelty beyond the common impulses of men. It is something that comes and goes, like a light that shines and is withdrawn, withdrawn so completely that one doubts if it has ever been. . . .

§ 6

I would mark with a curious interest the stray country member of the club up in town for a night or so. My mind would be busy with speculations about him, about his home, his family, his reading, his horizons, his innumerable fellows who didn't belong and never came up. I would fill in the outline of him with memories of my uncle and his Staffordshire neighbours. He was perhaps Alderman This or Councillor That down there, a great man in his ward, J.P. within seven miles of the boundary of the borough, and a God in his home. Here he was nobody, and very shy, and either rather too arrogant or rather too meek towards our very democratic mannered but still liveried waiters. Was he perhaps the backbone of England ? He over-ate himself lest he should appear mean, went through our Special Dinner conscientiously, drank, unless he was teetotal, of unfamiliar wines, and did his best, in spite of the rules, to tip.   Afterwards, in a state of flushed repletion, he would have old brandy, black coffee and a banded cigar, or in the name of temperance omit the brandy and have rather more coffee, in the smoking-room.   I would sit and watch that stiff dignity of self-indulgence, and wonder, wonder. . . .

An infernal clairvoyance would come to me.   I would have visions of him in relation to his wife, checking always, some-times bullying, sometimes being ostentatiously " kind " ;   I would see him glance furtively at his domestic servants upon his staircase, or stiffen his upper lips against the reluctant, pro-testing business employee.   We imaginative people are base enough, heaven knows, but it is only in rare moods of bitter penetration that we pierce down to the baser lusts, the viler shames, the everlasting lying and muddle-headed self-justifica-tion of the dull.

I would turn my eyes down the crowded room and see others of him and others.   What did he think he was up to ?   Did he for a moment realise that his presence under that ceramic glory of a ceiling with me meant, if it had any rational mean-ing at all, that we were jointly doing something with the nation and the empire and mankind ? . . .   How on earth could any one get hold of him, make any noble use of him ?   He didn't read beyond his newspaper.   He never thought, but only followed imaginings in his heart.   He never discussed.   At the first hint of discussion his temper gave way.   He was, I knew, a deep, thinly covered tank of resentments and quite irrational moral rages.   Yet withal I would have to resist an impulse to go over to him and nudge him and say to him, " Look here ! What indeed do you think we are doing with the nation and the empire and mankind ?   You know—*Mankind* ! "

I wonder what reply I should have got.

So far as any average could be struck and so far as any backbone could be located, it seemed to me that this silent, shy, replete, sub-angry, middle-class sentimentalist was in his endless species and varieties and dialects the backbone of our party.   So far as I could be considered as representing any-thing in the House, I pretended to sit for the elements of *him*. . . .

§ 7

For a time I turned towards the Socialists.   They at least had an air of coherent intentions.   At that time Socialism had come into politics again with a tremendous *éclat*, after a period of depression and obscurity.   There was visibly a following of Socialist members to Chris Robinson ;   mysteriously uncom-municative gentlemen in soft felt hats and short coats and square-toed boots who replied to casual advances a little surprisingly in rich North Country dialects. Members became aware of a " seagreen incorruptible," as Colonel Marlow put it to me, speaking on the Address, a slender twisted figure supporting itself on a stick and speaking with a fire that was altogether revolutionary. This was Philip Snowden, the member for Blackburn. They had come in nearly forty strong altogether, and with an air of presently meaning to come in much stronger. They were only one aspect of what seemed at that time a big national movement. Socialist societies, we gathered, were springing up all over the country, and every one was inquiring about Socialism and discussing Socialism. It had taken the Universities with particular force, and any youngster with the slightest intellectual pretension was either actively for or brilliantly against. For a time our Young Liberal group was ostentatiously sympathetic. . . .

When I think of the Socialists there comes a vivid memory of certain evening gatherings at our house. . . .

These gatherings had been organised by Margaret as the outcome of a discussion at the Baileys'. Altiora had been very emphatic and uncharitable upon the futility of the Socialist movement. It seemed that even the leaders fought shy of dinner-parties.

" They never meet each other," said Altiora, " much less people on the other side. How can they begin to understand politics until they do that ? "

" Most of them have totally unpresentable wives," said Altiora, " totally ! " and quoted instances, " and they *will* bring them. Or they won't come ! Some of the poor creatures have scarcely learned their table manners. They just make holes in the talk. . . ."

I thought there was a great deal of truth beneath Altiora's outburst. The presentation of the Socialist case seemed very greatly crippled by the want of a common intimacy in its leaders ; the want of intimacy didn't at first appear to be more than an accident, and our talk led to Margaret's attempt to get acquaintance and easy intercourse afoot among them and between them and the Young Liberals of our group. She gave a series of weekly dinners, planned, I think, a little too accurately upon Altiora's model, and after each we had as catholic a reception as we could contrive.

Our receptions were indeed, I should think, about as catholic as receptions could be. Margaret found herself with a weekly houseful of insoluble problems in intercourse. One did one's best, but one got a nightmare feeling as the evening wore on.

It was one of the few unanimities of these parties that every one should be slightly odd in appearance, funny about the hair or the tie or the shoes or more generally, and that bursts of violent aggression should alternate with an attitude entirely defensive. A number of our guests had an air of waiting for a clue that never came, and stood and sat about silently, mildly amused but not a bit surprised that we did not discover their distinctive Open-Sesames. There was a sprinkling of manifest seers and prophetesses in shapeless garments, far too many, I thought, for really easy social intercourse, and any conversation at any moment was liable to become oracular. One was in a state of tension from first to last ; the most innocent remark seemed capable of exploding resentment, and replies came out at the most unexpected angles. We Young Liberals went about puzzled but polite to the gathering we had evoked. The Young Liberals' tradition is on the whole wonderfully discreet, superfluous steam is let out far away from home in the Balkans or Africa, and the neat, stiff figures of the Cramptons, Bunting Harblow, and Lewis, either in extremely well-cut morning-coats indicative of the House, or in what is sometimes written of as " faultless evening dress," stood about on those evenings, they and their very quietly and simply and expensively dressed wives, like a datum line amidst lakes and mountains.

I didn't at first see the connection between systematic social reorganisation and arbitrary novelties in dietary and costume, just as I didn't realise why the most comprehensive constructive projects should appear to be supported solely by odd and exceptional personalities. On one of these evenings a group of rather jolly-looking pretty young people seated themselves for no particular reason in a large circle on the floor of my study, and engaged, so far as I could judge, in the game of Hunt the Meaning, the intellectual equivalent of Hunt the Slipper. It must have been that same evening I came upon an unbleached young gentleman before the oval mirror on the landing engaged in removing the remains of an anchovy sandwich from his protruded tongue—visible ends of cress having misled him into the belief that he was dealing with doctrinally permissible food. It was not unusual to be given hand-bills and printed matter by our guests, but there I had the advantage over Lewis, who was too tactful to refuse the stuff, too neatly dressed to pocket it, and had no writing-desk available upon which he could relieve himself in a manner flattering to the giver. So that his hands got fuller and fuller. A relentless, compact little woman in what Margaret declared to be an extremely expensive black dress has also printed herself on my memory ; she had set her heart upon my contributing to a weekly periodical in the lentil interest with which she was associated, and I spent much time and care in evading her.

Mingling with the more hygienic types were a number of Anti-Puritan Socialists, bulging with bias against temperance, and breaking out against austere methods of living all over their faces. Their manner was packed with heartiness. They were apt to choke the approaches to the buffet Margaret had set up downstairs, and there engage in discussions of Determinism—it always seemed to be Determinism—which became heartier and noisier, but never acrimonious even in the small hours. It seemed impossible to settle about this Determinism of theirs—ever. And there were worldly Socialists also. I particularly recall a large, active, buoyant, lady-killing individual with an eyeglass borne upon a broad black ribbon, who swam about us one evening. He might have been a slightly frayed actor, in his large frock-coat, his white waistcoat, and the sort of black-and-white check trousers that twinkle. He had a high-pitched voice with aristocratic intonations, and he seemed to be in a perpetual state of interrogation. " What are we all he-a for ? " he would ask only too audibly. " What are we doing he-a ? What's the connection ? "

What *was* the connection ?

We made a special effort with our last assembly in June 1907. We tried to get something like a representative collection of the parliamentary leaders of Socialism, the various exponents of Socialist thought and a number of Young Liberal thinkers into one room. Dorvil came, and Horatio Bulch ; Featherstonehaugh appeared for ten minutes and talked charmingly to Margaret and then vanished again ; there was Wilkins, the novelist, and Toomer and Dr. Tumpany. Chris Robinson stood about for a time in a new comforter, and Magdeberg and Will Pipes and five or six Labour members. And on our side we had our particular little group. Bunting Harblow, Crampton, Lewis, all looking as broad-minded and open to conviction as they possibly could, and even occasionally talking out from their bushes almost boldly. But the gathering as a whole refused either to mingle or dispute, and as an experiment in intercourse the evening was a failure. Unexpected dissociations appeared between Socialists one had supposed friendly. I could not have imagined it was possible for half so many people to turn their backs on everybody else in such small rooms as ours. But the unsaid things those backs expressed broke out, I remarked, with refreshed virulence in the various organs of the various sections of the party next week.

I talked, I remember, with Dr. Tumpany, a large young man in a still larger professional frock-coat, and with a great shock of very fair hair, who was candidate for some North Country constituency. We discussed the political outlook, and, like so many Socialists at that time, he was full of vague threatenings against the Liberal party. I was struck by a thing in him that I had already observed less vividly in many others of these Socialist leaders, and which gave me at last a clue to the whole business. He behaved exactly like a man in possession of valuable patent rights, who wants to be dealt with. He had an air of having a corner in ideas. Then it flashed into my head that the whole Socialist movement was an attempted corner in ideas. . . .

§ 8

Late that night I found myself alone with Margaret amid the débris of the gathering.

I sat before the fire, hands in pockets, and Margaret, looking white and weary, came and leaned upon the mantel.

" Oh, Lord ! " said Margaret.

I agreed. Then I resumed my meditation.

" Ideas," I said, " count for more than I thought in the world."

Margaret regarded me with that neutral expression behind which she was accustomed to wait for clues.

" When you think of the height and depth and importance and wisdom of the Socialist ideas, and see the men who are running them," I explained. . . . " A big system of ideas like Socialism grows up out of the obvious common sense of our present conditions. It's as impersonal as science. All these men—— They've given nothing to it. They're just people who have pegged out claims upon a big intellectual No-Man's-Land—and don't feel quite sure of the law. There's a sort of quarrelsome uneasiness. . . . If we professed Socialism do you think they'd welcome us ? Not a man of them ! They'd feel it was burglary. . . ."

" Yes," said Margaret, looking into the fire. " That is just what *I* felt about them all the evening. . . . Particularly Dr. Tumpany."

" We mustn't confuse Socialism with the Socialists," I said ; " that's the moral of it. I suppose if God were to find He had made a mistake in dates or something, and went back and annihilated everybody from Owen onwards who was in any way known as a Socialist leader or teacher, Socialism would be exactly where it is and what it is to-day—a growing realisation of constructive needs in every man's mind, and a little corner in party politics. So, I suppose, it will always be. . . . But they *were* a damned lot, Margaret ! "

I looked up at the little noise she made. " *Twice* ! " she said, smiling indulgently, " to-day ! " (Even the smile was Altiora's.)

I returned to my thoughts. They *were* a damned human lot. It was an excellent word in that connection. . . .

But the ideas marched on, the ideas marched on, just as though men's brains were no more than stepping-stones, just as though some great brain in which we are all little cells and corpuscles was thinking them ! . . .

" I don't think there is a man among them who makes me feel he is trustworthy," said Margaret ; " unless it is Featherstonehaugh."

I sat taking in this proposition.

" They'll never help us, I feel," said Margaret.

" Us ? "

" The Liberals."

" Oh, damn the Liberals ! " I said. " They'll never even help themselves."

" I don't think I could possibly get on with any of those people," said Margaret, after a pause.

She remained for a time looking down at me and, I could feel, perplexed by me, but I wanted to go on with my thinking, and so I did not look up, and presently she stooped to my forehead and kissed me and went rustling softly to her room.

I remained in my study for a long time with my thoughts crystallising out. . . .

It was then, I think, that I first apprehended clearly how that opposition to which I have already alluded of the immediate life and the mental hinterland of a man, can be applied to public and social affairs. The ideas go on—and no person or party succeeds in embodying them. The reality of human progress never comes to the surface, it is a power in the deeps, an undertow. It goes on in silence while men think, in studies where they write self-forgetfully, in laboratories under the urgency of an impersonal curiosity, in the rare illumination of honest talk, in moments of emotional insight, in thoughtful reading, but not in everyday affairs. Everyday affairs and whatever is made an everyday affair, are transactions of the ostensible self, the being of habits, interests, usage. Temper, vanity, hasty reaction to imitation, personal feeling, are their substance. No man can abolish his immediate self and specialise in the depths ; if he attempt that, he simply turns himself into something a little less than the common man. He may have an immense hinterland, but that does not absolve him from a frontage. That is the essential error of the specialist philosopher, the specialist teacher, the specialist publicist. They repudiate frontage ; claim to be pure hinterland. That is what bothered me about Codger, about those various schoolmasters who had prepared me for life, about the Baileys and their dream of an official ruling class. A human being who is a philosopher in the first place, a teacher in the first place, or a statesman in the first place, is thereby and inevitably, though he bring God-like gifts to the pretence—a quack. These are attempts to live deep-side shallow, inside out. They produce merely a new pettiness. To understand Socialism, again, is to gain a new breadth of outlook ; to join a Socialist organisation is to join a narrow cult which is not even tolerably serviceable in presenting or spreading the ideas for which it stands. . . .

I perceived I had got something quite fundamental here. It had taken me some years to realise the true relation of the great constructive ideas that swayed me not only to political parties, but to myself. I had been disposed to identify the formulæ of some one party with social construction, and to regard the other as necessarily anti-constructive, just as I had been in-

clined to follow the Baileys in the self-righteousness of suppos-
ing myself to be wholly constructive. But I saw now that every
man of intellectual freedom and vigour is necessarily constructive-minded nowadays, and that no man is disinterestedly
so. Each one of us repeats in himself the conflict of the race
between the splendour of its possibilities and its immediate
associations. We may be shaping immortal things, but we
must sleep and answer the dinner gong, and have our salt of
flattery and self-approval. In politics a man counts not for
what he is in moments of imaginative expansion, but for his
common workaday, selfish self ; and political parties are held
together not by a community of ultimate aims, but by the
stabler bond of an accustomed life. Everybody almost is for
progress in general, and nearly everybody is opposed to any
change, except in so far as gross increments are change, in his
particular method of living and behaviour. Every party
stands essentially for the interests and mental usages of some
definite class or group of classes in the existing community, and
every party has its scientific-minded and constructive leading
section, with well-defined hinterlands formulating its social
functions in a public-spirited form, and its superficial-minded
following confessing its meannesses and vanities and prejudices.
No class will abolish itself, materially alter its way of life, or
drastically reconstruct itself, albeit no class is indisposed to
co-operate in the unlimited socialisation of any other class. In
that capacity for aggression upon other classes lies the essential
driving force of modern affairs. The instincts, the persons, the
parties and vanities sway and struggle. The ideas and understandings march on and achieve themselves for all—in spite
of every one. . . .

The methods and traditions of British politics maintain the
form of two great parties, with rider groups seeking to gain
specific ends in the event of a small Government majority.
These two main parties are more or less heterogeneous in com-
position. Each, however, has certain necessary characteristics.
The Conservative party has always stood quite definitely for
the established propertied interests. The landowner, the big
lawyer, the Established Church, and latterly the huge private
monopoly of the liquor trade which has been created by
temperance legislation, are the essential Conservatives. Interwoven now with the native wealthy are the families of the
great international usurers, and a vast miscellaneous mass of
financial enterprise. Outside the range of resistance implied
by these interests, the Conservative party has always shown
itself just as constructive and collectivist as any other party.
The great landowners have been as well-disposed towards the
endowment of higher education, and as willing to co-operate
with the Church in protective and mildly educational legislation for children and the working class, as any political section.
The financiers, too, are adventurous-spirited and eager for

mechanical progress and technical efficiency. They are prepared to spend public money upon research, upon ports and harbours and public communications, upon sanitation and hygienic organisation. A certain rude benevolence of public intention is equally characteristic of the liquor trade. Provided his comfort leads to no excesses of temperance, the liquor trade is quite eager to see the common man prosperous, happy and with money to spend in a bar. All sections of the party are aggressively patriotic and favourably inclined to the idea of an upstanding, well-fed and well-exercised population in uniform. Of course there are reactionary landowners and old-fashioned country clergy, full of localised self-importance, jealous even of the cottager who can read, but they have neither the power nor the ability to retard the constructive forces in the party as a whole. On the other hand, when matters point to any definitely confiscatory proposal, to the public ownership and collective control of land, for example, or state mining and manufactures, or the nationalisation of the so-called public-house or extended municipal enterprise, or even to an increase of the taxation of property, then the Conservative party presents a nearly adamantine bar. It does not stand for, it *is*, the existing arrangement in these affairs.

Even more definitely a class party is the Labour party, whose immediate interest is to raise wages, shorten hours of labour, increase employment and make better terms for the working-man tenant and working-man purchaser. Its leaders are no doubt constructive minded, but the mass of the following is naturally suspicious of education and discipline, hostile to the higher education, and—except for an obvious antagonism to employers and property owners—almost destitute of ideas. What else can it be ? It stands for the expropriated multitude, whose whole situation and difficulty arise from its individual lack of initiative and organising power. It favours the nationalisation of land and capital with no sense of the difficulties involved in the process ; but, on the other hand, the equally reasonable socialisation of individuals which is implied by military service is steadily and quite naturally and quite illogically opposed by it. It is only in recent years that Labour has emerged as a separate party from the huge hospitable caravanserai of Liberalism, and there is still a very marked tendency to step back again into that multitudinous assemblage.

For multitudinousness has always been the Liberal characteristic. Liberalism never has been nor ever can be anything but a diversified crowd. Liberalism has to voice everything that is left out by these other parties. It is the party against the predominating interests. It is at once the party of the failing and of the untried ; it is the party of decadence and hope. From its nature it must be a vague and planless association in comparison with its antagonist, neither so constructive on the one hand, nor on the other so competent to hinder the inevitable constructions of the civilised state. Essentially it is the party of criticism, the "Anti" party. It is a system of hostilities and objections that somehow achieves at times an elusive common soul. It is a gathering together of all the smaller interests which find themselves at a disadvantage against the big established classes, the leasehold tenant as against the landowner, the retail tradesman as against the merchant and the moneylender, the Nonconformist as against the Churchman, the small employer as against the demoralising hospitable publican, the man without introductions and broad connections against the man who has these things. It is the party of the many small men against the fewer prevailing men. It has no more essential reason for loving the Collectivist state than the Conservatives ; the small dealer is doomed to absorption in that just as much as the large owner ; but it resorts to the state against its antagonists as in the Middle Ages common men pitted themselves against the barons by siding with the king. The Liberal party is the party against " class privilege " because it represents no class advantages, but it is also the party that is on the whole most set against Collective control because it represents no established responsibility. It is constructive only so far as its antagonism to the great owner is more powerful than its jealousy of the state. It organises only because organisation is forced upon it by the organisation of its adversaries. It lapses in and out of alliance with Labour as it sways between hostility to wealth and hostility to public expenditure. . . .

Every modern European state will have in some form or other these three parties : the resistant, militant, authoritative, dull and unsympathetic party of establishment and success, the rich party ; the confused, sentimental, spasmodic, numerous party of the small, struggling, various, undisciplined men, the poor man's party ; and a third party sometimes detaching itself from the second and sometimes reuniting with it, the party of the altogether expropriated masses, the proletarians, Labour. Change Conservative and Liberal to Republican and Democrat, for example, and you have the conditions in the United States. The Crown or a dethroned dynasty, the Established Church or a dispossessed church, nationalist secessions, the personalities of party leaders, may break up, complicate and confuse the self-expression of these three necessary divisions in the modern social drama, the analyst will make them out none the less for that. . . .

And then I came back as if I came back to a refrain ;—the ideas go on—as though we are all no more than little cells and corpuscles in some great brain beyond our understanding. . . .

So it was I sat and thought my problem out. . . . I still remember my satisfaction at seeing things plainly at last. It was like clouds dispersing to show the sky. Constructive ideas alone, of course, couldn't hold a party together, "interests and habits, not ideas," I had that now, and so the great constructive scheme of Socialism, invading and inspiring all parties, was necessarily claimed only by this collection of odds and ends, this residuum of disconnected and exceptional people. This was true not only of the Socialist idea, but of the scientific idea, the idea of veracity—of human confidence in humanity—of all that mattered in human life outside the life of individuals. . . . The only real party that would ever profess Socialism was the Labour party, and that in the entirely one-sided form of an irresponsible and non-constructive attack on property. Socialism in that mutilated form, the teeth and claws without the eyes and brain, I wanted as little as I wanted anything in the world.

Perfectly clear it was, perfectly clear, and why hadn't I seen it before ? . . . I looked at my watch, and it was half-past two.

I yawned, stretched, got up and went to bed.

§ 9

My ideas about statecraft have passed through three main phases to the final convictions that remain. There was the first immediacy of my dream of ports and harbours and cities, railways, roads and administered territories—the vision I had seen in the haze from that little church above Locarno. Slowly that had passed into a more elaborate legislative constructiveness, which had led to my uneasy association with the Baileys and the professedly constructive Young Liberals. To get that ordered life I had realised the need of organisation, knowledge, expertness, a wide movement of co-ordinated methods. On the individual side I thought that a life of urgent industry, temperance and close attention was indicated by my perception of these ends. I married Margaret and set to work. But something in my mind refused from the outset to accept these determinations as final. There was always a doubt lurking below, always a faint resentment, a protesting criticism, a feeling of vitally important omissions.

I arrived at last at the clear realisation that my political associates, and I in my association with them, were oddly narrow, priggish and unreal, that the Socialists with whom we were attempting co-operation were preposterously irrelevant to their own theories, that my political life didn't in some way comprehend more than itself, that rather perplexingly I was missing the thing I was seeking. Britten's footnotes to Altiora's self-assertions, her fits of energetic planning, her quarrels and rallies and vanities, his illuminating attacks on Cramptonism and the heavy-spirited triviality of such Liberalism as the Children's Charter, served to point my way to my present conclusions. I had been trying to deal all along with human progress as something immediate in life, something to be immediately attacked by political parties and groups pointing primarily to that end.   I now began to see that just as in my own being there was the rather shallow, rather vulgar, self-seeking careerist, who wore an admirable silk hat and bustled self-consciously through the lobby, and a much greater and indefinitely growing unpublished personality behind him —my hinterland, I have called it—so in human affairs generally the permanent reality is also a hinterland, which is never really immediate, which draws continually upon human experience and influences human action more and more, but which is itself never the actual player upon the stage.   It is the unseen dramatist who never takes a call.   Now it was just through the fact that our group about the Baileys didn't understand this, that with a sort of frantic energy they were trying to develop that sham expert officialdom of theirs to plan, regulate and direct the affairs of humanity, that the perplexing note of silliness and shallowness that I had always felt and felt now most acutely under Britten's gibes, came in.   They were neglecting human life altogether in social organisation.

In the development of intellectual modesty lies the growth of statesmanship.   It has been the chronic mistake of statecraft and all organising spirits to attempt immediately to scheme and arrange and achieve.   Priests, schools of thought, political schemers, leaders of men, have always slipped into the error of assuming that they can think out the whole—or at any rate completely think out definite parts—of the purpose and future of man, clearly and finally ; they have set themseves to legislate and construct on that assumption, and, experiencing the perplexing obduracy and evasions of reality, they have taken to dogma, persecution, training, pruning, secretive education ; and all the stupidities of self-sufficient energy.   In the passion of their good intentions they have not hesitated to conceal fact, suppress thought, crush disturbing initiatives and apparently detrimental desires.   And so it is blunderingly and wastefully, destroying with the making, that any extension of social organisation is at present achieved.

Directly, however, this idea of an emancipation from immediacy is grasped, directly the dominating importance of this critical, less personal, mental hinterland in the individual and of the collective mind in the race is understood, the whole problem of the statesman and his attitude towards politics gain a new significance, and becomes accessible to a new series of solutions.   He wants no longer to " fix up," as people say, human affairs, but to devote his forces to the development of that needed intellectual life without which all his shallow attempts at fixing up are futile.   He ceases to build on the sands, and sets himself to gather foundations.

You see, I began in my teens by wanting to plan and build

cities and harbours for mankind ; I ended in the middle
thirties by desiring only to serve and increase a general process
of thought, a process fearless, critical, real-spirited, that would
in its own time give cities, harbours, air, happiness, everything
at a scale and quality and in a light altogether beyond the
match-striking imaginations of a contemporary mind. I
wanted freedom of speech and suggestion, vigour of thought,
and the cultivation of that impulse of veracity that lurks more
or less discouraged in every man. With that I felt there
must go an emotion. I hit upon a phrase that became at last
something of a refrain in my speech and writings, to convey
the spirit that I felt was at the very heart of real human
progress—love and fine thinking.

(I suppose that nowadays no newspaper in England gets
through a week without the repetition of that phrase.)

My convictions crystallised more and more definitely upon
this. The more of love and fine thinking the better for men,
I said ; the less, the worse. And upon this fresh basis I set
myself to examine what I as a politician might do. I perceived I was at last finding an adequate expression for all
that was in me, for those forces that had rebelled at the crude
presentations of Bromstead, at the secrecies and suppressions
of my youth, at the dull unrealities of City Merchants, at the
conventions and timidities of the Pinky Dinkys, at the
philosophical recluse of Trinity and the phrases and tradition-
worship of my political associates. None of these things were
half alive, and I wanted life to be intensely alive and awake.
I wanted thought like an edge of steel and desire like a flame.
The real work before mankind now, I realised once and for
all, is the enlargement of human expression, the release and
intensification of human thought, the vivider utilisation of
experience and the invigoration of research—and whatever
one does in human affairs has or lacks value as it helps or
hinders that.

With that I had got my problem clear, and the solution, so
far as I was concerned, lay in finding out the point in the
ostensible life of politics at which I could most subserve these
ends. I was still against the muddles of Bromstead, but I
had hunted them down now to their essential form. The
jerry-built slums, the roads that went nowhere, the tarred
fences, litigious notice-boards and barbed wire fencing, the
litter and the heaps of dump, were only the outward appearances whose ultimate realities were jerry-built conclusions,
hasty purposes, aimless habits of thought and imbecile bars
and prohibitions in the thoughts and souls of men. How
are we through politics to get at that confusion ?

We want to invigorate and reinvigorate education. We
want to create a sustained counter effort to the perpetual
tendency of all educational organisations towards classicalism,
secondary issues and the evasion of life.

We want to stimulate the expression of life through art and literature, and its exploration through research.

We want to make the best and finest thought accessible to every one, and more particularly to create and sustain an enormous free criticism, without which art, literature and research alike degenerate into tradition or imposture.

Then all the other problems which are now so insoluble, destitution, disease, the difficulty of maintaining international peace, the scarcely faced possibility of making life generally and continually beautiful, become—*easy*. . . .

It was clear to me that the most vital activities in which I could engage would be those which most directly affected the Church, public habits of thought, education, organised research, literature and the channels of general discussion. I had to ask myself how my position as Liberal member for Kinghamstead squared with and conduced to this essential work.

CHAPTER TWO

SEEKING ASSOCIATES

§ 1

I HAVE told of my gradual abandonment of the pretensions and habits of party Liberalism. In a sense I was moving towards aristocracy. Regarding the development of the social and individual mental hinterland as the essential thing in human progress, I passed on very naturally to the practical assumption that we wanted what I may call " hinterlanders." Of course I do not mean by aristocracy the changing un-organised medley of rich people and privileged people who dominate the civilised world of to-day, but as opposed to this, a possibility of co-ordinating the will of the finer individuals, by habit and literature, into a broad common aim. We must have an aristocracy—not of privilege, but of understanding and purpose—or mankind will fail. I find this dawning more and more clearly when I look through my various writings of the years between 1903 and 1910. I was already emerging to plain statements in 1908.

I reasoned after this fashion. The line of human improve-ment and the expansion of human life lies in the direction of education and finer initiatives. If humanity cannot develop an education far beyond anything that is now provided, if it cannot collectively invent devices and solve problems on a much richer, broader scale than it does at the present time, it cannot hope to achieve any very much finer order or any more general happiness than it now enjoys. We must believe, therefore, that it *can* develop such a training and education, or we must abandon secular constructive hope. And here my peculiar difficulty as against crude democracy comes in. If humanity at large is capable of that high education and those creative freedoms our hope demands, much more must its better and more vigorous types be so capable. And if those who have power and leisure now, and freedom to respond to imaginative appeals, cannot be won to the idea of collective self-development, than the whole of humanity cannot be won to that. From that one passes to what has become my general conception in politics, the conception of the constructive im-agination working upon the vast complex of powerful people, clever people, enterprising people, influential people, amidst whom power is diffused to-day, to produce that self-conscious, highly selective, open-minded, devoted aristocratic culture, which seems to me to be the necessary next phase in the de-velopment of human affairs. I see human progress, not as the spontaneous product of crowds of raw minds swayed by ele-mentary needs, but as a natural but elaborate result of intricate human interdependencies, of human energy and curiosity liberated and acting at leisure, of human passions and motives, modified and redirected by literature and art. . . .

But now the reader will understand how it came about that, disappointed by the essential littleness of Liberalism, and disillusioned about the representative quality of the professed Socialists, I turned my mind more and more to a scrutiny of the big people, the wealthy and influential people, against whom Liberalism pits its forces. I was asking myself definitely whether, after all, it was not my particular job to work through them and not against them. Was I not altogether out of my element as an Anti-? Weren't there big bold qualities about these people that common men lack, and the possibility of far more splendid dreams? Were they really the obstacles, might they not be rather the vehicles of the possible new braveries of life?

§ 2

The faults of the Imperialist movement were obvious enough. The conception of the Boer War had been clumsy and puerile, the costly errors of that struggle appalling, and the subsequent campaign of Mr. Chamberlain for Tariff Reform seemed calculated to combine the financial adventurers of the Empire in one vast conspiracy against the consumer. The cant of Imperialism was easy to learn and use ; it was speedily adopted by all sorts of base enterprises and turned to all sorts of base ends. But a big child is permitted big mischief, and my mind was now continually returning to the persuasion that after all in some development of the idea of Imperial patriotism migh tbe found that wide, rough, politically acceptable expression of a constructive dream capable of sustaining a great educational and philosophical movement such as no formula of Liberalism supplied. The fact that it readily took vulgar forms only witnessed to its strong popular appeal. Mixed in with the noisiness and humbug of the movement there appeared a real regard for social efficiency, a real spirit of animation and enterprise. There suddenly appeared in my world—I saw them first, I think, in 1908—a new sort of little boy, a most agreeable development of the slouching, cunning, cigarette-smoking, town-bred youngster, a small boy in a khaki hat, and with bare knees and athletic bearing, earnestly engaged in wholesome and invigorating games up to and occasionally a little beyond his strength—the Boy Scout. I liked the Boy Scout, and I find it difficult to express how much it mattered to me, with my growing bias in favour of deliberate national training, that Liberalism hadn't been able to produce, and had indeed never attempted to produce, anything of this kind.

§ 3

In those days there existed a dining club called—there was some lost allusion to the exorcism of party feeling in its title—

the Pentagram Circle. It included Bailey and Dayton and myself, Sir Herbert Thorns, Lord Charles Kindling, Minns the poet, Gerbault the big railway man, Lord Gane, fresh from the settlement of Framboya, and Rumbold, who later became Home Secretary and left us. We were men of all parties and very various experiences, and our object was to discuss the welfare of the Empire in a disinterested spirit. We dined monthly at the Mermaid in Westminster, and for a couple of years we kept up an average attendance of ten out of fourteen. The dinner-time was given up to desultory conversation, and it is odd how warm and good the social atmosphere of that little gathering became as time went on ; then over the dessert, so soon as the waiters had swept away the crumbs and ceased to fret us, one of us would open with perhaps fifteen or twenty minutes' exposition of some specially prepared question, and after him we would deliver ourselves in turn, each for three or four minutes. When every one present had spoken once talk became general again, and it was rare we emerged upon Hendon Street before midnight. Sometimes, as my house was conveniently near, a knot of men would come home with me and go on talking and smoking in my dining-room until two or three. We had Fred Neal, that wild Irish journalist, among us towards the end, and his stupendous flow of words materially prolonged our closing discussions and made our continuance impossible.

I learned very much and very many things at those dinners, but more particularly did I become familiarised with the habits of mind of such men as Neal, Crupp, Gane, and the one or two other New Imperialists who belonged to us. They were nearly all like Bailey—Oxford men, though mostly of a younger generation, and they were all mysteriously and inexplicably advocates of Tariff Reform, as if it were the principal instead of at best a secondary aspect of constructive policy. They seemed obsessed by the idea that streams of trade could be diverted violently so as to link the parts of the Empire by common interests, and they were persuaded, I still think mistakenly, that Tariff Reform would have an immense popular appeal. They were also very keen on military organisation, and with a curious little martinet twist in their minds that boded ill for that side of public liberty. So much against them. But they were disposed to spend money much more generously on education and research of all sorts than our formless host of Liberals seemed likely to do ; and they were altogether more accessible than the Young Liberals to bold, constructive ideas affecting the universities and upper classes. The Liberals are abjectly afraid of the universities. I found myself constantly falling into line with these men in our discussions, and more and more hostile to Dayton's sentimentalising evasions of definite schemes and Minns' trust in such things as the " Spirit of our People " and the " General Trend of Progress." It wasn't that I thought them very much righter than their opponents ; I believe all definite party " sides " at any time are bound to be about equally right and equally lop-sided ; but that I thought I could get more out of them and, what was more important to me, more out of myself if I co-operated with them. By 1908 I had already arrived at a point where I could be definitely considering a transfer of my political allegiance.

These abstract questions are inseparably interwoven with my memory of a shining long white table, and our hock bottles and burgundy bottles, and bottles of Perrier and St. Galmier and the disturbed central trophy of dessert, and scattered glasses and nut-shells and cigarette-ends and menu-cards used for memoranda. I see old Dayton sitting back and cocking his eye to the ceiling in a way he had while he threw warmth into the ancient platitudes of Liberalism, and Minns leaning forward, and a little like a cockatoo with a taste for confidences, telling us in a hushed voice of his faith in the Destiny of Mankind. Thorns lounges, rolling his round face and round eyes from speaker to speaker and sounding the visible depths of misery whenever Neal begins. Gerbault and Gane were given to conversation in undertones, and Bailey pursued mysterious purposes in lisping whispers. It was Crupp attracted me most. He had, as people say, his eye on me from the beginning. He used to speak at me, and drifted into a custom of coming home with me very regularly for an after-talk.

He opened his heart to me.

" Neither of us," he said, " is a duke, and neither of us is a horny-handed son of toil. We want to get hold of the handles ; and to do that, one must go where the power is, and give it just as constructive a twist as we can. That's *my* Toryism."

" Is it Kindling's or Gerbault's ? "

" No. But theirs is soft, and mine's hard. Mine will wear theirs out. You and I and Bailey are all after the same thing, and why aren't we working together ? "

" Are you a Confederate ? " I asked suddenly.

" That's a secret nobody tells," he said.

" What are the Confederates after ? "

" Making aristocracy work, I suppose. Just as, I gather, *you* want to do." . . .

The Confederates were being heard of at that time. They were at once attractive and repellent to me, an odd secret society whose membership nobody knew, pledged, it was said, to impose Tariff Reform and an ample constructive policy upon the Conservatives. In the press, at any rate, they had an air of deliberately organised power. I have no doubt the rumour of them greatly influenced my ideas. . . .

In the end I made some very rapid decisions, but for nearly two years I was hesitating. Hesitations were inevitable in such a matter. I was not dealing with any simple question of principle, but with elusive and fluctuating estimates of the trend of diverse forces and of the nature of my own powers. All through that period I was asking over and over again : how far are these Confederates mere dreamers ? How far— and this was more vital—are they rendering lip-service to social organisations ? Is it true they desire war because it confirms the ascendency of their class ? How far can Conservatism be induced to plan and construct before it resists the thrust towards change. Is it really in bulk anything more than a mass of prejudice and conceit, cynical indulgence, and a hard suspicion of and hostility to the expropriated classes in the community ?

That is a research which yields no statistics, an inquiry like asking what is the ruling colour of a chameleon. The shadowy answer varied with my health, varied with my mood and the conduct of the people I was watching. How fine can people be ? How generous ?—not incidentally, but all round ? How far can you educate sons beyond the outlook of their fathers, and how far lift a rich, proud, self-indulgent class above the protests of its business agents and solicitors and its own habits and vanity ? Is chivalry in a class possible ?—was it ever, indeed, or will it ever indeed be possible ? Is the progress that seems attainable in certain directions worth the retrogression that may be its price ?

§ 4

It was to the Pentagram Circle that I first broached the new conceptions that were developing in my mind. I count the evening of my paper the beginning of the movement that created the *Blue Weekly* and our wing of the present New Tory party. I do that without any excessive egotism, because my essay was no solitary man's production ; it was my reaction to forces that had come to me largely through my fellow-members ; its quick reception by them showed that I was, so to speak, merely the first of the chestnuts to pop. The atmospheric quality o fthe evening stands out very vividly in my memory. The night, I remember, was warmly foggy when after midnight we went to finish our talk at my house.

We had recently changed the rules of the club to admit visitors, and so it happened that I had brought Britten, and Crupp introduced Arnold Shoesmith, my former schoolfellow at City Merchants', and now the wealthy successor of his father and elder brother. I remember his heavy, inexpressibly handsome face lighting to his rare smile at the sight of me, and how little I dreamt of the tragic entanglement that was destined to involve us both. Gane was present, and Esmeer, a newly added member, but I think Bailey was absent. Either he was absent, or he said something so entirely characteristic and undistinguished that it has left no impression on my mind.

I had broken a little from the traditions of the club even in my title, which was deliberately a challenge to the liberal idea : it was, " The World Exists for Exceptional People." It is not the title I should choose now—for since that time I have got my phrase of " mental hinterlander " into journalistic use. I should say now, " The World Exists for Mental Hinterland."

The notes I made of that opening have long since vanished with a thousand other papers, but some odd chance has preserved and brought with me to Italy the menu for the evening, its back black with the scrawled notes I made of the discussion for my reply. I found it the other day among some letters from Margaret and a copy of the 1909 Report of the Poor Law Commission, also rich with pencilled marginalia.

My opening was a criticism of the democratic idea and method, upon lines such as I have already sufficiently indicated in the preceding sections. I remember how old Dayton fretted in his chair, and tushed and pished at that, even as I gave it, and afterwards we were treated to one of his platitudinous harangues, he sitting back in his chair with that small obstinate eye of his fixed on the ceiling, and a sort of cadaverous glow upon his face, repeating—quite regardless of all my reasoning and all that had been said by others in the debate—the sacred empty phrases that were his soul's refuge from reality. " You may think it very clever," he said with a nod of his head to mark his sense of his point, " not to Trust in the People. *I* do." And so on. Nothing in his life or work had ever shown that he did trust in the people, but that was beside the mark. He was the party Liberal, and these were the party incantations.

After my preliminary attack on vague democracy I went on to show that all human life was virtually aristocratic ; people must either recognise aristocracy in general or else follow leaders, which is aristocracy in particular, and so I came to my point that the reality of human progress lay necessarily through the establishment of freedoms for the human best and a collective receptivity and understanding. There was a disgusted grunt from Dayton, " Superman rubbish—Nietzsche. Shaw ! Ugh ! " I sailed on over him to my next propositions. The prime essential in a progressive civilisation was the establishment of a more effective selective process for the privilege of higher education, and the very highest educational opportunity for the educable. We were too apt to patronise scholarship winners, as though a scholarship was toffee given as a reward for virtue. It wasn't any reward at all ; it was an invitation to capacity. We had no more right to drag in virtue, or any merit but quality, than we had to involve it in a search for the tallest man. We didn't want a mere process for the selection of good as distinguished from gifted and able boys— " No, you *don't*," from Dayton—we wanted all the brilliant stuff in the world concentrated upon the development of the world. Just to exasperate Dayton further I put in a plea for gifts as against character in educational, artistic and legislative work. " Good teaching," I said, " is better than good conduct. We are becoming idiotic about character."

Dayton was too moved to speak. He slewed round upon me an eye of agonised aversion.

I expatiated on the small proportion of the available ability that is really serving humanity to-day. " I suppose to-day all the thought, all the art, all the increments of knowledge that matter, are supplied so far as the English-speaking community is concerned by—how many ?—by three or four thousand individuals. (' Less,' said Thorns.) To be more precise, by the mental hinterlands of three or four thousand individuals. We who know some of the band entertain no illusions as to their innate rarity. We know that they are just the few out of many, the few who got in our world of chance and confusion, the timely stimulus, the apt suggestion at the fortunate moment, the needed training, the leisure. The rest are lost in the crowd, fail through the defects of their qualities, become commonplace workmen and second-rate professional men, marry commonplace wives, are as much waste as the driftage of superfluous pollen in a pine forest is waste."

" Decent honest lives'! " said Dayton to his bread-crumbs, with his chin in his necktie. " *Waste !* "

" And the people who do get what we call opportunity get it usually in extremely limited and cramping forms. No man lives a life of intellectual productivity alone ; he needs not only material and opportunity, but helpers, resonators. Round and about what I might call the *real* men, you want the sympathetic co-operators, who help by understanding. It isn't that our—*salt* of three or four thousand is needlessly rare ; it is sustained by far too small and undifferentiated a public. Most of the good men we know are not really doing the very best work of their gifts ; nearly all are a little adapted, most are shockingly adapted to some second-best use. Now I take it this is the very centre and origin of the muddle, futility and unhappiness that distresses us ; it's the cardinal problem of the state—to discover, develop and use the exceptional gifts of men. And I see that best done—I drift more and more away from the common stuff of legislative and administrative activity—not only by a quite revolutionary development of the educational machinery, but by a still more unprecedented attempt to keep science going, to keep literature going, and to keep what is the necessary spur of all science and literature, an intelligent and appreciative criticism going. You know none of these things have ever been kept going hitherto ; they've come unexpectedly and inexplicably."

" Hear, hear ! " from Dayton, cough, nodding of the head, and an expression of mystical profundity.

" They've lit up a civilisation and vanished, to give place to darkness again. Now the modern state doesn't mean to go back to darkness again—and so it's got to keep its light burning." I went on to attack the present organisation of our schools and universities, which seemed elaborately designed to turn the well-behaved, uncritical and uncreative men of each generation into the authoritative leaders of the next, and I suggested remedies upon lines that I have already indicated in the earlier chapters of this story. . . .

So far I had the substance of the club with me, but I opened new ground and set Crupp agog by confessing my doubt from which party or combination of groups these developments of science and literature and educational organisation could most reasonably be expected. I looked up to find Crupp's dark little eye intent upon me.

There I left it to them.

We had an astonishingly good discussion ; Neal burst once, but we emerged from this flood after a time, and Dayton had his interlude. The rest was all close, keen examination of my problem.

I see Crupp now with his arm bent before him on the table in a way he had, as though it was jointed throughout its length like a lobster's antenna, his plump, short-fingered hand crushing up a walnut shell into smaller and smaller fragments. "Remington," he said, "has given us the data for a movement, a really possible movement. It's not only possible, but necessary—urgently necessary, I think, if the Empire is to go on."

"We're working altogether too much at the social basement in education and training," said Gane. "Remington is right about our neglect of the higher levels."

Britten made a good contribution with an analysis of what he called the spirit of a country and what made it. "The modern community needs its serious men to be artistic and its artists to be taken seriously," I remember his saying. "The day has gone by for either dull responsibility or merely witty art."

I remember very vividly how Shoesmith harped on an idea I had thrown out of using some sort of review or weekly to express and elaborate these conceptions of a new, severer, aristocratic culture.

"It would have to be done amazingly well," said Britten, and my mind went back to my school-days and that ancient enterprise of ours, and how Cossington had rushed it. Well, Cossington had too many papers nowadays to interfere with us, and we perhaps had learned some defensive devices.

"But this thing has to be linked to some political party," said Crupp, with his eye on me. "You can't get away from that. The Liberals," he added, "have never done anything for research or literature."

"They had a Royal Commission on the Dramatic Censorship," said Thorns, with a note of minute fairness. "It shows what they were made of," he added.

"It's what I've told Remington again and again," said

Crupp, " we've got to pick up the tradition of aristocracy, re-organise it, and make it work.   But he's certainly suggested a method."

"There won't be much aristocracy to pick up," said Dayton, darkly to the ceiling, " if the House of Lords throws out the Budget."

" All the more reason for picking it up," said Neal.   " For we can't do without it."

" Will they go to the bad, or will they rise from the ashes, aristocrats indeed—if the Liberals come in overwhelmingly ? " said Britten.

" It's we who might decide that," said Crupp, insidiously.

" I agree," said Gane.

" No one can tell," said Thorns.   " I doubt if they will get beaten."

It was an odd, fragmentary discussion that night.   We were all with ideas in our minds at once fine and imperfect.   We threw out suggestions that showed themselves at once for in-adequate, and we tried to qualify them by minor self-contra-dictions.   Britten, I think, got more said than any one.   " You seem all to think you want to organise people, particular groups and classes of individuals," he insisted.   " It isn't that. That's the standing error of politicians.   You want to organise a culture.   Civilisation isn't a matter of concrete groupings ; it's a matter of prevailing ideas.   The problem is how to make bold, clear ideas prevail.   The question for Remington and us is just what groups of people will most help this culture forward."

" Yes, but how are the Lords going to behave ? " said Crupp. " You yourself were asking that a little while ago."

" If they win or if they lose," Gane maintained, " there will be a movement to reorganise aristocracy—Reform of the House of Lords, they'll call the political form of it."

" Bailey thinks that," said some one.

" The labour people want abolition," said some one.

" Let 'em," said Thorns.

He became audible, sketching a possibility of action.

" Suppose all of us were able to work together.   It's just one of those indeterminate, confused, eventful times ahead when a steady jet of ideas might produce enormous results."

" Leave me out of it," said Dayton, " *if* you please."

" We should," said Thorns under his breath.

I took up Crupp's initiative, I remember, and expanded it.

" I believe we could do—extensive things," I insisted.

" Revivals and revisions of Toryism have been tried so often," said Thorns.   " from the Young England movement onward."

" Not one but has produced its enduring effects," I said. " It's the peculiarity of English conservatism that it's per-sistently progressive and rejuvenescent."

I think it must have been about that point that Dayton fled our presence, after some clumsy sentence that I decided upon reflection was intended to remind me of my duty to my party.

Then I remember Thorns firing doubts at me obliquely across the table. "You can't run a country through its spoiled children," he said. "What you call aristocrats are really spoiled children. They've had too much of everything, except bracing experience."

"Children can always be educated," said Crupp.

"I said *spoiled* children," said Thorns.

"Look here, Thorns!" said I. "If this Budget row leads to a storm, and these big people get their power clipped, what's going to happen? Have you thought of that? When they go out lock, stock and barrel, who comes in?"

"Nature abhors a Vacuum," said Crupp, supporting me.

"Bailey's trained officials," suggested Gane.

"Quacks with a certificate of approval from Altiora," said Thorns. "I admit the horrors of the alternative. There'd be a massacre in three years."

"One may go on trying possibilities for ever," I said. "One thing emerges. Whatever accidents happen, our civilisation needs, and almost consciously needs, a culture of fine creative minds, and all the necessary tolerances, opennesses, considerations that march with that. For my own part, I think that is the Most Vital Thing. Build your ship of state as you will; get your men as you will; I concentrate on what is clearly the affair of my sort of man—I want to ensure the quality of the quarter-deck."

"Hear, hear!" said Shoesmith, suddenly—his first remark for a long time. "A first-rate figure," said Shoesmith, gripping it.

"Our danger is in missing that," I went on. "Muddle isn't ended by transferring power from the muddle-headed few to the muddle-headed many, and then cheating the many out of it again in the interests of a bureaucracy of sham experts. But that seems the limit of the liberal imagination. There is no real progress in a country, except a rise in the level of its free intellectual activity. All other progress is secondary and dependent. If you take on Bailey's dreams of efficient machinery and a sort of fanatical discipline with no free-moving brains behind it, confused ugliness becomes rigid ugliness—that's all. No doubt things are moving from looseness to discipline, and from irresponsible controls to organised controls—and also and rather contrariwise everything is becoming as people say, democratised; but all the more need in that, for an ark in which the living element may be saved."

"Hear, hear!" said Shoesmith, faint but pursuing.

It must have been in my house afterwards that Shoesmith became noticeable. He seemed trying to say something vague and difficult that he didn't get said at all on that occasion.

"We could do immense things with a weekly," he repeated, echoing Neal, I think. And there he left off and became a mute expressiveness, and it was only afterwards, when I was in bed, that I saw we had our capitalist in our hands. . . .

We parted that night on my doorstep in a tremendous glow —but in that sort of glow one doesn't act upon without much reconsideration, and it was some months before I made my decision to follow up the indications of that opening talk.

§ 5

I find my thoughts lingering about the Pentagram Circle. In my development it played a large part, not so much by starting new trains of thought as by confirming the practicability of things I had already hesitatingly entertained. Discussion with these other men so prominently involved in current affairs endorsed views that otherwise would have seemed only a little less remote from actuality than the guardians of Plato or the labour laws of More. Among other questions that were never very distant from our discussions, that came apt to every topic, was the true significance of democracy, Tariff Reform as a method of international hostility, and the imminence of war. On the first issue I can still recall little Bailey, glib and winking, explaining that democracy was really just a dodge for getting assent to the ordinances of the expert official by means of the polling booth. " If they don't like things," said he, " they can vote for the opposition candidate and see what happens then—and that, you see, is why we don't want proportional representation to let in the wild men." I opened my eyes—the lids had dropped for a moment under the caress of those smooth sounds—to see if Bailey's artful forefinger wasn't at the side of his predominant nose.

The international situation exercised us greatly. Our meetings were pervaded by the feeling that all things moved towards a day of reckoning with Germany, and I was largely instrumental in keeping up the suggestion that India was in a state of unstable equilibrium, that sooner or later something must happen there—something very serious to our Empire. Dayton frankly detested these topics. He was full of that old Middle Victorian persuasion that whatever is inconvenient or disagreeable to the English mind could be annihilated by not thinking about it. He used to sit low in his chair and look mulish. " Militarism," he would declare in a tone of the utmost moral fervour, " is a curse. It's an unmitigated curse." Then he would cough shortly and twitch his head back and frown, and seem astonished beyond measure that after this conclusive statement we could still go on talking of war.

All our Imperialists were obsessed by the thought of international conflict, and their influence revived for a time those uneasinesses that had been aroused in me for the first time by my continental journey with Willersley and by Meredith's

One of Our Conquerors. That quite justifiable dread of a punishment for all the slackness, mental dishonesty, presumption, mercenary respectability and sentimentalised commercialism of the Victorian period, at the hands of the better organised, more vigorous and now far more highly civilised peoples of Central Europe, seemed to me to have both a good and bad series of consequences. It seemed the only thing capable of bracing English minds to education, sustained constructive effort and research ; but on the other hand it produced the quality of a panic, hasty preparation, impatience of thought, a wasteful and sometimes quite futile immediacy. In 1909, for example, there was a vast clamour for eight additional Dreadnoughts—

> " We want eight
> And we won't wait,"

but no clamour at all about our national waste of inventive talent, our mean standard of intellectual attainment, our disingenuous criticism, and the consequent failure to distinguish men of the quality needed to carry on the modern type of war. Almost universally we have the wrong men in our places of responsibility and the right men in no place at all, almost universally we have poorly qualified, hesitating and resentful subordinates, because our criticism is worthless and, so habitually as to be now almost unconsciously, dishonest. Germany is beating England in every matter upon which competition is possible, because she attended sedulously to her collective mind for sixty pregnant years, because in spite of tremendous defects she is still far more anxious for quality in achievement than we are. I remember saying that in my paper. From that, I remember, I went on to an image that had flashed into my mind. " The British Empire," I said, " is like some of those early vertebrated monsters, the Brontosaurus and the Atlantosaurus and such-like ; it sacrifices intellect to character ; its backbone, that is to say—especially in the visceral region—is bigger than its cranium. It's no accident that things are so. We've worked for backbone. We brag about backbone, and if the joints are anchylosed so much the better. We're still but only half awake to our error. You can't change that suddenly."

" Turn it round and make it go backwards," interjected Thorns.

" It's trying to do that," I said, " in places."

And afterwards Crupp declared I had begotten a nightmare which haunted him of nights ; he was trying desperately and belatedly to blow a brain as one blows soap-bubbles on such a mesozoic saurian as I had conjured up, while the clumsy monster's fate, all teeth and brains, crept nearer and nearer. . . .

I've grown, I think, since those days out of the urgency of that apprehension. I still think a European war, and conceivably a very humiliating war for England, may occur at no very distant date, but I do not think there is any such heroic quality in our governing class as will make that war catastrophic. The prevailing spirit in English life—it is one of the essential secrets of our imperial endurance—is one of underbred aggression in prosperity and diplomatic compromise in moments of danger ; we bully haughtily where we can and assimilate where we must. It is not for nothing that our upper- and middle-class youth is educated by teachers of the highest character, scholars and gentlemen, men who can pretend quite honestly that Darwinism hasn't upset the historical fall of man, that cricket is moral training, and that socialism is an outrage upon the teachings of Christ. A sort of dignified dexterity of evasion is the national reward. Germany, with a larger population, a vigorous and irreconcilable proletariat, a bolder intellectual training, a harsher spirit, can scarcely fail to drive us at last to a realisation of intolerable strain. So we may never fight at all. The war of preparations that has been going on for thirty years may end like a sham-fight at last in an umpire's decision. We shall proudly but very firmly take the second place. For my own part, since I love England as much as I detest her present lethargy of soul, I pray for a chastening war—I wouldn't mind her flag in the dirt if only her spirit would come out of it. So I was able to shake off that earlier fear of some final and irrevocable destruction truncating all my schemes. At the most, a European war would be a dramatic episode in the reconstruction I had in view.

In India, too, I no longer foresee, as once I was inclined to see, disaster. The English rule in India is surely one of the most extraordinary accidents that has ever happened in history. We are there like a man who has fallen off a ladder on to the neck of an elephant, and doesn't know what to do or how to get down. Until something happens he remains. Our functions in India are absurd. We English do not own that country, do not even rule it. We make nothing happen ; at the most we prevent things happening. We suppress our own literature there. Most English people cannot even go to this land they possess ; the authorities would prevent it. If Messrs. Perowne or Cook organised a cheap tour of Manchester operatives, it would be stopped. No one dare bring the average English voter face to face with the reality of India, or let the Indian native have a glimpse of the English voter. In my time I have talked to English statesman, Indian officials and ex-officials, viceroys, soldiers, every one who might be supposed to know what India signifies, and I have prayed them to tell me what they thought we were up to there. I am not writing without my book in these matters. And beyond a phrase or so about " even-handed justice "—and look at our sedition trials !—they told me nothing. Time after time I have heard of that apocryphal native ruler in the north-west, who, when asked what would happen if we left India, replied that in a week his men would be in the saddle, and in six months not a rupee nor a virgin would be left in Lower Bengal. That is always given as our conclusive justification. But is it our business to preserve the rupees and virgins of Lower Bengal in a sort of magic inconclusiveness ? Better plunder than paralysis, better fire and sword than futility. Our flag is spread over the peninsula, without plans, without intentions—a vast preventive. The sum total of our policy is to arrest any discussion, any conferences that would enable the Indians to work out a tolerable scheme of the future for themselves. But that does not arrest the resentment of men held back from life. Consider what it must be for the educated Indian sitting at the feast of contemporary possibilities with his mouth gagged and his hands bound behind him ! The spirit of insurrection breaks out in spite of espionage and seizures. Our conflict for inaction develops stupendous absurdities. The other day the British Empire was taking off and examining printed cotton stomach wraps for seditious emblems and inscriptions. . . .

In some manner we shall have to come out of India. We have had our chance, and we have demonstrated nothing but the appalling dullness of our national imagination. We are not good enough to do anything with India. Codger and Flack, and Gates and Dayton, Cladingbowl in the club, and the *Home Churchman* in the home, cant about " character," worship of strenuous force and contempt of truth ; for the sake of such men and things as these, we must abandon in fact, if not in appearance, that empty domination. Had we great schools and a powerful teaching, could we boast great men, had we the spirit of truth and creation in our lives, then indeed it might be different. But a race that bears a sceptre must carry gifts to justify it.

It does not follow that we shall be driven catastrophically from India. That was my earlier mistake. We are not proud enough in our bones to be ruined by India as Spain was by her empire. We may be able to abandon India with an air of still remaining there. It is our new method. We train our future rulers in the public schools to have a very wholesome respect for strength, and as soon as a power arises in India in spite of us, be it a man or a culture, or a native state, we shall be willing to deal with it. We may or may not have a war, but our governing class will be quick to learn when we are beaten. Then they will repeat our South African diplomacy, and arrange for some settlement that will abandon the reality, such as it is, and preserve the semblance of power. The conqueror *de facto* will become the new " loyal Briton," and the democracy at home will be invited to celebrate our recession —triumphantly. I am no believer in the imminent dissolution of our Empire ; I am less and less inclined to see in either India or Germany the probability of an abrupt truncation of those slow intellectual and moral constructions which are the essentials of statecraft.

§ 6

I sit writing in this little loggia to the sound of dripping water—this morning we had rain, and the roof of our little casa is still not dry, there are pools in the rocks under the sweet chestnuts, and the torrent that crosses the salita is full and boastful—and I try to recall the order of my impressions during that watching, dubious time, before I went over to the Conservative party. I was trying—chaotic task !—to gauge the possibilities inherent in the quality of the British aristocracy. There comes a broad spectacular effect of wide parks, diversified by woods and bracken valleys, and dappled with deer ; of great smooth lawns shaded by ancient trees ; of big façades of sunlit buildings dominating the country-side ; of large fine rooms full of handsome, easy-mannered people. As a sort of representative picture to set off against those other pictures of Liberals and of Socialists I have given, I recall one of those huge assemblies the Duchess of Clynes inaugurated at Stamford House. The place itself is one of the vastest private houses in London, a huge clustering mass of white and gold saloons with polished floors and wonderful pictures, and staircases and galleries on a Gargantuan scale. And there she sought to gather all that was most representative of English activities, and did, in fact, in those brilliant nocturnal crowds, get samples of nearly every section of our social and intellectual life, with a marked predominance upon the political and social side.

I remember sitting in one of the recesses at the end of the big saloon with Mrs. Redmondson, one of those sharp-minded, beautiful rich women one meets so often in London, who seem to have done nothing and to be capable of everything, and we watched the crowd—uniforms and splendours were streaming in from a State ball—and exchanged information. I told her about the politicians and intellectuals, and she told me about the aristocrats, and we sharpened our wit on them and counted the percentage of beautiful people among the latter, and wondered if the general effect of tallness was or was not an illusion.

They were, we agreed, for the most part bigger than the average of people in London, and a handsome lot, even when they were not subtly individualised. " They look so well nurtured," I said, " well cared for. I like their quiet, well-trained movements, their pleasant consideration for each other."

" Kindly, good-tempered and at bottom utterly selfish," she said, " like big, rather carefully trained, rather pampered children. What else can you expect from them ? "

" They are good-tempered, anyhow," I witnessed, " and that's an achievement. I don't think I could ever be content under a bad-tempered, sentimentalising, strenuous Government. That's why I couldn't stand the Roosevelt *régime* in America. One's chief surprise when one comes across these big people for the first time is their admirable easiness and a real personal modesty. I confess I admire them. Oh ! I like them. I wouldn't at all mind, I believe, giving over the country to this aristocracy—given *something*——"

" Which they haven't got."

" Which they haven't got—or they'd be the finest sort of people in the world."

" That something ? " she inquired.

" I don't know. I've been puzzling my wits to know. They've done all sorts of things——"

" That's Lord Wrassleton," she interrupted, " whose leg was broken—you remember ?—at Spion Kop."

" It's healed very well. I like the gold lace and the white glove resting, with quite a nice awkwardness, on the sword. When I was a little boy I wanted to wear clothes like that. And the stars ! He's got the V.C. Most of these people here have at any rate shown pluck, you know—brought something off."

" Not quite enough," she suggested.

" I think that's it," I said. " Not quite enough—not quite hard enough," I added.

She laughed and looked at me. " You'd like to make us," she said.

" What ? "

" Hard."

" I don't think you'll go on if you don't get hard."

" We shan't be so pleasant if we do."

" Well, there my puzzled wits come in again. I don't see why an aristocracy shouldn't be rather hard trained, and yet kindly. I'm not convinced that the resources of education are exhausted. I want to better this, because it already looks so good."

" How are we to do it ? " asked Mrs. Redmondson.

" Oh, there you have me ! I've been spending my time lately in trying to answer that ! It makes me quarrel with " —I held up my fingers and ticked the items off—" the public schools, the private tutors, the army exams., the Universities, the Church, the general attitude of the country towards science and literature——"

" We all do," said Mrs. Redmondson. " We can't begin again at the beginning," she added.

" Couldn't one," I nodded at the assembly in general, " start a movement ? "

" There's the Confederates," she said, with a faint smile that masked a gleam of curiosity. . . . " You want," she said, " to say to the aristocracy, ' Be aristocrats. *Noblesse oblige.*' Do you remember what happened to the monarch who was told to ' Be a King ' ? ''

" Well," I said, " I want an aristocracy."

" This," she said, smiling, " is the pick of them. The backwoodsmen are off the stage. These are the brilliant ones—the smart and the blues. . . . They cost a lot of money, you know."

So far Mrs. Redmondson, but the picture remained full of things not stated in our speech. They were on the whole handsome people, charitable-minded, happy and easy. They led spacious lives, and there was something free and fearless about their bearing that I liked extremely. The women particularly were wide-reading, fine-thinking. Mrs. Redmondson talked as fully and widely and boldly as a man, and with those flashes of intuition, those startling, sudden delicacies of perception few men display. I liked, too, the relations that held between women and men, their general tolerance, their antagonism to the harsh jealousies that are the essence of the middle-class order. . . .

After all, if one's aim resolved itself into the development of a type and culture of men, why shouldn't one begin at this end ?

It is very easy indeed to generalise about a class of human beings, but much harder to produce a sample. Was old Lady Forthundred, for instance, fairly a sample ? I remember her as a smiling, magnificent presence, a towering accumulation of figure and wonderful shimmering blue silk and black lace and black hair, and small fine features and chins and chins and chins, disposed in a big cane chair with wraps and cushions upon the great terrace of Champneys. Her eye was blue and hard, and her accent and intonation were exactly what you would expect from a rather commonplace dressmaker pretending to be aristocratic. I was, I am afraid, posing a little as the intelligent but respectful inquirer from below investigating the great world, and she was certainly posing as my informant. She affected a cynical coarseness. She developed a theory on the governance of England, beautifully frank and simple. " Give 'um all a peerage when they get twenty thousand a year," she maintained. " That's my remedy."

In my new rôle of theoretical aristocrat I felt a little abashed.

" Twenty thousand," she repeated with conviction.

It occurred to me that I was in the presence of the aristocratic theory currently working as distinguished from my as yet unformulated intentions.

" You'll get a lot of loafers and scamps among 'um," said Lady Forthundred. " You get loafers and scamps everywhere, but you'll get a lot of men who'll work hard to keep things together, and that's what we're all after, isn't ut ? ''

" It's not an ideal arrangement."

" Tell me anything better," said Lady Forthundred.

On the whole, and because she refused emphatically to believe in education, Lady Forthundred scored.

We had been discussing Cossington's recent peerage, for Cossington, my old schoolfellow at City Merchants' and my victor in the affair of the magazine, had clambered to an amazing wealth up a piled heap of energetically pushed penny and halfpenny magazines, and a group of daily newspapers. I had expected to find the great lady hostile to the newcomer, but she accepted him, she gloried in him.

" We're a peerage," she said, " but none of us have ever had any nonsense about nobility."

She turned and smiled down on me. " We English," she said, " are a practical people. We assimilate 'um."

" Then, I suppose, they don't give trouble ? "

" Then they don't give trouble."

" They learn to shoot ? "

" And all that," said Lady Forthundred. " Yes. And things go on. Sometimes better than others, but they go on —somehow. It depends very much on the sort of butler who pokes 'um about."

I suggested that it might be possible to get a secure twenty thousand a year by at least detrimental methods—socially speaking.

" We must take the bad and the good of 'um," said Lady Forthundred, courageously. . . .

Now, was she a sample ? It happened she talked. What was there in the brains of the multitude of her first, second, third, fourth and fifth cousins, who didn't talk, who shone tall and bearing themselves finely, against a background of deft, attentive maids and valets, on every spacious social scene ? How did things look to them ?

§ 7

Side by side with Lady Forthundred, it is curious to put Evesham with his tall, bent body, his little-featured almost elvish face, his unequal mild brown eyes, his gentle manner, his sweet, amazing oratory. He led all these people wonderfully. He was always curious and interested about life, wary beneath a pleasing frankness—and I tormented my brain to get to the bottom of him. For a long time he was the most powerful man in England under the throne ; he had the Lords in his hand, and a great majority in the Commons, and the discontents and intrigues that are the concomitants of an overwhelming party advantage broke against him as waves break against a cliff. He foresaw so far in these matters that it seemed he scarcely troubled to foresee. He brought political art to the last triumph of naturalness. Always for me he has been the typical aristocrat, so typical and above the mere forms of aristocracy, that he remained a commoner to the end of his days.

I had met him at the beginning of my career ; he read some early papers of mine, and asked to see me, and I conceived a flattered liking for him that strengthened to a very strong feeling indeed. He seemed to me to stand alone without an equal, the greatest man in British political life. Some men one sees through and understands, some one cannot see into or round because they are of opaque clay, but about Evesham I had a sense of things hidden as it were by depth and mists, because he was so big and atmospheric a personality. No other contemporary has had that effect upon me. I've sat beside him at dinners, stayed in houses with him—he was in the big house-party at Champneys—talked to him, sounded him, watching him as I sat beside him. I could talk to him with extraordinary freedom and a rare sense of being understood. Other men have to be treated in a special manner ; approached through their own mental dialect, flattered by a minute regard for what they have said and done. Evesham was as widely and charitably receptive as any man I have ever met. The common politicians beside him seemed like rows of stuffy little rooms looking out upon the sea.

And what was he up to ? What did *he* think we were doing with Mankind ? That I thought worth knowing.

I remember his talking on one occasion at the Hartsteins', at a dinner so tremendously floriferous and equipped that we were almost forced into duologues, about the possible common constructive purpose in politics.

" I feel so much," he said, " that the best people in every party converge. We don't differ at Westminster as they do in the country towns. There's a sort of extending common policy that goes on under every government, because on the whole it's the right thing to do, and people know it. Things that used to be matters of opinion became matters of science— and cease to be party questions."

He instanced education.

" Apart," said I, " from the religious question."

" Apart from the religious question."

He dropped that aspect with an easy grace, and went on with his general theme that political conflict was the outcome of un-certainty. " Directly you get a thing established, so that people can say, ' Now this is Right,' with the same conviction that people can say water is a combination of oxygen and hydrogen, there's no more to be said. The thing has to be done. . . ."

And to put against this effect of Evesham, broad and humanely tolerant, posing as the minister of a steadily developing constructive conviction, there are other memories.

Have I not seen him in the House, persistent, persuasive, in-defatigable, and by all my standards wickedly perverse, leaning over the table with those insistent movements of his hand upon it, or swaying forward with a grip upon his coat lapel, fighting with a diabolical skill to preserve what are in effect religious tests, tests he must have known would outrage and humiliate and injure the consciences of a quarter—and that perhaps the best quarter—of the youngsters who come to the work of elementary education ?

In playing for points in the game of party advantage Evesham displayed at times the completest unscrupulousness in the use of his subtle mind. I would sit on the Liberal benches and watch him, and listen to his urbane voice, fascinated by him. Did he really care ? Did anything matter to him ? And if it really mattered nothing, why did he trouble to serve the narrowness and passion of his side ? Or did he see far beyond my scope, so that this petty iniquity was justified by greater, remoter ends of which I had no intimation ?

They accused him of nepotism. His friends and family were certainly well cared for. In private life he was full of an affectionate intimacy ; he pleased by being charmed and pleased. One might think at times there was no more of him than a clever man happily circumstanced, and finding an interest and occupation in politics. And then came a glimpse of thought, of imagination, like the sight of a soaring eagle through a staircase skylight. Oh, beyond question he was great ! No other contemporary politician had his quality. In no man have I perceived so sympathetically the great contrast between warm, personal things and the white dream of statecraft ? Except that he had it seemed no hot passions, but only interests and fine affections and indolences, he paralleled the conflict of my life. He saw and thought widely and deeply ; but at times it seemed to me his greatness stood over and behind the reality of his life, like some splendid servant, thinking his own thoughts, who waits behind a lesser master's chair. . . .

§ 8

Of course, when Evesham talked of this ideal of the organised state becoming so finely true to practicability and so clearly stated as to have the compelling conviction of physical science, he spoke quite after my heart. Had he really embodied the attempt to realise that, I could have done no more than follow him blindly. But neither he nor I embodied that, and there lies the gist of my story. And when it came to a study of others among the leading Tories and Imperialists the doubt increased, until with some at last it was possible to question whether they had any imaginative conception of constructive statecraft at all ; whether they didn't opaquely accept the world for what it was, and set themselves single-mindedly to make a place for themselves and cut a figure in it.

There were some very fine personalities among them : there were the great peers who had administered Egypt, India, South Africa, Framboya—Cromer, Kitchener, Curzon, Milner, Gane, for example. So far as that easier task of holding sword and scales had gone, they had shown the finest qualities, but they had returned to the perplexing and exacting problem of the home country, a little glorious, a little too simply bold. They wanted to arm and they wanted to educate, but the habit of immediate necessity made them far more eager to arm than to educate, and their experience of heterogeneous controls made them overrate the need for obedience in a homogeneous country. They didn't understand raw men, ill-trained men, uncertain minds and intelligent women ; and these are the things that matter in England. . . . There were also the great business adventurers, from Cranber to Cossington (who was now Lord Paddockhurst). My mind remained unsettled, and went up and down the scale between a belief in their far-sighted purpose and the perception of crude vanities, coarse ambitions, vulgar competitiveness, and a mere habitual persistence in the pursuit of gain. For a time I saw a good deal of Cossington— I wish I had kept a diary of his talk and gestures, to mark how he could vary from day to day between a *poseur*, a smart tradesman, and a very bold and wide-thinking political schemer. He had a vanity of sweeping actions, motor-car pounces, Napoleonic rushes, that led to violent ineffectual changes in the policy of his papers, and a haunting pursuit by parallel columns in the Liberal press that never abashed him in the slightest degree. By an accident I plumbed the folly in him—but I feel I never plumbed his wisdom. I remember him one day after a lunch at the Barhams' saying suddenly, out of profound meditation over the end of a cigar, one of those sentences that seem to light the whole interior being of a man. " Some day," he said softly, rather to himself than to me, and *à propos* of nothing—" some day I will raise the country."

" Why not ? " I said, after a pause, and leaned across him for the little silver spirit-lamp, to light my cigarette. . . .

Then the Tories had for another section the ancient creations, and again there were the financial peers, men accustomed to reserve, and their big lawyers, accustomed to—well, qualified statement. And below the giant personalities of the party were the young bloods, young, adventurous men of the type of Lord Tarvrille, who had seen service in South Africa, who had travelled and hunted ; explorers, keen motorists, interested in aviation, active in army organisation. Good, brown-faced stuff they were, but impervious to ideas outside the range of their activities, more ignorant of science than their chauffeurs, and of the quality of English people than welt-politicians ; contemptuous of school and university by reason of the Gateses and Flacks and Codgers who had come their way, witty, light-hearted, patriotic at the Kipling level, with a certain aptitude for bullying. They varied in insensible gradations between the noble sportsmen on the one hand, and men like Gane and the Tories of our Pentagram Club on the other. You perceive how a man might exercise his mind in the attempt to strike an average of public serviceability in this miscellany ! And mixed up with these, mixed up sometimes in the same man, was the pure reactionary, whose predominant idea was that the village schools should confine themselves to teaching the catechism, hat-touching and curtseying, and be given a holiday whenever beaters were in request. . . .

I find now in my mind as a sort of counterpoise to Evesham the figure of old Lord Wardingham, asleep in the largest arm-chair in the library of Stamford Court after lunch. One foot rested on one of those things—I think they are called gout stools. He had been playing golf all the morning and wearied a weak instep ; at lunch he had sat at my table and talked in the overbearing manner permitted to irascible important men whose insteps are painful. Among other things he had flouted the idea that women would ever understand statecraft or be more than a nuisance in politics, denied flatly that Hindoos were capable of anything whatever except excesses in popula-tion, regretted he could not censor picture-galleries and cir-culating libraries, and declared that dissenters were people who pretended to take theology seriously with the express purpose of upsetting the entirely satisfactory compromise of the Estab-lished Church. " No sensible people, with anything to gain or lose, argue about religion," he said. " They mean mischief." Having delivered his soul upon these points, and silenced the little conversation to the left of him from which they had arisen, he became, after an appreciative encounter with a sanguinary woodcock, more amiable, responded to some respectful initia-tives of Crupp's, and related a number of classical anecdotes of those blighting snubs, vindictive retorts and scandalous mis-carriages of justice that are so dear to the forensic mind. Now he reposed. He was breathing heavily with his mouth slightly open and his head on one side. One whisker was turned back against the comfortable padding. His plump strong hands gripped the arms of his chair, and his frown was a little assuaged. How tremendously fed-up he looked ! Honours, wealth, influence, respect, he had them all. How scornful and hard it had made his unguarded expression !

I note without comment that it didn't even occur to me then to wake him up and ask him what *he* was up to with mankind.

§ 9

One countervailing influence to my drift to Toryism in those days was Margaret's quite religious faith in the Liberals. I realised that slowly and with a mild astonishment. It set me, indeed, even then questioning my own change of opinion. We came at last incidentally, as our way was, to an exchange of views. It was as nearly a quarrel as we had before I came over to the Conservative side. It was at Champneys, and I think during the same visit that witnessed my exploration of

Lady Forthundred. It arose indirectly, I think, out of some comments of mine upon our fellow-guests, but it is one of those memories of which the scene and quality remain more vivid than the things said, a memory without any very definite beginning or end. It was afternoon, in the pause between tea and the dressing-bell, and we were in Margaret's big silver-adorned, chintz-bright room, looking out on the trim Italian garden. . . . Yes, the beginning of it has escaped me altogether, but I remember it as an odd exceptional little wrangle.

At first we seem to have split upon the moral quality of the aristocracy, and I had an odd sense that in some way too feminine for me to understand our hostess had aggrieved her. She said, I know, that Champneys distressed her ; made her " eager for work and reality again."

" But aren't these people real ? "

" They're so superficial, so extravagant ! "

I said I was not shocked by their unreality. They seemed the least affected people I had ever met. " And are they really so extravagant ? " I asked, and put it to her that her dresses cost quite as much as any other woman's in the house.

" It's not only their dresses," Margaret parried. " It's the scale and spirit of things."

I questioned that. " They're cynical," said Margaret, staring before her out of the window.

I challenged her, and she quoted the Brabants, about whom there had been an ancient scandal. She'd heard of it from Altiora, and it was Altiora, too, who'd given her a horror of Lord Carnaby, who was also with us. " You know his reputation," said Margaret. " That Normandy girl. Every one knows about it. I shiver when I look at him. He seems— oh ! like something not of *our* civilisation. He *will* come and say little things to me."

" Offensive things ? "

" No, politenesses and things. Of course his manners are— quite right. That only makes it worse, I think. It shows he might have helped—all that happened. I do all I can to make him see I don't like him. But none of the others make the slightest objection to him."

" Perhaps these people imagine something might be said for him."

" That's just it," said Margaret.

" Charity," I suggested.

" I don't like that sort of toleration."

I was oddly annoyed. " Like eating with publicans and sinners," I said. " No ! . . ."

But scandals, and the contempt for rigid standards their condonation displayed, weren't more than the sharp edge of the trouble. " It's their whole position, their selfish predominance, their class conspiracy against the mass of people," said Margaret. " When I sit at dinner in that splendid room, with its glitter and white reflections and candlelight, and its flowers and its wonderful service and its candelabra of solid gold, I seem to feel the slums and the mines and the over-crowded cottages stuffed away under the table."

I reminded Margaret that she was not altogether innocent of unearned increment.

" But aren't we doing our best to give it back ? " she said.

I was moved to question her. " Do you really think," I asked, " that the Tories and peers and rich people are to blame for social injustice as we have it to-day ? Do you really see politics as a struggle of light on the Liberal side against dark-ness on the Tory ? "

" They *must* know," said Margaret.

I found myself questioning that. I see now that to Margaret it must have seemed the perversest carping against manifest things, but at the time I was concentrated simply upon the elucidation of her view and my own ; I wanted to get at her conception in the sharpest, hardest lines that were possible. It was perfectly clear that she saw Toryism as the diabolical element in affairs. The thing showed in its hopeless untruth all the clearer for the fine, clean emotion with which she gave it out to me. My sleeping peer in the library at Stamford Court and Evesham talking luminously behind the Hartstein flowers embodied the devil, and my replete citizen sucking at his cigar in the National Liberal Club, Willie Crampton discuss-ing the care and management of the stomach over a specially hygienic lemonade, and Dr. Tumpany in his aggressive frock-coat pegging out a sort of copyright in socialism, were the centre and wings of the angelic side. It was nonsense. But how was I to put the truth to her ?

" I don't see things at all as you do," I said. " I don't see things in the same way."

" Think of the poor," said Margaret, going off at a tangent.

" Think of every one," I said. " We Liberals have done more mischief through well-intentioned benevolence than all the selfishness in the world could have done. We built up the liquor interest."

" *We* ! " cried Margaret. " How can you say that ? It's against us."

" Naturally. But we made it a monopoly in our clumsy efforts to prevent people drinking what they liked, because it interfered with industrial regularity——"

" Oh ! " cried Margaret, stung ; and I could see she thought I was talking mere wickedness.

" That's it," I said.

" But would you have people drink whatever they pleased ? "

" Certainly. What right have I to dictate to other men and women ? "

" But think of the children ! "

" Ah ! there you have the folly of modern Liberalism, its

half-cunning, half-silly way of getting at everything in a roundabout fashion. If neglecting children is an offence, and it *is* an offence, then deal with it as such, but don't go badgering and restricting people who sell something that may possibly in some cases lead to a neglect of children. If drunkenness is an offence, punish it, but don't punish a man for selling honest drink that perhaps after all won't make any one drunk at all. Don't intensify the viciousness of the public-house by assuming the place isn't fit for women and children. That's either spite or folly. Make the public-house *fit* for women and children. Make it a real public-house. If we Liberals go on as we are going, we shall presently want to stop the sale of ink and paper because those things tempt men to forgery. We do already threaten the privacy of the post because of betting touts' letters. The drift of all that kind of thing is narrow, unimaginative, mischievous, stupid. . . ."

I stopped short and walked to the window and surveyed a pretty fountain, facsimile of one in Verona, amidst trim-cut borderings of yew. Beyond, and seen between the stems of ilex trees, was a great blaze of yellow flowers. . . .

" But prevention," I heard Margaret behind me, " is the essence of our work."

I turned. " There's no prevention but education. There's no antiseptics in life but love and fine thinking. Make people fine, make fine people. Don't be afraid. These Tory leaders are better people individually than the average ; why cast them for the villains of the piece ? The real villain in the piece—in the whole human drama—is muddle-headedness, and it matters very little if it's virtuous-minded or wicked. I want to get at muddle-headedness. If I could do that I could let all that you call wickedness in the world run about and do what it jolly well pleased. It would matter about as much as a slightly neglected dog—in an otherwise well-managed home."

My thoughts had run away with me.

" I can't understand you," said Margaret, in the profoundest distress. " I can't understand how it is you are coming to see things like this."

§ 10

The moods of a thinking man in politics are curiously evasive and difficult to describe. Neither the public nor the historian will permit the statesman moods. He has from the first to assume he has an Aim, a definite Aim, and to pretend to an absolute consistency with that. Those subtle questionings about the very fundamentals of life which plague us all so relentlessly nowadays are supposed to be silenced. He lifts his chin and pursues his Aim explicitly in the sight of all men. Those who have no real political experience can scarcely imagine the immense mental and moral strain there is between one's everyday acts and utterances on the one hand and the

" thinking-out " process on the other. It is perplexingly difficult to keep in your mind, fixed and firm, a scheme essentially complex, to keep balancing a swaying possibility while at the same time under jealous, hostile and stupid observation you tread your part in the platitudinous, quarrelsome, ill-presented march of affairs. . . .

The most impossible of all autobiographies is an intellectual autobiography. I have thrown together in the crudest way the elements of the problem I struggled with, but I can give no record of the subtle details ; I can tell nothing of the long vacillations between Protean values, the talks and re-talks, the meditations, the bleak lucidities of sleepless nights. . . .

And yet these things I have struggled with must be thought out, and, to begin with, they must be thought out in this muddled, experimenting way. To go into a study to think about statecraft is to turn your back on the realities you are constantly needing to feel and test and sound if your thinking is to remain vital ; to choose an aim and pursue it in despite of all subsequent questionings is to bury the talent of your mind. It is no use dealing with the intricate as though it were simple, to leap haphazard at the first course of action that presents itself ; the whole world of politicians is far too like a man who snatches a poker to a failing watch. It is easy to say he wants to " get something done," but the only sane thing to do for the moment is to put aside that poker and take thought and get a better implement. . . .

One of the results of these fundamental preoccupations of mine was a curious irritability towards Margaret that I found difficult to conceal. It was one of the incidental cruelties of our position that this should happen. I was in such doubt myself, that I had no power to phrase things for her in a form she could use. Hitherto I had stage-managed our " serious " conversations. Now I was too much in earnest and too uncertain to go on doing this. I avoided talk with her. Her serene, sustained confidence in vague formulæ and sentimental aspirations exasperated me ; her want of sympathetic apprehension made my few efforts to indicate my changing attitudes distressing and futile. It wasn't that I was always thinking right, and that she was always saying wrong. It was that I was struggling to get hold of a difficult thing that was, at any rate, half true, I could not gauge how true, and that Margaret's habitual phrasing ignored these elusive elements of truth, and without premeditation fitted into the weaknesses of my new intimations, as though they had nothing but weaknesses. It was, for example, obvious that these big people, who were the backbone of Imperialism and Conservatism, were temperamentally lax, much more indolent, much more sensuous, than our deliberately virtuous Young Liberals. I didn't want to be reminded of that, just when I was in full effort to realise the finer elements in their composition. Margaret classed them and disposed of them. It was our incurable differences in habits and gestures of thought coming between us again.

The desert of misunderstanding widened. I was forced back upon myself and my own secret councils. For a time I went my way alone; an unmixed evil for both of us. Except for that Pentagram evening, a series of talks with Isabel Rivers, who was now becoming more and more important in my intellectual life, and the arguments I maintained with Crupp, I never really opened my mind at all during that period of indecisions, slow abandonments and slow acquisitions.

CHAPTER THREE

SECESSION

§ 1

A<small>T</small> last, out of a vast accumulation of impressions, decision distilled quite suddenly. I succumbed to Evesham and that dream of the right thing triumphant through expression. I determined I would go over to the Conservatives, and use my every gift and power on the side of such forces on that side as made for educational reorganisation, scientific research, literature, criticism and intellectual development. That was in 1909. I judged the Tories were driving straight at a conflict with the country, and I thought them bound to incur an electoral defeat. I underestimated their strength in the counties. There would follow, I calculated, a period of profound reconstruction in method and policy alike. I was entirely at one with Crupp in perceiving in this an immense opportunity for the things we desired. An aristocracy quickened by conflict and on the defensive, and full of the idea of justification by reconstruction, might prove altogether more apt for thought and high professions than Mrs. Redmondson's spoiled children. Behind the now inevitable struggle for a reform of the House of Lords, there would be great heart searchings and educational endeavour. On that we reckoned. . . .

At last we talked it out to the practical pitch, and Crupp and Shoesmith, and I and Gane, made our definite agreement together. . . .

I emerged from enormous silences upon Margaret one evening.

She was just back from the display of some new musicians at the Hartsteins'. I remember she wore a dress of golden satin, very rich-looking and splendid. About her slender neck there was a rope of gold-set amber beads. Her hair caught up and echoed and returned these golden notes. I, too, was in evening dress, but where I had been escapes me—some forgotten dinner, I suppose. I went into her room. I remember I didn't speak for some moments. I went across to the window and pulled the blind aside, and looked out upon the railed garden of the square, with its shrubs and shadowed turf gleaming pallidly and irregularly in the light of the big electric standard in the corner.

" Margaret," I said, " I think I shall break with the party."

She made no answer. I turned presently, a movement of inquiry.

" I was afraid you meant to do that," she said.

" I'm out of touch," I explained. " Altogether."

" Oh ! I know."

" It places me in a difficult position," I said.

Margaret stood at her dressing-table, looking steadfastly at herself in the glass, and with her fingers playing with a litter of stoppered bottles of tinted glass. " I was afraid it was coming to this," she said.

" In a way," I said, " we've been allies. I owe my seat to you. I couldn't have gone into Parliament . . ."

" I don't want considerations like that to affect us," she interrupted.

There was a pause. She sat down in a chair by her dressing-table, lifted an ivory hand-glass, and put it down again.

" I wish," she said, with something like a sob in her voice, " it were possible that you shouldn't do this." She stopped abruptly, and I did not look at her, because I could feel the effort she was making to control herself.

" I thought," she began again, " when you came into Parliament——"

There came another silence. " It's all gone so differently," she said. " Everything has gone so differently."

I had a sudden memory of her, shining triumphant after the Kinghampstead election, and for the first time I realised just how perplexing and disappointing my subsequent career must have been to her.

" I'm not doing this without consideration," I said.

" I know," she said, in a voice of despair, " I've seen it coming. But—I still don't understand it. I don't understand how you can go over."

" My ideas have changed and developed," I said.

I walked across to her bearskin hearthrug, and stood by the mantel.

" To think that you," she said, " you who might have been leader——" She could not finish it. " All the forces of reaction," she threw out.

" I don't think they are the forces of reaction," I said. " I think I can find work to do—better work on that side."

" Against us ! " she said. " As if progress wasn't hard enough ! As if it didn't call upon every able man ! "

" I don't think Liberalism has a monopoly of progress."

She did not answer that. She sat quite still looking in front of her. " *Why* have you gone over ? " she asked abruptly as though I had said nothing.

There came a silence that I was impelled to end. I began a stiff dissertation from the hearthrug. " I am going over, because I think I may join in an intellectual renascence on the Conservative side. I think that in the coming struggle there will be a partial and altogether confused and demoralising victory for democracy, that will stir the classes which now dominate the Conservative party into an energetic revival. They will set out to win back, and win back. Even if my estimate of contemporary forces is wrong and they win, they

will still be forced to reconstruct their outlook. A war abroad
will supply the chastening if home politics fail. The effort at
renascence is bound to come by either alternative. I believe
I can do more in relation to that effort than in any other connection in the world of politics at the present time. That's
my case, Margaret."

She certainly did not grasp what I said. "And so you will
throw aside all the beginnings, all the beliefs and pledges——"
Again her sentence remained incomplete. "I doubt if even,
once you have gone over, they will welcome you."

"That hardly matters."

I made an effort to resume my speech.

"I came into Parliament, Margaret," I said, "a little pre-
maturely. Still—I suppose it was only by coming into Parliament that I could see things as I do now in terms of personality
and imaginative range. . . ." I stopped. Her stiff, unhappy,
unlistening silence broke up my disquisition.

"After all," I remarked, "most of this has been implicit in
my writings."

She made no sign of admission.

"What are you going to do ? " she asked.

"Keep my seat for a time and make the reasons of my
breach clear. Then either I must resign or—probably this new
Budget will lead to a General Election. It's evidently meant
to strain the Lords and provoke a quarrel."

"You might, I think, have stayed to fight for the Budget."

"I'm not," I said, "so keen against the Lords."

On that we halted.

"But what are you going to do ? " she asked.

"I shall make my quarrel over some points in the Budget.
I can't quite tell you yet where my chance will come. Then I
shall either resign my seat—or if things drift to dissolution I
shall stand again."

"It's political suicide."

"Not altogether."

"I can't imagine you out of Parliament again. It's just
like—like undoing all we have done. What will you do ? "

"Write. Make a new, more definite place for myself. You
know, of course, there's already a sort of group about Crupp
and Gane."

Margaret seemed lost for a time in painful thought.

"For me," she said at last, "our political work has been a
religion—it has been more than a religion."

I heard in silence. I had no form of protest available
against the implications of that.

"And then I find you turning against all we aimed to do—
talking of going over, almost lightly—to those others." . . .

She was white-lipped as she spoke. In the most curious
way she had captured the moral values of the situation. I
found myself protesting ineffectually against her fixed con-

viction. " It's because I think my duty lies in this change that I make it," I said.

" I don't see how you can say that," she replied quietly.

There was another pause between us.

" Oh ! " she said and clenched her hand upon the table. " That it should have come to this ! "

She was extraordinarily dignified and extraordinarily absurd. She was hurt and thwarted beyond measure. She had no place in her ideas, I thought, for me. I could see how it appeared to her, but I could not make her see anything of the intricate process that had brought me to this divergence. The opposition of our intellectual temperaments was like a gag in my mouth. What was there for me to say ? A flash of intuition told me that behind her white dignity was a passionate disappointment, a shattering of dreams that needed before everything else the relief of weeping.

" I've told you," I said awkwardly, " as soon as I could."

There was another long silence. " So that is how we stand," I said with an air of having things defined. I walked slowly to the door.

She had risen and stood now staring in front of her.

" Good-night," I said, making no movement towards our habitual kiss.

" Good-night," she answered in a tragic note. . . .

I closed the door softly. I remained for a moment or so on the big landing, hesitating between my bedroom and my study. As I did so I heard the soft rustle of her movement and the click of the key in her bedroom door. Then everything was still. . . .

She hid her tears from me. Something gripped my heart at the thought.

" Damnation ! " I said, wincing. " Why the devil can't people at least *think* in the same manner ? "

§ 2

And that insufficient colloquy was the beginning of a prolonged estrangement between us. It was characteristic of our relations that we never reopened the discussion. The thing had been in the air for some time ; we had recognised it now ; the widening breach between us was confessed. My own feelings were curiously divided. It is remarkable that my very real affection for Margaret only became evident to me with this quarrel. The changes of the heart are very subtle changes. I am quite unaware how or when my early romantic love for her purity and beauty and high-principled devotion evaporated from my life ; but I do know that quite early in my parliamentary days there had come a vague, unconfessed resentment at the tie that seemed to hold me in servitude to her standards of private living and public act. I felt I was caught, and none the less so because it had been my own act

to rivet on my shackles. So long as I still held myself bound
to her that resentment grew. Now, since I had broken my
bonds and taken my line it withered again, and I could think
of Margaret with a returning kindliness.

But I still felt embarrassment with her. I felt myself
dependent upon her for house room and food and social
support, as it were under false pretences. I would have liked
to have separated our financial affairs altogether. But I knew
that to raise the issue would have seemed a last brutal in-
delicacy. So I tried almost furtively to keep my personal
expenditure within the scope of the private income I made by
writing, and we went out together in her motor brougham,
dined and made appearances, met politely at breakfast—
parted at night with a kiss upon her cheek. The locking of her
door upon me, which at that time I quite understood, which
I understand now, became for a time in my mind, through
some obscure process of the soul, an offence. I never crossed
the landing to her room again.

In all this matter, and, indeed, in all my relations with
Margaret, I perceive now I behaved badly and foolishly. My
manifest blunder is that I, who was several years older than
she, much subtler and in many ways wiser, never in any
measure sought to guide and control her. After our marriage
I treated her always as an equal, and let her go her way ; held
her responsible for all the weak and ineffective and unfortunate
things she said and did to me. She wasn't clever enough to
justify that. It wasn't fair to expect her to sympathise,
anticipate and understand. I ought to have taken care of
her, roped her to me when it came to crossing the difficult
places. If I had loved her more, and wiselier and more
tenderly, if there had not been the consciousness of my financial
dependence on her always stiffening my pride, I think she
would have moved with me from the outset and left the
Liberals with me. But she did not get any inkling of the ends
I sought in my change of sides. It must have seemed to her
inexplicable perversity. She had, I knew—for surely I knew
it then !—an immense capacity for loyalty and devotion.
There she was with these treasures untouched, neglected and
perplexed. A woman who loves wants to give. It is the
duty and business of the man she has married for love to help
her to help and give. But I was stupid. My eyes had never
been opened. I was stiff with her and difficult to her, because
even on my wedding morning there had been, deep down in my
soul, voiceless though present, something weakly protesting,
a faint perception of wrong-doing, the infinitesimally small,
slow-multiplying germs of shame.

§ 3

I made my breach with the party on the Budget.

In many ways I was disposed to regard the 1909 Budget as

a fine piece of statecraft. Its production was certainly a very unexpected display of vigour on the Liberal side. But, on the whole, this movement towards collectivist organisation on the part of the Liberals rather strengthened than weakened my resolve to cross the floor of the House. It made it more necessary, I thought, to leaven the purely obstructive and reactionary elements that were at once manifest in the opposition. I assailed the land taxation proposals in one main speech, and a series of minor speeches in committee. The line of attack I chose was that the land was a great public service that needed to be controlled on broad and far-sighted lines. I had no objection to its nationalisation, but I did object most strenuously to the idea of leaving it in private hands, and attempting to produce beneficial social results through the pressure of taxation upon the land-owning class. That might break it up in an utterly disastrous way. The drift of the Government proposals was all in the direction of sweating the landowner to get immediate values from his property, and such a course of action was bound to give us an irritated and vindictive land-owning class, the class upon which we had hitherto relied—not unjustifiably—for certain broad, patriotic services and an influence upon our collective judgments that no other class seemed prepared to exercise. Abolish landlordism if you will, I said, buy it out, but do not drive it to a defensive fight, and leave it still sufficiently strong and wealthy to become a malcontent element in your state. You have taxed and controlled the brewer and the publican until the outraged Liquor Interest has become a national danger. You now propose to do the same thing on a larger scale. You turn a class which has many fine and truly aristocratic traditions towards revolt, and there is nothing in these or any other of your proposals that shows any sense of the need for leadership to replace these traditional leaders you are ousting. This was the substance of my case, and I hammered at it not only in the House, but in the Press. . . .

The Kinghampstead division remained for some time insensitive to my defection.

Then it woke up suddenly, and began, in the columns of the *Kinghampstead Guardian*, an indignant, confused outcry. I was treated to an open letter, signed " Junius Secundus," and I replied in provocative terms. There were two thinly attended public meetings at different ends of the constituency, and then I had a correspondence with my old friend Parvill, the photographer, which ended in my seeing a deputation.

My impression is that it consisted of about eighteen or twenty people. They had had to come upstairs to me and they were manifestly full of indignation and a little short of breath. There was Parvill himself, J.P., dressed wholly in black—I think to mark his sense of the occasion—and curiously suggestive in his respect for my character and his concern for the honourableness of the *Kinghampstead Guardian* editor, of Mark Antony at the funeral of Cæsar. There was Mrs. Bulger, also in mourning; she had never abandoned the widow's streamers since the death of her husband ten years ago, and her loyalty to Liberalism of the severest type was part as it were of her weeds. There was a nephew of Sir Roderick Newton, a bright young Hebrew of the graver type, and a couple of dissenting ministers in high collars and hats that stopped half-way between the bowler of this world and the shovel-hat of heaven. There was also a young solicitor from Lurky done in the horsey style, and there was a very little nervous man with a high brow and a face contracting below as though the jaw-bones and teeth had been taken out and the features compressed. The rest of the deputation, which included two other public-spirited ladies and several ministers of religion, might have been raked out of any omnibus going Strandward during the May meetings. They thrust Parvill forward as spokesman, and manifested a strong disposition to say " Hear, hear ! " to his more strenuous protests provided my eye wasn't upon them at the time.

I regarded this appalling deputation as Parvill's apologetic but quite definite utterances drew to an end. I had a moment of vision. Behind them I saw the wonderful array of skeleton forces that stand for public opinion, that are as much public opinion as exists indeed at the present time. The whole process of politics which bulks so solidly in history seemed for that clairvoyant instant but a froth of petty motives above abysms of indifference. . . .

Some one had finished. I perceived I had to speak.

" Very well," I said, " I won't keep you long in replying. I'll resign if there isn't a dissolution before next February, and if there is I shan't stand again. You don't want the bother and expense of a bye-election (approving murmurs) if it can be avoided. But I may tell you plainly now that I don't think it will be necessary for me to resign, and the sooner you find my successor the better for the party. The Lords are in a corner ; they've got to fight now or never, and I think they will throw out the Budget. Then they will go on fighting. It is a fight that will last for years. They have a sort of social discipline, and you haven't. You Liberals will find yourselves with a country behind you, vaguely indignant perhaps, but totally unprepared with any ideas whatever in the matter, face to face with the problem of bringing the British constitution up to date. Anything may happen, provided only that it is sufficiently absurd. If the King backs the Lords—and I don't see why he shouldn't—you have no Republican movement whatever to fall back upon. You lost it during the Era of Good Taste. The country, I say, is destitute of ideas, and you have no ideas to give it. I don't see what you will do. . .

For my own part, I mean to spend a year or so between a
window and my writing-desk."

I paused. " I think, gentlemen," began Parvill, " that we
hear all this with very great regret. . . ."

§ 4

My estrangement from Margaret stands in my memory
now as something that played itself out within the four walls
of our house in Radnor Square, which was, indeed, confined
to those limits. I went to and fro between my house and the
House of Commons, and the dining-rooms and clubs and
offices in which we were preparing our new developments, in
a state of aggressive and energetic dissociation, in the nascent
state, as a chemist would say. I was free now, and greedy for
fresh combination. I had a tremendous sense of released
energies. I had got back to the sort of thing I could do, and
to the work that had been shaping itself for so long in my
imagination. Our purpose now was plain, bold and extraordinarily congenial. We meant no less then to organise a
new movement in English thought and life, to resuscitate a
Public Opinion and prepare the ground for a revised and
renovated ruling culture.

For a time I seemed quite wonderfully able to do whatever
I wanted to do. Shoesmith responded to my first advances.
We decided to create a weekly paper as our nucleus, and
Crupp and I set to work forthwith to collect a group of writers
and speakers, including Esmeer, Britten, Lord Gane, Neal, and
one or two younger men, which should constitute a more or
less definite editorial council about me, and meet at a weekly
lunch on Tuesday to sustain our general co-operations. We
marked our claim upon Toryism even in the colour of our
wrapper, and spoke of ourselves collectively as the Blue
Weeklies. But our lunches were open to all sorts of guests,
and our deliberations were never of a character to control me
effectively in my editorial decisions. My only influential
councillor at first was old Britten, who became my sub-editor.
It was curious how we two had picked up our ancient intimacy
again and resumed the easy give and take of our speculative
dreaming schoolboy days.

For a time my life centred altogether upon this journalistic
work. Britten was an experienced journalist, and I had most
of the necessary instincts for the business. We meant to make
the paper right and good down to the smallest detail, and we
set ourselves at this with extraordinary zeal. It wasn't our
intention to show our political motives too markedly at first,
and through all the dust-storm and tumult and stress of the
political struggle of 1910, we made a little intellectual oasis of
good art criticism and good writing. It was the firm belief of
nearly all of us that the Lords were destined to be beaten

badly in 1910, and our game was the longer game of reconstruction that would begin when the shouting and tumult of
that immediate conflict were over.   Meanwhile we had to get
into touch with just as many good minds as possible.

As we felt our feet, I developed slowly and carefully a
broadly conceived and consistent political attitude.   As I will
explain later, we were feminist from the outset, though that
caused Shoesmith and Gane great searching of heart ; we
developed Esmeer's House of Lords reform scheme into a
general cult of the aristocratic virtues, and we did much to
humanise and liberalise the narrow excellencies of that Break-
up of the Poor Law agitation, which had been organised
originally by Beatrice and Sidney Webb.   In addition, without
any very definite explanation to any one but Esmeer and
Isabel Rivers, and as if it was quite a small matter, I set myself
to secure a uniform philosophical quality in our columns.

That, indeed, was the peculiar virtue and characteristic of
the *Blue Weekly*.   I was now very definitely convinced that
much of the confusion and futility of contemporary thought
was due to the general need of metaphysical training. . . .
The great mass of people—and not simply common people,
but people active and influential in intellectual things—are
still quite untrained in the methods of thought and absolutely
innocent of any criticism of method ; it is scarcely a caricature
to call their thinking a crazy patchwork, discontinuous and
chaotic.   They arrive at conclusions by a kind of accident,
and do not suspect any other way may be found to their
attainment.   A stage above this general condition stands that
minority of people who have at some time or other discovered
general terms and a certain use for generalisations.   They are
—to fall back on the ancient technicality—Realists of a crude
sort.   When I say Realist of course I mean Realist as opposed
to Nominalist, and not Realist in the almost diametrically
different sense of opposition to Idealist.   Such are the Baileys ;
such, to take their great prototype, was Herbert Spencer (who
couldn't read Kant) ; such are whole regiments of prominent
and entirely self-satisfied contemporaries.   They go through
queer little processes of definition and generalisation and
deduction with the completest belief in the validity of the
intellectual instrument they are using.   They are Realists—
Cocksurists—in matter of fact ; sentimentalists in behaviour.
The Baileys having got to this glorious stage in mental development—it is glorious because it has no doubts—were
always talking about training " Experts " to apply the same
simple process to all the affairs of mankind.   Well, Realism
isn't the last word of human wisdom.   Modest-minded people,
doubtful people, subtle people, and the like—the kind of
people William James writes of as " tough-minded," go on
beyond this methodical happiness, and are for ever after
critical of premises and terms.   They are truer—and less con-

fident.   They have reached scepticism and the artistic method.
They have emerged into the new Nominalism.

Both Isabel and I believe firmly that these differences of intellectual method matter profoundly in the affairs of mankind,
that the collective mind of this intricate complex modern
state can only function properly upon neo-Nominalist lines.
This has always been her side of our mental co-operation rather
than mine.   Her mind has the light movement that goes so
often with natural mental power ; she has a wonderful art in
illustration, and, as the reader probably knows already, she
writes of metaphysical matters with a rare charm and vividness.   So far there has been no collection of her papers published, but they are to be found not only in the *Blue Weekly*
columns but scattered about the monthlies ; many people must
be familiar with her style.   It was an intention we did much
to realise before our private downfall, that we would use the
Blue Weekly to maintain a stream of suggestion against crude
thinking, and at last scarcely a week passed but some popular
distinction, some large imposing generalisation, was touched
to flaccidity by her pen or mine. . . .

I was at great pains to give my philosophical, political and
social matter the best literary and critical backing we could get
in London.   I hunted sedulously for good descriptive writing
and good criticism ; I was indefatigable in my readiness to
hear and consider, if not to accept advice ; I watched every
corner of the paper, and had a dozen men alert to get me special
matter of the sort that draws in the unattached reader.   The
chief danger on the literary side of a weekly is that it should fall
into the hands of some particular school, and this I watched for
closely.   It seems almost impossible to get vividness of apprehension and breadth of view together in the same critic.   So it
falls to the wise editor to secure the first and impose the second.
Directly I detected the shrill partisan note in our criticism, the
attempt to puff a poor thing because it was " in the right
direction," or damn a vigorous piece of work because it wasn't,
I tackled the man and had it out with him.   Our pay was good
enough for that to matter a good deal. . . .

Our distinctive little blue and white poster kept up its neat
persistent appeal to the public eye, and before 1911 was out,
the *Blue Weekly* was printing twenty pages of publishers' advertisements, and went into all the clubs in London and three-
quarters of the country houses where week-end parties gather
together.   Its sale by newsagents and bookstalls grew steadily.
One got more and more the reassuring sense of being discussed,
and influencing discussion.

§ 5

Our office was at the very top of a big building near the end
of Adelphi Terrace ; the main window beside my desk, a big
undivided window of plate glass, looked out upon Cleopatra's

Needle, the corner of the Hotel Cecil, the fine arches of Waterloo Bridge, and the long sweep of south bank with its shot
towers and chimneys, past Bankside to the dimly seen piers of
the great bridge below the Tower. The dome of St. Paul's
just floated into view on the left against the hotel façade. By
night and day, in every light and atmosphere, it was a beautiful
and various view, alive as a throbbing heart ; a perpetual flow
of traffic ploughed and splashed the streaming silver of the
river, and by night the shapes of things became velvet black
and grey, and the water a shining mirror of steel, wearing corus-
cating gems of light. In the foreground the Embankment
trams sailed glowing by, across the water advertisements
flashed and flickered, trains went and came and a rolling drift of
smoke reflected unseen fires. By day that spectacle was sometimes a marvel of shining wet and wind-cleared atmosphere,
sometimes a mystery of drifting fog, sometimes a miracle of
crowded details, minutely fine.

As I think of that view, so variously spacious in effect, I am
back there, and this sunlit paper might be lamp-lit and lying on
my old desk. I see it all again, feel it all again. In the foreground is a green shaded lamp and crumpled galley slips and
paged proofs and letters, two or three papers in manuscript,
and so forth. In the shadows are chairs and another table
bearing papers and books, a rotating bookcase dimly seen, a
long window-seat black in the darkness, and then the cool un-
broken spectacle of the window. How often I would watch
some tram-car, some string of barges go from me slowly out of
sight. The people were black animalculæ by day, clustering,
collecting, dispersing ; by night they were phantom face-
specks coming, vanishing, stirring obscurely between light and
shade.

I recall many hours at my desk in that room before the crisis
came, hours full of the peculiar happiness of effective strenuous
work. Once some piece of writing went on, holding me intent
and forgetful of time until I looked up from the warm circle of
my electric lamp to see the eastward sky above the pale silhouette of the Tower Bridge, flushed and banded brightly with
the dawn.

CHAPTER FOUR

THE BESETTING OF SEX

§ 1

ART is selection and so is most autobiography. But I am concerned with a more tangled business than selection, I want to show a contemporary man in relation to the state and social usage, and the social organism in relation to that man. To tell my story at all I have to simplify. I have given now the broad lines of my political development, and how I passed from my initial liberal-socialism to the conception of a constructive aristocracy. I have tried to set that out in the form of a man discovering himself. Incidentally that self-development led to a profound breach with my wife. One has read stories before of husband and wife speaking severally two different languages and coming to an understanding. But Margaret and I began in her dialect, and, as I came more and more to use my own, diverged.

I had thought when I married that the matter of womankind had ended for me. I have tried to tell all that sex and women had been to me up to my married life with Margaret and our fatal entanglement, tried to show the queer, crippled, embarrassed and limited way in which these interests break upon the life of a young man under contemporary conditions. I do not think my lot was a very exceptional one. I missed the chance of sisters and girl playmates, but that is not an uncommon misadventure in an age of small families; I never came to know any woman at all intimately until I was married to Margaret. My earlier love affairs were encounters of sex, under conditions of furtiveness and adventure that made them things in themselves, restricted and unilluminating. From a boyish disposition to be mystical and worshipping towards women I had passed into a disregardful attitude, as though women were things inferior or irrelevant, disturbers in great affairs. For a time Margaret had blotted out all other women; she was so different and so near; she was like a person who stands suddenly in front of a little window through which one has been surveying a crowd. She didn't become womankind for me so much as eliminate womankind from my world. . . . And then came this secret separation. . . .

Until this estrangement and the rapid and uncontrollable development of my relations with Isabel which chanced to follow it, I seemed to have solved the problem of women by marriage and disregard. I thought these things were over. I went about my career with Margaret beside me, her brow slightly knit, her manner faintly strenuous, helping, helping; and if we had not altogether abolished sex we had at least so circumscribed and isolated it that it would not have affected the general tenor of our lives in the slightest degree if we had.

And then, clothing itself more and more in the form of Isabel and her problems, this old, this fundamental obsession of my life returned. The thing stole upon my mind so that I was unaware of its invasion and how it was changing our long intimacy. I have already compared the lot of the modern publicist to Machiavelli writing in his study ; in his day women and sex were as disregarded in these high affairs as, let us say, the chemistry of air or the will of the beasts in the fields ; in ours the case has altogether changed, and woman has come now to stand beside the tall candles, half in the light, half in the mystery of the shadows, besetting, interrupting, demanding unrelentingly an altogether unprecedented attention. I feel that in these matters my life has been almost typical of my time. Woman insists upon her presence. She is no longer a mere physical need, an æsthetic byplay, a sentimental background ; she is a moral and intellectual necessity in a man's life. She comes to the politician and demands, Is she a child or a citizen ? Is she a thing or a soul ? She comes to the individual man, as she came to me, and asks, Is she a cherished weakling or an equal mate, an unavoidable helper ? Is she to be tried and trusted or guarded and controlled, bond or free ? For if she is a mate, one must at once trust more and exact more, exacting toil, courage, and the hardest, most necessary thing of all, the clearest, most shameless, explicitness of understanding. . . .

§ 3

In all my earlier imaginings of statecraft I had tacitly assumed either that the relations of the sexes were all right or that anyhow they didn't concern the state. It was a matter they, whoever " they " were, had to settle among themselves. That sort of disregard was possible then. But even before 1906 there were endless intimations that the dams holding back great reservoirs of discussion were crumbling. We political schemers were ploughing wider than any one had ploughed before in the field of social reconstruction. We had also, we realised, to plough deeper. We had to plough down at last to the passionate elements of sexual relationship and examine and decide upon them.

The signs multiplied. In a year or so half the police of the metropolis were scarce sufficient to protect the House from one clamorous aspect of the new problem. The members went about Westminster with an odd, new sense of being beset. A good proportion of us kept up the pretence that the Vote for Women was an isolated fad, and the agitation an epidemic madness that would presently pass. But it was manifest to any one who sought more than comfort in the matter that the

streams of women and sympathisers and money forthcoming
marked far deeper and wider things than an idle fancy for the
franchise.   The existing laws and conventions of relationship
between Man and Woman were just as unsatisfactory a disorder, as anything else in our tumbled confusion of a world,
and that also was coming to bear upon statecraft.

My first parliament was the parliament of the Suffragettes.
I don't propose to tell here of that amazing campaign, with its
absurdities and follies, its courage and devotion.   There were
aspects of that unquenchable agitation that were absolutely
heroic and aspects that were absolutely pitiful.   It was unreasonable, unwise, and, except for its one central insistence,
astonishingly incoherent.   It was amazingly effective.   The
very incoherence of the demand witnessed, I think, to the forces
that lay behind it.   It wasn't a simple argument based on a
simple assumption ; it was the first crude expression of a great
mass and mingling of convergent feelings, of a widespread,
confused persuasion among modern educated women that the
conditions of their relations with men were oppressive, ugly,
dishonouring, and had to be altered.   They had not merely
adopted the Vote as a symbol of equality ; it was fairly manifest to me that, given it, they meant to use it, and to use it
perhaps even vindictively and blindly, as a weapon against
many things they had every reason to hate. . . .

I remember with exceptional vividness that great night early
in the session of 1909 when—I think it was—fifty or sixty
women went to prison.   I had been dining at the Barhams',
and Lord Barham and I came down from the direction of St.
James's Park into a crowd and a confusion outside the Caxton
Hall.   We found ourselves drifting with an immense multitude
towards Parliament Square and parallel with a silent, close-
packed column of girls and women, for the most part white-
faced and intent.   I still remember the effect of their faces
upon me.   It was quite different from the general effect of
staring about and divided attention one gets in a political procession of men.   There was an expression of heroic tension.

There had been a pretty deliberate appeal on the part of the
women's organisers to the Unemployed, who had been demon-
strating throughout that winter, to join forces with the movement, and the result was shown in the quality of the crowd
upon the pavement.   It was an ugly, dangerous-looking crowd,
but as yet good-tempered and sympathetic.   When at last we
got within sight of the House the square was a seething sea of
excited people, and the array of police on horse and on foot
might have been assembled for a revolutionary outbreak.
There were dense masses of people up Whitehall, and right on
to Westminster Bridge.   The scuffle that ended in the arrests
was the poorest explosion to follow such stupendous preparations. . . .

§ 3

Later on in that year the women began a new attack. Day and night, and all through the long nights of the Budget sittings, at all the piers of the gates of New Palace Yard and at St. Stephen's Porch, stood women pickets, and watched us silently and reproachfully as we went to and fro. They were women of all sorts, though of course the independent worker-class predominated. There were grey-headed old ladies standing there, sturdily charming in the rain; battered-looking, ambiguous women, with something of the desperate bitterness of battered women showing in their eyes; north-country factory girls; cheaply-dressed suburban women; trim, comfortable mothers of families; valiant-eyed girl graduates and undergraduates; lank, hungry-looking creatures, who stirred one's imagination; one very dainty little woman in deep mourning, I recall, grave and steadfast, with eyes fixed on distant things. Some of those women looked defiant, some timidly aggressive, some full of the stir of adventure, some drooping with cold and fatigue. The supply never ceased. I had a mortal fear that somehow the supply might halt or cease. I found that continual siege of the legislature extraordinarily impressive—infinitely more impressive than the feeble-forcible " ragging " of the more militant section. I thought of the appeal that must be going through the country, summoning the women from countless scattered homes, rooms, colleges, to Westminster.

I remember too the petty little difficulty I felt whether I should ignore these pickets altogether, or lift a hat as I hurried past with averted eyes, or look them in the face as I did so. Towards the end the House evoked an etiquette of salutation.

§ 4

There was a tendency, even on the part of its sympathisers, to treat the whole suffrage agitation as if it were a disconnected issue, irrelevant to all other broad developments of social and political life. We struggled, all of us, to ignore the indicating finger it thrust out before us. " Your schemes, for all their bigness," it insisted to our reluctant, averted minds, " still don't go down to the essential things. . . ."

We have to go deeper, or our inadequate children's insufficient children will starve amidst harvests of earless futility. That conservatism which works in every class to preserve in its essentials the habitual daily life is all against a profounder treatment of political issues. The politician, almost as absurdly as the philosopher, tends constantly, in spite of magnificent preludes, vast intimations, to specialise himself out of the reality he has so stupendously summoned—he bolts back to littleness. The world has to be moulded anew, he continues to admit, but without, he adds, any risk of upsetting his week-end visits, his morning cup of tea.

The discussion of the relations of men and women disturbs every one. It reacts upon the private life of every one who attempts it. And at any particular time only a small minority have a personal interest in changing the established state of affairs. Habit and interest are in a constantly recruited majority against conscious change and adjustment in these matters. Drift rules us. The great mass of people, and an overwhelming proportion of influential people, are people who have banished their dreams and made their compromise. Wonderful and beautiful possibilities are no longer to be thought about. They have given up any aspirations for intense love, for splendid offspring, for keen delights, have accepted a culti-vated kindliness and an uncritical sense of righteousness as their compensation. It's a settled affair with them, a settled, dangerous affair. Most of them fear, and many hate, the slightest reminder of those abandoned dreams. As Dayton once said to the Pentagram Circle, when we were discussing the problem of a universal marriage and divorce law through-out the Empire, " I am for leaving all these things alone." And then, with a groan in his voice, " Leave them alone ! Leave them all alone ! "

That, in a note of suppressed passion, was his whole speech for the evening ; and presently, against all our etiquette, he got up and went out.

For some years after my marriage, I too was for leaving them alone. I developed a dread and dislike for romance, for emotional music, for the human figure in art—turning my heart to landscape. I wanted to sneer at lovers and their ecstasies, and was uncomfortable until I found the effective sneer. In matters of private morals these were my most uncharitable years. I didn't want to think of these things any more for ever. I hated the people whose talk or practice showed they were not of my opinion. I wanted to believe that their views were immoral and objectionable and contemptible, because I had decided to treat them as at that level. I was, in fact, falling into the attitude of the normal decent man.

And yet one cannot help thinking ! The sensible moralised man finds it hard to escape the stream of suggestion that there are still dreams beyond these commonplace acquiescences—the appeal of beauty suddenly shining upon one, the mothlike stirrings of serene summer nights, the sweetness of distant music. . . .

It is one of the paradoxical factors in our public life at the present time, which penalises abandonment to love so abun-dantly and so heavily, that power, influence and control fall largely to unencumbered people and sterile people and people who have married for passionless purposes, people whose very deficiency in feeling has left them free to follow ambition, people beauty-blind, who don't understand what it is to fall in love, what it is to desire children or have them, what it is to feel in their blood and bodies the supreme claim of good births and selective births above all other affairs in life, people almost of necessity averse from this most fundamental aspect of existence. . . .

§ 5

It wasn't, however, my deepening sympathy with and understanding of the position of women in general, or the change in my ideas about all these intimate things my fast friendship with Isabel was bringing about, that led me to the heretical views I have in the last five years dragged from the region of academic and timid discussion into the field of practical politics. Those influences, no doubt, have converged to the same end, and given me a powerful emotional push upon my road, but it was a broader and colder view of things that first determined me in my attempt to graft the Endowment of Motherhood in some form or other upon British Imperialism. Now that I am exiled from the political world, it is possible to estimate just how effectually that grafting has been done.

I have explained how the ideas of a trained aristocracy and a universal education grew to paramount importance in my political scheme. It is but a short step from this to the question of the quantity and quality of births in the community, and from that again to these forbidden and fear-beset topics of marriage, divorce and the family organisation. A sporadic discussion of these aspects had been going on for years, a Eugenic society existed, and articles on the Falling Birth Rate, and the Rapid Multiplication of the Unfit were staples of the monthly magazines. But beyond an intermittent scolding of prosperous childless people in general—one never addressed them in particular—nothing was done towards arresting those adverse processes. Almost against my natural inclination, I found myself forced to go into these things. I came to the conclusion that under modern conditions the isolated private family, based on the existing marriage contract, was failing in its work. It wasn't producing enough children, and children good enough and well trained enough for the demands of the developing civilised state. Our civilisation was growing outwardly, and decaying in its intimate substance ; and unless it was presently to collapse, some very extensive and courageous reorganisation was needed. The old haphazard system of pairing, qualified more and more by worldly discretions, no longer secures a young population numerous enough or good enough for the growing needs and possibilities of our Empire. Statecraft sits weaving splendid garments, no doubt, but with a puny, ugly, insufficient baby in the cradle.

No one so far has dared to take up this problem as a present question for statecraft, but it comes unheralded, unadvocated, and sits at every legislative board. Every improvement is provisional except the improvement of the race, and it became more and more doubtful to me if we were improving the race at all! Splendid and beautiful and courageous people must come together and have children, women with their fine senses and glorious devotion must be freed from the net that compels them to be celibate, compels them to be childless and useless, or to bear children ignobly to men whom need and ignorance and the treacherous pressure of circumstances have forced upon them. We all know that, and so few dare even to whisper it for fear that they should seem, in seeking to save the family, to threaten its existence. It is as if a party of pigmies in a not too capacious room had been joined by a carnivorous giant—and decided to go on living happily by cutting him dead. . . .

The problem the developing civilised state has to solve is how it can get the best possible increase under the best possible conditions. I became more and more convinced that the independent family unit of to-day, in which the man is master of the wife and owner of the children, in which all are dependent upon him, subordinated to his enterprises and liable to follow his fortunes up or down, does not supply anything like the best conceivable conditions. We want to modernise the family footing altogether. An enormous premium both in pleasure and competitive efficiency is put upon voluntary childlessness, and enormous inducements are held out to women to subordinate instinctive and selective preferences to social and material considerations.

The practical reaction of modern conditions upon the old tradition of the family is this : that beneath the pretence that nothing is changing, secretly and with all the unwholesomeness of secrecy, everything is changed. Offspring fall away, the birth-rate falls, and falls most among just the most efficient and active and best adapted classes in the community. The species is recruited from among its failures and from among less civilised aliens. Contemporary civilisations are in effect burning the best of their possible babies in the furnaces that run the machinery. In the United States the native Anglo-American strain has scarcely increased at all since 1830, and in most Western European countries the same is probably true of the ablest and most energetic elements in the community. The women of these classes still remain legally and practically dependent and protected, with the only natural excuse for their dependence gone. . . .

The modern world becomes an immense spectacle of unsatisfactory groupings ; here childless couples bored to death in the hopeless effort to sustain an incessant honeymoon, here homes in which a solitary child grows unsocially, here small two- or three-child homes that do no more than continue the culture of the parents at a great social cost, here numbers of unhappy, educated but childless married women, here careless, decivilised fecund homes, here orphanages and asylums for the heedlessly begotten. It is just the disorderly proliferation of Bromstead over again, in lives instead of in houses.

What is the good, what is the common sense, of rectifying boundaries, pushing research and discovery, building cities, improving all the facilities of life, making great fleets, waging wars, while this aimless decadence remains the quality of the biological outlook ? . . .

It is difficult now to trace how I changed from my early aversion until I faced this mass of problems. But so far back as 1910 I had it clear in my mind that I would rather fail utterly than participate in all the surrenders of mind and body that are implied in Dayton's snarl of " Leave it alone ; leave it all alone ! " Marriage and the beginning and care of children, is the very ground substance in the life of the community. In a world in which everything changes, in which fresh methods, fresh adjustments and fresh ideas perpetually renew the circumstances of life, it is preposterous that we should not even examine into these matters, should rest content to be ruled by the uncriticised traditions of a barbaric age.

Now it seems to me that the solution of this problem is also the solution of the woman's individual problem. The two go together, are right and left of one question. The only conceivable way out from our *impasse* lies in the recognition of parentage, that is to say of adequate mothering, as no longer a chance product of individual passions but a service rendered to the State. Women must become less and less subordinated to individual men, since this works out in a more or less complete limitation, waste and sterilisation of their essentially social function ; they must become more and more subordinated as individually independent citizens to the collective purpose. Or to express the thing by a familiar phrase, the highly organised, scientific state we desire must, if it is to exist at all, base itself not upon the irresponsible man-ruled family, but upon the matriarchal family, the citizenship and freedom of women and the public endowment of motherhood.

After two generations of confused and experimental revolt it grows clear to modern women that a conscious, deliberate motherhood and mothering is their special function in the State, and that a personal subordination to an individual man with an unlimited power of control over this intimate and supreme duty is a degradation. No contemporary woman of education put to the test is willing to recognise any claim a man can make upon her but the claim of her freely-given devotion to him. She wants the reality of her choice and she means " family " while a man too often means only possession. This alters the spirit of the family relationships fundamentally. Their form remains just what it was when woman was esteemed a pretty, desirable and incidentally a child-producing, chattel.

Against these time-honoured ideas the new spirit of woman-hood struggles in shame, astonishment, bitterness and tears. . . .

I confess myself altogether feminist. I have no doubts in the matter. I want this coddling and brow-beating of women to cease. I want to see women come in, free and fearless, to a full participation in the collective purpose of mankind. Women, I am convinced, are as fine as men ; they can be as wise as men ; they are capable of far greater devotion than men. I want to see them citizens, with a marriage law framed primarily for them and for their protection and the good of the race, and not for men's satisfactions. I want to see them bearing and rearing good children in the State as a generously rewarded public duty and service, choosing their husbands freely and discerningly, and in no way enslaved by or sub-ordinated to the men they have chosen. The social conscious-ness of women seems to me an unworked, an almost untouched mine of wealth for the constructive purpose of the world. I want to change the respective values of the family group alto-gether, and make the home indeed the woman's kingdom and the mother the owner and responsible guardian of her children.

It is no use pretending that this is not novel and revolu-tionary ; it is. The Endowment of Motherhood implies a new method of social organisation, a rearrangement of the social unit, untried in human experience—as untried as electric traction or flying was in 1800. Of course, it may work out to modify men's ideas of marriage profoundly. To me that is a secondary consideration. I do not believe that particular assertion myself, because I am convinced that a practical monogamy is a psychological necessity to the mass of civilised people. But even if I did believe it I should still keep to my present line, because it is the only line that will prevent a highly organised civilisation from ending in biological decay. The public Endowment of Motherhood is the only possible way which will ensure the permanently developing civilised state at which all constructive minds are aiming. A point is reached in the life-history of a civilisation when either this re-construction must be effected or the quality and *morale* of the population prove insufficient for the needs of the developing organisation. It is not so much moral decadence that will destroy us as moral inadaptability. The old code fails under the new needs. The only alternative to this profound recon-struction is a decay in human quality and social collapse. Either this unprecedented rearrangement must be achieved by our civilisation, or it must presently come upon a phase of disorder and crumble and perish, as Rome perished, as France declines, as the strain of the Pilgrim Fathers dwindles out of America. Whatever hope there may be in the attempt therefore, there is no alternative to the attempt.

§ 6

I wanted political success now dearly enough, but not at the price of constructive realities. These questions were no doubt monstrously dangerous in the political world ; there wasn't a politician alive who didn't look scared at the mention of " The Family," but if raising these issues was essential to the social reconstructions on which my life was set, that did not matter. It only implied that I should take them up with deliberate caution. There was no release because of risk or difficulty.

The question of whether I should commit myself to some open project in this direction was going on in my mind concurrently with my speculations about a change of party, like bass and treble in a complex piece of music. The two drew to a conclusion together. I would not only go over to Imperialism, but I would attempt to biologise Imperialism.

I thought at first that I was undertaking a monstrous uphill task. But as I came to look into the possibilities of the matter, a strong persuasion grew up in my mind that this panic fear of legislative proposals affecting the family basis was excessive, that things were much riper for development in this direction than old experienced people out of touch with the younger generation imagined, that to phrase the thing in a parliamentary fashion, "something might be done in the constituencies " with the Endowment of Motherhood forthwith, provided only that it was made perfectly clear that anything a sane person could possibly intend by "morality " was left untouched by these proposals.

I went to work very carefully. I got Roper of the *Daily Telephone* and Burkett of the *Dial* to try over a silly-season discussion of State Help for Mothers, and I put a series of articles on eugenics, upon the fall in the birth-rate, and similar topics in the *Blue Weekly*, leading up to a tentative and generalised advocacy of the public endowment of the nation's children. I was more and more struck by the acceptance won by a sober and restrained presentation of this suggestion.

And then, in the fourth year of the *Blue Weekly's* career, came the Handitch election, and I was forced by the clamour of my antagonist, and very willingly forced, to put my convictions to the test. I returned triumphantly to Westminster with the Public Endowment of Motherhood as part of my open profession and with the full approval of the party press. Applauding benches of Imperialists cheered me on my way to the table between the whips.

That second time I took the oath I was not one of a crowd of new members, but salient, an event, a symbol of profound changes and new purposes in the national life.

Here it is my political book comes to an end, and in a sense my book ends altogether. For the rest is but to tell how I was swept out of this great world of political possibilities. I close this Third Book as I opened it, with an admission of difficulties and complexities ; but now with a pile of manuscript before me I have to confess them unsurmounted and still entangled.

Yet my aim was a final simplicity.   I have sought to show my growing realisation that the essential quality of all political and social effort is the development of a great race mind behind the interplay of individual lives.   That is the collective human reality, the basis of morality, the purpose of devotion. To that our lives must be given, from that will come the perpetual fresh release and further ennoblement of individual lives. . . .

I have wanted to make that idea of a collective mind play in this book the part United Italy plays in Machiavelli's *Prince*.   I have called it the hinterland of reality, shown it accumulating a dominating truth and rightness which must force men's now sporadic motives more and more into a disciplined and understanding relation to a plan.   And I have tried to indicate how I sought to serve this great clarification of our confusions. . . .

Now I come back to personality and the story of my self-betrayal, and how it is I have had to leave all that far-reaching scheme of mine, a mere project and beginning for other men to take or leave as it pleases them.

Book Four

Isabel

CHAPTER ONE

LOVE AND SUCCESS

§ 1

I COME to the most evasive and difficult part of my story, which is to tell how Isabel and I have made a common wreck of our joint lives.

It is not the telling of one simple disastrous accident. There was a vein in our natures that led to this collapse, gradually and at this point, and that it crept to the surface. One may indeed see our destruction—for politically we could not be more extinct if we had been shot dead—in the form of a catastrophe as disconnected and conclusive as a meteoric stone falling out of heaven upon two friends and crushing them both. But I do not think that is true to our situation or ourselves. We were not taken by surprise. The thing was in us and not from without, it was akin to our way of thinking and our habitual attitudes ; it had, for all its impulsive effect, a certain necessity. We might have escaped, no doubt, as two men at a hundred yards may shoot at each other with pistols for a considerable time and escape. But it isn't particularly reasonable to talk of the contrariety of fate if they both get hit.

Isabel and I were dangerous to each other for several years of friendship, and not quite unwittingly so.

In writing this, moreover, there is a very great difficulty in steering my way between two equally undesirable tones in the telling. In the first place I do not want to seem to confess my sins with a penitence I am very doubtful if I feel. Now that I have got Isabel we can no doubt count the cost of it and feel unquenchable regrets ; but I am not sure, if we could be put back now into such circumstances as we were in a year ago or two years ago, whether with my eyes fully open I should not do over again very much as I did. And on the other hand I do not want to justify the things we have done. We are two bad people—if there is to be any classification of good and bad at all, we have acted badly ; and quite apart from any other considerations we've largely wasted our own very great possibilities. But it is part of a queer humour that underlies all this, that I find myself slipping again and again into a sentimental treatment of our case that is as unpremeditated as it is insincere. When I am growing tired after a morning's writing I find the faint suggestion getting into every other sentence that our blunders and misdeeds embodied, after the fashion of the prophet Hosea, profound moral truths. Indeed, I feel so little confidence in my ability to keep this altogether out of my book that I warn the reader here that in spite of anything he may read elsewhere in the story, intimating however shyly an esoteric and exalted virtue in our proceedings, the plain truth of this business is that Isabel and I wanted each other with a want entirely formless, inconsiderate and overwhelming. And though I could tell you countless delightful and beautiful things about Isabel, were this a book in her praise, I cannot either analyse that want or account for its extreme intensity.

I will confess that deep in my mind there is a belief in a sort of wild rightness about any love that is fraught with beauty, but that eludes me and vanishes again, and is not, I feel, to be put with the real veracities and righteousness and virtues in the paddocks and menageries of human reason. . . .

We have already a child, and Margaret was childless, and I find myself prone to insist upon that as if it was a justification. But indeed when we became lovers there was small thought of Eugenics between us. Ours was a mutual and not a philoprogenitive passion. Old Nature behind us may have had such purposes with us, but it is not for us to annex her intentions by a moralising afterthought. There isn't, in fact, any decent justification for us whatever—at that the story must stand.

But if there is no justification there is at least a very effective excuse in the mental confusedness of our time. The evasion of that passionately thorough exposition of belief and of the grounds of morality, which is the outcome of the mercenary religious compromises of the late Victorian period, the stupid suppression of anything but the most timid discussion of sexual morality in our literature and drama, the pervading cultivated and protected muddle-headedness, leaves mentally vigorous people with relatively enormous possibilities of destruction and little effective help. They find themselves confronted by the habits and prejudices of manifestly commonplace people, and by that extraordinary patched-up Christianity, the cult of a " Bromsteadised " deity, diffused, scattered and aimless, which hides from examination and any possibility of faith behind the plea of good taste. A god about whom there is delicacy is far worse than no god at all. We are *forced* to be laws unto ourselves and to live experimentally. It is inevitable that a considerable fraction of just that bolder, more initiatory section of the intellectual community, the section that can least be spared from the collective life in a period of trial and change, will drift into such emotional crises and such disaster as overtook us. Most perhaps will escape, but many will go down, many more than the world can spare. It is the unwritten law of all our public life, and the same holds true of America, that an honest open scandal ends a career. England in the last quarter of a century has wasted half a dozen statesmen on this score ; she would, I believe, reject Nelson now if he sought to serve her. Is it wonderful that to us fretting here in exile this should seem the cruellest as well as the most foolish elimination of a necessary social element ?

It destroys no vice ; for vice hides by nature. It not only rewards dullness as if it were positive virtue, but sets an enormous premium upon hypocrisy. That is my case, and that is why I am telling this side of my story with so much explicitness.

§ 2

Ever since the Kinghamstead election I had maintained what seemed a desultory friendship with Isabel. At first it was rather Isabel kept it up than I. Whenever Margaret and I went down to that villa, with its three or four acres of garden and shrubbery about it, which fulfilled our election promise to live at Kinghamstead, Isabel would turn up in a state of frank cheerfulness, rejoicing at us, and talk all she was reading and thinking to me, and stay for the rest of the day. In her shameless liking for me she was as natural as a savage. She would exercise me vigorously at tennis, while Margaret lay and rested her back in the afternoon, or guide me for some long ramble that dodged the suburban and congested patches of the constituency with amazing skill. She took possession of me in that unabashed, straight-minded way a girl will sometimes adopt with a man, chose my path or criticised my game with a motherly solicitude for my welfare that was absurd and delightful. And we talked. We discussed and criticised the stories of novels, scraps of history, pictures, social questions, socialism, the policy of the Government. She was young and most unevenly informed, but she was amazingly sharp and quick and good. Never before in my life had I known a girl of her age, or a woman of her quality. I had never dreamt there was such talk in the world. Kinghamstead became a lightless place when she went to Oxford. Heaven knows how much that may not have precipitated my abandonment of the seat !

She went to Ridout College, Oxford, and that certainly weighed with me when presently after my breach with the Liberals various little undergraduate societies began to ask for lectures and discussions. I favoured Oxford. I declared openly I did so because of her. At that time I think we neither of us suspected the possibility of passion that lay like a coiled snake in the path before us. It seemed to us that we had the quaintest, most delightful friendship in the world ; she was my pupil, and I was her guide, philosopher and friend. People smiled indulgently—even Margaret smiled indulgently —at our attraction for one another.

Such friendships are not uncommon nowadays among easy-going, liberal-minded people. For the most part there's no sort of harm, as people say, in them. The two persons concerned are never supposed to think of the passionate love that hovers so close to the friendship, or if they do, then they banish the thought. I think we kept the thought as permanently in exile as any one could do. If it did in odd moments come into our heads we pretended elaborately it wasn't there.

Only we were both very easily jealous of each other's attention, and tremendously insistent upon each other's preference.

I remember once during the Oxford days an intimation that
should have set me thinking and, I suppose, discreetly disentangling myself. It was one Sunday afternoon, and it must
have been about May, for the trees and shrubs of Ridout
College were gay with blossom, and fresh with the new sharp
greens of spring. I had walked, talking with Isabel and a
couple of other girls, through the wide gardens of the place,
seen and criticised the new brick pond, nodded to the daughter
of this friend and that in the hammocks under the trees, and
picked a way among the scattered tea-parties on the lawn to
our own circle on the grass under a Siberian crab near the
great bay window. There I sat and ate great quantities of
cake, and discussed the tactics of the Suffragettes. I had
made some comments upon the spirit of the movement in an
address to the men in Pembroke, and it had got abroad, and a
group of girls and women dons were now having it out with me.

I forget the drift of the conversation, or what it was made
Isabel interrupt me. She did interrupt me. She had been
lying prone on the ground at my right hand, chin on fists,
listening thoughtfully, and I was sitting beside old Lady
Evershead on a garden seat. I turned to Isabel's voice, and
saw her face uplifted, and her dear cheeks and nose and forehead all splashed and barred with sunlight and the shadows of
the twigs of the trees behind me. And something—an infinite
tenderness, stabbed me. It was a keen physical feeling, like
nothing I had ever felt before. It had a quality of tears in it.
For the first time in my narrow and concentrated life another
human being had really thrust into my being and gripped my
very heart.

Our eyes met perplexed for an extraordinary moment.
Then I turned back and addressed myself a little stiffly to the
substance of her intervention. For some time I couldn't
look at her again.

From that time forth I knew I loved Isabel beyond measure.

Yet it is curious that it never occurred to me for a year or
so that this was likely to be a matter of passion between us.
I have told how definitely I put my imagination into harness
in those matters at my marriage, and I was living now in a
world of big interests, where there is neither much time nor
inclination for deliberate love-making. I suppose there is a
large class of men who never meet a girl or a woman without
thinking of sex, who meet a friend's daughter and decide :
" Mustn't get friendly with her—wouldn't *do*," and set invisible bars between themselves and all the wives in the world.
Perhaps that is the way to live. Perhaps there is no other
method than this effectual annihilation of half—and the most
sympathetic and attractive half—of the human beings in the
world, so far as any frank intercourse is concerned. I am

quite convinced anyhow that such a qualified intimacy as ours, such a drifting into the sense of possession, such untrammelled conversation with an invisible, implacable limit set just where the intimacy glows, is no kind of tolerable compromise. If men and women are to go so far together, they must be free to go as far as they may want to go, without the vindictive destruction that has come upon us. On the basis of the accepted codes the jealous people are right, and the liberal-minded ones are playing with fire. If people are not to love, then they must be kept apart. If they are not to be kept apart, then we must prepare for an unprecedented toleration of lovers.

Isabel was as unforeseeing as I to begin with, but sex marches into the life of an intelligent girl with demands and challenges far more urgent than the mere call of curiosity and satiable desire that comes to a young man. No woman yet has dared to tell the story of that unfolding. She attracted men, and she encouraged them and watched them and tested them and dismissed them, and concealed the substance of her thoughts about them in the way that seems instinctive in a natural-minded girl. There was even an engagement—amidst the protests and disapproval of the college authorities. I never saw the man, though she gave me a long history of the affair, to which I listened with a forced and insincere sympathy. She struck me oddly as taking the relationship for a thing in itself, and regardless of its consequences. After a time she became silent about him, and then threw him over ; and by that time, I think, for all that she was so much my junior, she knew more about herself and me than I was to know for several years to come.

We didn't see each other for some months after my resignation, but we kept up a frequent correspondence. She said twice over that she wanted to talk to me, that letters didn't convey what one wanted to say, and I went up to Oxford pretty definitely to see her—though I combined it with one or two other engagements—somewhere in February. Insensibly she had become important enough for me to make journeys for her.

But we didn't see very much of one another on that occasion. There was something in the air between us that made a faint embarrassment ; the mere fact, perhaps, that she had asked me to come up.

A year before she would have dashed off with me quite unscrupulously to talk alone, carried me off to her room for an hour with a minute of chaperonage to satisfy the rules. Now there was always some one or other near us that it seemed impossible to exorcise.

We went for a walk on the Sunday afternoon with old Fortescue, K.C., who'd come up to see his two daughters, both great friends of Isabel's, and some mute inglorious don whose name I forget, but who was in a state of marked admiration for her. The six of us played a game of conversational en-

tanglements throughout, and mostly I was impressing the
Fortescue girls with the want of mental concentration possible
in a rising politician. We went down Carfax, I remember, to
Folly Bridge, and inspected the Barges, and then back by way
of Merton to the Botanic Gardens and Magdalen Bridge. And
in the Botanic Gardens she got almost her only chance with me.

"Last months at Oxford," she said.

"And then ? " I asked.

"I'm coming to London," she said.

"To write ? "

She was silent for a moment. Then she said abruptly, with
that quick flush of hers and a sudden boldness in her eyes :
"I'm going to work with you. Why shouldn't I ? "

§ 3

Here, again, I suppose I had a fair warning of the drift of
things. I seem to remember myself in the train to Padding-
ton, sitting with a handful of papers—galley proofs for the
Blue Weekly, I suppose—on my lap, and thinking about her
and that last sentence of hers, and all that it might mean to me.

It is very hard to recall even the main outline of anything so
elusive as a meditation. I know that the idea of working with
her gripped me, fascinated me. That my value in her life
seemed growing filled me with pride and a kind of gratitude. I
was already in no doubt that her value in my life was tremendous. It made it none the less, that in those days I was obsessed by the idea that she was transitory, and bound to go
out of my life again. It is no good trying to set too fine a face
upon this complex business, there is gold and clay and sunlight
and savagery in every love-story, and a multitude of elvish
elements peeped out beneath the fine rich curtain of affection
that masked our future. I've never properly weighed how
immensely my vanity was gratified by her clear preference for
me. Nor can I for a moment determine how much deliberate
intention I hide from myself in this affair.

Certainly I think some part of me must have been saying in
the train : "Leave go of her. Get away from her. End this
now." I can't have been so stupid as not to have had that in
my mind. . . .

If she had been only a beautiful girl in love with me, I think
I could have managed the situation. Once or twice since my
marriage and before Isabel became of any significance in my
life, there had been incidents with other people, flashes of
temptation—no telling is possible of the thing resisted. I think
that mere beauty and passion would not have taken me. But
between myself and Isabel things were incurably complicated
by the intellectual sympathy we had, the jolly march of our
minds together. That has always mattered enormously. I
should have wanted her company nearly as badly if she had
been some crippled old lady ; we would have hunted shoulder

to shoulder, as two men. Only two men would never have had the patience and readiness for one another we two had. I had never for years met any one with whom I could be so carelessly sure of understanding or to whom I could listen so easily and fully. She gave me, with an extraordinary completeness, that rare, precious effect of always saying something fresh, and yet saying it so that it filled into and folded about all the little recesses and corners of my mind with an infinite, soft familiarity. It is impossible to explain that. It is like trying to explain why her voice, her voice heard speaking to any one—heard speaking in another room—pleased my ears.

She was the only Oxford woman who took a first that year. She spent the summer in Scotland and Yorkshire, writing to me continually of all she now meant to do, and stirring my imagination. She came to London for the autumn session. For a time she stayed with old Lady Colbeck, but she fell out with her hostess when it became clear she wanted to write, not novels, but journalism ; and then she set every one talking by taking a flat near Victoria and installing as her sole protector an elderly German governess she had engaged through a scholastic agency. She began writing, not in that copious flood the undisciplined young woman of gifts is apt to produce, but in exactly the manner of an able young man, experimenting with forms, developing the phrasing of opinions, taking a definite line. She was, of course, tremendously discussed. She was disapproved of, but she was invited out to dinner. She got rather a reputation for the management of elderly distinguished men. It was an odd experience to follow Margaret's soft rustle of silk into some big drawing-room and discover my snub-nosed girl in the blue sack transformed into a shining creature in the soft splendour of pearls and ivory-white and lace, and with a silver band about her dusky hair.

For a time we did not meet very frequently, though always she professed an unblushing preference for my company, and talked my views and sought me out. Then her usefulness upon the *Blue Weekly* began to link us closelier. She would come up to the office, and sit by the window and talk over the proofs of the next week's articles, going through my intentions with a keen investigatory scalpel. Her talk always puts me in mind of a steel blade. Her writing became rapidly very good ; she had a wit and a turn of the phrase that was all her own. We seemed to have forgotten the little shadow of embarrassment that had fallen over our last meeting at Oxford. Everything seemed natural and easy between us in those days ; a little unconventional, but that made it all the brighter.

We developed something like a custom of walks, about once a week or so, and letters and notes became frequent. I won't pretend things were not keenly personal between us, but they had an air of being innocently mental. She used to call me " Master " in our talks, a monstrous and engaging flattery, and

I was inordinately proud to have her as my pupil. Who
wouldn't have been ? And we went on at that distance for a
long time—until within a year of the Handitch election.

After Lady Colbeck threw her up as altogether too " intellectual " for comfortable control, Isabel was taken up by the
Balfes in a less formal and compromising manner, and week-
ended with them and their cousin Leonora Sparling, and spent
large portions of her summer with them in Herefordshire.
There was a lover or so in that time, men who came a little
timidly at this brilliant young person with the frank manner
and the Amazonian mind, and, she declared, received her kindly
refusals with manifest relief. And Arnold Shoesmith struck
up a sort of friendship that oddly imitated mine. She took a
liking to him because he was clumsy and shy and inexpressive ;
she embarked upon the dangerous interest of helping him to
find his soul. I had some twinges of jealousy about that. I
didn't see the necessity of him. He invaded her time, and I
thought that might interfere with her work. If their friendship stole some hours from Isabel's writing, it did not for a long
while interfere with our walks or our talks, or the close intimacy we had together.

§ 4

Then suddenly Isabel and I found ourselves passionately in love.
The change came so entirely without warning or intention
that I find it impossible now to tell the order of its phases.
What disturbed pebble started the avalanche I cannot trace.
Perhaps it was simply that the barriers between us and this
masked aspect of life had been wearing down unperceived.

And there came a change in Isabel. It was like some change
in the cycle of nature, like the onset of spring—a sharp brightness, an uneasiness. She became restless with her work ;
little encounters with men began to happen, encounters not
quite in the quality of the earlier proposals ; and then came
an odd incident of which she told me, but somehow, I felt,
didn't tell me completely. She told me all she was able to tell
me. She had been at a dance at the Ropers', and a man, rather
well known in London, had kissed her. The thing amazed her
beyond measure. It was the sort of thing immediately possible
between any man and any woman, that one never expects to
happen until it happens. It had the surprising effect of a
judge generally known to be bald suddenly whipping off his
wig in court. No absolutely unexpected revelation could have
quite the same quality of shock. She went through the whole
thing to me with a remarkable detachment, told me how she
had felt—and the odd things it seemed to open to her.

" I *want* to be kissed, and all that sort of thing," she avowed.
" I suppose every woman does."

She added after a pause : " And I don't want any one to
do it."

This struck me as queerly expressive of the woman's attitude to these things. "Some one presently will—solve that," I said.

"Some one will perhaps."

I was silent.

"Some one will," she said, almost viciously. "And then we'll have to stop these walks and talks of ours, dear Master. . . . I'll be sorry to give them up."

"It's part of the requirements of the situation," I said, "that he should be—oh, very interesting ! He'll start, no doubt, all sorts of new topics, and open no end of attractive vistas. . . . You can't, you know, always go about in a state of pupilage."

"I don't think I can," said Isabel. "But it's only just recently I've begun to doubt about it."

I remember these things being said, but just how much we saw and understood, and just how far we were really keeping opaque to each other then, I cannot remember. But it must have been quite soon after this that we spent nearly a whole day together at Kew Gardens, with the curtains up and the barriers down, and the thing that had happened plain before our eyes. I don't remember we ever made any declaration. We just assumed the new footing. . . .

It was a day early in that year—I think in January, because there was thin, crisp snow on the grass, and we noted that only two other people had been to the Pagoda that day. I've a curious impression of greenish colour, hot, moist air and huge palm fronds about very much of our talk, as though we were nearly all the time in the Tropical House. But I also remember very vividly looking at certain orange and red spray-like flowers from Patagonia, which could not have been there. It is a curious thing that I do not remember we made any profession of passionate love for one another ; we talked as though the fact of our intense love for each other had always been patent between us. There was so long and frank an intimacy between us that we talked far more like brother and sister or husband and wife than two people engaged in the war of the sexes. We wanted to know what we were going to do, and whatever we did we meant to do in the most perfect concert. We both felt an extraordinary accession of friendship and tenderness then, and, what again is curious, very little passion. But there was also, in spite of the perplexities we faced, an immense satisfaction about that day. It was as if we had taken off something that had hindered our view of each other, like people who unvizard to talk more easily at a masked ball.

I've had since to view our relations from the standpoint of the ordinary observer. I find that vision in the most preposterous contrast with all that really went on between us. I suppose there I should figure as a wicked seducer, while an unprotected girl succumbed to my fascinations. As a matter of fact, it didn't occur to us that there was any personal inequality between us. I knew her for my equal mentally ; in so many things she was beyond comparison cleverer than I ; her courage out went mine. The quick leap of her mind evoked a flash of joy in mine like the response of an induction wire ; her way of thinking was like watching sunlight reflected from little waves upon the side of a boat, it was so bright, so mobile, so variously and easily true to its law. In the back of our minds we both had a very definite belief that making love is full or joyous, splendid, tender, and exciting possibilities, and we had to discuss why we shouldn't be to the last degree lovers.

Now what I should like to print here, if it were possible, in all the screaming emphasis of red ink, is this : that the circumstances of my upbringing and the circumstances of Isabel's upbringing had left not a shadow of belief or feeling that the utmost passionate love between us was in itself intrinsically *wrong*. I've told with the fullest particularity just all that I was taught or found out for myself in these matters ; and Isabel's reading and thinking, and the fierce silences of her governesses and the breathless warnings of teachers, and all the social and religious influences that had been brought to bear upon her, had worked out to the same void of conviction. The code had failed with us altogether. We didn't for a moment consider anything but the expediency of what we both, for all our quiet faces and steady eyes, wanted most passionately to do.

Well, here you have the state of mind of whole brigades of people, and particularly of young people, nowadays. The current morality hasn't gripped them ; they don't really believe in it at all. They may render it lip-service, but that is quite another thing. There are scarcely any tolerable novels to justify its prohibitions ; its prohibitions do, in fact, remain unjustified amongst these ugly suppressions. You may, if you choose, silence the admission of this in literature and current discussion ; you will not prevent it working out in lives. People come up to the great moments of passion crudely unaware, astoundingly unprepared as no really civilised and intelligently planned community would let any one be unprepared. They find themselves hedged about with customs that have no organic hold upon them, and mere discretions all generous spirits are disposed to despise.

Consider the infinite absurdities of it ! Multitudes of us are trying to run this complex modern community on a basis of " Hush " without explaining to our children or discussing with them anything about love and marriage at all. Doubt and knowledge creep about in enforced darknesses and silences. We are living upon an ancient tradition which everybody doubts and nobody has ever analysed. We affect a tremendous and cultivated shyness and delicacy about imperatives of the most arbitrary appearance. What ensues ? What did ensue with us, for example ? On the one hand was a great desire, robbed of any appearance of shame and grossness by the power of love, and on the other hand, the possible jealousy of so-and-so, the disapproval of so-and-so, material risks and dangers. It is only in the retrospect that we have been able to grasp something of the effectual case against us. The social prohibition lit by the intense glow of our passion, presented itself as preposterous, irrational, arbitrary and ugly, a monster fit only for mockery. We might be ruined ! Well, there is a phase in every love-affair, a sort of heroic hysteria, when death and ruin are agreeable additions to the prospect. It gives the business a gravity, a solemnity. Timid people may hesitate and draw back with a vague instinctive terror of the immensity of the oppositions they challenge, but neither Isabel nor I are timid people.

We weighed what was against us. We decided just exactly as scores of thousands of people have decided in this very matter, that if it were possible to keep this thing to ourselves, there was nothing against it. And so we took our first step. With the hunger of love in us, it was easy to conclude we might be lovers, and still keep everything to ourselves. That cleared our minds of the one persistent obstacle that mattered to us— the haunting presence of Margaret.

And then we found, as all those scores of thousands of people scattered about us have found, that we could not keep it to ourselves. Love will out. All the rest of this story is the chronicle of that. Love with sustained secrecy cannot be love. It is just exactly the point people do not understand.

§ 5

But before things came to that pass, some months and many phases and a sudden journey to America intervened.

" This things spells disaster," I said. " You are too big and I am too big to attempt this secrecy. Think of the intolerable possibility of being found out ! At any cost we have to stop —even at the cost of parting."

" Just because we may be found out ! "

" Just because we may be found out."

" Master, I shouldn't in the least mind being found out with you. I'm afraid—I'd be proud."

" Wait till it happens."

There followed a struggle of immense insincerity between us. It is hard to tell who urged and who resisted.

She came to me one night to the editorial room of the *Blue Weekly*, and argued and kissed me with wet salt lips, and wept in my arms ; she told me that now passionate longing for me and my intimate life possessed her, so that she could not work, could not think, could not endure other people for the love of me. . . .

I fled absurdly. That is the secret of the futile journey to America that puzzled all my friends.

I ran away from Isabel. I took hold of the situation with all my strength, put in Britten with sketchy, hasty instructions to edit the paper, and started with luggage from which, among other articles, my shaving things were omitted, upon a tour round the world.

Preposterous flight that was ! I remember as a thing almost farcical my explanations to Margaret, and how frantically anxious I was to prevent the remote possibility of her coming with me, and how I crossed in the *Tuscan*, a bad, wet boat, and mixed sea-sickness with ungovernable sorrow. I wept—tears. It was inexpressibly queer and ridiculous—and, good God ! how I hated my fellow-passengers !

New York inflamed and excited me for a time, and when things slackened, I whirled westward to Chicago—eating and drinking, I remember, in the train from shoals of little dishes, with a sort of desperate voracity. I did the queerest things to distract myself—no novelist would dare to invent my mental and emotional muddle. Chicago also held me at first, amazing lapse from civilisation that the place is ! and then abruptly, with hosts expecting me and everything settled for some days in Denver, I found myself at the end of my renunciations, and turned and came back headlong to London.

Let me confess it wasn't any sense of perfect and incurable trust and confidence that brought me back, or any idea that now I had strength to refrain. It was a sudden realisation that after all the separation might succeed ; some careless phrasing in one of her jealously read letters set that idea going in my mind—the haunting perception that I might return to London and find it empty of the Isabel who had pervaded it. Honour, discretion, the careers of both of us, became nothing at the thought. I couldn't conceive my life resuming there without Isabel. I couldn't, in short, stand it.

I don't even excuse my return. It is inexcusable. I ought to have kept upon my way westward—and held out. I couldn't. I wanted Isabel, and I wanted her so badly now that everything else in the world was phantom-like until that want was satisfied. Perhaps you have never wanted anything like that. I went straight to her.

But here I come to untellable things. There is no describing the reality of love. The shapes of things are nothing, the actual happenings are nothing, except that somehow there falls a light upon them and a wonder. Of how we met, and the thrill of the adventure, the curious bright sense of defiance, the joy of having dared, I can't tell—I can but hint of just one aspect, of what an amazing *lark*—it's the only word—it seemed to us. The beauty which was the essence of it, which justifies it so far as it will bear justification, eludes statement.

What can a record of contrived meetings, of sundering difficulties evaded and overcome, signify here ? Or what can it convey to say that one looked deep into two dear, steadfast eyes, or felt a heart throb and beat, or gripped soft hair softly in a trembling hand ? Robbed of encompassing love, these things are of no more value than the taste of good wine or the sight of good pictures, or the hearing of music—just sensuality and no more. No one can tell love—we can only tell the gross facts of love and its consequences. Given love—given mutuality, and one has effected a supreme synthesis and come to a new level of life—but only those who know can know. This business has brought me more bitterness and sorrow than I had ever expected to bear, but even now I will not say that I regret that wilful home-coming altogether. We loved—to the uttermost. Neither of us could have loved any one else as we did and do love one another. It was ours, that beauty ; it existed only between us when we were close together, for no one in the world ever to know save ourselves.

My return to the office sticks out in my memory with an extreme vividness, because of the wild eagle of pride that screamed within me. It was Tuesday morning, and though not a soul in London knew of it yet except Isabel, I had been back in England a week. I came in upon Britten and stood in the doorway.

" God ! " he said at the sight of me.

" I'm back," I said.

He looked at my excited face with those red-brown eyes of his. Silently I defied him to speak his mind.

" Where did you turn back ? " he said at last.

§ 6

I had to tell what were, so far as I can remember, my first positive lies to Margaret in explaining that return. I had written to her from Chicago and again from New York, saying that I felt I ought to be on the spot in England for the new session, and that I was coming back—presently. I concealed the name of my boat from her, and made a calculated prevarication when I announced my presence in London. I telephoned before I went back for my rooms to be prepared. She was, I knew, with the Bunting Harblows in Durham, and when she came back to Radnor Square I had been at home a day.

I remember her return so well.

My going away and the vivid secret of the present had wiped out from my mind much of our long estrangement. Something, too, had changed in her. I had had some hint of it in her letters, but now I saw it plainly. I came out of my study upon the landing when I heard the turmoil of her arrival below, and she came upstairs with a quickened gladness. It was a cold March, and she was dressed in unfamiliar dark furs that suited her extremely and reinforced the delicate flush of her sweet face. She held out both her hands to me, and drew me to her unhesitatingly and kissed me.

" So glad you are back, dear," she said. " Oh! so very glad you are back."

I returned her kiss with a queer feeling at my heart, too undifferentiated to be even a definite sense of guilt or meanness. I think it was chiefly amazement—at the universe—at myself.

" I never knew what it was to be away from you," she said.

I perceived suddenly that she had resolved to end our estrangement. She put herself so that my arm came caressingly about her.

" These are jolly furs," I said.

" I got them for you."

The parlourmaid appeared below dealing with the maid and the luggage cab.

" Tell me all about America," said Margaret. " I feel as though you'd been away six years."

We went arm in arm into our little sitting-room, and I took off the furs for her and sat down upon the chintz-covered sofa by the fire. She had ordered tea, and came and sat by me. I don't know what I had expected, but of all things I had certainly not expected this sudden abolition of our distances.

" I want to know all about America," she repeated, with her eyes scrutinising me. " Why did you come back ? "

I repeated the substance of my letters rather lamely, and she sat listening.

" But why did you turn back—without going to Denver ? "

" I wanted to come back. I was restless."

" Restlessness," she said, and thought. " You were restless in Venice. You said it was restlessness took you to America."

Again she studied me. She turned a little awkwardly to her tea-things, and poured needless water from the silver kettle into the teapot. Then she sat still for some moments looking at the equipage with expressionless eyes. I saw her hand upon the edge of the table tremble slightly. I watched her closely. A vague uneasiness possessed me. What might she not know or guess ?

She spoke at last with an effort. " I wish you were in Parliament again," she said. " Life doesn't give you events enough."

" If I was in Parliament again, I should be on the Conservative side."

" I know," she said, and was still more thoughtful.

" Lately," she began, and paused. " Lately I've been reading—you."

I didn't help her out with what she had to say. I waited.

" I didn't understand what you were after. I had misjudged. I didn't know. I think perhaps I was rather stupid." Her eyes were suddenly shining with tears. " You didn't give me much chance to understand."

She turned upon me suddenly with a voice full of tears.

" Husband," she said abruptly, holding her two hands out to me, " I want to begin over again."

I took her hands, perplexed beyond measure. " My
dear ! " I said.

" I want to begin over again."

I bowed my head to hide my face, and found her hand in
mine and kissed it.

" Ah ! " she said, and slowly withdrew her hand. She
leaned forward with her arm on the sofa-back, and looked very
intently into my face. I felt the most damnable scoundrel
in the world as I returned her gaze. The thought of Isabel's
darkly shining eyes seemed like a physical presence between
us. . . .

" Tell me," I said presently, to break the intolerable tension,
" tell me plainly what you mean by this."

I sat a little away from her, and then took my teacup in
hand, with an odd effect of defending myself. " Have you
been reading that old book of mine ? " I asked.

" That and the paper. I took a complete set from the beginning down to Durham with me. I have read it over, thought
it over. I didn't understand—what you were teaching."

There was a pause.

" It all seems so plain to me now," she said, " and so true."

I was profoundly disconcerted. I put down my teacup,
stood up in the middle of the hearth-rug, and began talking.
" I'm tremendously glad, Margaret, that you've come to see
I'm not altogether perverse," I began. I launched out into a
rather trite and windy exposition of my views, and she sat
close to me on the sofa, looking up into my face, hanging on
my words, a deliberate and invincible convert.

" Yes," she said, " yes." . . .

I had never doubted my new conceptions before ; now I
doubted them profoundly. But I went on talking. It's the
grim irony in the lives of all politicians, writers, public teachers,
that once the audience is at their feet, a new loyalty has
gripped them. It isn't their business to admit doubt and im-
perfections. They have to go on talking. And I was now
so accustomed to Isabel's vivid interruptions, qualifications,
restatements and confirmations. . . .

Margaret and I dined together at home. She made me open
out my political projects to her. " I have been foolish," she
said. " I want to help."

And by some excuse I have forgotten she made me come to
her room. I think it was some book I had to take her, some
American book I had brought back with me, and mentioned
in our talk. I walked in with it, and put it down on the
table and turned to go.

" Husband ! " she cried, and held out her slender arms to
me. I was compelled to go to her and kiss her, and she
twined them softly about my neck and drew me to her and
kissed me. I disentangled them very gently, and took each
wrist and kissed it, and the backs of her hands.

" Good-night," I said.   There came a little pause.   " Good-night, Margaret," I repeated, and walked very deliberately and with a kind of sham preoccupation to the door.

I did not look at her, but I could feel her standing, watching me.   If I had looked up, she would, I knew, have held out her arms to me. . . .

At the very outset that secret, which was to touch no one but Isabel and myself, had reached out to stab another human being.

§ 7

The whole world had changed for Isabel and me ; and we tried to pretend that nothing had changed except a small matter between us.   We believed quite honestly at that time that it was possible to keep this thing that had happened from any reaction at all, save perhaps through some magically enhanced vigour in our work, upon the world about us !   Seen in retrospect, one can realise the absurdity of this belief ; within a week I realised it ; but that does not alter the fact that we did believe as much, and that people who are deeply in love and unable to marry will continue to believe so to the very end of time.   They will continue to believe out of existence every consideration that separates them until they have come together.   Then they will count the cost, as we two had to do.

I am telling a story, and not propounding theories in this book ; and chiefly I am telling of the ideas and influences and emotions that have happened to me—me as a sort of sounding-board for my world.   The moralist is at liberty to go over my conduct with his measure and say, " At this point or at that you went wrong, and you ought to have done "—so-and-so. The point of interest to the statesman is that it didn't for a moment occur to us to do so-and-so when the time for doing it came.   It amazes me now to think how little either of us troubled about the established rights or wrongs of the situation.   We hadn't an atom of respect for them, innate or acquired.   The guardians of public morals will say we were very bad people ;   I submit in defence that they are very bad guardians—provocative guardians. . . . And when at last there came a claim against us that had an effective validity for us, we were in the full tide of passionate intimacy.

I had a night of nearly sleepless perplexity after Margaret's return.   She had suddenly presented herself to me like something dramatically recalled, fine, generous, infinitely capable of feeling.   I was amazed how much I had forgotten her.   In my contempt for vulgarised and conventionalised honour I had forgotten that for me there was such a reality as honour.   And here it was, warm and near to me, living, breathing, unsuspecting.   Margaret's pride was my honour, that I had had no right even to imperil.

I do not now remember if I thought at that time of going to Isabel and putting this new aspect of the case before her.

Perhaps I did.   Perhaps I may have considered even then the possibility of ending what had so freshly and passionately begun.   If I did, it vanished next day at the sight of her. Whatever regrets came in the darkness, the daylight brought an obstinate confidence in our resolution again.   We would, we declared, "pull the thing off."   Margaret must not know. Margaret should not know.   If Margaret did not know, then no harm whatever would be done.   We tried to sustain that. . . .

For a brief time we had been like two people in a magic cell, magically cut off from the world and full of a light of its own, and then we began to realise that we were not in the least cut off, that the world was all about us and pressing in upon us, limiting us, threatening us, resuming possession of us.   I tried to ignore the injury to Margaret of her unreciprocated advances. I tried to maintain to myself that this hidden love made no difference to the now irreparable breach between husband and wife.   But I never spoke of it to Isabel or let her see that aspect of our case.   How could I ?   The time for that had gone. . . .

Then in new shapes and relations came trouble.   Distressful elements crept in by reason of our unavoidable furtiveness ; we ignored them, hid them from each other, and attempted to hide them from ourselves.   Successful love is a thing of abounding pride, and we had to be secret.   It was delightful at first to be secret, a whispering, warm conspiracy ; then presently it became irksome and a little shameful.   Her essential frankness of soul was all against the masks and false-hoods that many women would have enjoyed.   Together in our secrecy we relaxed, then in the presence of other people again it was tiresome to have to watch for the careless, too easy phrase, to snatch back one's hand from the limitless betrayal of a light, familiar touch.

Love becomes a poor thing, at best a poor beautiful thing, if it develops no continuing and habitual intimacy.   We were always meeting, and most gloriously loving and beginning— and then we had to snatch at remorseless ticking watches, hurry to catch trains, and go back to this or that.   That is all very well for the intrigues of idle people perhaps, but not for an intense personal relationship.   It is like lighting a candle for the sake of lighting it, over and over again, and each time blowing it out.   That, no doubt, must be very amusing to children playing with the matches, but not to people who love warm light, and want it in order to do fine and honourable things together.   We had achieved—I give the ugly phrase that expresses the increasing discolouration in my mind— " illicit intercourse."   To end at that, we now perceived, wasn't in our style.   But where were we to end ? . . .

Perhaps we might at this stage have given it up.   I think if we could have seen ahead and around us we might have done so.   But the glow of our cell blinded us. . . . I wonder what might have happened if at that time we had given it up. . . . We propounded it, we met again in secret to discuss it, and our overpowering passion for one another reduced that meeting to absurdity. . . .

Presently the idea of children crept between us. It came in from all our conceptions of life and public service ; it was, we found, in the quality of our minds that physical love without children is a little weak, timorous, more than a little shameful. With imaginative people there very speedily comes a time when that realisation is inevitable. We hadn't thought of that before —it isn't natural to think of that before. We hadn't known. There is no literature in English dealing with such things.

There is a necessary sequence of phases in love. These came in their order, and with them, unanticipated tarnishings on the first bright perfection of our relations. For a time these developing phases were no more than a secret and private trouble between us, little shadows spreading by imperceptible degrees across that vivid and luminous cell.

§ 8

The Handitch election flung me suddenly into prominence.

It is still only two years since that struggle, and I will not trouble the reader with a detailed history of events that must be quite sufficiently present in his mind for my purpose already. Huge stacks of journalism have dealt with Handitch and its significance. For the reader very probably, as for most people outside a comparatively small circle, it meant my emergence from obscurity. We obtruded no editor's name in the *Blue Weekly* ; I had never as yet been on the London hoardings. Before Handitch I was a journalist and writer of no great public standing ; after Handitch, I was definitely a person in the little group of persons who stood for the Young Imperialist movement. Handitch was, to a very large extent, my affair. I realised then, as a man comes to do, how much one can still grow after seven-and-twenty. In the second election I was a man taking hold of things ; at Kinghamstead I had been simply a young candidate, a party unit, led about the constituency, told to do this and that, and finally washed in by the great Anti-Imperialist flood, like a starfish rolling up a beach.

My feminist views had earned the mistrust of the party, and I do not think I should have got the chance of Handitch or indeed any chance at all of Parliament for a long time, if it had not been that the seat with its long record of Liberal victories and its Liberal majority of 3642 at the last election, offered a hopeless contest. The Liberal dissensions and the belated but by no means contemptible Socialist candidate were providential interpositions. I think, however, the conduct of Gane, Crupp, and Tarvrille in coming down to fight for me, did count tremendously in my favour. " We aren't going to win, perhaps," said Crupp, " but we are going to talk." And until the very eve of victory, we treated Handitch not so much as a battlefield as a hoarding. And so it was the Endowment of Motherhood as a practical form of eugenics got into English politics.

Plutus, our agent, was scared out of his wits when the thing began.

"They're ascribing all sorts of queer ideas to you about the Family," he said.

"I think the Family exists for the good of the children," I said ; "is that queer ?"

"Not when you explain it—but they won't let you explain it. And about marriage—— ?"

"I'm all right about marriage—trust me."

"Of course, if *you* had children," said Plutus, rather inconsiderately. . . .

They opened fire upon me in a little electioneering rag called the *Handitch Sentinel*, with a string of garbled quotations and misrepresentations that gave me an admirable text for a speech. I spoke for an hour and ten minutes with a more and more crumpled copy of the *Sentinel* in my hand, and I made the fullest and completest exposition of the idea of endowing motherhood that I think had ever been made up to that time in England. Its effect on the Press was extraordinary. The Liberal papers gave me quite unprecedented space under the impression that I had only to be given rope to hang myself ; the Conservatives cut me down or tried to justify me ; the whole country was talking. I had had a pamphlet in type upon the subject, and I revised this carefully and put it on the book-stalls within three days. It sold enormously and brought me bushels of letters. We issued over three thousand in Handitch alone. At meeting after meeting I was heckled upon nothing else. Long before polling day Plutus was converted.

"It's catching on like old-age pensions," he said. "We've dished the Liberals ! To think that such a project should come from our side !"

But it was only with the declaration of the poll that my battle was won. No one expected more than a snatch victory, and I was in by over fifteen hundred. At one bound Cossington's papers passed from apologetics varied by repudiation to triumphant praise. "A renascent England, breeding men," said the leader in his chief daily on the morning after the polling, and claimed that the Conservatives had been ever the pioneers in sanely bold constructive projects.

I came up to London with a weary but rejoicing Margaret by the night train.

CHAPTER TWO

THE IMPOSSIBLE POSITION

§ 1

To any one who did not know of that glowing secret between Isabel and myself, I might well have appeared at that time the most successful and enviable of men. I had recovered rapidly from an uncongenial start in political life ; I had become a considerable force through the *Blue Weekly*, and was shaping an increasingly influential body of opinion ; I had re-entered Parliament with quite dramatic distinction, and in spite of a certain faltering on the part of the orthodox Conservatives towards the bolder elements in our propaganda, I had loyal and unenvious associates who were making me a power in the party. People were coming to our group, understandings were developing. It was clear we should play a prominent part in the next general election, and that, given a Conservative victory, I should be assured of office. The world opened out to me brightly and invitingly. Great schemes took shape in my mind, always more concrete, always more practicable ; the years ahead seemed falling into order, shining with the credible promise of immense achievement.

And at the heart of it all, unseen and unsuspected, was the secret of my relations with Isabel—like a seed that germinates and thrusts, thrusts relentlessly.

From the onset of the Handitch contest onward, my meetings with her had been more and more pervaded by the discussion of our situation. It had innumerable aspects. It was very present to us that we wanted to be together as much as possible—we were beginning to long very much for actual living together in the same house, so that one could come as it were carelessly—unawares—upon the other, busy perhaps about some trivial thing. We wanted to feel each other in the daily atmosphere. Preceding our imperatively sterile passion, you must remember, outside it, altogether greater than it so far as our individual lives were concerned, there had grown and still grew an enormous affection and intellectual sympathy between us. We brought all our impressions and all our ideas to each other, to see them in each other's light. It is hard to convey that quality of intellectual unison to any one who has not experienced it. I thought more and more in terms of conversation with Isabel ; her possible comments upon things would flash into my mind—oh ! with the very sound of her voice.

I remember, too, the odd effect of seeing her in the distance going about Handitch, like any stranger canvasser ; the queer emotion of her approach along the street, the greeting as she passed. The morning of the polling she vanished from the constituency. I saw her for an instant in the passage behind our Committee rooms.

" Going ? " said I.

She nodded.

" Stay it out. I want you to see the fun. I remember— the other time."

She didn't answer for a moment or so, and stood with face averted.

" It's Margaret's show," she said abruptly. " If I see her smiling there like a queen by your side—— ! She did—last time. I remember." She caught at a sob and dashed her hand across her face impatiently. " Jealous fool, mean and petty, jealous fool ! . . . Good luck, old man, to you ! You're going to win. But I don't want to see the end of it all the same. . . ."

" Good-bye ! " said I, clasping her hand as some supporter appeared in the passage. . . .

I came back to London victorious, and a little flushed and coarse with victory ; and so soon as I could break away I went to Isabel's flat and found her white and worn, with the stain of recent weeping about her eyes. I came into the room to her and shut the door.

" You said I'd win," I said, and held out my arms.

She hugged me closely for a moment.

" My dear," I whispered, " it's nothing—without you— nothing ! "

We didn't speak for some seconds. Then she slipped from my hold. " Look ! " she said, smiling like winter sunshine. " I've had in all the morning papers—the pile of them, and you—resounding."

" It's more than I dared hope."

" Or I."

She stood for a moment still smiling bravely, and then she was sobbing in my arms. " The bigger you are—the more you show," she said—" the more we are parted. I know, I know——"

I held her close to me, making no answer.

Presently she became still. " Oh, well," she said, and wiped her eyes and sat down on the sofa by the fire ; and I sat down beside her.

" I didn't know all there was in love," she said, staring at the coals, " when we went love-making."

I put my arm behind her and took a handful of her dear soft hair in my hand and kissed it.

" You've done a great thing this time," she said. " Han- ditch will make you."

" It opens big chances," I said. " But why are you weeping, dear one ? "

"Envy," she said, " and love."

"You're not lonely ? "

"I've plenty to do—and lots of people."

"Well ? "

"I want you."

"You've got me."

She put her arm about me and kissed me. "I want you," she said, "just as if I had nothing of you. You don't under-stand—how a woman wants a man. I thought once if I just gave myself to you it would be enough. It was nothing—it was just a step across the threshold. My dear, every moment you are away I ache for you—ache ! I want to be about when it isn't love-making or talk. I want to be doing things for you, and watching you when you're not thinking of me. All those safe, careless, intimate things. And something else——" She stopped. "Dear, I don't want to bother you. I just want you to know I love you. . . ."

She caught my head in her hands and kissed it, then stood up abruptly.

I looked up at her, a little perplexed.

"Dear heart," said I, "isn't this enough ? You're my councillor, my colleague, my right hand, the secret soul of my life——"

"And I want to darn your socks," she said, smiling back at me.

"You're insatiable."

She smiled. "No," she said. "I'm not insatiable, Master. But I'm a woman in love. And I'm finding out what I want, and what is necessary to me—and what I can't have. That's all."

"We get a lot."

"We want a lot. You and I are greedy people for the things we like, Master. It's very evident we've got nearly all we can ever have of one another—and I'm not satisfied."

"What more is there ? "

"For you—very little. I wonder. For me—everything. Yes—everything. You didn't mean it, Master ; you didn't know any more than I did when I began, but love between a man and a woman is sometimes very one-sided. Fearfully one-sided ! That's all. . . .

"Don't you ever want children ? " she said abruptly.

"I suppose I do."

"You don't ! "

"I haven't thought of them."

"A man doesn't, perhaps. But I have. . . . I want them —like hunger. Your children, and home with you. Really, continually you ! That's the trouble. . . . I can't have 'em, Master, and I can't have you."

She was crying, and through her tears she laughed.

"I'm going to make a scene," she said, "and get this over.

I'm so discontented and miserable ; I've got to tell you. It would come between us if I didn't. I'm in love with you, with everything—with all my brains. I'll pull through all right. I'll be good, Master, never you fear. But to-day I'm crying out with all my being. This election—— You're going up ; you're going on. In these papers—you're a great big fact. It's suddenly come home to me. At the back of my mind I've always had the idea I was going to have you somehow presently for myself—I mean to have you to go long tramps with, to keep house for, to get meals for, to watch for of an evening. It's a sort of habitual background to my thought of you. And it's nonsense—utter nonsense ! " She stopped. She was crying and choking. " And the child, you know—the child ! "

I was troubled beyond measure, but Handitch and its intimations were clear and strong.

" We can't have that," I said.

" No," she said, " we can't have that."

" We've got our own things to do."

" *Your* things," she said.

" Aren't they yours too ? "

" Because of you," she said.

" Aren't they your very own things ? "

" Women don't have that sort of very own thing. Indeed, it's true ! And think ! You've been down there preaching the goodness of children, telling them the only good thing in a state is happy, hopeful children, working to free mothers and children——"

" And we give our own children to do it ? " I said.

" Yes," she said. " And sometimes I think it's too much to give—too much altogether. . . . Children get into a woman's brain—when she mustn't have them, especially when she must never hope for them. Think of the child we might have now !—the soft, tender skin, the little hands and feet ! At times it haunts me. It comes and says, Why wasn't I given life ? I can hear it in the night. . . . The world is full of such ghosts, dear lover—little things that asked for life and were refused. They clamour to me. It's like a small fist beating at my heart. Love children, beautiful children. Oh, my heart and my lord ! " She was holding my arm with both her hands and weeping against it, and now she drew herself to my shoulder and wept and sobbed in my embrace. " I shall never sit with your child on my knee and you beside me—never, and I am a woman and your lover ! "

§ 2

But the profound impossibility of our relation was now becoming more and more apparent to us. We found ourselves seeking justification, clinging passionately to a situation that was coldly, pitilessly impossible and fated. We wanted quite intensely to live together and have a child, but also we wanted very many other things that were incompatible with these desires. It was extraordinarily difficult to weigh our political and intellectual ambitions against those intimate wishes. The weights kept altering according as one found oneself grasping this valued thing or that. It wasn't as if we could throw everything aside for our love, and have that as we wanted it. Love such as we bore one another isn't altogether, or even chiefly, a thing in itself—it is for the most part a value set upon things. Our love was interwoven with all our other interests ; to go out of the world and live in isolation seemed to us like killing the best parts of each other ; we loved the sight of each other engaged finely and characteristically, we knew each other best as activities. We had no delusions about material facts ; we didn't want each other alive or dead, we wanted each other fully alive. We wanted to do big things together, and for us to take each other openly and desperately would leave us nothing in the world to do. We wanted children indeed passionately, but children with every helpful chance in the world ; and children born in scandal would be handicapped at every turn. We wanted to share a home, and not a solitude.

And when we were at this stage of realisation, began the intimations that were found out, and that scandal was afoot against us. . . .

I heard it first from Esmeer ; who deliberately mentioned it, with that steady grey eye of his watching me, as an instance of the preposterous falsehoods people will circulate. It came to Isabel almost simultaneously through a married college friend, who made it her business to demand either confirmation or denial. It filled us both with consternation. In the surprise of the moment Isabel admitted her secret, and her friend went off " reserving her freedom of action."

Discovery broke out in every direction. Friends with grave faces and an atmosphere of infinite tact invaded us both. Other friends ceased to invade either of us. It was manifest we had become—we knew not how—a private scandal, a subject for duologues, an amazement, a perplexity, a vivid interest. In a few brief weeks it seemed London passed from absolute unsuspiciousness to a chattering exaggeration of its knowledge of our relations.

It was just the most inappropriate time for that disclosure. The long smouldering antagonism to my endowment of motherhood ideas had flared up into an active campaign in the *Expurgator*, and it would be altogether disastrous to us if I should be convicted of any personal irregularity. It was just because of the manifest and challenging respectability of my position that I had been able to carry the thing as far as I had done. Now suddenly my fortunes had sprung a leak, and scandal was pouring in. . . . It chanced, too, that a wave of moral intolerance was sweeping through London, one of those waves

in which the bitterness of the consciously just finds an ally in
the panic of the undiscovered.   A certain Father Blodgett had
been preaching against social corruption with extraordinary
force, and had roused the Church of England people to a kind
of competition in denunciation.   The old methods of the anti-
socialist campaign had been renewed, and had offered far too
wide a scope and too tempting an opportunity for private
animosity to be restricted to the private affairs of the socialists.
I had intimations of an extensive circulation of " private and
confidential " letters. . . .

I think there can be nothing else in life quite like the un-
nerving realisation that rumour and scandal are afoot about
one.   Abruptly one's confidence in the solidity of the universe
disappears.   One walks silenced through a world that one feels
to be full of inaudible accusations.   One cannot challenge the
assault, get it out into the open, separate truth and falsehood.
It slinks from you, turns aside its face.   Old acquaintances
suddenly evaded me, made extraordinary excuses ; men who
had presumed on the verge of my world and pestered me with an
intrusive enterprise, now took the bold step of flat repudiation.
I became doubtful about the return of a nod, retracted all
those tentacles of easy civility that I had hitherto spread to the
world.   I still grow warm with amazed indignation when I
recall that Edward Crampton, meeting me full on the steps of
the Climax Club, cut me dead.   " By God ! " I cried, and came
near catching him by the throat and wringing out of him what
of all good deeds and bad could hearten him, a younger man
than I and empty beyond comparison, to dare to play the
judge to me.   And then I had an open slight from Mrs. Millingham, whom I had counted on as one counts upon the sunrise.   I had not expected things of that sort ; they were
enormously disconcerting ; it was as if the world were giving
way beneath my feet, as though something failed in the essential confidence of life, as though a hand of wet ice had touched
my heart.   Similar things were happening to Isabel.   Yet we
went on working, visiting, meeting, trying to ignore this gathering of implacable forces against us.

For a time I was perplexed beyond measure to account for
this campaign.   Then I got a clue.   The centre of diffusion
was the Bailey household.   The Baileys had never forgiven me
my abandonment of the young Liberal group they had done so
much to inspire and organise ; their dinner-table had long been
a scene of hostile depreciation of the *Blue Weekly* and all its
allies ; week after week Altiora proclaimed that I was " doing
nothing," and found other causes for our bye-election triumphs;
I counted Chambers Street a dangerous place for me.   Yet,
nevertheless, I was astonished to find them using a private
scandal against me.   They did.   I think Handtich had filled
up the measure of their bitterness, for I had not only abandoned
them, but I was succeeding beyond even their power of mis-

representation. Always I had been a wasp in their spider's web, difficult to claim as a tool, uncritical, antagonistic. I admired their work and devotion enormously, but I had never concealed my contempt for a certain childish vanity they displayed, and for the frequent puerility of their political intrigues ; I suppose contempt galls more than injuries, and anyhow they had me now. They had me. Bailey, I found, was warning fathers of girls against me as a " reckless libertine," and Altiora, flushed, roguish and dishevelled, was sitting on her fender curb after dinner, and pledging little parties of five or six women at a time with infinite gusto not to let the matter go further. Our cell was open to the world, and a bleak, distressful daylight streaming in.

I had in the reports that came to me a gleam of a more intimate motive in Altiora. Isabel had been doing a series of five or six articles in the *Political Review* in support of our campaign, the *Political Review* which had hitherto been loyally Baileyite. Quite her best writing, up to the present at any rate, is in those papers ; and no doubt Altiora had had not only to read her in those invaded columns, but listen to her praises in the mouths of the tactless influential. Altiora, like so many people who rely on gesture and vocal insistence in conversation, writes a poor and slovenly prose and handles an argument badly ; Isabel has her University training behind her and wrote from the first with the stark power of a clear-headed man. " Now we know," said Altiora, with just a gleam of malice showing through her brightness, " now we know who helps with the writing ! "

She revealed astonishing knowledge.

For a time I couldn't for the life of me discover her sources. I had, indeed, a desperate intention of challenging her, and then I bethought me of a youngster named Curmain, who had been my supplemental typist and secretary for a time, and whom I had sent on to her before the days of our breach. " Of course ! " said I, " Curmain ! " He was a tall, drooping, side-long youth with sandy hair, a little forward head, and a long thin neck. He stole stamps and, I suspected, rifled my private letter drawer, and I found him one day on a turn of the stairs looking guilty and ruffled with a pretty Irish housemaid of Margaret's manifestly in a state of hot indignation. I saw nothing, but I felt everything in the air between them. I hate this pestering of servants, but at the same time I didn't want Curmain wiped out of existence ; so I had packed him off without unnecessary discussion to Altiora. He was quick and cheap anyhow, and I thought her general austerity ought to redeem him if anything could ; the Chambers Street housemaid wasn't for any man's kissing and showed it, and the stamps and private letters were looked after with an efficiency altogether surpassing mine. And Altiora, I've no doubt left now whatever, pumped this young undesirable about me, and scenting a story, had him to dinner alone one evening to get to the bottom of the matter. She got quite to the bottom of it—it must have been a queer duologue. She read Isabel's careless, intimate letters to me, so to speak, by this proxy, and she wasn't ashamed to use this information in the service of the bitterness that had sprung up in her since our political breach. It was essentially a personal bitterness ; it helped no public purpose of theirs to get rid of me. My downfall in any public sense was sheer waste—the loss of a man. She knew she was behaving badly, and so, when it came to remonstrance, she behaved worse. She'd got names and dates and places ; the efficiency of her information was irresistible. And she set to work at it marvellously. Never before, in all her pursuit of efficient ideals, had Altiora achieved such levels of efficiency. I wrote a protest that was perhaps ill-advised and angry, I went to her and tried to stop her. She wouldn't listen, she wouldn't think, she denied and lied, she behaved like a naughty child of six years old which has made up its mind to be hurtful. It wasn't only, I think, that she couldn't bear our political and social influence ; she also, I realised at that interview, couldn't bear our loving. It seemed to her the sickliest thing—a thing quite unendurable. While such things were, the virtue had gone out of her world.

I've the vividest memory of that call of mine. She'd just come in and taken off her hat, and she was grey and dishevelled and tired, and in a business-like dress of black and crimson that didn't suit her and was muddy about the skirts ; she had a cold in her head and sniffed penetratingly, she avoided my eye as she talked and interrupted everything I had to say ; she kept stabbing fiercely at the cushions of her sofa with a long hat-pin and pretending she was overwhelmed with grief at the *débâcle* she was deliberately organising.

"Then part," she cried, "part. If you don't want a smashing up—part. You two have got to be parted. You've got never to see each other ever, never to speak." There was a zest in her voice. "We're not circulating stories," she denied. "No ! And Curmain never told us anything—Curmain is an *excellent* young man ; oh ! a quite excellent young man. You misjudged him altogether." . . .

I was equally unsuccessful with Bailey. I caught the little wretch in the League Club, and he wriggled and lied. He wouldn't say where he had got his facts, he wouldn't admit he had told any one. When I gave him the names of two men who had come to me astonished and incredulous, he attempted absurdly to make me think they had told *him*. He did his horrible little best to suggest that honest old Quackett, who had just left England for the Cape, was the real scandalmonger. That struck me as mean, even for Bailey. I've still the odd vivid impression of his fluting voice, excusing the inexcusable, his big, shifty face evading me, his perspiration-beaded forehead, the shrugging shoulders, and the would-be exculpatory

288 THE NEW MACHIAVELLI

gestures—Houndsditch gestures—of his enormous ugly hands. "I can assure you, my dear fellow," he said ; "I can assure you we've done everything to shield you—everything." . . .

§ 3

Isabel came after dinner one evening and talked in the office. She made a white-robed, dusky figure against the deep blues of my big window. I sat at my desk and tore a quill pen to pieces as I talked.

"The Baileys don't intent to let this drop," I said. "They mean that every one in London is to know about it."

"I know."

"Well ? " I said.

"Dear heart," said Isabel, facing it, "it's no good waiting for things to overtake us ; we're at the parting of the ways."

"What are we to do ? "

"They won't let us go on."

"Damn them ! "

"They are *organising* scandal."

"It's no good waiting for things to overtake us," I echoed ; "they have overtaken us." I turned on her. "What do you want to do ? "

"Everything," she said. "Keep you and have our work. Aren't we Mates ? "

"We can't."

"And we can't ! "

"I've got to tell Margaret," I said.

"Margaret ! "

"I can't bear the idea of any one else getting in front with it. I've been wincing about Margaret secretly——"

"I know. You'll have to tell her—and make your peace with her."

She leaned back against the bookcases under the window.

"We've had some good times, Master," she said, with a sigh in her voice.

And then for a long time we stared at one another in silence.

"We haven't much time left," she said.

"Shall we bolt ? " I said.

"And leave all this ? " she asked, with her eyes going round the room. "And that ? " And her head indicated Westminster. "No ! "

I said no more of bolting.

"We've got to screw ourselves up to surrender," she said.

"Something."

"A lot."

"Master," she said, "it isn't all sex and stuff between us ? "

"No ! "

"I can't give up the work. Our work's my life."

We came upon another long pause.

" No one will believe we've ceased to be lovers—if we simply do," she said.

" We shouldn't."

" We've got to do something more parting than that."

I nodded, and again we paused. She was coming to something.

" I could marry Shoesmith," she said abruptly.

" But——" I objected.

" He knows. It wasn't fair. I told him."

" Oh, that explains," I said. " There's been a kind of sulkiness—— But—you told him ? "

She nodded. " He's rather badly hurt," she said. " He's been a good friend to me. He's curiously loyal. But something, something he said one day—forced me to let him know. . . . That's been the beastliness of all this secrecy. That's the beastliness of all secrecy. You have to spring surprises on people. But he keeps on. He's steadfast. He'd already suspected. He wants me very badly to marry him. . . ."

" But you don't want to marry him ? "

" I'm forced to think of it."

" But does he want to marry you at that ? Take you as a present from the world at large ?—against your will and desire ? . . . I don't understand him."

" He cares for me."

" How ? "

" He thinks this is a fearful mess for me. He wants to pull it straight."

We sat for a time in silence, with imaginations that obstinately refused to take up the realities of this proposition.

" I don't want you to marry Shoesmith," I said at last.

" Don't you like him ? "

" Not as your husband."

" He's a very clever and sturdy person—and very generous and devoted to me."

" And me ? "

" You can't expect that. He thinks you are wonderful—and, naturally, that you ought not to have started this."

" I've a curious dislike to any one thinking that but myself. I'm quite ready to think it myself."

" He'd let us be friends—and meet."

" Let us be friends ! " I cried, after a long pause. " You and me ! "

" He wants me to be engaged soon. Then, he says, he can go round fighting these rumours, defending us both—and force a quarrel on the Baileys."

" I don't understand him," I said, and added, " I don't understand you."

I was staring at her face. It seemed white and set in the dimness.

" Do you really mean this, Isabel ? " I asked.

"What else is there to do, my dear?—what else is there to do at all? I've been thinking day and night. You can't go away with me. You can't smash yourself suddenly in the sight of all men. I'd rather die than that should happen. Look what you are becoming in the country! Look at all you've built up!—me helping. I wouldn't let you do it if you could. I wouldn't let you—if it were only for Margaret's sake. *This* . . . closes the scandal, closes everything."

"It closes all our life together," I cried.

She was silent.

"It never ought to have begun," I said.

She winced. Then abruptly she was on her knees before me, with her hands upon my shoulder and her eyes meeting mine.

"My dear," she said very earnestly, "don't misunderstand me! Don't think I'm retreating from the things we've done! Our love is the best thing I could ever have had from life. Nothing can ever equal it; nothing could ever equal the beauty and delight you and I have had together. Never! You have loved me; you do love me. . . .

"No one could ever know how to love you as I have loved you; no one could ever love me as you have loved me, my king. And it's just because it's been so splendid, dear; it's just because I'd die rather than have a tithe of all this wiped out of my life again—for it's made me, it's all I am—dear, it's years since I began loving you—it's just because of its goodness that I want not to end in wreckage now, not to end in the smashing up of all the big things I understand in you and love in you. . . .

"What is there for us if we keep on and go away?" she went on. "All the big interests in our lives will vanish—everything. We shall become specialised people—people overshadowed by a situation. We shall be an elopement, a romance—all our breadth and meaning gone! People will always think of it first when they think of us; all our work and aims will be warped by it and subordinated to it. Is it good enough, dear? Just to specialise. . . . I think of you. We've got a case, a passionate case, the best of cases, but do we want to spend all our lives defending it and justifying it? And there's that other life. I know now you care for Margaret —you care more than you think you do. You have said fine things of her. I've watched you about her. Little things have dropped from you. She's given her life for you; she's nothing without you. You feel that to your marrow all the time you are thinking about these things. Oh, I'm not jealous, dear. I love you for loving her. I love you in relation to her. But there it is, an added weight against us, another thing worth saving."

Presently, I remember, she sat back on her heels and looked up into my face. "We've done wrong—and parting's paying.

It's time to pay. We needn't have paid, if we'd kept to the track. . . . You and I, Master, we've got to be men."

"Yes," I said ; "we've got to be men."

§ 4

I was driven to tell Margaret about our situation by my intolerable dread that otherwise the thing might come to her through some stupid and clumsy informant. She might even meet Altiora, and have it from her.

I can still recall the feeling of sitting at my desk that night in that large study of mine in Radnor Square, waiting for Margaret to come home. It was oddly like the feeling of a dentist's reception-room ; only it was for me to do the dentistry with clumsy, cruel hands. I had left the door open so that she would come in to me.

I heard her silken rustle on the stairs at last, and then she was in the doorway. "May I come in ? " she said.

"Do," I said, and turned round to her.

"Working ? " she said.

"Hard," I answered. "Where have *you* been ? "

"At the Vallerys'. Mr. Evesham was talking about you. They were all talking. I don't think everybody knew who I was. Just Mrs. Mumble I'd been to them. Lord Wardenham doesn't like you."

"He doesn't."

"But they all feel you're rather big, anyhow. Then I went on to Park Lane to hear a new pianist and some other music at Eva's."

"Yes."

"Then I looked in at the Brabants' for some midnight tea before I came on here. They'd got some writers—and Grant was there."

"You *have* been flying round. . . ."

There was a little pause between us.

I looked at her pretty, unsuspecting face, and at the slender grace of her golden-robed body. What gulfs there were between us ! "You've been amused," I said.

"It's been amusing. You've been at the House ? "

"The Medical Education Bill kept me." . . .

After all, why should I tell her ? She'd got to a way of living that fulfilled her requirements. Perhaps she'd never hear. But all that day and the day before I'd been making up my mind to do the thing.

"I want to tell you something," I said. "I wish you'd sit down for a moment or so." . . .

Once I had begun, it seemed to me I had to go through with it.

Something in the quality of my voice gave her an intimation of unusual gravity. She looked at me steadily for a

moment and sat down slowly in my armchair. "What is
it ?" she said.

I went on awkwardly. "I've got to tell you—something
extraordinarily distressing," I said.

She was manifestly altogether unaware.

"There seems to be a good deal of scandal abroad—I've
only recently heard of it—about myself—and Isabel."

"Isabel !"

I nodded.

"What do they say ?" she asked.

It was difficult, I found, to speak.

"They say she's my mistress."

"Oh ! How abominable !"

She spoke with the most natural indignation. Our eyes met.

"We've been great friends," I said.

"Yes. And to make *that* of it. My poor dear ! But how
can they ?" She paused and looked at me. "It's so incredible. How can any one believe it ? I couldn't."

She stopped, with her distressed eyes regarding me. Her
expression changed to dread. There was a tense stillness for
a second, perhaps.

I turned my face towards the desk, and took up and dropped
a handful of paper fasteners.

"Margaret," I said, "I'm afraid you'll have to believe it."

§ 5

Margaret sat very still. When I looked at her again, her
face was very white, and her distressed eyes scrutinised me.
Her lips quivered as she spoke. "You really mean—*that* ?"
she said.

I nodded.

"I never dreamt."

"I never meant you to dream."

"And that is why—we've been apart ?"

I thought. "I suppose it is."

"Why have you told me now ?"

"Those rumours. I didn't want any one else to tell you."

"Or else it wouldn't have mattered ?"

"No."

She turned her eyes from me to the fire. Then for a moment
she looked about the room she had made for me, and then
quite silently, with a childish quivering of her lips, with a sort
of dismayed distress upon her face, she was weeping. She sat
weeping in her dress of cloth of gold, with her bare slender
arms dropped limp over the arms of her chair, and her eyes
averted from me, making no effort to stay or staunch her
tears. "I am sorry, Margaret," I said. "I was in love. . . .
I did not understand. . . ."

Presently she asked : "What are you going to do ?"

"You see, Margaret, now it's come to be your affair—I want to know what you—what you want."

"You want to leave me?"

"If you want me to, I must."

"Leave Parliament—leave all the things you are doing—all this fine movement of yours?"

"No." I spoke sullenly. "I don't want to leave anything. I want to stay on. I've told you, because I think we—Isabel and I, I mean—have got to drive through a storm of scandal anyhow. I don't know how far things may go, how much people may feel, and I can't, I can't have you unconscious, unarmed, open to any revelation——"

She made no answer.

"When the thing began—I know it was stupid but I thought it was a thing that wouldn't change, wouldn't be anything but itself, wouldn't unfold—consequences. . . . People have got hold of these vague rumours. . . . Directly it reached any one else but—but us two—I saw it had to come to you."

I stopped. I had that distressful feeling I have always had with Margaret, of not being altogether sure she heard, of being doubtful if she understood. I perceived that once again I had struck at her and shattered a thousand unsubstantial pinnacles. And I couldn't get at her to help her, or touch her mind! I stood up, and at my movement she moved. She produced a dainty little handkerchief, and made an effort to wipe her face with it, and held it to her eyes. "Oh, my Husband!" she sobbed.

"What do you mean to do?" she said, with her voice muffled by her handkerchief.

"We're going to end it," I said.

Something gripped me tormentingly as I said that. I drew a chair beside her and sat down. "You and I, Margaret, have been partners," I began. "We've built up this life of ours together; I couldn't have done it without you. We've made a position, created a work——"

She shook her head. "You," she said.

"You helping. I don't want to shatter it—if you don't want it shattered. I can't leave my work. I can't leave you. I want you to have—all that you have ever had. I've never meant to rob you. I've made an immense and tragic blunder. You don't know how things took us, how different they seemed! My character and accident have conspired—— We'll pay—in ourselves, not in our public service."

I halted again. Margaret remained very still.

"I want you to understand that the thing is at an end. It is definitely at an end. We—we talked—yesterday. We mean to end it altogether." I clenched my hands. "She's —she's going to marry Arnold Shoesmith."

I wasn't looking now at Margaret any more, but I heard the rustle of her movement as she turned on me.

" It's all right," I said, clinging to my explanation. " We're
doing nothing shabby. He knows. He will. It's all as right
—as things can be now. We're not cheating any one, Margaret.
We're doing things straight—now. Of course, you know . . .
we shall—we shall have to make sacrifices. Give things up
pretty completely. Very completely. . . . We shall have
not to see each other for a time, you know. Perhaps not a long
time. Two or three years. Or write—or just any of that
sort of thing ever——"

Some subconscious barrier gave way in me. I found myself
crying uncontrollably—as I have never cried since I was a
little child. I was amazed and horrified at myself. And
wonderfully, Margaret was on her knees beside me, with her
arms about me, mingling her weeping with mine. " Oh, my
Husband ! " she cried, " my poor Husband ! Does it hurt
you so ? I would do anything ! Oh, the fool I am ! Dear,
I love you. I love you over and away and above all these
jealous little things ! "

She drew down my head to her as a mother might draw
down the head of a son. She caressed me, weeping bitterly
with me. " Oh ! my dear," she sobbed, " my dear ! I've
never seen you cry ! I've never seen you cry. Ever ! I
didn't know you could. Oh ! my dear ! Can't you have her,
my dear, if you want her ? I can't bear it ! Let me help you,
dear. Oh ! my Husband ! My Man ! I can't bear to have
you cry ! " For a time she held me in silence.

" I've thought this might happen. I dreamt it might
happen. You two, I mean. It was dreaming put it into my
head. When I've seen you together, so glad with each other.
. . . Oh ! Husband mine, believe me ! believe me ! I'm
stupid, I'm cold, I'm only beginning to realize how stupid and
cold, but all I want in all the world is to give my life to
you." . . .

§ 6

" We can't part in a room," said Isabel.

" We'll have one last talk together," I said, and planned
that we should meet for half a day between Dover and Walmer
and talk ourselves out. I still recall that day very well, recall
even the curious exaltation of grief that made our mental
atmosphere distinctive and memorable. We had seen so
much of one another, had become so intimate, that we talked
of parting even as we parted with a sense of incredible remote-
ness. We went together up over the cliffs, and to a place
where they fall towards the sea, past the white, quaint-
lanterned lighthouses of the South Foreland. There, in a
kind of niche below the crest, we sat talking. It was a spacious
day, serenely blue and warm, and on the wrinkled water
remotely below a black tender and six hooded submarines came
presently, and engaged in mysterious manoeuvres. Shrieking

gulls and chattering jackdaws circled over us and below us,
and dived and swooped ; and a skerry of weedy, fallen chalk
appeared, and gradually disappeared again, as the tide fell
and rose.

We talked and thought that afternoon on every aspect of
our relations. It seems to me now we talked so wide and far
that scarcely an issue can arise in the life between man and
woman that we did not at least touch upon. Lying there at
Isabel's feet, I have become for myself a symbol of all this
world-wide problem between duty and conscious, passionate
love the world has still to solve. Because it isn't solved ;
there's a wrong in it either way. . . . The sky, the wide horizon,
seemed to lift us out of ourselves until we were something representative and general. She was womanhood become
articulate, talking to her lover.

" I ought," I said, " never to have loved you."

" It wasn't a thing planned," she said.

" I ought never to have let our talk slip to that, never to
have turned back from America."

" I'm glad we did it," she said. " Don't think I repent."

I looked at her.

" I will never repent," she said. " Never ! " as though
she clung to her life in saying it.

I remember we talked for a long time of divorce. It seemed
to us then, and it seems to us still, that it ought to have been
possible for Margaret to divorce me, and for me to marry
without the scandalous and ugly publicity, the taint and
ostracism that follow such a readjustment. We went on to
the whole perplexing riddle of marriage. We criticised the
current code, how muddled and conventionalised it had become, how modified by subterfuges and concealments and
new necessities, and the increasing freedom of women. " It's
all like Bromstead when the building came," I said ; for I had
often talked to her of that early impression of purpose dis-
solving again into chaotic forces. " There is no clear right in
the world any more. The world is Byzantine. The justest
man to-day must practise a tainted goodness."

These questions need discussion—a magnificent frankness
of discussion—if any standards are again to establish an
effective hold upon educated people. Discretions, as I have
said already, will never hold any one worth holding—longer
than they held us. Against every " shalt not " there must be
a " why not " plainly put—the " why not " largest and
plainest, the law deduced from its purpose. " You and I,
Isabel," I said, " have always been a little disregardful of duty,
partly at least because the idea of duty comes to us so ill-
clad. Oh ! I know there's an extravagant insubordinate
strain in us, but that wasn't all. I wish humbugs would leave
duty alone. I wish all duty wasn't covered with slime.
That's where the real mischief comes in. Passion can always con-

trive to clothe itself in beauty, strips itself splendid. That carried us. But for all its mean associations there *is* this duty. . . ."

" Don't we come rather late to it ? "

" Not so late that it won't be atrociously hard to do."

" It's queer to think of now," said Isabel. " Who could believe we did all we have done honestly ? Well, in a manner honestly. Who could believe we thought this might be hidden ? Who could trace it all step by step from the time when we found that a certain boldness in our talk was pleasing ? We talked of love. . . . Master, there's not much for us to do in the way of Apologia that any one will credit. And yet if it were possible to tell the very heart of our story. . .

" Does Margaret really want to go on with you ? " she asked —" shield you—knowing of . . . *this*? "

" I'm certain. I don't understand—just as I don't understand Shoesmith, but she does. These people walk on solid ground which is just thin air to us. They've got something we haven't got. Assurances ? I wonder." . . .

Then it was, or later, we talked of Shoesmith, and what her life might be with him.

" He's good," she said ; " he's kindly. He's everything but magic. He's the very image of the decent, sober, honourable life. You can't say a thing against him, or I—except that something—something in his imagination, something in the tone of his voice—fails for me. Why don't I love him ?— he's a better man than you ! Why don't you ? *Is* he a better man than you ? He's usage, he's honour, he's the right thing, he's the breed and the tradition—a gentleman. You're your erring, incalculable self. I suppose we women will trust his sort and love your sort to the very end of time. . . ."

We lay side by side and nibbled at grass stalks as we talked. It seemed enormously unreasonable to us that two people who had come to the pitch of easy and confident affection and happiness that held between us should be obliged to part and shun one another, or murder half the substance of their lives. We felt ourselves crushed and beaten by an indiscriminating machine which destroys happiness in the service of jealousy. " The mass of people don't feel these things in quite the same manner as we feel them," she said. " Is it because they're different in grain, or educated out of some primitive instinct ? "

" It's because we've explored love a little, and they know no more than the gateway," I said. " Lust and then jealousy ; their simple conception—and we have gone past all that and wandered hand in hand. . . ."

I remember that for a time we watched two of that larger sort of gull whose wings are brownish-white, circle and hover against the blue. And then we lay and looked at a band of water mirror—clear far out to sea, and wondered why the breeze that rippled all the rest should leave it so serene.

" And in this State of ours," I resumed.

" Eh ! " said Isabel, rolling over into a sitting posture and looking out at the horizon. " Let's talk no more of things we can never see. Talk to me of the work you are doing and all we shall do—after we have parted. We've said too little of that. We've had our red life, and it's over. Thank Heaven !—though we stole it ! Talk about your work, dear, and the things we'll go on doing—just as though we were still together. We'll still be together in a sense—through all these things we have in common."

And so we talked of politics and our outlook. We were interested to the pitch of self-forgetfulness. We weighed persons and forces, discussed the probabilities of the next general election, the steady drift of public opinion in the north and west away from Liberalism towards us. It was very manifest that in spite of Wardenham and the *Expurgator*, we should come into the new Government strongly. The party had no one else, all the young men were formally or informally with us ; Esmeer would have office, Lord Tarville, I . . . and very probably there would be something for Shoesmith. " And for my own part," I said, " I count on backing on the Liberal side. For the last two years we've been forcing competition in constructive legislation between the parties. The Liberals have not been long in following up our Endowment of Motherhood lead. They'll have to give votes and lip-service anyhow. Half the readers of the *Blue Weekly*, they say, are Liberals. . . .

" I remember talking about things of this sort with old Willersley," I said, " ever so many years ago. It was some place near Locarno, and we looked down the lake that shone weltering—just as now we look over the sea. And then we dreamt in an indistinct featureless way of all that you and I are doing now."

" I ! " said Isabel, and laughed.

" Well, of some such thing," I said, and remained for a while silent, thinking of Locarno.

I recalled once more the largeness, the release from small personal things that I had felt in my youth ; statecraft became real and wonderful again with the memory, the gigantic handling of gigantic problems. I began to talk out my thoughts, sitting up beside her, as I could never talk of them to any one but Isabel ; began to recover again the purpose that lay under all my political ambitions and adjustments and anticipations. I saw the State, splendid and wide as I had seen it in that first travel of mine, but now it was no mere distant prospect of spires and pinnacles, but populous with fine-trained, bold-thinking, bold-doing people. It was as if I had forgotten for a long time and now remembered with amazement.

At first, I told her, I had been altogether at a loss how I

could do anything to battle against the aimless muddle of our world ; I had wanted a clue—until she had come into my life questioning, suggesting, unconsciously illuminating. " But I have done nothing," she protested. I declared she had done everything in growing to education under my eyes, in reflecting again upon all the processes that had made myself, so that instead of abstractions and blue-books and bills and devices, I had realised the world of mankind as a crowd needing before all things fine women and men. We'd spoiled ourselves in learning that, but anyhow we had our lesson. Before her advent I was in a nineteenth-century darkness, dealing with the nation as if it were a crowd of selfish men, forgetful of women and children and that shy wild thing in the hearts of men, love, which must be drawn upon as it has never been drawn upon before, if the State is to live. I saw now how it is possible to bring the loose factors of a great realm together, to create a mind of literature and thought in it, and the expres- sion of a purpose to make it self-conscious and fine. I had it all clear before me, so that at a score of points I could presently begin. The *Blue Weekly* was a centre of force. Already we had given Imperialism a criticism, and leavened half the press from our columns. Our movement consolidated and spread. We should presently come into power. Everything moved towards our hands. We should be able to get at the schools, the services, the universities, the church ; enormously increase the endowment of research, and organise what was sorely wanted, a criticism of research ; contrive a closer contact between the press and creative intellectual life ; foster litera- ture, clarify, strengthen the public consciousness, develop social organisation and a sense of the State. Men were coming to us every day, brilliant young peers like Lord Dentonhill, writers like Carnot and Cresswell. It filled me with pride to win such men. " We stand for so much more than we seem to stand for," I said. I opened my heart to her, so freely that I hesitate to open my heart even to the reader, telling of pro- jects and ambitions I cherished, of my consciousness of great powers and widening opportunities. . . .

Isabel watched me as I talked.

She too, I think, had forgotten these things for a while. For it is curious and I think a very significant thing that since we had become lovers, we had talked very little of the broader things that had once so strongly gripped our imaginations.

" It's good," I said, " to talk like this to you, to get back to youth and great ambitions with you. There have been times lately when politics has seemed the pettiest game played with mean tools for mean ends—and none the less so that the happiness of three hundred million people might be touched by our follies. I talk to no one else like this. . . . And now I think of parting, I think but of how much more I might have talked to you." . . .

Things drew to an end at last, but after we had spoken of a thousand things.

" We've talked away our last half-day," I said, staring over my shoulder at the blazing sunset sky behind us. " Dear, it's been the last day of our lives for us. . . . It doesn't seem like the last day of our lives. Or any day."

" I wonder how it will feel ? " said Isabel.

" It will be very strange at first—not to be able to tell you things."

" I've a superstition that after—after we've parted—if ever I go into my room and talk, you'll hear. You'll be—somewhere."

" I shall be in the world—yes."

" I don't feel as though these days ahead were real. Here we are, here we remain."

" Yes, I feel that. As though you and I were two immortals, who didn't live in time and space at all, who never met, who couldn't part, and here we lie on Olympus. And those two poor creatures who did meet, poor little Richard Remington and Isabel Rivers, who met and loved too much and had to part, they part and go their ways, and we lie here and watch them, you and I. She'll cry, poor dear."

" She'll cry. She's crying now ! "

" Poor little beasts ! I think he'll cry too. He winces. He could—for tuppence. I didn't know he had lachrymal glands at all until a little while ago. I suppose all love is hysterical—and a little foolish. Poor mites ! Silly little pitiful creatures ! How we have blundered ! Think how we must look to God ! Well, we'll pity them, and then we'll inspire him to stiffen up again—and do as we've determined he shall do. We'll see it through—we who lie here on the cliff. They'll be mean at times, and horrid at times ; we know them ! Do you see her, a poor little fine lady in a great house—she sometimes goes to her room and writes."

" She writes for his *Blue Weekly* still."

" Yes. Sometimes—I hope. And he's there in the office with a bit of her copy in his hand."

" Is it as good as if she still talked it over with him before she wrote it ? Is it ? "

" Better, I think. Let's play it's better—anyhow. It may be that talking over was rather mixed with love-making. After all, love-making is joy rather than magic. Don't let's pretend about that even. . . . Let's go on watching him. (I don't see why her writing shouldn't be better. Indeed I don't.) See ! There he goes down along the Embankment to Westminster just like a real man, for all that he's smaller than a grain of dust. What is running round inside that speck of a head of his ? Look at him going past the policemen, specks too—selected large ones from the country. I think he's going to dinner with the Speaker—some old thing like that. Is his face harder or commoner or stronger ?—I can't quite see. . . . And now he's up and speaking in the House. Hope he'll hold on to the thread. He'll have to plan his speeches to the very end of his days—and learn the headings."

" Isn't she up in the women's gallery to hear him ? "

" No. Unless it's by accident."

" She's there," she said.

" Well, by accident it happens. Not too many accidents, Isabel. Never any more adventures for us, dear, now. No ! . . . They play the game, you know. They've begun late, but now they've got to. You see it's not so very hard for them since you and I, my dear, are here always, always faithfully here on this warm cliff of love accomplished, watching and helping them under high heaven. It isn't so *very* hard. Rather good in some ways. Some people *have* to be broken a little. Can you see Altiora down there, by any chance ? "

" She's too little to be seen," she said.

" Can you see the sins they once committed ? "

" I can only see you here beside me, dear—for ever. For all my life, dear, till I die. Was that—the sin ? " . . .

I took her to the station, and after she had gone I was to drive to Dover, and cross to Calais by the night boat. I couldn't, I felt, return to London. We walked over the crest and down to the little station of Martin Mill side by side, talking at first in broken fragments, for the most part of unimportant things.

" None of this," she said abruptly, " seems in the slightest degree real to me. I've got no sense of things ending."

" We're parting," I said.

" We're parting—as people part in a play. It's distressing. But I don't feel as though you and I were really never to see each other again for years. Do you ? "

I thought. " No," I said.

" After we've parted I shall look to talk it over with you."

" So shall I."

" That's absurd."

" Absurd."

" I feel as if you'd always be there, just about where you are now. Invisible, perhaps, but there. We've spent so much of our lives joggling elbows." . . .

" Yes. Yes. I don't in the least realise it. I suppose I shall begin to when the train goes out of the station. Are we wanting in imagination, Isabel ? "

" I don't know. We've always assumed it was the other way about."

" Even when the train goes out of the station—— ! I've seen you into so many trains."

" I shall go on thinking of things to say to you—things to put in your letters. For years to come. How can I ever stop thinking in that way now? We've got into each other's brains."

"It isn't real," I said; "nothing is real. The world's no more than a fantastic dream. Why are we parting, Isabel?"

"I don't know. It seems now supremely silly. I suppose we have to. Can't we meet?—don't you think we shall meet even in dreams?"

"We'll meet a thousand times in dreams," I said.

"I wish we could dream at the same time," said Isabel. . . . "Dream walks. I can't believe, dear, I shall never have a walk with you again."

"If I'd stayed six months in America," I said, "we might have walked long walks and talked long talks for all our lives."

"Not in a world of Baileys," said Isabel. "And any-how——"

She stopped short. I looked interrogation.

"We've loved," she said.

I took her ticket, saw to her luggage, and stood by the door of the compartment. "Good-bye," I said a little stiffly, conscious of the people upon the platform. She bent above me, white and dusky, looking at me very steadfastly.

"Come here," she whispered. "Never mind the porters. What can they know? Just one time more—I must."

She rested her hand against the door of the carriage and bent down upon me, and put her cold, moist lips to mine.

CHAPTER THREE

THE BREAKING POINT

§ 1

AND then we broke down. We broke our faith with both Margaret and Shoesmith, flung career and duty out of our lives, and went away together.

It is only now, almost a year after these events, that I can begin to see what happened to me. At the time it seemed to me I was a rational, responsible creature, but indeed I had not parted from her two days before I became a monomaniac to whom nothing could matter but Isabel. Every truth had to be squared to that obsession, every duty. It astounds me to think how I forgot Margaret, forgot my work, forgot everything but that we two were parted. I still believe that with better chances we might have escaped the consequences of the emotional storm that presently seized us both. But we had no foresight of that, and no preparation for it, and our circumstances betrayed us. It was partly Shoesmith's unwisdom in delaying his marriage until after the end of the session—partly my own amazing folly in returning within four days to Westminster. But we were all of us intent upon the defeat of scandal and the complete restoration of appearances. It seemed necessary that Shoesmith's marriage should not seem to be hurried, still more necessary that I should not vanish inexplicably. I had to be visible with Margaret in London just as much as possible ; we went to restaurants, we visited the theatre ; we could even contemplate the possibility of my presence at the wedding. For that, however, we had schemed a week-end visit to Wales, and a fictitious sprained ankle at the last moment which would justify my absence. . . .

I cannot convey to you the intolerable wretchedness and rebellion of my separation from Isabel. It seemed that in the past two years all my thoughts had spun commissures to Isabel's brain and I could think of nothing that did not lead me surely to the need of the one intimate I had found in the world. I came back to the House and the office and my home, I filled all my days with appointments and duty, and it did not save me in the least from a lonely emptiness such as I had never felt before in all my life. I had little sleep. In the daytime I did a hundred things, I even spoke in the House on two occasions, and by my own low standards spoke well, and it seemed to me that I was going about in my own brain like a hushed survivor in a house whose owner lies dead upstairs.

I came to a crisis after that wild dinner of Tarvrille's. Something in that stripped my soul bare.

It was an occasion made absurd and strange by the odd

accident that the house caught fire upstairs while we were dining below. It was a men's dinner—" a dinner of all sorts," said Tarvrille, when he invited me ; " everything from Evesham and Gane to Wilkins the author, and Heaven knows what will happen ! " I remember that afterwards Tarvrille was accused of having planned the fire to make his dinner a marvel and a memory. It was indeed a wonderful occasion, and I suppose if I had not been altogether drenched in misery, I should have found the same wild amusement in it that glowed in all the others. There were one or two university dons, Lord George Fester, the racing man, Panmure, the artist, two or three big City men, Weston Massinghay and another prominent Liberal whose name I can't remember, the three men Tarvrille had promised and Esmeer, Lord Wrassleton, Waulsort, the member for Monckton, Neal and several others. We began a little coldly, with duologues ; but the conversation was already becoming general—so far as such a long table permitted—when the fire asserted itself.

It asserted itself first as a penetrating and emphatic smell of burning rubber—it was caused by the fusing of an electric wire. The reek forced its way into the discussion of the Pekin massacres that had sprung up between Evesham, Waulsort and the others at the end of the table. " Something burning," said the man next to me.

" Something must be burning," said Panmure.

Tarvrille hated undignified interruptions. He had a particularly imperturbable butler with a cadaverous sad face and an eye of rigid disapproval. He spoke to this individual over his shoulder. " Just see, will you," he said, and caught up the pause in the talk to his left.

Wilkins was asking questions, and I, too, was curious. The story of the siege of the Legations in China in the year 1900 and all that followed upon that, is just one of those disturbing interludes in history that refuse to join on to that general scheme of protestation by which civilisation is maintained. It is a break in the general flow of experience as disconcerting to statecraft as the robbery of my knife and the scuffle that followed it had been to me when I was a boy at Penge. It is like a tear in a curtain revealing quite unexpected backgrounds. I had never given the business a thought for years ; now this talk brought back a string of pictures to my mind ; how the reliefs arrived and the plundering began, how section after section of the International Army was drawn into murder and pillage, how the infection spread upward until the wives of Ministers were busy looting, and the very sentinels stripped and crawled like snakes into the Palace they were set to guard. It did not stop at robbery, men were murdered, women, being plundered, were outraged, children were butchered, strong men had found themselves with arms in a lawless, defenceless city, and this had followed. Now it was all recalled.

" Respectable ladies addicted to district-visiting at home were as bad as any one," said Panmure. " Glazebrook told me of one—flushed like a woman at a bargain sale, he said—and when he pointed out to her that the silk she'd got was blood-stained, she just said, " Oh, bother ! " and threw it aside, and went back. . . ."

We became aware that Tarville's butler had returned. We tried not to seem to listen.

" Beg pardon, m'lord," he said. " The house *is* on fire, m'lord.

" Upstairs, m'lord.

" Just overhead, m'lord.

The maids are throwing water, m'lord, and I've telephoned *fire*.

" No, m'lord, no immediate danger."

" It's all right," said Tarville to the table generally. " Go on ! It's not a general conflagration, and the fire brigade won't be five minutes. Don't see that it's our affair. The stuff's insured. They say old Lady Paskershortly was dreadful. Like a harpy. The Dowager Empress had shown her some little things of hers. Pet things—hidden away. Susan went straight for them—used to take an umbrella for the silks. Born shoplifter."

It was evident he didn't want his dinner spoiled, and we played up loyally.

" This is recorded history," said Wilkins—" practically. It makes one wonder about unrecorded history. In India, for example."

But nobody touched that.

" Thompson," said Tarville to the imperturbable butler, and indicating the table generally, " champagne. Champagne. Keep it going."

" M'lord," and Thompson marshalled his assistants.

Some man I didn't know began to remember things about Mandalay. " It's queer," he said, " how people break out at times " ; and told his story of an army doctor, brave, public-spirited, and, as it happened, deeply religious, who was caught one evening by the excitement of plundering—and stole and hid, twisted the wrist of a boy until it broke, and was afterwards overcome by wild remorse.

I watched Evesham listening intently. " Strange," he said, " very strange. We are such stuff as thieves are made of. And in China, too, they murdered people—for the sake of murdering. Apart, so to speak, from mercenary considerations. I'm afraid there's no doubt of it in certain cases. No doubt at all. Young soldiers—fresh from German high schools and English homes ! "

" Did *our* people ? " asked some patriot.

" Not so much. But I'm afraid there were cases. . . . Some of the Indian troops were pretty bad."

Gane picked up the tale with confirmations.

It is all printed in the vividest way as a picture upon my memory, so that were I painter I think I could give the deep rich browns and warm greys beyond the brightly lit table, the various distinguished faces, strongly illuminated, interested and keen, above the black and white of evening dress, the alert men-servants with their heavier, clean-shaved faces indistinctly seen in the dimness behind. Then this was coloured emotionally for me by my aching sense of loss and sacrifice, and by the chance trend of our talk to the breaches and unrealities of the civilised scheme. We seemed a little transitory circle of light in a universe of darkness and violence ; an effect to which the diminishing smell of burning rubber, the trampling of feet overhead, the swish of water, added enormously. Everybody —unless, perhaps, it was Evesham—drank rather carelessly because of the suppressed excitement of our situation, and talked the louder and more freely.

" But what a flimsy thing our civilisation is ! " said Evesham ; " a mere thin net of habits and associations ! "

" I suppose those men came back," said Wilkins.

" Lady Paskershortly did ! " chuckled Evesham.

" How do they fit it in with the rest of their lives ? " Wilkins speculated. " I suppose there's Pekin-stained police officers, Pekin-stained J.P.'s—trying petty pilferers in the severest manner." . . .

Then for a time things became preposterous. There was a sudden cascade of water by the fireplace, and then absurdly the ceiling began to rain upon us, first at this point and then that. " My new suit ! " cried some one. " Perrrrrr-up pe-rr "—a new vertical line of blackened water would establish itself and form a spreading pool upon the gleaming cloth. The men nearest would arrange catchment areas of plates and flower bowls. " Draw up ! " said Tarville, " draw up. That's the bad end of the table ! " He turned to the imperturbable butler. " Take round bath towels," he said ; and presently the men behind us were offering—with inflexible dignity—" Port wine, Sir. Bath towel, Sir ! " Waulsort, with streaks of blackened water on his forehead, was suddenly reminded of a wet year when he had followed the French army manœuvres. An animated dispute sprang up between him and Neal about the relative efficiency of the new French and German field-guns. Wrassleton joined in and a little drunken shrivelled Oxford don of some sort with a black-splashed shirt-front who presently silenced them all by the immensity and particularity of his knowledge of field artillery. Then the talk drifted to Sedan and the effect of dead horses upon drinking water, which brought Wrassleton and Weston Massinghay into a dispute of great vigour and emphasis. " The trouble in South Africa," said Weston Massinghay, " wasn't that we didn't boil our water. It was that we didn't boil our men.

The Boers drank the same stuff we did. *They* didn't get dysentery."

That argument went on for some time. I was attacked across the table by a man named Burshort about my Endowment of Motherhood schemes, but in the gaps of that debate I could still hear Weston Massinghay at intervals repeat in a rather thickened voice : " *They* didn't get dysentery."

I think Evesham went early. The rest of us clustered more and more closely towards the drier end of the room, the table was pushed along, and the area beneath the extinguished conflagration abandoned to a tinkling, splashing company of pots and pans and bowls and baths. Everybody was now disposed to be hilarious and noisy, to say startling and aggressive things ; we must have sounded a queer clamour to a listener in the next room. The devil inspired them to begin baiting me. " Ours isn't the Tory party any more," said Burshort. " Remington has made it the Obstetric party."

" That's good ! " said Weston Massinghay, with all his teeth gleaming ; " I shall use that against you in the House ! "

" I shall denounce you for abusing private confidences if you do," said Tarvrille.

" Remington wants us to give up launching Dreadnoughts and launch babies instead," Burshort urged. " For the price of one Dreadnought——"

The little shrivelled don who had been omniscient about guns joined in the baiting, and displayed himself a venomous creature. Something in his eyes told me he knew of Isabel and hated me for it. " Love and fine thinking," he began, a little thickly, and knocking over a wine-glass with a too easy gesture. " Love and fine thinking. Two things don't go together. No ph'losophy worth a damn ever came out of excesses of love. Salt Lake City—Piggott—Ag—Agapemone again—no works to matter."

Everybody laughed.

" Got to rec'nise these facts," said my assailant. " Love and fine think'n pretty phrase—attractive. Suitable for p'litical dec'rations. Postcard, Christmas, gilt lets, in a wreath of white flow's. Not oth'wise valu'ble."

I made some remark, I forget what, but he overbore me.

" Real things we want are Hate—Hate and *coarse* think'n. I b'long to the school of Mrs. F.'s Aunt——"

" What ? " said some one, intent.

" In *Little Dorrit*," explained Tarvrille ; " go on ! "

" Hate a fool," said my assailant.

Tarvrille glanced at me. I smiled to conceal the loss of my temper.

" Hate," said the little man, emphasising his point with a clumsy fist. " Hate's the driving force. What's m'rality ?— hate of rotten goings on. What's patriotism ?—hate of int'loping foreigners. What's Radicalism ?—hate of lords.

What's Toryism ?—hate of disturbance. It's all hate—hate
from top to bottom. Hate of a mess. Remington owned it
the other day, said he hated a—mu'll. There you are ! If
you couldn't get hate into an election, damn it (hic) people
wou'n't poll. Poll for love !—no' me ! "

He paused, but before any one could speak he had resumed.
" Then this about fine thinking. Like going into a bear pit
armed with a tagle—talgent—talgent galv'nometer. Like
going to fight a mad dog with Shasepeare and the Bible. Fine
thinking—what we want is the thickes' thinking we can get.
Thinking that stands up alone. Taf Reform means work for
all—thassort of thing."

The gentleman from Oxford paused. " *You* a flag ! " he
said. " I'd as soon go to ba'ell und' wet tissue-paper ! "

My best answer on the spur of the moment was : " The
Japanese did." Which was absurd.

I went on to some other reply, I forget exactly what, and the
talk of the whole table drew round me. It was an extraordinary revelation to me. Every one was unusually careless
and outspoken, and it was amazing how manifestly they
echoed the feeling of this old Tory spokesman. They were
quite friendly to me, they regarded me and the *Blue Weekly*
as valuable party assets for Toryism, but it was clear they
attached no more importance to what were my realities than
they did to the remarkable therapeutic claims of Mrs. Eddy.
They were flushed and amused, perhaps they went a little too
far in their resolves to draw me, but they left the impression on
my mind of men irrevocably set upon narrow and cynical views
of political life. For them the political struggle was a game,
whose counters were human hate and human credulity ; their
real aim was just every one's aim, the preservation of the class
and way of living to which their lives were attuned. They did
not know how tired I was, how exhausted mentally and
morally, nor how cruel their convergent attack on me chanced
to be. But my temper gave way, I became tart and fierce,
perhaps my replies were a trifle absurd, and Tarville, with
that quick eye and sympathy of his, came to the rescue.
Then for a time I sat silent and drank port wine while the
others talked. The disorder of the room, the still dripping
ceiling, the noise, the displaced ties and crumpled shirts of my
companions, jarred on my tormented nerves. . . .

It was long past midnight when we dispersed. I remember
Tarville coming with me into the hall, and then suggesting
we should go upstairs to see the damage. A man-servant
carried up two flickering candles for us. One end of the room
was gutted, curtains, hangings, several chairs and tables were
completely burned, the panelling was scorched and warped,
three smashed windows made the candles flare and gutter, and
some scraps of broken china still lay on the puddled floor.

As we surveyed this, Lady Tarville appeared, back from

some party, a slender, white-cloaked, satin-footed figure with amazed blue eyes beneath her golden hair. I remember how stupidly we laughed at her surprise.

§ 2

I parted from Panmure at the corner of Aldington Street, and went my way alone. But I did not go home, I turned westward and walked for a long way, and then struck northward aimlessly. I was too miserable to go to my house.

I wandered about that night like a man who has discovered his gods are dead. I can look back now detached yet sympathetic upon that wild confusion of moods and impulses, and by it I think I can understand, oh ! half the wrong-doing and blundering in the world.

I do not feel now the logical force of the process that must have convinced me then that I had made my sacrifice and spent my strength in vain. At no time had I been under any illusion that the Tory party had higher ideals than any other party, yet it came to me like a thing newly discovered that the men I had to work with had for the most part no such dreams, no sense of any collective purpose, no atom of the faith I held. They were just as immediately intent upon personal ends, just as limited by habits of thought, as the men in any other group or party. Perhaps I had slipped unawares for a time into the delusions of a party man—but I do not think so.

No, it was the mood of profound despondency that had followed upon the abrupt cessation of my familiar intercourse with Isabel, that gave this fact that had always been present in my mind its quality of devastating revelation. It seemed as though I had never seen before nor suspected the stupendous gap between the chaotic aims, the routine, the conventional acquiescences, the vulgarisations of the personal life, and that clearly conscious development and service of a collective thought and purpose at which my efforts aimed. I had thought them but a little way apart, and now I saw they were separated by all the distance between earth and heaven. I saw now in myself and every one around me, a concentration upon interests close at hand, an inability to detach oneself from the provocations, tendernesses, instinctive hates, dumb lusts and shy timidities that touched one at every point ; and, save for rare exalted moments, a regardlessness of broader aims and remoter possibilities that made the white passion of statecraft seem as unearthly and irrelevant to human life as the story an astronomer will tell, half proven but altogether incredible, of habitable planets and answering intelligences, suns' distances uncounted across the deep. It seemed to me I had aspired too high and thought too far, had mocked my own littleness by presumption, had given the uttermost dear reality of life for a theoriser's dream.

All through that wandering agony of mine that night a

dozen threads of thought interwove ; now I was a soul speaking in protest to God against a task too cold and high for it, and now I was an angry man, scorned and pointed upon, who had let life cheat him of the ultimate pride of his soul. Now I was the fool of ambition, who opened his box of gold to find blank emptiness, and now I was a spinner of flimsy thoughts, whose web tore to rags at a touch. I realised for the first time how much I had come to depend upon the mind and faith of Isabel, how she had confirmed me and sustained me, how little strength I had to go on with our purposes now that she had vanished from my life. She had been the incarnation of those great abstractions, the saving reality, the voice that answered back. There was no support that night in the things that had been. We were alone together on the cliff for ever more ! —that was very pretty in its way, but it had no truth whatever that could help me now, no ounce of sustaining value. I wanted Isabel that night, no sentiment or memory of her, but Isabel alive—to talk to me, to touch me, to hold me together. I wanted unendurably the dusky gentleness of her presence, the consolation of her voice.

We were alone together on the cliff ! I startled a passing cabman into interest by laughing aloud at that magnificent and characteristic sentimentality. What a lie it was, and how satisfying it had been ! That was just where we shouldn't remain. We of all people had no distinction from that humanity whose lot is to forget. We should go out to other interests, new experiences, new demands. That tall and intricate fabric of ambitious understandings we had built up together in our intimacy would be the first to go ; and last perhaps to endure with us would be a few gross memories of sights and sounds, and trivial incidental excitements. . . .

I had a curious feeling that night that I had lost touch with life for a long time, and had now been reminded of its quality. That infernal little don's parody of my ruling phrase, " Hate and coarse thinking," stuck in my thoughts like a poisoned dart, a centre of inflammation. Just as a man who is debilitated has no longer the vitality to resist an infection, so my mind, slackened by the crisis of my separation from Isabel, could find no resistance to his emphatic suggestion. It seemed to me that what he had said was overpoweringly true, not only of contemporary life, but of all possible human life. Love is the rare thing, the treasured thing ; you lock it away jealously and watch, and well you may ; hate and aggression and force keep the streets and rule the world. And fine thinking is, in the rough issues of life, weak thinking, is a balancing indecisive process, discovers with disloyal impartiality a justice and a defect on each disputing side. " Good honest men," as Dayton calls them, rule the world, with a way of thinking out decisions like shooting cart-loads of bricks, and with a steadfast pleasure in hostility. Dayton liked to call his antagonists

" blaggards and scoundrels "—it justified his opposition—the
Lords were " scoundrels," all people richer than he were
" scoundrels," all socialists, all troublesome poor people ; he
liked to think of jails and justice being done. His public
spirit was saturated with the sombre joys of conflict and the
pleasant thought of condign punishment for all recalcitrant
souls. That was the way of it, I perceived. That had survival
value, as the biologists say. He was fool enough in politics to
be a consistent and happy politician. . . .

Hate and coarse thinking ; how the infernal truth of the
phrase beat me down that night ! I couldn't remember that
I had known this all along, and that it did not really matter
in the slightest degree. I had worked it all out long ago in
other terms, when I had seen how all parties stood for interests
inevitably, and how the purpose in life achieves itself, if it
achieves itself at all, as a bye-product of the war of individuals
and classes. Hadn't I always known that science and philosophy elaborate themselves in spite of all the passion and
narrowness of men, in spite of the vanities and weakness of
their servants, in spite of all the heated disorder of contemporary things ? Wasn't it my own phrase to speak of " that
greater mind in men, in which we are but moments and
transitorily lit cells ? " Hadn't I known that the spirit of
man still speaks like a thing that struggles out of mud and
slime, and that the mere effort to speak means choking and
disaster ? Hadn't I known that we who think without fear
and speak without discretion will not come to our own for the
next two thousand years ?

It was the last was most forgotten, of all that faith mislaid.
Before mankind, in my vision that night, stretched new centuries of confusion, vast stupid wars, hastily conceived laws,
foolish contemporary triumphs of order, lapses, set-backs,
despairs, catastrophes, new beginnings, a multitudinous wilderness of time, a nigh plotless drama of wrong-headed energies.
In order to assuage my parting from Isabel we had set ourselves
to imagine great rewards for our separation, great personal
rewards ; we had promised ourselves success visible and shining
in our lives. To console ourselves in our separation we had
made out of the *Blue Weekly* and our young Tory movement
preposterously enormous things—as though those poor
fertilising touches at the soil were indeed the germinating seeds
of the millennium, as though a million lives such as ours had not
to contribute before the beginning of the beginning. That
poor pretence had failed. That magnificent proposition
shrivelled to nothing in the black loneliness of that night.

I saw that there were to be no such compensations. So far
as my real services to mankind were concerned I had to live
an unrecognised and unrewarded life. If I made successes it
would be by the way. Our separation would alter nothing of
that. My scandal would cling to me now for all my life, a

thing affecting relationships, embarrassing and hampering my spirit. I should follow the common lot of those who live by the imagination, and follow it now in infinite loneliness of soul ; the one good comforter, the one effectual familiar, was lost to me for ever ; I should do good and evil together, no one caring to understand ; I should produce much weary work, much bad-spirited work, much absolute evil ; the good in me would be too often ill-expressed and missed or misinterpreted. In the end I might leave one gleaming flake or so amidst the slag-heaps for a moment of post-mortem sympathy. I was afraid beyond measure of my derelict self. Because I believed with all my soul in love and fine thinking that did not mean that I should necessarily either love steadfastly or think finely. I remember how I fell talking to God—I think I talked out loud. " Why do I care for these things ? " I cried, " when I can do so little ! Why am I apart from the jolly thoughtless fighting life of men ? These dreams fade to nothingness, and leave me bare ! "

I scolded. " Why don't you speak to a man, show yourself ? I thought I had a gleam of you in Isabel—and then you take her away. Do you really think I can carry on this game alone, doing your work in darkness and silence, living in muddled conflict, half living, half dying ? "

Grotesque analogies arose in my mind. I discovered a strange parallelism between my now tattered phrase of " Love and fine thinking " and the " Love and the Word " of Christian thought. Was it possible the Christian propaganda had at the outset meant just that system of attitudes I had been feeling my way towards from the very beginning of my life ? Had I spent a lifetime making my way back to Christ ? It mocks humanity to think how Christ has been overlaid. I went along now, recalling long-neglected phrases and sentences ; I had a new vision of that great central figure preaching love with hate and coarse thinking even in the disciples about Him, rising to a tidal wave at last in that clamour for Barabbas, and the public satisfaction in His fate.

It's curious to think that hopeless love and a noisy disordered dinner should lead a man to these speculations, but they did. " He *did* mean that ! " I said, and suddenly thought what a bludgeon they'd made of His Christianity. Athwart that perplexing, patient enigma sitting inaudibly among publicans and sinners, danced and gibbered a long procession of the champions of orthodoxy. " He wasn't human," I said, and remembered that last despairing cry, " My God ! My God ! why hast Thou forsaken Me ? "

" Oh, *He* forsakes every one," I said, flying out as a tired mind will, with an obvious repartee. . . .

I passed at a bound from such monstrous theology to a towering rage against the Baileys. In an instant and with no sense of absurdity I wanted—in the intervals of love and fine thinking—to fling about that strenuously virtuous couple ; I wanted to kick Keyhole of the *Peepshow* into the gutter and make a common massacre of all the preposterous rascaldom that makes a trade and rule of virtue. I can still feel that transition. In a moment I had reached that phase of weakly decisive anger which is for people of my temperament the concomitant of exhaustion.

" I will have her," I cried. " By Heaven ! I *will* have her ! Life mocks me and cheats me. Nothing can be made good to me again. . . . Why shouldn't I save what I can ? I can't save myself without her. . . ."

I remember myself—as a sort of anticlimax to that—rather tediously asking my way home. I was somewhere in the neighbourhood of Holland Park. . . .

It was then between one and two. I felt that I could go home now without any risk of meeting Margaret. It had been the thought of returning to Margaret that had sent me wandering that night. It is one of the ugliest facts I recall about that time of crisis, the intense aversion I felt for Margaret. No sense of her goodness, her injury and nobility, and the enormous generosity of her forgiveness, sufficed to mitigate that. I hope now that in this book I am able to give something of her silvery splendour, but all through this crisis I felt nothing of that. There was a triumphant kindliness about her that I found intolerable. She meant to be so kind to me, to offer unstinted consolation, to meet my needs, to supply just all she imagined Isabel had given me.

When I left Tarville's, I felt I could anticipate exactly how she would meet my home-coming. She would be perplexed by my crumpled shirt front, on which I had spilt some drops of wine ; she would overlook that by an effort, explain it sentimentally, resolve it should make no difference to her. She would want to know who had been present, what we had talked about, show the alertest interest in whatever it was—it didn't matter what. . . . No, I couldn't face her.

So I did not reach my study until two o'clock.

There, I remember, stood the new and very beautiful old silver candlesticks that she had set there two days since to please me—the foolish kindliness of it ! But in her search for expression, Margaret heaped presents upon me. She had fitted these candlesticks with electric lights, and I must, I suppose, have lit them to write my note to Isabel. " Give me a word— the world aches without you," was all I scrawled, though I fully meant that she should come to me. I knew, though I ought not to have known, that now she had left her flat, she was with the Balfes—she was to have been married from the Balfes'— and I sent my letter there. And I went out into the silent square and posted the note forthwith, because I knew quite clearly that if I left it until morning I should never post it at all.

§ 3

I had a curious revulsion of feeling that morning of our meeting. (Of all places for such a clandestine encounter she had chosen the bridge opposite Buckingham Palace.) Overnight I had been full of self-pity, and eager for the comfort of Isabel's presence. But the ill-written scrawl in which she had replied had been full of the suggestion of her own weakness and misery. And when I saw her, my own selfish sorrows were altogether swept away by a wave of pitiful tenderness. Something had happened to her that I did not understand. She was manifestly ill. She came towards me wearily, she who had always borne herself so bravely ; her shoulders seemed bent, and her eyes were tired, and her face white and drawn. All my life has been a narrow self-centred life ; no brothers, no sisters or children or weak things had ever yet made any intimate appeal to me, and suddenly—I verily believe for the first time in my life !—I felt a great passion of protective ownership ; I felt that here was something that I could die to shelter, something that meant more than joy or pride or splendid ambitions or splendid creation to me, a new kind of hold upon me, a new power in the world. Some sealed fountain was opened in my breast. I knew that I could love Isabel broken, Isabel beaten, Isabel ugly and in pain, more than I could love any sweet or delightful or glorious thing in life. I didn't care any more for anything in the world but Isabel, and that I should protect her. I trembled as I came near her, and could scarcely speak to her for the emotion that filled me. . . .

" I had your letter," I said.

" I had yours."

" Where can we talk ? "

I remember my lame sentences. " We'll have a boat. That's best here."

I took her to the little boat-house, and there we hired a boat, and I rowed in silence under the bridge and into the shade of a tree. The square grey stone masses of the Foreign Office loomed through the twigs, I remember, and a little space of grass separated us from the pathway and the scrutiny of passers-by. And there we talked.

" I had to write to you," I said.

" I had to come."

" When are you to be married ? "

" Thursday week."

" Well ? " I said. " But—can we ? "

She leaned forward and scrutinised my face with eyes wide open. " What do you mean ? " she said at last in a whisper.

" Can we stand it ? After all ? "

I looked at her white face. " Can you ? " I said.

She whispered. " Your career ? "

Then suddenly her face was contorted—she wept silently,

exactly as a child tormented beyond endurance might suddenly weep. . . .

"Oh! I don't care," I cried, "now. I don't care. Damn the whole system of things! Damn all this patching of the irrevocable! I want to take care of you, Isabel! and have you with me."

"I can't stand it," she blubbered.

"You needn't stand it. I thought it was best for you. . . . I thought indeed it was best for you. I thought even you wanted it like that."

"Couldn't I live alone—as I meant to do?"

"No," I said, "you couldn't. You're not strong enough. I've thought of that. I've got to shelter you."

"And I want you," I went on, "I'm not strong enough—I can't stand life without you."

She stopped weeping, she made a great effort to control herself, and looked at me steadfastly for a moment. "I was going to kill myself," she whispered. "I was going to kill myself quietly—somehow. I meant to wait a bit and have an accident. I thought—you didn't understand. You were a man, and couldn't understand. . . ."

"People can't do as we thought we could do," I said. "We've gone too far together."

"Yes," she said, and I stared into her eyes.

"The horror of it," she whispered. "The horror of being handed over. It's just only begun to dawn upon me, seeing him now as I do. He tries to be kind to me. . . . I didn't know. I felt adventurous before. . . . It makes me feel like all the women in the world who have ever been owned and subdued. . . . It's not that he isn't the best of men, it's because I'm a part of you. . . . I can't go through with it. If I go through with it, I shall be left—robbed of pride—outraged—a woman beaten. . . ."

"I know," I said, "I know."

"I want to live alone. . . . I don't care for anything now but just escape. If you can help me. . . ."

"I must take you away. There's nothing for us but to go away together."

"But your work," she said; "your career! Margaret! Our promises!"

"We've made a mess of things, Isabel—or things have made a mess of us. I don't know which. Our flags are in the mud, anyhow. It's too late to save those other things! They have to go. You can't make terms with defeat. I thought it was Margaret needed me most. But it's you. And I need you. I didn't think of that either. I haven't a doubt left in the world now. We've got to leave everything rather than leave each other. I'm sure of it. Now we have gone so far. We've got to go right down to earth and begin again. . . . Dear, I *want* disgrace with you. . . ."

So I whispered to her as she sat crumpled together on the faded cushions of the boat, this white and weary young woman who had been so valiant and careless a girl. " I don't care," I said. " I don't care for anything, if I can save you out of the wreckage we have made together."

§ 4

The next day I went to the office of the *Blue Weekly* in order to get as much as possible of its affairs in working order before I left London with Isabel. I just missed Shoesmith in the lower office. Upstairs I found Britten amidst a pile of outside articles, methodically reading the title of each and sometimes the first half-dozen lines, and either dropping them in a growing heap on the floor for a clerk to return, or putting them aside for consideration. I interrupted him, squatted on the window-sill of the open window, and sketched out my ideas for the session.

" You're far-sighted," he remarked at something of mine which reached out ahead.

" I like to see things prepared," I answered.

" Yes," he said, and ripped open the envelope of a fresh aspirant.

I was silent while he read.

" You're going away with Isabel Rivers," he said abruptly.

" Well ! " I said, amazed.

" I know," he said, and lost his breath. " Not my business. Only——"

It was queer to find Britten afraid to say a thing.

" It's not playing the game," he said.

" What do you know ? "

" Everything that matters."

" Some games," I said, " are too hard to play."

There came a pause between us.

" I didn't know you were watching all this," I said.

" Yes," he answered, after a pause, " I've watched."

" Sorry—sorry you don't approve."

" It means smashing such an infernal lot of things, Remington."

I did not answer.

" You're going away then ? "

" Yes."

" Soon ? "

" Right away."

" There's your wife."

" I know."

" Shoesmith—whom you're pledged to in a manner. You've just picked him out and made him conspicuous. Every one will know. Oh ! of course—it's nothing to you. Honour——"

" I know."

" Common decency."

I nodded.

" All this movement of ours. That's what *I* care for most. . . . It's come to be a big thing, Remington."

" That will go on."

" We have a use for you—no one else quite fills it. No one. . . . I'm not sure it will go on."

" Do you think I haven't thought of all these things ? "

He shrugged his shoulders, and rejected two papers unread.

" I knew," he remarked, " when you came back from America. You were alight with it." Then he let his bitterness gleam for a moment. " But I thought you would stick to your bargain."

" It's not so much choice as you think," I said.

" There's always a choice."

" No," I said.

He scrutinised my face.

" I can't live without her—I can't work. She's all mixed up with this—and everything. And besides, there's things you can't understand. There's feelings you've never felt. . . . You don't understand how much we've been to one another."

Britten frowned and thought.

" Some things one's *got* to do," he threw out.

" Some things one can't do."

" These infernal institutions——"

" Some one must begin," I said.

He shook his head. " Not *you*," he said. " No ! "

He stretched out his hands on the desk before him, and spoke again.

" Remington," he said, " I've thought of this business day and night too. It matters to me. It matters immensely to me. In a way—it's a thing one doesn't often say to a man— I've loved you. I'm the sort of man who leads a narrow life. . . . But you've been something fine and good for me, since that time, do you remember ? when we talked about Mecca together."

I nodded.

" Yes. And you'll always be something fine and good for me anyhow. I know things about you—qualities—no mere act can destroy them. . . . Well, I can tell you, you're doing wrong. You're going on now like a man who is hypnotised and can't turn round. You're piling wrong on wrong. It was wrong for you two people ever to be lovers."

He paused.

" It gripped us hard," I said.

" Yes !—but in your position ! And hers ! It was vile ! "

" You've not been tempted."

" How do you know ? Anyhow—having done that, you ought to have stood the consequences and thought of other people. You could have ended it at the first pause for reflection. You didn't. You blundered again. You kept on.

You owed a certain secrecy to all of us ! You didn't keep it. You were careless. You made things worse. This engagement and this publicity !—Damn it, Remington ! "

" I know," I said, with smarting eyes. " Damn it !—with my all heart ! It came of trying to patch. . . . You *can't* patch."

" And now, as I care for anything under heaven, Remington, you two ought to stand these last consequences—and part. You ought to part. Other people have to stand things ! Other people have to part. You ought to. You say—what do you say ? It's loss of so much life to lose each other. So is losing a hand or a leg. But it's what you've incurred. Amputate. Take your punishment—— After all, you chose it."

" Oh, damn ! " I said, standing up and going to the window.

" Damn by all means. I never knew a topic so full of justifiable damns. But you two did choose it. You ought to stick to your undertaking."

I turned upon him with a snarl in my voice. " My dear Britten ! " I cried. " Don't I *know* I'm doing wrong ? Aren't I in a net ? Suppose I don't go ! Is there any right in that ? Do you think we're going to be much to ourselves or any one after this parting ? I've been thinking all last night of this business, trying it over and over again from the beginning. How was it we went wrong ? Since I came back from America —I grant you *that*—but *since*, there's never been a step that wasn't forced, that hadn't as much right in it or more, as wrong. You talk as though I was a thing of steel that could bend this way or that and never change. You talk as though Isabel was a cat one could give to any kind of owner. . . . We two are things that change and grow and alter all the time. We're—so interwoven that being parted now will leave us just misshapen cripples. . . . You don't know the motives, you don't know the rush and feel of things, you don't know how it was with us, and how it is with us. You don't know the hunger for the mere sight of one another ; you don't know anything."

Britten looked at his finger-nails closely. His red face puckered to a wry frown. " Haven't we all at times wanted the world put back ? " he grunted, and looked hard and close at one particular nail.

There was a long pause.

" I want her," I said, " and I'm going to have her. I'm too tired for balancing the right or wrong of it any more. You can't separate them. I saw her yesterday. . . . She's— ill. . . . I'd take her now, if death were just outside the door waiting for us."

" Torture ? "

I thought. " Yes."

" For her ? "

" There isn't," I said.

" If there was ? "

I made no answer.

" It's blind Want. And there's nothing ever been put into you to stand against it. What are you going to do with the rest of your lives ? "

" No end of things."

" Nothing."

" I don't believe you are right," I said. " I believe we can save something——"

Britten shook his head. " Some scraps of salvage won't excuse you," he said.

His indignation rose. " In the middle of life ! " he said. " No man has a right to take his hand from the plough ! "

He leaned forward on his desk and opened an argumentative palm. " You know, Remington," he said, " and I know, that if this could be fended off for six months—if you could be clapped in prison, or got out of the way somehow—until this marriage was all over and settled down for a year, say—you know then you two could meet, curious, happy, as friends. Saved ! You *know* it."

I turned and stared at him. " You're wrong, Britten," I said. " And does it matter if we could ? "

I found that in talking to him I could frame the apologetics I had not been able to find for myself alone.

" I am certain of one thing, Britten. It is our duty not to hush up this scandal."

He raised his eyebrows. I perceived now the element of absurdity in me, but at the time I was as serious as a man who is burning.

" It's our duty," I went on, " to smash now openly in the sight of every one. Yes ! I've got that as clean and plain—as prison whitewash. I am convinced that we have got to be public to the uttermost now—I mean it—until every corner of our world knows this story, knows it fully, adds it to the Parnell story and the Ashton Dean story and the Carmel story and the Witterslea story, and all the other stories that have picked man after man out of English public life, the men with active imaginations, the men of strong initiative. To think this tottering old woman-ridden Empire should dare to waste a man on such a score ! You say I ought to be penitent——"

Britten shook his head and smiled very faintly.

" I'm boiling with indignation," I said. " I lay in bed last night and went through it all. What in God's name was to be expected of us but what has happened ? I went through my life bit by bit last night, I recalled all I've had to do with virtue and women, and all I was told and how I was prepared. I was born into cowardice and debasement. We all are. Our generation's grimy with hypocrisy. I came to the most beautiful things in life—like Peeping Tom of Coventry. I was never given a light, never given a touch of natural manhood by all this dingy, furtive, canting, humbugging English world. Thank God ! I'll soon be out of it ! The shame of it ! The very savages in Australia initiate their children better than the English do to-day. Neither of us was ever given a view of what they call morality that didn't make it show as shabby subservience, as the meanest discretion, an abject submission to unreasonable prohibitions ! meek surrender of mind and body to the dictation of pedants and old women and fools. We weren't taught—we were mumbled at ! And when we found that the thing they called unclean, unclean, was Pagan beauty—God ! it was a glory to sin, Britten, it was a pride and splendour like bathing in the sunlight after dust and grime ! "

" Yes," said Britten. " That's all very well——"

I interrupted him. " I know there's a case—I'm beginning to think it a valid case against us ; but we never met it ! There's a steely pride in self-restraint, a nobility of chastity, but only for those who see and think and act—untrammelled and unafraid. The other thing, the current thing, why ! it's worth as much as the chastity of a monkey kept in a cage by itself ! " I put my foot on a chair, and urged my case upon him. " This is a dirty world, Britten, simply because it is a muddled world, and the thing you call morality is dirtier now than the thing you call immorality. Why don't the moralists pick their stuff out of the slime if they care for it, and wipe it ?—damn them ! I am burning now to say : ' Yes, we did this and this,' to all the world. All the world ! . . . I will ! "

Britten rubbed the palm of his hand on the corner of his desk. " That's all very well, Remington," he said. " You mean to go."

He stopped and began again. " If you didn't know you were in the wrong you wouldn't be so damned rhetorical. You're in the wrong. It's as plain to you as it is to me. You're leaving a big work, you're leaving a wife who trusted you, to go and live with your jolly mistress. . . . You won't see you're a statesman that matters, that no single man, maybe, might come to such influence as you in the next ten years. You're throwing yourself away and accusing your country of rejecting you."

He swung round upon his swivel at me. " Remington," he said, " have you forgotten the immense things our movement means ? "

I thought. " Perhaps I am rhetorical," I said.

" But the things we might achieve ! If you'd only stay now—even now ! Oh ! you'd suffer a little socially, but what of that ? You'd be able to go on—perhaps all the better for hostility of the kind you'd get. You know, Remington—you *know*."

I thought and went back to his earlier point. " If I am

rhetorical, at any rate it's a living feeling behind it. Yes, I remember all the implications of our aims—very splendid, very remote. But just now it's rather like offering to give a freezing man the sunlit Himalayas from end to end in return for his camp-fire. When you talk of me and my jolly mistress, it isn't fair. That misrepresents everything. I'm not going out of this—for delights. That's the sort of thing men like Snuffles and Keyhole imagine—that excites them ! When I think of the things these creatures think ! Ugh ! But *you* know better ? You know that physical passion that burns like a fire—ends clean. I'm going for love, Britten—if I sinned for passion. I'm going, Britten, because when I saw her the other day she *hurt* me. She hurt me damnably, Britten. . . . I've been a cold man—I've led a rhetorical life—you hit me with that word !—I put things in a windy way, I know, but what has got hold of me at last is her pain. She's ill. Don't you understand ? She's a sick thing—a weak thing. She's no more a goddess than I'm a god. . . . I'm not in love with her now ; I'm *raw* with love for her. I feel like a man that's been flayed. I have been flayed. . . . You don't begin to imagine the sort of helpless solicitude. . . . She's not going to do things easily ; she's ill. Her courage fails. . . . It's hard to put things when one isn't rhetorical, but it's this, Britten—there are distresses that matter more than all the delights or achievements in the world. . . . I made her what she is—as I never made Margaret. I've made her—I've broken her. . . . I'm going with my own woman. The rest of my life and England, and so forth, must square itself to that. . . ."

For a long time, as it seemed, we remained silent and motionless. We'd said all we had to say. My eyes caught a printed slip upon the desk before him, and I came back abruptly to the paper.

I picked up this galley proof. It was one of Winter's essays. "This man goes on doing first-rate stuff," I said. " I hope you will keep him going."

He did not answer for a moment or so. "I'll keep him going," he said at last with a sigh.

§ 5

I have a letter Margaret wrote me within a week of our flight. I cannot resist transcribing some of it here, because it lights things as no word of mine can do. It is a string of nearly inconsecutive thoughts written in pencil in a fine, tall, sprawling hand. Its very inconsecutiveness is essential. Many words are underlined. It was in answer to one from me ; but what I wrote has passed utterly from my mind. . . .

"Certainly," she says, " I want to hear from you, but I do not want to see you. There's a sort of abstract *you* that I want to go on with. Something I've made *out* of you. . . . I want to know things about you—but I don't want to see or feel or imagine. When some day I have got rid of my intolerable sense of proprietorship, it may be different. Then perhaps we may meet again. I think it is even more the loss of our political work and dreams that I am feeling than the loss of your presence. Aching loss. I thought so much of the things we were *doing* for the world—had given myself so unreservedly. You've left me with nothing to *do*. I am suddenly at loose ends. . . .

" We women are trained to be so dependent on a man. I've got no life of my own at all. It seems now to me that I wore my clothes even for you and your schemes. . . .

" After I have told myself a hundred times why this has happened, I ask again, ' Why did he give things up ? Why did he give things up ? ' . . .

" It is just as though you were wilfully dead. . . .

" Then I ask again and again whether this thing need have happened at all, whether if I had had a warning, if I had understood better, I might not have adapted myself to your restless mind and made this catastrophe impossible. . . .

" Oh, my dear ! why hadn't you the pluck to hurt me at the beginning, and tell me what you thought of me and life ? You didn't give me a chance ; not a chance. I suppose you couldn't. All these things you and I stood away from. You let my first repugnances repel you. . . .

" It is strange to think after all these years that I should be asking myself, do I love you ? have I loved you ? In a sense I think I *hate* you. I feel you have taken my life, dragged it in your wake for a time, thrown it aside. I am resentful. Unfairly resentful, for why should I exact that you should watch and understand my life, when clearly I have understood so little of yours. But I am savage—savage at the wrecking of all you were to do.

" Oh, why—why did you give things up ?

" No human being is his own to do what he likes with. You were not only pledged to my tiresome, ineffectual companionship, but to great purposes. They *are* great purposes. . . .

" If only I could take up your work as you leave it, with the strength you had—then indeed I feel I could let you go—you and your young mistress. . . . All that matters so little to me. . . .

" Yet I think I must indeed love you yourself in my slower way. At times I am mad with jealousy at the thought of all I hadn't the wit to give you. . . . I've always hidden my tears from you—and what was in my heart. It's my nature to hide —and you, you want things brought to you to see. You are so curious as to be almost cruel. You don't understand reserves. You have no mercy with restraints and reservations. You are not really a *civilised* man at all. You hate pretences—and not only pretences but decent coverings. . . .

" It's only after one has lost love and the chance of loving

that slow people like myself find what they might have done.
Why wasn't I bold and reckless and abandoned ? It's as
reasonable to ask that, I suppose, as to ask why my hair is
fair. . . .

"I go on with these perhapses over and over again here
when I find myself alone. . . .

"My dear, my dear, you can't think of the desolation of
things—— I shall never go back to that house we furnished
together, that was to have been the laboratory (do you remember calling it a laboratory ?) in which you were to forge
so much of the new order. . . .

"But, dear, if I can help you—even now—in any way—
help both of you, I mean. . . . It tears me when I think of you
poor and discredited. You will let me help you if I can—it
will be the last wrong not to let me do that. . . .

"You had better not get ill. If you do, and I hear of it—I
shall come after you with a troupe of doctors and nurses. If I
am a failure as a wife, no one has ever said I was anything but a
success as a district visitor. . . ."

There are other sheets, but I cannot tell whether they were
written before or after the ones from which I have quoted.
And most of them have little things too intimate to set down.
But this oddly penetrating analysis of our differences must, I
think, be given.

"There are all sorts of things I can't express about this and
want to. There's this difference that has always been between
us, that you like nakedness and wildness, and I, clothing and
restraint. It goes through everything. You are always *talking* of order and system, and the splendid dream of the order
that might replace the muddled system you hate, but by a
sort of instinct you seem to want to break the law. I've
watched you so closely. Now *I* want to obey laws, to make
sacrifices, to follow rules. I don't want to make, but I do want
to keep. You are at once makers and rebels, you and Isabel
too. You're bad people—criminal people, I feel, and yet full
of something the world must have. You're so much better
than me, and so much viler. It may be there is no making
without destruction, but it seems to me sometimes that it is
nothing but an instinct for lawlessness that drives you. You
remind me—do you remember ?—of that time we went from
Naples to Vesuvius, and walked over the hot new lava there.
Do you remember how tired I was ? I know it disappointed
you that I was tired. One walked there in spite of the heat
because there was a crust ; like custom, like law. But directly
a crust forms on things, you are restless to break down to the
fire again. You talk of beauty, both of you, as something
terrible, mysterious, imperative. *Your* beauty is something
altogether different from anything I know or feel. It has pain
in it. Yet you always speak as though it was something I
ought to feel and am dishonest not to feel. *My* beauty is a

quiet thing. You have always laughed at my feeling for old-fashioned chintz and blue china and Sheraton. But I like all these familiar *used* things. My beauty is *still* beauty, and yours, is excitement. I know nothing of the fascination of the fire, or why one should go deliberately out of all the decent fine things of life to run dangers and be singed and tormented and destroyed. I don't understand. . . ."

§ 6

I remember very freshly the mood of our departure from London, the platform of Charing Cross with the big illuminated clock overhead, the bustle of porters and passengers with luggage, the shouting of news-boys and boys with flowers and sweets, and the groups of friends seeing travellers off by the boat train. Isabel sat very quiet and still in the compartment, and I stood upon the platform with the door open, with a curious reluctance to take the last step that should sever me from London's ground. I showed our tickets, and bought a handful of red roses for her. At last came the guards crying : "Take your seats," and I got in and closed the door on me. We had, thank Heaven ! a compartment to ourselves. I let down the window and stared out.

There was a bustle of final adieux on the platform, a cry of "Stand away, please, stand away !" and the train was gliding slowly and smoothly out of the station.

I looked out upon the river as the train rumbled with slowly gathering pace across the bridge, at the bobbing black heads of the pedestrians in the footway, and the curve of the river and the glowing great hotels, and the lights and reflections and blacknesses of that old, familiar spectacle. Then with a common thought, we turned our eyes westward to where the pinnacles of Westminster and the shining clock-tower rose hard and clear against the still, luminous sky.

"They'll be in Committee on the Reformatory Bill to-night," I said, a little stupidly.

"And so," I added, " good-bye to London ! "

We said no more, but watched the south-side streets below— bright gleams of lights and movement, and the dark, dim, monstrous shapes of houses and factories. We ran through Waterloo Station, London Bridge, New Cross, St. John's. We said never a word. It seemed to me that for a time we had exhausted our emotions. We had escaped, we had cut our knot, we had accepted the last penalty of that headlong return of mine from Chicago a year and a half ago. That was all settled. That harvest of feelings we had reaped. I thought now only of London, of London as the symbol of all we were leaving and all we had lost in the world. I felt nothing now but an enormous and overwhelming regret. . . .

The train swayed and rattled on its way. We ran through old Bromstead, where once I had played with cities and armies on the nursery floor. The sprawling suburbs with their scattered lights gave way to dim tree-set country under a cloud-veiled, intermittently shining moon. We passed Card-caster Place. Perhaps old Wardingham, that pillar of the old Conservatives, was there, fretting over his unsuccessful struggle with our young Toryism. Little he recked of this new turn of the wheel and how it would confirm his contempt of all our novelties. Perhaps some faint intimation drew him to the window to see behind the stems of the young fir-trees that bordered his domain, the little string of lighted carriage windows gliding southward. . . .

Suddenly I began to realise just what it was we were doing.

And now, indeed, I knew what London had been to me, London where I had been born and educated, the slovenly mother of my mind and all my ambitions, London and the empire ! It seemed to me we must be going out to a world that was utterly empty. All our significance fell from us—and before us was no meaning any more. We were leaving London ; my hand, which had gripped so hungrily upon its complex life, had been forced from it, my fingers left their hold. That was over. I should never have a voice in public affairs again. The inexorable, unwritten law which forbids overt scandal sentenced me. We were going out to a new life, a life that appeared in that moment to be a mere shrivelled remnant of me, a mere residuum of sheltering and feeding and seeing amidst alien scenery and the sound of unfamiliar tongues. We were going to live cheaply in a foreign place, so cut off that I meet now the merest stray tourist, the commonest tweed-clad stranger with a mixture of shyness and hunger. . . . And suddenly all the schemes I was leaving appeared fine and ad-venturous and hopeful as they had never done before. How great was this purpose I had relinquished, this bold and subtle remaking of the English will ! I had doubted so many things, and now suddenly I doubted my unimportance, doubted my right to this suicidal abandonment. Was I not a trusted messenger, greatly trusted and favoured, who had turned aside by the way ? Had I not, after all, stood for far more than I had thought ; was I not filching from that dear great city of my birth and life, some vitally necessary thing, a key, a link, a reconciling clue in her political development, that now she might seek vaguely for in vain ? What is one life against the State ? Ought I not to have sacrificed Isabel and all my passion and sorrow for Isabel, and held to my thing—stuck to my thing ?

I heard as though he had spoken it in the carriage Britten's " It *was* a good game. No end of a game." And for the first time I imagined the faces and voices of Crupp and Esmeer and Gane when they learned of this secret flight, this flight of which they were quite unwarned. And Shoesmith might be there in the house—Shoesmith who was to have been married in four days—the thing might hit him full in front of any kind of people. Cruel eyes might watch him. Why the devil hadn't I written letters to warn them all? I could have posted them five minutes before the train started. I had never thought to that moment of the immense mess they would be in; how the whole edifice would clatter about their ears. I had a sudden desire to stop the train and go back for a day, for two days, to set that negligence right. My brain for a moment brightened, became animated and prolific of ideas. I thought of a brilliant line we might have taken on that confounded Reformatory Bill. . . .

That sort of thing was over. . . .

What indeed wasn't over? I passed to a vaguer, more multitudinous perception of disaster, the friends I had lost already since Altiora began her campaign, the ampler remnant whom now I must lose. I thought of people I had been merry with, people I had worked with and played with, the companions of talkative walks, the hostesses of houses that had once glowed with welcome for us both. I perceived we must lose them all. I saw life like a tree in late autumn that had once been rich and splendid with friends—and now the last brave dears would be hanging on doubtfully against the frosty chill of facts, twisting and tortured in the universal gale of indignation, trying to evade the cold blast of the truth. I had betrayed my party, my intimate friend, my wife, the wife whose devotion had made me what I was. For a while the figure of Margaret, remote, wounded, shamed, dominated my mind, and the thought of my immense ingratitude. Damn them! they'd take it out of her too. I had a feeling that I wanted to go straight back and grip some one by the throat, some one talking ill of Margaret. They'd blame her for not keeping me, for letting things go so far. . . . I wanted the whole world to know how fine she was. I saw in imagination the busy, excited dinner-tables at work upon us all, rather pleasantly excited, brightly indignant, merciless.

Well, it's the stuff we are! . . .

Then suddenly, stabbing me to the heart, came a vision of Margaret's tears and the sound of her voice saying, "Husband mine! Oh! Husband mine! To see you cry!" . . .

I came out of a cloud of thoughts to discover the narrow compartment with its feeble lamp overhead and our rugs and hand-baggage swaying on the rack, and Isabel, very still in front of me, gripping my wilting red roses tightly in her bare and ringless hand.

For a moment I could not understand her attitude, and then I perceived she was sitting bent together with her head averted from the light to hide the tears that were streaming down her face. She had not got her handkerchief out for fear that I should see this, but I saw her tears, dark drops of tears, upon her sleeve. . . .

I suppose she had been watching my expression, divining my thoughts.

For a time I stared at her and was motionless, in a sort of still and weary amazement. Why had we done this injury to one another ? *Why ?* Then something stirred within me.

" *Isabel* ! " I whispered.

She made no sign.

" Isabel ! " I repeated, and then crossed over to her and crept closely to her, put my arm about her, and drew her wet cheek to mine.

THE FOOD OF
THE GODS

CONTENTS

Book One

The Dawn of the Food

Book Two

The Food in the Village

Book Three

The Harvest of the Food

Book One

The Dawn of the Food

CHAPTER ONE

THE DISCOVERY OF THE FOOD

I

IN the middle years of the nineteenth century there first became abundant in this strange world of ours a class of men, men tending for the most part to become elderly, who are called, and who, though they dislike it extremely, are very properly called " Scientists." They dislike that word so much that from the columns of *Nature*, which was from the first their distinctive and characteristic paper, it is as carefully excluded as if it were—that other word which is the basis of all really bad language in this country. But the Great Public and its Press know better, and " Scientists " they are, and when they emerge to any sort of publicity, " distinguished scientists " and " eminent scientists " and " well-known scientists " is the very least we call them.

Certainly both Mr. Bensington and Professor Redwood quite merited any of these terms long before they came upon the marvellous discovery of which this story tells. Mr. Bensington was a Fellow of the Royal Society and a former president of the Chemical Society, and Professor Redwood was Professor of Physiology in the Bond Street College of the London University and had been grossly libelled by the anti-vivisectionists time after time. And both had led lives of academic distinction from their very earliest youth.

They were of course quite undistinguished-looking men, as indeed all true Scientists are. There is more personal distinction about the mildest-mannered actor alive than there is about the entire Royal Society. Mr. Bensington was short and very, very bald, and he stooped slightly ; he wore gold-rimmed spectacles and cloth boots that were abundantly cut open because of his numerous corns, and Professor Redwood was entirely ordinary in his appearance. Until they happened upon the Food of the Gods (as I must insist upon calling it) they led lives of such eminent and studious obscurity that it is hard to find anything whatever to tell the reader about them.

Mr. Bensington won his spurs (if one may use such an expression of a gentleman in boots of slashed cloth) by his splendid researches upon the More Toxic Alkaloids, and Professor Redwood rose to eminence—I do not clearly remember how he rose to eminence. I know he was very eminent, and that's all. But I fancy it was a voluminous work on Reaction Times with numerous plates of sphygmograph tracings (I write subject to correction) and an admirable new terminology, that did the thing for him.

The general public saw little or nothing of either of these

gentlemen. Sometimes at such places as the Royal Institution and the Society of Arts it did in a sort of way see Mr. Bensington, or at least his blushing baldness and something of his collar and coat, and hear fragments of a lecture or paper that he imagined himself to be reading audibly ; and once I remember—one midday in the vanished past—when the British Association was at Dover, coming on Section C or D or some such letter, which had taken up its quarters in a public-house, and following, out of mere curiosity, two serious-looking ladies with paper parcels through a door labelled " Billiards " and " Pool " into a scandalous darkness, broken only by a magic-lantern circle of Redwood's tracings.

I watched the lantern slides come and go, and listened to a voice (I forget what it was saying) which I believe was the voice of Professor Redwood, and there was a sizzling from the lantern and another sound that kept me there, still out of curiosity, until the lights were unexpectedly turned up. And then I perceived that this sound was the sound of the munching of buns and sandwiches and things that the assembled British Associates had come there to eat under cover of the magic-lantern darkness.

And Redwood, I remember, went on talking all the time the lights were up and dabbing at the place where his diagram ought to have been visible on the screen—and so it was again so soon as the darkness was restored. I remember him then as a most ordinary, slightly nervous-looking dark man, with an air of being preoccupied with something else and doing what he was doing just then under an unaccountable sense of duty.

I heard Bensington also once—in the old days—at an educational conference in Bloomsbury. Like most eminent chemists and botanists, Mr. Bensington was very authoritative upon teaching—though I am certain he would have been scared out of his wits by an average Board School class in half an hour —and so far as I can remember now, he was propounding an improvement of Professor Armstrong's Heuristic method, whereby at the cost of three or four hundred pounds' worth of apparatus, a total neglect of all other studies and the undivided attention of a teacher of exceptional gifts, an average child might with a peculiar sort of thumby thoroughness acquire in the course of ten or twelve years almost as much chemistry as one could learn from one of those objectionable shilling text-books that were then so common. . . .

Quite ordinary persons you perceive, both of them, outside their science. Or if anything on the unpractical side of ordinary. And that you will find is the case with " scientists " as a class all the world over. What there is great about them is an annoyance to their fellow scientists and a mystery to the general public, and what is not is evident.

There is no doubt about what is not great, no race of men have such obvious littlenesses. They live, so far as their human intercourse goes, in a narrow world ; their researches involve infinite attention and an almost monastic seclusion ; and what is left over is not very much.   To witness some queer, shy, misshapen, grey-headed, self-important little discoverer of great discoveries, ridiculously adorned with the wide ribbon of an order of chivalry and holding a reception of his fellow-men, or to read the anguish of *Nature* at the " neglect of science " when the angel of the birthday honours passes the Royal Society by, or to listen to one indefatigable lichenologist commenting on the work of another indefatigable lichenologist, such things force one to realise the unfaltering littleness of men.

And withal the reef of science that these little " scientists " built and are yet building is so wonderful, so portentous, so full of mysterious half-shapen promises for the mighty future of man !   They do not seem to realise the things they are doing ! No doubt long ago even Mr. Bensington, when he chose this calling, when he consecrated his life to the alkaloids and their kindred compounds, had some inkling of the vision—more than an inkling.   Without some great inspiration, for such glories and positions only as a " scientist " may expect, what young man would have given his life to this work, as young men do ? No, they *must* have seen the glory, they must have had the vision, but so near that it has blinded them.   The splendour has blinded them, mercifully, so that for the rest of their lives they can hold the light of knowledge in comfort—that we may see.

And perhaps it accounts for Redwood's touch of preoccupation that—there can be no doubt of it now—he among his fellows was different ; he was different inasmuch as something of the vision still lingered in his eyes.

II

The Food of the Gods I call it, this substance that Mr. Bensington and Professor Redwood made between them ; and having regard now to what it has already done and all that it is certainly going to do, there is surely no exaggeration in the name.   But Mr. Bensington would no more have called it by that named in cold blood than he would have gone out from his flat in Sloane Street clad in regal scarlet and a wreath of laurel. The phrase was a mere first cry of astonishment from him.   He called it the Food of the Gods in his enthusiasm, and for an hour or so at the most altogether.   After that he decided he was being absurd.   When he first thought of the thing he saw, as it were, a vista of enormous possibilities—literally enormous possibilities, but upon this dazzling vista, after one stare of amazement, he resolutely shut his eyes even as a conscientious " scientist " should.   After that, the Food of the Gods sounded blatant to the pitch of indecency.   He was surprised he had used the expression.   Yet for all that something of that clear-eyed moment hung about him and broke out ever and again. . . .

"Really, you know," he said, rubbing his hands together and laughing nervously, "it has more than a theoretical interest.

"For example," he confided, bringing his face close to the Professor's and dropping to an undertone, "it would perhaps, if suitably handled, sell. . . .

"Precisely," he said, walking away—"as a Food. Or at least a food ingredient.

"Assuming of course that it is palatable. A thing we cannot know till we have prepared it."

He turned upon the hearthrug, and studied the carefully designed slits upon his cloth shoes.

"Name ? " he said, looking up in response to an inquiry. "For my part I incline to the good old classical allusion. It —it makes Science res—— Gives it a touch of old-fashioned dignity. I have been thinking . . . I don't know if you will think it absurd of me. . . . A little fancy is surely occasionally permissible. . . . Herakleophorbia. Eh ? The nutrition of a possible Hercules ? You know it *might*. . . .

"Of course if you think *not*——"

Redwood reflected with his eyes on the fire and made no objection.

"You think it would do ? "

Redwood moved his head gravely.

"It might be Titanophorbia, you know. Food of Titans. . . . You prefer the former ?

"You're quite sure you don't think it a little *too*——"

"No."

"Ah ! I'm glad."

And so they called it Herakleophorbia throughout their investigations, and in their report—the report that was never published, because of the unexpected developments that upset all their arrangements, it is invariably written in that way. There were three kindred substances prepared before they hit on the one their speculations had foretold, and these they spoke of as Herakleophorbia I., Herakleophorbia II., and Herakleophorbia III. It is Herakleophorbia IV. which I— insisting upon Bensington's original name—call here the Food of the Gods.

III

The idea was Mr. Bensington's. But as it was suggested to him by one of Professor Redwood's contributions to the Philosophical Transactions, he very properly consulted that gentleman before he carried it further. Besides which it was, as a research, a physiological quite as much as a chemical inquiry.

Professor Redwood was one of those scientific men who are addicted to tracings and curves. You are familiar—if you are at all the sort of reader I like—with the sort of scientific paper I mean. It is a paper you cannot make head nor tail of, and at the end come five or six long folded diagrams that open out and show peculiar zigzag tracings, flashes of lightning over-done, or sinuous inexplicable things called " smoothed curves " set up on ordinates and rooting in abscissae—and things like that.   You puzzle over the thing for a long time and end with the suspicion that not only do you not understand it but that the author does not understand it either.   But really you know many of these scientific people understand the meaning of their own papers quite well, it is simply a defect of expression that raises the obstacle between us.

I am inclined to think that Redwood thought in tracings and curves.   And after his monumental work upon Reaction Times (the unscientific reader is exhorted to stick to it for a little bit longer and everything will be as clear as daylight) Redwood began to turn out smoothed curves and sphygmographeries upon Growth, and it was one of his papers upon Growth that really gave Mr. Bensington his idea.

Redwood, you know, had been measuring growing things of all sorts, kittens, puppies, sunflowers, mushrooms, bean plants and (until his wife put a stop to it) his baby, and he showed that growth went on, not at a regular pace, or, as he put it, so

but with bursts and intermissions of this sort,

and that apparently nothing grew regularly and steadily, and so far as he could make out nothing could grow regularly and steadily ; it was as if every living thing had first to accumulate force to grow, grew with vigour only for a time and then had to wait for a space before it could go on growing again.   And in the muffled and highly technical language of the really careful " scientist," Redwood suggested that the process of growth probably demanded the presence of a considerable quantity of some necessary substance in the blood that was only formed very slowly, and that when this substance was used up by growth, it was only very slowly replaced, and that meanwhile the organism had to mark time.   He compared his unknown substance to oil in machinery.   A growing animal was rather like an engine, he suggested, that can move a certain distance and must then be oiled before it can run again.   (" But why shouldn't one oil the engine from without ? " said Mr. Bensington, when he read the paper.)   And all this, said Redwood, with the delightful nervous inconsecutiveness of his class, might very probably be found to throw a light upon the mystery of certain of the ductless glands. As though they had anything to do with it at all !

In a subsequent communication Redwood went further. He gave a perfect Brock's benefit of diagrams—exactly like rocket trajectories they were, and the gist of it—so far as it had any gist—was that the blood of puppies and kittens and the sap of sunflowers and the juice of mushrooms in what he called the " growing phase " differed as to the proportions of certain elements from their blood and sap on the days when they were not particularly growing.

And when Mr. Bensington, after holding the diagrams sideways and upside down, began to see what this difference was, a great amazement came upon him. Because, you see, the difference might probably be due to the presence of just the very substance he had recently been trying to isolate in his researches upon such alkaloids as are most stimulating to the nervous system. He put down Redwood's paper on the patent reading-desk that swung inconveniently from his armchair, took off his gold-rimmed spectacles, breathed on them and wiped them very carefully.

" By Jove ! " said Mr. Bensington.

Then replacing his spectacles again he turned to the patent reading-desk, which immediately, as his elbow came against its arm, gave a coquettish squeak and deposited the paper, with all its diagrams in a dispersed and crumpled state, on the floor. " By Jove ! " said Mr. Bensington, straining his stomach over the armchair with a patient disregard of the habits of this convenience, and then, finding the pamphlet still out of reach, he went down on all-fours in pursuit. It was on the floor that the idea of calling it the Food of the Gods came to him. . . .

For you see, if he was right and Redwood was right, then by injecting or administering this new substance of his in food, he would do away with the " resting phase," and instead of growth going on in this fashion

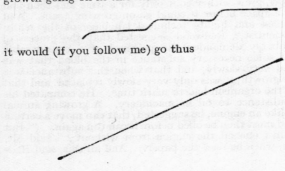

it would (if you follow me) go thus

IV

The night after his conversation with Redwood, Mr. Bensington could sleep scarcely a wink.   He did seem once to get into a sort of doze, but it was only for a moment, and then he dreamt he had dug a deep hole into the earth and poured in tons and tons of the Food of the Gods and the earth was swelling and swelling, and all the boundaries of the countries were bursting, and the Royal Geographical Society was all at work like one mighty guild of tailors letting out the equator.

That of course was a ridiculous dream ; but it shows the state of mental excitement into which Mr. Bensington got and the real value he attached to his idea, much better than any of the things he said or did when he was awake and on his guard. Or I should not have mentioned it, because as a general rule it is not I think at all interesting for people to tell each other about their dreams.

By a singular coincidence Redwood also had a dream that night, and his dream was this :—

It was a diagram done in fire upon a long scroll of the abyss. And he (Redwood) was standing on a planet before a sort of black platform lecturing about the new sort of growth that was now possible, to the More than Royal Institution of Primordial Forces, forces which had always previously, even in the growth of races, empires, planetary systems and worlds, gone so :—

And even in some cases so :—

And he was explaining to them quite lucidly and convincingly that these slow, these even retrogressive methods would be very speedily quite put out of fashion by his discovery.

Ridiculous of course.   But that too shows—

That either dream is to be regarded as in any way significant or prophetic beyond what I have categorically said, I do not for one moment suggest.

CHAPTER TWO

THE EXPERIMENTAL FARM

I

MR. BENSINGTON proposed originally to try this stuff, so soon as he was really able to prepare it, upon tadpoles. One always does try this sort of thing upon tadpoles to begin with ; that being what tadpoles are for. And it was agreed that he should conduct the experiments and not Redwood, because Redwood's laboratory was occupied with the ballistic apparatus and animals necessary for an investigation into the Diurnal Variation in the Butting Frequency of the Young Bull Calf, an investigation that was yielding curves of an abnormal and very perplexing sort, and the presence of glass globes of tadpoles was extremely undesirable while this particular research was in progress.

But when Mr. Bensington conveyed to his cousin Jane something of what he had in mind, she put a prompt veto upon the importation of any considerable number of tadpoles, or any such experimental creatures, into their flat. She had no objection whatever to his use of one of the rooms of the flat for the purposes of a non-explosive chemistry that so far as she was concerned, came to nothing ; and she let him have a gas furnace and a sink and a dust-tight cupboard of refuge from the weekly storm of cleaning she would not forgo. And having known people addicted to drink, she regarded his solicitude for distinction in learned societies as an excellent substitute for the coarser form of depravity. But any sort of living things in quantity, " wriggly " as they were bound to be alive, and " smelly " dead, she could not and would not abide. She said these things were certain to be unhealthy, and Bensington was notoriously a delicate man—it was nonsense to say he wasn't. And when Bensington tried to make the enormous importance of this possible discovery clear, she said that it was all very well, but if she consented to his making everything nasty and unwholesome in the place (and that was what it all came to) then she was certain he would be the first to complain.

And Mr. Bensington went up and down the room, regardless of his corns, and spoke to her quite firmly and angrily without the slightest effect. He said that nothing ought to stand in the way of the Advancement of Science, and she said that the Advancement of Science was one thing and having a lot of tadpoles in a flat was another ; he said that in Germany it was an ascertained fact that a man with an idea like his would at once have twenty thousand properly-fitted cubic feet of laboratory placed at his disposal, and she said she was glad

and always had been glad that she was not a German ; he
said that it would make him famous for ever, and she said it
was much more likely to make him ill to have a lot of tadpoles
in a flat like theirs ; he said he was master in his own house,
and she said that rather than wait on a lot of tadpoles she'd go
as matron to a school ; and then he asked her to be reasonable,
and she asked *him* to be reasonable then and give up all this
about tadpoles ; and he said she might respect his ideas, and
she said not if they were smelly she wouldn't ; and then he
gave way completely and said—in spite of the classical remarks
of Huxley upon the subject—a bad word. Not a very bad
word it was, but bad enough.

And after that she was greatly offended and had to be
apologised to, and the prospect of ever trying the Food of the
Gods upon tadpoles in their flat at any rate vanished completely
in the apology.

So Bensington had to consider some other way of carrying
out these experiments in feeding that would be necessary to
demonstrate his discovery, so soon as he had his substance
isolated and prepared. For some days he meditated upon the
possibility of boarding out his tadpoles with some trustworthy
person, and then the chance sight of the phrase in a newspaper
turned his thoughts to an Experimental Farm.

And chicks. Directly he thought of it, he thought of it as
a poultry farm. He was suddenly taken with a vision of
wildly growing chicks. He conceived a picture of coops and
runs, outsize and still more outsize coops, and runs progres-
sively larger. Chicks are so accessible, so easily fed and observed, so much drier to handle and measure, that for his
purpose tadpoles seemed to him now, in comparison with
them, quite wild and uncontrollable beasts. He was quite
puzzled to understand why he had not thought of chicks instead
of tadpoles from the beginning. Among other things it would
have saved all this trouble with his cousin Jane. And when
he suggested this to Redwood, Redwood quite agreed with
him.

Redwood said he was convinced that in working so much
upon needlessly small animals experimental physiologists
made a great mistake. It is exactly like making experiments
in chemistry with an insufficient quantity of material ; errors
of observation and manipulation become disproportionately
large. It was of extreme importance just at present that
scientific men should assert their right to have their material
big. That was why he was doing his present series of experiments at the Bond Street College upon Bull Calves, in spite of
a certain amount of inconvenience to the students and pro-
fessors of other subjects caused by their incidental levity in
the corridors. But the curves he was getting were quite exceptionally interesting, and would, when published, amply justify
his choice. For his own part, were it not for the inadequate

endowment of science in this country, he would never, if he could avoid it, work on anything smaller than a whale. But a Public Vivarium on a scale sufficient to render this possible was, he feared, at present, in this country at any rate, a Utopian demand. In Germany——etc.

As Redwood's bull calves needed his daily attention, the selection and equipment of the Experimental Farm fell largely on Bensington. The entire cost also, it was understood, was to be defrayed by Bensington, at least until a grant could be obtained. Accordingly he alternated his work in the laboratory of his flat with farm-hunting up and down the lines that run southward out of London, and his peering spectacles, his simple baldness, and his lacerated cloth shoes filled the owners of numerous undesirable properties with vain hopes. And he advertised in several daily papers and *Nature* for a responsible couple (married), punctual, active, and used to poultry, to take entire charge of an Experimental Farm of three acres.

He found the place he seemed in need of at Hickleybrow, near Urshot in Kent. It was a queer little isolated place, in a dell surrounded by old pine woods that were black and forbidding at night. A humped shoulder of down cut it off from the sunset, and a gaunt well with a shattered penthouse dwarfed the dwelling. The little house was creeperless, several windows were broken, and the cart-shed had a black shadow at midday. It was a mile and a half from the end house of the village, and its loneliness was very doubtfully relieved by an ambiguous family of echoes.

The place impressed Bensington as being eminently adapted to the requirements of scientific research. He walked over the premises sketching out coops and runs with a sweeping arm, and he found the kitchen capable of accommodating a series of incubators and foster mothers with the very minimum of alteration. He took the place then and there ; on his way back to London he stopped at Dunton Green and closed with an eligible couple that had answered his advertisements, and that same evening he succeeded in isolating a sufficient quantity of Herakleophorbia I. to more than justify these engagements.

The eligible couple who were destined under Mr. Bensington to be the first almoners on earth of the Food of the Gods, were not only very perceptibly aged, but also extremely dirty. This latter point Mr. Bensington did not observe, because nothing destroys the powers of general observation quite so much as a life of experimental science. They were named Skinner, Mr. and Mrs. Skinner, and Mr. Bensington interviewed them in a small room with hermetically sealed windows, a spotted overmantel looking-glass, and some ailing calceolarias.

Mrs. Skinner was a very little old woman, capless, with dirty white hair drawn back very very tightly from a face that had

begun by being chiefly, and was now through the loss of teeth
and chin and the wrinkling up of everything else, ending by
being almost exclusively—nose. She was dressed in slate
colour (so far as her dress had any colour) slashed in one place
with red flannel. She let him in and talked to him guardedly
and peered at him round and over her nose, while Mr. Skinner
she alleged made some alteration in his toilette. She had one
tooth that got into her articulation, and she held her two long
wrinkled hands nervously together. She told Mr. Bensington
that she had managed fowls for years, and knew all about
incubators ; in fact, they themselves had run a Poultry Farm
at one time, and it had only failed at last through the want of
pupils. " It's the pupils as pay," said Mrs. Skinner.

Mr. Skinner, when he appeared, was a large-faced man with
a lisp, and a squint that made him look over the top of your
head, slashed slippers that appealed to Mr. Bensington's
sympathies, and a manifest shortness of buttons. He held
his coat and shirt together with one hand and traced patterns
on the black and gold tablecloth with the index finger of the
other, while his disengaged eye watched Mr. Bensington's
sword of Damocles, so to speak, with an expression of sad
detachment. " You don't want to run thith Farm for profit.
No, Thir. Ith all the thame, Thir. Ekthperimenth !
Prethithely.'"

He said they could go to the farm at once. He was doing
nothing at Dunton Green except a little tailoring. " It ithn't
the thmart plathe I thought it wath, and what I get thent
thkarthely worth having," he said, " tho that if ith any con-
venienth to you for uth to come. . . ."

And in a week Mr. and Mrs. Skinner were installed in the
farm, and the jobbing carpenter from Hickleybrow was
diversifying the task of erecting runs and henhouses with a
systematic discussion of Mr. Bensington.

" I haven't theen much of 'im yet," said Mr. Skinner.
" But ath far ath I can make 'im out 'e theemth to be a
thtewpid o' fool."

" *I* thought 'e seemed a bit dotty," said the carpenter from
Hickleybrow.

" 'E fanthieth 'imthelf about poultry," said Mr. Skinner.
" O my goodneth ! You'd think nobody knew nothin' about
poultry thept 'im."

" 'E *looks* like a 'en," said the carpenter from Hickleybrow ;
" what with them spectacles of 'is."

Mr. Skinner came closer to the carpenter from Hickleybrow
and spoke in a confidential manner, and one sad eye regarded
the distant village and one was bright and wicked. " Got to
be meathured every blethed day—every blethed 'en, 'e thayth.
Tho' ath to thee they grow properly. What oh . . . eh ?
Every blethed 'en—every blethed day."

And Mr. Skinner put up his hand to laugh behind it in a

refined and contagious manner, and humped his shoulders very much—and only the other eye of him failed to participate in his laughter. Then doubting if the carpenter had quite got the point of it, he repeated in a penetrating whisper: " *Meathured !* "

" 'E's worse than our old guvnor ; I'm dratted if 'e ain't," said the carpenter from Hickleybrow.

II

Experimental work is the most tedious thing in the world (unless it be the reports of it in the *Philosophical Transactions*), and it seemed a long time to Mr. Bensington before his first dream of enormous possibilities was replaced by a crumb of realisation. He had taken the Experimental Farm in October, and it was May before the first inklings of success began. Herakleophorbia I. and II. and III. had to be tried, and failed ; there was trouble with the rats of the Experimental Farm, and there was trouble with the Skinners. The only way to get Skinner to do anything he was told to do was to dismiss him. Then he would rub his unshaven chin—he was always unshaven most miraculously and yet never bearded—with a flattened hand, and look at Mr. Bensington with one eye, and over him with the other, and say, " Oo, of courthe, Thir—if you're *theriouth* . . . ! "

But at last success dawned. And its herald was a letter in the long slender handwriting of Mr. Skinner.

" The new Brood are out," wrote Mr. Skinner, " and don't quite like the look of them. Growing very rank—quite unlike what the similar lot was before your last directions was given. The last before the cat got them was a very nice stocky chick, but these are Growing like thistles. I never saw. They peck so hard, striking above boot top, that am unable to give exact Measures as requested. They are regular Giants and eating as such. We shall want more corn very soon, for you never saw such chicks to eat. Bigger than Bantams. Going on at this rate they ought to be a bird for show, rank as they are. Plymouth Rocks won't be in it. Had a scare last night thinking that cat was at them, and when I looked out at the window could have sworn I see her getting in under the wire. The chicks was all awake and pecking about hungry when I went out, but could not see anything of the cat. So gave them a peck of corn, and fastened up safe. Shall be glad to know if the Feeding to be continued as directed. Food you mixed is pretty near all gone, and do not like to mix any more myself on account of the accident with the pudding. With best wishes from us both, and soliciting continuance of esteemed favours.   Respectfully yours,
" ALFRED NEWTON SKINNER."

The allusion towards the end referred to a milk pudding with which some Herakleophorbia II. had got itself mixed, with painful and very nearly fatal results to the Skinners.

But Mr. Bensington, reading between the lines, saw in this rankness of growth the attainment of his long-sought goal. The next morning he alighted at Urshot station, and in the bag in his hand he carried, sealed in three tins, a supply of the Food of the Gods sufficient for all the chicks in Kent.

It was a bright and beautiful morning late in May, and his corns were so much better that he resolved to walk through Hickleybrow to his farm.   It was three miles and a half altogether, through the park and village and then along the green glades of the Hickleybrow preserves.   The trees were all dusted with the green spangles of high spring, the hedges were full of stitchwort and campion and the woods of blue hyacinths and purple orchid, and everywhere there was a great noise of birds, thrushes, blackbirds, robins, finches, and many more ; and in one warm corner of the park some bracken was unrolling, and there was a leaping and rushing of fallow deer.

These things brought back to Mr. Bensington his early and forgotten delight in life ; before him the promise of his discovery grew bright and joyful, and it seemed to him that indeed he must have come upon the happiest day in his life.   And when in the sunlit run by the sandy bank under the shadow of the pine trees he saw the chicks that had eaten the food he had mixed for them, gigantic and gawky, bigger already than many a hen that is married and settled ; and still growing, still in their first soft yellow plumage (just faintly marked with brown along the back), he knew indeed that his happiest day had come.

At Mr. Skinner's urgency he went into the run ; but after he had been pecked through the cracks in his shoes once or twice he got out again, and watched these monsters through the wire netting.   He peered close to the netting, and followed their movements as though he had never seen a chick before in his life.

" Whath they'll be when they're grown up ith impothible to think," said Mr. Skinner.

" Big as a horse," said Mr. Bensington.

" Pretty near," said Mr. Skinner.

" Several people could dine off a wing ! " said Mr. Bensington.   " They'd cut up into joints like butcher's meat."

" They won't go on growing at thith pathe though," said Mr. Skinner.

" No ? " said Mr. Bensington.

" No," said Mr. Skinner.   " I know thith thort.   They begin rank, but they don't go on, bleth you !   No."

There was a pause.

" Itth management," said Mr. Skinner modestly.

Mr. Bensington turned his glasses on him suddenly.

" We got 'em almoth ath big at the other plathe," said Mr. Skinner, with his better eye piously uplifted and letting himself go a little ; " me and the mithith."

Mr. Bensington made his usual general inspection of the premises, but he speedily returned to the new run. It was, you know, in truth ever so much more than he had dared to expect. The course of science is so tortuous and so slow ; after the clear promises and before the practical realisation arrives there comes almost always year after year of intricate contrivance, and here—here was the Food of the Gods arriving after less than a year of testing ! It seemed too good—too good. That Hope Deferred which is the daily food of the scientific imagination was to be his no more ! So at least it seemed to him then. He came back and stared at these stupendous chicks of his time after time.

" Let me see," he said. " They're ten days old. And by the side of an ordinary chick I should fancy—about six or seven times as big. . . ."

" Itth about time we artht for a rithe in thkrew," said Mr. Skinner to his wife. " He'th ath pleathed ath Punth about the way we got thothe chickth on in the further run—pleathed ath Punth he ith."

He bent confidentially towards her. " Thinkth it'th that old food of hith," he said behind his hand, and made a noise of suppressed laughter in his pharyngeal cavity. . . .

Mr. Bensington was indeed a happy man that day. He was in no mood to find fault with details of management. The sunshine certainly brought out the accumulating slovenliness of the Skinner couple more vividly than he had ever seen it before. But his comments were of the gentlest. The fencing of many of the runs was out of order, but he seemed to consider it quite satisfactory when Mr. Skinner explained that it was a " fokth or a dog or thomething " did it. He pointed out that the incubator had not been cleaned.

" That it 'asn't, Sir," said Mrs. Skinner with her arms folded, smiling coyly behind her nose. " We don't seem to have had time to clean it not since we been 'ere. . . ."

He went upstairs to see some ratholes that Skinner said would justify a trap—they certainly were enormous—and discovered that the room in which the Food of the Gods was mixed with meal and bran was in a quite disgraceful disorder. The Skinners were the sort of people who find a use for cracked saucers and old cans and pickle jars and mustard boxes, and the place was littered with these. In one corner a great pile of apples that Skinner had saved was decaying ; and from a nail in the sloping part of the ceiling hung several rabbit skins upon which he proposed to test his gift as a furrier. (" There ithn't mutth about furth and thingth that *I* don't know," said Skinner.)

Mr. Bensington certainly sniffed critically at this disorder,

but he made no unnecessary fuss, and even when he found a
wasp regaling itself in a gallipot half full of Herakleophorbia IV.,
he simply remarked mildly that his substance was better sealed
from the damp than exposed to the air in that manner.

And he turned from these things at once to remark—what
had been for some time in his mind—" I *think*, you know,
Skinner—I shall kill one of these chicks—as a specimen. I
think we will kill it this afternoon, and I will take it back with
me to London."

He pretended to peer into another gallipot and then took off
his spectacles to wipe them.

" I should like," he said, " I should like very much to have
some relic—some memento—of this particular brood at this
particular day.

" By the bye," he said, " you don't give those little chicks
meat ? "

" Oh ! *no*, Thir," said Skinner, " I can athure you, Thir, we
know far too much about the management of fowlth of all
dethcriptionth to do anything of that thort."

" Quite sure you don't throw your dinner refuse—I thought
I noticed the bones of a rabbit scattered about the far corner
of the run——"

But when they came to look at them they found they were
the larger bones of a cat picked very clean and dry.

III

" *That's* no chick," said Mr. Bensington's cousin Jane.

" Well, I should *think* I knew a chick when I saw it," said
Mr. Bensington's cousin Jane hotly.

" It's too big for a chick, for one thing, and besides you can
see perfectly well it isn't a chick."

" It's more like a bustard than a chick."

" For my part," said Redwood, reluctantly allowing Bensington to drag him into the argument, " I must confess that, considering all the evidence——"

" Oh ! if you do *that*," said Mr. Bensington's cousin Jane,
" instead of using your eyes like a sensible person——"

" Well, but really, Miss Bensington—— ! "

" Oh ! Go *on* ! " said cousin Jane. " You men are all
alike."

" Considering all the evidence, this certainly falls within the
definition—no doubt it's abnormal and hypertrophied, but still
—especially since it was hatched from the egg of a normal hen
—yes, I think, Miss Bensington, I must admit—this, so far as
one can call it anything, is a sort of chick."

" You mean it's a chick ? " said cousin Jane.

" I *think* it's a chick," said Redwood.

" What NONSENSE ! " said Mr. Bensington's cousin Jane, and
' Oh *!* " directed at Redwood's head, " I haven't patience with

you," and then suddenly she turned about and went out of the room with a slam.

"And it's a very great relief for me to see it, too, Bensington," said Redwood, when the reverberation of the slam had died away. "In spite of its being so big."

Without any urgency from Mr. Bensington he sat down in the low armchair by the fire and confessed to proceedings that even in an unscientific man would have been indiscreet. "You will think it very rash of me, Bensington, I know," he said, "but the fact is I put a little—not very much of it—but some —into Baby's bottle very nearly a week ago!"

"But suppose——!" cried Mr. Bensington.

"I know," said Redwood, and glanced at the giant chick upon the plate on the table.

"It's turned out all right, thank goodness," and he felt in his pocket for his cigarettes.

He gave fragmentary details. "Poor little chap wasn't putting on weight . . . desperately anxious.—Winkles, a frightful duffer . . . former pupil of mine . . . no good. . . . Mrs. Redwood—unmitigated confidence in Winkles. . . . *You* know, man with a manner like a cliff—towering. . . . No confidence in *me*, of course. . . . Taught Winkles. . . . Scarcely allowed in the nursery. . . . Something had to be done. . . . Slipped in while the nurse was at breakfast . . . got at the bottle."

"But he'll grow," said Mr. Bensington.

"He's growing. Twenty-seven ounces last week. . . . You should hear Winkles. It's management, he said."

"Dear me! That's what Skinner says!"

Redwood looked at the chick again. "The bother is to keep it up," he said. "They won't trust me in the nursery alone, because I tried to get a growth curve out of Georgina Phyllis— you know—and how I'm to give him a second dose——"

"Need you?"

"He's been crying two days—can't get on with his ordinary food again, anyhow. He wants some more now."

"Tell Winkles."

"Hang Winkles!" said Redwood.

"You might get at Winkles and give him powders to give the child——"

"That's about what I shall have to do," said Redwood, resting his chin on his fist and staring into the fire.

Bensington stood for a space smoothing the down on the breast of the giant chick. "They will be monstrous fowls," he said.

"They will," said Redwood, still with his eyes on the glow.

"Big as horses," said Bensington.

"Bigger," said Redwood. "That's just it!"

Bensington turned away from the specimen. "Redwood," he said, "these fowls are going to create a sensation."

Redwood nodded his head at the fire.

" And by Jove ! " said Bensington, coming round suddenly with a flash in his spectacles, " so will your little boy ! "

" That's just what I'm thinking of," said Redwood.

He sat back, sighed, threw his unconsumed cigarette into the fire and thrust his hands deep into his trouser pockets. " That's precisely what I'm thinking of. This Herakleophorbia is going to be queer stuff to handle. The pace that chick must have grown at—— ! "

" A little boy growing at that pace," said Mr. Bensington slowly, and stared at the chick as he spoke.

" I *say* ! " said Bensington, " he'll be Big."

" I shall give him diminishing doses," said Redwood. " Or at any rate Winkles will."

" It's rather too much of an experiment."

" Much."

" Yet still, you know, I must confess—— . . . Some baby will sooner or later have to try it."

" Oh, we'll try it on *some* baby—certainly."

" Exactly so," said Bensington, and came and stood on the hearthrug and took off his spectacles to wipe them.

" Until I saw these chicks, Redwood, I don't think I *began* to realise—anything—of the possibilities of what we were making. It's only beginning to dawn upon me . . . the possible consequences. . . ."

And even then, you know, Mr. Bensington was far from any conception of the mine that little train would fire.

IV

That happened early in June. For some weeks Bensington was kept from revisiting the Experimental Farm by a severe imaginary catarrh, and one necessary flying visit was made by Redwood. He returned an even more anxious-looking parent than he had gone. Altogether there were seven weeks of steady, uninterrupted growth. . . .

And then the Wasps began their career.

It was late in July and nearly a week before the hens escaped from Hickleybrow that the first of the big wasps was killed. The report of it appeared in several papers, but I do not know whether the news reached Mr. Bensington, much less whether he connected it with the general laxity of method that prevailed at the Experimental Farm.

There can be but little doubt now, that while Mr. Skinner was plying Mr. Bensington's chicks with Herakleophorbia IV., a number of wasps were just as industriously—perhaps more industriously—carrying quantities of the same paste to their early summer broods in the sand-banks beyond the adjacent pine woods. And there can be no dispute whatever that these early broods found just as much growth and benefit in the substance as Mr. Bensington's hens. It is in the nature of the wasp to attain to effective maturity before the domestic fowl, and of all the creatures that through the generous carelessness of the Skinners were partaking of the benefits Mr. Bensington heaped upon his hens, the wasps were the first to make any sort of figure in the world.

It was a keeper named Godfrey on the estate of Lieutenant-Colonel Rupert Hick, near Maidstone, who encountered and had the luck to kill the first of these monsters of whom history has any record. He was walking knee-high in bracken across an open space in the beechwoods that diversify Lieutenant-Colonel Hick's park, and he was carrying his gun—very fortunately for him a double-barrelled gun—over his shoulder, when he first caught sight of the thing. It was, he says, coming down against the light so that he could not see it very distinctly, and as it came it made a drone " like a motor-car." He admits he was frightened. It was evidently as big or bigger than a barn owl, and to his practised eye its flight, and particularly the misty whirl of its wings, must have seemed weirdly unbird-like. The instinct of self-defence, I fancy, mingled with long habit when, as he says, he " let fly, right away."

The queerness of the experience probably affected his aim ; at any rate most of his shot missed, and the thing merely dropped for a moment with an angry " Wuzzzz " that revealed the wasp at once, and then rose again with all its stripes shining against the light. He says it turned on him. At any rate, he fired his second barrel at less than twenty yards and threw down his gun, ran a pace or so, and ducked to avoid it.

It flew, he is convinced, within a yard of him ; struck the ground, rose again, came down again perhaps thirty yards away, and rolled over with its body wriggling and its sting stabbing out and back in its last agony. He emptied both barrels into it again before he ventured to go near.

When he came to measure the thing, he found it was twenty-seven and a half inches across its open wings, and its sting was three inches long. The abdomen was blown clean off from its body, but he estimated the length of the creature from head to sting as eighteen inches—which is very nearly correct. Its compound eyes were the size of penny pieces.

That is the first authenticated appearance of the giant wasps. The day after, a cyclist riding feet up down the hill between Sevenoaks and Tonbridge, very narrowly missed running over a second of these giants that was crawling across the roadway. His passage seemed to alarm it, and it rose with a noise like a sawmill. His bicycle jumped the footpath in the emotion of the moment, and when he could look back the wasp was soaring away above the woods towards Westerham.

After riding unsteadily for a little time, he put on his brake, dismounted—he was trembling so violently that he fell over his machine in doing so—and sat down by the roadside to recover. He had intended to ride to Ashford, but he did not get beyond Tonbridge that day. . . .

After that, curiously enough, there is no record of any big wasps being seen for three days. I find on consulting the meteorological record of those days that they were overcast and chilly with local showers, which may perhaps account for this intermission. Then on the fourth day came blue sky and brilliant sunshine, and such an outburst of wasps as the world had surely never seen before.

How many big wasps came out that day it is impossible to guess. There are at least fifty accounts of their apparition. There was one victim, a grocer, who discovered one of these monsters in a sugar-cask and very rashly attacked it with a spade as it rose. He struck it to the ground for a moment, and it stung him through the boot as he struck at it again and cut its body in halves. He was first dead of the two. . . .

The most dramatic of the fifty appearances was certainly that of the wasp that visited the British Museum about mid-day, dropping out of the blue serene upon one of the innumerable pigeons that feed in the courtyard of that building, and flying up to the cornice to devour its victim at leisure. After that it crawled for a time over the museum roof, entered the dome of the reading-room by a skylight, buzzed about inside it for some little time—there was a stampede among the readers—and at last found another window and vanished again with a sudden silence from human observation.

Most of the other reports were of mere passings or descents. A picnic party was dispersed at Aldington Knoll and all its sweets and jam consumed, and a puppy was killed and torn to pieces near Whitstable under the very eyes of its mistress. . . .

The streets that evening resounded with the cry, the newspaper placards gave themselves up exclusively in the biggest of letters to the " Gigantic Wasps in Kent." Agitated editors and assistant editors ran up and down tortuous staircases bawling things about wasps. And Professor Redwood, emerging from his college in Bond Street at five, flushed from a heated discussion with his committee about the price of bull calves, bought an evening paper, opened it, changed colour, forgot about bull calves and committee forthwith, and took a hansom headlong for Bensington's flat.

V

The flat was occupied, it seemed to him, to the exclusion of all other sensible objects by Mr. Skinner and his voice, if indeed you can call either him or it a sensible object !

The voice was up very high slopping about among the notes of anguish. " Itth impothible for uth to thtop, Thir. We've thtopped on hoping thingth would get better and they've only got worth, Thir. It ithn't on'y the waptheth, Thir—thereth big earwighth, Thir—big ath that, Thir. (He indicated all his

hand, and about three inches of fat dirty wrist.)   " They pretty
near give Mithith Thkinner fitth, Thir.   And the thtinging
nettleth by the runth, Thir, *they're* growing, Thir, and the
canary creeper, Thir, what we thowed near the think, Thir—it
put itth tendril through the window in the night, Thir, and very
nearly caught Mithith Thkinner by the legth, Thir.   Itth that
food of yourth, Thir.   Wherever we thplathed it about, Thir,
a bit, it'th thet everything growing ranker, Thir, than I ever
thought anything could grow.   Itth impothible to thtop a
month, Thir.   Itth more than our liveth are worth, Thir.
Even if the waptheth don't thting uth, we thall be thuffocated
by the creeper, Thir.   You can't imagine, Thir—unleth you
come down to thee, Thir——"

He turned his superior eye to the cornice above Redwood's
head.   "'Ow do we know the ratth 'aven't got it, Thir !
That 'th what I think of motht, Thir.   I 'aven't theen any big
ratth, Thir, but 'ow do I know, Thir.   We been frightened for
dayth becauth of the earwigth we've theen—like lobthterth
they wath—two of 'em, Thir—and the frightful way the canary
creeper wath growing, and directly I heard the waptheth—
directly I 'eard 'em, Thir, I underthood.   I didn't wait for
nothing exthept to thow on a button I'd lortht, and then I
came on up.   Even now, Thir, I'm arf wild with angthiety,
Thir.   'Ow do *I* know watth happenin' to Mithith Thkinner,
Thir !   Thereth the creeper growing all over the plathe like a
thnake, Thir—thwelp me but you 'ave to watch it, Thir, and
jump out of itth way !—and the earwigth gettin' bigger and
bigger, and the waptheth—— She 'athen't even got a Blue
Bag, Thir—if anything thould happen, Thir ! "

" But the hens," said Mr. Bensington ; " how are the hens?"

" We fed 'em up to yethterday, thwelp me," said Mr.
Skinner.   " But thith morning we didn't *dare*, Thir.   The
noithe of the waptheth wath—thomething awful, Thir.   They
wath coming out—dothenth.   Ath big ath 'enth.   I thayth
to 'er, I thayth you juth thow me on a button or two, I thayth,
for I can't go to London like thith, I thayth, and I'll go up to
Mither Benthington, I thayth, and ekthplain thingth to 'im.
And you thtop in thith room till I come back to you, I thayth,
and keep the windowth thhut jutht ath tight ath ever you can,
I thayth."

" If you hadn't been so confoundedly untidy——" began
Redwood.

" Oh ! don't thay *that*, Thir," said Skinner.   " Not now,
Thir.   Not with me tho diththrethed, Thir, about Mithith
Thkinner, Thir !   Oh, *don't*, Thir !   I 'aven't the 'eart to
argue with you.   Thwelp me, Thir, I 'aven't !   Itth the ratth
I keep a thinking of—'Ow do I know they 'aven't got at Mithith
Thkinner while I been up 'ere ? "

" And you haven't got a solitary measurement of all these
beautiful growth curves ! " said Redwood.

" I been too upthet, Thir," said Mr. Skinner. " If you knew
what we been through—me and the mithith ! All thith latht
month. We 'aven't known what to make of it, Thir. What
with the henth gettin' tho rank, and the earwighth, and the
canary creeper. I dunno if I told you, Thir—the canary
creeper . . ."

" You've told us all that," said Redwood. " The thing is,
Bensington, what are we to do ? "

" What are *we* to do ? " said Mr. Skinner.

" You'll have to go back to Mrs. Skinner," said Redwood.
" You can't leave her there alone all night."

" Not alone, Thir, I don't. Not if there wath a dothen
Mithith Thkinnerth. Itth Mithter Benthington——"

" Nonsense," said Redwood. " The wasps will be all right
at night. And the earwigs will get out of your way——"

" But about the ratth ? "

" There aren't any rats," said Redwood.

VI

Mr. Skinner might have foregone his chief anxiety. Mrs.
Skinner did not stop out her day.

About eleven the canary creeper, which had been quietly
active all the morning, began to clamber over the window and
darken it, and the darker it got the more and more clearly Mrs.
Skinner perceived that her position would speedily become un-
tenable. And also that she had lived many ages since Skinner
went. She peered out of the darkling window through the
stirring tendrils for some time, and then went very cautiously
and opened the bedroom door and listened. . . .

Everything seemed quiet ; and so, tucking her skirts high
about her, Mrs. Skinner made a bolt for the bedroom, and
having first looked under the bed and locked herself in, proceeded with the methodical rapidity of an experienced woman
to pack for departure. The bed had not been made, and the
room was littered with pieces of the creeper that Skinner had
hacked off in order to close the window overnight, but these
disorders she did not heed. She packed in a decent sheet.
She packed all her own wardrobe and a velveteen jacket that
Skinner wore in his finer moments, and she packed a jar of
pickles that had not been opened, and so far she was justified
in her packing. But she also packed two of the hermetically
closed tins containing Herakleophorbia IV. that Mr. Bensington had brought on his last visit. (She was honest, good
woman—but she was a grandmother, and her heart had burned
within her to see such good growth lavished on a lot of dratted
chicks.)

And having packed all these things, she put on her bonnet
took off her apron, tied a new bootlace round her umbrella, and
after listening for a long time at door and window, opened the
door and sallied out into a perilous world. The umbrella was

under her arm and she clutched the bundle with two gnarled and resolute hands.   It was her best Sunday bonnet she wore, and the two poppies that reared their heads amidst its splendours of band and bead seemed instinct with the same tremulous courage that possessed her.

The features about the roots of her nose wrinkled with determination.   She had had enough of it!   All alone there! Skinner might come back there if he liked.

She went out by the front door, going that way not because she wanted to go to Hickleybrow (her goal was Cheasing Eyebright where her married daughter resided), but because the back door was impassable on account of the canary creeper that had been growing so furiously ever since she upset the can of food near its roots.   She listened for a space and closed the front door very carefully behind her.   At the corner of the house she paused and reconnoitered. . . .

An extensive sandy scar upon the hillside beyond the pine woods marked the nest of the giant Wasps, and this she studied very earnestly.   The coming and going of the morning was over, not a wasp chanced to be in sight then, and except for a sound scarcely more perceptible than a steam wood-saw at work amidst the pines would have been, everything was still. As for earwigs, she could see not one.   Down among the cabbages indeed something was stirring, but it might just as probably be a cat stalking birds.   She watched this for a time.

She went a few paces past the corner, came in sight of the run containing the giant chicks and stopped again.   " Ah ! " she said, and shook her head slowly at the sight of them.   They were at that time about the height of emus, but of course much thicker in the body—a larger thing altogether.   They were all hens and five all told, now that the two cockerels had killed each other.   She hesitated at their drooping attitudes.   " Poor dears ! " she said, and put down her bundle ;   " they've got no water.   And they've 'ad no food these twenty-four hours ! And such appetites, too, as they 'ave ! "   She put a lean finger to her lips and communed with herself.

Then this dirty old woman did what seems to me a quite heroic deed of mercy.   She left her bundle and umbrella in the middle of the brick path, and went to the well and drew no fewer than three pailfuls of water for the chickens' empty trough, and then while they were all crowding about that, she undid the door of the run very softly, after which she became extremely active, resumed her package, got over the hedge at the bottom of the garden, crossed the rank meadows (in order to avoid the wasps' nest) and toiled up the winding path towards Cheasing Eyebright.

She panted up the hill ; and as she went she paused ever and again to rest her bundle and get her breath and stare back at the little cottage beside the pinewood below.   And when at last, as she was nearing the crest of the hill, she saw afar off three several wasps dropping heavily westward, it helped her greatly on her way.

She soon got out of the open and into the high banked lane beyond (which seemed a safer place to her) and so up by Hickleybrow Coombe to the downs. There at the foot of the downs where a big tree gave an air of shelter she rested for a space on a stile.

Then on again very resolutely. . . .

You figure her, I hope, with her white bundle, a sort of erect black ant, hurrying along the little white path-thread athwart the downland slopes under the hot sun of the summer afternoon. On she struggled after her resolute indefatigable nose, and the poppies in her bonnet quivered perpetually and her spring side boots grew whiter and whiter with the downland dust. Flip, flap, flip, flap went her footfalls through the still heat of the day, and persistently, incurably, her umbrella sought to slip from under the elbow that retained it. The mouth wrinkle under her nose was pursed to an extreme resolution, and ever and again she told her umbrella to come up or gave her tightly clutched bundle a vindictive jerk. And at times her lips mumbled with fragments of some foreseen argument between herself and Skinner.

And far away, miles and miles away, a steeple and a hanger grew insensibly out of the vague blue to mark more and more distinctly the quiet corner where Cheasing Eyebright sheltered from the tumult of the world, recking little or nothing of the Herakleophorbia concealed in that white bundle that struggled so persistently towards its orderly retirement.

VII

So far as I can gather, the pullets came into Hickleybrow about three o'clock in the afternoon. Their coming must have been a brisk affair, though nobody was out in the street to see it. The violent bellowing of little Skelmersdale seems to have been the first announcement of anything out of the way. Miss Durgan of the Post Office was at the window as usual, and saw the hen that had caught the unhappy child, in violent flight up the street with its victim, closely pursued by two others. You know that swinging stride of the emancipated athletic latter-day pullet ! You know the keen insistence of the hungry hen ! There was Plymouth Rock in these birds, I am told, and even without Herakleophorbia that is a gaunt and striking strain.

Probably Miss Durgan was not altogether taken by surprise. In spite of Mr. Bensington's insistence upon secrecy, rumours of the great chicken Mr. Skinner was producing had been about the village for some weeks. " Lor ! " she cried, " it's what I expected."

She seems to have behaved with great presence of mind. She snatched up the sealed bag of letters that was waiting to go on to Urshot, and rushed out of the door at once. Almost simultaneously Mr. Skelmersdale himself appeared down the village, gripping a watering-pot by the spout and very white in the face. And of course in a moment or so every one in the village was rushing to the door or window.

The spectacle of Miss Durgan all across the road, with the entire day's correspondence of Hickleybrow in her hand, gave pause to the pullet in possession of Master Skelmersdale. She halted through one instant's indecision and then turned for the open gates of Fulcher's yard. That instant was fatal. The second pullet ran in neatly, captured the child by a well-directed peck, and went over the wall into the vicarage garden.

" Charawk, chawk, chawk, chawk, chawk, chawk ! " shrieked the hindmost hen, hit smartly by the watering-can Mr. Skelmersdale had thrown, and fluttered wildly over Mrs. Glue's cottage and so into the doctor's field, while the rest of those Gargantuan birds pursued the pullet in possession of the child across the vicarage lawn.

" Good heavens ! " cried the curate, or (as some say) something much more manly, and ran, whirling his croquet mallet and shouting, to head off the chase.

" Stop, you wretch ! " cried the curate, as though giant hens were the commonest facts in life.

And then, finding he could not possibly intercept her, he hurled his mallet with all his might and main, and out it shot in a gracious curve within a foot or so of Master Skelmersdale's head and through the glass lantern of the conservatory. Smash ! The new conservatory ! The vicar's wife's beautiful new conservatory !

It frightened the hen. It might have frightened any one. She dropped her victim into a Portugal laurel (from which he was presently extracted, disordered but, save for his less delicate garments, uninjured), made a flapping leap for the roof of Fulcher's stables, put her foot through a weak place in the tiles, and descended, so to speak, out of the infinite into the contemplative quiet of Mr. Bumps the paralytic—who, it is now proved beyond all cavil, did, on this one occasion in his life, get down the entire length of his garden and indoors without any assistance whatever, bolt the door after him, and immediately relapse again into Christian resignation and helpless dependence upon his wife. . . .

The rest of the pullets were headed off by the other croquet players, and went through the vicar's kitchen garden into the doctor's field, to which rendezvous the fifth also came at last, clucking disconsolately after an unsuccessful attempt to walk on the cucumber frames at Mr. Witherspoon's.

They seem to have stood about in a hen-like manner for a time, and scratched a little and chirrawked meditatively, and then once pecked at and pecked over a hive of the doctor's bees, and after that they set off in a gawky jerky feathery fitful sort of way across the fields towards Urshot, and Hickleybrow street saw them no more. Near Urshot they really came upon commensurate food in a field of swedes, and pecked for a space with gusto, until their fame overtook them.

The chief immediate reaction of this astonishing irruption of gigantic poultry upon the human mind was to arouse an extraordinary passion to whoop and run and throw things, and in quite a little time almost all the available manhood of Hickleybrow, and several ladies, were out with a remarkable assortment of flappish and whangable articles in hand—to begin the scooting of the giant hens. They drove them into Urshot, where there was a Rural Fête, and Urshot took them as the crowning glory of a happy day. They began to be shot at near Findon Beeches, but at first only with a rook rifle. Of course birds of that size could absorb an unlimited quantity of small shot without inconvenience. They scattered somewhere near Sevenoaks, and near Tonbridge one of them fled clucking for a time in excessive agitation, somewhat ahead of and parallel with the afternoon boat express—to the great astonishment of every one therein.

And about half-past five two of them were caught very cleverly by a circus proprietor at Tunbridge Wells, who lured them into a cage rendered vacant through the death of a widowed dromedary, by scattering cakes and bread. . . .

VIII

When the unfortunate Skinner got out of the South-Eastern train at Urshot that evening it was already nearly dusk. The train was late, but not inordinately late—and Mr. Skinner remarked as much to the stationmaster. Perhaps he saw a certain pregnancy in the stationmaster's eye. After the briefest hesitation and with a confidential movement of his hand to the side of his mouth he asked if "anything" had happened that day.

"How d'yer *mean* ? " said the stationmaster, a man with a hard emphatic voice.

"Thethe 'ere waptheth and thingth."

"We 'aven't 'ad much time to think of *waptheth*," said the stationmaster agreeably. "We've been too busy with your brasted 'ens," and he broke the news of the pullets to Mr. Skinner as one might break the window of an adverse politician.

"You ain't 'eard anything of Mithith Thkinner ? " asked Skinner, amidst that missile shower of pithy information and comment.

"No fear ! " said the stationmaster—as though even he drew the line somewhere in the matter of knowledge.

"I mutht make inquirieth 'bout thith," said Mr. Skinner, edging out of reach of the stationmaster's concluding generalisations about the responsibility attaching to the excessive nurture of hens. . . .

Going through Urshot Mr. Skinner was hailed by a lime-burner from the pits over by Hankey and asked if he was looking for his hens.

"You ain't 'eard anything of Mithith Thkinner?" he asked.

The lime-burner—his exact phrases need not concern us—expressed his superior interest in hens. . . .

It was already dark—as dark at least as a clear night in the English June can be—when Skinner—or his head at any rate—came into the bar of the Jolly Drovers and said: "Ello! You 'aven't 'eard anything of thith 'ere thtory 'bout my 'enth, 'ave you?"

"Oh, '*aven't* we!" said Mr. Fulcher. "Why, part of the story's been and bust into my stable roof and one chapter smashed a 'ole in Missis Vicar's green-'ouse—I beg 'er pardon—Conservarratory."

Skinner came in. "I'd like thomething a little comforting," he said, "'ot gin and water'th about my figure," and everybody began to tell him things about the pullets.

"*Grathuth* me!" said Skinner.

"You 'aven't 'eard anything about Mithith Thkinner, 'ave you?" he asked in a pause.

"That we 'aven't!" said Mr. Witherspoon. "We 'aven't thought of 'er. We ain't thought nothing of either of you."

"Ain't you been 'ome to-day?" asked Fulcher over a tankard.

"If one of those brasted birds 'ave pecked 'er," began Mr. Witherspoon, and left the full horror to their unaided imaginations. . . .

It appeared to the meeting at the time that it would be an interesting end to an eventful day to go on with Skinner and see if anything *had* happened to Mrs. Skinner. One never knows what luck one may have when accidents are at large. But Skinner, standing at the bar and drinking his hot gin and water, with one eye roving over the things at the back of the bar and the other fixed on the Absolute, missed the psychological moment.

"I thuppothe there 'athn't been any trouble with any of thethe big waptheth to-day anywhere?" he asked, with an elaborate detachment of manner.

"Been too busy with your 'ens," said Fulcher.

"I thuppothe they've all gone in now anyhow," said Skinner.

"What—the 'ens?"

"I wath thinking of the waptheth more particularly," said Skinner.

And then with an air of circumspection that would have awakened suspicion in a week-old baby, and laying the accent heavily on most of the words he chose, he asked, "I *thuppothe nobody* 'athn't '*eard* of any other *big* thingth about, 'ave they? Big *dogth* or *catth* or anything of *that* thort? Theemth to me if thereth big henth and big waptheth comin' on——"

He laughed with a fine pretence of talking idly.

But a brooding expression came upon the faces of the Hickleybrow men. Fulcher was the first to give their condensing thought the concrete shape of words.

" A cat to match them 'ens——" said Fulcher.

" Aye ! " said Witherspoon, " a cat to match they 'ens."

" 'Twould be a tiger," said Fulcher.

" More'n a tiger," said Witherspoon. . . .

When at last Skinner followed the lonely footpath over the swelling field that separated Hickleybrow from the sombre pine-shaded hollow in whose black shadows the gigantic canary creeper grappled silently with the Experimental Farm, he followed it alone.

He was distinctly seen to rise against the skyline, against the warm clear immensity of the northern sky—for so far public interest followed him—and to descend again into the night, into an obscurity from which it would seem he will nevermore emerge. He passed—into a mystery. No one knows to this day what happened to him after he crossed the brow. When later on the two Fulchers and Witherspoon, moved by their own imaginations, came up the hill and stared after him, the night had swallowed him up altogether.

The three men stood close. There was not a sound out of the wooded blackness that hid the Farm from their eyes.

" It's all right," said young Fulcher ending a silence.

" Don't see any lights," said Witherspoon.

" You wouldn't from here."

" It's misty," said the elder Fulcher.

They meditated for a space.

" 'E'd 'ave come back if anything was wrong," said young Fulcher, and this seemed so obvious and conclusive that presently old Fulcher said " Well," and the three went home to bed—thoughtfully I will admit. . . .

A shepherd out by Huckster's Farm heard a squealing in the night that he thought was foxes, and in the morning one of his lambs had been killed, dragged half-way towards Hickleybrow and partially devoured. . . .

The inexplicable part of it all is the absence of any indisputable remains of Skinner !

Many weeks after, amidst the charred ruins of the Experimental Farm, there was found something which may or may not have been a human shoulder-blade, and in another part of the ruins a long bone greatly gnawed and equally doubtful. Near the stile going up towards Eyebright there was found a glass eye, and many people discovered thereupon that Skinner owed much of his personal charm to such a possession. It stared out upon the world with that same inevitable effect of detachment, that same severe melancholy that had been the redemption of his else worldly countenance.

And about the ruins industrious research discovered the

metal rings and charred coverings of two linen buttons, three shanked buttons entire, and one of that metallic sort which is used in the less conspicuous sutures of the human Œconomy. These remains have been accepted by persons in authority as conclusive of a destroyed and scattered Skinner, but for my own entire conviction, and in view of his distinctive idiosyncrasy, I must confess I should prefer fewer buttons and more bones.

The glass eye of course has an air of extreme conviction, but if it really *is* Skinner's—and even Mrs. Skinner did not certainly know if that immobile eye of his was glass—something has changed it from a liquid brown to a serene and confident blue. That shoulder-blade is an extremely doubtful document, and I would like to put it side by side with the gnawed scapulæ of a few of the commoner domestic animals before I admitted its humanity.

And where were Skinner's boots, for example ? Perverted and strange as a rat's appetite must be, is it conceivable that the same creatures that could leave a lamb only half eaten, would finish up Skinner, hair, bones, teeth, and boots ?

I have closely questioned as many as I could of those who knew Skinner at all intimately, and they one and all agree that they cannot imagine *anything* eating him. He was the sort of man, as a retired seafaring person living in one of Mr. W. W. Jacobs' cottages at Dunton Green told me, with a guarded significance of manner not uncommon in those parts, who would " get washed up anyhow," and as regards *the* devouring element was " fit to put a fire out." He considered that Skinner would be as safe on a raft as anywhere. The retired seafaring man added that he wished to say nothing whatever against Skinner ; facts were facts. And rather than have his clothes made by Skinner, the retired seafaring man remarked he would take his chance of being locked up. These observations certainly do not present Skinner in the light of an appetising object.

To be perfectly frank with the reader, I do not believe he ever went back to the Experimental Farm. I believe he hovered through long hesitations about the fields of the Hickleybrow glebe ; and finally, when that squealing began, took the line of least resistance out of his perplexities into the Incognito.

And in the Incognito, whether of this or of some other world unknown to us, he obstinately and quite indisputably has remained to this day. . . .

CHAPTER THREE

THE GIANT RATS

I

IT was two nights after the disappearance of Mr. Skinner that the Podbourne doctor was out late near Hankey, driving in his buggy. He had been up all night assisting another undistinguished citizen into this curious world of ours ; and his task accomplished, he was driving homeward in a drowsy mood enough. It was about two o'clock in the morning, and the waning moon was rising. The summer night had gone cold ; and there was a low-lying whitish mist that made things indistinct. He was quite alone—for his coachman was ill in bed—and there was nothing to be seen on either hand but a drifting mystery of hedge running athwart the yellow glare of his lamps, and nothing to hear but the clitter, clatter of his horse and the gride and hedge echo of his wheels. His horse was as trustworthy as himself, and one does not wonder that he dozed. . . .

You know that intermittent drowsing as one sits, the drooping of the head, the nodding to the rhythm of the wheels, then chin upon breast, and at once the sudden start up again.

Pitter, litter, patter.

" What was that ? "

It seemed to the doctor he had heard a thin shrill squeal close at hand. For a moment he was quite awake. He said a word or two of undeserved rebuke to his horse, and looked about him. He tried to persuade himself that he had heard the distant squeal of a fox—or perhaps a young rabbit gripped by a ferret.

Swish, swish, swish, pitter, patter, swish—— . . .

" What was that ? "

He felt he was getting fanciful. He shook his shoulders and told his horse to get on. He listened and heard nothing.

" Or was it nothing ? "

He had the queerest impression that something had just peeped over the hedge at him, a queer big head. With round ears ! He peered hard, but he could see nothing.

" Nonsense," said he.

He sat up with an idea that he had dropped into a nightmare, gave his horse the slightest touch of the whip, spoke to it and peered again over the hedge. The glare of his lamp, however, together with the mist, rendered things indistinct, and he could distinguish nothing. It came into his head, he says, that there could be nothing there, because if there was his horse would have shied at it. Yet for all that his senses remained nervously awake.

361

Then he heard quite distinctly a soft pattering of feet in pursuit along the road.

He would not believe his ears about that. He could not look round, for the road just there had a sinuous curve. He whipped up his horse and glanced sideways again. And then he saw quite distinctly where a ray from his lamp leapt a low stretch of hedge, the curved back of—some big animal, he couldn't tell what, going along in quick convulsive leaps.

He says he thought of the old tales of witchcraft—the thing was so utterly unlike any animal he knew, and he tightened his hold on the reins for fear of the fear of his horse. Educated man as he was, he admits he asked himself if this could be something that his horse could not see.

Ahead, and drawing near in silhouette against the rising moon, was the outline of the little hamlet of Hankey, comforting, though it showed never a light, and he cracked his whip and spoke again and then in a flash the rats were at him !

He had passed a gate, and as he did so, the foremost rat came leaping over into the road. The thing sprang upon him out of vagueness into the utmost clearness, the sharp, eager, round-eared face, the long body exaggerated by its movement ; and what particularly struck him, the pink webbed forefeet of the beast. What must have made it more horrible to him at the time, was that he had no idea the thing was any created beast he knew. He did not recognise it as a rat, because of its size. His horse gave a bound as the thing dropped into the road beside it. The little lane woke into tumult at the report of the whip and the doctor's shout. The whole thing suddenly went fast.

Rattle-clatter, clash, clatter.

The doctor, one gathers, stood up, shouted to his horse, and slashed with all his strength. The rat winced and swerved most reassuringly at his blow—in the glare of his lamp he could see the fur furrow under the lash—and he slashed again and again, heedless and unaware of the second pursuer that gained upon his offside.

He let the reins go, and glanced back to discover the third rat in pursuit behind. . . .

His horse bounded forward. The buggy leapt high at a rut. For a frantic minute perhaps everything seemed to be going in leaps and bounds. . . .

It was sheer good luck the horse came down in Hankey and not either before or after the houses had been passed.

No one knows how the horse came down, whether it stumbled or whether the rat on the offside really got home with one of those slashing down strokes of the incisors (given with the full weight of the body) ; and the doctor never discovered that he himself was bitten until he was inside the brickmaker's house, much less did he discover when the bite occurred, though bitten he was and badly—a long slash like the slash of a double tomahawk that had cut two parallel ribbons of flesh from his left shoulder.

He was standing up in his buggy at one moment, and in the next he had leapt to the ground, and with his ankle, though he did not know it, badly sprained, he was cutting furiously at a third rat that was flying directly at him. He scarcely remembers the leap he must have made over the top of the wheel as the buggy came over, so obliteratingly hot and swift did his impressions rush upon him. I think myself the horse reared up with the rat biting again at its throat, and fell sideways, and carried the whole affair over ; and that the doctor sprang, as it were, instinctively. As the buggy came down, the receiver of the lamp smashed, and suddenly poured a flare of blazing oil, a thud of white flame into the struggle.

That was the first thing the brickmaker saw.

He had heard the clatter of the doctor's approach and—though the doctor's memory has nothing of this—wild shouting. He had got out of bed hastily, and as he did so came the terrific smash, and up shot the glare outside the rising blind. "It was brighter than day," he says. He stood, blind cord in hand, and stared out of the window at a nightmare transformation of the familiar road before him. The black figure of the doctor with its whirling whip danced out against the flame. The horse kicked indistinctly, half hidden by the blaze, with a rat at its throat. In the obscurity against the churchyard wall, the eyes of a second monster shone wickedly. Another —a mere dreadful blackness with red-lit eyes and flesh-coloured hands—clutched unsteadily on the wall coping to which it had leapt at the flash of the exploding lamp.

You know the keen face of a rat, those two sharp teeth, those pitiless eyes. Seen magnified to near six times its linear dimensions, and still more magnified by darkness and amazement and the leaping fancies of a fitful blaze, it must have been an ill sight for the brickmaker—still more than half asleep.

Then the doctor had grasped the opportunity, that momentary respite the flare afforded, and was out of the brickmaker's sight below battering the door with the butt of his whip. . . .

The brickmaker would not let him in until he had got a light.

There are those who have blamed the man for that, but until I know my own courage better, I hesitate to join their number.

The doctor yelled and hammered. . . .

The brickmaker says he was weeping with terror when at last the door was opened.

"Bolt," gasped the doctor, "bolt," and could say no more. He tried to move to the door to help, and sank down on the chair beside the clock while the brickmaker fastened the door.

"I don't know what they *are* !" he repeated several times. "I don't know what they *are*"—with a high note on the "are."

The brickmaker would have got him whisky, but the doctor

would not be left alone with nothing but a flickering light just then.

It was long before the brickmaker could get him to go upstairs. . . .

And when the fire was out the giant rats came back, took the dead horse, dragged it across the churchyard into the brickfield and ate at it it until it was dawn, none even then daring to disturb them. . . .

II

Redwood went round to Bensington about eleven the next morning with the "second edition" of three evening papers in his hand.

Bensington looked up from a despondent meditation over the forgotten pages of the most distracting novel the Brompton Road librarian had been able to find him. "Anything fresh ? " he asked.

"Two men stung near Chartham."

"They ought to let us smoke out that nest. They really did. It's their own fault."

"It's their own fault, certainly," said Redwood.

"Have you heard anything—about buying the farm ? "

"The House Agent," said Redwood, "is a thing with a big mouth and made of dense wood. It pretends some one else is after the house—it always does, you know—and won't understand there's a hurry. "This is a matter of life and death," I said, "don't you understand ? " It drooped its eyes half shut and said, "Then why don't you go the other two hundred pounds ? " I'd rather live in a world of solid wasps than give in to the stonewalling stupidity of that offensive creature. I——"

He paused, feeling that a sentence like that might very easily be spoiled by its context.

"It's too much to hope," said Bensington, "that one of the wasps——"

"The wasp has no more idea of public utility than a—than a House Agent," said Redwood.

He talked for a little while about house agents and solicitors and people of that sort, in the unjust, unreasonable way that so many people do somehow get to talk of these business calculi ("Of all the oranky things in this cranky world, the most cranky of all tc my mind is that while we expect honour, courage, efficiency from a doctor or a soldier as a matter of course, a solicitor or a house agent is not only permitted but expected to display nothing but a sort of greedy, greasy, obstructive, over-reaching imbecility——" etc.)—and then, greatly relieved, he went to the window and stared out at the Sloane Street traffic.

Bensington had put the most exciting novel conceivable on the little table that carried his electric standard. He joined the fingers of his opposed hands very carefully and regarded them. " Redwood," he said. " Do they say much about *Us* ? "

" Not so much as I should expect."

" They don't denounce us at all ? "

" Not a bit. But, on the other hand, they don't back up what I point out must be done. I've written to *The Times*, you know, explaining the whole thing——"

" We take the *Daily Chronicle*," said Bensington.

" And *The Times* has a long leader on the subject—a very high-class, well-written leader—with three pieces of *Times* Latin—*status quo* is one—and it reads like the voice of Some-body Impersonal of the Greatest Importance suffering from Influenza Headache and talking through sheets and sheets of felt without getting any relief from it whatever. Reading between the lines, you know, it's pretty clea that *The Times* considers it is useless to mince matters and that something (indefinite of course) has to be done at once. Otherwise still more undesirable consequences—*Times* English, you know, for more wasps and stings. Thoroughly statesmanlike article ! "

" And meanwhile this Bigness is spreading in all sorts of ugly ways."

" Precisely."

" I wonder if Skinner was right about those big rats——"

" Oh no ! That would be too much," said Redwood.

He came and stood by Bensington's chair.

" By the bye," he said, with a slightly lowered voice, " how does *she*—— ? "

He indicated the closed door.

" Cousin Jane ? She simply knows nothing about it. Doesn't connect us with it and won't read the articles. ' Gig-antic wasps ! ' she says, ' I haven't patience to read the papers.' "

" That's very fortunate," said Redwood.

" I suppose—Mrs. Redwood—— ? "

" No,' said Redwood, " just at present it happens—she's terribly worried about the child. You know, he keeps on."

" Growing ? "

" Yes. Put on forty-one ounces in ten days. Weighs nearly four stone. And only six months old ! Naturally rather alarming."

" Healthy ? "

" Vigorous. His nurse is leaving because he kicks so forc-ibly. And everything, of course, shockingly outgrown. Every-thing, you know, has had to be made fresh, clothes and every-thing. Perambulator—light affair—broke one wheel, and the youngster had to be brought home on the milkman's hand-truck. Yes. Quite a crowd. . . . And we've put Georgina Phyllis back into his cot and put him into the bed of Georgina Phyllis. His mother—naturally alarmed. Proud at first and inclined to praise Winkles.   Not now.   Feels the thing *can't* be wholesome.   *You* know."

" I imagined you were going to put him on diminishing doses."

" I tried it."

" Didn't it work ? "

" Howls.   In the ordinary way the cry of a child is loud and distressing ; it is for the good of the species that this should be so—but since he has been on the Herakleophorbia treatment——"

" Mm," said Bensington, regarding his fingers with more resignation than he had hitherto displayed.

" Practically the thing *must* come out.   People will hear of this child, connect it up with our hens, and the whole thing will come round to my wife. . . .   How she will take it I haven't the remotest idea."

" It *is* difficult," said Mr. Bensington, " to form any plan—certainly."

He removed his glasses and wiped them carefully.

" It is another instance," he generalised, " of the thing that is continually happening.   We—if indeed I may presume to the adjective—*scientific* men—we work of course always for a theoretical result—a purely theoretical result.   But incidentally we do set forces in operation—*new* forces.   We mustn't control them—and nobody else *can*.   Practically, Redwood, the thing is out of our hands.   *We* supply the material——"

" And they," said Redwood, turning to the window, " get the experience."

" So far as this trouble down in Kent goes I am not disposed to worry further."

" Unless they worry us."

" Exactly.   And if they like to muddle about with solicitors and pettifoggers and legal obstructions and weighty considerations of the tomfool order, until they have got a number of new gigantic species of vermin well established——   Things always *have* been in a muddle, Redwood."

Redwood traced a twisted, tangled line in the air.

" And our real interest lies at present with your boy."

Redwood turned about and came and stared at his collaborator.

" What do you think of him, Bensington ?   You can look at this business with a greater detachment than I can.   What am I to do about him ? "

" Go on feeding him."

" On Herakleophorbia ? "

" On Herakleophorbia."

" And then he'll grow."

" He'll grow, as far as I can calculate from the hens and the wasps, to the height of about five and thirty feet—with everything in proportion——"

" And then what'll he do ? "

" That," said Mr. Bensington, " is just what makes the whole thing so interesting."

" Confound it, man ! Think of his clothes."

" And when he's grown up," said Redwood, " he'll only be one solitary Gulliver in a pigmy world."

Mr. Bensington's eye over his gold rim was pregnant.

" Why solitary ? " he said, and repeated still more darkly. " *Why* solitary ? "

" But you don't propose—— ? "

" I said," said Mr. Bensington, with the self-complacency of a man who has produced a good significant saying, " Why solitary ? "

" Meaning that one might bring up other children—— ? "

" Meaning nothing beyond my inquiry."

Redwood began to walk about the room. " Of course," he said, " one might—— But still ! What are we coming to ? "

Bensington evidently enjoyed his line of high intellectual detachment. " The thing that interests me most, Redwood, of all this, is to think that his brain at the top of him will also, so far as my reasoning goes, be five and thirty feet or so above our level. . . . What's the matter ? "

Redwood stood at the window and stared at a news placard on a paper-cart that rattles up the street,

" What's the matter ? " repeated Bensington, rising.

Redwood exclaimed violently.

" What is it ? " said Bensington.

" Get a paper," said Redwood, moving doorward.

" Why ? "

" Get a paper. Something—I didn't quite catch—Gigantic rats—— ! "

" Rats ? "

" Yes, rats. Skinner was right after all ! "

" What do you mean ? "

" How the Deuce am *I* to know till I see a paper ? Great Rats ! Good Lord ! I wonder if he's been eaten ! " He glanced for his hat, and decided to go hatless.

As he rushed downstairs two steps at a time, he could hear along the street the mighty howlings to and fro of the Hooligan paper-sellers making a Boom.

" 'Orrible affair in Kent—'orrible affair in Kent. Doctor . . . eaten by rats. 'Orrible affair—'orrible affair—rats— eaten by Stchewpendous rats. Full perticulers—'orrible affair."

III

Cossar, the well-known civil engineer, found them in the great doorway of the flat mansions, Redwood holding out the damp pink paper and Bensington on tiptoe, reading over his arm. Cossar was a large-bodied man with gaunt inelegant limbs placed casually at convenient corners of his body and a face like a carving abandoned at an early stage as altogether too unpromising for completion. His nose had been left square, and his lower jaw projected beyond his upper. He breathed audibly. Few people considered him handsome. His hair was entirely tangential, and his voice, which he used sparingly was pitched high, and had commonly a quality of bitter protest. He wore a grey cloth jacket suit and a silk hat on all occasions. He plumbed an abysmal trouser pocket with a vast red hand, paid his cabman, and came panting resolutely up the steps, a copy of the pink paper clutched about the middle like Jove's thunderbolt in his hand.

" Skinner ? " Bensington was saying, regardless of his approach.

" Nothing about him," said Redwood. " Bound to be eaten. Both of them. It's too horrible. . . . Hallo! Cossar ! "

" This your stuff ? " asked Cossar, waving the paper.

" Well, why don't you stop it ? " he demanded.

" *Can't*, be Jiggered ! " said Cossar.

" *Buy the place* ? " he cried. " What nonsense ! Burn it. I knew you chaps would fumble this. *What are you to do ?* Why—what I tell you ! "

" *You ?* Do ? Why ! Go up the street to the gunsmith's, of course. *Why ?* For guns ! Yes—there's only one shop. Get eight guns ! Rifles. Not elephant guns—no ! Too big. Not army rifles—too small. Say it's to kill—kill a bull. Say it's to shoot buffalo ! See ? Eh ? Rats ? No ! How the deuce are they to understand that ? . . . Because we *want* eight. Get a lot of ammunition. Don't gets guns without ammunition—No ! Take the lot in a cab to—where's the place ? *Urshot ?* Charing Cross, then. There's a train— Well, the first train that starts after two. Think you can do it ? All right. Licence ? Get eight at a post-office, of course. Gun licences, you know. Not game. Why ? It's rats, man. You—Bensington. Got a telephone ? Yes. I'll ring up five of my chaps from Ealing. *Why* five ? Because it's the right number ! "

" Where you going, Redwood ? Get a hat ! *Nonsense.* Have mine. You want guns, man—not hats. Got money ? Enough ? All right. So long.

" Where's the telephone, Bensington ? "

Bensington wheeled about obediently and led the way.

Cossar used and replaced the instrument. " Then there's the wasps," he said. " Sulphur and nitre'll do that. Obviously. Plaster of Paris. You're a chemist. Where can I get sulphur by the ton in portable sacks ? *What* for ? Why, Lord *bless* my heart and soul !—to smoke out the nest, of course ! I suppose it must be sulphur, eh ? You're a chemist. Sulphur best, eh ? "

" Yes, I should *think* sulphur."

" Nothing better ? "

" Right. That's your job. That's all right. Get as much sulphur as you can—saltpetre to make it burn. Sent ? Charing Cross. Right away. See they do it. Follow it up. Anything ? "

He thought a moment.

" Plaster of Paris—any sort of plaster—bung up nest—holes —you know. That *I'd* better get."

" How much ? "

" How much what ? "

" Sulphur."

" Ton. See ? "

Bensington tightened his glasses with a hand tremulous with determination. " Right," he said, very curtly.

" Money in your pocket ? " asked Cossar.

" Hang cheques. They may not know you. Pay cash. Obviously. Where's your bank ? All right. Stop on the way and get forty pounds—notes and gold."

Another meditation. " If we leave this job for public officials we shall have all Kent in tatters," said Cossar. " Now is there—anything ? *No ! HI !* "

He stretched a vast hand towards a cab that became convulsively eager to serve him (" Cab, Sir ? " said the cabman. " Obviously," said Cossar) ; and Bensington, still hatless, paddled down the steps and prepared to mount.

" I *think*," he said with his hand on the cab apron, and a sudden glance up at the windows of his flat, " I *ought* to tell my cousin Jane——"

" More time to tell her when you come back," said Cossar, thrusting him in with a vast hand expanded over his back. . . .

" Clever chaps," remarked Cossar, " but no initiative whatever. Cousin Jane indeed ! I know her. Rot, these cousin Janes ! Country infested with 'em. I suppose I shall have to spend the whole blessed night seeing they do what they know perfectly well they ought to have done all along. I wonder if it's Research makes 'em like that or cousin Jane or what ? "

He dismissed this obscure problem, meditated for a space upon his watch, and decided there would be just time to drop into a restaurant and get some lunch before he hunted up the plaster of Paris and took it to Charing Cross.

The train started at five minutes past three, and he arrived at Charing Cross at a quarter to three, to find Bensington in heated argument between two policemen and his van-driver outside, and Redwood in the luggage office involved in some technical obscurity about his ammunition. Everybody was pretending, in the way dear to South-Eastern officials when they catch you in a hurry, neither to know anything nor to have any authority.

" Pity they can't shoot all these officials and get a new lot," remarked Cossar with a sigh. But the time was too limited for anything fundamental, and so he swept through these minor controversies, disinterred what may or may not have been the stationmaster from some obscure hiding-place, walked about the premises holding him and giving orders in his name, and was out of the station with everybody and everything aboard before that official was fully awake to the breaches in the most sacred routines and regulations that were being committed.

"Who *was* he ?" said the high official, caressing the arm Cossar had gripped, and smiling with knit brows.

"'E was a gentleman, Sir," said a porter, "anyhow. 'Im and all 'is party travelled first class."

"Well, we got him and his stuff off pretty sharp—whoever he was," said the high official, rubbing his arm with something approaching satisfaction.

And as he walked slowly back, blinking in the unaccustomed daylight, towards that dignified retirement in which the higher officials at Charing Cross shelter from the importunity of the vulgar, he still smiled at his unaccustomed energy. It was a very gratifying revelation of his own possibilities, in spite of the stiffness of his arm. He wished some of those confounded armchair critics of railway management could have seen it.

IV

By five o'clock that evening this amazing Cossar, with no appearance of hurry at all, had got all the stuff for his fight with insurgent Bigness out of Urshot and on the road to Hickleybrow. Two barrels of paraffin and a load of dry brushwood he had bought in Urshot ; plentiful sacks of sulphur, eight big game guns and ammunition, three light breech-loaders, with small-shot ammunition for the wasps, a hatchet, two billhooks, a pick and three spades, two coils of rope, some bottled beer, soda and whisky. One gross of packets of rat poison and cold provisions for three days had come down from London. All these things he had sent on in a coal trolley and a hay waggon in the most businesslike way, except the guns and ammunition, which were stuck under the seat of the Red Lion waggonette appointed to bring on Redwood and the five picked men who had come up from Ealing at Cossar's summons.

Cossar conducted all these transactions with an invincible air of commonplace, in spite of the fact that Urshot was in a panic about the rats, and all the drivers had to be specially paid. All the shops were shut in the place, and scarcely a soul abroad in the street, and when he banged at a door a window was apt to open. He seemed to consider that the conduct of business from open windows was an entirely legitimate and obvious method. Finally he and Bensington get the Red Lion dog-cart and set off with the waggonette, to overtake the baggage. They did this a little beyond the cross-roads, and so reached Hickleybrow first.

Bensington, with a gun between his knees, sitting beside Cossar in the dog-cart, developed a long-germinated amazement. All they were doing was, no doubt, as Cossar insisted, quite the obvious thing to do, only——! In England one so rarely does the obvious thing. He glanced from his neighbour's feet to the boldly sketched hands upon the reins. Cossar had apparently never driven before, and he was keeping the line of least resistance down the middle of the road by some no doubt quite obvious but certainly unusual light of his own.

"Why don't we all do the obvious?" thought Bensington. "How the world would travel if one did! I wonder for instance why I don't do such a lot of things I know would be all right to do—things I *want* to do. Is everybody like that, or is it peculiar to me!" He plunged into obscure speculation about the Will. He thought of the complex organised futilities of the daily life, and in contrast with them the plain and manifest things to do, the sweet and splendid things to do, that some incredible influences will never permit us to do. Cousin Jane? Cousin Jane he perceived was important in the question, in some subtle and difficult way. Why should we after all eat, drink, and sleep, remain unmarried, go here, abstain from going there, all out of deference to cousin Jane? She became symbolical without ceasing to be incomprehensible. . . .

A stile and a path across the fields caught his eye and reminded him of that other bright day, so recent in time, so remote in its emotions, when he had walked from Urshot to the Experimental Farm to see the giant chicks. . . .

Fate plays with us.

"Tcheck, Tcheck," said Cossar. "Get up."

It was a hot midday afternoon, not a breath of wind, and the dust was thick on the roads. Few people were about, but the deer beyond the park palings browsed in profound tranquillity. They saw a couple of big wasps stripping a gooseberry bush just outside Hickleybrow, and another was crawling up and down the front of the little grocer's shop in the village street trying to find an entry. The grocer was dimly visible within, with an ancient fowling-piece in hand, watching its endeavours. The driver of the waggonette pulled up outside the Jolly Drovers and informed Redwood that his part of the bargain was done. In this contention he was presently joined by the drivers of the waggon and the trolley. Not only did they maintain this, but they refused to let the horses be taken further.

"Them big rats is nuts on 'orses," the trolley driver kept on repeating.

Cossar surveyed the controversy for a moment.

"Get the things out of that waggonette," he said, and one of his men, a tall fair dirty engineer, obeyed.

"Gimme that shot gun," said Cossar.

He placed himself between the drivers. "We don't want *you* to drive," he said.

" You can say what you like," he conceded, " but we want these horses."

They began to argue, but he continued speaking.

" If you try and assault us I shall, in self-defence, let fly at your legs. The horses are going on."

He treated the incident as closed. " Get up on the waggon, Flack," he said to a thick-set, wiry little man. " Boon, take the trolley."

The two drivers blustered.

" You've done your duty to your employers," said Redwood. " You stop in this village until we come back. No one will blame you, seeing we've got guns. We've no wish to do anything unjust or violent, but this business is pressing. I'll pay if anything happens to the horses, never fear.

" *That's* all right," said Cossar, who rarely promised.

They left the waggonette behind, and the men who were not driving went afoot. Over each shoulder sloped a gun. It was the oddest little expedition for an English country road, more like a Yankee party trekking west in the good old Indian days.

They went up the road until at the crest by the stile they came into sight of the Experimental Farm. They found a little group of men there with a gun or so—the two Fulchers were among them—and one man, a stranger from Maidstone, stood out before the others and watched the place through an opera-glass.

These men turned about and stared at Redwood's party.

" Anything fresh ? " said Cossar.

" The waspses keeps a-comin' and a-goin'," said old Fulcher. " Can't see as they bring anything."

" The Canary Creeper's got in among the pine trees now," said the man with the lorgnette. " It wasn't there this morning. You can see it grow while you watch it."

He took out a handkerchief and wiped his object-glasses with careful deliberation.

" I reckon you're going down there," ventured Skelmersdale

" Will you come ? " said Cossar.

Skelmersdale seemed to hesitate.

" It's an all-night job."

Skelmersdale decided that he wouldn't.

" Rats about ? " asked Cossar.

" One was up in the pines this morning—rabbiting, we reckon."

Cossar slouched on to overtake his party.

Bensington, regarding the Experimental Farm under his hand, was able to gauge now the vigour of the Food. His first impression was that the house was smaller than he had thought, very much smaller; his second was to perceive that all the vegetation between the house and the pine wood had become extremely large. The roof over the well peeped amidst tussocks of grass a good eight feet high, and the Canary Creeper wrapped about the chimney stack and gesticulated with stiff tendrils towards the heavens. Its flowers were vivid yellow splashes, distinctly visible as separate specks this mile away. A great green cable had writhed across the big wire enclosures of the giant hens' run, and flung twining leaf stems about two outstanding pines. Fully half as tall as these was the grove of nettles running round behind the cart-shed. The whole prospect, as they drew nearer, became more and more suggestive of a raid of pigmies upon a doll's house that has been left in a neglected corner of some great garden.

There was a busy coming and going from the wasps' nest, they saw. A swarm of black shapes interlaced in the air above the rusty hill-front beyond the pine cluster, and ever and again one of these would dart up into the sky with incredible swiftness and soar off upon some distant quest. Their humming became audible at more than half a mile's distance from the Experimental Farm. Once a yellow-striped monster dropped towards them and hung for a space watching them with its great compound eyes, but at an ineffectual shot from Cossar it darted off again. Down in a corner of the field, away to the right, several were crawling about over some ragged bones that were probably the remains of the lamb the rats had brought from Huxter's Farm. The horses became very restless as they drew near these creatures. None of the party was an expert driver, and they had to put a man to lead each horse and encourage it with the voice.

They could see nothing of the rats as they came up to the house, and everything seemed perfectly still except for the rising and falling " whoozzzzzzZZZ, whooozoo-oo " of the wasps' nest.

They led the horses into the yard, and one of Cossar's men, seeing the door open—the whole of the middle portion of the door had been gnawed out—walked into the house. Nobody missed him for the time, the rest being occupied with the barrels of paraffin, and the first intimation they had of his separation from them was the report of his gun and the whizz of his bullet. " Bang, bang," both barrels, and his first bullet it seems went through the cask of sulphur, smashed out a stave from the further side, and filled the air with yellow dust. Redwood had kept his gun in hand and let fly at something grey that leapt past him. He had a vision of the broad hind quarters, the long scaly tail and long soles of the hind feet of a rat, and fired his second barrel. He saw Bensington drop as the beast vanished round the corner.

Then for a time everybody was busy with a gun. For three minutes lives were cheap at the Experimental Farm, and the banging of guns filled the air. Redwood, careless of Bensington in his excitement, rushed in pursuit, and was knocked headlong by a mass of brick fragments, mortar, plaster, and rotten lath splinters that came flying out at him as a bullet whacked through the wall.

He found himself sitting on the ground with blood on his hands and lips, and a great stillness brooded over all about him

Then a flattish voice from within the house remarked : " Gee-whizz ! "

" Hullo ! " said Redwood.

" Hullo there ! " answered the voice.

And then : " Did you chaps get 'im ? "

A sense of the duties of friendship returned to Redwood. " Is Mr. Bensington hurt ? " he said.

The man inside heard imperfectly. " No one ain't to blame if I ain't," said the voice inside.

It became clearer to Redwood that he must have shot Bensington. He forgot the cuts upon his face, arose and came back to find Bensington seated on the ground and rubbing his shoulder. Bensington looked over his glasses. " We peppered him, Redwood," he said, and then : " He tried to jump over me, and knocked me down. But I let him have it with both barrels, and my ! how it has hurt my shoulder to be sure ! "

A man appeared in the doorway. " I got him once in the chest and once in the side," he said.

" Where's the waggons ? " said Cossar, appearing amidst a thicket of gigantic canary-creeper leaves.

It became evident, to Redwood's amazement, first, that no one had been shot, and, secondly, that the trolley and waggon had shifted fifty yards, and were now standing with interlocked wheels amidst the tangled distortions of Skinner's kitchen garden. The horses had stopped their plunging. Half-way towards them, the burst barrel of sulphur lay in the path with a cloud of sulphur dust above it. He indicated this to Cossar and walked towards it. " Has any one seen that rat ? " shouted Cossar, following. " I got him in between the ribs once, and once in the face as he turned on me."

They were joined by two men, as they worried at the locked wheels.

" I killed that rat," said one of the men.

" Have they got him ? " asked Cossar.

" Jim Bates has found him, beyond the hedge. I got him jest as he came round the corner. . . . Whack behind the shoulder. . . ."

When things were a little shipshape again, Redwood went and stared at the huge misshapen corpse. The brute lay on its side, with its body slightly bent. Its rodent teeth overhanging its receding lower jaw gave its face a look of colossal feebleness, of weak avidity. It seemed not in the least ferocious or terrible. Its fore paws reminded him of lank emaciated hands. Except for one neat round hole with a scorched rim on either side of its neck, the creature was

absolutely intact. He meditated over this fact for some time.
"There must have been two rats," he said at last, turning
away.

"Yes. And the one that everybody hit—got away."

"I am certain that my own shot——"

A canary-creeper leaf tendril, engaged in that mysterious
search for a holdfast which constitutes a tendril's search, bent
itself engagingly towards his neck and made him step aside
hastily.

"Whoo-z-z-z-z-z-z-Z-Z-Z," from the distant-wasps' nest,
"whoo-oo-zoo-oo."

V

The incident left the party alert but not unstrung.

They got their stores into the house, which had evidently
been ransacked by the rats after the flight of Mrs. Skinner,
and four of the men took the two horses back to Hickleybrow.
They dragged the dead rat through the hedge and into a
position commanded by the windows of the house, and incidentally came upon a cluster of giant earwigs in the ditch. These
creatures dispersed hastily, but Cossar reached out incalculable
limbs and managed to kill several with his boots and gun-butt.
Then two of the men hacked through several of the main
stems of the canary creeper—huge cylinders they were, a
couple of feet in diameter, that came out by the sink at the
back ; and while Cossar set the house in order for the night,
Bensington, Redwood, and one of the assistant electricians
went cautiously round by the fowl-runs in search of the
rat-holes.

They skirted the giant nettles widely, for these huge weeds
threatened them with poison-thorns a good inch long. Then
round beyond the gnawed dismantled stile they came abruptly
on the huge cavernous throat of the most westerly of the giant
rat-holes, an evil-smelling profundity that drew them up into
a line together.

"I *hope* they'll come out," said Redwood, with a glance at
the pent-house of the well.

"If they don't——" reflected Bensington.

"They will," said Redwood.

They meditated.

"We shall have to rig up some sort of flare if we *do* go in,"
said Redwood.

They went up a little path of white sand through the pine
wood and halted presently within sight of the wasp-holes.

The sun was setting now, and the wasps were coming home
for good ; their wings in the golden light made twirling haloes
about them. The three men peered out from under the trees
—they did not care to go right to the edge of the wood—and
watched these tremendous insects drop and crawl for a little
and enter and disappear. "They will be still in a couple of

hours from now," said Redwood. . . . "This is like being a boy again."

"We can't miss those holes," said Bensington, "even if the night is dark. By the bye—about the light——"

"Full moon," said the electrician. "I looked it up."

They went back and consulted with Cossar.

He said that "obviously" they must get the sulphur, nitre, and plaster of Paris through the wood before twilight, and for that they broke bulk and carried the sacks. After the necessary shouting of the preliminary directions, never a word was spoken, and as the buzzing of the wasps' nest died away there was scarcely a sound in the world but the noise of footsteps, the heavy breathing of burthened men, and the thud of the sacks. They all took turns at that labour except Mr. Bensington, who was manifestly unfit. He took post in the Skinners' bedroom with a rifle, to watch the carcass of the dead rat ; and of the others, they took turns to rest from sack-carrying and to keep watch two at a time upon the rat-holes behind the nettle grove. The pollen sacs of the nettles were ripe, and every now and then their vigil would be enlivened by the dehiscence of these, the bursting of the sacs sounding exactly like the crack of a pistol, and pollen grains as big as buckshot pattered all about them.

Mr. Bensington sat at his window on a hard horsehair-stuffed armchair, covered by a grubby antimacassar that had given a touch of social distinction to the Skinners' sitting-room for many years. His unaccustomed rifle rested on the sill, and his spectacles anon watched the dark bulk of the dead rat in the thickening twilight, anon wandered about him in curious meditation. There was a faint smell of paraffin without, for one of the casks leaked, and it mingled with a less unpleasant odour arising from the hacked and crushed creeper.

Within, when he turned his head, a blend of faint domestic scents, beer, cheese, rotten apples, and old boots as the leading *motifs*, was full of reminiscences of the vanished Skinners. He regarded the dim room for a space. The furniture had been greatly disordered—perhaps by some inquisitive rat— but a coat upon a clothes-peg on the door, a razor and some dirty scraps of paper, and a piece of soap that had hardened through years of disuse into a horny cube, were redolent of Skinner's distinctive personality. It came to Bensington's mind with a complete novelty of realisation that in all probability the man had been killed and eaten, at least in part, by the monster that now lay dead there in the darkling.

To think of all that a harmless-looking discovery in chemistry may lead to !

Here he was in homely England and yet in infinite danger, sitting out alone with a gun in a twilit, ruined house, remote from every comfort, his shoulder dreadfully bruised from a gun-kick, and—by Jove !

He grasped now how profoundly the order of the universe
had changed for him. He had come right away to this
amazing experience, *without even saying a word to his cousin
Jane* !

What must she be thinking of him ?

He tried to imagine it and he could not. He had an extraordinary feeling that she and he were parted for ever and would
never meet again. He felt he had taken a step and come into
a world of new immensities. What other monsters might not
those deepening shadows hide ? . . . The tips of the giant
nettles came out sharp and black against the pale green and
amber of the western sky. Everything was very still, very
still indeed. He wondered why he could not hear the others
away there round the corner of the house. The shadow in
the cart-shed was now an abysmal black.

Bang . . . *Bang* . . . *Bang*.

A sequence of echoes and a shout.

A long silence.

Bang and a *diminuendo* of echoes.

Stillness.

Then, thank goodness ! Redwood and Cossar were coming
out of the inaudible darknesses, and Redwood was calling
" Bensington ! "

" Bensington ! We've bagged another of the rats ! "

" Cossar's bagged another of the rats ! "

VI

When the Expedition had finished refreshment, the night
had fully come. The stars were at their brightest, and a
growing pallor towards Hankey heralded the moon. The
watch on the rat-holes had been maintained, but the watchers
had shifted to the hill slope above the holes, feeling this a
safer firing-point. They squatted there in a rather abundant
dew, fighting the damp with whisky. The others rested in the
house, and the three leaders discussed the night's work with
the men. The moon rose towards midnight, and as soon as
it was clear of the downs, every one except the rat-hole
sentinels started off in single file, led by Cossar, towards the
wasps' nest.

So far as the wasps' nest went, they found their task exceptionally easy, astonishingly easy. Except that it was a longer
labour, it was no graver affair than any common wasps' nest
might have been. Danger there was, no doubt, danger to
life, but it never so much as thrust its head out of that
portentous hillside. They stuffed in the sulphur and nitre,
they bunged the holes soundly, and fired their trains. Then
with a common impulse all the party but Cossar turned and
ran athwart the long shadows of the pines, and, finding Cossar
had stayed behind, came to a halt together in a knot, a hundred

yards away, convenient to a ditch that offered cover. Just for a minute or two the moonlit night, all black and white, was heavy with a suffocated buzz, that rose and mingled to a roar, a deep abundant note, and culminated and died, and then almost incredibly the night was still.

"By Jove!" said Bensington, almost in a whisper, "it's *done*!"

All stood intent. The hillside above the black point-lace of the pine shadows seemed as bright as day and as colourless as snow. The setting plaster in the holes positively shone. Cossar's loose framework moved towards them.

"So far——" said Cossar.

"Crack—bang!"

A shot from near the house and then—stillness.

"What's *that*?" said Bensington.

"One of the rats put its head out," suggested one of the men.

"By the bye, we left our guns up there," said Redwood.

"By the sacks."

Every one began to walk towards the hill again.

"That must be the rats," said Bensington.

"Obviously," said Cossar, gnawing his finger nails.

"*Bang!*"

"Hullo?" said one of the men.

Then abruptly came a shout, two shots, a loud shout that was almost a scream, three shots in rapid succession and a splintering of wood. All these sounds were very clear and very small in the immense stillness of the night. Then for some moments nothing but a minute muffled confusion from the direction of the rat-holes, and then again a wild yell. . . . Each man found himself running hard for the guns.

Two shots.

Bensington found himself, gun in hand, going hard through the pine-trees after a number of receding backs. It is curious that the thought uppermost in his mind at that moment was the wish that his cousin Jane could see him. His bulbous slashed boots flew out in wild strides and his face was distorted into a permanent grin, because that wrinkled his nose and kept his glasses in place. Also he held the muzzle of his gun projecting straight before him as he flew through the chequered moonlight. The man who had run away met them full tilt —he had dropped his gun.

"Hullo," said Cossar, and caught him in his arms. "What's this?"

"They came out together," said the man.

"The rats?"

"Yes, six of them."

"Where's Flack?"

"Down."

"What's he say?" panted Bensington, coming up, unheeded.

" Flack's down ? "

" He fell down."

" They came out one after the other."

" What ? "

" Made a rush. I fired both barrels first."

" You left Flack ? "

" They were on to us."

" Come on," said Cossar. " You come with us. Where's Flack ? Show us."

The whole party moved forward. Further details of the engagement dropped from the man who had run away. The others clustered about him, except Cossar, who led.

" Where are they ? "

" Back in their holes, perhaps. I cleared. They made a rush for their holes."

" What do you mean ? Did you get behind them ? "

" We got down by their holes. Saw 'em come out, you know, and tried to cut 'em off. They lollopped out—like rabbits. We ran down and let fly. They ran about wild after our first shot and suddenly came at us. *Went* for us."

" How many ? "

" Six or seven."

Cossar led the way to the edge of the pine wood and halted.

" D'yer mean they *got* Flack ? " asked some one.

" One of 'em was on to him."

" Didn't you shoot ? "

" How *could* I ? "

" Every one loaded ? " said Cossar over his shoulder.

There was a confirmatory movement.

" But Flack—— " said one.

" D'yer mean—Flack—— " said another.

" There's no time to lose," said Cossar, and shouted " Flack ! " as he led the way. The whole force advanced towards the rat-holes, the man who had run away a little to the rear. They went forward through the rank exaggerated weeds and skirted the body of the second dead rat. They were extended in a bunchy line, each man with his gun pointing forward, and they peered about them in the clear moonlight for some crumpled ominous shape, some crouching form. They found the gun of the man who had run away very speedily.

" Flack ! " cried Cossar. " Flack ! "

" He ran past the nettles and fell down," volunteered the man who ran away.

" Where ? "

" Round about there."

" Where did he fall ? "

He hesitated and led them athwart the long black shadows for a space and turned judicially. " About here, I think."

" Well, he's not here now."

" But his gun—— ? "

" Confound it ! " swore Cossar, " where's everything got to ? " He strode a step towards the black shadows on the hillside that masked the holes and stood staring. Then he swore again. " If they *have* dragged him in—— ! "

So they hung for a space tossing each other the fragments of thoughts. Bensington's glasses flashed like diamonds as he looked from one to the other. The men's faces changed from cold clearness to mysterious obscurity as they turned them to or from the moon. Every one spoke, no one completed a sentence. Then abruptly Cossar chose his line. He flapped limbs this way and that and expelled orders in pellets. It was obvious he wanted lamps. Every one except Cossar was moving towards the house.

" You're going into the holes ? " asked Redwood.

" Obviously," said Cossar.

He made it clear once more that the lamps of the cart and trolley were to be got and brought to him.

Bensington, grasping this, started off along the path by the well. He glanced over his shoulder and saw Cossar's gigantic figure standing out as if he were regarding the holes pensively. At the sight Bensington halted for a moment and half turned. They were all leaving Cossar—— !

Cossar was able to take care of himself, of course !

Suddenly Bensington saw something that made him shout a windless " HI ! " In a second three rats had projected themselves from the dark tangle of the creeper towards Cossar. For three seconds Cossar stood unaware of them, and then he had become the most active thing in the world. He didn't fire his gun. Apparently he had no time to aim, or to think of aiming ; he ducked a leaping rat, Bensington saw, and then smashed at the back of its head with the butt of his gun. The monster gave one leap and fell over itself.

Cossar's form went right down out of sight among the reedy grass, and then he rose again, running towards another of the rats and whirling his gun overhead. A faint shout came to Bensington's ears, and then he perceived the remaining two rats bolting divergently, and Cossar in pursuit towards the holes.

The whole thing was an affair of misty shadows ; all three fighting monsters were exaggerated and made unreal by the delusive clearness of the light. At moments Cossar was colossal, at moments invisible. The rats flashed athwart the eye in sudden unexpected leaps, or ran with a movement of the feet so swift, they seemed to run on wheels. It was all over in half a minute. No one saw it but Bensington. He could hear the others behind him still receding towards the house. He shouted something inarticulate and then ran back towards Cossar, while the rats vanished.

He came up to him outside the holes. In the moonlight the distribution of shadows that constituted Cossar's visage intimated calm. " Hullo," said Cossar, " back already ? Where's the lamps ? They're all back now in their holes. One I broke the neck of as it ran past me. . . . See ? There ! " And he pointed a gaunt finger.

Bensington was too astonished for conversation. . . .

The lamps seemed an interminable time in coming. At last they appeared, first one unwinking luminous eye, preceded by a swaying yellow glare, and then, winking now and then, and then shining out again, two others. About them came little figures with little voices, and then enormous shadows. This group made as it were a spot of inflammation upon the gigantic dreamland of moonshine.

" Flack," said the voices. " Flack."

An illuminating sentence floated up. " Locked himself in the attic."

Cossar was continually more wonderful. He produced great lumps of cotton-wool and stuffed them in his ears—Bensington wondered why. Then he loaded his gun with a quarter charge of powder. Who else could have thought of that ? Wonderland culminated with the disappearance of Cossar's twin realms of boot sole up the central hole.

Cossar was on all-fours with two guns, one trailing on each side from a string under his chin, and his most trusted assistant, a little dark man with a grave face, was to go in stooping behind him, holding a lantern over his head. Everything had been made as sane and obvious and proper as a lunatic's dream. The wool, it seemed, was on account of the concussion of the rifle ; the man had some, too. Obviously ! So long as the rats turned tail on Cossar no harm could come to him, and directly they headed for him he would see their eyes and fire between them. Since they would have to come down the cylinder of the hole, Cossar could hardly fail to hit them. It was, Cossar insisted, the obvious method, a little tedious perhaps, but absolutely certain. As the assistant stooped to enter, Bensington saw that the end of a ball of twine had been tied to the tail of his coat. By this he was to draw in the rope if it should be needed to drag out the bodies of the rats.

Bensington perceived that the object he held in his hand was Cossar's silk hat.

How had it got there ? . . .

It would be something to remember him by, anyhow.

At each of the adjacent holes stood a little group with a lantern on the ground shining up the hole, and with one man kneeling and aiming at the round void before him, waiting for anything that might emerge.

There was an interminable suspense.

Then they heard Cossar's first shot, like an explosion in a mine. . . .

Every one's nerves and muscles tightened at that, and bang ! bang ! bang ! the rats had tried a bolt, and two more were dead. Then the man who held the ball of twine reported a twitching. " He's killed one in there," said Bensington, " and he wants the rope."

He watched the rope creep into the hole, and it seemed as though it had become animated by a serpentine intelligence—for the darkness made the twine invisible. At last it stopped crawling, and there was a long pause. Then what seemed to Bensington the queerest monster of all crept slowly from the hole, and resolved itself into the little engineer emerging backwards. After him, and ploughing deep furrows, Cossar's boots thrust out, and then came his lantern-illuminated back. . . .

Only one rat was left alive now, and this poor, doomed wretch cowered in the inmost recesses until Cossar and the lantern went in again and slew it, and finally Cossar, that human ferret, went through all the runs to make sure.

" We got 'em," he said to his nearly awe-stricken company at last. " And if I hadn't been a mud-headed mucker I should have stripped to the waist. Obviously. Feel my sleeves, Bensington ! I'm wet through with perspiration. Jolly hard to think of everything. Only a halfway-up of whisky can save me from a cold."

VII

There were moments during that wonderful night when it seemed to Bensington that he was planned by nature for a life of fantastic adventure. This was particularly the case for an hour or so after he had taken a stiff whisky. " Shan' go back to Sloane Street," he confided to the tall, fair, dirty engineer.

" You won't, eh ? "

" No fear," said Bensington, nodding darkly.

The exertion of dragging the seven dead rats to the funeral pyre by the nettle grove left him bathed in perspiration, and Cossar pointed out the obvious physical reaction of whisky to save him from the otherwise inevitable chill. There was a sort of brigand's supper in the old bricked kitchen, with the row of dead rats lying in the moonlight against the hen-runs outside, and after thirty minutes or so of rest Cossar roused them all to the labours that were still to do. " Obviously," as he said, they had to " wipe the place out. No litter—no scandal. See ? " He stirred them up to the idea of making destruction complete. They smashed and splintered every fragment of wood in the house ; they built trails of chopped wood wherever big vegetation was springing ; they made a pyre for the rat bodies and soaked them in paraffin.

Bensington worked like a conscientious navvy. He had a sort of climax of exhilaration and energy towards two o'clock. When in the work of destruction he wielded an axe the bravest fled his neighbourhood. Afterwards he was a little sobered by the temporary loss of his spectacles, which were found for him at last in his side coat-pocket.

Men went to and fro about him—grimy, energetic men. Cossar moved amongst them like a god.

Bensington drank that delight of human fellowship that comes to happy armies, to sturdy expeditions—never to those who live the life of the sober citizens in cities. After Cossar had taken his axe away and set him to carry wood he went to and fro, saying they were all " good fellows." He kept on—long after he was aware of fatigue.

At last all was ready and the broaching of the paraffin began. The moon, robbed now of all its meagre night retinue of stars, shone high above the dawn.

" Burn everything," said Cossar, going to and fro, " burn the ground and make a clean sweep of it. See ? "

Bensington became aware of him, looking now very gaunt and horrible in the pale beginnings of the daylight, hurrying past with his lower jaw projected and a flaring torch of touch-wood in his hand.

" Come away ! " said some one, pulling Bensington's arm.

The still dawn—no birds were singing there—was suddenly full of a tumultuous crackling ; a little dull red flame ran about the base of the pyre, changed to blue upon the ground, and set out to clamber, leaf by leaf, up the stem of a giant nettle. A singing sound mingled with the crackling. . . .

They snatched their guns from the corner of the Skinners' living-room, and then every one was running. Cossar came after them with heavy strides. . . .

Then they were standing looking back at the Experimental Farm. It was boiling up ; the smoke and flames poured out like a crowd in a panic, from doors and windows and from a thousand cracks and crevices in the roof. Trust Cossar to build a fire ! A great column of smoke, shot with blood-red tongues and darting flashes, rushed up into the sky. It was like some huge giant suddenly standing up, straining upward and abruptly spreading his great arms out across the sky. It cast the night back upon them, utterly hiding and obliterating the incandescence of the sun that rose behind it. All Hickleybrow was soon aware of that stupendous pillar of smoke, and came out upon the crest, in various deshabille, to watch them coming.

Behind, like some fantastic fungus, this smoke pillar swayed and fluctuated, up, up, into the sky—making the Downs seem low and all other objects petty, and in the foreground, led by Cossar, the makers of this mischief followed the path, eight little black figures coming wearily, guns shouldered, across the meadow.

As Bensington looked back there came into his jaded brain, and echoed there, a familiar formula. What was it ? " You have lit to-day—— ? "   " You have lit to-day—— ? "

Then he remembered Latimer's words : " We have lit this day such a Candle in England as no man may ever put out again——"

What a man Cossar was, to be sure ! He admired his back view for a space and was proud to have held that hat. Proud ! Although he was an eminent investigator and Cossar only engaged in applied science.

Suddenly he fell shivering and yawning enormously and wishing he was warmly tucked away in bed in his little flat that looked out upon Sloane Street. (It didn't do even to think of cousin Jane.) His legs became cotton strands, his feet lead. He wondered if any one would get them coffee in Hickleybrow. He had never been up all night for three-and-thirty years.

VIII

And while these eight adventurers fought with rats about the Experimental Farm, nine miles away in the village of Cheasing Eyebright, an old lady with an excessive nose struggled with great difficulties by the light of a flickering candle. She gripped a sardine tin opener in one gnarled hand, and in the other she held a tin of Herakleophorbia, which she had resolved to open or die. She struggled indefatigably, grunting at each fresh effort, while through the flimsy partition the voice of the Caddles infant wailed.

" Bless 'is poor 'art," said Mrs. Skinner ; and then, with her solitary tooth biting her lip in an ecstasy of determination " Come *up* ! "

And presently, " *Jab* ! " a fresh supply of the Food of the Gods was let loose to wreak its powers of giantry upon the world.

CHAPTER FOUR

THE GIANT CHILDREN

I

FOR a time at least the spreading circle of residual consequences about the Experimental Farm must pass out of
the focus of our narrative, how for a long time a power
of bigness, in fungus and toadstool, in grass and weed, radiated
from that charred but not absolutely obliterated centre. Nor
can we tell here at any length how those mournful spinsters,
the two surviving hens, made a wonder of and a show, spent
their remaining years in eggless celebrity. The reader who is
hungry for fuller details in these matters is referred to the
newspapers of the period, to the voluminous, indiscriminate
files of the modern Recording Angel. Our business lies with
Mr. Bensington at the focus of the disturbance.

He had come back to London to find himself a quite terribly
famous man. In a night the whole world had changed with
respect to him. Everybody understood. Cousin Jane, it
seemed, knew all about it ; the people in the streets knew all
about it ; the newspapers all and more. To meet cousin Jane
was terrible, of course, but when it was over not so terrible
after all. The good woman had limits even to her power over
facts ; it was clear that she had communed with herself and
accepted the Food as something in the nature of things.

She took the line of huffy dutifulness. She disapproved
highly, it was evident, but she did not prohibit. The flight of
Bensington, as she must have considered it, may have shaken
her, and her worst was to treat him with bitter persistence for
a cold he had not çaught and fatigue he had long since forgotten,
and to buy him a new sort of hygienic all-wool combination
underwear that was as apt to get involved and turned partially
inside out and partially not, and as difficult to get into for an
absent-minded man, as—Society. And so for a space, and as
far as this convenience left him leisure, he still continued to
participate in the development of this new element in human
history, the Food of the Gods.

The public mind, following its own mysterious laws of selection, had chosen him as the one and only responsible Inventor
and Promoter of this new wonder ; it would hear nothing of
Redwood, and without a protest it allowed Cossar to follow his
natural impulse into a terribly prolific obscurity. Before he
was aware of the drift of these things, Mr. Bensington was, so to
speak, stark and dissected upon the hoardings. His baldness,
his curious general pinkness, and his golden spectacles had become a national possession. Resolute young men with large
expensive-looking cameras and a general air of complete author-

isation took possession of the flat for brief but fruitful periods, let off flashlights in it that filled it for hours with dense, intolerable vapour, and retired to fill the pages of the syndicated magazines with their admirable photographs of Mr. Bensington complete and at home in his second best jacket and his slashed shoes. Other resolute-mannered persons of various ages and sexes dropped in and told him things about Boomfood—it was *Punch* first called the stuff " Boomfood "—and afterwards reproduced what they had said as his own original contribution to the Interview. The thing became quite an obsession with Broadbeam, the Popular Humourist. He scented another confounded thing he could not understand, and he fretted dreadfully in his efforts to " laugh the thing down." One saw him in clubs, a great clumsy presence with the evidences of his midnight oil-burning manifest upon his large unwholesome face, explaining to every one he could buttonhole : " These Scientific chaps, you know, haven't a Sense of Humour, you know. That's what it is. This Science—kills it." His jests at Bensington became malignant libels. . . .

An enterprising press-cutting agency sent Bensington a long article about himself from a sixpenny weekly, entitled " A New Terror," and offered to supply one hundred such disturbances for a guinea ; and two extremely charming young ladies, totally unknown to him, called and, to the speechless indignation of cousin Jane, had tea with him and afterwards sent him their birthday books for his signature. He was speedily quite hardened to seeing his name associated with the most incongruous ideas in the public Press, and to discover in the reviews articles written about Boomfood and himself in a tone of the utmost intimacy by people he had never heard of. And whatever delusions he may have cherished in the days of his obscurity about the pleasantness of Fame were dispelled utterly and for ever.

At first—except for Broadbeam—the tone of the public mind was quite free from any touch of hostility. It did not seem to occur to the public mind as anything but a mere playful supposition that any more Herakleophorbia was going to escape again. And it did not seem to occur to the public mind that the growing little band of babies now being fed on the food would presently be growing more " up " than most of us ever grow. The sort of thing that pleased the public mind was caricatures of eminent politicians after a course of Boomfeeding, uses of the idea on hoardings, and such edifying exhibitions as the dead wasps that had escaped the fire and the remaining hens.

Beyond that the public did not care to look, until very strenuous efforts were made to turn its eyes to the remoter consequences ; and even then for a while its enthusiasm for action was partial. " There's always somethin' New," said the public—a public so glutted with novelty that it would hear of the earth being split as one splits an apple without surprise, and, " I wonder what they'll do next."

But there were one or two people outside the public, as it were, who did already take that further glance, and some it seems were frightened by what they saw there. There was young Caterham, for example, cousin of the Earl of Pewterstone, and one of the most promising of English politicians, who, taking the risk of being thought a faddist, wrote a long article in the *Nineteenth Century and After* to suggest the total suppression of the food. And—in certain of his moods, there was Bensington.

" They don't seem to realise——" he said to Cossar.

" No, they don't."

" And do we ? Sometimes, when I think of what it means—— This poor child of Redwood's—and, of course, your three. . . . Forty feet high, perhaps ! . . . After all, *ought* we to go on with it ? "

" Go on with it ! " cried Cossar, convulsed with inelegant astonishment and pitching his note higher than ever. " Of *course* you'll go on with it ! What d'you think you were made for ? Just to loaf about between meal-times ?

" Serious consequences," he screamed, " of course ! Enormous. Obviously. Ob-viously. Why, man, it's the only chance you'll ever get of a serious consequence ! And you want to shirk it ! " For a moment his indignation was speechless. " It's downright Wicked ! " he said at last, and repeated explosively, " Wicked ! "

But Bensington worked in his laboratory now with more emotion than zest. He couldn't tell whether he wanted serious consequences to his life or not ; he was a man of quiet tastes. It was a marvellous discovery, of course, quite marvellous, but—— He had already become the proprietor of several acres of scorched, discredited property near Hickleybrow, at a price of nearly £90 an acre ; and at times he was disposed to think this as serious a consequence of speculative chemistry as any unambitious man could wish. Of course he was Famous—terribly Famous. More than satisfying, altogether more than satisfying, was the Fame he had attained.

But the habit of Research was strong in him. . . .

And at moments, rare moments in the laboratory chiefly, he would find something else than habit and Cossar's arguments to urge him to his work. This little spectacled man, poised perhaps with his slashed shoes wrapped about the legs of his high stool and his hand upon the tweezer of his balance weights, would have again a flash of that adolescent vision, would have a momentary perception of the eternal unfolding of the seed that had been sown in his brain, would see as it were in the sky, behind the grotesque shapes and accidents of the present, the coming world of giants and all the mighty things the future has in store—vague and splendid, like some glittering palace seen suddenly in the passing of a sunbeam far away. . . . And presently it would be with him as though that distant splendour had never shone upon his brain, and he would perceive nothing ahead but sinister shadows, vast declivities and darknesses, inhospitable immensities, cold, wild, and terrible things.

II

Amidst the complex and confused happenings, the impacts from the great outer world that constituted Mr. Bensington's fame, a shining and active figure presently became conspicuous, became almost, as it were, a leader and marshal of these externalities in Mr. Bensington's eyes. This was Doctor Winkles, that convincing young practitioner, who has already appeared in this story as the means whereby Redwood was able to convey the Food to his son. Even before the great outbreak, it was evident that the mysterious powders Redwood had given him had awakened this gentleman's interest immensely, and so soon as the first wasps came he was putting two and two together.

He was the sort of doctor that is in manners, in morals, in methods and appearance, most succinctly and finally expressed by the word " rising." He was large and fair, with a hard, alert, superficial, aluminium-coloured eye and hair like chalk mud, even-featured and muscular about the clean-shaven mouth, erect in figure and energetic in movement, quick and spinning on the heel ; and he wore long frock coats, black silk ties and plain gold studs and chains, and his silk hats had a special shape and brim that made him look wiser and better than anybody. He looked as young or old as anybody grown up. And after that first wonderful outbreak he took to Bensington and Redwood and the Food of the Gods with such a convincing air of proprietorship, that at times, in spite of the testimony of the Press to the contrary, Bensington was disposed to regard him as the original inventor of the whole affair.

" These accidents," said Winkles, when Bensington hinted at the dangers of further escapes, " are nothing. Nothing. The discovery is everything. Properly developed, suitably handled, sanely controlled, we have—we have something very portentous indeed in this food of ours. . . . We must keep our eye on it. . . . We mustn't let it out of control again, and— we mustn't let it rest."

He certainly did not mean to do that. He was at Bensington's now almost every day. Bensington, glancing from the window, would see the faultless equipage come spanking up Sloane Street, and after an incredibly brief interval Winkles would enter the room with a light, strong motion, and pervade it, and protrude some newspaper and supply information and make remarks.

" Well," he would say, rubbing his hands, " how are we getting on ? " and so pass to the current discussion.

" Do you see," he would say for example, " that Caterham has been talking about our stuff at the Church Association ? "

" Dear me ! " said Bensington, " that's a cousin of the Prime Minister, isn't it ? "

" Yes," said Winkles, " a very able young man—very able. Quite wrong-headed, you know, violently reactionary—but thoroughly able. And he's evidently disposed to make capital out of this stuff of ours. Takes a very emphatic line. Talks of our proposal to use it in the elementary schools——"

" Our proposal to use it in the elementary schools ! "

" *I* said something about that the other day—quite in passing—little affair at a Polytechnic. Trying to make it clear the stuff was really highly beneficial. Not in the slightest degree dangerous, in spite of those first little accidents. Which cannot possibly occur again. . . . You know it *would* be rather good stuff—— But he's taken it up."

" What did you say ? "

" Mere obvious nothings. But as you see—— ! Takes it up with perfect gravity. Treats the thing as an attack. Says there is already a sufficient waste of public money in elementary schools without this. Tells the old stories about piano lessons again—*you* know. No one, he says, wishes to prevent the children of the lower classes obtaining an education suited to their condition, but to give them a food of this sort will be to destroy their sense of proportion utterly. Expands the topic. What Good will it do, he asks, to make poor people six-and-thirty feet high ? He really believes, you know, that they *will* be thirty-six feet high."

" So they would be," said Bensington, " if you gave them our food at all regularly. But nobody said anything——"

" *I* said something."

" But, my dear Winkles—— ! "

" They'll be Bigger, of course," interrupted Winkles, with an air of knowing all about it, and discouraging the crude ideas of Bensington. " Bigger indisputably. But listen to what he says ! Will it make them happier ? That's his point. Curious, isn't it ? Will it make them better ? Will they be more respectful to properly constituted authority ? Is it fair to the children themselves ? Curious how anxious his sort are for justice—so far as any future arrangements go. Even nowadays, he says, the cost of feeding and clothing children is more than many of their parents can contrive, and if this sort of thing is to be permitted—— ! Eh ?

" You see he makes my mere passing suggestion into a positive proposal. And then he calculates how much a pair of breeches for a growing lad of twenty feet high or so will cost. Just as though he really believed—— Ten pounds, he reckons, for the merest decency. Curious man, this Caterham ! So concrete ! The honest and struggling ratepayer will have to contribute to that, he says. He says we have to consider the

Rights of the Parent. It's all here. Two columns. Every
Parent has a right to have his children brought up in his own
Size. . . .

" Then comes the question of school accommodation, cost of
enlarged desks and forms for our already too greatly burthened
National Schools. And to get what ?—a proletariat of hungry
giants. Winds up with a very serious passage, says even if this
wild suggestion—mere passing fancy of mine, you know, and
misinterpreted at that—this wild suggestion about the schools
comes to nothing, that doesn't end the matter. This is a
strange food, so strange as to seem to him almost wicked. It
has been scattered recklessly—so he says—and it may be
scattered again. Once you've taken it, it's poison unless you
go on with it. (" So it is," said Bensington.) And in short
he proposes the formation of a National Society for the Preservation of the Proper Proportions of Things. Odd ? Eh ?
People are hanging on to the idea like anything."

" But what do they propose to do ? "

Winkles shrugged his shoulders and threw out his hands.
" Form a Society," he said, " and fuss. They want to make
it illegal to manufacture this Herakleophorbia—or at any rate
to circulate the knowledge of it. I've written about a bit
to show that Caterham's idea of the stuff is very much exaggerated, very much exaggerated indeed, but that doesn't
seem to check it. Curious how people are turning against it.
And the National Temperance Association, by the bye, has
founded a branch for Temperance in Growth."

" Hm," said Bensington, and stroked his nose.

" After all that has happened there's bound to be this uproar. On the face of it the thing's—*startling*."

Winkles walked about the room for a time, hesitated, and
departed.

It became evident there was something at the back of his
mind, some aspect of crucial importance to him, that he waited
to display. One day, when Redwood and Bensington were at
the flat together, he gave them a glimpse of this something in
reserve.

" How's it all going ? " he said, rubbing his hands together.

" We're getting together a sort of report."

" For the Royal Society ? "

" Yes."

" Hm," said Winkles, very profoundly, and walked to the
hearth-rug. " Hm. But—— Here's the point. *Ought*
you ? "

" Ought we—what ? "

" Ought you to publish ? "

" We're not in the Middle Ages," said Redwood.

" I know."

" As Cossar says, swapping wisdom—that's the true scientific
method."

" In most cases, certainly. But—— This is exceptional."

" We shall put the whole thing before the Royal Society in the proper way," said Redwood.

Winkles returned to that on a later occasion.

" It's in many ways an Exceptional Discovery."

" That doesn't matter," said Redwood.

" It's the sort of knowledge that could easily be subject to grave abuse—grave dangers, as Caterham puts it."

Redwood said nothing.

" Even carelessness, you know——

" If we were to form a committee of trustworthy people to control the manufacture of Boomfood—Herakleophorbia, I *should* say—we might——"

He paused, and Redwood, with a certain private discomfort, pretended that he did not see any sort of interrogation. . . .

Outside the apartments of Redwood and Bensington, Winkles, in spite of the incompleteness of his instructions, became a leading authority upon Boomfood. He wrote letters defending its use ; he made notes and articles explaining its possibilities ; he jumped up irrelevantly at the meetings of the scientific and medical associations to talk about it ; he identified himself with it. He published a pamphlet called *The Truth about Boomfood*, in which he minimised the whole of the Hickleybrow affair almost to nothing. He said that it was absurd to say Boomfood would make people thirty-seven feet high. That was " obviously exaggerated." It would make them Bigger, of course, but that was all. . . .

Within that intimate circle of two it was chiefly evident that Winkles was extremely anxious to help in the making of Herakleophorbia, help in correcting any proofs there might be of any paper there might be in preparation upon the subject, do anything indeed that might lead up to his participation in the details of the making of Herakleophorbia. He was continually telling them both that he felt it was a Big Thing, that it had big possibilities. If only they were——" safeguarded in some way." And at last one day he asked outright to be told just how it was made.

" I've been thinking over what you said," said Redwood.

" Well ? " said Winkles, brightly.

" It's the sort of knowledge that could easily be subject to grave abuse," said Redwood.

" But I don't see how that applies," said Winkles.

" It does," said Redwood.

Winkles thought it over for a day or so. Then he came to Redwood and said that he doubted if he ought to give powders about which he knew nothing to Redwood's little boy ; it seemed to him it was uncommonly like taking responsibility in the dark. That made Redwood thoughtful.

" You've seen that the Society for the Total Suppression of

Boomfood claims to have several thousand members," said Winkles, changing the subject.

"They've drafted a bill," said Winkles. "They've got young Caterham to take it up—readily enough. They're in earnest. They're forming local committees to influence candidates. They want to make it penal to prepare and store Herakleophorbia without special licence, and felony—matter of imprisonment without option—to administer Boomfood—that's what they call it, you know—to any person under one-and-twenty. But there's collateral societies, you know. All sorts of people. The Society for the Preservation of Ancient Statures is going to have Mr. Frederick Harrison on the council, they say. You know he's written an essay about it ; says it is vulgar, and entirely inharmonious with that Revelation of Humanity that is found in the teachings of Comte. It is the sort of thing the Eighteenth Century *couldn't* have produced even in its worst moments. The idea of the Food never entered the head of Comte—which shows how wicked it really is. No one, he says, who really understood Comte . . ."

"But you don't mean to say——" said Redwood, alarmed out of his disdain for Winkles.

"They'll not do all that," said Winkles. "But public opinion is public opinion, and votes are votes. Everybody can see you are up to a disturbing thing. And the human instinct is all against disturbance, you know. Nobody seems to believe Caterham's idea of people thirty-seven feet high, who won't be able to get inside a church, or a meeting-house, or any social or human institution. But for all that they're not so easy in their minds about it. They see there's something, something more than a common discovery——"

"There is," said Redwood, "in every discovery."

"Anyhow, they're getting—restive. Caterham keeps harping on what may happen if it gets loose again. I say over and over again it won't and it can't. But—there it is ! "

And he bounced about the room for a little while as if he meant to reopen the topic of the secret, and then thought better of it and went.

The two scientific men looked at one another. For a space only their eyes spoke.

"If the worst comes to the worst," said Redwood at last, in a strenuously calm voice, "I shall give the Food to my little Teddy with my own hands."

III

It was only a few days after this that Redwood opened his paper to find that the Prime Minister had promised a Royal Commission on Boomfood. This sent him, newspaper in hand, round to Bensington's flat.

"Winkles, I believe, is making mischief for the stuff. He

plays into the hands of Caterham. He keeps on talking about it, and what it is going to do, and alarming people. If he goes on, I really believe he'll hamper our inquiries. Even as it is—with this trouble about my little boy——"

Bensington wished Winkles wouldn't.

"Do you notice how he has dropped into the way of calling it Boomfood ?"

"I don't like that name," said Bensington, with a glance over his glasses.

"It is just so exactly what it is—to Winkles."

"Why does he keep on about it ? It isn't his ! "

"It's something called Booming," said Redwood. *I* don't understand. If it isn't his, everybody is getting to think it is. Not that *that* matters."

"In the event of this ignorant, this ridiculous agitation becoming—Serious," began Bensington.

"My little boy can't get on without the stuff," said Redwood. "I don't see how I can help myself now. If the worst comes to the worst——"

A slight bouncing noise proclaimed the presence of Winkles. He became visible in the middle of the room rubbing his hands together.

"I wish you'd knock," said Bensington, looking vicious over the gold rims.

Winkles was apologetic. Then he turned to Redwood. "I'm glad to find you here," he began ; "the fact is——"

"Have you seen about this Royal Commission ?" interrupted Redwood.

"Yes," said Winkles, thrown out. "Yes."

"What do you think of it ? "

"Excellent thing," said Winkles. "Bound to stop most of this clamour. Ventilate the whole affair. Shut up Caterham. But that's not what I came round for, Redwood. The fact is——"

"I don't like this Royal Commission," said Bensington.

"I can assure you it will be all right. I may say—I don't think it's a breach of confidence—that very possibly *I* may have a place on the commission——"

"Oom," said Redwood, looking into the fire.

"I can put the whole thing right. I can make it perfectly clear, first, that the stuff is controllable, and, secondly, that nothing short of a miracle is needed before anything like that catastrophe at Hickleybrow can possibly happen again. That is just what is wanted, an authoritative assurance. Of course, I could speak with more confidence if I knew—— But that's quite by the way. And just at present there's something else, another little matter, upon which I'm wanting to consult you. Ahem. The fact is—— Well—— I happen to be in a slight difficulty, and you can help me out."

Redwood raised his eyebrows and was secretly glad.

" The matter is—highly confidential."

" Go on," said Redwood.   " Don't worry about that."

" I have recently been entrusted with a child—the child of —of an Exalted Personage."

Winkles coughed.

" You're getting on," said Redwood.

" I must confess it's largely your powders—and the reputation of my success with your little boy.   There is, I cannot disguise, a strong feeling against its use.   And yet I find that among the more intelligent——   One must go quietly in these things, you know—little by little.   Still, in the case of Her Serene High—I mean this new little patient of mine.   As a matter of fact—the suggestion came from the parent.   Or I should never——"

He struck Redwood as being embarrassed.

" I thought you had a doubt of the advisability of using these powders," said Redwood.

" Merely a passing doubt."

" You don't propose to discontinue——"

" In the case of your little boy ?   Certainly not ! "

" So far as I can see, it would be murder."

" I wouldn't do it for the world."

" You shall have the powders," said Redwood.

" I suppose you couldn't——"

" No fear," said Redwood.   " There isn't a recipe.   It's no good, Winkles, if you'll pardon my frankness.   I'll make you the powders myself."

" Just as well, perhaps," said Winkles, after a momentary hard stare at Redwood, " just as well."   And then : " I can assure you I really don't mind in the least."

IV

When Winkles had gone, Bensington came and stood on the hearth-rug and looked down at Redwood.

" Her Serene Highness ! " he remarked.

" Her Serene Highness ! " said Redwood.

" It's the Princess of Weser Dreiburg ! "

" No further than a third cousin."

" Redwood," said Bensington ; " it's a curious thing to say, I know, but—do you think Winkles understands ? "

" What ? "

" Just what it is we have made.

" Does he really understand," said Bensington, dropping his voice and keeping his eye doorward, " that in the Family —the Family of his new patient——"

" Go on," said Redwood.

" Who have always been if anything a little *under*— *under*——"

" The Average ? "

" Yes.   And so *very* tactfully undistinguished in *any* way,

he is going to produce a royal personage—an outside royal
personage—of *that* size. You know, Redwood, I am not sure
whether there is not something almost—*treasonable* . . ."

He transferred his eyes from the door to Redwood.

Redwood flung a momentary gesture—index finger erect—
at the fire. " By Jove ! " he said, " he *doesn't* know !

"That man," said Redwood, "doesn't know anything.
That was his most exasperating quality as a student. Nothing.
He passed all his examinations, he had all his facts—and he
had just as much knowledge—as a rotating bookshelf containing the *Times Encyclopædia.* And he doesn't know anything
now. He's Winkles and incapable of really assimilating anything not immediately and directly related to his superficial
self. He is utterly void of imagination and, as a consequence,
incapable of knowledge. No one could possibly pass so many
examinations and be so well dressed, so well done, and so
successful as a doctor without that precise incapacity. That's
it. And in spite of all he's seen and heard and been told,
there he is—he has no idea whatever of what he has set going.
He has got a Boom on, he's working it well on Boomfood, and
some one has let him in to this new Royal Baby—and that's
Boomier than ever ! And the fact that Weser Dreiburg will
presently have to face the gigantic problem of a thirty-odd-
foot Princess not only hasn't entered his head, but couldn't
—it couldn't ! "

" There'll be a fearful row," said Bensington.

" In a year or so."

" So soon as they really see she is going on growing."

" Unless after their fashion—they hush it up."

" It's a lot to hush up."

" Rather ! "

" I wonder what they'll do ? "

" They never do anything—Royal tact."

" They're bound to do something."

" Perhaps *she* will."

" O Lord ! Yes."

" They'll suppress her. Such things have been known."

Redwood burst into desperate laughter. "The redundant
royalty—the bouncing babe in the Iron Mask ! " he said.
"They'll have to put her in the tallest tower of the old Weser
Dreiburg castle and make holes in the ceilings as she grows
from floor to floor ! . . . Well, I'm in the very same pickle.
And Cossar and his three boys. And—— Well, well."

" There'll be a fearful row," Bensington repeated, not
joining in the laughter. " A *fearful* row."

" I suppose," he argued, " you've really thought it out
thoroughly, Redwood. You're quite sure it wouldn't be wiser
to warn Winkles, wean your little boy gradually and—rely
upon the Theoretical Triumph ? "

" I wish to goodness you'd spend half an hour in my nursery

when the Food's a little late," said Redwood, with a note of exasperation in his voice, " then you wouldn't talk like that, Bensington. Besides—fancy warning Winkles ! . . . No ! The tide of this thing has caught us unawares, and whether we're frightened or whether we're not—*we've got to swim* ! "

" I suppose we have," said Bensington, staring at his toes. " Yes. We've got to swim. And your boy will have to swim, and Cossar's boys—he's given it to all three of them. Nothing partial about Cossar—all or nothing ! And Her Serene Highness. And everything. We are going on making the Food. Cossar also. We're only just in the dawn of the beginning, Redwood. It's evident all sorts of things are to follow. Monstrous great things. But I can't imagine them, Redwood. Except——"

He scanned his finger nails. He looked up at Redwood with eyes bland through his glasses.

" I've half a mind," he adventured, " that Caterham is right. At times. It's going to destroy the Proportions of Things. It's going to dislocate—— What isn't it going to dislocate ? "

" Whatever it dislocates," said Redwood, " my little boy must have the Food."

They heard some one falling rapidly upstairs. Then Cossar put his head into the flat. " Hullo ! " he said at their expressions, and entering, " Well ? "

They told him about the Princess.

" *Difficult question* ! " he remarked. " Not a bit of it. *She'll* grow. Your boy'll grow. All the others you give it to 'll grow. Everything. Like anything. What's difficult about that ? That's all right. A child could tell you that. Where's the bother ? "

They tried to make it clear to him.

" *Not go on with it* ! " he shrieked. " But—— ! You can't help yourselves now. It's what you're for. It's what Winkles is for. It's all right. Often wondered what Winkles was for. *Now* it's obvious. What's the trouble ?

" *Disturbance ?* Obviously. *Upset things ?* Upset everything. Finally—upset every human concern. Plain as a pikestaff. They're going to try and stop it, but they're too late. It's their way to be too late. You go on and start as much of it as you can. Thank God he has a use for you ! "

" But the conflict ! " said Bensington, " the stress ! I don't know if you have imagined——"

" You ought to have been some sort of little vegetable, Bensington," said Cossar, " that's what you ought to have been. Something growing over a rockery. Here you are, fearfully and wonderfully made, and all you think you're made for is just to sit about and take your vittles. D'you think this world was made for old women to mop about in ? Well, anyhow, you can't help yourselves now, you've *got* to go on."

" I suppose we must," said Redwood.   " Slowly——"

" No," said Cossar, in a huge shout.   " No ! Make as much as you can and as soon as you can. Spread it about ! "

He was inspired to a stroke of wit. He parodied one of Redwood's curves with a vast upward sweep of his arm.

" Redwood ! " he said, to point the allusion, " make it SO ! "

V

There is, it seems, an upward limit to the pride of maternity, and this in the case of Mrs. Redwood was reached when her offspring completed his sixth month of terrestrial existence, broke down his high-class bassinet-perambulator and was brought home, bawling, in the milk-truck. Young Redwood at that time weighed fifty-nine and a half pounds, measured forty-eight inches in height, and gripped about sixty pounds. He was carried upstairs to the nursery by the cook and house-maid. After that, discovery was only a question of days. One afternoon Redwood came home from his laboratory to find his unfortunate wife deep in the fascinating pages of *The Mighty Atom*, and at the sight of him, she put the book aside and ran violently forward and burst into tears on his shoulder.

" Tell me what you have *done* to him," she wailed. " Tell me what you have done."

Redwood took her hand and led her to the sofa, while he tried to think of a satisfactory line of defence.

" It's all right, my dear," he said ; " it's all right. You're only a little overwrought. It's that cheap perambulator. I've arranged for a bath-chair man to come round with something stouter to-morrow——"

Mrs. Redwood looked at him tearfully over the top of her handkerchief.

" A baby in a bath-chair ? " she sobbed.

" Well, why not ? "

" It's like a cripple."

" It's like a young giant, my dear, and you've no cause to be ashamed of him."

" You've done something to him, Dandy," she said. " I can see it in your face."

" Well, it hasn't stopped his growth, anyhow," said Redwood heartlessly.

" I *knew*," said Mrs. Redwood, and clenched her pocket-handkerchief ball fashion in one hand. She looked at him with a sudden change to severity. " What have you done to our child, Dandy ? "

" What's wrong with him ? "

" He's so big. He's a monster."

" Nonsense. He's as straight and clean a baby as ever a woman bore. What's wrong with him ? "

" Look at his size."

" That's all right.   Look at the puny little brutes about us !   He's the finest baby——"

" He's *too* fine," said Mrs. Redwood.

" It won't go on," said Redwood reassuringly ;   " it's just a start he's taken."

But he knew perfectly well it would go on.   And it did. By the time this baby was twelve months old he measured just one inch under five feet high and scaled eight stone three he was as big in fact as a *San Pietro in Vaticano* cherub, and his affectionate clutch at the hair and features of visitors became the talk of West Kensington.   They had an invalid's chair to carry him up and down to his nursery, and his special nurse, a muscular young person just out of training, used to take him for his airings in a Panhard 8-h.p. hill-climbing perambulator specially made to meet his requirements.   It was lucky in every way that Redwood had his expert-witness connection in addition to his professorship.

When one got over the shock of little Redwood's enormous size, he was, I am told by people who used to see him almost daily teufteufing slowly about Hyde Park, a singularly bright and pretty baby.   He rarely cried or needed a comforter. Commonly he clutched a big rattle, and sometimes he went along hailing the bus-drivers and policemen along the road outside the railings as " Dadda ! " and " Babba ! " in a sociable democratic way.

" There goes that there great Boomfood baby," the bus-driver used to say.

" Looks 'ealthy," the forward passenger would remark.

" Bottle fed," the bus-driver would explain.   " They say it 'olds a gallon and 'ad to be specially made for 'im."

" Very 'ealthy child anyhow," the forward passenger would conclude.

When Mrs. Redwood realised that his growth was indeed going on indefinitely and logically—and this she really did for the first time when the motor-perambulator arrived—she gave way to a passion of grief.   She declared she never wished to enter her nursery again, wished she was dead, wished the child was dead, wished everybody was dead, wished she had never married Redwood, wished no one ever married anybody. Ajaxed a little, and retired to her own room, where she lived almost exclusively on chicken broth for three days.   When Redwood came to remonstrate with her, she banged pillows about and wept and tangled her hair.

" *He's* all right," said Redwood.   " He's all the better for being big.   You wouldn't like him smaller than other people's children."

" I want him to be *like* other children, neither smaller nor bigger.   I wanted him to be a nice little boy, just as Georgina Phyllis is a nice little girl, and I wanted to bring him up nicely in a nice way, and here he is "—and the unfortunate woman's voice broke—" wearing number four grown-up shoes and being wheeled about by—booboo !—Petroleum !

" I can never love him," she wailed, " never ! He's too much for me ! I can never be a mother to him, such as I meant to be ! "

But at last they contrived to get her into the nursery, and there was Edward Monson Redwood (" Pantagruel " was only a later nickname) swinging in a specially strengthened rocking-chair and smiling and talking " goo " and " wow." And the heart of Mrs. Redwood warmed again to her child, and she went and held him in her arms and wept.

" They've done something to you," she sobbed, " and you'll grow and grow, dear, but whatever I can do to bring you up nice I'll do for you, whatever your father may say."

And Redwood, who had helped bring her to the door, went down the passage much relieved.

(Eh ! but it's a base job this being a man—with women as they are !)

VI

Before the year was out there were, in addition to Redwood's pioneer vehicle, quite a number of motor-perambulators to be seen in the west of London. I am told there were as many as eleven ; but the most careful inquiries yield trustworthy evidence of only six within the Metropolitan area at that time. It would seem the stuff acted differently upon different types of constitution. At first Herakleophorbia was not adapted to injection, and there can be no doubt that quite a considerable proportion of human beings are incapable of absorbing this substance in the normal course of digestion. It was given, for example, to Winkles' youngest boy ; but he seems to have been as incapable of growth as, if Redwood was right, his father was incapable of knowledge. Others again, according to the Society for the Total Suppression of Boomfood, became in some inexplicable way corrupted by it, and perished at the onset of infantile disorders. The Cossar boys took to it with amazing avidity.

Of course a thing of this kind never comes with absolute simplicity of application into the life of man ; growth in particular is a complex thing, and all generalisations must needs be a little inaccurate. But the general law of the Food would seem to be this, that when it could be taken into the system in any way it stimulated it in very nearly to the same degree in all cases. It increased the amount of growth from six to seven times, and it did not go beyond that whatever amount of the Food was taken in excess. Excess of Herakleophorbia indeed beyond the necessary minimum led, it was found, to morbid disturbances of nutrition, to cancer and tumours, ossifications and the like. And once growth upon the large scale had begun it was soon evident that it could only continue upon that scale,

and that the continuous administration of Herakleophorbia in
small but sufficient doses was imperative.

If it was discontinued while growth was still going on, there
was first a vague restlessness and distress, then a period of
voracity—as in the case of the young rats at Hankey—and then
the growing creature had a sort of exaggerated anæmia and
sickened and died. Plants suffered in a similar way. This,
however, applied only to the growth period. So soon as adolescence was attained—in plants this was represented by the
formation of the first flower-buds—the need and appetite for
Herakleophorbia diminished, and so soon as the plant or animal
was fully adult, it became altogether independent of any further
supply of the food. It was, as it were, completely established
on the new scale. It was so completely established on the new
scale that, as the thistles about Hickleybrow and the grass of
the down side already demonstrated, its seed produced giant
offspring after its kind.

And presently little Redwood, pioneer of the new race, first
child of all who ate the food, was crawling about his nursery,
smashing furniture, biting like a horse, pinching like a vice, and
bawling gigantic baby talk at his " Nanny " and " Mammy "
and the rather scared and awe-stricken " Daddy," who had set
this mischief going.

The child was born with good intentions. " Padda be good,
be good," he used to say as the breakables flew before him.
" Padda " was his rendering of Pantagruel, the nickname Redwood imposed on him. And Cossar, disregarding certain
Ancient Lights that presently led to trouble, did, after a conflict with the local building regulations, get building on a vacant
piece of ground adjacent to Redwood's home, a comfortable
well-lit playroom, schoolroom, and nursery for their four boys ;
sixty feet square about this room was, and forty feet high.

Redwood fell in love with that great nursery as he and Cossar
built it, and his interest in curves faded, as he had never dreamt
it could fade, before the pressing needs of his son. " There is
much," he said, " in fitting a nursery. Much."

" The walls, the things in it, they will all speak to this new
mind of ours, a little more, a little less eloquently, and teach
it or fail to teach it a thousand things."

" Obviously," said Cossar, reaching hastily for his hat.

They worked together harmoniously, but Redwood supplied
most of the educational theory required. . . .

They had the walls and woodwork painted with a cheerful
vigour ; for the most part a slightly warmed white prevailed,
but there were bands of bright clean colour to enforce the simple
lines of construction. " Clean colours we *must* have," said
Redwood, and in one place had a neat horizontal band of
squares, in which crimson and purple, orange and lemon, blues
and greens, in many hues and many shades, did themselves
honour. These squares the giant children should arrange and

rearrange to their pleasure. "Decorations must follow," said Redwood ; "let them first get the range of all the tints and then this may go away. There is no reason why one should bias them in favour of any particular colour or design."

Then, "The place must be full of interest," said Redwood. "Interest is food for a child and blankness torture and starvation. He must have pictures galore." There were no pictures hung about the room for any permanent service, however, but blank frames were provided into which new pictures would come and pass thence into a portfolio so soon as their fresh interest had passed. There was one window that looked down the length of a street, and in addition, for an added interest, Redwood had contrived above the roof of the nursery a camera-obscura that watched the Kensington High Street and not a little of the Gardens.

In one corner that most worthy implement, an Abacus, four feet square, a specially strengthened piece of ironmongery with rounded corners, awaited the young giants' incipient computations. There were few woolly lambs and such-like idols, but instead Cossar, without explanation, had brought one day in three four-wheelers a great number of toys (all just too big for the coming children to swallow) that could be piled up, arranged in rows, rolled about, bitten, made to flap and rattle, smacked together, felt over, pulled out, opened, closed and mauled and experimented with to an interminable extent. There were many bricks of wood in diverse colours, oblong and cuboid, bricks of polished china, bricks of transparent glass and bricks of india-rubber ; there were slabs and slates ; there were cones, truncated cones and cylinders ; there were oblate and prolate spheroids, balls of varied substances, solid and hollow, many boxes of diverse size and shape, with hinged lids and screw lids and fitting lids, and one or two to catch and lock ; there were bands of elastic and leather, and a number of rough and sturdy little objects of a size together that could stand up steadily and suggest the shape of a man. "Give 'em these," said Cossar. "One at a time."

These things Redwood arranged in a locker in one corner. Along one side of the room, at a convenient height for a six or eight foot child, there was a blackboard on which the youngsters might flourish in white and coloured chalk ; and near by a sort of drawing-block from which sheet after sheet might be torn, and on which they could draw in charcoal ; and a little desk there was, furnished with great carpenter's pencils of varying hardness and a copious supply of paper, on which the boys might first scribble and then draw more neatly. And moreover Redwood gave orders, so far ahead did his imagination go, for specially large tubes of liquid paint and boxes of pastels against the time when they should be needed. He laid in a cask or so of plasticine and modelling clay. "At first he and his tutor shall model together," he said, "and when he is more skilful he shall copy casts and perhaps animals. And that reminds me, I must also have made for him a box of tools !

"Then books. I shall have to look out a lot of books to put in his way, and they'll have to be big type. Now what sort of books will he need ? There is his imagination to be fed. That, after all, is the crown of every education. The crown—as sound habits of mind and conduct are the throne. No imagination at all is brutality ; a base imagination is lust and cowardice ; but a noble imagination is God walking the earth again. He must dream, too, of a dainty fairy-land and of all the quaint little things of life, in due time. But he must feed chiefly on the splendid real ; he shall have stories of travel through all the world, travels and adventures and how the world was won ; he shall have stories of beasts, great books splendidly and clearly done of animals and birds and plants and creeping things, great books about the deeps of the sky and the mystery of the sea ; he shall have histories and maps of all the empires the world has seen, pictures and stories of all the tribes and habits and customs of men. And he must have books and pictures to quicken his sense of beauty, subtle Japanese pictures to make him love the subtler beauties of bird and tendril and falling flower ; and western pictures too, pictures of gracious men and women, sweet groupings, and broad views of land and sea. He shall have books on the building of houses and palaces ; he shall plan rooms and invent cities——

"I think I must give him a little theatre.

"Then there is music ! "

Redwood thought that over and decided that his son might best begin with a very pure-sounding harmonicon of one octave, to which afterwards there could be an extension. "He shall play with this first, sing to it and give names to the notes," said Redwood, "and afterwards—— ? "

He stared up at the window-sill overhead and measured the size of the room with his eye.

"They'll have to build his piano in here," he said. "Bring it in in pieces."

He hovered about amidst his preparations, a pensive dark little figure. If you could have seen him there he would have looked to you like a ten-inch man amidst common nursery things. A great rug—indeed it was a Turkey carpet—four hundred square feet of it, upon which young Redwood was soon to crawl, stretched to the grill-guarded electric radiator that was to warm the whole place. A man from Cossar's hung amidst scaffolding overhead, fixing the great frame that was to hold the transitory pictures. A blotting-paper book for plant specimens as big as a house door leant against the wall, and from it projected a gigantic stalk, a leaf edge or so and one flower of chickweed, all of that gigantic size that was soon to make Urshot famous throughout the botanical world. . . .

A sort of incredulity came to Redwood as he stood among these things.

" If it really *is* going on——" said Redwood, staring up to the remote ceiling.

From far away came a sound like the bellowing of a Mafficking bull, almost as if in answer.

" It's going on all right," said Redwood.   " Evidently."

There followed resounding blows upon a table, followed by a vast crowing shout, " Gooloo !   Boo-zoo !   Bzz . . ."

" The best thing I can do," said Redwood, following out some divergent line of thought," is to teach him myself."

That beating became more insistent. For a moment it seemed to Redwood that it caught the rhythm of an engine's throbbing, the engine he could have imagined of some great train of events that bore down upon him.   Then a descendant flight of sharper beats broke up that effect, and were repeated.

" Come in," he cried, perceiving that some one rapped, and the door that was big enough for a cathedral opened slowly a little way. The new winch ceased to creak, and Bensington appeared in the crack, gleaming benevolently under his protruded baldness and over his glasses.

" I've ventured round to *see*," he whispered in a confidentially furtive manner.

" Come in," said Redwood, and he did, shutting the door behind him.

He walked forward, hands behind his back, advanced a few steps, and peered up with a birdlike movement at the dimensions about him. He rubbed his chin thoughtfully.

" Every time I come in," he said, with a subdued note in his voice, " it strikes me as—' Big.' "

" Yes," said Redwood, surveying it all again also, as if in an endeavour to keep hold of the visible impression.   " Yes. They're going to be big, too, you know."

" I know," said Bensington, with a note that was nearly awe.   " *Very* big."

They looked at one another, almost, as it were, apprehensively.

" Very big indeed," said Bensington, stroking the bridge of his nose, and with one eye that watched Redwood doubtfully for a confirmatory expression.   " All of them, you know— fearfully Big. I don't seem able to imagine—even with this —just how big they're all going to be."

CHAPTER FIVE

THE MINIMIFICENCE OF MR. BENSINGTON

I

IT was while the Royal Commissioner on Boomfood was preparing its report that Herakleophorbia really began to demonstrate its capacity for leakage. And the earliness of this second outbreak was the more unfortunate, from the point of view of Cossar at any rate, since the draft report still in existence shows that the Commission had, under the tutelage of that most able member, Doctor Stephen Winkles (F.R.S., M.D., F.R.C.P., D.Sc., J.P., D.L., etc.), already quite made up its mind that accidental leakages were impossible, and was prepared to recommend that to entrust the preparation of Boomfood to a qualified committee (Winkles chiefly), with an entire control over its sale, was quite enough to satisfy all reasonable objections to its free diffusion. This committee was to have an absolute monopoly. And it is, no doubt, to be considered as a part of the irony of life that the first and most alarming of this second series of leakages occurred within fifty yards of a little cottage at Keston occupied during the summer months by Doctor Winkles.

There can be little doubt now that Redwood's refusal to acquaint Winkles with the composition of Herakleophorbia IV. had aroused in that gentleman a novel and intense desire towards analytical chemistry. He was not an expert manipulator, and for that reason probably he saw fit to do his work not in the excellently equipped laboratories that were at his disposal in London, but without consulting any one, and almost with an air of secrecy, in a rough little garden laboratory at the Keston establishment. He does not seem to have shown either great energy or great ability in this quest; indeed one gathers he dropped the inquiry after working at it intermittently for about a month.

This garden laboratory, in which the work was done, was very roughly equipped, supplied by a stand-pipe tap with water, and draining into a pipe that ran down into a swampy rush-bordered pool under an alder tree in a secluded corner of the common just outside the garden hedge. The pipe was cracked, and the residuum of the Food of the Gods escaped through the crack into a little puddle amidst clumps of rushes, just in time for the spring awakening.

Everything was astir with life in that scummy little corner. There was frog spawn adrift, tremulous with tadpoles just bursting their gelatinous envelopes; there were little pond snails creeping out into life, and under the green skin of the rush stems the larvæ of a big Water Beetle were struggling out of their egg cases. I doubt if the reader knows the larva of the beetle called (I know not why) Dytiscus. It is a jointed, queer-looking thing, very muscular and sudden in its movements, and given to swimming head downward with its tail out of water ; the length of a man's top thumb joint it is, and more —two inches, that is, for those who have not eaten the Food— and it has two sharp jaws that meet in front of its head, tubular jaws with sharp points, through which its habit is to suck its victim's blood.

The first things to get at the drifting grains of the Food were the tapdoles and the water snails ; the little wriggling tadpoles in particular, once they had the taste of it, took to it with zest. But scarcely did one of them begin to grow into a conspicuous position in that tadpole world and try a smaller brother or so as an aid to a vegetarian dietary, when nip ! one of the Beetle larvæ had its curved bloodsucking prongs gripping into his heart, and with that red stream went Herakleophorbia IV., in a state of solution, into the being of a new client. The only thing that had a chance with these monsters to get any share of the Food were the rushes and slimy green scum in the water and the seedling weeds in the mud at the bottom. A clean-up of the study presently washed a fresh spate of the Food into the puddle, overflowed it, and carried all this sinister expansion of the struggle for life into the adjacent pool under the roots of the alder. . . .

The first person to discover what was going on was a Mr. Lukey Carrington, a special science teacher under the London Education Board, and, in his leisure, a specialist in fresh-water algæ, and he is certainly not to be envied his discovery. He had come down to Keston Common for the day to fill a number of specimen tubes for subsequent examination, and he came, with a dozen or so of corked tubes clanking faintly in his pocket, over the sandy crest and down towards the pool, spiked walking-stick in hand. A garden lad standing on the top of the kitchen steps clipping Doctor Winkles' hedge saw him in this unfrequented corner, and found him and his occupation sufficiently inexplicable and interesting to watch him pretty closely.

He saw Mr. Carrington stoop down by the side of the pool, with his hand against the old alder stem, and peer into the water, but of course he could not appreciate the surprise and pleasure with which Mr. Carrington beheld the big unfamiliar-looking blobs and threads of the algae scum at the bottom. There were no tadpoles visible—they had all been killed by that time—and it would seem Mr. Carrington saw nothing at all unusual except the excessive vegetation. He bared his arm to the elbow, leant forward, and dipped deep in pursuit of a specimen. His seeking hand went down. Instantly there flashed out of the cool shadow under the tree roots something——

Flash ! It had buried its fangs deep into his arm—a bizarre shape it was, a foot long and more, brown and jointed like a scorpion.

Its ugly apparition, and the sharp amazing painfulness of its bite, was too much for Mr. Carrington's equilibrium. He felt himself going and yelled aloud. Over he toppled, face foremost, splash ! into the pool.

The boy saw him vanish, and heard the splashing of his struggle in the water. The unfortunate man emerged again into the boy's field of vision, hatless and streaming with water, and screaming !

Never before had the boy heard screams from a man.

This astonishing stranger appeared to be tearing at something on the side of his face There appeared streaks of blood there. He flung out his arms as if in despair, leapt in the air like a frantic creature, ran violently ten or twelve yards and then fell and rolled on the ground and over and out of sight of the boy.

The lad was down the steps and through the hedge in a trice —happily with the garden shears still in hand. As he came crashing through the gorse bushes, he says he was half minded to turn back, fearing he had to deal with a lunatic, but the possession of the shears reassured him. " I could 'ave jabbed his eyes," he explained, " anyhow." Directly Mr. Carrington caught sight of him, his demeanour became at once that of a sane but desperate man. He struggled to his feet, stumbled, stood up and came to meet the boy.

" Look ! " he cried, " I can't get 'em off ! "

And with a qualm of horror the boy saw that attached to Mr. Carrington's cheek, to his bare arm, and to his thigh, and lashing furiously with their lithe brown muscular bodies, were three of these horrible larvæ, their great jaws buried deep in his flesh and sucking for dear life. They had the grip of bulldogs, and Mr. Carrington's efforts to detach the monster from his face had only served to lacerate the flesh to which it had attached itself, and streak face and neck and coat with living scarlet.

" I'll cut 'im," cried the boy ; " 'old on, Sir."

And with the zest of his age in such proceedings, he severed one by one the heads from the bodies of Mr. Carrington's assailants. " Yup," said the boy with a wincing face as each one fell before him. Even then, so tough and determined was their grip that the severed heads remained for a space, still fiercely biting home and still sucking, with the blood streaming out of their necks behind. But the boy stopped that with a few more slashes of his scissors—in one of which Mr. Carrington was implicated.

" I couldn't get 'em off ! " repeated Carrington, and stood for a space, swaying and bleeding profusely. He dabbed feeble hands at his injuries and examined the result upon his palms.

Then he gave way at the knees and fell headlong in a dead faint at the boy's feet, between the still leaping bodies of his defeated foes. Very luckily it didn't occur to the boy to splash water on his face—for there were still more of these horrors under the alder roots—and instead he passed back by the pond and went into the garden with the intention of calling assistance. And there he met the gardener-coachman and told him of the whole affair.

When they got back to Mr. Carrington he was sitting up, dazed and weak, but able to warn them against the danger in the pool.

II

Such were the circumstances by which the world had its first notification that the Food was loose again. In another week Keston Common was in full operation as what naturalists call a centre of distribution. This time there were no wasps or rats, no earwigs and no nettles, but there were at least three water-spiders, several dragon-fly larvæ which presently became dragon-flies, dazzling all Kent with their hovering sapphire bodies, and a nasty gelatinous, scummy growth that swelled over the pond margin, and sent its slimy green masses surging half-way up the garden path to Doctor Winkles' house. And there began a growth of rushes and equisetum and potamogeton that ended only with the drying of the pond.

It speedily became evident to the public mind that this time there was not simply one centre of distribution, but quite a number of centres. There was one at Ealing, there can be no doubt now, and from that came the plague of flies and red spiders ; there was one at Sunbury, productive of ferocious great eels, that could come ashore and kill sheep ; and there was one in Bloomsbury that gave the world a new strain of cockroaches of a quite terrible sort—an old house it was in Bloomsbury, and much inhabited by undesirable things. Abruptly the world found itself confronted with the Hickley-brow experiences all over again, with all sorts of queer exaggerations of familiar monsters in the place of the giant hens and rats and wasps. Each centre burst out with its own characteristic local fauna and flora. . . .

We know now that every one of these centres corresponded to one of the patients of Doctor Winkles, but that was by no means apparent at the time. Doctor Winkles was the last person to incur any odium in the matter. There was a panic quite naturally, a passionate indignation ; but it was indignation not against Doctor Winkles but against the Food, and not so much against the Food as against the unfortunate Bensington, whom from the very first the popular imagination had insisted upon regarding as the sole and only person responsible for this new thing.

The attempt to lynch him that followed is just one of those explosive events that bulk largely in history and are in reality the least significant of occurrences.

The history of the outbreak is a mystery. The nucleus of the crowd certainly came from an Anti-Boomfood meeting in Hyde Park organised by extremists of the Caterham party, but there seems no one in the world who actually first proposed, no one who ever first hinted a suggestion of the outrage at which so many people assisted. It is a problem for M. Gustave le Bon, a mystery in the psychology of crowds. The fact emerges that about three o'clock on Sunday afternoon a remarkably big and ugly London crowd, entirely out of hand, came rolling down Thursday Street intent on Bensington's exemplary death as a warning to all scientific investigators, and that it came nearer accomplishing its object than any London crowd has ever come since the Hyde Park railings came down in remote middle Victorian times. This crowd came so close to its object indeed, that for the space of an hour or more a word would have settled the unfortunate gentleman's fate.

The first intimation he had of the thing was the noise of the people outside. He went to the window and peered, realising nothing of what impended. For a minute perhaps he watched them seething about the entrance, disposing of an ineffectual dozen of policemen who barred their way, before he fully realised his own importance in the affair. It came upon him in a flash—that that roaring, swaying multitude was after him. He was all alone in the flat—fortunately perhaps—his cousin Jane having gone down to Ealing to have tea with a relation on her mother's side, and he had no more idea of how to behave under such circumstances than he had of the etiquette of the Day of Judgment. He was still dashing about the flat asking his furniture what he should do, turning keys in locks and then unlocking them again, making darts at door and window and bedroom—when the floor clerk came to him.

"There isn't a moment, Sir," he said. "They've got your number from the board in the hall! They're coming straight up!"

He ran Mr. Bensington out into the passage, already echoing with the approaching tumult from the great staircase, locked the door behind them, and led the way into the opposite flat by means of his duplicate key.

"It's our only chance now," he said.

He flung up a window which opened on a ventilating shaft, and showed that the wall was set with iron staples that made the rudest and most perilous of wall ladders to serve as a fire escape from the upper flats. He shoved Mr. Bensington out of the window, showed him how to cling on, and pursued him up the ladder, goading and jabbing his legs with a bunch of keys whenever he desisted from climbing. It seemed to Bensington at times that he must climb that vertical ladder for evermore.

Above, the parapet was inaccessibly remote, a mile perhaps; below—— He did not care to think of things below.

"Steady on!" cried the clerk, and gripped his ankle. It was quite horrible having his ankle gripped like that, and Mr. Bensington tightened his hold on the iron staple above to a drowning clutch and gave a faint squeal of terror.

It became evident the clerk had broken a window, and then it seemed he had leapt a vast distance sideways, and there came the noise of a window-frame sliding in its sash. He was bawling things.

Mr. Bensington moved his head round cautiously until he could see the clerk. "Come down six steps," the clerk commanded.

All this moving about seemed very foolish, but very, very cautiously Mr. Bensington lowered a foot.

"Don't pull me!" he cried, as the clerk made to help him from the open window.

It seemed to him that to reach the window from the ladder would be a very respectable feat for a flying fox, and it was rather with the idea of a decent suicide than in any hope of accomplishing it that he made the step at last, and quite ruthlessly the clerk pulled him in. "You'll have to stop here," said the clerk; "my keys are no good here. It's an American lock. I'll get out and slam the door behind me and see if I can find the man of this floor. You'll be locked in. Don't go to the window, that's all. It's the ugliest crowd I've ever seen. If only they think you're out they'll probably content themselves by breaking up your stuff——"

"The indicator said In," said Bensington.

"The devil it did! Well, anyhow, I'd better not be found——"

He vanished with a slam of the door.

Bensington was left to his own initiative again.

It took him under the bed.

There presently he was found by Cossar.

Bensington was almost comatose with terror when he was found, for Cossar had burst the door in with his shoulder by jumping at it across the breadth of the passage.

"Come out of it, Bensington," he said. "It's all right. It's me. We've got to get out of this. They're setting the place on fire. The porters are all clearing out. The servants are gone. It's lucky I caught the man who knew.

"Look here!"

Bensington, peering from under the bed, became aware of some unaccountable garments on Cossar's arm, and, of all things, a black bonnet in his hand!

"They're having a clear-out," said Cossar. "If they don't set the place on fire they'll come here. Troops may not be here for an hour yet. Fifty per cent. hooligans in the crowd, and the more furnished flats they go into the better they'll like it. Obviously. . . . They mean a clear-out. You put this skirt and bonnet on, Bensington, and clear out with me."

" D'you *mean*—— ? " began Bensington, protruding a head, tortoise fashion.

" I mean, put 'em on and come ! Obviously." And with a sudden vehemence he dragged Bensington from under the bed, and began to dress him for his new impersonation of an elderly woman of the people.

He rolled up his trousers and made him kick off his slippers, took off his collar and tie and coat and vest, slipped a black skirt over his head, and put on a red flannel bodice and a body over the same. He made him take off his all too characteristic spectacles, and clapped the bonnet on his head. " You might have been born an old woman," he said as he tied the strings. Then came the spring-side boots—a terrible wrench for corns —and the shawl, and the disguise was complete. " Up and down," said Cossar, and Bensington obeyed.

" You'll do," said Cossar.

And in this guise it was, stumbling awkwardly over his unaccustomed skirts, shouting womanly imprecations upon his own head in a weird falsetto to sustain his part, and to the roaring note of a crowd bent upon lynching him, that the original discoverer of Herakleophorbia IV. proceeded down the corridor of Chesterfield Mansions, mingled with that inflamed disorderly multitude, and passed out altogether from the thread of events that constitutes our story.

Never once after that escape did he meddle again with the stupendous development of the Food of the Gods, he of all men had done most to begin.

III

This little man who started the whole thing passes out of the story, and after a time he passed altogether out of the world of significant activities. But because he started the whole thing it is seemly to give his exit an intercalary page of attention. One may picture him in his later days at Tunbridge Wells came to know him. For it was at Tunbridge Wells he reappeared after a temporary obscurity, so soon as he fully realised how transitory, how quite exceptional and unmeaning that fury of rioting was. He reappeared under the wing of cousin Jane, treating himself for nervous shock to the exclusion of all other interests, and totally indifferent, as it seemed, to the battles that were raging then about those new centres of distribution, and about the baby Children of the Food.

He took up his quarters at the Mount Glory Hydro-therapeutic Hotel, where there are quite extraordinary facilities for baths ; Carbonated Baths, Creosote Baths, Galvanic and Faradic Treatment, Massage, Pine Baths, Starch and Hemlock Baths, Radium Baths, Light Baths, Heat Baths, Bran and Needle Baths, Tar and Birdsdown Baths, all sorts of baths ;

and he devoted his mind to the development of that system of curative treatment that was still imperfect when he died.   And sometimes he would go out in a hired vehicle and a sealskin-trimmed coat, and sometimes, when his feet permitted, he would walk to the Pantiles, and there he would sip chalybeate water under the eye of his cousin Jane.

His stooping shoulders, his pink appearance, his beaming glasses, became a " feature " of Tunbridge Wells.   No one was the least bit unkind to him, and indeed the place and the Hotel seemed very glad to have the distinction of his presence. Nothing could rob him of that distinction now.   And though he preferred not to follow the development of his great invention in the daily papers, yet when he crossed the Lounge of the Hotel or walked down the Pantiles and heard the whisper, " There he is !   That's him ! " it was not dissatisfaction that softened his mouth and gleamed for a moment in his eye.

This little figure, this minute little figure, launched the Food of the Gods upon the world !   One does not know which is the most amazing, the greatness or the littleness of these scientific and philosophical men.   There you have him on the Pantiles, in the overcoat trimmed with fur.   He stands under that chinaware window where the spring spouts, and holds and sips the glass of chalybeate water in his hand.   One bright eye over the gilt rim is fixed, with an expression of inscrutable severity, on cousin Jane.   " M," he says, and sips.

So we make our souvenir, so we focus and photograph this discoverer of ours for the last time, and leave him, a mere dot in our foreground, and pass to the greater picture that has developed about him, to the story of his Food, how the scattered Giant Children grew up day by day into a world that was all too small for them, and how the net of Boomfood Laws and Boomfood Conventions, which the Boomfood Commission was weaving even then, drew closer and closer upon them with every year of their growth.   Until——

Book Two

The Food in the Village

CHAPTER ONE

THE COMING OF THE FOOD

I

OUR theme, which began so compactly in Mr. Bensington's study, has already spread and branched until it points this way and that, and henceforth our whole story is one of dissemination. To follow the Food of the Gods further is to trace the ramifications of a perpetually branching tree ; in a little while, in the quarter of a lifetime, the Food had trickled and increased from its first spring in the little farm near Hickleybrow until it had spread, it and the report, and shadow of its power, throughout the world. It spread beyond England very speedily. Soon in America, all over the continent of Europe, in Japan, in Australia, at last all over the world, the thing was working towards its appointed end. Always it worked slowly, by indirect courses and against resistance. It was bigness insurgent. In spite of prejudice, in spite of law and regulation, in spite of all that obstinate conservatism that lies at the base of the formal order of mankind, the Food of the Gods, once it had been set going, pursued its subtle and invincible progress.

The Children of the Food grew steadily through all these years ; that was the cardinal fact of the time. But it is the leakages make history. The children who had eaten grew, and soon there were other children growing ; and all the best intentions in the world could not stop further leakages and still further leakages. The Food insisted on escaping with the pertinacity of a thing alive. Flour treated with the stuff crumbled in dry weather almost as if by intention into an impalpable powder, and would lift and travel before the lightest breeze. Now it would be some fresh insect won its way to a temporary fatal new development, now some fresh outbreak from the sewers of rats and such-like vermin. For some days the village of Pangbourne in Berkshire fought with giant ants. Three men were bitten and died. There would be a panic, there would be a struggle, and the salient evil would be fought down again, leaving always something behind, in the obscurer things of life—changed for ever. Then again another acute and startling outbreak, a swift upgrowth of monstrous weedy thickets, a drifting dissemination about the world of inhumanly growing thistles, of cockroaches men fought with shot-guns, or a plague of mighty flies.

There were some strange and desperate struggles in obscure places. The Food begot heroes in the cause of littleness. . . .

And men took such happenings into their lives, and met them by the expedients of the moment, and told one another there was " no change in the essential order of things." After

the first great panic, Caterham, in spite of his power of eloquence, became a secondary figure in the political world,
remained in men's minds as the exponent of an extreme view.

Only slowly did he win a way towards a central position in
affairs. "There was no change in the essential order of
things"—that eminent leader of modern thought, Doctor
Winkles, was very clear upon this—and the exponents of what
was called in those days Progressive Liberalism grew quite
sentimental upon the essential insincerity of their progress.
Their dreams, it would appear, ran wholly on little nations,
little languages, little households, each self-supported on its
little farm. A fashion for the small and neat set in. To be big
was to be "vulgar," and dainty, neat, mignon, miniature,
"minutely perfect," became the key words of critical
approval. . . .

Meanwhile, quietly, taking their time as children must, the
Children of the Food, growing into a world that changed to
receive them, gathered strength and stature and knowledge,
became individual and purposeful, rose slowly towards the
dimensions of their destiny. Presently they seemed a natural
part of the world ; all these stirrings of bigness seemed a
natural part of the world, and men wondered how things had
been before their time. There came to men's ears stories of
things the giant boys could do, and they said "Wonderful !"
—without a spark of wonder. The popular papers would tell
of the three sons of Cossar, and how these amazing children
would lift great cannons, hurl masses of iron for hundreds of
yards, and leap two hundred feet. They were said to be
digging a well, deeper than any well or mine that man had
ever made, seeking, it was said, for treasures hidden in the
earth since ever the earth began.

These Children, said the popular magazines, will level
mountains, bridge seas, tunnel your earth to a honeycomb.
"Wonderful !" said the little folks, "isn't it ? What a lot of
conveniences we shall have !" and went about their business
as though there was no such thing as the Food of the Gods on
earth. And indeed these things were no more than the first
hints and promises of the powers of the Children of the Food.
It was still no more than child's play with them, no more than
the first use of a strength in which no purpose had arisen.
They did not know themselves for what they were. They
were children, slow-growing children of a new race. The giant
strength grew day by day—the giant will had still to grow
into purpose and an aim.

Looking at it in a shortened perspective of time, those years
of transition have the quality of a single consecutive occurrence ; but indeed no one saw the coming of Bigness in the
world, as no one in all the world till centuries had passed saw,
as one happening, the Decline and Fall of Rome. They who
lived in those days were too much among these developments

to see them together as a single thing.   It seemed even to wise men that the Food was giving the world nothing but a crop of unmanageable, disconnected irrelevancies, that might shake and trouble indeed, but could do no more to the established order and fabric of mankind.

To one observer at least the most wonderful thing throughout that period of accumulating stress is the invincible inertia of the great mass of people, their quiet persistence in all that ignored the enormous presences, the promises of still more enormous things, that grew among them.   Just as many a stream will be at its smoothest, will look most tranquil, running deep and strong, at the very verge of a cataract, so all that is most conservative in man seemed settling quietly into a serene ascendency during these latter days.   Reaction became popular, there was talk of the bankruptcy of science, of the dying of Progress, of the advent of the Mandarins, talk of such things amidst the echoing footsteps of the Children of the Food.   The fussy pointless Revolutions of the old time, a vast crowd of silly little people chasing some silly little monarch and the like, had indeed died out and passed away ;   but Change had not died out.   It was only Change that had changed.   The New was coming in its own fashion and beyond the common understanding of the world.

To tell fully of its coming would be to write a great history, but everywhere there was a parallel chain of happenings.   To tell therefore of the manner of its coming in one place is to tell something of the whole.   It chanced one stray seed of Immensity fell into the pretty petty village of Cheasing Eyebright in Kent, and the story of its queer germination there and of the tragic futility that ensued, one may attempt—following one thread, as it were, to show the direction in which the whole great interwoven fabric rolled off the loom of Time.

II

Cheasing Eyebright had of course a Vicar.   There are vicars and vicars, and of all sorts I love an innovating vicar, a piebald progressive professional reactionary, the least.   But the Vicar of Cheasing Eyebright was one of the least innovating of vicars, a most worthy, plump, ripe, and conservative-minded little man.   It is becoming to go back a little in our story to tell of him.   He matched his village, and one may figure them best together as they used to be, on the sunset evening when Mrs. Skinner—you will remember her flight !—brought the Food with her all unsuspected into these rustic serenities.

The village was looking its very best just then, under that western light.   It lay down along the valley beneath the beechwoods of the Hanger, a beading of thatched and red-tiled cottages, cottages with trellised porches and pyracanthus-lined faces, that clustered closer and closer as the road dropped from the yew trees by the church towards the bridge.   The vicarage peeped not too ostentatiously between the trees beyond the inn, an early Georgian front ripened by time, and the spire of the church rose happily in the depression made by the valley in the outline of the hills. A winding stream, a thin intermittency of sky-blue and foam, glittered amidst a thick margin of reeds and loose-strife and overhanging willows, along the centre of a sinuous pennant of meadow. The whole prospect had that curiously English quality of ripened cultivation, that look of still completeness that apes perfection, under the sunset warmth.

And the Vicar, too, looked mellow. He looked habitually and essentially mellow, as though he had been a mellow baby born into a mellow class, a ripe and juicy little boy. One could see, even before he mentioned it, that he had gone to an ivy-clad public school in its anecdotage, with magnificent traditions, aristocratic associations and no chemical laboratories, and proceeded thence to a venerable college in the very ripest Gothic. Few books he had younger than a thousand years ; of these, Yarrow and Ellis and good pre-Methodist sermons made the bulk. He was a man of moderate height, a little shortened in appearance by his equatorial dimensions, and a face that had been mellow from the first was now climacterically ripe. The beard of a David hid his redundancy of chin ; he wore no watch chain out of refinement, and his modest clerical garments were made by a West End tailor. . . . And he sat with a hand on either shin, blinking at his village in beatific approval. He waved a plump palm towards it. His burthen sang out again. What more could any one desire ?

" We are fortunately situated," he said, putting the thing tamely.

" We are in a fastness of the hills," he expanded.

He explained himself at length. " We are out of it all."

For they had been talking, he and his friend, of the Horrors of the Age, of Democracy, and Secular Education, and Sky Scrapers, and Motor Cars, and the American Invasion, the Scrappy Reading of the Public, and the disappearance of any Taste at all.

" We are out of it all," he repeated, and even as he spoke, the footsteps of some one coming smote upon his ear and he rolled over and regarded her.

You figure the old woman's steadfastly tremulous advance, the bundle clutched in her gnarled lank hand, her nose (which was her countenance) wrinkled with breathless resolution. You see the poppies nodding fatefully on her bonnet, and the dust-white spring-sided boots beneath her skimpy skirts, pointing with an irrevocable slow alternation east and west. Beneath her arm, a restive captive, waggled and slipped a scarcely valuable umbrella. What was there to tell the Vicar that this grotesque old figure was—so far as his village was concerned at any rate—no less than Fruitful Chance and the Unforeseen,

the Hag weak men call Fate. But for us, you understand,
no more than Mrs. Skinner.

As she was too much encumbered for a curtsey, she pretended
not to see him and his friend at all, and so passed flip, flop,
within three yards of them, onward down towards the village.
The Vicar watched her slow transit in silence, and ripened a
remark the while. . . .

The incident seemed to him of no importance whatever.
Old womenkind, *aere perennius*, has carried bundles since the
world began. What difference has it made ?

"We are out of it all," said the Vicar. "We live in an
atmosphere of simple and permanent things, Birth and Toil,
simple seed-time and simple harvest. The Uproar passes us
by." He was always very great upon what he called the permanent things. "Things change," he would say, "but
Humanity—*aere perennius.*"

Thus the Vicar. He loved a classical quotation subtly
misapplied. Below, Mrs. Skinner, inelegant but resolute, had
involved herself curiously with Wilmerding's stile.

III

No one knows what the Vicar made of the Giant Puff-Balls.
No doubt he was among the first to discover them. They
were scattered at intervals up and down the path between the
near down and the village end, a path he frequented daily in
his constitutional round. Altogether, of these abnormal fungi
there were, from first to last, quite thirty. The Vicar seems
to have stared at each severally and to have prodded most of
them with his stick once or twice. Once he attempted to
measure with his arms, but it burst at his Ixion embrace.

He spoke to several people about them and said they were
" marvellous ! " and he related to at least seven different persons the well-known story of the flagstone that was lifted from
the cellar floor by a growth of fungi beneath. He looked up
his Sowerby to see if it was *Lycoperdon coelatum* or *giganteum*—
like all his kind since Gilbert White became famous, he Gilbert-
Whited. He cherished a theory that *giganteum* is unfairly
named.

One does not know if he observed that those white spheres
lay in the very track that old woman of yesterday had followed,
or if he noted that the last of the series swelled not a score of
yards from the gate of the Caddles' cottage. If he observed
these things, he made no attempt to place his observation on
record. His observation in matters botanical was what the
inferior sort of scientific people call a " trained observation "
—you look for certain definite things and neglect everything
else. And he did nothing to link this phenomenon with the
remarkable expansion of the Caddles' baby that had been
going on now for some weeks, indeed ever since Caddles walked
over one Sunday afternoon a month or more ago to see his

mother-in-law and hear Mr. Skinner (since defunct) brag about
his management of hens.

IV

The growth of the puff-balls following on the expansion of
the Caddles' baby really ought to have opened the Vicar's
eyes.   The latter fact had already come right into his arms at
the christening—almost overpoweringly. . . .

The youngster bawled with deafening violence when the cold
water that sealed its divine inheritance and its right to the
name of " Albert Edward Caddles " fell upon its brow.   It was
already beyond maternal porterage, and Caddles, staggering
indeed, but grinning triumphantly at quantitatively inferior
parents, bore it back to the free-sitting occupied by his party.

" I never saw such a child ! " said the Vicar.

This was the first public intimation that the Caddles' baby,
which had begun its earthly career a little under seven pounds,
did after all intend to be a credit to its parents.   Very soon it
was clear it meant to be not only a credit but a glory.   And
within a month their glory shone so brightly as to be in connection with people in the Caddles' position, improper.

The butcher weighed the infant eleven times.   He was a
man of few words, and he soon got through with them.   The
first time he said, " 'E's a good 'un " ; the next time he
said, " My word ! " the third time he said, " *Well*, mum," and
after that he simply blew enormously each time, scratched his
head, and looked at his scales with an unprecedented mistrust.
Every one came to see the Big Baby—so it was called by
universal consent—and most of them said, " 'E's a Bouncer,"
and almost all remarked to him, " *Did* they ? "   Miss Fletcher
came and said she " never *did*," which was perfectly true.

Lady Wondershoot, the village tyrant, arrived the day after
the third weighing, and inspected the phenomenon narrowly
through glasses that filled it with howling terror.   " It's an
unusually Big child," she told its mother, in a loud instructive
voice.   " You ought to take unusual care of it, Caddles.   Of
course it won't go on like this, being bottle fed, but we must
do what we can for it.   I'll send you down some more flannel."

The doctor came and measured the child with a tape, and
put the figures in a notebook, and old Mr. Drifthassock, who
farmed by Up Marden, brought a manure traveller two miles
out of their way to look at it.   The traveller asked the child's
age three times over, and said finally that he was blowed.   He
left it to be inferred how and why he was blowed ; apparently
it was the child's size blowed him.   He also said it ought to be
put into a baby show.   And all day long, out of school hours,
little children kept coming and saying, " Please, Mrs. Caddles,
mum, may we have a look at your baby, please, mum," until
Mrs. Caddles had to put a stop to it.   And amidst all these
scenes of amazement came Mrs. Skinner, and stood and smiled,

standing somewhat in the background, with each sharp elbow in a lank gnarled hand, and smiling, smiling under and about her nose, with a smile of infinite profundity.

" It makes even that old wretch of a grandmother look quite pleasant," said Lady Wondershoot. " Though I'm sorry she's come back to the village."

Of course, as with almost all cottagers' babies, the eleemosynary element had already come in, but the child soon made it clear by colossal bawling, that so far as the filling of its bottle went, it hadn't come in yet nearly enough.

The baby was entitled to a nine days' wonder, and every one wondered happily over its amazing growth for twice that time and more. And then you know, instead of its dropping into the background and giving place to other marvels, it went on growing more than ever !

Lady Wondershoot heard Mrs. Greenfield, her housekeeper, with infinite amazement.

" Caddles downstairs again. No food for the child ! My dear Greenfield, it's impossible. The creature eats like a hippopotamus ! I'm sure it can't be true."

" I'm sure I hope you're not being imposed upon, my lady," said Mrs. Greenfield.

" It's so difficult to tell with these people," said Lady Wondershoot. " Now I do wish, my good Greenfield, that you'd just go down there yourself this afternoon and *see*—see it have its bottle. Big as it is, I cannot imagine that it needs more than six pints a day."

" It hasn't no business to, my lady," said Mrs. Greenfield.

The hand of Lady Wondershoot quivered, with that C.O.S. sort of emotion, that suspicious rage that stirs in all true aristocrats, at the thought that possibly the meaner classes are after all—as mean as their betters, and—where the sting lies— scoring points in the game.

But Mrs. Greenfield could observe no evidence of peculation, and the order for an increasing daily supply to the Caddles' nursery was issued. Scarcely had the first instalment gone, when Caddles was back again at the great house in a state abjectly apologetic.

" We took the greates' care of 'em, Mrs. Greenfield, I do assure you, mum, but he's regular burst em ! They flew with such vilence, mum, that one button broke a pane of the window, mum, and one hit me a regular stinger jest 'ere, mum."

Lady Wondershoot, when she heard that this amazing child had positively burst out of its beautiful charity clothes, decided that she must speak to Caddles herself. He appeared in her presence with his hair hastily wetted and smoothed by hand, breathless and clinging to his hat brim as though it was a lifebelt, and he stumbled at the carpet edge out of sheer distress of mind.

Lady Wondershoot liked bullying Caddles. Caddles was her

deal lower-class person, dishonest, faithful, abject, industrious, and inconceivably incapable of responsibility. She told him it was a serious matter, the way his child was going on.

"It's 'is appetite, my ladyship," said Caddles, with a rising note.

"Check 'im, my ladyship, you can't," said Caddles. "There 'e lies, my ladyship, and kicks out 'e does, and 'owls, that distressin'. We 'aven't the 'eart, my ladyship. If we 'ad—the neighbours would interfere. . . ."

Lady Wondershoot consulted the parish doctor.

"What I want to know," said Lady Wondershoot, "is it *right* this child should have such an extraordinary quantity of milk ? "

"The proper allowance for a child of that age," said the parish doctor, "is a pint and a half to two pints in the twenty-four hours. I don't see that you are called upon to provide more. If you do, it is your own generosity. Of course we might try the legitimate quantity for a few days. But the child, I must admit, seems for some reason to be physiologically different. Possibly what is called a Sport. A case of General Hypertrophy."

"It isn't fair to the other parish children," said Lady Wondershoot. "I am certain we shall have complaints if this goes on."

"I don't see that any one can be expected to give more than the recognised allowance. We might insist on its doing with that or if it wouldn't, send it as a case into the Infirmary."

"I suppose," said Lady Wondershoot, reflecting, "that apart from the size and the appetite, you don't find anything else abnormal—nothing monstrous ? "

"No. No, I don't. But no doubt if this growth goes on, we shall find grave moral and intellectual deficiencies. One might almost prophesy that from Max Nordau's law. A most gifted and celebrated philosopher, Lady Wondershoot. He discovered that the abnormal is—abnormal, a most valuable discovery, and well worth bearing in mind. I find it of the utmost help in practice. When I come upon anything abnormal, I say at once, This is abnormal." His eyes became profound, his voice dropped, his manner verged upon the intimately confidential. He raised one hand stiffly. "And I treat it in that spirit," he said.

V

"Tut, tut ! " said the Vicar to his breakfast-things—the day after the coming of Mrs. Skinner. "Tut, tut ! what's this ? " and poised his glasses at his paper with a general air of remonstrance.

"Giant wasps ! What's the world coming to ? . . . American journalists, I suppose ! Hang these Novelties ! Giant gooseberries are good enough for me.

" Nonsense ! " said the Vicar, and drank off his coffee at a
gulp, eyes steadfast on the paper, and smacked his lips incredulously.

" Bosh ! " said the Vicar, rejecting the hint altogether.

But the next day there was more of it, and the light came.
Not all at once, however. When he went for his constitutional that day he was still chuckling at the absurd story his
paper would have had him believe. Wasps indeed—killing a
dog ! Incidentally as he passed by the site of that first crop
of puff-balls he remarked that the grass was growing very rank
there, but he did not connect that in any way with the matter
of his amusement. "We should certainly have heard something
of it," he said ; "Whitstable can't be twenty miles from here."

Beyond he found another puff-ball, one of the second crop,
rising like a roc's egg out of the abnormally coarsened turf.

The thing came upon him in a flash.

He did not take his usual round that morning. Instead he
turned aside by the second stile and came round to the Caddles'
cottage. " Where's that baby ? " he demanded, and at the
sight of it, " Goodness me ! "

He went up the village blessing his heart and met the doctor
full tilt coming down. He grasped his arm. " What does
this *mean* ? " he said. " Have you seen the paper these last
few days ? "

The doctor said he had.

" Well, what's the matter with that child ? What's the
matter with everything, wasps, puff-balls, babies, eh ? What's
making them grow so big ? This is most unexpected. In
Kent, too ! If it was America now——"

" It's a little difficult to say just what it is," said the doctor.
" So far as I can grasp the symptoms——"

" Yes ? "

" It's Hypertrophy—General Hypertrophy."

" Hypertrophy ? "

" Yes. General—affecting all the bodily structures—all the
organism. I may say that in my own mind, between ourselves,
I'm very nearly convinced it's that. . . . But one has to be
careful."

" Ah," said the Vicar, a good deal relieved to find the doctor
equal to the situation. " But how is it it's breaking out in
this fashion, all over the place ? "

" That again," said the doctor, " is difficult to say."

" Urshot. Here. It's a pretty clear case of spreading."

" Yes," said the doctor. " Yes. I think so. It has a
strong resemblance at any rate to some sort of epidemic.
Probably Epidemic Hypertrophy will meet the case."

" Epidemic ! " said the Vicar. " You don't mean it's
contagious ? "

The doctor smiled gently and rubbed one hand against the
other. " That I couldn't say," he said.

" But—— ! " cried the Vicar, round-eyed.   " If it's *catching*
—it—it affects *us* ! "

He made a stride up the road and turned about.

" I've just been there," he cried.   " Hadn't I better—— ?
I'll go home at once and have a bath and fumigate my clothes."

The doctor regarded his retreating back for a moment and
then turned about and went towards his own house. . . .

But on the way he reflected that one case had been in the
village a month without any one catching the disease, and
after a pause of hesitation decided to be as brave as a doctor
should be and take the risks like a man.

And indeed he was well advised by his second thoughts.
Growth was the last thing that could ever happen to him again.
He could have eaten—and the Vicar could have eaten—Herak-
leophorbia by the truckful.   For growth had done with them.
Growth had done with these two gentlemen for evermore.

VI

It was a day or so after this conversation, a day or so that
is after the burning of the Experimental Farm, that Winkles
came to Redwood and showed him an insulting letter.   It was
an anonymous letter, and an author should respect his character's secrets.   " You are only taking credit for a natural
phenomenon," said the letter, " and trying to advertise yourself by your letter to *The Times*.   You and your Boomfood !
Let me tell you, this absurdly named food of yours has only
the most accidental connection with those big wasps and rats.
The plain fact is there is an epidemic of Hypertrophy—Contagious Hypertrophy—which you have about as much claim
to control as you have to control the solar system.   The thing
is as old as the hills.   There was Hypertrophy in the family of
Anak.   Quite outside your range, at Cheasing Eyebright, at
the present time there is a baby——"

" Shaky up-and-down writing.   Old gentleman apparently," said Redwood.   " But it's odd a baby——"

He read a few lines further and had an inspiration.

" By Jove ! " said he.   " That's my missing Mrs. Skinner ! "

He descended upon her suddenly in the afternoon of the
following day.

She was engaged in pulling onions in the little garden before
her daughter's cottage when she saw him coming through the
garden gate.   She stood for a moment " consternated," as the
country folks say, and then folded her arms, and with the little
bunch of onions held defensively under her left elbow, awaited
his approach.   Her mouth opened and shut several times ; she
mumbled her remaining tooth, and once quite suddenly she
curtsied, like the blink of an arc-light.

" I thought I should find you," said Redwood.

" I thought you might, Sir," she said, without joy.

" Where's Skinner ? "

" 'E ain't never written to me, Sir, not once, nor come nigh of me since I came here, Sir."

" Don't you know what's become of him ? "

" Him not having written, no, Sir," and she edged a step towards the left with an imperfect idea of cutting off Redwood from the barn door.

" No one knows what has become of him," said Redwood.

" I dessay 'e knows," said Mrs. Skinner.

" He doesn't tell."

" He was always a great one for looking after 'imself and leaving them that was near and dear to 'im in trouble, was Skinner. Though clever as could be," said Mrs. Skinner. . . .

" Where's this child ? " asked Redwood abruptly.

She begged his pardon.

" This child I hear about, the child you've been giving our stuff to—the child that weighs two stone."

Mrs. Skinner's hands worked and she dropped the onions " Reely, Sir," she protested, " I don't hardly know, Sir, what you mean. My daughter, Sir, Mrs. Caddles, *as* a baby, Sir." And she made an agitated curtsey and tried to look innocently inquiring by tilting her nose to one side.

" You'd better let me see that baby, Mrs. Skinner," said Redwood.

Mrs. Skinner unmasked an eye at him as she led the way towards the barn. " Of course, Sir, there may 'ave been a *little*, in a little can of Nicey I give his father to bring over from the farm, or a little perhaps what I happened to bring about with me, so to speak. Me packing in a hurry and all. . . ."

" Um ! " said Redwood, after he had cluckered to the infant for a space. " Oom ! "

He told Mrs. Caddles the baby was a very fine child indeed, a thing that was getting well home to her intelligence—and he ignored her altogether after that. Presently she left the barn —through sheer insignificance.

" Now you've started him, you'll have to keep on with him, you know," he said to Mrs. Skinner.

He turned on her abruptly. " Don't splash it about *this* time," he said.

" Splash it about, Sir ? "

" Oh ! *you* know."

She indicated knowledge by convulsive gestures.

" You haven't told these people here ? The parents, the squire and so on at the big house, the doctor, no one ? "

Mrs. Skinner shook her head.

" I wouldn't," said Redwood. . . .

He went to the door of the barn and surveyed the world about him. The door of the barn looked between the end of the cottage and some disused piggeries through a five-barred gate upon the high road. Beyond was a high red brick wall rich with ivy and wallflower and pennywort and set along the top with broken glass. Beyond the corner of the wall, a sunlit notice-board amidst green and yellow branches reared itself above the rich tones of the first fallen leaves and announced that " Trespassers in these Woods will be Prosecuted." The dark shadow of a gap in the hedge threw a stretch of barbed wire into relief.

" Um," said Redwood, then in a deeper note, " Oom ! "

There came a clatter of horses and the sound of wheels and Lady Wondershoot's greys came into view. He marked the faces of coachman and footman as the equipage approached. The coachman was a very fine specimen, full and fruity, and he drove with a sort of sacramental dignity. Others might doubt their calling and position in the world, he at any rate was sure— he drove her ladyship. The footman sat beside him with folded arms and a face of inflexible certainties. Then the great lady herself became visible, in a hat and mantle disdainfully inelegant, peering through her glasses. Two young ladies protruded necks and peered also.

The Vicar passing on the other side swept off the hat from his David's brow unheeded. . . .

Redwood remained standing in the doorway for a long time after the carriage had passed, his hands folded behind him. His eyes went to the green-grey upland of down, and into the cloud-curdled sky, and came back to the glass-set wall. He turned upon the cool shadows within and amidst spots and blurs of colour regarded the giant child amidst that Rembrandtesque gloom, naked except for a swathing of flannel, seated upon a huge truss of straw and playing with its toes.

" I begin to see what we have done," he said.

He mused, and young Caddles and his own child and Cossar's brood mingled in his musing.

He laughed abruptly. " Good Lord ! " he said at some passing thought.

He roused himself presently and addressed Mrs. Skinner. " Anyhow he mustn't be tortured by a break in his food. That at least we can prevent. I shall send you a can every six months. That ought to do for him all right."

Mrs. Skinner mumbled something about " if you think so, Sir," and " probably got packed by mistake. . . . Thought no harm in giving him a little," and so by the aid of various aspen gestures indicated that she understood.

So the child went on growing.

And growing.

" Practically," said Lady Wondershoot, " he's eaten up every calf in the place. If I have any more of this sort of thing from that man Caddles——"

VII

But even so secluded a place as Cheasing Eyebright could not rest for long in the theory of Hypertrophy—Contagious or not

—in view of the growing hubbub about the Food. In a little while there were painful explanations for Mrs. Skinner—explanations that reduced her to speechless mumblings of her remaining tooth—explanations that probed her and ransacked her and exposed her—until at last she was driven to take refuge from a universal convergence of blame in the dignity of inconsolable widowhood. She turned her eye—which she constrained to be watery—upon the angry Lady of the Manor, and wiped suds from her hands.

" You forget, my lady, what I'm bearing up under."

And she followed up this warning note with a slightly defiant :

" It's 'IM I think of, my lady, night *and* day."

She compressed her lips and her voice flattened and faltered :

" Bein 'et, my lady."

And having established herself on these grounds, she repeated the affirmation her ladyship had refused before. " I 'ad no more idea what I was giving the child, my lady, than any one *could* 'ave. . . ."

Her ladyship turned her mind in more hopeful directions, wigging Caddles of course tremendously by the way. Emissaries, full of diplomatic threatenings, entered the whirling lives of Bensington and Redwood. They presented themselves as Parish Councillors, stolid and clinging phonographically to prearranged statements. " We hold you responsible, Mr. Bensington, for the injury inflicted upon our parish, Sir. We hold you responsible."

A firm of solicitors, with a snake of a style, Banghurst, Brown, Flapp, Codlin, Brown, Tedder, and Snoxton, they called themselves, and appeared invariably in the form of a small rufous cunning-looking gentleman with a pointed nose, said vague things about damages, and there was a polished personage, her ladyship's agent, who came in suddenly upon Redwood one day and asked, " Well, Sir, and what do you propose to do ? "

To which Redwood answered that he proposed to discontinue supplying the food for the child, if he or Bensington were bothered any further about the matter. " I give it for nothing as it is," he said, " and the child will yell your village to ruins before it dies if you don't let it have the stuff. The child's on your hands and you have to keep it. Lady Wondershoot can't always be Lady Bountiful and Earthly Providence of her parish without sometimes meeting a responsibility, you know."

" The mischief's done," Lady Wondershoot decided when they told her—with expurgations—what Redwood had said.

" The mischief's done," echoed the Vicar.

Though indeed as a matter of fact the mischief was only beginning.

CHAPTER TWO

THE BRAT GIGANTIC

I

THE giant child was ugly—the Vicar would insist. "He always had been ugly—as all excessive things must be." The Vicar's views had carried him out of sight of just judgment in this matter. The child was much subjected to snapshots even in that rustic retirement, and their net testimony is against the Vicar, testifying that the young monster was at first almost pretty, with a copious curl of hair reaching to his brow and a great readiness to smile. Usually Caddles, who was slightly built, stands smiling behind the baby, perspective emphasising his relative smallness.

After the second year the good looks of the child became more subtle and more contestable. He began to grow, as his unfortunate grandfather would no doubt have put it, "rank." He lost colour and developed an increasing effect of being somehow, albeit colossal, yet slight. He was vastly delicate. His eyes and something about his face grew finer, grew, as people say, "interesting." His hair, after one cutting, began to tangle into a mat. "It's the degenerate strain coming out in him," said the parish doctor, marking these things, but just how far he was right in that, and just how far the youngster's lapse from ideal healthfulness was the result of living entirely in a white-washed barn upon Lady Wondershoot's sense of charity tempered by justice, is open to question.

The photographs of him that present him from three to six show him developing into a round-eyed, flaxen-haired youngster with a truncated nose and a friendly stare. There lurks about his lips that never very remote promise of a smile that all the photographs of the early giant children display. In summer he wears loose garments of ticking tacked together with string ; there is usually one of those straw baskets upon his head that workmen use for their tools, and he is barefooted. In one picture he grins broadly and holds a bitten melon in his hand.

The winter pictures are less numerous and satisfactory. He wears huge sabots, no doubt of beechwood, and (as fragments of the inscription "John Stickells, Iping" show) sacks for socks, and his trousers and jacket are unmistakably cut from the remains of a gaily patterned carpet. Underneath that there were rude swathings of flannel ; five or six yards of flannel are tied comforter fashion about his neck. The thing on his head is probably another sack. He stares, sometimes smiling, sometimes a little ruefully, at the camera. Even when he was only five years old, one sees that half-whimsical wrinkling over his soft brown eyes that characterised his face.

He was from the first, the Vicar always declared, a terrible nuisance about the village. He seems to have had a proportionate impulse to play, much curiosity and sociability, and in addition there was a certain craving within him—I grieve to say— for more to eat. In spite of what Mrs. Greenfield called an " *excessively* generous " allowance of food from Lady Wondershoot, he displayed what the doctor perceived at once was the " Criminal Appetite." It carries out only too completely Lady Wondershoot's worst experiences of the lower classes, that in spite of an allowance of nourishment inordinately beyond what is known to be the maximum necessity even of an adult human being, the creature was found to steal. And what he stole he ate with an inelegant voracity. His great hand would come over garden walls ; he would covet the very bread in the baker's carts. Cheeses went from Marlow's store loft, and never a pig trough was safe from him. Some farmer walking over his field of swedes would find the great spoor of his feet and the evidence of his nibbling hunger, a root picked here, a root picked there, and the holes, with childish cunning, heavily erased. He ate a swede as one devours a radish. He would stand and eat apples from a tree, if no one was about, as normal children eat blackberries from a bush. In one way at any rate this shortness of provisions was good for the peace of Cheasing Eyebright—for many years he ate up every grain very nearly of the Food of the Gods that was given him. . . .

Indisputably the child was troublesome and out of place. " He was always about," the Vicar used to say. He could not go to school ; he could not go to church by virtue of the obvious limitations of its cubical content. There was some attempt to satisfy the spirit of that " most foolish and destructive law "— I quote the Vicar—the Elementary Education Act of 1870, by getting him to sit outside the open window while instruction was going on within. But his presence there destroyed the discipline of the other children. They were always popping up and peering at him, and every time he spoke they laughed together. His voice was so odd ! So they let him stay away.

Nor did they persist in pressing him to come to church, for his vast proportions were of little help to devotion. Yet there they might have had an easier task ; there are good reasons for guessing there were the germs of religious feeling somewhere in that big carcass. The music perhaps drew him. He was often in the churchyard on a Sunday morning, picking his way softly among the graves after the congregation had gone in, and he would sit the whole service out beside the porch, listening as one listens outside a hive of bees.

At first he showed a certain want of tact ; the people inside would hear his great feet crunch restlessly round their place of worship, or become aware of his dim face peering in through the stained glass, half curious, half envious, and at times some simple hymn would catch him unawares and he would howl lugubriously in a gigantic attempt at unison. Whereupon little Sloppet, who was organ-blower and verger and beadle and sexton and bell-ringer on Sundays, besides being postman and chimney-sweep all the week, would go out very briskly and valiantly and send him mournfully away. Sloppet, I am glad to say, felt it—in his more thoughtful moments at any rate. It was like sending a dog home when you start out for a walk, he told me.

But the intellectual and moral training of young Caddles, though fragmentary, was explicit. From the first, Vicar, mother, and all the world, combined to make it clear to him that his giant strength was not for use. It was a misfortune that that he had to make the best of. He had to mind what was told him, do what was set him, be careful never to break anything nor hurt anything. Particularly he must not go treading on things or jostling against things or jumping about. He had to salute the gentlefolks respectfully and be grateful for the food and clothing they spared him out of their riches. And he learnt all these things submissively, being by nature and habit a teachable creature and only by food and accident gigantic.

For Lady Wondershoot, in these early days, he displayed the profoundest awe. She found she could talk to him best when she was in short skirts and had her dog-whip, and she gesticulated with that and was always a little contemptuous and shrill. But sometimes the Vicar played master, a minute, middle-aged, rather breathless David pelting a childish Goliath with reproof and reproach and dictatorial command. The monster was now so big that it seems it was impossible for any one to remember he was after all only a child of seven, with all a child's desire for notice and amusement and fresh experience, with all a child's craving for response, attention, and affection, and all a child's capacity for dependence and unrestricted dulness and misery.

The Vicar, walking down the village road some sunlit morning, would encounter an ungainly eighteen feet of the Inexplicable, as fantastic and unpleasant to him as some new form of Dissent, as it padded fitfully along with craning neck, seeking, always seeking the two primary needs of childhood, something to eat and something with which to play.

There would come a look of furtive respect into the creature's eyes and an attempt to touch the matted forelock.

In a limited way the Vicar had an imagination—at any rate, the remains of one—and with young Caddles it took the line of developing the huge possibilities of personal injury such vast muscles must possess. Suppose a sudden madness—— ! Suppose a mere lapse into disrespect—— ! However, the truly brave man is not the man who does not feel fear but the man who overcomes it. Every time and always the Vicar got his imagination under. And he used always to address young Caddles stoutly in a good clear service tenor.

" Being a good boy, Albert Edward ? "

And the young giant, edging closer to the wall and blushing deeply, would answer, " Yessir—trying."

" Mind you do," said the Vicar and would go past him with at most a slight acceleration of his breathing. And out of respect for his manhood he made it a rule, whatever he might fancy, never to look back at the danger, when once it was passed.

In a fitful manner the Vicar would give young Caddles private tuition. He never taught the monster to read—it was not needed—but he taught him the more important points of the Catechism, his duty to his neighbour for example, and of that Deity who would punish Caddles with extreme vindictiveness if ever he ventured to disobey the Vicar and Lady Wondershoot. The lessons would go on in the Vicar's yard, and passers-by would hear that great cranky childish voice droning out the essential teachings of the Established Church.

" To onner 'n 'bey the King and allooer put 'nthority under 'im. To s'bmit meself t'all my gov'ners, teachers, spir'shall pastors an' masters. To order myself lowly 'n rev'rently t'all my betters——"

Presently it became evident that the effect of the growing giant on unaccustomed horses was like that of a camel, and he was told to keep off the high road, not only near the shrubbery (where the oafish smile over the wall had exasperated her ladyship extremely), but altogether. That law he never completely obeyed, because of the vast interest the high road had for him. But it turned what had been his constant resort into a stolen pleasure. He was limited at last almost entirely to old pasture and the Downs.

I do not know what he would have done if it had not been for the Downs. There there were spaces where he might wander for miles, and over these spaces he wandered. He would pick branches from trees and make insane vast nosegays there until he was forbidden, take up sheep and put them in neat rows from which they immediately wandered (at this he invariably laughed very heartily) until he was forbidden, dig away the turf, great wanton holes, until he was forbidden. . . .

He would wander over the Downs as far as the hill above Wreckstone, but not farther, because there he came upon cultivated land, and the people by reason of his depredations upon their root crops, and inspired moreover by a sort of hostile timidity his big unkempt appearance frequently evoked, always came out against him with yapping dogs to drive him away. They would threaten him and lash at him with cart whips. I have heard that they would sometimes fire at him with shot-guns. And in the other direction he ranged within sight of Hickleybrow. From above Thursley Hanger he could get a glimpse of the London, Chatham, and Dover railway, but ploughed fields and a suspicious hamlet prevented his nearer access.

And after a time there came boards, great boards with red letters that debarred him every direction. He could not read what the letters said : " Out of Bounds," but in a little while he understood. He was often to be seen in those days, by the railway passengers, sitting, chin on knees, perched up on the Down hard by the Thursley chalk pits, where afterwards he was set working. The train seemed to inspire a dim emotion of friendliness in him, and sometimes he would wave an enormous hand at it, and sometimes give it a rustic incoherent hail.

" Big," the peering passenger would say. " One of these Boom children. They say, Sir, quite unable to do anything for itself—little better than an idiot in fact, and a great burden on the locality."

" Parents quite poor, I'm told."

" Lives on the charity of the local gentry."

Every one would stare intelligently at that distant squatting monstrous figure for a space.

" Good thing that was put a stop to," some spacious thinking mind would suggest. " Nice to 'ave a few thousand of *them* on the rates, eh ? "

And usually there was some one wise enough to tell this philosopher : " You're about Right there, Sir," in hearty tones.

II

He had his bad days.

There was, for example, that trouble with the river.

He made little boats out of whole newspapers, an art he learnt by watching the Spender boy, and he set them sailing down the stream, great paper cocked hats. When they vanished under the bridge which marks the boundary of the strictly private grounds about Eyebright House, he would give a great shout and run round and across Tormat's new field— Lord ! how Tormat's pigs did scamper to be sure, and turn their good fat into lean muscle !—and so to meet his boats by the ford. Right across the nearer lawns these paper boats of his used to go, right in front of Eyebright House, right under Lady Wondershoot's eyes ! Disorganising folded newspaper ! A pretty thing !

Gathering enterprise from impunity, he began babyish hydraulic engineering. He delved a huge port for his paper fleets with an old shed door that served him as a spade, and, no one chancing to observe his operations just then, he devised an ingenious canal that incidentally flooded Lady Wondershoot's ice-house, and finally he dammed the river. He dammed it right across with a few vigorous doorfuls of earth —he must have worked like an avalanche—and down came a most amazing spate through the shrubbery and washed away Miss Spinks and her easel and the most promising water-colour sketch she had ever begun, or, at any rate, it washed away her easel and left her wet to the knees and dismally tucked up in flight to the house, and thence the waters rushed through the kitchen garden and so by the green door into the lane and down into the river-bed again by Short's ditch.

Meanwhile, the Vicar, interrupted in conversation with the blacksmith, was amazed to see distressful stranded fish leaping out of a few residual pools, and heaped green weed in the bed of the stream where ten minutes before there had been eight feet and more of clear cool water.

After that, horrified at his own consequences, young Caddles fled his home for two days and nights. He returned only at the insistent call of hunger, to bear with stoical calm an amount of violent scolding that was more in proportion to his size than anything else that had ever before fallen to his lot in the Happy Village.

III

Immediately after that affair Lady Wondershoot, casting about for exemplary additions to the abuse and fastings she had inflicted, issued a Ukase. She issued it first to her butler and very suddenly, so that she made him jump. He was clearing away the breakfast-things and she was staring out of the tall window on the terrace where the fawns would come to be fed. " Jobbet," she said, in her most imperial voice, " Jobbet, this Thing must work for its living."

And she made it quite clear not only to Jobbet (which was easy), but to every one else in the village, including young Caddles, that in this matter, as in all things, she meant what she said.

" Keep him employed," said Lady Wondershoot. " That's the tip for Master Caddles."

"It's the Tip, I fancy, for all Humanity," said the Vicar. " The simple duties, the modest round, seed-time and harvest——"

" Exactly," said Lady Wondershoot. " What *I* always say. Satan finds some mischief still for idle hands to do. At any rate among the labouring classes. We bring up our under-housemaids on that principle, always. What shall we set him to do ? "

That was a little difficult. They thought of many things, and meanwhile they broke him in to labour a bit by using him instead of a horse messenger to carry telegrams and notes when extra speed was needed, and he also carried luggage and packing-cases and things of that sort very conveniently in a big net they found for him. He seemed to like employment, regarding it as a sort of game, and Kinkle, Lady Wondershoot's agent, seeing him shift a rockery for her one day, was struck by the brilliant idea of putting him into her chalk quarry at Thursley Hanger hard by Hickleybrow. This idea was carried out, and it seemed they had settled his problem.

He worked in the chalk pit, at first with the zest of a playing child, and afterwards with an effect of habit, delving, loading, doing all the haulage of the trucks, running the full ones down the lines towards the siding, and hauling the empty ones up by the wire of a great windlass : working the entire quarry at last single-handed.

I am told that Kinkle made a very good thing indeed out of him for Lady Wondershoot, consuming as he did scarcely anything but his food, though that never restrained her denunciation of " the Creature " as a gigantic parasite upon her charity. . . .

At that time he used to wear a sort of smock of sacking, trousers of patched leather, and iron-shod sabots. Over his head was sometimes a queer thing, a worn-out beehive straw chair it was, but usually he went bareheaded. He would be moving about the pit with a powerful deliberation, and the Vicar on his constitutional round would get there about midday to find him shamefully eating his vast need of food with his back to all the world.

His food was brought to him every day, a mess of grain in the husk, in a truck, a small railway truck, like one of the trucks he was perpetually filling with chalk, and this load he used to char in an old lime kiln and then devour. Sometimes he would mix with it a bag of sugar. Sometimes he would sit licking a lump of such salt as is given to cows, or eating a huge lump of dates, stones and all, such as one sees in London on barrows. For drink he walked to the rivulet beyond the burnt-out site of the Experimental Farm at Hickleybrow and put down his face to the stream. It was from his drinking in that way after eating that the Food of the Gods did at last get loose, spreading first of all in huge weeds from the river-side, then in big frogs, bigger trout and stranding carp, and at last in a fantastic exuberance of vegetation all over the little valley.

And after a year or so the queer monstrous grub things in the field before the blacksmith's grew so big and developed into such frightful skipjacks and cockchafers—motor cockchafers the boys called them—that they drove Lady Wondershoot abroad.

IV

But soon the Food was to enter upon a new phase of its work in him. In spite of the simple instructions of the Vicar, instructions intended to round off the modest natural life befitting a giant peasant, in the most complete and final manner, he began to ask questions, to inquire into things, to *think*. As he grew from boyhood to adolescence it became increasingly evident that his mind had processes of its own—out of the Vicar's control. The Vicar did his best to ignore this distressing phenomenon, but still—he could feel it there.

The young giant's material for thought lay about him.

Quite involuntarily, with his spacious views, his constant over-looking of things, he must have seen a good deal of human life, and as it grew clearer to him that he, too, save for this clumsy greatness of his, was also human, he must have come to realise more and more just how much was shut against him by his melancholy distinction. The social hum of the school, the mystery of religion that was partaken in such finery, and which exhaled so sweet a strain of melody, the jovial chorusing from the Inn, the warmly glowing rooms, candle-lit and fire-lit, into which he peered out of the darkness, or again the shouting excitement, the vigour of flannelled exercise upon some imperfectly understood issue that centred about the cricket-field, all these things must have cried aloud to his companion-able heart. It would seem that as his adolescence crept upon him, he began to take a very considerable interest in the pro-ceedings of lovers, in those preferences and pairings, those close intimacies that are so cardinal in life.

One Sunday, just about that hour when the stars and the bats and the passions of rural life come out, there chanced to be a young couple " kissing each other a bit " in Love Lane, the deep-hedged lane that runs out back towards the Upper Lodge. They were giving their little emotions play, as secure in the warm still twilight as any lovers could be. The only conceivable interruption they thought possible must come pacing visibly up the lane ; the twelve-foot hedge towards the silent Downs seemed to them an absolute guarantee.

Then suddenly—incredibly—they were lifted and drawn apart.

They discovered themselves held up, each with a finger and thumb under the armpits, and with the perplexed brown eyes of young Caddles scanning their warm flushed faces. They were naturally dumb with the emotions of their situation.

" *Why* do you like doing that ? " asked young Caddles.

I gather the embarrassment continued until the swain, remembering his manhood, vehemently, with loud shouts, threats, and virile blasphemies, such as became the occasion, bade young Caddles under penalties put them down. Where-upon young Caddles, remembering his manners, did put them down politely and very carefully, and conveniently near for a resumption of their embraces, and having hesitated above them for a while, vanished again into the twilight. . . .

" But I felt precious silly," the swain confided to me. " We couldn't 'ardly look at one another. Bein' caught like that.

" Kissing we was—*you* know.

" And the cur'ous thing is, she blamed it all on to me," said the swain.

" Flew out something outrageous, and wouldn't 'ardly speak to me all the way 'ome. . . ."

The giant was embarking upon investigations, there could be no doubt. His mind, it became manifest, was throwing up questions. He put them to few people as yet, but they troubled him. His mother, one gathers, sometimes came in for cross-examination.

He used to come into the yard behind his mother's cottage, and, after a careful inspection of the ground for hens and chicks, he would sit down slowly with his back against the barn. In a minute the chicks, who liked him, would be pecking all over him at the mossy chalk mud in the seams of his clothing, and if it was blowing up for wet, Mrs. Caddles' kitten, who never lost her confidence in him, would assume a sinuous form and start scampering into the cottage, up to the kitchen fender, round, out, up his leg, up his body, right up to his shoulder, meditative moment, and then scat! back again, and so on. Sometimes she would stick her claws in his face out of sheer gaiety of heart, but he never dared to touch her because of the uncertain weight of his hand upon a creature so frail. Besides, he rather liked to be tickled. And after a time he would put some clumsy questions to his mother.

" Mother," he would say, " if it's good to work, why doesn't every one work ? "

His mother would look up at him and answer, " It's good for the likes of us."

He would meditate, " *Why* ? "

And going unanswered, " What's work *for*, mother ? Why do I cut chalk and you wash clothes, day after day, while Lady Wondershoot goes about in her carriage, mother, and travels off to those beautiful foreign countries you and I mustn't see, mother ? "

" She's a lady," said Mrs. Caddles.

" Oh," said young Caddles, and meditated profoundly.

" If there wasn't gentlefolks to make work for us to do," said Mrs. Caddles, " how should we poor people get a living ? "

This had to be digested.

" Mother," he tried again, " if there wasn't any gentlefolks, wouldn't things belong to people like me and you, and if they did——"

" Lord sakes and *drat* the Boy ! " Mrs. Caddles would say— she had with the help of a good memory become quite a florid and vigorous individuality since Mrs. Skinner died. " Since your poor dear grandma was took, there's no abiding you. Don't you arst no questions and you won't be told no lies. If once I was to start out answerin' you *serious*, y'r father'd 'ave to go and arst some one else for 'is supper—let alone finishin' the washin'."

" All right, mother," he would say, after a wondering stare at her. " I didn't mean to worry."

And he would go on thinking.

V

He was thinking, too, four years after, when the Vicar, now no longer ripe but over-ripe, saw him for the last time of all. You figure the old gentleman visibly a little older now, slacker in his girth, a little coarsened and a little weakened in his thought and speech, with a quivering shakiness in his hand and a quivering shakiness in his convictions, but his eye still bright and merry for all the trouble the Food had caused his village and himself. He had been frightened at times and disturbed, but was he not alive still and the same still ?—and fifteen long years, a fair sample of eternity—had turned the trouble into use and wont.

"It was a disturbance, I admit," he would say, "and things are different. Different in many ways. There was a time when a boy could weed, but now a man must go out with axe and crowbar—in some places down by the thickets at least. And it's a little strange still to us old-fashioned people for all this valley, even what used to be the river-bed before they irrigated, to be under wheat—as it is this year—twenty-five feet high. They used the old-fashioned scythe here twenty years ago, and they would bring home the harvest on a wain —rejoicing in a simple honest fashion. A little simple drunkenness, a little innocent dalliance perhaps, to conclude. . . . Poor dear Lady Wondershoot—she didn't like these innovations. Very conservative, poor dear lady ! A touch of the eighteenth century about her, I always said. Her language for example. . . . Bluff vigour. . . .

"She died comparatively poor. These big weeds got into her garden. She was not one of these gardening women, but she liked her garden in order—things growing where they were planted and as they were planted—under control. . . . The way things grew was unexpected—upset her ideas. . . . She didn't like the perpetual invasion of this young monster—at least she began to fancy he was always gaping at her over her wall. . . . She didn't like his being nearly as high as her house. . . . Jarred with her sense of proportion. Poor dear lady ! I had hoped she would last my time. It was the big cock-chafers we had for a year or so that decided her. They came from the giant larvæ—nasty things as big as rats—in the valley turf. . . .

"And the ants no doubt weighed with her also.

"Since everything was upset and there was no peace and quietness anywhere now, she said she thought she might just as well be at Monte Carlo as anywhere else. And she went.

"She played pretty boldly, I'm told. Died in an hotel there. Very sad end. . . . Exile. . . . Not—not what one considers meet. . . . A natural leader of our English people. . . . Uprooted. So ! . . .

"Yet after all," harped the Vicar, "it comes to very little.

A nuisance of course. Children cannot run about so freely as they used to do, what with ant bites and so forth. Perhaps it's as well. . . . There used to be talk—as though this stuff would revolutionise everything. . . . But there is something that defies all these forces of the New. . . . I don't know of course. I'm not one of your modern philosophers—explain everything with ether and atoms. Evolution. Rubbish like that. What I mean is something the 'Ologies don't include. Matter of reason—not understanding. Ripe wisdom. Human nature. *Aere perennius.* . . Call it what you will."

And so at last it came to the last time.

The Vicar had no intimation of what lay so close upon him. He did his customary walk, over by Farthing Down, as he had done it for more than a score of years, and so to the place whence he would watch young Caddles. He did the rise over by the chalk pit crest a little puffily—he had long since lost the Muscular Christian stride of early days—but Caddles was not at his work, and then, as he skirted the thicket of giant bracken that was beginning to obscure and overshadow the Hanger, he came upon the monster's huge form seated on the hill—brooding as it were upon the world. Caddles' knees were drawn up, his cheek was on his hand, his head a little aslant. He sat with his shoulder towards the Vicar, so that those perplexed eyes could not be seen. He must have been thinking very intently, at any rate he was sitting very still. . . .

He never turned round. He never knew that the Vicar, who had played so large a part in shaping his life, looked then at him for the very last of innumerable times—did not know even that he was there. (So it is so many partings happen.) The Vicar was struck at the time by the fact that, after all, no one on earth had the slighest idea of what this great monster thought about when he saw fit to rest from his labours. But he was too indolent to follow up that new theme that day ; he fell back from its suggestion into his older grooves of thought.

" *Aere perennius,*" he whispered, walking slowly homeward by a path that no longer ran straight athwart the turf after its former fashion, but wound circuitously to avoid new sprung tussocks of giant grass. " No ! nothing is changed. Dimensions are nothing. The simple round, the common task——"

And that night, quite painlessly, and all unknowing, he himself went the common way—out of this Mystery of Change he had spent his life in denying.

They buried him in the churchyard of Cheasing Eyebright, near to the largest yew, and the modest tombstone bearing his epitaph—it ended with : *Ut in Principio, nunc est et semper*—was almost immediately hidden from the eye of man by a spread of giant grey tasselled grass too stout for scythe or sheep, that came sweeping like a fog over the village out of the germinating moisture of the valley meadows in which the Food of the Gods had been working.

Book Three

The Harvest of the Food

CHAPTER ONE

THE ALTERED WORLD

I

CHANGE played in its new fashion with the world for twenty years. To most men the new things came little by little and day by day, remarkably enough, but not so abruptly as to overwhelm. But to one man at least the full accumulation of those two decades of the Food's work was to be revealed suddenly and amazingly in one day. For our purpose it is convenient to take him for that one day and to tell something of the things he saw.

This man was a convict, a prisoner for life—his crime is no concern of ours—whom the law saw fit to pardon after twenty years. One summer morning this poor wretch, who had left the world a young man of three-and-twenty, found himself thrust out again from the grey simplicity of toil and discipline that had become his life, into a dazzling freedom. They had put unaccustomed clothes upon him ; his hair had been growing for some weeks, and he had parted it now for some days, and there he stood, in a sort of shabby and clumsy newness of body and mind, blinking with his eyes and blinking indeed with his soul, *outside* again, trying to realise one incredible thing, that after all he was again for a little while in the world of life, and for all other incredible things, totally unprepared. He was so fortunate as to have a brother who cared enough for their distant common memories to come and meet him and clasp his hand, a brother he had left a little lad and who was now a bearded prosperous man—whose very eyes were unfamiliar. And together he and this stranger from his kindred came down into the town of Dover saying little to one another and feeling many things.

They sat for a space in a public-house, the one answering the questions of the other about this person and that, reviving queer old points of view, brushing aside endless new aspects and new perspectives, and then it was time to go to the station and take the London train. Their names and the personal things they had to talk of do not matter to our story, but only the changes and all the strangeness that this poor returning soul found in the once familiar world.

In Dover itself he remarked little except the goodness of beer from pewter—never before had there been such a draught of beer, and it brought tears of gratitude to his eyes. " Beer's as good as ever," said he, believing it infinitely better. . . .

It was only as the train rattled them past Folkestone that he could look out beyond his more immediate emotions, to see what had happened to the world. He peered out of the window.

" It's sunny," he said for the twelfth time.   " I couldn't a' had
better weather."   And then for the first time it dawned upon
him that there were novel disproportions in the world.   " Lord
sakes," he cried, sitting up and looking animated for the first
time, " but them's mortal great thissels growing out there on
the bank by that broom.   If so be they *be* thissels ?   Or 'ave
I been forgetting ? "

But they were thistles, and what he took for tall bushes of
broom was the new grass, and amidst these things a company
of British soldiers—red-coated as ever—was skirmishing in accordance with the directions of the drill book that had been
partially revised after the Boer War.   Then whack ! into a
tunnel, and then into Sandling Junction, which was now em-
bedded and dark—its lamps were all alight—in a great thicket
of rhododendron that had crept out of some adjacent gardens
and grown enormously up the valley.   There was a train of
trucks on the Sandgate siding piled high with rhododendron
logs, and here it was the returning citizen heard first of Boomfood.

As they sped out again into a country that seemed absolutely
unchanged, the two brothers were hard at their explanations.
The one was full of eager, dull questions, the other had never
thought, had never troubled to see the thing as a single fact,
and he was allusive and difficult to follow.   " It's this here
Boomfood stuff," he said, touching his bottom rock of knowledge.   " Don't you know ?   'Aven't they told you, any of
'em ?   Boomfood !   You know—Boomfood.   What all the
election's about.   Scientific sort of stuff.   'Asn't no one ever
told you ? "

He thought prison had made his brother a fearful duffer not
to know that.

They made wide shots at each other by way of question and
answer.   Between these scraps of talk were intervals of window
gazing.   At first the man's interest in things was vague and
general.   His imagination had been busy with what old so-and-
so would say, how so-and-so would look, how he would say to
all and sundry certain things that would present his " putting
away " in a mitigated light.   This Boomfood came in at first
as it were a thing in an odd paragraph of the newspaper, then
as a source of intellectual difficulty with his brother.   But it
came to him presently that Boomfood was persistently coming
in upon any topic he began.

In those days the world was a patchwork of transition, so
that this great new fact came to him in a series of shocks of
contrast.   The process of change had not been uniform ; it
had spread from one centre of distribution here and another
centre there.   The country was in patches : great areas where
the Food was still to come, and areas where it was already in
the soil and in the air, sporadic and contagious.   It was a bold
new motif creeping in among ancient and venerable airs.

The contrast was very vivid indeed along the line from Dover to London at that time. For a space they traversed just such a countryside as he had known since his childhood, the small oblongs of field, hedge-lined, of a size for pigmy horses to plough, the little roads three cart widths wide, the elms and oaks and poplars dotting these fields about, little thickets of willow beside the streams, ricks of hay no higher than a giant's knees, dolls' cottages with diamond panes, brickfields, and straggling village streets, the larger houses of the petty great, flower-grown railway banks, garden-set stations, and all the little things of the vanished nineteenth century still holding out against Immensity. Here and there would be a patch of wind-sown, wind-tattered giant thistle defying the axe ; here and there a ten-foot puff-ball or the ashen stems of some burnt-out patch of monster grass ; but that was all there was to hint at the coming of the Food.

For a couple of score of miles there was nothing else to fore-shadow in any way the strange bigness of the wheat and of the weeds that were hidden from him not a dozen miles from his route just over the hills in the Cheasing Eyebright valley. And then presently, the traces of the Food would begin. The first striking thing was the great new viaduct at Tonbridge, where the swamp of the choked Medway (due to a giant variety of *Chara*) began in those days. Then again the little country, and then, as the petty multitudinous immensity of London spread out under its haze, the traces of man's fight to keep out greatness became abundant and incessant.

In that south-eastern region of London at that time, and all about where Cossar and his children lived, the Food had become mysteriously insurgent at a hundred points ; the little life went on amidst daily portents that only the deliberation of their increase, the slow parallel growth of usage to their presence, had robbed of their warning. But this returning citizen peered out to see for the first time the facts of the Food strange and predominant, scarred and blackened areas, big unsightly defences and preparations, barracks and arsenals that this subtle persistent influence had forced into the life of men.

Here on an ampler scale the experience of the first Experimental Farm had been repeated time and again. It had been in the inferior and accidental things of life—under foot and in waste places, irregularly and irrelevantly—that the coming of a new force and new issues had first declared itself. There were great evil-smelling yards and enclosures where some invincible jungle of weed furnished fuel for gigantic machinery (little cockneys came to stare at its clangorous oiliness and tip the men a sixpence) ; there were roads and tracks for big motors and vehicles, roads made of the interwoven fibres of hypertrophied hemp ; there were towers containing steam sirens that could yell at once and warn the world against any new insurgence of vermin, or, what was queerer, venerable church towers conspicuously fitted with a mechanical scream. There were little red painted refuge huts and garrison shelters, each with its 300-yard rifle range, where the riflemen practised daily with soft-nosed ammunition at targets in the shape of monstrous rats.

Six times since the day of the Skinners there had been outbreaks of giant rats—each time from the south-west London sewers, and now they were as much an accepted fact there as tigers in the delta by Calcutta. . . .

His brother had bought a paper in a heedless sort of way at Sandling, and at last this chanced to catch the eye of the released man. He opened the unfamiliar sheets—they seemed to him to be smaller, more numerous, and different in type from the papers of the times before—and he found himself confronted with innumerable pictures about things so strange as to be uninteresting, and with tall columns of printed matter whose headings, for the most part, were as unmeaning as though they had been written in a foreign tongue—"Great Speech by Mr. Caterham"; "The Boomfood Laws."

"Who's this here Caterham?" he asked, in an attempt to make conversation.

"*He's* all right," said his brother.

"Ah! Sort of politician, eh?"

"Goin' to turn out the Government. Jolly well time he did."

"Ah!" He reflected. "I suppose all the lot *I* used to know, Chamberlain, Rosebery, all that lot—— *What?*"

His brother had grasped his wrist and pointed out of the window.

"That's the Cossars!" The eyes of the released prisoner followed the finger's direction and saw——

"My Gawd!" he cried, for the first time really overcome with amazement. The paper dropped into final forgottenness between his feet. Through the trees he could see very distinctly, standing in an easy attitude, the legs wide apart and the hand grasping a ball as if about to throw it, a gigantic human figure a good forty feet high. The figure glittered in the sunlight, clad in a suit of woven white metal and belted with a broad belt of steel. For a moment it focussed all attention, and then the eye was wrested to another more distant Giant who stood prepared to catch, and it became apparent that the whole area of that great bay in the hills just north of Sevenoaks had been scarred to gigantic ends.

A hugely banked entrenchment overhung the chalk pit, in which stood the house, a monstrous squat Egyptian shape that Cossar had built for his sons when the Giant Nursery had served its turn, and behind was a great dark shed that might have covered a cathedral, in which a spluttering incandescence came and went, and from out of which came a Titanic hammering to beat upon the ear. Then the attention leapt back to the giant as the great ball of iron-bound timber soared up out of his hand.

The two men stood up and stared. The ball seemed as big as a cask.

" Caught ! " cried the man from prison, as a tree blotted out the thrower.

The train looked on these things only for the fraction of a minute and then passed behind trees into the Chislehurst tunnel. " My Gawd ! " said the man from prison again as the darkness closed about them. " Why ! that chap was as 'igh as a 'ouse."

" That's them young Cossars," said his brother, jerking his head allusively, " what all this trouble's about. . . ."

They emerged again to discover more siren surmounted towers, more red huts, and then the clustering villas of the outer suburbs. The art of bill-sticking had lost nothing in the interval, and from countless tall hoardings, from house ends, from palings, and a hundred such points of vantage came the polychromatic appeals of the great Boomfood election. " Caterham," " Boomfood," and " Jack the Giant-killer " again and again and again, and monstrous caricatures and distortions, a hundred varieties of misrepresentations of those great and shining figures they had passed so nearly only a few minutes before. . . .

II

It had been the purpose of the younger brother to do a very magnificent thing, to celebrate this return to life by a dinner at some restaurant of indisputable quality, a dinner that should be followed by all that glittering succession of impressions the Music Halls of those days were so capable of giving. It was a worthy plan to wipe off the more superficial stains of the prison house by this display of free indulgence ; but so far as the second item went the plan was changed. The dinner stood, but there was a desire already more powerful than the appetite for shows, already more efficient in turning the man's mind away from his grim prepossession with his past than any theatre could be, and that was an enormous curiosity and perplexity about this Boomfood and these Boom children, this new portentous giantry that seemed to dominate the world. " I 'aven't the 'ang of 'em," he said. " They disturve me."

His brother had that fineness of mind that can even set aside a contemplated hospitality. " It's *your* evening, dear old boy," he said. " We'll try to get into the mass meeting at the People's Palace."

And at last the man from prison had the luck to find himself wedged into a packed multitude and staring from afar at a little brightly lit platform under an organ and a gallery. The organ had been playing something that had set boots tramping as the people swarmed in ; but that was over now.

Hardly had the man from prison settled into place and done his quarrel with an importunate stranger who elbowed, before Caterham came. He walked out of a shadow towards the middle of the platform, the most insignificant little pigmy, away there in the distance, a little black figure with a pink dab for a face—in profile one saw his quite distinctive aquiline nose —a little figure that trailed after it, most inexplicably, a cheer. A cheer it was that began away there and grew and spread. A little spluttering of voices about the platform at first that suddenly leapt up into a flame of sound and swept athwart the whole mass of humanity within the building and without. How they cheered ! Hooray ! Hoo-ray !

No one in all those myriads cheered like the man from prison. The tears poured down his face, and he only stopped cheering at last because the thing had choked him. You must have been in prison as long as he before you can understand, or even begin to understand, what it means to a man to let his lungs go in a crowd. (But for all that he did not even pretend to himself that he knew what all this emotion was about.) Hooray ! O God !—Hoo-ray !

And then a sort of silence. Caterham had subsided to a conspicuous patience, and subordinate and inaudible persons were saying and doing formal and insignificant things. It was like hearing voices through the noise of leaves in spring. " Wawawawa——" What did it matter ? People in the audience talked to one another. " Wawawawawa——" the thing went on. Would that grey-headed duffer never have done ? Interrupting ? Of course they were interrupting. " Wa, wa, wa, wa——" But shall we hear Caterham any better ?

Meanwhile at any rate there was Caterham to stare at, and one could stand and study the distant prospect of the great man's features. He was easy to draw was this man, and already the world had him to study at leisure on lamp chimneys and children's plates, on Anti-Boomfood medals and Anti-Boomfood flags, on the selvedges of Caterham silks and cottons and in the linings of Good Old English Caterham hats. He pervades all the caricature of that time. One sees him as a sailor standing to an old-fashioned gun, a port-fire labelled " New Boomfood Laws " in his hand ; while in the sea wallows that huge ugly threatening monster, " Boomfood " ; or he is cap-à-pie in armour, St. George's cross on shield and helm, and a cowardly titanic Caliban sitting amidst desecrations at the mouth of a horrid cave declines his gauntlet of the " New Boomfood Regulations " ; or he comes flying down as Perseus and rescues a chained and beautiful Andromeda (labelled distinctly about her belt as " Civilisation ") from a wallowing waste of sea monster bearing upon its various necks and claws " Irreligion," " Trampling Egotism," " Mechanism," " Monstrosity," and the like. But it was as " Jack the Giant-

killer " that the popular imagination considered Caterham
most correctly cast, and it was in the vein of a Jack the Giant-
killer poster that the man from prison enlarged that distant
miniature.

The " Wawawawa " came abruptly to an end.

He's done. He's sitting down. Yes ! No ! Yes ! It's
Caterham !   " Caterham ! "   " Caterham ! "   And then came
the cheers.

It takes a multitude to make such a stillness as followed that
disorder of cheering.   A man alone in a wilderness—it's stillness of a sort no doubt, but he hears himself breathe, he hears
himself move, he hears all sorts of things.   Here the voice of
Caterham was the one single thing heard, a thing very bright
and clear, like a little light burning in a black velvet recess.
Hear indeed !   One heard him as though he spoke at one's
elbow.

It was stupendously effective to the man from prison, that
gesticulating little figure in a halo of light, in a halo of rich and
swaying sounds ; behind it, partially effaced as it were, sat its
supporters on the platform, and in the foreground was a wide
perspective of innumerable backs and profiles, a vast multitudinous attention.   That little figure seemed to have
absorbed the substance from them all.

Caterham spoke of our ancient institutions.   " Earearear,"
roared the crowd.   " Ear ! ear ! " said the man from prison.
He spoke of our ancient spirit of order and justice.   " Earearear ! " roared the crowd.   " Ear !   Ear ! " cried the man from
prison, deeply moved.   He spoke of the wisdom of our forefathers, of the slow growth of venerable institutions, of moral
and social traditions, that fitted our English national characteristics as the skin fits the hand.   " Ear !   Ear ! " groaned
the man from prison, with tears of excitement on his cheeks.
And now all these things were to go into the melting pot.   Yes,
into the melting pot !   Because three men in London twenty
years ago had seen fit to mix something indescribable in a
bottle, all the order and sanctity of things—— Cries of
" No ! No ! "— Well, if it was not to be so, they must exert
themselves, they must say good-bye to hesitation—— Here
there came a gust of cheering.   They must say good-bye to
hesitation and half-measures.

" We have heard, gentlemen," cried Caterham, " of nettles
that become giant nettles.   At first they are no more than
other nettles, little plants that a firm hand may grasp and
wrench away ; but if you leave them—if you leave them, they
grow with such a power of poisonous expansion that at last
you must needs have axe and rope, you must needs have
danger to life and limb, you must needs have toil and distress
—men may be killed in their felling, man may be killed in
their felling——"

There came a stir and interruption and then the man from

prison heard Caterham's voice again, ringing clear and strong :
" Learn about Boomfood from Boomfood itself and——" He
paused—" *Grasp your nettle before it is too late ?* "

He stopped and stood wiping his lips. " A crystal," cried
some one, " a crystal," and then came that same strange swift
growth to thunderous tumult, until the whole world seemed
cheering. . . .

The man from prison came out of the hall at last, marvellously stirred, and with that in his face that marks those who
have seen a vision. He knew, every one knew ; his ideas
were no longer vague. He had come back to a world in crisis,
to the immediate decision of a stupendous issue. He must
play his part in the great conflict like a man—like a free
responsible man. The antagonism presented itself as a
picture. On the one hand those easy gigantic mail-clad figures
of the morning—one saw them now in a different light—on
the other this little black-clad gesticulating creature under the
limelight, that pigmy thing with its ordered flow of melodious
persuasion, its little marvellously penetrating voice, John
Caterham—" Jack the Giant-killer." They must all unite to
" grasp the nettle " before it was " too late."

III

The tallest and strongest and most regarded of all the
children of the Food were the three sons of Cossar. The mile
or so of land near Sevenoaks in which their boyhood passed
became so trenched, so dug out and twisted about, so covered
with sheds and huge working models and all the play of their
developing powers, it was like no other place on earth. And
long since it had become too little for the things they sought
to do. The eldest son was a mighty schemer of wheeled
engines ; he had made himself a sort of giant bicycle that no
road in the world had room for, no bridge could bear. There
it stood, a great thing of wheels and engines, capable of two
hundred and fifty miles an hour, useless save that now and
then he would mount it and fling himself backwards and forwards across that cumbered work-yard. He had meant to go
around the little world with it ; he had made it with that
intention, while he was still no more than a dreaming boy.
Now its spokes were rusted deep red like wounds, wherever
the enamel had been chipped away.

" You must make a road for it first, Sonnie," Cossar had
said, " before you can do that."

So one morning about dawn the young giant and his brothers
had set to work to make a road about the world. They seem
to have had an inkling of opposition impending, and they had
worked with remarkable vigour. The world had discovered
them soon enough, driving that road as straight as a flight of
a bullet towards the English Channel, already some miles of it
levelled and made and stamped hard. They had been stopped

before midday by a vast crowd of excited people, owners of land, land agents, local authorities, lawyers, policemen, soldiers even.

" We're making a road," the biggest boy had explained.

" Make a road by all means," said the leading lawyer on the ground, " but please respect the rights of other people. You have already infringed the private rights of twenty-seven private proprietors ; let alone the special privileges and property of an urban district board, nine parish councils, a county council, two gas works, and a railway company. . . ."

" Goodney ! " said the elder boy Cossar.

" You will have to stop it."

" But don't you want a nice straight road in the place of all these rotten rutty little lanes ? "

" I won't say it wouldn't be advantageous, but——"

" It isn't to be done," said the eldest Cossar boy, picking up his tools.

" Not in this way," said the lawyer, " certainly."

" How is it to be done ? "

The leading lawyer's answer had been complicated and vague.

Cossar had come down to see the mischief his children had done, and reproved them severely and laughed enormously and seemed to be extremely happy over the affair. " You boys must wait a bit," he shouted up to them, " before you can do things like that."

" The lawyer told us we must begin by preparing a scheme, and getting special powers and all sorts of rot. Said it would take us years."

" *We'll* have a scheme before long, little boy," cried Cossar, hands to his mouth as he shouted, " never fear. For a bit you'd better play about and make models of the things you want to do."

They did as he told them like obedient sons.

But for all that the Cossar lads brooded a little.

" It's all very well," said the second to the first, " but I don't always want just to play about and plan. I want to do something *real*, you know. We didn't come into this world so strong as we are, just to play about in this messy little bit of ground, you know, and take little walks and keep out of the towns "—for by that time they were forbidden all boroughs and urban districts. " Doing nothing's just wicked. Can't we find out something the little people *want* done and do it for them—just for the fun of doing it ?

" Lots of them haven't houses fit to live in," said the second boy. " Let's go and build 'em a house close up to London that will hold heaps and heaps of them and be ever so comfortable and nice, and let's make 'em a nice little road to where they all go and do business—a nice straight little road, and make it all as nice as nice. We'll make it all so clean and pretty that won't any of them be able to live grubby and beastly like most of them do now. Water enough for them to wash with, we'll have—you know they're so dirty now that nine out of ten of their houses haven't even baths in them, the filthy little skunks! You know, the ones that have baths spit insults at the ones that haven't, instead of helping them to get them—and call 'em the Great Unwashed—*You* know. We'll alter all that. And we'll make electricity light and cook and clean up for them, and all. Fancy! They make their women—women who are going to be mothers—crawl about and scrub floors!

"We could make it all beautifully. We could bank up a valley in that range of hills over there and make a nice reservoir, and we could make a big place here to generate our electricity and have it all simply lovely. Couldn't we? . . . And then perhaps they'd let us do some other things."

"Yes," said the elder brother, "we could do it *very* nice for them."

"Then *let's*," said the second brother.

"*I* don't mind," said the elder brother, and looked about for a handy tool.

And that led to another dreadful bother.

Agitated multitudes were at them in no time, telling them for a thousand reasons to stop, telling them to stop for no reason at all—babbling, confused, and varied multitudes. The place they were building was too high—it couldn't possibly be safe. It was ugly; it interfered with the letting of proper-sized houses in the neighbourhood; it ruined the tone of the neighbourhood; it was unneighbourly; it was contrary to the Local Building Regulations; it infringed the right of the local authority to muddle about with a minute expensive electric supply of its own; it interfered with the concerns of the local water company.

Local Government Board clerks roused themselves to judicial obstruction. The little lawyer turned up again to represent about a dozen threatened interests; local landowners appeared in opposition; people with mysterious claims claimed to be bought off at exorbitant rates; the Trades Unions of all the building trades lifted up collective voices; and a ring of dealers in all sorts of building material became a bar. Extraordinary associations of people with prophetic visions of æsthetic horrors rallied to protect the scenery of the place where they would build the great house, of the valley where they would bank up the water. These last people were absolutely the worst asses of the lot, the Cossar boys considered. In no time that beautiful house of the Cossar boys was just like a walking-stick thrust into a wasp's nest.

"I never did!" said the elder boy.

"We can't go on," said the second brother.

"Rotten little beasts they are," said the third of the brothers; "we can't do *anything*!"

"Even when it's for their own comfort. Such a *nice* place we'd have made for them too."

"They seem to spend their silly little lives getting in each other's way," said the eldest boy. "Rights and laws and regulations and rascalities : it's like a game of spellicans. . . . Well anyhow, they'll have to live in their grubby dirty silly little houses for a bit longer. It's very evident *we* can't go on with this."

And the Cossar children left that great house unfinished, a mere hole of foundations and the beginning of a wall, and sulked back to their big enclosure. After a time the hole was filled with water and with stagnation, and weeds and vermin ; and the Food, either dropped there by the sons of Cossar or blowing thither as dust, set growth going in its usual fashion. Water voles came out over the country and did infinite havoc, and one day a farmer caught his pigs drinking there, and instantly and with great presence of mind—for he knew of the great hog of Oakham—slew them all. And from that deep pool it was the mosquitoes came, quite terrible mosquitoes, whose only virtue was that the sons of Cossar, after being bitten for a little, could stand it no longer, and chose a moonlight night when law and order were abed, and drained the water clean away into the river by Brook.

But they left the big weeds and the big water voles and all sorts of big undesirable things still living and breeding on the site they had chosen, the site on which the fair great house of the little people might have towered to heaven. . . .

IV

That had been in the boyhood of the Sons, but now they were nearly men. And the chains had been tightening upon them and tightening with every year of growth. Each year they grew and the Food spread and great things multiplied, each year the stress and tension rose. The Food had been at first for the great mass of mankind a distant marvel, and now it was coming home to every threshold and threatening, pressing against and distorting the whole order of life. It blocked this, it overturned that, it changed natural products, and by changing natural products it stopped employments and threw men out of work by the hundred thousand ; it swept over boundaries and turned the world of trade into a world of cataclysms ; no wonder mankind hated it.

And since it is easier to hate animate than inanimate things, animals more than plants, and one's fellow-men more completely than any animals, the fear and trouble engendered by giant nettles and six-foot grass blades, awful insects and tiger-like vermin, grew all into one great power of detestation that aimed itself with a simple directness at that scattered band of great human beings, the Children of the Food. That hatred had become the central force in political affairs. The old party lines had been traversed and effaced altogether under the insistence of these newer issues, and the conflict lay now between the party of the temporisers, who were for setting little political men to control and regulate the Food, and the party of reaction, for whom Caterham spoke, speaking always with a more sinister ambiguity, crystallising his intention first in one threatening phrase and then another, now that men must " prune the bramble growths," now that they must find a " cure for elephantiasis," and at last upon the eve of the election that they must " Grasp the nettle."

One day the three sons of Cossar, who were now no longer boys but men, sat among the masses of their futile work and talked together after their fashion of all these things. They had been working all day at one of a series of great and complicated trenches their father had bid them make, and now it was sunset and they sat in the little garden space before the great house and looked at the world and rested, until the little servants within should say their food was ready.

You must figure these mighty forms, forty feet high the least of them was, reclining on a patch of turf that would have seemed a stubble of reeds to a common man. One sat up and chipped earth from his huge boots with an iron girder he grasped in his hand ; the second rested on his elbow ; the third whittled a pine-tree into shape making the air aromatic with resin. They were clothed not in cloth but in under-garments of woven rope and outer clothes of felted aluminium wire ; they were shod with timber and iron and the links and buttons and belts of their clothing were all of plated steel. The great single-storeyed house they lived in, Egyptian in its massiveness, half built of monstrous blocks of chalk and half excavated from the living rock of the hill, had a front a full hundred feet in height, and beyond, the chimneys and wheels, the cranes and covers of their work-sheds rose marvellously against the sky. Through a circular window in the house there was visible a spout from which some white-hot metal dripped and dripped in measured drops into a receptacle out of sight. The place was enclosed and rudely fortified by monstrous banks of earth backed with steel both over the crests of the Downs above, and across the dip of the valley. It needed something of common size to mark the nature of the scale. The train that came rattling from Sevenoaks athwart their vision, and presently plunged into the tunnel out of their sight, looked by contrast with them like a small automatic toy.

" They have made all the woods this side of Ightham out of bounds," said one, " and moved the board that was out by Knockholt two miles and more this way."

" It is the least they could do," said the youngest, after a pause. " They are trying to take the wind out of Caterham's sails."

"It's not enough for that and—it is almost too much for us," said the third.

"They are cutting us off from Brother Redwood. Last time I went to him the red notices had crept a mile in, either way. The road to him along the Downs is no more than a narrow lane."

The speaker thought. "What has come to our Brother Redwood?"

"Why?" said the eldest brother.

The speaker hacked a bough from his pine. "He was like—as though he wasn't awake. He didn't seem to listen to what I had to say. And he said something of—love."

The youngest tapped his girder on the edge of his iron sole and laughed. "Brother Redwood," he said, "has dreams."

Neither spoke for a space. Then the eldest brother said, "This cooping up and cooping up grows more than I can bear. At last, I believe, they will draw a line round our boots and tell us to live on that."

The middle brother swept aside a heap of pine boughs with one hand and shifted his attitude. "What they do now is nothing to what they will do when Caterham has power."

"If he gets power," said the youngest brother, smiting the ground with his girder.

"As he will," said the eldest, staring at his feet.

The middle brother ceased his lopping and his eye went to the great banks that sheltered them about. "Then, brothers," he said, "our youth will be over and as Father Redwood said to us long ago, we must quit ourselves like men."

"Yes," said the eldest; "but what exactly does that mean? Just what does it mean—when that day of trouble comes?"

He too glanced at those rude vast suggestions of entrenchment about them, looking not so much at them as through them and over the hills to the innumerable multitudes beyond. Something of the same sort came into all their minds, a vision of little people coming out to war, in a flood, the little people inexhaustible, incessant, malignant. . . .

"They are little," said the youngest brother; "but they have numbers beyond counting, like the sands of the sea."

"They have arms—they have weapons even, that our brothers in Sunderland have made."

"Besides, Brothers, except for vermin, except for little accidents with evil things, what have we seen of killing?"

"I know," said the eldest brother. "For all that—we are what we are. When the day of trouble comes we must do the thing we have to do."

He closed his knife with a snap—the blade was the length of a man—and used his new pine staff to help himself rise. He stood up and turned towards the squat grey immensity of the house. The crimson of the sunset caught him as he rose, caught the mail and clasps about his neck and the woven metal of his arms, and to the eyes of his brother it seemed as though he was suddenly suffused with blood. . . .

As the young giant rose a little black figure became visible to him against that western incandescence on the top of the embankment that towered above the summit of the down. The black limbs waved in ungainly gestures. Something in the fling of the limbs suggested haste to the young giant's mind. He waved his pine mast in reply, filled the whole valley with his vast Hallo ! threw a " Something's up " to his brothers, and set off in twenty-foot strides to meet and help his father.

V

It chanced too that a young man who was not a giant was delivering his soul about these sons of Cossar just at that same time. He had come over the hills beyond Sevenoaks, he and his friend, and he it was did the talking. In the hedge as they came along they had heard a pitiful squealing and had intervened to rescue three nestling tits from the attack of a couple of giant ants. That adventure it was had set him talking.

" Reactionary ! " he was saying, as they came within sight of the Cossar encampment. " Who wouldn't be reactionary ? Look at that square of ground, that space of God's earth that was once sweet and fair, torn, desecrated, disembowelled ! Those sheds ! That great wind-wheel ! That monstrous wheeled machine ! Those dykes ! Look at those three monsters squatting there, plotting some ugly devilment or other ! Look—look at all the land ! "

His friend glanced at his face. " You have been listening to Caterham," he said.

" Using my eyes. Looking a little into the peace and order of the past we leave behind. This foul Food is the last shape of the Devil, still set as ever upon the ruin of our world. Think what the world must have been before our days, what it was still when our mothers bore us, and see it now ! Think how these slopes once smiled under the golden harvest, how the hedges, full of sweet little flowers, parted the modest portion of this man from that, how the ruddy farmhouses dotted the land and the voice of the church bells from yonder tower stilled the whole world each Sabbath into Sabbath prayer. And now, every year, still more and more of monstrous weeds, of monstrous vermin, and these giants growing all about us, straddling over us, blundering against all that is subtle and sacred in our world. Why here—— Look ! "

He pointed, and his friend's eyes followed the line of his white finger.

" One of their footmarks. See ! It has smashed itself three feet deep and more, a pitfall for horses and rider, a trap to the unwary. There is a briar rose smashed to death ; there is grass uprooted and a teazle crushed aside, a farmer's rain-pipe snapped and the edge of the pathway broken down. Destruction ! So they are doing all over the world, all over the order and decency the world of men has made. Trampling on all things. Reaction ! What else ? "

" But—reaction. What do you hope to do ? "

" Stop it ! " cried the young man from Oxford. " Before it is too late."

" But——"

" It's *not* impossible," cried the young man from Oxford, with a jump in his voice. " We want the firm hand ; we want the subtle plan, the resolute mind. We have been mealy-mouthed and weak-handed ; we have trifled and temporised, and the Food has grown and grown. Yet even now——"

He stopped for a moment. " This is the echo of Caterham," said his friend.

" Even now. Even now there is hope—abundant hope, if only we make sure of what we want and what we mean to destroy. The mass of people are with us, much more with us than they were a few years ago ; the law is with us, the constitution and order of society, the spirit of the established religions, the customs and habits of mankind are with us—and against the Food. Why should we temporise ? Why should we lie ? We hate it, we don't want it ; why then should we have it ? Do you mean to just grizzle and obstruct passively and do nothing—till the sands are out ? "

He stopped short and turned about. " Look at that grove of nettles there. In the midst of them are homes—deserted—where once familes of simple men played out their honest lives !

" And there ! " he swung round to where the young Cossars muttered to one another of their wrongs.

" Look at them ! And I know their father, a brute, a sort of brute beast with an intolerant loud voice, a creature who has run amuck in our all too merciful world for the last thirty years and more. An engineer ! To him all that we hold dear and sacred is nothing. Nothing ! The splendid traditions of our race and land, the noble institutions, the venerable order, the broad slow march from precedent to precedent that has made our English people great and this sunny island free—it is all an idle tale, told and done with. Some claptrap about the Future is worth all these sacred things. . . . This sort of man who would run a tramway over his mother's grave if he thought that was the cheapest line the tramway could take. . . . And you think to temporise, to make some scheme of compromise, that will enable you to live in your way while that—that machinery—lives in its. I tell you it is hopeless—hopeless. As well make treaties with a tiger ! They want things monstrous—we want them sane and sweet. It is one thing or the other."

" But what can you do ? "

" Much ! All ! Stop the Food ! They are still scattered, these giants, still immature and disunited. Chain them, gag them, muzzle them. At any cost stop them. It is their world or ours ! Stop the Food. Shut up these men who make it. Do anything to stop Cossar ! You don't seem to remember—one generation—only one generation needs holding down and then—— Then we could level those mounds there, fill up their footsteps, take the ugly sirens from our church towers, smash all our elephant guns, and turn our faces again to the old order, the ripe old civilisation for which the soul of man is fitted."

" It's a mighty effort."

" For a mighty end. And if we don't ? Don't you see the prospect before us clear as day ? Everywhere the giants will increase and multiply ; everywhere they will make and scatter the Food. The grass will grow gigantic in our fields, the weeds in our hedges, the vermin in the thickets, the rats in the drains. More and more and more. This is only a beginning. The insect world will rise on us, the plant world, the very fishes in the sea will swamp and drown our ships. Tremendous growths will obscure and hide our houses, smother our churches, smash and destroy all the order of our cities, and we shall become no more than a feeble vermin under the heels of the new race. Mankind will be swamped and drowned in things of its own begetting ! And all for nothing ! Size ! Mere size ! Enlargement and *da capo*. Already we go picking our way among the first beginnings of the coming time. And all we do is to say ' How inconvenient ! ' To grumble and do nothing. *No !* "

He raised his hand.

" Let them do the thing they have to do ! So also will I. I am for Reaction—unstinted and fearless Reaction. Unless you mean to take this Food also, what else is there to do in all the world ? We have trifled in the middle ways too long. You ! Trifling in the middle ways is your habit, your circle of existence, your space and time. So, not I. I am against the Food, with all my strength and purpose against the Food."

He turned on his companion's grunt of dissent. " Where are you ? "

" It's a complicated business——"

" Oh !—Driftwood ! " said the young man from Oxford, very bitterly, with a fling of all his limbs. " The middle way is nothingness. It is one thing or the other. Eat or destroy. Eat or destroy ! What else is there to do ? "

CHAPTER TWO

THE GIANT LOVERS

I

Now it chanced in the days when Caterham was campaigning against the Boom-children before the General Election that was—amidst the most tragic and terrible circumstances—to bring him into power, that the giant Princess, that Serene Highness whose early nutrition had played so great a part in the brilliant career of Doctor Winkles, had come from the kingdom of her father to England, on an occasion that was deemed important. She was affianced for reasons of state to a certain Prince—and the wedding was to be made an event of international significance. There had arisen mysterious delays. Rumour and Imagination collaborated in the story and many things were said. There were suggestions of a recalcitrant Prince who declared he would not be made to look like a fool—at least to this extent. People sympathised with him. That is the most significant aspect of the affair.

Now it may seem a strange thing, but it is a fact that the giant Princess, when she came to England, knew of no other giants whatever. She had lived in a world where tact is almost a passion and reservations the air of one's life. They had kept the thing from her; they had hedged her about from sight or suspicion of any gigantic form, until her appointed coming to England was due. Until she met young Redwood she had no inkling that there was such a thing as another giant in the world.

In the kingdom of the father of the Princess there were wild wastes of upland and mountains where she had been accustomed to roam freely. She loved the sunrise and the sunset and all the great drama of the open heavens more than anything else in the world, but among a people at once so democratic and so vehemently loyal as the English her freedom was much restricted. People came in brakes, in excursion trains, in organised multitudes to see her; they would cycle long distances to stare at her, and it was necessary to rise betimes if she would walk in peace. It was still near the dawn that morning when young Redwood came upon her.

The Great Park near the Palace where she lodged stretched, for a score of miles and more, west and south of the western palace gates. The chestnut trees of its avenues reached high above her head. Each one as she passed it seemed to proffer a more abundant wealth of blossom. For a time she was content with sight and scent, but at last she was won over by these offers, and set herself so busily to choose and pick that she did not perceive young Redwood until he was close upon her.

457

She moved among the chestnut trees, with the destined lover drawing near to her, unanticipated, unsuspected. She thrust her hands in among the branches, breaking them and gathering them. She was alone in the world. Then——

She looked up, and in that moment she was mated.

We must needs put our imaginations to his stature to see the beauty he saw. That unapproachable greatness that prevents our immediate sympathy with her did not exist for him. There she stood, a gracious girl, the first created being that had ever seemed a mate for him, light and slender, lightly clad, the fresh breeze of the dawn moulding the subtly folding robe upon her against the soft strong lines of her form, and with a great mass of blossoming chestnut branches in her hands. The collar of her robe opened to show the whiteness of her neck and a soft shadowed roundness that passed out of sight towards her shoulders. The breeze had stolen a strand or so of her hair, too, and strained its red-tipped brown across her cheek. Her eyes were open blue, and her lips rested always in the promise of a smile as she reached among the branches.

She turned upon him, with a start, saw him and for a space they regarded one another. For her, the sight of him was so amazing, so incredible, as to be, for some moments at least, terrible. He came to her with the shock of a supernatural apparition ; he broke all the established law of her world. He was a youth of one-and-twenty then, slenderly built, with his father's darkness and his father's gravity. He was clad in a sober soft brown leather, close-fitting easy garments, and in brown hose that shaped him bravely. His head went uncovered in all weathers. They stood regarding one another— she incredulously amazed, and he with his heart beating fast. It was a moment without a prelude, the cardinal meeting of their lives.

For him there was less surprise. He had been seeking her and yet his heart beat fast. He came towards her, slowly with his eyes upon her face.

" You are the Princess," he said. " My father has told me. You are the Princess who was given the Food of the Gods."

" I am the Princess—yes," she said, with eyes of wonder. " But—what are you ? "

" I am the son of the man who made the Food of the Gods."

" The Food of the Gods ! "

" Yes, the Food of the Gods."

" But—— "

Her face expressed infinite perplexity.

" What ?   I don't understand. The Food of the Gods ? "

" You have not heard ? "

" The Food of the Gods ! *No !* "

She found herself trembling violently. The colour left her face. " I did not know," she said. " Do you mean—— ? "

He waited for her.

" Do you mean there are other—giants ? "

He repeated. " Did you not know ? "

And she answered with the growing amazement of realisation " No ! "

The whole world and all the meaning of the world was changing for her. A branch of chestnut slipped from her hand. " Do you mean to say," she repeated stupidly, " that there are other giants in the world ? That some food—— ? "

He caught her amazement.

" You know nothing ? " he cried. " You have never heard of us ? You, whom the Food has made akin to us ! "

There was terror still in the eyes that stared at him. Her hand rose towards her throat and fell again. She whispered " No."

It seemed to her that she must weep or faint. Then in a moment she had rule over herself and she was speaking and thinking clearly. " All this has been kept from me," she said. " It is like a dream. I have dreamt—— I have dreamt such things. But waking—— No. Tell me ! Tell me ! What are you ? What is this Food of the Gods ? Tell me slowly— and clearly. Why have they kept it from me, that I am not alone ? "

II

" Tell me," she said, and young Redwood, tremulous and excited, set himself to tell her—it was poor and broken telling for a time—of the Food of the Gods and the giant children who were scattered over the world.

You must figure them both, flushed and startled in their bearing, getting at one another's meaning through endless half-heard, half-spoken phrases, repeating, making perplexing breaks and new departures—a wonderful talk, in which she awakened from the ignorance of all her life. And very slowly it became clear to her that she was no exception to the order of mankind, but one of a scattered brotherhood, who had all eaten the Food and grown for ever out of the little limits of the folk beneath their feet. Young Redwood spoke of his father, of Cossar, of the Brothers scattered throughout the country, of the great dawn of wider meaning that had come at last into the history of the world. " We are in the beginning of a beginning," he said ; " this world of theirs is only the prelude to the world the Food will make.

" My father believes—and I also believe—that a time will come when littleness will have passed altogether out of the world of man. When giants shall go freely about this earth— their earth—doing continually greater and more splendid things. But that—that is to come. We are not even the first generation of that—we are the first experiments."

" And of these things," she said, " I knew nothing ! "

" There are times when it seems to me almost as if we had

come too soon. Some one, I suppose, had to come first. But the world was unprepared for our coming and for the coming of all the lesser great things that drew their greatness from the Food. There have been blunders ; there have been conflicts. The little people hate our kind. . . .

"They are hard towards us because they are so little. . . . And because our feet are heavy on the things that make their lives. But at any rate they hate us now ; they will have none of us—only if we could shrink back to the common size of them would they begin to forgive. . . .

"They are happy in houses that are prison cells to us ; their cities are too small for us ; we go in misery along their narrow ways ; we cannot worship in their churches. . . .

"We see over their walls and over their protections ; we look inadvertently into their upper windows ; we look over their customs ; their laws are no more than a net about our feet. . . .

"Every time we stumble we hear them shouting ; every time we blunder against their limits or stretch out to any spacious act. . . .

"Our easy paces are wild flights to them, and all they deem great and wonderful no more than doll's pyramids to us. Their pettiness of method and appliance and imagination hampers and defeats our powers. There are no machines to the power of our hands, no helps to fit our needs. They hold our greatness in servitude by a thousand invisible bands. We are stronger, man for man, a hundred times, but we are disarmed ; our very greatness makes us debtors ; they claim the land we stand upon ; they tax our ampler need of food and shelter, and for all these things we must toil with the tools these dwarfs can make us—and to satisfy their dwarfish fancies. . . .

"They pen us in, in every way. Even to live one must cross their boundaries. Even to meet you here to-day I have passed a limit. All that is reasonable and desirable in life they make out of bounds for us. We may not go into the towns ; we may not cross the bridges ; we may not step on their ploughed fields or into the harbours of the game they kill. I am cut off now from all our Brethren except the three sons of Cossar, and even that way the passage narrows day by day. One could think they sought occasion against us to do some more evil thing. . . ."

"But we are strong," she said.

"We should be strong—yes. We feel, all of us—you too I know must feel—that we have power, power to do great things, power insurgent in us. But before we can do any-thing——"

He flung out a hand that seemed to sweep away a world.

"Though I thought I was alone in the world," she said, after a pause, "I have thought of these things. They have taught me always that strength was almost a sin, that it was

better to be little than great, that all true religion was to
shelter the weak and little, encourage the weak and little, help
them to multiply and multiply until at last they crawled over
one another, to sacrifice all our strength in their cause.   But
. . . always I have doubted the things they taught."

"This life," he said, "these bodies of ours, are not for
dying."

"No."

"Nor to live in futility.   But if we would not do that, it is
already plain to all our Brethren a conflict must come.   I
know not what bitterness of conflict must presently come,
before the little folks will suffer us to live as we need to live.
All the Brethren have thought of that.   Cossar, of whom I
told you ; he too has thought of that."

"They are very little and weak."

"In their way.   But you know all the means of death are
in their hands, and made for their hands.   For hundreds of
thousands of years, these little people, whose world we invade,
have been learning how to kill one another.   They are very
able at that.   They are able in many ways.   And besides,
they can deceive and change suddenly. . . . I do not know.
. . . There comes a conflict.   You—you perhaps are different
from us.   For us, assuredly, the conflict comes. . . . The
thing they call War.   We know it.   In a way we prepare for
it.   But you know—those little people !—we do not know how
to kill, at least we do not want to kill——"

"Look," she interrupted, and he heard a yelping horn.

He turned in the direction of her eyes, and found a bright
yellow motor-car, with dark goggled driver and fur-clad
passengers, whooping, throbbing, and buzzing resentfully at his
heel.   He moved his foot, and the mechanism, with three angry
snorts, resumed its fussy way towards the town.   "Filling up
the roadway ! " floated up to him.

Then some one said, "Look !   Did you see ?   There is the
monster Princess over beyond the trees ! " and all their goggled
faces came round to stare.

"I say," said another.   "*That* won't do. . . ."

"All this," she said, "is more amazing than I can tell."

"That they should not have told you," he said, and left his
sentence incomplete.

"Until you came upon me, I had lived in a world where I
was great—alone.   I had made myself a life—for that.   I had
thought I was the victim of some strange freak of nature.   And
now my world has crumbled down, in half an hour, and I see
another world, other conditions, wider possibilities—fellowship——"

"Fellowship," he answered.

"I want you to tell me more yet, and much more," she said.
"You know this passes through my mind like a tale that is
told.   You even. . . . In a day perhaps, or after several days,

462 · THE FOOD OF THE GODS

I shall believe in you. Now—— Now I am dreaming. . . . Listen ! "

The first stroke of a clock above the palace offices far away had penetrated to them. Each counted mechanically "Seven."

"This," she said, "should be the hour of my return. They will be taking my bowl of coffee into the hall where I sleep. The little officials and servants—you cannot dream how grave they are—will be stirring about their little duties.

"They will wonder. . . . But I want to talk to you."

She thought. "But I want to think too. I want now to think alone, and think out this change in things, think away the old solitude, and think you and those others into my world. . . . I shall go. I shall go back to-day to my place in the castle, and to-morrow, as the dawn comes, I shall come again—here."

"I shall be here waiting for you."

"All day I shall dream and dream of this new world you have given me. Even now, I can scarcely believe——"

She took a step back and surveyed him from the feet to the face. Their eyes met and locked for a moment.

"Yes," she said, with a little laugh that was half a sob. "You are real. But it is very wonderful ! Do you think— indeed—— ? Suppose to-morrow I come and find you—a pigmy like the others ! . . . Yes, I must think. And so for to-day—as the little people do——"

She held out her hand, and for the first time they touched one another. Their hands clasped firmly and their eyes met again.

"Good-bye," she said, "for to-day. Good-bye ! Good-bye, Brother Giant ! "

He hesitated with some unspoken thing, and at last he answered her simply, "Good-bye."

For a space they held each other's hands, studying each the other's face. And many times after they had parted, she looked back half doubtfully at him, standing still in the place where they had met. . . .

She walked into her apartments across the great yard of the Palace like one who walks in a dream, with a vast branch of chestnut trailing from her hand.

III

These two met altogether fourteen times before the beginning of the end. They met in the Great Park, or on the heights and among the gorges of the rusty-roaded, heathery moorland, set with dusky pine woods, that stretched to the south-west. Twice they met in the great avenue of chestnuts, and five times near the broad ornamental water the king, her great-grand-father, had made. There was a place where a great trim lawn, set with tall conifers, sloped graciously to the water's edge, and there she would sit, and he would lie at her knees and look up in her face and talk, telling of all the things that had been, and of the work his father had set before him, and of the great and spacious dream of what the giant people should one day be. Commonly they met in the early dawn, but once they met there in the afternoon, and found presently a multitude of peering eavesdroppers about them, cyclists, pedestrians, peeping from the bushes, rustling (as sparrows will rustle about one in the London parks) amidst the dead leaves in the woods behind, gliding down the lake in boats towards a point of view, trying to get nearer to them and hear.

It was the first hint that offered of the enormous interest the countryside was taking in their meetings. And once—it was the seventh time, and it precipitated the scandal—they met out upon the breezy moorland under a clear moonlight, and talked in whispers there, for the night was warm and still.

Very soon they had passed from the realisation that in them and through them a new world of giantry shaped itself in the earth, from the contemplation of the great struggle between big and little, in which they were clearly destined to participate, to interests at once more personal and more spacious. Each time they met and talked and looked on one another, it crept a little more out of their subconscious being towards recognition, that something more dear and wonderful than friendship was between them, and walked between them and drew their hands together. And in a little while they came to the word itself and found themselves lovers, the Adam and Eve of a new race in the world.

They set foot side by side into the wonderful valley of love, with its deep and quiet places. The world changed about them with their changing mood, until presently it had become, as it were, a tabernacular beauty about their meetings, and the stars were no more than flowers of light beneath the feet of their love, and the dawn and sunset the coloured hangings by the way. They ceased to be beings of flesh and blood to one another and themselves ; they passed into a bodily texture of tenderness and desire. They gave it first whispers and then silence, and drew close and looked into one another's moonlit and shadowy faces under the infinite arch of the sky. And the still black pine trees stood about them like sentinels.

The beating steps of time were hushed into silence, and it seemed to them the universe hung still. Only their hearts were audible, beating. They seemed to be living together in a world where there is no death, and indeed so it was with them then. It seemed to them that they sounded, and indeed they sounded, such hidden splendours in the very heart of things as none have ever reached before. Even for mean and little souls, love is the revelation of splendours. And these were giant lovers who had eaten the Food of the Gods. . . .

You may imagine the spreading consternation in this ordered world when it became known that the Princess who was affianced to the Prince, the Princess, Her Serene Highness! with royal blood in her veins! met—frequently met—the hypertrophied offspring of a common professor of chemistry, a creature of no rank, no position, no wealth, and talked to him as though there were no Kings and Princes, no order, no reverence—nothing but Giants and Pigmies in the world, talked to him and, it was only too certain, held him as her lover.

" If those newspaper fellows get hold of it ! " gasped Sir Arthur Poodle Bootlik. . . .

" I am told——" whispered the old Bishop of Frumps. . . .

" New story upstairs," said the first footman, as he nibbled among the dessert things.   " So far as I can make out this here giant Princess——"

" They say——" said the lady who kept the stationer's shop by the main entrance to the Palace, where the little Americans get their tickets for the State Apartments. . . .

And then :

" We are authorised to deny——" said " Picaroon " in *Gossip.*

And so the whole trouble came out.

IV

" They say that we must part," the Princess said to her lover.

" But why ? " he cried.   " What new folly have these people got into their heads ? "

" Do you know," she asked, " that to love me—is high treason ? "

" My dear," he cried ; " but does it matter ?   What is their right—right without a shadow of reason—and their treason and their loyalty to us ? "

" You shall hear," she said, and told him of the things that had been told to her.

" It was the queerest little man who came to me—with a soft beautifully modulated voice, a softly moving little gentleman who sidled into the room like a cat and put his pretty white hand up so, whenever he had anything significant to say.   He is bald, but not of course nakedly bald, and his nose and face are chubby rosy little things and his beard is trimmed to a point in quite the loveliest way.   He pretended to have emotions several times and made his eyes shine.   You know he is quite a friend of the real royal family here, and he called me his dear young lady and was perfectly sympathetic even from the beginning.   ' My dear young lady,' he said, ' you know— *you mustn't,*' several times, and then, ' you owe a duty.' "

" Where do they make such men ? "

" He likes it," she said.

" But I don't see——"

" He told me serious things."

"You don't think," he said, turning on her abruptly, "that there's anything in the sort of thing he said?"

"There's something in it quite certainly," said she.

"You mean——?"

"I mean that without knowing it we have been trampling on the most sacred conceptions of the little folks. We who are royal are a class apart. We are worshipped prisoners, processional toys. We pay for worship by losing—our elementary freedom. And I was to have married that Prince—— You know nothing of him though. Well, a pigmy Prince. He doesn't matter. . . . It seems it would have strengthened the bonds between my country and another. And this country also—was to profit. Imagine it!—strengthening the bonds!"

"And now?"

"They want me to go on with it—as though there was nothing between us two."

"Nothing!"

"Yes. But that isn't all. He said——"

"Your specialist in Tact?"

"Yes. He said, it would be better for you, better for all the giants, if we two—abstained from conversation. That was how he put it."

"But what can they do if we don't?"

"He said you might have your freedom."

"I!"

"He said, with a stress, 'My dear young lady, it would be better, it would be more dignified, if you parted willingly.' That was all he said. With a stress on willingly."

"But——! What business is it of these little wretches, where we love, how we love! What have they and their world to do with us?"

"They do not think that."

"Of course," he said, "you disregard all this."

"It seems utterly foolish to me."

"That their laws should fetter us! That we, at the first spring of life, should be tripped by their old engagements, their aimless institutions! Oh——! We disregard it."

"I am yours. So far—yes."

"So far? Isn't that all?"

"But they—— If they want to part us——"

"What can they do?"

"I don't know. What can they do?"

"Who cares what they can do, or what they will do? I am yours and you are mine. What is there more than that? I am yours and you are mine—for ever. Do you think I will stop for their little rules, for their little prohibitions, their scarlet boards indeed!—and keep from you?"

"Yes. But still, what can they do?"

"You mean," he said, "what are we to do?"

"Yes."

" We ? We can go on."

" But if they seek to prevent us ? "

He clenched his hands. He looked round as if the little people were already coming to prevent them. Then turned away from her and looked about the world. " Yes," he said. " Your question was the right one. What can they do ? "

" Here in this little land," she said and stopped.

He seemed to survey it all. " They are everywhere."

" But we might——"

" Whither ? "

" We could go. We could swim the seas together. Beyond the seas—— "

" I have never been beyond the seas."

" There are great and desolate mountains amidst which we should seem no more than little people, there are remote and deserted valleys, there are hidden lakes and snow-girdled uplands untrodden by the feet of men. *There*—— "

" But to get there we must fight our way day after day through millions and millions of mankind."

" It is our only hope. In this crowded land there is no fastness, no shelter. What place is there for us among these multitudes ? They who are little can hide from one another, but where are we to hide ? There is no place where we could eat, no place where we could sleep. If we fled—night and day they would pursue our footsteps."

A thought came to him.

" There is one place," he said, " even in this island."

" Where ? "

" The place our Brothers have made over beyond there. They have made great banks about their house, north and south and east and west ; they have made deep pits and hidden places and even now—one came over to me quite recently. He said—I did not altogether heed what he said then. But he spoke of arms. It may be—there—we should find shelter. . . ."

" For many days," he said, after a pause, " I have not seen our Brothers. . . . Dear ! I have been dreaming. I have been forgetting ! The days have passed and I have done nothing but look to see you again. . . . I must go to them and talk to them and tell them of you and of all the things that hang over us. If they will help us, they can help us. Then indeed we might hope. I do not know how strong their place is, but certainly Cossar will have made it strong. Before all this— before you came to me, I remember now—there was trouble brewing. There was an election—when all the little people settled things by counting heads. It must be over now. There were threats against all our race, against all our race, that is, but you. I must see our Brothers. I must tell them all that has happened between us and all that threatens now."

V

He did not come to their next meeting until she had waited
some time. They were to meet that day about midday in a
great space of park that fitted into a bend of the river, and as
she waited, looking ever southward under her hand, it came to
her that the world was very still, that indeed it was broodingly
still. And then she perceived that, spite of the lateness of the
hour, her customary retinue of voluntary spies had failed her.
Left and right, when she came to look, there was no one in
sight, and there was never a boat upon the silver curve of the
Thames. She tried to find a reason for this strange stillness in
the world. . . .

Then, a grateful sight for her, she saw young Redwood far
away over a gap in the tree masses that bounded her view.

Immediately the trees hid him and presently he was thrusting through them and in sight again. She could see there was
something different, and then she saw that he was hurrying
unusually and then that he limped. He gestured to her and
she walked towards him. His face became clearer, and she
saw with infinite concern that he winced at every stride.

She was running now towards him, her mind full of questions
and vague fear. He drew near to her and spoke without a
greeting.

" Are we to part ? " he panted.

" No," she answered. " Why ? What is the matter ? "

" But if we do not part—— ! It is *now*."

" What is the matter ? "

" I do not want to part," he said. " Only——"

He broke off abruptly to ask, " You will not part from me ? "

She met his eyes with a steadfast look. " What has
happened ? " she pressed.

" Not for a time ? "

" What time ? "

" Years perhaps."

" Part ! No ! "

" You have thought ? " he insisted.

" I will not part." She took his hand. " If this meant
death, *now*, I would not let you go."

" If it meant death," he said, and she felt his grip upon her
fingers.

He looked about him as if he feared to see the little people
coming as he spoke. And then : " It may mean death."

" Now tell me," she said.

" They tried to stop my coming."

" How ? "

" And as I came out of my workshop where I make the
Food of the Gods for the Cossars to store in their camp, I
found a little officer of police—a man in blue with white clean
gloves—who beckoned me to stop. ' This way is closed ! '

said he.   I thought little of that ; I went round my workshop
to where another road runs west, and there was another
officer.   ' This road is closed ! ' he said, and added : ' all the
roads are closed ! ' "

" And then ? "

" I argued with him a little.   ' They are public roads ! ' "
I said.

" ' That's it,' said he.   ' You spoil them for the public.'

" ' Very well,' said I, ' I'll take the fields,' and then up leapt
others from behind a hedge and said, ' These fields are private.'

" ' Curse your public and private,' I said, ' I'm going to my
Princess,' and I stooped down and picked him up very gently
—kicking and shouting—and put him out of my way.   In a
minute all the fields about me seemed alive with running men.
I saw one on horseback galloping beside me and reading something as he rode—shouting it.   He finished and turned and
galloped away from me—head down.   I couldn't make it out.
And then behind me I heard the crack of guns."

" Guns ! "

" Guns—just as they shoot at the rats.   The bullets came
through the air with a sound like things tearing : one stung
me in the leg."

" And you ? "

" Came on to you here and left them shouting and running
and shooting behind me.   And now——"

" Now ? "

" It is only the beginning.   They mean that we shall part.
Even now they are coming after me."

" We will not."

" No.   But if we are not to part—then you must come with
me to our Brothers."

" Which way ? " she said.

" To the east.   Yonder is the way my pursuers will be
coming.   This then is the way we must go.   Along this avenue
of trees.   Let me go first, so that if they are waiting——"

He made a stride, but she had seized his arm.

" No," cried she.   " I come close to you, holding you.
Perhaps I am royal, perhaps I am sacred.   If I hold you——
Would God we could fly with my arms about you !—it may
be, they will not shoot at you——"

She clasped his shoulder and seized his hand as she spoke ;
she pressed herself nearer to him.   " It may be they will not
shoot you," she repeated, and with a sudden passion of
tenderness he took her into his arms and kissed her cheek.
For a space he held her.

" Even if it is death," she whispered.

She put her arms about his neck and lifted her face to his.
" Dearest, kiss me once more."

He drew her to him.   Silently they kissed one another on
the lips, and for another moment clung to one another.   Then

hand in hand, and she striving always to keep her body near to his, they set forward if haply they might reach the camp of refuge the sons of Cossar had made, before the pursuit of the little people overtook them.

And as they crossed the great spaces of the park behind the castle there came horsemen galloping out from among the trees and vainly seeking to keep pace with their giant strides. And presently ahead of them were houses and men with guns running out of the houses. At the sight of that, though he sought to go on and was even disposed to fight and push through, she made him turn aside towards the south.

As they fled a bullet whipped by them overhead.

CHAPTER THREE

YOUNG CADDLES IN LONDON

I

ALL unaware of the trend of events, unaware of the laws that were closing in upon all the Brethren, unaware indeed that there lived a Brother for him on the earth, young Caddles chose this time to come out of his chalk pit and see the world. His brooding came at last to that. There was no answer to all his questions in Cheasing Eyebright; the new Vicar was less luminous even than the old, and the riddle of his pointless labour grew at last to the dimensions of exasperation. "Why should I work in this pit day after day?" he asked. "Why should I walk within bounds and be refused all the wonders of the world beyond there? What have I done, to be condemned to this?"

And one day he stood up, straightened his back, and said in a loud voice, "No!

"I won't," he said, and then with great vigour cursed the pit.

Then having few words he sought to express his thought in acts. He took a truck half filled with chalk, lifted it and flung it, smash, against another. Then he grasped a whole row of empty trucks and spun them down a bank. He sent a huge boulder of chalk bursting among them, and then ripped up a dozen yards of rail with a mighty plunge of his foot. So he began the conscientious wrecking of the pit.

"Work all my days," he said, "at this!"

It was an astonishing five minutes for the little geologist he had, in his preoccupation, overlooked. This poor little creature having dodged two boulders by a hairsbreadth, got out by the westward corner and fled athwart the hill, with flapping rucksack and twinkling knickerbockered legs, leaving a trail of Cretaceous echinoderms behind him, while young Caddles, satisfied with the destruction he had achieved, came striding out to fulfil his purpose in the world.

"Work in that old pit, until I die and rot and stink! . . . What worm did they think was living in my giant body? Dig chalk for God knows what foolish purpose! Not *I*!"

The trend of road and railway perhaps, or mere chance it was, turned his face to London; and thither he came striding over the Downs and athwart the meadows, through the hot afternoon, to the infinite amazement of the world. It signified nothing to him that torn posters in red and white bearing various names flapped from every wall and barn; he knew nothing of the electoral revolution that had flung Caterham, "Jack the Giant-killer," into power. It signified nothing to

him that every police station along his route had what was
known as Caterham's ukase upon its notice-board that afternoon, proclaiming that no giant, no person whatever over
eight feet in height, should go more than five miles from his
" place of location " without a special permission.   It signified
nothing to him that on his wake belated police officers, not a
little relieved to find themselves belated, shook warning hand-
bills at his retreating back.   He was going to see what the
world had to show him, poor incredulous blockhead, and he
did not mean that occasional spirited persons shouting " Hi ! "
at him should stay his course.   He came on down by Rochester
and Greenwich towards an ever-thickening aggregation of
houses, walking rather slowly now, staring about him and
swinging his huge chopper.

People in London had heard something of him before, how
that he was idiotic but gentle, and wonderfully managed by
Lady Wondershoot's agent and the Vicar ; how in his dull
way he revered these authorities and was grateful to them for
their care of him, and so forth.   So that when they learnt
from the newspaper placards that afternoon that he also was
" on strike," the thing appeared to many of them as a
deliberate concerted act.

" They mean to try our strength," said the men in the
trains going home from business.

" Lucky we have Caterham."

" It's in answer to his proclamation."

The men in the clubs were better informed.   They clustered
round the tape or talked in groups in their smoking-rooms.

" He has no weapons.   He would have gone to Sevenoaks
if he had been put up to it."

" Caterham will handle him. . . ."

The shopmen told their customers.   The waiters in
restaurants snatched a moment for an evening paper between
the courses.   The cabmen read it immediately after the
betting news. . . .

The placards of the chief government evening paper were
conspicuous with " Grasping the Nettle."   Others relied for
effect on : " Giant Redwood continues to meet the Princess."
The *Echo* struck a line of its own with : " Rumoured Revolt
of Giants in the North of England.   The Sunderland Giants
Start for Scotland."   The *Westminster Gazette* sounded its
usual warning note.   " Giants Beware," said the *Westminster
Gazette*, and tried to make a point out of it that might perhaps
serve towards uniting the Liberal party—at that time greatly
torn between seven intensely egotistical leaders.   The later
newspapers dropped into uniformity.   " The Giant in the
New Kent Road," they proclaimed.

" What I want to know," said the pale young man in the
tea-shop, " is why we aren't getting any news of the young
Cossars.   You'd think they'd be in it most of all. . . ."

"They tell me there's another of them young giants got loose," said the barmaid, wiping out a glass. "I've always said they was dangerous things to 'ave about. Right away from the beginning. . . . It ought to be put a stop to. Any'ow, I 'ope 'e won't come along 'ere."

"I'd like to 'ave a look at 'im," said the young man at the bar recklessly, and added, "I *seen* the Princess."

"D'you think they'll 'urt 'im ?" said the barmaid.

"May 'ave to," said the young man at the bar, finishing his glass.

Amidst a hum of ten million such sayings young Caddles came to London. . . .

II

I think of young Caddles always as he was seen in the New Kent Road, the sunset warm upon his perplexed and staring face. The Road was thick with its varied traffic, omnibuses, trams, vans, carts, trolleys, cyclists, motors, and a marvelling crowd — loafers, women, nursemaids, shopping women, children, venturesome hobbledehoys—gathered behind his gingerly moving feet. The hoardings were untidy everywhere with the tattered election paper. A babblement of voices surged about him. One sees the customers and shopmen crowding in the doorways of the shops, the faces that came and went at the windows, the little street boys running and shouting, the policemen taking it all quite stiffly and calmly, the workmen knocking off upon scaffoldings, the seething miscellany of the little folks. They shouted to him, vague encouragement, vague insults, the imbecile catch-words of the day, and he stared down at them, at such a multitude of living creatures as he had never before imagined in the world.

Now that he had fairly entered London he had had to slacken his pace more and more, the little folks crowded so mightily upon him. The crowd grew denser at every step, and at last, at a corner where two great ways converged, he came to a stop and the multitude flowed about him and closed him in.

There he stood, with his feet a little apart, his back to a big corner gin palace that towered twice his height and ended in a sky sign, staring down at the pigmies and wondering, trying, I doubt not, to collate it all with the other things of his life, with the valley among the downlands, the nocturnal lovers, the singing in the church, the chalk he hammered daily, and with instinct and death and the sky, trying to get it all together coherent and significant. His brows were knit. He put up his huge paw to scratch his coarse hair, and groaned aloud.

"I don't see it," he said.

His accent was unfamiliar. A great babblement went across the open space, a babblement amidst which the gongs of the trams, ploughing their obstinate way through the mass,

rose like red poppies amidst corn. " What did he say ? "
" Said he didn't see." " Said, where is the sea ? " Said,
where is a seat ? " " He wants a seat." " Can't the brasted
fool sit on a 'ouse or somethin' ? "

" What are ye for, ye swarming little people ? What are
ye all doing, what are ye all for ?

" What are ye doing up here, ye swarming little people, while
I'm a-cuttin' chalk for ye, down in the chalk pits there ? "

His queer voice, the voice that had been so bad for school
discipline at Cheasing Eyebright, smote the multitude to
silence while it sounded and splashed them all to tumult at the
end. Some wit was audible screaming " Speech, speech ! "
" What's he saying ? " was the burthen of the public mind,
and an opinion was abroad that he was drunk. " Hi, hi, hi,"
bawled the omnibus drivers, threading a dangerous way. A
drunken American sailor wandered about tearfully inquiring,
" What's he want anyhow ? " A leathery-faced rag-dealer
upon a little pony-drawn cart soared up over the tumult by
virtue of his voice. " Garn 'ome, you Brasted Giant ! " he
brawled, " Garn 'ome ! You Brasted Great Dangerous
Thing ! Can't you see you're a-frightening the 'orses ? Go
'ome with you ? 'Asn't any one 'ad the sense to tell you the
law ? " And over all this uproar young Caddles stared,
perplexed, expectant, saying no more.

Down a side road came a little string of solemn policemen,
and threaded itself ingeniously into the traffic. " Stand back,"
said the little voices ; " keep moving, please."

Young Caddles became aware of a little dark blue figure
thumping at his shin.

He looked down. " *What ?* " he said, bending forward.

" Can't stand about here," shouted the inspector.

" No ! You can't stand about here," he repeated.

" But where am I to go ? "

" Back to your village. Place of location. Anyhow, now—
you've got to move on. You're obstructing the traffic."

" What traffic ? "

" Along the road."

" But where is it going ? Where does it come from ? What
does it mean ? They're all around me. What do they want ?
What are they doin' ? I want to understand. I'm tired of
cuttin' chalk and bein' all alone. What are they doin' for me
while I'm a-cuttin' chalk ? I may just as well understand
here and now, as anywhere."

" Sorry. But we aren't here to explain things of that sort.
I must arst you to move on."

" Don't you know ? "

" I must arst you to move on—*if* you please. . . . I'd
strongly advise you to get off 'ome. We've 'ad no special instructions yet—but it's against the law. . . . Clear away there.
Clear a-way."

The pavement to his left became invitingly bare, and young Caddles went slowly on his way. But now his tongue was loosened.

" I don't understand," he muttered. " I don't understand." He would appeal brokenly to the changing crowd that ever trailed beside him and behind. " I didn't know there were such places as this. What are all you people doing with yourselves ? What's it all for ? What is it all for and where do I come in ? "

He had already begotten a new catch-word. Young men of wit and spirit addressed each other in this manner, " Ullo Arry O'Cock. Wot's it all *for* ? Eh ? Wot's it all bloomin' well *for* ? "

To which there sprang up a competing variety of repartees, for the most part impolite. The most popular and best adapted for general use appears to have been " *Shut* it," or, in a voice of scornful detachment—

" *Garn !* "

III

What was he seeking ? He wanted something the pigmy world did not give, some end which the pigmy world prevented his attaining, prevented even his seeing clearly, which he was never to see clearly. It was the gigantic social side of this lonely dumb monster crying out for his race, for the things akin to him, for something he might love and something he might serve, for a purpose he might comprehend and a command he could obey. And, you know, all this was *dumb*, raged dumbly within him, could not even had he met a fellow-giant have found outlet and expression in speech. All the life he knew was the dull round of the village, all the speech he knew was the talk of the cottage, that failed and collapsed at the bare outline of his least gigantic need. He knew nothing of money, this monstrous simpleton, nothing of trade, nothing of the complex pretences upon which the social fabric of the little folks was built. He needed, he needed—— Whatever he needed, he never found his need.

All through the day and the summer night he wandered, growing hungry but as yet untired, marking the varied traffic of the different streets, the inexplicable businesses of all these infinitesimal beings. In the aggregate it had no other colour than confusion for him. . . .

He is said to have plucked a lady from her carriage in Kensington, a lady in evening dress of the smartest sort, to have scrutinised her closely, train and shoulder blades, and to have replaced her—a little carelessly—with the profoundest sigh. For that I cannot vouch. For an hour or so he watched people fighting for places in the omnibuses at the end of Piccadilly. He was seen looming over Kennington Oval for some moments in the afternoon, but when he saw these dense thousands were engaged with the mystery of cricket and quite regardless of him, he went his way with a groan.

He came back to Piccadilly Circus between eleven and twelve at night and found a new sort of multitude. Clearly they were very intent : full of things they, for inconceivable reasons, might do, and of others they might not do. They stared at him and jeered at him and went their way. The cabmen, vulture-eyed, followed one another continually along the edge of the swarming pavement. People emerged from the restaurants or entered them, grave, intent, dignified, or gently and agreeably excited, or keen and vigilant—beyond the cheating of the sharpest waiter born. The great giant, standing at his corner, peered at them all. "What is it all for ? " he murmured in a mournful vast undertone, " What is it all for ? They are all so earnest. What is it I do not understand ? "

And none of them seemed to see, as he could do, the drink-sodden wretchedness of the painted women at the corner, the ragged misery that sneaked along the gutters, the infinite futility of all this employment. The infinite futility ! None of them seemed to feel the shadow of that giant's need, that shadow of the future, that lay athwart their paths. . . .

Across the road high up mysterious letters flamed and went, that might, could he have read them, have measured for him the dimensions of human interest, have told him of the fundamental needs and features of life as the little folks conceived it. First would come a flaming

T ;

Then U would follow.

T U ;

Then P,

T U P ;

Until at last there stood complete, across the sky, this cheerful message to all who felt the burthen of life's earnestness :

TUPPER'S TONIC WINE FOR VIGOUR.

Snap ! and it had vanished into night, to be followed in the same slow development by a second universal solicitude :

BEAUTY SOAP.

Not, you remark, mere cleansing chemicals, but something, as they say, "ideal " ; and then, completing the tripod of the little life :

YANKER'S YELLOW PILLS.

After that there was nothing for it but Tupper again, in flaming crimson letters, snap, snap, across the void :

T   U   P   P   :   :   :   :

Early in the small hours it would seem that young Caddles came to the shadowy quiet of Regent's Park, stepped over the railings and lay down on a grassy slope near where the people skate in winter-time, and there he slept an hour or so. And about six o'clock in the morning he was talking to a draggled woman he had found sleeping in a ditch near Hampstead Heath, asking her very earnestly what she thought she was for. . . .

IV

The wandering of Caddles about London came to a head on the second day in the morning. For then his hunger overcame him. He hesitated where the hot-smelling loaves were being tossed into a cart, and then very quietly knelt down and commenced robbery. He emptied the cart while the baker's man fled for the police, and then his great hand came into the shop and cleared counter and cases. Then with an armful, still eating, he went his way, looking for another shop to go on with his meal. It happened to be one of those seasons when work is scarce and food dear, and the crowd in that quarter was sympathetic even with a giant who took the food they all desired. They applauded the second phase of his meal, and laughed at his stupid grimace at the policeman.

" I woff hungry," he said, with his mouth full.

" Brayvo ! " cried the crowd. " Brayvo ! "

Then when he was beginning his third baker's shop, he was stopped by half a dozen policemen hammering with truncheons at his shins. " Look here, my fine giant, you come along o' me," said the officer in charge. " You ain't allowed away from home like this. You come off home with me."

They did their best to arrest him. There was a trolley, I am told, chasing up and down the streets at that time, bearing rolls of chain and ships' cable to play the part of handcuffs in that great arrest. There was no intention then of killing him. " He is no party to the plot," Caterham had said. " I will not have innocent blood upon my hands."

At first Caddles did not understand the import of these attentions. When he did, he told the policemen not to be fools and set off in great strides that left them all behind. The bakers' shops had been in the Harrow Road, and he went through canal London to St. John's Wood and sat down in a private garden there to pick his teeth and be speedily assailed by another posse of constables.

" You lea' me alone," he growled, and slouched through the gardens—spoiling several lawns and kicking down a fence or so, while the energetic little policemen followed him up, some through the gardens, some along the road in front of the houses. Here there were one or two with guns, but they made no use of them. When he came out into the Edgware Road there was a new note and a new movement in the crowd, and a mounted policeman rode over his foot and got upset for his pains.

"You lea' me alone," said Caddles, facing the breathless crowd. "I've done nothing to you!"

At that time he was unarmed, for he had left his chalk chopper in Regent's Park. But now, poor wretch, he seems to have felt the need of some weapon. He turned back towards the goods yard of the Great Western Railway, wrenched up the standard of a tall arc light, a formidable mace for him, and flung it over his shoulder. And finding the police still turning up to pester him, he went back along the Edgware Road, towards Cricklewood, and struck off sullenly to the north.

He wandered as far as Waltham, and then turned back westward and then again towards London, and came by the cemeteries and over the crest of Highgate about midday into view of the greatness of the city again. He turned aside, and sat down in a garden with his back to a house that overlooked all London. He was breathless, and his face was lowering, and now the people no longer crowded upon him as they had done when first he came to London, but lurked in the adjacent garden, and peeped from cautious securities. They knew by now the thing was grimmer than they had thought. "Why can't they lea' me alone," growled young Caddles. "I *mus'* eat. Why can't they lea' me alone."

He sat with a darkling face, gnawing at his knuckles and looking down over London. All the fatigue, worry, perplexity, and impotent wrath of his wanderings was coming to a head in him. "They mean nothing," he whispered. "They mean nothing. And they *won't* let me alone, and they *will* get in my way." And again, over and over to himself, "meanin' nothing.

"Ugh! the little people!"

He bit harder at his knuckles and his scowl deepened. "Cuttin' chalk for 'em," he whispered. "And all the world is theirs! *I* don't come in—anywhere."

Presently with a spasm of sick anger he saw the now familiar form of a policeman astride the garden wall.

"Leave me alone," grunted the giant. "Leave me alone."

"I got to do my duty," said the little policeman, with a face that was white and resolute.

"You leave me alone. I got to live as well as you. I got to think. I got to eat. You lea' me alone."

"It's the Law," said the little policeman, coming no further. "We never made the Law."

"Nor me," said young Caddles. "Your little people made all that before I was born. You and your law! What I must and what I mustn't. No food for me to eat unless I work a slave, no rest, no shelter, nothin', and you tell me——"

"I ain't got no business with that," said the policeman. "I'm not one to argue. All I got to do is to carry out the

law." And he brought his second leg over the wall and seemed
disposed to get down. Other policemen appeared behind him.

"I got no quarrel with *you*—mind," said young Caddles,
with his grip tight upon his huge mace of iron, his face pale,
and a lank explanatory great finger to the policeman. "I got
no quarrel with you. But—*you lea' me alone*."

The policeman tried to be calm and commonplace, with a
monstrous tragedy clear before his eyes. "Give me the proclamation," he said to some unseen follower, and a little white
paper was handed to him.

"Lea' me alone," said Caddles, scowling, tense, and drawn
together.

"This means," said the policeman before he read, "go 'ome.
Go 'ome to your chalk pit. If not, you'll be hurt."

Caddles gave an inarticulate growl.

Then when the proclamation had been read, the officer made
a sign. Four men with rifles came into view and took up
positions of affected ease along the wall. They wore the uniform of the rat police. At the sight of the guns, young Caddles
blazed into anger. He remembered the sting of the Wreckstone farmers' shot-guns. "You going to shoot off those at
me?" he said, pointing, and it seemed to the officer he must
be afraid.

"If you don't march back to your pit——"

Then in an instant the officer had slung himself back over
the wall, and sixty feet above him the great electric standard
whirled down to his death. Bang, bang, bang, went the heavy
guns, and smash! the shattered wall, the soil and sub-soil of
the garden flew. Something flew with it, that left red drops on
one of the shooter's hands. The riflemen dodged this way and
that and turned valiantly to fire again. But young Caddles,
already shot twice through the body, had spun about to find
who it was had hit him so heavily in the back. Bang! Bang!
He had a vision of houses and greenhouses and gardens, of
people dodging at windows, the whole swaying fearfully and
mysteriously. He seems to have made three stumbling strides,
to have raised and dropped his huge mace, and to have clutched
his chest. He was stung and wrenched by pain.

What was this, warm and wet, on his hand? . . .

One man peering from a bedroom window saw his face, saw
him staring, with a grimace of weeping dismay, at the blood
upon his hand, and then his knees bent under him, and he
came crashing to the earth, the first of the giant nettles to fall
to Caterham's resolute clutch, the very last that he had
reckoned would come into his hand.

CHAPTER FOUR

REDWOOD'S TWO DAYS

I

So soon as Caterham knew the moment for grasping his nettle had come, he took the law into his own hands and sent to arrest Cossar and Redwood.

Redwood was there for the taking. He had been undergoing an operation in the side, and the doctors had kept all disturbing things from him until his convalescence was assured. Now they had released him. He was just out of bed, sitting in a fire-warmed room with a heap of newspapers about him, reading for the first time of the agitation that had swept the country into the hands of Caterham, and of the trouble that was darkening over the Princess and his son. It was in the morning of the day when young Caddles died, and when the policeman tried to stop young Redwood on his way to the Princess. The latest newspapers Redwood had did but vaguely prefigure these imminent things. He was re-reading these first adumbrations of disaster with a sinking heart, reading the shadow of death more and more perceptibly into them, reading to occupy his mind until further news should come. When the officers followed the servant into his room, he looked up eagerly.

" I thought it was an early evening paper," he said.

Then standing up, and with a swift change of manner : " What's this ? . . ."

After that Redwood had no news of anything for two days.

They had come with a vehicle to take him away, but when it became evident that he was ill, it was decided to leave him for a day or so until he could be safely removed, and his house was taken over by the police and converted into a temporary prison. It was the same house in which Giant Redwood had been born and in which Herakleophorbia had for the first time been given to a human being, and Redwood had now been a widower and had lived alone in it eight years.

He had become an iron-grey man, with a little pointed grey beard and still active brown eyes. He was slender and soft-voiced, as he had ever been, but his features had now that indefinable quality that comes of brooding over mighty things. To the arresting officer his appearance was in impressive contrast to the enormity of his offences. " Here's this feller," said the officer in command to his next subordinate, " has done his level best to bust up everything, and 'e's got a face like a quiet country gentleman ; and here's Judge Hangbrow keepin' everything nice and in order for every one, and 'e's got a 'ead like a 'og. Then their manners! One all consideration and the other snort and grunt. Which just shows you, doesn't it, that appearances aren't to be gone upon, whatever else you do."

But his praise of Redwood's consideration was presently dashed. The officers found him troublesome at first until they had made it clear that it was useless for him to ask questions or beg for papers. They made a sort of inspection of his study indeed and cleared away even the papers he had. Redwood's voice was high and expostulatory. "But don't you see," he said over and over again, "it's my son, my only son, that is in this trouble. It isn't the Food I care for, but my son."

"I wish indeed I could tell you, Sir," said the officer.

"But our orders are strict."

"Who gave the orders?" cried Redwood.

"Ah, *that*, Sir——" said the officer, and moved towards the door. . . .

"'E's going up and down 'is room," said the second officer, when his superior came down. "That's all right. He'll walk it off a bit."

"I hope 'e will," said the chief officer. "The fact is I didn't see it in that light before, but this here Giant what's been going on with the Princess, you know, is this man's son."

The two regarded one another and the third policeman for a space.

"Then it is a bit rough on him," the third policeman said.

It became evident that Redwood had still imperfectly apprehended the fact that an iron curtain had dropped between him and the outer world. They heard him go to the door, try the handle and rattle the lock, and then the voice of the officer who was stationed on the landing telling him it was no good to do that. Then afterwards they heard him at the windows and saw the men outside looking up. "It's no good that way," said the second officer. Then Redwood began upon the bell. The senior officer went up and explained very patiently that it could do no good to ring the bell like that, and if it was rung for nothing now it might have to be disregarded presently when he had need of something. "Any reasonable attendance, Sir," the officer said. "But if you ring it just by way of protest we shall be obliged, Sir, to disconnect."

The last word the officer heard was Redwood's high-pitched, "But at least you might tell me if my son——"

II

After that Redwood spent most of his time at the windows. But the windows offered him little of the march of events outside. It was a quiet street at all times, and that day it was unusually quiet. Scarcely a cab, scarcely a tradesman's cart passed all that morning. Now and then men went by—without any distinctive air of events—now and then a little group of children, a nursemaid and a woman going shopping, and so forth. They came on to the stage right or left, up or down the street, with an exasperating suggestion of indifference to any concerns more spacious than their own ; they would discover the police-guarded house with amazement and exit in the opposite direction, where the great trusses of a giant hydrangea hung across the pavement, staring back or pointing. Now and then a man would come and ask one of the policemen a question and get a curt reply. . . .

Opposite the houses seemed dead. A housemaid appeared once at a bedroom window and stared for a space, and it occurred to Redwood to signal to her. For a time she watched his gestures as if with interest and made a vague response to them, then looked over her shoulder suddenly and turned and went away. An old man hobbled out of Number 37 and came down the steps and went off to the right, altogether without looking up. For ten minutes the only occupant of the road was a cat. . . .

With such events that interminable momentous morning lengthened out.

About twelve there came a bawling of newsvendors from the adjacent road ; but it passed. Contrary to their wont they left Redwood's street alone, and a suspicion dawned upon him that the police were guarding the end of the street. He tried to open the window, but this brought a policeman into the room forthwith. . . .

The clock of the parish church struck twelve, and after an abyss of time—one.

They mocked him with lunch.

He ate a mouthful and tumbled the food about a little in order to get it taken away, drank freely of whisky, and then took a chair and went back to the window. The minutes expanded into grey immensities, and for a time perhaps he slept. . . .

He awoke with a vague impression of remote concussions. He perceived a rattling of the windows like the quiver of an earthquake, that lasted for a minute or so and died away. Then after a silence it returned. . . . Then it died away again. He fancied it might be merely the passage of some heavy vehicle along the main road. What else could it be ? . . .

After a time he began to doubt whether he had heard this sound.

He began to reason interminably with himself. Why after all was he seized ? Caterham had been in office two days— just long enough—to grasp his Nettle ! Grasp his Nettle ! Grasp his Giant Nettle ! The refrain once started, sang through his mind and would not be dismissed.

What after all could Caterham do ? He was a religious man. He was bound in a sort of way by that not to do violence without a cause.

Grasp his Nettle ! Perhaps for example the Princess was to be seized and sent abroad. There might be trouble with his son. In which case—— ! But why had he been arrested ? Why was it necessary to keep him in ignorance of a thing like that ? The thing suggested—something more extensive.

Perhaps, for example—they meant to lay all the giants by the heels. They were all to be arrested together. There had been hints of that in the election speeches. And then ?

No doubt they had got Cossar also !

Caterham was a religious man. Redwood clung to that. The back of his mind was a black curtain, and on that curtain there came and went a word—a word written in letters of fire. He struggled perpetually against that word. It was always as it were beginning to get written on the curtain and never getting completed.

He faced it at last. " Massacre ! " There was the word in its full brutality.

No ! No ! No ! It was impossible ! Caterham was a religious man, a civilised man. And besides after all these years, after all these hopes !

Redwood sprang up ; he paced the room. He spoke to himself ; he shouted.

" No ! "

Mankind was surely not so mad as that—surely not ! It was impossible, it was incredible, it could not be. What good would it do, to kill the giant human when the gigantic in all the lower things had now inevitably come ? They could not be so mad as that !

" I must dismiss such an idea," he said aloud ; " dismiss such an idea ! Absolutely ! "

He pulled up short. What was that ?

Certainly the windows had rattled. He went to look out into the street. Opposite he saw the instant confirmation of his ears. At a bedroom at Number 35 was a woman, towel in hand, and at the dining-room of Number 37 a man was visible behind a great vase of hypertrophied maidenhair fern, both staring out and up, both disquieted and curious. He could see now, too, quite clearly that the policeman on the pavement had heard it also. The thing was not his imagination.

He turned to the darkling room.

" Guns," he said.

He brooded.

" Guns ? "

They brought him in strong tea, such as he was accustomed to have. It was evident his housekeeper had been taken into consultation. After drinking it, he was too restless to sit any longer at the window and he paced the room. His mind became more capable of consecutive thought.

The room had been his study for four-and-twenty years. It had been furnished at his marriage, and all the essential equipment dated from then, the large complex writing-desk, the rotating chair, the easy chair at the fire, the rotating bookcase, the fixture of indexed pigeon-holes that filled the farther recess. The vivid Turkey carpet, the later Victorian rugs and curtains had mellowed now to a rich dignity of effect, and copper and brass shone warm about the open fire. Electric lights had replaced the lamp of former days ; that was the chief alteration in the original equipment. But among these things his connection with the Food had left abundant traces. Along one wall, above the dado, ran a crowded array of blackframed photographs and photogravures, showing his son and Cossar's sons and others of the Boom-children at various ages and amidst various surroundings. Even young Caddles' vacant visage had its place in that collection. In the corner stood a sheaf of the tassels of gigantic meadow grass from Cheasing Eyebright, and on the desk there lay three empty poppy heads as big as hats. The curtain rods were grass stems. And the tremendous skull of the great hog of Oakham hung, a portentous ivory overmantel, with a Chinese jar in either eye socket, snout down above the fire. . . .

It was to the photographs that Redwood went, and in particular to the photographs of his son.

They brought back countless memories of things that had passed out of his mind, of the early days of the Food, of Bensington's timid presence, of his cousin Jane, of Cossar and the night work at the Experimental Farm. These things came to him now very little and bright and distinct, like things seen through a telescope on a sunny day. And then there was the giant nursery, the giant childhood, the young giant's first efforts to speak, his first clear signs of affection.

Guns ?

It flowed in on him, irresistibly, overwhelmingly, that outside there, outside this accursed silence and mystery, his son and Cossar's sons and all these glorious first fruits of a greater age were even now—fighting. Fighting for life ! Even now his son might be in some dismal quandary, cornered, wounded, overcome. . . .

He swung away from the pictures and went up and down the room gesticulating. " It cannot be," he cried, " it cannot be ! It cannot end like that !

" What was that ? "

He stopped, stricken rigid.

The trembling of the windows had begun again, and then had come a thud—a vast concussion that shook the house. The concussion seemed to last for an age. It must have been very near. For a moment it seemed that something had struck the house above him—an enormous impact that broke into a tinkle of falling glass and then a stillness that ended at last with a minute clear sound of running feet in the street below.

Those feet released him from his rigor. He turned towards the window and saw it starred and broken.

His heart beat high with a sense of crisis, of conclusive occurrence, of release. And then again, his realisation of impotent confinement fell about him like a curtain !

He could see nothing outside except that the small electric lamp opposite was not lighted ; he could hear nothing after the first suggestion of a wide alarm. He could add nothing to interpret or enlarge that mystery except that presently there came a reddish fluctuating brightness in the sky towards the south-east.

This light waxed and waned. When it waned he doubted if it had ever waxed. It had crept upon him very gradually with the darkling. It became the predominant fact in his long night of suspense. Sometimes it seemed to him it had the quiver one associates with dancing flames ; at others he fancied it was no more than the normal reflection of the evening lights. It waxed and waned through the long hours and only vanished at last when it was submerged altogether under the rising tide of dawn. Did it mean—— ? What could it mean ? Almost certainly it was some sort of fire, near or remote, but he could not even tell whether it was smoke or cloud drift that streamed across the sky. But about one o'clock there began a flickering of searchlights athwart that ruddy tumult, a flickering that continued for the rest of the night. That too might mean many things ? What could it mean ? What did it mean ? Just this stained unrestful sky he had and the suggestion of a huge explosion to occupy his mind. There came no further sounds, no further running, nothing but a shouting that might have been only the efforts of distant drunken men. . . .

He did not turn up his lights ; he stood at his draughty broken window a distressful, slight black outline to the officer who looked ever and again into the room and exhorted him to rest.

All night Redwood remained at his window peering up at the ambiguous drift of the sky, and only with the coming of the dawn did he obey his fatigue and lie down upon the little bed they had prepared for him between his writing-desk and the sinking fire in the fireplace under the great hog's skull.

III

For thirty-six long hours did Redwood remain imprisoned, closed in and shut off from the great drama of the Two Days, while the little people in the dawn of greatness fought against the Children of the Food. Then abruptly the iron curtain rose again and he found himself near the very centre of the struggle. That curtain rose as unexpectedly as it had fallen. In the late afternoon he was called to the window by the clatter of a cab, that stopped without. A young man descended and in another minute stood before him in the room, a slightly built young man of thirty perhaps, clean shaven, well dressed, well mannered.

"Mr. Redwood, Sir," he began, "would you be willing to come to Mr. Caterham ? He needs your presence very urgently."

"Needs my presence ! . . ." There leapt a question into Redwood's mind, that for a moment he could not put. He hesitated. Then in a voice that broke he asked, "What has he done to my son ? " and stood breathless for the reply.

"Your son, Sir ? Your son is doing well. So at least we gather."

"Doing well ? "

He was wounded, Sir, yesterday. Have you not heard ? "

Redwood smote these pretences aside. His voice was no longer coloured by fear, but by anger. "You know I have not heard. You know I have heard nothing."

"Mr. Caterham feared, Sir—— It was a time of upheaval. Every one—taken by surprise. He arrested you to save you, Sir, from any misadventure——"

"He arrested me to prevent my giving any warning or advice to my son. Go on. Tell me what has happened. Have you succeeded ? Have you killed them all ? "

The young man made a pace or so towards the window, and turned.

"No, Sir," he said concisely.

"What have you to tell me ? "

"It's our proof, Sir, that this fighting was not planned by us. They found us . . . totally unprepared."

"You mean ? "

"I mean, Sir, the giants have—to a certain extent—held their own."

The world changed for Redwood. For a moment something like hysteria had the muscles of his face and throat. Then he gave vent to a profound "Ah ! " His heart bounded towards exultation. "The giants have held their own ! "

"There has been terrible fighting—terrible destruction. It is all a most hideous misunderstanding. . . . In the north and midlands giants have been killed. . . . Everywhere."

"They are fighting now ? "

"No, Sir. There was a flag of truce."

"From them ? "

"No, Sir. Mr. Caterham sent a flag of truce. The whole thing is a hideous misunderstanding. That is why he wants to talk to you, and put his case before you. They insist, Sir, that you should intervene——"

Redwood interrupted. "Do you know what happened to my son ? " he asked.

"He was wounded."

"Tell me ! Tell me ! "

" He and the Princess came—before the—the movement to surround the Cossar camp was complete—the Cossar pit at Chislehurst. They came suddenly, Sir, crashing through a dense thicket of giant oats, near River, upon a column of infantry. . . . Soldiers had been very nervous all day, and this produced a panic."

" They shot him ? "

" No, Sir. They ran away. Some shot at him—wildly—against orders."

Redwood gave a note of denial.

" It's true, Sir. Not on account of your son, I won't pretend, but on account of the Princess."

" Yes. That's true."

" The two giants ran shouting towards the encampment. The soldiers ran this way and that, and then some began firing. They say they saw him stagger——"

" Ugh ! "

" Yes, Sir. But we know he is not badly hurt."

" How ? "

" He sent the message, Sir, that he was doing well ! "

" To me ? "

" Who else, Sir ? "

Redwood stood for nearly a minute with his arms tightly folded, taking this in. Then his indignation found a voice.

" Because you were fools in doing the thing, because you miscalculated and blundered, you would like me to think you are not murderers in intention. And besides—— The rest ? "

The young man looked interrogation.

" The other giants ? "

The young man made no further pretence of misunderstanding. His tone fell. " Thirteen, Sir, are dead."

" And others wounded ? "

" Yes, Sir."

" And Caterham," he gasped, " wants to meet me ! . . . Where are the others ? "

" Some got to the encampment during the fighting, Sir. . . . They seem to have known——"

" Well, of course they did. If it hadn't been for Cossar—— Cossar is there ? "

" Yes, Sir. And all the surviving giants are there—the ones who didn't get to the camp in the fighting have gone, or are going now under the flag of truce."

" That means," said Redwood, " that you are beaten."

" We are not beaten. No, Sir. You cannot say we are beaten. But your sons have broken the rules of war. Once last night, and now again. After our attack had been withdrawn. This afternoon they began to bombard London——"

" That's legitimate ! "

" They have been firing shells filled with—poison."

" Poison ? "

" Yes. Poison. The Food——"

" Herakleophorbia ? "

" Yes, Sir. Mr. Caterham, Sir——"

" You are beaten ! Of course that beats you. It's Cossar ! What can you hope to do now ? What good is it to do anything now ? You will breathe it in the dust of every street. What is there to fight for more ? Rules of war, indeed ! And now Caterham wants to humbug me to help him bargain. Good heavens, man ! Why should I come to your exploded windbag ? He has played his game . . . murdered and muddled. Why should I ? "

The young man stood with an air of vigilant respect.

" It is a fact, Sir," he interrupted, " that the giants insist that they shall see you. They will have no ambassador but you. Unless you come to them, I am afraid, Sir, there will be more bloodshed."

" On *your* side, perhaps."

" No, Sir—on both sides. The world is resolved the thing must end."

Redwood looked about the study. His eyes rested for a moment on the photograph of his boy. He turned and met the expectation of the young man.

" Yes," he said at last, " I will come."

IV

His encounter with Caterham was entirely different from his anticipation. He had seen the man only twice in his life, once at dinner and once in the lobby of the House, and his imagination had been active not with the man but with the creation of the newspapers and caricaturists, the legendary Caterham, Jack the Giant-Killer, Perseus, and all the rest of it. The element of a human personality came in to disorder all that.

Here was not the face of the caricatures and portraits, but the face of a worn and sleepless man, lined and drawn, yellow in the whites of the eyes, a little weakened about the mouth. Here, indeed, were the red-brown eyes, the black hair, the distinctive aquiline profile of the great demagogue, but here was also something else that smote any premeditated scorn and rhetoric aside. This man was suffering ; he was suffering acutely ; he was under enormous stress. From the beginning he had an air of impersonating himself. Presently, with a single gesture, the slightest movement, he revealed to Redwood that he was keeping himself up with drugs. He moved a thumb to his waistcoat pocket, and then, after a few sentences more, threw concealment aside, and slipped the little tabloid to his lips.

Moreover, in spite of the stresses upon him, in spite of the fact that he was in the wrong, and Redwood's junior by a dozen years, that strange quality in him, the something—personal magnetism one may call it for want of a better name—that had won his way for him to this eminence of disaster was with him still. On that also Redwood had failed to reckon. From the first, so far as the course and conduct of their speech went, Caterham prevailed over Redwood. All the quality of the first phase of their meeting was determined by him, all the tone and procedure was his. That happened as if it was a matter of course. All Redwood's expectations vanished at his presence. He shook hands before Redwood remembered that he meant to parry that familiarity ; he pitched the note of their conference from the outset, sure and clear, as a search for expedients under a common catastrophe.

If he made any mistake it was when ever and again his fatigue got the better of his immediate attention, and the habit of the public meeting carried him away. Then he drew himself up—through all their interview both men stood—and looked away from Redwood, and began to fence and justify. Once even he said " Gentlemen ! "

Quietly, expandingly, he began to talk. . . .

There were moments when Redwood ceased even to feel himself an interlocutor, when he became the mere auditor of a monologue. He became the privileged spectator of an extraordinary phenomenon. He perceived something almost like a specific difference between himself and this being whose beautiful voice enveloped him, who was talking, talking. This mind before him was so powerful and so limited. From its driving energy, its personal weight, its invincible oblivion to certain things, there sprang up in Redwood's mind the most grotesque and strange of images. Instead of an antagonist who was a fellow-creature, a man one could hold morally responsible, and to whom one could address reasonable appeals, he saw Caterham as something, something like a monstrous rhinoceros, as it were, a civilised rhinoceros begotten of the jungle of democratic affairs, a monster of irresistible onset and invincible resistance. In all the crashing conflicts of that tangle he was supreme. And beyond ? This man was a being supremely adapted to make his way through multitudes of men. For him there was no fault so important as self-contradiction, no science so significant as the reconciliation of " interests." Economic realities, topographical necessities, the barely touched mines of scientific expedients existed for him no more than railways or rifled guns or geographical literature exist for his animal prototype. What did exist were gatherings, and caucuses, and votes—above all votes. He was votes incarnate—millions of votes.

And now in the great crisis, with the giants broken but not beaten, this vote-monster talked.

It was so evident that even now he had everything to learn. He did not know there were physical laws and economic laws, quantities and reactions that all humanity voting *nemine contradicente* cannot vote away, and that are disobeyed only at the price of destruction. He did not know there are moral laws that cannot be bent by any force of glamour, or are bent only to fly back with vindictive violence. In the face of shrapnel or the Judgment Day, it was evident to Redwood that this man would have sheltered behind some curiously dodged vote of the House of Commons.

What most concerned his mind now was not the powers that held the fastness away there to the south, not defeat and death, but the effect of these things upon his Majority, the cardinal reality in his life. He had to defeat the giants or go under. He was by no means absolutely despairful. In this hour of his utmost failure, with blood and disaster upon his hands, and the rich promise of still more horrible disaster, with the gigantic destinies of the world towering and toppling over him, he was capable of a belief that by sheer exertion of his voice, by explaining and qualifying and restating, he might yet reconstitute his power. He was puzzled and distressed no doubt, fatigued and suffering, but if only he could keep up, if only he could keep talking——

As he talked he seemed to Redwood to advance and recede, to dilate and contract. Redwood's share of the talk was of the most subsidiary sort, wedges as it were suddenly thrust in. "That's all nonsense." "No." "It's no use suggesting that." "Then why did you begin?"

It is doubtful if Caterham really heard him at all. Round such interpolations Caterham's speech flowed indeed like some swift stream about a rock. There this incredible man stood, on his official hearthrug, talking, talking with enormous power and skill, talking as though a pause in his talk, his explanations, his presentation of standpoints and lights, of considerations and expedients, would permit some antagonistic influence to leap into being—into vocal being, the only being he could comprehend. There he stood amidst the slightly faded splendours of that official room in which one man after another had succumbed to the belief that a certain power of intervention was the creative control of an empire. . . .

The more he talked the more certain Redwood's sense of stupendous futility grew. Did this man realise that while he stood and talked there, the whole great world was moving, that the invincible tide of growth flowed and flowed, that there were any hours but parliamentary hours, or any weapons in the hands of the Avengers of Blood? Outside, darkling the whole room, a single leaf of giant Virginian creeper tapped unheeded on the pane.

Redwood became anxious to end this amazing monologue, to escape to sanity and judgment, to that beleaguered camp, the fastness of the future, where, at the very nucleus of greatness, the Sons were gathered together. For that this talking was endured. He had a curious impression that unless this monologue ended he would presently find himself carried away by it, that he must fight against Caterham's voice as one fights against a drug. Facts had altered and were altering beneath that spell.

What was the man saying?

Since Redwood had to report it to the Children of the Food in a sort of way he perceived it did matter. He would have to listen and guard his sense of realities as well as he could.

Much about bloodguiltiness. That was eloquence. That didn't matter. Next?

He was suggesting a convention!

He was suggesting that the surviving Children of the Food should capitulate and go apart and form a community of their own. There were precedents, he said, for this. " We would assign them territory——"

" Where?" interjected Redwood, stooping to argue.

Caterham snatched at that concession. He turned his face to Redwood's and his voice fell to a persuasive reasonableness. That could be determined. That he contended was a quite subsidiary question. Then he went on to stipulate: " And except for them and where they are we must have absolute control, the Food and all the Fruits of the Food must be stamped out——"

Redwood found himself bargaining: " The Princess?"

" She stands apart."

" No," said Redwood, struggling to get back to the old footing. " That's absurd."

" That afterwards. At any rate we are agreed that the making of the Food must stop——"

" I have agreed to nothing. I have said nothing——"

" But on one planet, to have two races of men, one great, one small! Consider what has happened! Consider that is but a little foretaste of what might presently happen if this Food has its way! Consider all you have already brought upon this world! If there is to be a race of giants, increasing and multiplying——"

" It is not for me to argue," said Redwood. " I must go to our sons. I want to go to my son. That is why I have come to you. Tell me exactly what you offer."

Caterham made a speech upon his terms.

The Children of the Food were to be given a great reservation—in North America perhaps or Africa—in which they might live out their lives in their own fashion.

" But it's nonsense," said Redwood. " There are other giants now abroad. All over Europe—here and there!"

" There could be an international convention. It's *not* impossible. Something of the sort indeed has already been spoken of. . . . But in this reservation they can live out their own lives in their own way. They may do what they like ; they may make what they like. We shall be glad if they will make us things. They may be happy. Think!"

" Provided there are no more children."

" Precisely. The children are for us. And so, Sir, we shall save the world, we shall save it abolsutely from the fruits of your terrible discovery. It is not too late for us. Only we are eager to temper expediency with mercy. Even now we are burning and searing the places their shells hit yesterday. We can get it under. Trust me we shall get it under. But in that way, without cruelty, without injustice——"

" And suppose the Children do not agree ? "

For the first time Caterham looked Redwood fully in the face.

" They must ! "

" I don't think they will."

" Why should they not agree ? " he asked, in richly toned amazement.

" Suppose they don't ? "

" What can it be but war ? We cannot have the thing go on. We cannot, Sir. Have you scientific men *no* imagination ? Have you no mercy ? We cannot have our world trampled under a growing herd of such monsters and monstrous growths as your food has made. We cannot and we cannot ! I ask you, Sir, what can it be but war ? And remember—this that has happened is only a beginning ! *This* was a skirmish. A mere affair of police. Believe me, a mere affair of police. Do not be cheated by perspective, by the immediate bigness of these newer things. Behind us is the nation —is humanity. Behind the thousands who have died there are millions. Were it not for the fear of bloodshed, Sir, behind our first attacks there would be forming other attacks, even now. Whether we can kill this Food or not, most assuredly we can kill your sons ! You reckon too much on the things of yesterday, on the happenings of a mere score of years, on one battle. You have no sense of the slow course of history. I offer this convention for the sake of lives, not because it can change the inevitable end. If you think that your poor two dozen of giants can resist all the forces of our people and of all the alien peoples who will come to our aid ; if you think you can change Humanity at a blow, in a single generation, and alter the nature and stature of Man——"

He flung out an arm. " Go to them now, Sir ! See them, for all the evil they have done, crouching among their wounded——"

He stopped, as though he had glanced at Redwood's son by chance.

There came a pause.

" Go to them," he said.

" That is what I want to do."

" Then go now. . . ."

He turned and pressed the button of a bell ; without, in immediate response, came a sound of opening doors and hastening feet.

The talk was at an end.   The display was over.   Abruptly Caterham seemed to contract, to shrivel up into a yellow-faced, fagged-out, middle-sized, middle-aged man.   He stepped forward, as if he were stepping out of a picture, and with a complete assumption of that friendliness that lies behind all the public conflicts of our race, he held out his hand to Redwood.

As if it were a matter of course, Redwood shook hands with him for the second time.

CHAPTER FIVE

I

PRESENTLY Redwood found himself in a train going south over the Thames. He had a brief vision of the river shining under its lights, and of the smoke still going up from the place where the shell had fallen on the north bank, and where a vast multitude of men had been organised to burn the Herakleophorbia out of the ground. The southern bank was dark, for some reason even the streets were not lit ; all that was clearly visible were the outlines of the tall alarm-towers and the dark bulks of flats and schools, and after a minute of peering scrutiny he turned his back on the window and sank into thought. There was nothing more to see or do until he saw the Sons. . . .

He was fatigued by the stresses of the last two days ; it seemed to him that his emotions must needs be exhausted, but he had fortified himself with strong coffee before starting, and his thoughts ran thin and clear. His mind touched many things. He reviewed again, but now in the enlightenment of accomplished events, the manner in which the Food had entered and unfolded itself in the world.

" Bensington thought it might be an excellent food for infants," he whispered to himself, with a faint smile. Then there came into his mind as vivid as if they were still unsettled his own horrible doubts after he had committed himself by giving it to his own son. From that, with a steady unfaltering expansion, in spite of every effort of men to help and hinder, the Food had spread through the whole world of man. And now ?

" Even if they kill them all," Redwood whispered, " the thing is done."

The secret of its making was known far and wide. That had been his own work. Plants, animals, a multitude of distressful growing children would conspire irresistibly to force the world to revert again to the Food, whatever happened in the present struggle. " The thing is done," he said, with his mind swinging round beyond all his controlling to rest upon the present fate of the Children and his son. Would he find them exhausted by the efforts of the battle, wounded, starving, on the verge of defeat; or would he find them still stout and hopeful, ready for the still grimmer conflict of the morrow ? . . . His son was wounded ! But he had sent a message !

His mind came back to his interview with Caterham.

He was roused from his thoughts by the stopping of his train in Chislehurst station. He recognised the place by the

493

huge rat-alarm tower that crested Camden Hill, and the row of blossoming giant hemlocks that lined the road. . . .

Caterham's private secretary came to him from the other carriage and told him that half a mile farther the line had been wrecked and that the rest of the journey was to be made in a motor-car. Redwood descended upon a platform lit only by a hand lantern and swept by the cool night breeze. The quiet of that derelict, wood-set, weed-embedded suburb—for all the inhabitants had taken refuge in London at the outbreak of yesterday's conflict—became instantly impressive. His conductor took him down the steps to where a motor-car was waiting with blazing lights—the only lights to be seen—handed him over to the care of the driver and bade him farewell.

"You will do your best for us," he said, with an imitation of his master's manner, as he held Redwood's hand.

So soon as Redwood could be wrapped about, they started out into the night. At one moment they stood still, and then the motor-car was rushing softly and swiftly down the station incline. They turned one corner and another, followed the windings of a lane of villas, and then before them stretched the road. The motor droned up to its topmost speed, and the black night swept past them. Everything was very dark under the starlight, and the whole world crouched mysteriously and was gone without a sound. Not a breath stirred the flying things by the wayside ; the deserted, pallid white villas on either hand with their black unlit windows reminded him of a noiseless procession of skulls. The driver beside him was a silent man, or stricken into silence by the conditions of his journey. He answered Redwood's brief questions in monosyllables, and gruffly. Athwart the southern sky the beams of searchlights waved noiseless passes ; the sole strange evidences of life they seemed in all that derelict world about the hurrying machine.

The road was presently bordered on either side by gigantic blackthorn shoots that made it very dark, and by tall grass and big campions, huge giant dead-nettles as high as trees, flickering past darkly in silhouette overhead. Beyond Keston they came to a rising hill, and the driver went slow. At the crest he stopped. The engine throbbed and became still. "There," he said, and his big gloved finger pointed, a black misshapen thing, before Redwood's eyes.

Far away as it seemed the great embankment, crested by the blaze from which the searchlights sprang, rose up against the sky. Those beams went and came among the clouds and the hilly land about them as if they traced mysterious incantations.

"I don't know," said the driver at last, and it was clear he was afraid to go on.

Presently a searchlight swept down the sky to them, stopped as it were with a start, scrutinised them, a blinding stare confused rather than mitigated by an intervening monstrous weed stem or so. They sat with their gloves held over their eyes, trying to look under them and meet that light.

" Go on," said Redwood after a while.

The driver still had his doubts ; he tried to express them and died down to " I don't know " again.

At last he ventured on. " Here goes," he said, and roused his machinery to motion again, followed intently by that great white eye.

To Redwood it seemed for a long time they were no longer on earth, but passing in a state of palpitating hurry through a luminous cloud. Teuf, teuf, teuf, teuf, went the machine, and ever and again—obeying I know not what nervous impulse—the driver sounded his horn.

They passed into the welcome darkness of a high-fenced lane, and down into a hollow and past some houses into that blinding stare again. Then for a space the road ran naked across a down, and they seemed to hang throbbing in immensity. Once more giant weeds rose about them and whirled past. Then quite abruptly close upon them loomed the figure of a giant, shining brightly where the searchlight caught him below and black against the sky above. " Hullo, there ! " he cried, and " stop ! There's no more road beyond. . . . Is that Father Redwood ? "

Redwood stood up and gave a vague shout by way of answer, and then Cossar was in the road beside him, gripping both hands with both of his and pulling him out of the car.

" What of my son ? " asked Redwood.

" He's all right," said Cossar. " They've hurt nothing serious in *him*."

" And your lads ? "

" Well. All of them, well. But we've had to make a fight for it."

The giant was saying something to the motor driver. Redwood stood aside as the machine wheeled round, and then suddenly Cossar vanished, everything vanished, and he was in absolute darkness for a space. The glare was following the motor back to the crest of the Keston hill. He watched the little conveyance receding in that white halo. It had a curious effect, as though it was not moving at all and the halo was. A group of war-blasted giant elder trees flashed into gaunt scarred gesticulations and were swallowed again by the night. . . . Redwood turned to Cossar's dim outline again and clasped his hand. " I have been shut up and kept in ignorance," he said, " for two whole days."

" We fired the Food at them," said Cossar. " Obviously ! Thirty shots. Eh ! "

" I come from Caterham."

" I know you do." He laughed with a note of bitterness. " I suppose he's wiping it up."

II

" Where is my son ? " said Redwood.

" He is all right.   The giants are waiting for your message."

" Yes, but my son——— . . ."

He passed with Cossar down a long slanting tunnel that was lit red for a moment and then became dark again, and came out presently into the great pit of shelter the giants had made.

Redwood's first impression was of an enormous arena bounded by very high cliffs and with its floor greatly encumbered.   It was in darkness save for the passing reflections of the watchman's searchlights that whirled perpetually high overhead, and for a red glow that came and went from a distant corner where two giants worked together amidst a metallic clangour.   Against the sky, as the glare came about, his eye caught the familiar outline of the old worksheds and playsheds that were made for the Cossar boys.   They were hanging now, as it were, at a cliff brow, and strangely twisted and distorted with the guns of Caterham's bombardment. There were suggestions of huge gun emplacements above there, and nearer were piles of mighty cylinders that were perhaps ammunition.   All about the wide space below, the forms of great engines and incomprehensible bulks were scattered in vague disorder.   The giants appeared and vanished among these masses and in the uncertain light ; great shapes they were, not disproportionate to the things amidst which they moved.   Some were actively employed, some sitting and lying as if they courted sleep, and one near at hand, whose body was bandaged, lay on a rough litter of pine boughs and was certainly asleep.   Redwood peered at these dim forms ; his eyes went from one stirring outline to another.

" Where is my son, Cossar ? "

Then he saw him.

His son was sitting under the shadow of a great wall of steel.   He presented himself as a black shape recognisable only by his pose—his features were invisible.   He sat chin upon hand, as though weary or lost in thought.   Beside him Redwood discovered the figure of the Princess, the dark suggestion of her merely, and then, as the glow from the distant iron returned, he saw for an instant, red-lit and tender, the infinite kindliness of her shadowed face.   She stood looking down upon her lover with her hand resting against the steel.   It seemed that she whispered to him.

Redwood would have gone towards them.

" Presently," said Cossar.   " First there is your message."

" Yes," said Redwood, " but——— "

He stopped.   His son was now looking up and speaking to the Princess, but in too low a tone for them to hear.   Young Redwood raised his face and she bent down towards him, and glanced aside before she spoke.

" But if we are beaten," they heard the whispered voice of
young Redwood.

She paused, and the red blaze showed her eyes bright with
unshed tears. She bent nearer him and spoke still lower.
There was something so intimate and private in their bearing,
in their soft tones, that Redwood, Redwood who had thought
for two whole days of nothing but his son, felt himself intrusive
there. Abruptly he was checked. For the first time in his
life perhaps he realised how much more a son may be to his
father than a father can ever be to a son ; he realised the full
predominance of the future over the past. Here between
these two he had no part. His part was played. He turned
to Cossar, in the instant realisation. Their eyes met. His
voice was changed to the tone of a grey resolve.

" I will deliver my message now," he said. " Afterwards—— . . . It will be soon enough then."

The pit was so enormous and so encumbered that it was a
long and tortuous route to the place from which Redwood
could speak to them all.

He and Cossar followed a steeply descending way that
passed beneath an arch of interlocking machinery, and so
came into a vast deep gangway that ran athwart the bottom
of the pit. This gangway, wide and vacant, and yet relatively
narrow, conspired with everything about it to enhance Redwood's sense of his own littleness. It became as it were an
excavated gorge. High overhead, separated from him by
cliffs of darkness, the searchlights wheeled and blazed, and
the shining shapes went to and fro. Giant voices called to one
another above there, calling the giants together to the Council
of War, to hear the terms that Caterham had sent. The
gangway still inclined downward towards black vastnesses,
towards shadows and mysteries and inconceivable things, into
which Redwood went slowly with reluctant footsteps and
Cossar with a confident stride. . . .

Redwood's thoughts were busy.

The two men passed into the completest darkness, and
Cossar took his companion's wrist. They went now slowly
perforce.

Redwood was moved to speak. " All this," he said, " is
strange."

" Big," said Cossar.

" Strange. And strange that it should be strange to me—I
who am, in a sense, the beginning of it all. It's——"

He stopped, wrestling with his elusive meaning, and threw
an unseen gesture at the cliff.

" I have not thought of it before. I have been busy, and
the years have passed. But here I see—— It is a new
generation, Cossar, and new emotions and new needs. All
this, Cossar——"

Cossar saw now his dim gesture to the things about them.

"All this is Youth."

Cossar made no answer, and his irregular footfalls went striding on.

"It isn't *our* youth, Cossar. They are taking things over. They are beginning upon their own emotions, their own experiences, their own way. We have made a new world, and it isn't ours. This great place——"

"I planned it," said Cossar, his face close.

"But now?"

"Ah! I have given it to my sons."

Redwood could feel the loose wave of the arm that he could not see.

"That is it. We are over—or almost over."

"Your message!"

"Yes. And then——"

"We're over."

"Well—— ?"

"Of course we are out of it, we two old men," said Cossar, with his familiar note of sudden anger. "Of course we are. Obviously. Each man for his own time. And now—it's *their* time beginning. That's all right. Excavator's gang. We do our job and go. See? That is what Death is for. We work out all our little brains and all our little emotions, and then this lot begins afresh. Fresh and fresh! Perfectly simple. What's the trouble?"

He paused to guide Redwood to some steps.

"Yes," said Redwood, "but one feels——"

He left his sentence incomplete.

"That is what Death is for." He heard Cossar insisting below him. "How else could the thing be done? That is what Death is for."

III

After devious windings and ascents they came out upon a projecting ledge from which it was possible to see over the greater extent of the giant's pit, and from which Redwood might make himself heard by the whole of their assembly. The giants were already gathered below and about him at different levels, to hear the message he had to deliver. The eldest son of Cossar stood on the bank overhead watching the revelations of the searchlights, for they feared a breach of the truce. The workers at the great apparatus in the corner stood out clear in their own light; they were near stripped; they turned their faces towards Redwood, but with a watchful reference ever and again to the castings that they could not leave. He saw these nearer figures with a fluctuating indistinctness, by lights that came and went, and the remoter ones still less distinctly. They came from and vanished again into the depths of great obscurities. For these giants had no more light than they could help in the pit, that their eyes might be ready to see effectually any attacking force that might spring upon them out of the darknesses around.

Ever and again some chance glare would pick out and display this group or that of tall and powerful forms, the giants from Sunderland clothed in overlapping metal plates, and the others clad in leather, in woven rope or in woven metal, as their conditions had determined. They sat amidst or rested their hands upon, or stood erect among machines and weapons as mighty as themselves, and all their faces, as they came and went from visible to invisible, had steadfast eyes.

He made an effort to begin and did not do so. Then for a moment his son's face glowed out in a hot insurgence of the fire, his son's face looking up to him, tender as well as strong ; and at that he found a voice to reach them all, speaking across a gulf as it were to his son.

" I come from Caterham," he said. " He sent me to you, to tell you the terms he offers."

He paused. " They are impossible terms I know, now that I see you here all together ; they are impossible terms, but I brought them to you, because I wanted to see you all—and my son. Once more. . . . I wanted to see my son. . . ."

" Tell them the terms," said Cossar.

" This is what Caterham offers. He wants you to go apart and leave his world ! "

" Where ? "

" He does not know. Vaguely somewhere in the world a great region is to be set apart. . . . And you are to make no more of the Food, to have no children of your own, to live in your own way for your own time, and then to end for ever."

He stopped.

" And that is all ? "

" That is all."

There followed a great stillness. The darkness that veiled the giants seemed to look thoughtfully at him.

He felt a touch at his elbow, and Cossar was holding a chair for him—a queer fragment of doll's furniture amidst these piled immensities. He sat down and crossed his legs, and then put one across the knee of the other, and clutched his boot nervously, and felt small and self-conscious and acutely visible and absurdly placed.

Then at the sound of a voice he forgot himself again.

" You have heard, Brothers," said this voice out of the shadows.

And another answered, " We have heard."

" And the answer, Brothers ? "

" To Caterham ? "

" Is No ! "

" And then ? "

There was a silence for the space of some seconds.

Then a voice said : " These people are right. After their

lights, that is. They have been right in killing all that grew larger than its kind, beast and plant and all manner of great things that arose. They were right in trying to massacre us. They are right now in saying we must not marry our kind. According to their lights they are right. They know—it is time that we also knew—that you cannot have pigmies and giants in one world together. Caterham has said that again and again—clearly—their world or ours."

" We are not half a hundred now," said another, " and they are endless millions."

" So it may be. But the thing is as I have said."

Then another long silence.

" And are we to die then ? "

" God forbid ! "

" Are they ? "

" No."

" But that is what Caterham says ! He would have us live out our lives, die one by one, till only one remains, and that one at last would die also, and they would cut down all the giant plants and weeds, kill all the giant underlife, burn out the traces of the Food—make an end to us and to the Food for ever. Then the little pigmy world would be safe. They would go on—safe for ever, living their little pigmy lives, doing pigmy kindnesses and pigmy cruelties each to the other ; they might even perhaps attain a sort of pigmy millennium, make an end to war, make an end to over-population, sit down in a world-wide city to practise pigmy arts, worshipping one another till the world begins to freeze. . . ."

In a corner a sheet of iron fell in thunder to the ground.

" Brothers, we know what we mean to do."

In a spluttering of light from the searchlights Redwood saw earnest youthful faces turning to his son.

" It is easy now to make the Food. It would be easy for us to make Food for all the world."

" You mean, Brother Redwood," said a voice out of the darkness, " that it is for the little people to eat the Food."

" What else is there to do ? "

" We are not half a hundred and they are many millions."

" But we held our own."

" So far."

" If it is God's will, we may still hold our own."

" Yes. But think of the dead ! "

Another voice took up the strain. " The dead," it said. " Think of the unborn. . . ."

" Brothers," came the voice of young Redwood, " what can we do but fight them, and if we beat them, make them take the Food ? They cannot help but take the Food now. Suppose we were to resign our heritage and do this folly that Caterham suggests ! Suppose we could ! Suppose we give up this great thing that stirs within us, repudiate this thing our fathers did for us, that *you*, Father, did for us, and pass, when our time has come, into decay and nothingness ! What then ? Will this little world of theirs be as it was before ? They may fight against greatness in us who are the children of men, but can they conquer ? Even if they should destroy us every one, what then ? Would it save them ? No ! For greatness is abroad, not only in us, not only in the Food, but in the purpose of all things ! It is in the nature of all things, it is part of space and time. To grow and still to grow, from first to last that is Being, that is the law of life. What other law can there be ? ''

" To help others ? ''

" To grow. It is still, to grow. Unless we help them to fail. . . .''

" They will fight hard to overcome us,'' said a voice.

And another, " What of that ? ''

" They will fight,'' said young Redwood. " If we refuse these terms, I doubt not they will fight. Indeed I hope they will be open and fight. If after all they offer peace, it will be only the better to catch us unawares. Make no mistake, Brothers ; in some way or other they will fight. The war has begun, and we must fight to the end. Unless we are wise, we may find presently we have lived only to make them better weapons against our children and our kind. This, so far, has been only the dawn of battle. All our lives will be a battle. Some of us will be killed in battle, some of us will be waylaid. There is no easy victory, no victory whatever that is not more than half defeat for us. Be sure of that. What of that ? If only we keep a foothold, if only we leave behind us a growing host to fight when we are gone ! ''

" And to-morrow ? ''

" We will scatter the Food ; we will saturate the world with the Food.''

" Suppose they come to terms ? ''

" Our terms are the Food. It is not as though little and great could live together in any perfection of compromise. It is one thing or the other. What right have parents to say, my child shall have no light but the light I have had, shall grow no greater than the greatness to which I have grown ? Do I speak for you, Brothers ? ''

Assenting murmurs answered him.

" And to the children who will be women as well as to the children who will be men,'' said a voice from the darkness.

" Even more so—to be mothers of a new race. . . .''

" But for the next generation there must be great and little,'' said Redwood, with his eyes on his son's face.

" For many generations. And the little will hamper the great and the great press upon the little. So it must needs be, Father.''

" There will be conflict.''

" Endless conflict. Endless misunderstanding. All life is that. Great and little cannot understand one another. But in every child born of man, Father Redwood, lurks some seed of greatness—waiting for the Food."

" Then I am to go to Caterham again and tell him——"

" You will stay with us, Father Redwood. Our answer goes to Caterham at dawn."

" He says that he will fight. . . ."

" So be it," said young Redwood, and his brethren murmured assent.

" *The iron waits*," cried a voice, and the two giants who were working in the corner began a rhythmic hammering that made a mighty music to the scene. The metal glowed out far more brightly than it had done before, and gave Redwood a clearer view of the encampment than had yet come to him. He saw the oblong space to its full extent, with the great engines of warfare ranged ready to hand. Beyond, and at a higher level, the house of the Cossars stood. About him were the young giants, huge and beautiful, glittering in their mail, amidst the preparations for the morrow. The sight of them lifted his heart. They were so easily powerful ! They were so tall and gracious ! They were so steadfast in their movements ! There was his son amongst them, and the first of all giant women, the Princess. . . .

There leapt into his mind the oddest contrast, a memory of Bensington, very bright and little—Bensington with his hand amidst the soft breast feathers of that first great chick, standing in that conventionally furnished room of his, peering over his spectacles dubiously as cousin Jane banged the door. . . .

It had all happened in a yesterday of one-and-twenty years.

Then suddenly a strange doubt took hold of him, that this place and present greatness were but the texture of a dream ; that he was dreaming and would in an instant wake to find himself in his study again, the giants slaughtered, the Food suppressed, and himself a prisoner locked in. What else indeed was life but that—always to be a prisoner locked in ! This was the culmination and end of his dream. He would wake through bloodshed and battle, to find his Food the most foolish of fancies, and his hopes and faith of a greater world to come no more than the coloured film upon a pool of bottomless decay. Littleness invincible ! . . .

So strong and deep was this wave of despondency, this suggestion of impending disillusionment, that he started to his feet. He stood and pressed his clenched fists into his eyes, and so for a moment remained, fearing to open them again and see, lest the dream should already have passed away.

The voice of the giant children spoke to one another, an undertone to that clangorous melody of the smiths. His tide of doubt ebbed. He heard the giant voices ; he heard their movements about him still. It was real, surely it was real—

as real as spiteful acts ! More real, for these great things, it may be, are the coming things, and the littleness, bestiality, and infirmity of men are the things that go. He opened his eyes.

"Done," cried one of the two ironworkers, and they flung their hammers down.

A voice sounded above. The son of Cossar standing on the great embankment had turned and was now speaking to them all.

"It is not that we would oust the little people from the world," he said, " in order that we, who are no more than one step upwards from their littleness, may hold their world for ever. It is the step we fight for and not ourselves. . . . We are here, Brothers, to what end ? To serve the spirit and the purpose that has been breathed into our lives. We fight not for ourselves—for we are but the momentary hands and eyes of the Life of the World. So you, Father Redwood, taught us. Through us and through the little folk the Spirit looks and learns. From us by word and birth and act it must pass—to still greater lives. This earth is no resting place ; this earth is no playing place, else indeed we might put our throats to the little people's knife, having no greater right to live than they. And they in their turn might yield to the ants and vermin. We fight not for ourselves but for growth, growth that goes on for ever. To-morrow, whether we live or die, growth will conquer through us. That is the law of the spirit for evermore. To grow according to the will of God ! To grow out of these cracks and crannies, out of these shadows and darknesses, into greatness and the light ! Greater," he said, speaking with slow deliberation, " greater, my Brothers ! And then—still greater. To grow and again—to grow. To grow at last into the fellowship and understanding of God. Growing. . . . Till the earth is no more than a footstool. . . . Till the spirit shall have driven fear into nothingness, and spread. . . ." He swung his arms heavenward—" *There !* "

His voice ceased. The white glare of one of the searchlights wheeled about, and for a moment fell upon him, standing out gigantic with hand upraised against the sky.

For one instant he shone, looking up fearlessly into the starry deeps, mail-clad, young and strong, resolute and still. Then the light had passed and he was no more than a great black outline against the starry sky, a great black outline that threatened with one mighty gesture the firmament of heaven and all its multitude of stars.